Praise for Helen Hollick's Novels

"Compelling, convincing, and unforgettable."

—Sharon Kay Penman

"A spellbinding novel...a fabulous read and one to be recommended unreservedly. If only all historical fiction could be this good."

—*Historical Novels Review*

"An epic retelling of the events leading to the Norman Conquest...most impressive."

—*The Lady*

"Hollick juggles a large cast of characters and a bloody, tangled plot with great skill...spirited retelling of the final days of King Arthur's court."

—*Publishers Weekly*

"Don't miss Helen Hollick's colourful re-creation of the events leading up to the Norman Conquest in *Harold the King*."

—*Daily Mail*

"Helen Hollick has written a spellbinder of a historical novel, meaty and colourful."

—*Northern Echo*

"Uniquely compelling…bound to have a resounding and lasting impact on Arthurian fiction."

—*Books* magazine

"Helen Hollick joins the ranks of Rosemary Sutcliff, Mary Stewart, and Marion Bradley with this splendid novel."

—*Pendragon* magazine

"Masterly and colourful re-creation."

—*Bolton Evening News*

"A novel of enormous emotional power…Helen Hollick is a fabulous writer of historical fiction."

—Elizabeth Chadwick

I am
The Chosen King

HELEN HOLLICK

Previously published in the UK as *Harold the King*

Published by Sourcebooks Landmark, an imprint of Sourcebooks, Inc.
P.O. Box 4410, Naperville, Illinois 60567-4410
(630) 961-3900
Fax: (630) 961-2168
www.sourcebooks.com

Originally published as *Harold the King* in the UK by William Heinemann in 2000.

Library of Congress Cataloging-in-Publication Data

Hollick, Helen.
  I am the chosen king / by Helen Hollick.
      p. cm.
   1. Harold, King of England, 1022?-1066--Fiction. 2. Great Britain--History-- Anglo-Saxon period, 449-1066--Fiction. I. Title.
   PR6058.O4464I24 2011
   823'.914--dc22
                                    2010048508

                    Printed and bound in Canada.
                    WC 10 9 8 7 6 5 4 3 2 1

Also by Helen Hollick

Acknowledgments

Author Elizabeth Chadwick has been a staunch friend, and Sharon Kay Penman an encouraging ally throughout my writing career. I am indebted to both of them.

My gratitude to the entire team at Sourcebooks—Shana, Danielle—and Dominque Raccah for their enthusiasm and their faith in my books.

I must also thank another, sadly now deceased author, who was such an influence on my writing career—Rosemary Sutcliff. Her novels of Roman Britain, especially, inspired me to write. Running through many of her novels is the presence of a ring that has a flaw, shaped like a dolphin, in the stone. Hence the name of one of the ships that appears in this book. My small, personal, tribute to her.

And to my family, Ron and Kathy, thank you for not minding the preoccupation I have for my writing. Neither of them complain that I forget to do the laundry or the shopping or prepare dinner—although Kathy, now that she is grown up, has mastered the art of survival and learned to cook.

Kathy is not only my daughter but my best friend. This book is dedicated to her, even though because of her severe dyslexia she will not be able to read it. The opening verse used for the section headings was written by Kathy several years ago when she was at school; because of her difficulties, she experienced an enormous lack of confidence and low self-esteem. She wrote it to express her feelings, and I felt it appropriate to use it in this novel.

I felt as proud of her courage and bravery then as I do now.

Helen Hollick
November 2010

My heart may fight for power and my head can fight for tears, but nothing can stop my anger, nor my fears.

K.V.H.

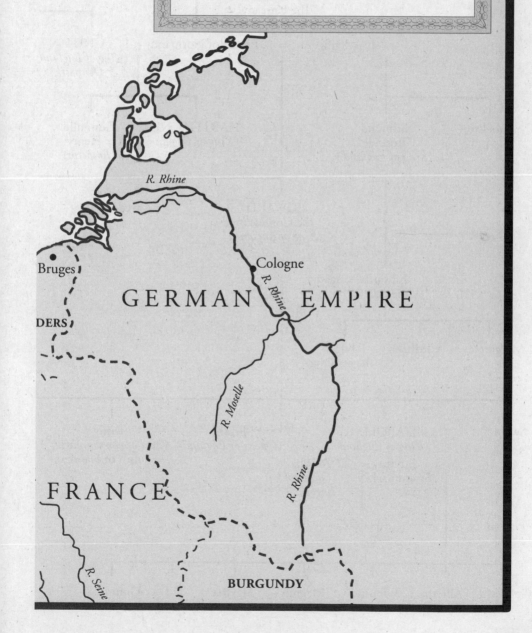

R. Rhine

Cologne

R. Rhine

Bruges

GERMAN EMPIRE

DERS

R. Moselle

R. Rhine

FRANCE

R. Seine

BURGUNDY

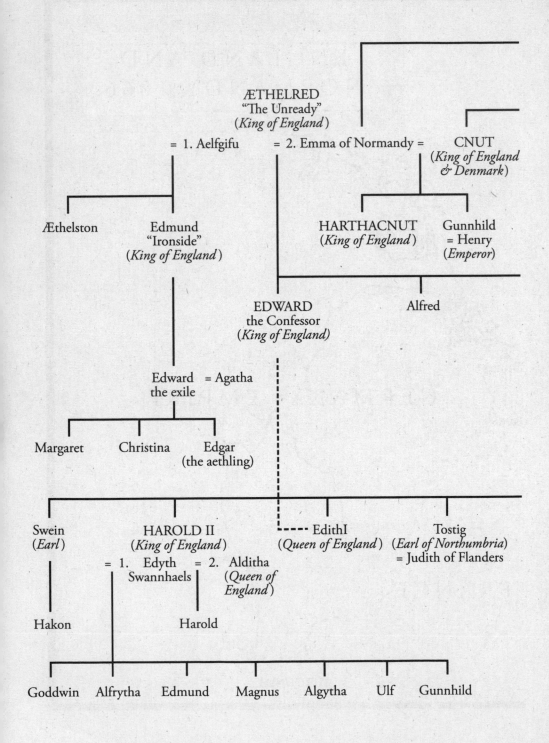

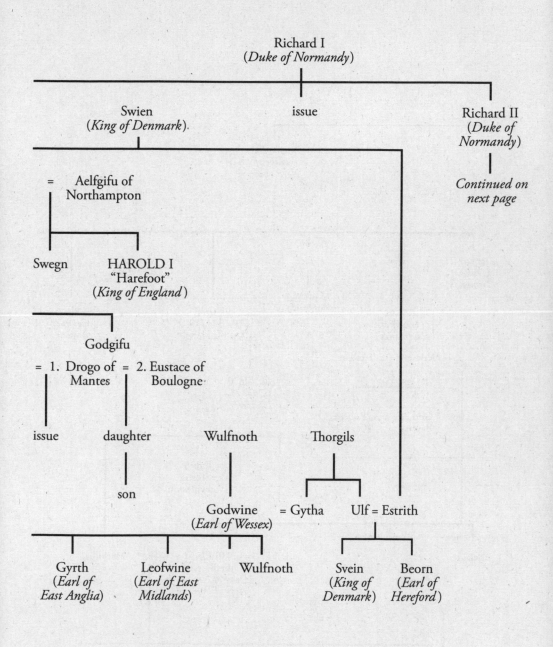

Richard I
(*Duke of Normandy*)

Swien
(*King of Denmark*).

issue

Richard II
(*Duke of Normandy*)

Continued on next page

= Aelfgifu of Northampton

Swegn

HAROLD I
"Harefoot"
(*King of England*)

Godgifu

= 1. Drogo of Mantes

= 2. Eustace of Boulogne

issue

daughter

Wulfnoth

Thorgils

son

Godwine
(*Earl of Wessex*)

= Gytha

Ulf = Estrith

Gyrth
(*Earl of East Anglia*)

Leofwine
(*Earl of East Midlands*)

Wulfnoth

Svein
(*King of Denmark*)

Beorn
(*Earl of Hereford*)

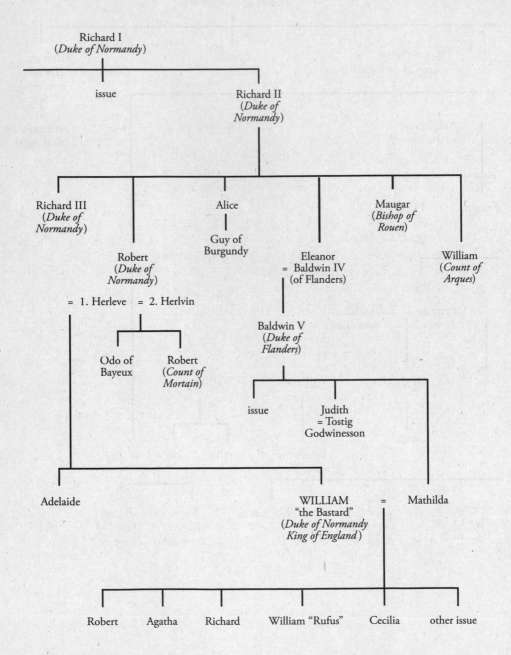

Part One

Fight for Power

I

⤳

Winchester—April 1043

Emma, twice married, twice widowed, Dowager Queen of England, watched her only surviving son dance, tripping and prancing with dainty steps among the boisterous twirl of men and women. With the solemnity of the coronation ritual completed, and the pomp of the banquet ended, this evening's celebration and merry-making came most welcome to the guests here within the King's Hall at Winchester. A pity that the crowned king had to be Edward.

Emma sipped at her wine to disguise the flare of contempt. Edward, her first-born son, crowned and anointed this day as King of England. She would have to learn to accept it. She took another sip, savouring the richness of the red grape as it warmed her throat, overcoming the taste of bile that rose from her stomach. Accept it, maybe, but she would never come to like it! Edward was as weak and shallow as his incompetent father, Æthelred, had been. How well had the clerics who wrote the history of these things mocked that name! Æthelred, *Noble-Counsel*—and how soon into his dithering, floundering reign had that been altered to *un-raed*, ill-counselled?

A thunder of laughter from the far end of the crowded Hall drew her attention. Godwine's two eldest sons, Swegn and Harold, stood among a group of fine-dressed young men sharing some, no doubt lewd, jest between them. For all their faults—and where the Earl and his brood were concerned, there were faults a-plenty—they were sons to be proud of. Swegn might be wild, more interested in the pursuit of enjoyment rather than the demands of decision-making, but these faults were outweighed by better traits. All Earl Godwine's sons were strong, courageous and manly, aye, even young Leofwine, who was but seven years of age. Where was the manliness in her son Edward?

Unable to keep her thoughts to herself, Emma spoke to the man sitting beside her, his hand tapping out the merry rhythm-beat of the dance on his knee. "I have been wife, and queen, to two men who have ruled England." Her words oozed contempt. "You would have thought one of them could have sired upon me a man worthy to be called son."

"Harthacnut, your last-born—" Godwine began, but Emma irritably waved him silent.

"My second husband, Cnut, gave me a child of each sex, both of whom had the constitution and life-span of a mayfly." Briefly, an expression of regret clouded Emma's face. To be queen for over two score years, to rule as regent, survive attempts of murder and the harsh bitterness of exile: such a woman needed to shield her weaknesses from those who would, at the drop of an autumn leaf, oppose her. But Godwine knew Emma well, better perhaps than either of her husbands. Harthacnut, her youngest son, she had genuinely adored. A boy like his father, wise and disciplined, with a sense of duty and purpose; strong of body and mind. How much had she endured for that lad! And for what? For him to die of a seizure when he was but three and twenty and crowned king for less than two short years.

"The life of the wrong son was ended," she said softly. Godwine assumed she referred to Harthacnut's untimely death, winced as she murmured, "It ought have been Edward killed, not Alfred."

Godwine made no comment to that. Emma had borne two sons to Æthelred: Edward and Alfred, and Alfred was a name that still conjured difficult memories that brought the blood stealing into Godwine's cheeks. As young men, exiled from England, the brothers had tried and failed in a pathetic attempt to claim their right of succession after Cnut's death. Captured, the boy Alfred had been placed in Godwine's care. It had not been good care for the lad had fallen into the murdering clutch of Cnut's illegitimate son, Harold Harefoot. Imprisoned and cruelly blinded, Alfred had not survived the torture. Ever since, Godwine had carried the blame for that wicked death.

But such was the fate of young men who tried to take by force a crown from the one who was already, rightly or wrongly, wearing it.

Earl Godwine's hawk-sighted blue eyes followed Emma's narrowed gaze. Edward was an elegant fine-featured man, two years short of forty years of age, tall and slender, dressed in bright-coloured, extravagant clothing.

Disdainfully, Emma snorted. "A pious weakling with neither brain nor balls."

"Give him time, my Lady. He has been almost thirty years an exile. He was but eight when forced to flee to your birthplace in Normandy."

Aye, it must have been hard for the lad and his brother Alfred, when they left London, muffled by the concealing darkness of night, bundled into a boat and taken, alone and frightened, across the sea to live among those of a foreign tongue and way of life. Never knowing when they would return to their mother, and England. Knowing, later, that when she agreed marriage with their father's usurper, Cnut, that the "when" would not come until the Danish conqueror met with death. And even then, only if their place had not been superseded by other sons.

"Look at his hands! Too delicate to wield a sword," Emma announced with scorn. "I pity England if she is ever again faced with invasion. At least Alfred, for all his childhood mewling and whimpering, had the stomach for a fight once he was grown."

Godwine refrained from answering. Alfred, as king, would not have survived beyond the turn of a season, not against experienced, battle-hardened men such as Magnus of Norway or Svein Estrithson of Denmark—those two Viking seafarers had always been far too concerned with England's affairs. But at least the roving greed of their ancestral cousins, Emma's kindred the dukes of Normandy, were of no consequence to England's future. The present Duke, William, was yet a boy. He would have problems enough keeping his head attached to his shoulders.

With tact, Godwine commented, "Edward is amenable. He listens to his elders and accepts the wisdom of the Witan, his council."

"He does not listen to me! I came into this world nigh on four and fifty years past. I have been Queen of England from the age of thirteen when I was wed to that weak fool Æthelred. I ruled as regent for Cnut, when his duties as king of Denmark and Norway took him across the seas. I guided Harthacnut through his brief but glorious reign—yet this whelp Edward, the first-born son of my womb, publicly spits on me and calls me an interfering hag!"

She glared at Godwine, but fell silent as the whirling dance finished amid laughter and excited applause. She watched as Godwine's sons were joined by a few of the breathless dancers, Harold swirling a fair-haired young girl into his arms.

His sister laughed back at him, her eyes bright with youth and excitement, her cheeks flushed pink from exertion and the heat of the crowded Hall. Edith was a resourceful girl, determined to enjoy herself whenever opportunity presented itself. Watching her, one eyebrow raised, Emma had a suspicion that she might also have high-reaching ambitions, and the shrewdness to take full advantage of those offered opportunities. Pride was as ripe in the daughter as it was in the sons. Edith would make a good wife for some power-seeking young earl. Or...Emma sucked the inside of her cheek, then sipped again from her silvered goblet. Or perhaps Edith, only daughter of the noble lord Earl Godwine of Wessex, would marry higher?

Edward was talking, all light smiles and expressive hands, to that odious man, Robert Champart, one-time Abbot of Jumièges. Emma was Norman by birth, daughter to the illustrious Duke Richard of Normandy, great-granddaughter of the Viking, Rollo, the first acclaimed duke of the North Men, the Normans. She ought to feel an affinity for her fellow countryman, but there was nothing but dislike in her for this one. A secretive, scheming, cunning, snide little man, too ambitious and arrogant to be a man of God. Her son, the fool, doted on him like a youth suffering the pangs of first love.

"You are fortunate, Godwine," she said, and again that hint of regret edged into her voice. "Your sons are men worthy to be called sons." She stared straight at the Earl. Unblinking, and perfectly serious, she added, "I would that I had trusted you when I was young enough to take a lover to my bed. Your seed, or either of my lawful husbands' to sire my sons?" She locked her ageing brown gaze into the vividness of his blue. "In hindsight," she finished candidly, "would yours not have been preferable to theirs?"

Godwine was not often flustered, but her words left him speechless, his heart fluttering, his manhood stirring. For the most part he remained loyal to Gytha his wife, save for the occasional rut with a tavern whore or village maid when campaign of war, or requirements of court, kept him overlong from home. She was a good woman, Gytha.

Emma? Ah, he had always wanted Emma.

But a man who valued his life, and his privates, did not openly lust after the woman who had twice been queen.

2

Waltham

To Harold, in his happiness, the sky was a bright blue and the sun shone with the full warmth of midsummer. No matter that in reality the spring day was dull, with a distinct damp chill, accompanied by a wind that tugged at his cloak with the persistence of a bored child trying to attract attention. He was the new-acclaimed Earl of East Anglia, and no grey clouds or sullen spatter of rain was going to spoil his delight. The prestigious title had been bestowed upon him with full honour during the two days of Council following Edward's coronation at Winchester—Earl! The two eldest sons of Godwine of Wessex were now made earl—a fine reward indeed for a family so loyal to the royal line.

The smile beamed wide upon Harold's face as he rode with his father, brothers Swegn and Tostig, and all their escort, beside the ambling river. In his one and twentieth year he was now set equal to Swegn, his elder by two years, and to those proud, dominating lords at court, most especially the Earls of Northumbria and Mercia, both sharp rivals and vociferous opponents of Harold's father.

Of course, Leofric of Mercia had denounced Harold's election. There was already an imbalance, he had protested; Godwine was Earl of Wessex and his first-born, Swegn, Earl of the Welsh Borders—and now the second son was to be granted East Anglia, Essex, Cambridgeshire and Huntingdonshire? Harold ran his hand along his stallion's crested neck and grinned. Earl of East Anglia, Essex, Cambridgeshire and Huntingdonshire…ah, did that not have a splendid ring to his ears!

Disregarding the opposition, Edward had awarded the earldom where he and the rest of his council had seen fit. The alternative? Leofric's son. Godwine, for all his obsession with protocol and duty, was preferable to the ill-humoured Lord of Mercia and his scowling son. Edward might spend over-much time on his knees before God's altar, and prefer the thrill of hunting deer to the necessary duties of state, but he was no fool regarding Mercia. Leofric's seed would never be as trusted as Godwine's brood, for all their inter-family squabbling and petty rivalry.

There were some who privately whispered, and as many who openly scoffed, that the Godwines—father and six sons, the daughter counted for naught—sought only power and wealth, and would lie and murder and cheat without pause for their own gain. Hah! With the recent swinging changes of kingship and the chances available for anyone who could think straight, ride fast and use a sword to its best advantage—who would not?

Godwine and his sons shared another advantage, one that Leofric and all the others did not. Earl Godwine, or so his Saxon mother had claimed, held Wessex blood in his veins. Not as thick or potently royal as that of this recent-crowned king, but it was there, she had insisted. Watered down, blended and subdued by time it might be, but Godwine could claim, albeit distantly, to be kindred to the Great King Alfred and, through his lineage, could trace back to the dawn-time of the Saxon kings, to the first king of Wessex, Cerdic himself. There were some who still told the story around the hearth fires on a blustery winter's night, that Cerdic was descended from a noble king of the British. From a time before the Saxons had come to England in their longships from across the sea, before they had built their new farmsteadings, raised new-planted crops and nurtured their new-born children. That British king, the tale-tellers said in their light, sing-song voices, had been called Arthur. Harold had no idea whether Arthur belonged to the realm of reality or myth. Whichever, his was a good story, passed from father to son, mother to daughter. It was cheering to know that your blood might carry a trace of such a heroic lord.

"Look at that little slut hiding beneath the trees! Does she think we are so blind that we cannot see her?"

Harold's idling thoughts interrupted, the glow of pleasure dimmed as he glanced to where his brother Swegn pointed. Beneath the sweep of willows dressed in their new, spring-bright array, on the far bank of the Lea river, a girl, huddled small, with legs curled beneath her, fingers clamped around the muzzle of a rough-coated dog to keep it from barking, Harold had already seen her a few moments past; had watched her scurry beneath the shelter of the trees, dragging the dog with her, intent on not being seen by the group of men on horseback. Trust Swegn to notice her also.

"Some lazy servant girl I would wager, lurking here to meet a secret lover. Hah, I would have her whipped." As ever, Swegn's words were snarled; he said little that did not have an edge of sneering contempt to it. His expression was always puckered, as if there were some putrid smell constantly beneath his nose.

The younger of the three, Tostig, lobbed an insult back at him. "Only whip her, brother? What? Would you not force her first?"

Anger instantly aroused, Swegn raised his riding whip. Earl Godwine's rumble of disapproval coming as immediate. "Calm your fire, boy, and you." He turned with a glare to his third-born son. "Keep your moralistic tongue to yourself."

The two brothers glowered at each other, but the petty argument was ended. None of the brood would dare oppose their father; all had tasted the sting of his belt across their backs merely for a wrong word, a wrong glance. Godwine was the son of Wulfnoth, a Saxon thegn turned pirate, who ruled his family with a sternness that would have put his father's seafaring hard-headedness to shame.

They looked much alike, these three eldest sons, had the same slight-curled fair hair, wore the same style moustache, although Tostig's had yet to mature to its full lustre and thickness. Blue eyes, firm chins, muscular but lean bodies. Like their father, they were tall men, although perhaps Harold stood an inch or so the tallest. Only their characters made it difficult to believe that the three had been born from the same womb, set there by the same seed. Harold, despite his love of hunting and tendency to follow the easiest course through life, was conscientious, just and even-tempered. He was quick to laugh and the first to admit his own many faults. Tostig, at eighteen, was impatient to grow into the responsibilities of manhood, but was not as quick-witted as others of the family and resented the advantages held by his two elder brothers; while Swegn, arrogant and sour in mind and tongue, was contemptuous of all who dared cast a shadow over his path. Some maggot had surely wormed its way in with his begetting! Swegn was brash and quick to reach for anger, and often, coming close behind, for a dagger or sword.

Harold's fist had tightened round the rein, jerking his stallion's head higher. Twice already this day Swegn and Tostig had come close to exchanging blows. Harold was becoming sickened of these squabbles. He had only glimpsed the girl, the river was five and forty—fifty—yards across, yet he had clearly seen the alarm on her face, and that she was no drab of a serving girl. There had been a flash of gold from bracelets on her arms and her cloak, bright-coloured, was surely fine-woven.

The dogs, sniffing and circling ahead of the horses, set a brace of wild duck into a shrill of whirring wings and raucous quacking. The brindle bitch snapped at tail feathers, her darker, quicker daughter fastening her jaws around the other bird's neck. Tostig and Swegn spurred their horses forward, beat at the dogs with their whips, the younger man leaping from his horse to retrieve the bird before it became too torn and bloody. He tossed the carcass to a servant, remounted. They were a distance further along the track by now, the horses jogging and prancing at the sudden scatter of excitement, the girl forgotten. Harold was the only one to turn round, take a last look at those secretive willows that rippled beside the ambling waters. She had gone, taking her chance to dart through the sweep of leaf and branch.

And then he saw her again, briefly, as she ran across the new green of the common-land meadows, heading for a thicker belt of forest trees, a protection of oak and beach and hornbeam. His smile returned, and the happiness bounced back into his chest. He was an earl and he had come to see for himself the lands that had been granted him. A nuisance that his father and brothers had insisted on riding with him, but for all that, the days ahead beckoned with a promise of excitement and adventure.

They would rest tonight with the thegn Eadric of Nazeing and when Harold had toured all his earldom and seen all there was to see he would consider where to build a house. A fine manor, an estate fit for a new, young earl.

And maybe he would also find a wife to give that manor the necessary comforts of a home…or at least, if not a wife, a suitable woman to keep the bed-place warm.

The dog, a great-pawed, tawny-coloured hound, bounded at the girl's side, ears flapping, tail whipping. The girl ran fast, her skirt gathered in her hand. Her legs, Harold fancied, would be long and slender. A slim ankle, a shapely calf.

She ran with a swirl of fine, sun-gold hair and fluttering from her shoulders a cloak that was coloured as bright, and as bold, as the startling blue of a kingfisher's feathers.

3

Nazeing

That the riders were the guests expected by her father Edyth had no doubt. Looking back from her vantage point halfway up the hillside, she saw them cross the river by way of the stone bridge and take the eastward track. To entertain Earl Godwine and his sons was an honour—three earls would bed beneath their humble roof this night—but Edyth could not suppress the thought that, surely, her father was not the only thegn in all Essex who had fought with Godwine twenty and five years ago? Was there not some other steading they could have made use of?

She would never reach home before them; they were mounted on good horses and she had over three miles to walk, much of it uphill. She should never have come so far, of course, not when her mother had so much to prepare for the arrival of these important visitors. The quiet of the river had always been so alluring, though, and anyway, Thor had needed the exercise. He was a big dog, prone to boredom and a fat belly, the former a fault shared by Edyth herself.

She ought to be as pleased at their coming as was her father, but she could only think of these brash, hard-voiced men as an intrusion. Her mother was flustered and anxious, the servants and slaves scuttling about…the peace of the farm had been shattered so carelessly by the arrival of a messenger, last evening, on his big, black horse.

Guilt and the knowledge that her mother would have sharp words waiting for her made Edyth run at first, arms pumping, head back, her long legs covering the ground, fair hair tossing like wind-strewn dandelion seeds. Thor bounded at her side, enjoying the excitement, but the ground was rising and Edyth soon slowed to a jog, a walk, then an amble. The dog paddled into a ditch to drink; absently Edyth put her hand to his great head as he came back beside her, water dripping from his lolling tongue, her fingers fondling the silk of his ears. For eleven years they had roamed these woods and fields together, swum in the river, dozed in the heat of the sun or sat, shivering with fear, beneath the boom of a wild thunderstorm. Thor was a trusted friend, who had listened to her dreams and doubts, shared her laughter and tears. Although, perhaps, he had been more attentive to scratching at his fleas than to the sound of her voice. Her father had put him, a rain-sodden, lost and frightened pup, into her lap when she was just turned four years of age. Edyth loved her dog, but was not much interested in men. There would be more of them sniffing around, keen to claim her dowry, she supposed, now that she was fifteen. The Hall would be full of guests tonight: would her father listen to any who took advantage of this opportunity to speak for her? Perhaps not: he would be too occupied with his important visitors.

Her father proudly boasted that he had once saved Earl Godwine's life, when they had fought in support of the old king's claim to the English crown. Cnut, that had been, Cnut the Dane. He was fond of storytelling, her father, entertaining the household well on those long winter evenings, when it seemed that the sun had forgotten to return, although, as Edyth's mother the Lady Ælfthryth often remarked, he had an inclination to imagine gold where there was only copper or bronze. Edyth assumed, however, that there was an element of truth to the tale of how her father's axe had turned a sword from a blow that would have split Godwine's head in two. He had certainly been granted a handsome reward: raised to the status of thegn and awarded sufficient gold coin to leave his meagre acreage in Wessex and set himself up instead within the fertile farmland of this, the Lea Valley. A prudent man, a good farmer and a careful lord, he had soon acquired more land and enough wealth for Edyth, his only child, to become a prize worth the winning.

Godwine and his sons—one of them the new-made Earl of East Anglia—would be at the steading by now. Her father would have come out to greet them, his smile and arms wide. The horses would be settled in the stables; wine, bread and cheese offered—the main meal of the day would come later, at dusk. She ought to have been there for their arrival. Her father would be annoyed with her, for he liked to show off his daughter. She had not minded that when his friends had merely smiled at her with the distracted indulgence of an adult to a child, but since her body had flowered into young womanhood, she had not much liked the new look that had come into their eyes, nor the surreptitious groping of her buttocks or breasts whenever her father or mother were not watching. A few months past—Yule, it had been—a freeholder from a neighbouring farm had cornered her around the back of the barn, pinned her against the wall and planted his wet, slobbering lips over hers.

Edyth scowled. He would not try that again in a hurry! She had brought her knee up, sharp, into where it had hurt. The scowl twitched into an amused smile that swarmed into a burst of laughter. Her father had never understood why the wretched man had gone off down the lane hobbling and howling without the courtesy of a farewell. She broke into a jog-trot again, Thor racing ahead. From behind the copse of trees she could see the dancing trails of hearth and cooking-fire smoke, curling and weaving up to meet the sullen, lead-grey sky.

The yard, muddy and rain-puddled, was busy with slaves and servants. Goodness, but the presence of these three earls was stirring up a nest of ants! Edyth picked her way through the ruts, sidestepping horse and cattle dung. Twice, servants warned her that her parents had been seeking her.

"You'll be in trouble, lass, if you don't get inside quick!" Cuthbert, the herds-man, chided her as she skipped past. For all his scolding, his eyes twinkled and his lips smiled.

"I could tell them I was delayed helping you with the cows," she retorted with an impudent grin.

"Aye, you could, but you will not."

Edyth smiled, put up her hand to push open the great oak door that led into her father's modest-built Hall. No, she would not. Her father—and Cuthbert—had tutored her well. As the sole heir to wealth and land she could read and write, reckon the accounts and speak the Danish tongue as well as her own English. From her mother she knew how to weave a cloak and sew a garment; what herbs were needed to flavour a venison stew or cure a wound or cough. She knew the scriptures of Christ and that the highest sin was the dishonour of a lie.

Thor padded into the high-roofed timbered building beside her, his body pressing tighter against her skirts as he scented the presence of strangers. Edyth tucked her hair behind her ears, took a breath to steady her nerve and set a brave smile to her lips. She bobbed a curtsey as the men turned, wine in hand, to stare at her, her father exclaiming, "Why, here she is at last, my wayward imp!"

There were many hastily invited guests gathered within; prominent among them a tall, broad-shouldered man, his stomach showing the first signs of a paunch that was beginning to climb over his tunic belt, his face, firm-jowled and moustached, framed by waves of fair, slightly curled hair, his blue, piercing eyes staring from a gruff expression. Earl Godwine it must be. Not a man to cross. Beside him, three young men; from their likeness to him, his sons. One, the youngest, was scowling. His boredom evident, he turned away as he realised the newcomer was a girl, no one of interest.

Forcing her smile to remain wide and welcoming Edyth walked forward, her fingers brushing Thor's rough coat for reassurance. Why was she so shy of men? The other girls from down in the village of Nazeing, the daughters of farmers and servants, were so at ease with the opposite sex. Some, indecently so. Elsa, Gunnor's daughter, no more than a few months her senior—unwed—was with child. Edyth would never have the courage to be so intimate with a man! She dreaded the prospect of marriage.

The two elder sons were taller than their father by two or three fingers, leaner, one with hair a shade darker than the usual Danish corn-gold colouring. Their mother, Godwine's wife, was from Denmark, her brother had been husband to Cnut's sister. Earls in their own right and blood kindred of Viking nobility—no wonder these two had such presence. Edyth wondered which one of them was Earl of East Anglia.

The darker-haired one twitched a mild smile at her, but the other brother, peering from beneath heavy, frowning eyebrows, gestured at her with his tankard, slopping wine over the brim. "By God, you're the whore we saw by the river!"

Sound and movement ceased. Servants froze. Lady Ælfthryth audibly caught her breath, pressing her fingertips to her lips. Eadric stood, his mouth open, the words that had been about to introduce his beloved daughter stilled. The insult burned red into Edyth's cheeks, the silence stretching into an embarrassment of eternity.

Then the man with the darker hair tactfully brushed his brother aside, stepped up to the girl, took her hand and formally bowed. His smile was genuine, more than just an upturn of the mouth, coming from the laughter that glistened behind his penetrating eyes. "No, brother, you are mistaken," he said, his voice rumbling, pleasant and soothing, like the sound of rippling waves caressing the shore. This is no village whore I see before me. With these sapphire eyes and flawless white skin, this lady has the beauty of a swan-maid." He took her hand, brushed her palm, lightly, with his lips. "I am Earl Harold." His gaze touched hers, lingered for a long moment, before he bowed again. "Your servant, my Lady."

And all was well, the noise of chatter and laughter resuming. The Hall was full of Eadric's neighbours from the valley and the upland forest who had come, eager, to meet their new overlord, Harold Godwinesson. Land-folk, freehold farmers, a few of Eadric's own tenants, the priest from the village of Nazeing and Abbot Osbert from the little chapel at Waltham; the smith, a giant of a man with muscles as strong as an oak tree. The potter, the cooper and the fuller, the stench of his occupation forever clinging to him. Servants bustled about their duties, pouring wine, setting the trestle tables and benches, where soon the guests would sit and eat and drink. A forgotten hen scratched at the earth floor in the far corner, the dogs jostled for the best places beneath the tables or near the hearth fire.

Edyth blushed, ducked her head from Harold's gaze. Liked the warm, excited feel that he roused within her.

❧

Swegn lurched into the side of the barn, cursed as a prominent timber-edge stabbed his shoulder, the oath followed by a belch. He would say one thing for Eadric the thegn, he certainly hosted a fine table!

After the brightness within doors it was dark out here, the night overcast, carrying a threat of more rain. The cool air slapped his hot cheeks, sobering him slightly as he strode along the narrow path, but it was slippery, and after only two unsteady paces his foot skidded in the mud. The latrine pit was somewhere over to the left, beside the high boundary fence, too far to walk in this slime. Swegn turned to face the barn wall, relieved himself against its timbers.

"So, you persist in bringing discredit to our host. Could you not hold yourself until you reached the proper place?"

Swegn looked up, but made no effort to stop the stream of urine. Finished, he readjusted his clothing and said caustically to his brother, "I care not for muddying my boots. What difference is there between a dog or a man piddling against a wall?"

Harold's smile as he walked on was sardonic. "In your instance, none at all."

Swegn took a few steps away from the barn, heading back towards the Hall and another goblet of Eadric's fine-brewed ale. Many guests had already returned to their homes, for the feasting was finished and it was growing late; only a few remained, those who lived close by, or who had elected to curl into their cloaks before the hearth fire. For those who warranted them the servants had already set the bed-places ready, hay-stuffed mattresses laid within the alcoves that ran to either side of the aisled Hall. Swegn intended to sit drinking with his father and their host for most of the night. If there was no woman to companion him, what point in seeking a bed?

He stopped, then pivoted to call to his brother's back, the night masking the ugly sneer on his face. "Then we run as a pack, you and I. Your tail has been wagging at that little swannhaels, that swan-maid bitch, all evening, has it not?"

Harold ignored him. Deep in his drink Swegn was an unpleasant man; sober, he was not much improved. The shy lass, Edyth, had amused Harold. A quiet, gentle child—no, young lady—who had blushed whenever he had caught her looking at him. It had amused him to intercept her frequent glances when he reached for bread, salt, ale or meat. Easy to make that rush of crimson flood into her pretty cheeks. All he had to do, it seemed, was smile at her. He had deliberately teased her, although it had been unfair of him, a man of his age, tormenting a young lass so. Trust Swegn, seated to the left of their own father, also to notice her flush. Whistling, Harold sauntered down the hill to the latrine. Aye, the path was muddy and only dim lit, but he would not dishonour his host's steading by piddling against the barn wall.

Reflecting on the feasting, Harold decided he very much liked the man Eadric—as his father had told him he would. Liked, also, the respect and courtesy that had been offered him from the thegn and his guests. Liked the importance that this earldom brought him. As the second-born son of the King's most senior adviser, he had expected to be granted such a position at some time in the future, but he was still young. To be awarded the responsibility of an area the size of East Anglia was a daunting prospect, which would be made easier if the thegns and minor nobles all turned out to be as pleasant, and welcoming, as Eadric.

There was another man relieving himself in the cesspit. Harold joined him at its turfed edge, wrinkling his nose at the noisome smell. Tomorrow, after so many had used it, the place would be filled, a new hole dug. A sobering thought passed through Harold's mind. Some men were born to higher status than others, some with more wit, others with greater strength and ability, but when all was weighed in the sight of God, all men, whether earl or servant, needed to piss into the same latrine.

⚭

Opening the side door, Swegn, already ruffled from bruising his shoulder and from his brother's chiding, growled as he found his path blocked by someone coming the opposite way. A dog thrust past his legs. Swegn stood, glowering, refusing to move. He was an earl. He did not step aside, especially not for a chit of a girl.

Edyth flushed. There were far too many disconcerting men here this night! The fierce but kindly Earl Godwine; Earl Harold whose laughing eyes made her stomach twist into perplexing somersaults; and Earl Swegn who made her heart lurch with fright. How could two brothers be so different, she wondered, as she flattened herself to the side of the narrow porchway, her head dipped, eyes lowered? Thor had squeezed ahead as the door had opened; she could hear him barking at her father's hunting dogs shut within the kennels.

"Excuse me my Lord," she apologised. "I did not know you were there."

Swegn pushed arrogantly past. "Keep that damned dog under control," he snapped. "He almost had me over."

"I will my Lord, I'm sorry."

Swegn's hand swung aside the doe-hide curtain, hung to deter the persistent draught, let it fall behind him, and stood for a moment within the Hall, the many smells and sounds assaulting his nostrils and ears. Sweat and other human odours mingled with the lingering aroma of stale wine, ale and food; of wood smoke, hot candle-wax, and the sawdust of the timbers of the Hall itself. The faint scent of herbs, scattered and crushed underfoot among the layers of floor rushes. His father was seated beside the hearth fire, feet resting, crossed at the ankles, on the low wall of enclosing bricks. He was laughing, his hand going forward to slap his friend Eadric's shoulder, wine slopping from a goblet clutched in his other hand. Tostig was not there; he would have found himself a bed. Tostig was not one for drinking and whoring.

Whirling around, Swegn ducked out through the curtain again, kicking the door beyond open with his boot. Damn it, why should his brother monopolise the girl? Beside being the eldest, was he not the better-looking of the two? The more experienced, the better endowed?

Edyth's heartbeat was still pounding as she crossed the courtyard. God's love but she would be pleased when these guests of her father's moved on, north-wards, tomorrow. Admittedly, it was exciting having all these people here, sharing with them a feast that, in her memory, had never before been so lavish, not even for the celebration of Yule. Exciting, but so very wearying. Oh, her father was enjoying himself, but her mother had looked flustered for most of the evening; would the wine and ale last? Would there be enough to eat, the boar and ox roasted evenly? Would Earl Godwine be comfortable in the big wooden-built box bed that sufficed for her and her husband? Huh, another thing that riled Edyth: her mother and father had given up their private chamber to the north end of the Hall for Earl Godwine; she herself had been moved out of her smaller adjoining room for the Earls Harold and Swegn. She did not much like the thought of that gruff-voiced man, Swegn, using her bed.

She kicked at a stone, sending it bouncing and tumbling ahead of her, gasped as a hand clamped her waist and fingers caught at her hair, spinning her round. A man's mouth fixed over hers, stemming the scream. He smelt of ale and sweat. His lips were wet, his moustache rough and hard against her skin. He let go of her hair, began fumbling at the lacings of her bodice. Edyth kicked, her boot slamming into his shin; his mouth left hers as he yelled at the sudden pain, but his hand tightened about her waist, pulling her body closer into his own. It gave her the opportunity to scream though, a piercing call cut off abruptly as his knuckles rammed across her cheek. She cried out, expecting a second blow and tried to break free of his grip, but a shape, huge and strong, rough-coated, silent and fast, leapt at the man. The dog's weight and impetus knocked Swegn backwards, sending him sprawling into the mud and scattered piles of dung.

As he fell, Swegn's fingers were already drawing his dagger from its leather sheath; the dog, snarling and growling, had his teeth fixed firmly into his lower leg. The padding of the cross-gaitered leggings protected the flesh, but those jaws were clamped as tight as a snare. Lying sprawled on his back, Swegn tried to shake the beast off, cursing and shouting.

Men were coming from the Hall, another running from the path beside the barn. Swegn managed to bring his weapon up, ripped it through the dog's throat. The animal yelped, blood sluicing in a gush of red stickiness. Edyth, standing with her hands over her mouth, screamed again, her anguish thundering up to the rain-laden clouds. She ran forward, falling to her knees, cradling Thor as he whimpered, tried to lick her face. Died.

Tears cascading her cheeks, she cried, "You bastard! You bastard! You've killed my dog!"

"Bloody thing attacked me!" Swegn was scrabbling to his feet, men and women from the Hall, from outbuildings, the kitchen place, gathering round with solemn faces. Godwine was there, pushing his way through the crowd; Eadric; Edyth's mother, her hair unbound for she had been preparing herself for her bed, a pace behind, a woollen cloak flung carelessly around her shoulders.

"Damn thing was vicious!" Swegn said again.

"He was protecting the girl!" Harold was there, angry. "Protecting her from you," he repeated, taking a step nearer, jaw clenched.

Swegn ostentatiously sheathed his dagger, spread his hands, protesting his innocence. "Nonsense. I was merely intending to—"

Harold brought his left hand up, the knuckles balling into a fist, ploughing into Swegn's face, sending him sprawling on to his backside. "I saw what you were doing, saw it all. You disgust me! You, my own brother, bring dishonour to me. Disgrace me before these good people who have freely offered hospitality. How dare you?" Bending, Harold's fingers tightened around Swegn's tunic neckband and dragged him to his feet. "Someone saddle his horse!" he ordered. "You will leave here, now."

When a man is caught in the wrong, often his only defence is anger. Swegn turned on his brother, his dagger coming automatically back into his hand. He hurled his own left fist into Harold's belly and, almost within the same movement, brought his knee up into his groin. Harold doubled over, let go his hold of the neckband, air whooshing from his mouth, and Swegn leapt forward, the blade stabbing down, ripping through Harold's cloak and tunic, gouging a diagonal path of blood that instantly welled and oozed through the torn fabric.

Bellowing, Godwine clamped his broad hands on to his eldest son's shoulders, threw him to his knees, snatched the weapon from his hand. "Do you dare disgrace me also?" he roared. "Drawing a blade on your own brother? Brawling like some gutter-slave? Get you to your horse and go!"

"I'll not be ordered about by a younger brother…"

"It is not a younger brother who commands you," Harold gasped, stumbling to his feet, his right hand clutching at his left shoulder.

"It is the Earl of East Anglia who speaks. You will leave my earldom or face a charge of incitement to war and therefore answer to the King. A charge that carries the penalty of treason."

Swegn glowered at his father. "Are you going to allow him to treat me like this? Let him insult me, accuse me, before all these people?"

Godwine answered his eldest son with a brusque snap of undisputed authority. "He is earl of these people, not I. It is his word to be obeyed here, not mine."

A servant had run for the stables, saddled Swegn's horse and brought him out, followed by the four men of Swegn's personal guard, his accompanying housecarls. Swegn swung into the saddle and, angrily pulling the horse's head round, spurred it into a canter. As he rode towards the opening gate he shouted defiantly, "Have the little whore for yourself then, brother. I hope she carries the pox!"

Harold winced. So, this was something else that he had gained from being given the honour of an earldom. He had position and wealth, coupled with respect and admiration, but from his younger brother, Tostig, there were signs of emerging jealousy and from his elder brother a declaration of dislike that had passed beyond the petty squabbling of siblings. Harold had acquired authority and, in this instance, did not much like its company.

The girl was bent over the dog, cradling his warm body, her head buried into his rough coat, shoulders heaving as she sobbed. Ignoring the blood running down his arm, Harold hunkered down beside her, did not know what to say. "I'm sorry, lass," was all he could think of. It did not seem adequate. He was not surprised that he received no reply.

4

Wilton Nunnery

Earl Godwine's daughter, Edith, skipped excitedly down the three steps that led from the guest apartments, her white linen veil fluttering, her arms spread wide. If the abbess had seen her, she would have been sharply reprimanded. Ladies, especially within the confines of the nunnery, did not run nor did they raise their voices, unless singing praise to God.

"Harold!" Edith shouted, breaking into a faster run as her feet touched the paving of the courtyard. "Where have you been? You are the last to arrive, all the others are here. We have been waiting for you!"

The man entering through the far gateway, leading his stallion out of deference to the holy sisters, looked up and smiled. Edith always had been an exuberant child. Wilton was the best scholastic institution in all England for the rearing of titled young ladies; she received a fine education here, could read and write Latin, Greek, French and English, speak Danish and Gaelic with fluency; could sew and weave, sing, and play music—but never, Harold maintained, would she learn the discipline of modesty.

"Sister!" he responded, passing the reins to his servant and lengthening his stride to meet the running girl halfway across the wide expanse of the paved courtyard. A few early-fallen autumn leaves, hustled by the boisterous wind, whirled in a brief dance, while the stately elm trees, marching behind the east wall, rustled with its passing. Away to the left the rooks were noisily squabbling and the delicious smell of new-baked bread wafted from the bakehouse. Wilton was a welcoming place, serene, yet homely. "I am certain you have grown since I saw you last in Winchester at Easter!" Harold declared, catching Edith around the waist and whirling her high in the air.

She was a pretty girl with unblemished skin, wide blue eyes, fair hair and a mouth that could form easily into a smile. Edith put her hands on her brother's broad shoulders, squealed with indignation as he swung her upwards.

"Put me down!" she demanded, wagging an admonishing finger as he set her on her feet. "You must not do that. I am no longer a child to be tossed and played with, I am come to fourteen years of age this day." He ought not to have to be reminded of such an important matter!

Suitably chastised, Harold nodded gravely. "Indeed, you are becoming too old for childhood games. Too old for presents also, I assume?"

Her frown instantly disappearing, Edith ran to the servant's packhorse and began to rummage at the intriguing bundles strapped to its back. "What have you brought me?" she asked, breathless. "Father and Mother have given me a fine ruby necklace and Swegn"—she turned to look at Harold, her eyes sparkling— "Swegn has brought me a pony! It comes from the mountains of Wales. The best birthing-day present I have ever had!"

Harold said nothing as he began unlacing one of the larger bundles. It was inevitable that Swegn would be here to celebrate their sister's special day, but Harold had half hoped that the eldest-born might have been busy elsewhere, snared by duties within his own earldom of the Welsh border Marches.

The quarrel that had occurred between them at Easter had not ceased. That insult to their host and his daughter—the insult and injury to Harold—had been unacceptable. The wound had been deep, slow to mend, and had left a scar that slanted from collarbone to shoulder. Harold had been justified in demanding Swegn leave East Anglia, but was it justifiable to continue this displeasure at his brother's drunken behaviour?

Hopping from foot to foot, impatient for Harold to untie the cloth-wrapped package, Edith told him of the pony: "I have called him Hafren, after the Welsh name for the border river. He is a grey, neat little ears and a long mane and tail. Very placid-tempered."

"Hah! He's not like the rest of the Welsh then! Nor the brother who gave him to you," Harold remarked sarcastically. He lifted the rolled bundle down and passed it to his sister. "I trust he is in a more agreeable humour than when I last saw him?"

Edith ignored the comment. From Tostig's frequent letters she knew of the rift between her two eldest brothers. He had, no doubt, elaborated the facts, but even allowing for Tostig's exaggeration, for two men to fight over a dead dog…oh, for heaven's sake! But then, the two brothers rarely needed much of an excuse to be at each other's throats.

Edith unrolled the parcel to disclose a fur cloak. Tossing its weight around her shoulders, she stroked the softness. "I can wear it when I am riding my pony," she said, delighted.

"It's marten," Harold protested gently. "Very expensive."

"So was the pony," growled a man's voice from behind them, Harold swung round, came face to face with his brother Swegn. For a long moment they regarded each other through narrowed eyes. Was the argument over?

"So, the new earl comes in all his glory," Swegn observed, fingering the rich cloth and fur trimmings of Harold's own mantle. "East Anglia's taxes are of benefit it seems."

"My revenue is no greater than is yours, brother."

"Maybe not, but you do not have to supervise an unsettled border that has heathen Welsh regularly swarming across it to raid, burn and steal."

"Things appear calm enough if you can purchase their ponies."

"Ah!" Swegn barked. "The Welsh make sport out of annoying us English, but equally, they seize any chance to part us from our gold!" With the knack that Swegn had of abruptly changing mood, he clapped Harold's shoulder and then elaborately embraced him. The dispute was over then, Harold returned the embrace and together they walked towards the guest chambers, Edith trotting happily between them, chattering about the entertainment planned for her visiting family. A cynical thought crossed Harold's mind, but he shrugged it aside. What was Swegn after? Something important enough for him to swallow his pride and admit he had been in the wrong? It might not have been much of an apology, that embrace, but it had been, without doubt, a gesture of repentance. It would be churlish not to accept the peace offering; all the same, the suspicion that had come so easily into Harold's mind stayed there.

⤙⤙⤚

A young novice crept into the guest hall where the Godwine family and the Abbess of Wilton were seated, engaged in the easy conversation that flows between long-term friends and kindred. She dipped a reverence before the Abbess, whispered a message into her ear. The lady listened, nodded. For a few seconds she sat, fingers interlaced, thoughtful. Noticing, Earl Godwine asked with concern, "My Lady? Is anything amiss?"

The Abbess smiled warmly and stood. Out of courtesy to her status the men in the room, Godwine and his sons, rose also. "No, nothing is amiss, merely"—she laughed lightly—"a little awkward." She spread her hands, her smile remaining wide. "It seems that the Queen is to arrive at Wilton, seeking accommodation for the night."

Godwine too smiled, although no one else in the room echoed his pleasure. "My Lady Emma, arriving here? This is indeed a pleasant coincidence!" He turned to his daughter. "Edith, get you out into the courtyard to greet her. The Queen will not be aware that it is your birthing-day, she must be invited to join our family celebration. One of you boys go also." Godwine flapped his hand at his group of sons who exchanged rueful glances. Harold shrugged good-naturedly. Obedient, but with a sullen scowl, Edith left the room, accompanied by the novice and Harold.

The Countess Gytha, Godwine's Danish-born wife, had already realised the dilemma this posed the Abbess, even if her husband had not. She rose to her feet. A placid, genial woman, Gytha was doubly blessed with handsome looks and an alert mind. Evening was an hour or so away; soon the abbey gates would be closed and locked, the nuns seeking the solitude of prayer and then their beds. The guest apartments would be lit with candles and torches, supper served and wine brought; talk and laughter would last, in this quarter of the nunnery, well into the late hours of darkness. "The Abbess, my dear," she said, threading her arm through her husband's, "is placed in a somewhat difficult domestic position. The Queen will be requiring the principal bed-chamber."

Godwine frowned, not understanding her.

"Husband, it has already been allotted to us."

With gallantry, embarrassed that he had not immediately seen the problem for himself, Godwine stepped forward and raised the Abbess's hand, touching his lips to her ring. "My good Lady, there is no difficulty. We will remove ourselves to a different chamber this instant."

"My Lord Earl, that is most kind of you, but where can I put you? Your sons have our other chambers." The Abbess's concern showed clearly in her expression. Wilton was a place that relied heavily on noble patronage; it could not afford to offend anyone, least of all the King's mother or the Earls Godwine, Swegn and Harold.

"One of them will share," Godwine gazed expectantly across the room at his eldest, Swegn, whose answering, lazy smile was uncharacteristically co-operative.

"No problem, I'll go in with Harold."

⁓

Within the half of an hour the Earl's personal belongings were removed from one chamber to another and Emma was settling herself, washing her face and hands from a bowl of warmed, rose-scented water, changing travel-stained garments for fresh robes. Her journey to Wilton had been annoyingly interrupted by a series of delays ranging from a lame horse to a fallen bridge, washed away by the recent rain. Her intention had been to arrive earlier in the afternoon, preferably before Earl Godwine—but no matter, as long as her meeting with him appeared to be by chance…

Emma contemplated her reflection, distorted slightly by the curve of the silver hand mirror. She was still a handsome woman, despite four and fifty years of more disappointments than happiness. The lines creased around her blue eyes, mouth and chin, and the predominance of silver in what had once been sun-gold hair, added wisdom to her looks, not age. Her cheeks were more hollow than a few years ago, and her long, slender hands were wrinkled and brown-flecked, with knuckles that were beginning to bend and ache. But her mind was as alert as ever it had been; her thoughts as quick, her expectations as high.

The succession of tragedies, the broken hopes, the faded dreams, had all taken their toll of her energy, and occasionally her will to go on. But Emma was descended from a warrior race, the North Men, the Viking seafarers, and like those infamous ancestors she was a fighter, one who would unflinchingly face death rather than admit to the shame of defeat.

And she would not, *would not*, be defeated by the spineless toad-spawn that was her only surviving son, Edward!

She flicked her fingers at her handmaid, indicating that she was ready to have her veil fastened in place and leave her chamber, to join Godwine and his family. With a smile that barely touched her lips, she took a small, moderately valuable brooch from her jewel box. A gift for Edith. Nothing, no action, no word, must give the impression that this meeting was anything but coincidence. Edward had his spies, he mistrusted her as much as she did him—perhaps he was not so much the fool after all? Left to make his own decisions, he was an incompetent, but as king he had the benefit of older and wiser men to advise him. Men like the Earls of Mercia and Northumbria, shrewd men, who mistrusted the easy friendship that existed between Godwine and the woman who had once held the reins of power in England. And, despite his personal inadequacies, Edward knew only too well the extent of his mother's capabilities. Aye, if the Queen wished to have a confidential word with Earl Godwine it must be done with great care.

Just in case Edward found the sense to listen to advice and had employed someone to watch her.

⟨⟩

The bed-chamber door closed with a shuddering bang, the ensuing draught sending the lamplight twisting and flickering. As he entered and crossed to a table on the far side, Swegn's distorted shadow leapt grotesquely against the richly embroidered wall coverings. "Wine?" he asked, his voice loud in the quiet of the room. Not waiting for an answer, he poured two generous goblets.

Harold closed the bed fur tighter round his body, willing sleep to return.

"You're not asleep, are you?" Swegn turned to face the bed, incredulous; it was not yet the tenth hour. He strode across the room, pulled back one of the partially drawn bed curtains and roughly shook the mound that was Harold. "I want to speak with you."

Emerging from the furs, Harold blinked wearily. He had known sharing a chamber with Swegn would not be a good idea. "I'm tired." He yawned. "Today I had a long ride, tomorrow I have another. The lure of sleep, Swegn, is more enticing than conversation with you. Can it not wait until morning?"

Swegn proffered the goblet in his hand. Harold sighed, swung his legs from the bed and pulled one of the furs around his shoulders. With the brazier offering only a dull, half-hearted glow, the room was chill and draughty, with tendrils of a northerly wind scurrying beneath the ill-fitting door and through numerous cracks in the timber walls. Several of the tapestries were rippling, restless, nudged by the constant irritation.

Swegn selected wood from the pile and chivvied the reluctant fire into life. Going back to the table, he lifted his own goblet, took a deep swallow, licked his lips and wiped the residue from the trail of his moustache with the back of his hand. He had already drunk well all evening, but there was always room in his belly for more. "Wilton has two things worth this annual, tedious family reunion." He drank again, belched. "The lure of untouched virgins and the best wine in all England."

Harold sipped at the goblet in his own hand, tucking the fur tighter around his legs. He wore woollen braies and stockings, but still his feet were cold. With his brother's second comment he could not disagree, but for the first? Ah, Swegn had never been one for minding his manners.

"What is it you want?" Harold queried. Another yawn, wide and lingering, rippled through him. He brushed bleary tears of tiredness from his eyes.

"Want? I want nothing." Swegn's protest came too quickly. "I wish to talk, brother to brother." His accompanying smile was intended to be reassuring; to Harold it was more of a leer. "Earl to earl."

Harold did not believe a word of it. "Talk? About what?" When had they ever talked, as opposed to quarrelled? As young men? Harold could not remember a time when the two had exchanged conversation for the simple pleasure of it. As boys? Incessant squabbling in childhood, mostly at Swegn's instigation, had put an end to any prospect of brotherly companionship. If they had never been friends as children, what hope had they, as grown men, of seeing eye to eye?

"How are you finding East Anglia? It is a rich earldom, is it not?" Swegn hooked the room's only stool nearer the brazier with his foot, seated himself close to its meagre warmth. His next comment held a tinge of the jealousy that had ever haunted his life. "You have ample opportunity for expanding your purse, I would wager."

Harold did not rise to the jibe. "Aye," he said indifferently, "wool, salt and corn, among other industries, provide well enough for a king's revenue."

The King's revenue. Taxation. Two inescapable curses of both rich and poor: famine, and taxes. Only a king was certain of a full belly and enough gold to fill the household coffers. And in return for overseeing their designated portions of the King's realm the earls—providing they stayed in favour—received a handsome share of those taxes. Except, in Swegn's considered opinion, some had a more prosperous share than others.

East Anglia, because of its greater size and location, was wealthier than his own fluctuating Borders. Trade flourished in East Anglia, an area of wide skies sailing above fertile land, land which abutted the eastward coast, with safe harbours and bustling ports; land traversed by tranquil rivers and dotted with established, profitable farmsteadings. What had he, Swegn, to his name? Hostile forests and isolated towns cowering behind timber fortifications, all overshadowed by the damned, persistent raiding of the Welsh. And drenched by incessant rain.

"Constant patrolling ensures that my purse remains thin." Swegn swilled the last dregs of wine around his goblet, watching the pattern of red liquid swirl against the silver. He looked up at his brother, the accusation there behind his voice. "Edward favoured you more than me when he gave you the peaceful fenlands of East Anglia."

Harold's angry response came unchecked. He leapt to his feet, sending wine splashing over the rim of his cup. "Peaceful? The Fens? Do you know how many Viking raiding parties we chased offshore last month? Do you know how much trade has been lost to pirates cruising my coast, like basking whales? Three families were butchered but last week at Maldon…"

"Only three?" Swegn retorted with a sneer. "I have lost more than three and twenty to the Welsh!" He had been about to jump to his feet also, but he fought down the impulse. He could not, on this occasion, afford to quarrel with his brother. Taking a deep breath, he patted the air soothingly with a palm. "Nay, I do not want argument. Of course you have problems with our Scandinavian cousins, but you have a fair income to counterbalance your costs. Between them, the two Welsh princes of north and south are bleeding me dry. Gryffydd ap Rhydderch, of the south, Deheubarth, is the worst offender."

In no mood for hard words, Harold sank back on to the bed. It was late, he wanted to sleep. "Can you not contain the border raiding? Surely, with the men of the fyrd, you have adequate resources to keep watch on those few crossing places over the Severn river?"

"What? The whole year round? There is a limit to how many weeks the fyrd will be called out and these Welsh are wild mountain men, brother, they do not respect inclement weather, as would you or I." Swegn drained his wine. "What I need to do is hit at them, hard. Burn a few of their farms, slaughter their cattle, take their women and children as slaves." Swegn stood, walked with quick strides to stand before his brother. "I need to take an English army into Wales, teach Gryffydd a lesson that he will not forget."

"Good idea," Harold mumbled drowsily.

Swegn reached forward to grasp his brother's arm. "I have just come from the Queen, from Emma. She has promised me handsome financial aid. If you provide the additional men I need, I can—"

Harold jerked awake, sat up. "What!"

"I need men. Your men. I have not the ability to furnish an army from my own paltry earldom. With Emma's promised aid I can have gold to arm them, to feed them, all I need is the men…"

Harold thrust Swegn aside, scrabbling to his feet. "Are you moon-mad?"

"How else can I protect my wealth? I do not have the easy picking that you have been given, brother!" The rage was swelling, red and blotched, over Swegn's face.

Ignoring the last insult, for in his anger he had barely heard it, Harold bellowed an answer. "And what will the King make of such an army?"

"To protect his realm from the heathen Welsh?" Swegn's retort was scathing. "He will welcome it!"

"Two earls of the same kindred combining their power? Aided by his mother's gold? You fool!" Harold stormed to the far side of the room, as if to distance himself from his brother's stupidity. "Edward will assume us—you—to be gathering an army against him."

Swegn flapped a hand dismissively. "Nonsense."

"Are you so inane? Why do you think Emma is here at the same time as our father? She knows full well that we come to Wilton on this date to visit our sister. Her arrival was no coincidence—though Edward would be hard pushed to prove it so. She will fund you, Swegn, but not to furnish an army for Wales. When Edward decides to move against his mother's meddling in royal affairs our father must side with the King. She is here, mark my words, with the hope of enticing the most powerful earl in all England to support her." Harold crossed back to the bed, retrieved his boots from where he had left them beneath it, lifted his cloak and scabbard from a hook in a timber wall post. "I would prefer to spend the night with our youngest brothers. They sleep more soundly than do you." He strode to the door, opened it, looked back over his shoulder, said, "I would assume our father has already rejected the Queen's plea for aid. You, on the other hand, by supplying her with an army, have walked right into her political web." He stepped through the door, adding, as he began to walk again, "Treason, when kings come to hear of it, is not rewarded well, brother. Think on that."

5

London

King Edward sat huddled beneath the heavy weight of his cloak, his hands stuffed beneath his armpits in a futile attempt to keep the bite of cold from his fingers. He was certain his toes had already dropped off, for he could no longer feel them, although his doe-hide boots, like the cloak, were well lined with warm squirrel fur. A swirl of wind-driven rain spattered down the smoke hole in the thatched roof of this, his King's Hall, the curl of smoke from the hearth fire billowing in sullen clouds beneath the high dust and cobweb-draped rafters. The glistening drops of rain sizzled and hissed into the sulking flames below. This was a dismal place, Edward thought, a creaking, smoke-blackened, wind-battered, timber-built archaic old building. The palace of London—huh! He had never much liked it, nor even as a child when his father, Æthelred, had sat here in this very same royal chair. All those years ago he had regarded this Hall as cold and unwelcoming. A king's palace? Peasant's bothy more like! In Normandy the grand dukes built their fortified residences of stone. Stone that was hard to penetrate by wind and army. Stone that displayed strength and grandeur. And permanence. He would build in stone one day, when he could muster the funding. When his damned mother let go her clutch over the royal treasury.

He dabbed at his nose with the edge of his cloak, certain he was beginning a head cold; his throat felt sore and dry, nose running and swollen, his temples throbbed. Mind, his head always ached whenever Emma was present.

Glowering, Edward looked across at her, seated on her queen's throne a few yards to his left, sited, at his ordering, as far along the dais as was possible. She sat erect, resplendent in her robes, precious jewels sparkling. The council of earls and nobles sat arrayed semicircular before the dais, most eyes not on him, but fixed on the figure of the Queen. He shifted, on this uncomfortable, hard-backed, hard-seated throne, shivering, pulling the cloak tighter around his chest, as the debate swirled around him. Each speaker disagreed with the last, the argument going fruitlessly round and round. Not one of them bothered to ask him, the King, for his opinion on the matter. All seemed to defer to his mother's view, even those who usually disagreed with her as a matter of course—notably Siward and Leofric. Irritated at being ignored, Edward pouted. "I do not want Stigand to be appointed as bishop of East Anglia, Mother. He is of your choosing, not mine."

The talk faded as eyes and attention turned to the King. Emma exhaled slowly, holding hard to her patience. What did he know of the delicate task of appointing a new bishop? If the wrong man were to be put in the wrong place—God's breath, such ineptitude could, overnight, deliver irretrievable power direct into the hands of Rome!

"My Lord King," she said, a thick mask of honey disguising her annoyance, "I do but use my years of acquired wisdom to advise you. Stigand is a talented and able cleric with an acute grasp of politics." She smiled pleasantly at her son, though the expression was difficult to maintain. Her fingers itched to slap the peevish defiance from his sullen cheeks; to control her hands she curled her grip around the lioness-heads that formed the carved arms of her chair. Cnut had ordered it made for her, soon after their marriage. He had been a magnificent king, Cnut, strong in body, wise, determined yet open to well-constructed argument. Would England ever see his like again? Not in her son, that was for certain.

"My Lord." With a modest cough to attract attention, Godwine came to his feet. "This matter has now been discussed at great length. We all"—and he swept his hand around the semicircle of men—"agree that you require a man whose loyalty can be relied upon without question—"

"Loyalty?" Edward interjected with a stab of petulant sarcasm. "To whom?"

"Why"—Godwine spread his hands, innocently puzzled—"to you, Lord. You are the King. To you, and to England."

"Huh! To my mother, more like." Edward muttered, slumping further into the cocoon of his cloak.

Giving a small acknowledging bow, Earl Harold stood. Godwine granted him precedence by resuming his seat. Harold had grown in confidence since the Easter festivities, the responsibility of overseeing such a great earldom igniting his abilities. He took his duties seriously—although the lure of a comely woman or the thrill of the hunt could still divert his attention a little too easily. For over an hour the deciding who ought to be bishop had rumbled on and although the inclement weather outside was hardly enticing, Harold had much to do. If he did not leave for Essex soon, he would need delay the journey until the morrow. Another night in this dreary royal stronghold? His groan of dismay at the thought was almost audible. "Sire," he coaxed with a warm smile, "the coastal lands of East Anglia are under severe threat from Magnus of Norway. It is highly probable that the present irregular sea raids may escalate next spring into full-scale invasion. Magnus regards his claim to your throne as just and valid. I need strong men of influence at my back if I am to maintain authority and calm among the populace of that part of your kingdom." Harold put as much emphasis on his point as he could. Come the passing of winter, England could well be at war with Norway, and East Anglia or the coast of Kent would be Magnus's battleground.

Stigand was a shrewd and politically capable man. Despite his personal dislike of him, Harold knew he would be an effective bishop. A man who could keep a firm hand on the greed of certain prelates within the church hierarchy, would be equally capable of instilling trust into the land-folk and the men who would be called upon to make up the army of the fyrd. What more could he add to the argument already put forward? "I support the recommendation of Stigand; he would be welcome in my earldom." Harold, glancing ruefully at his father, sat.

Wind battered against the window shutters—which, closed, did little to keep out the draught, but effectively barred light—rapping as if demanding entrance. Dusk would be falling within three hours. Earl Siward of Northumbria glanced at his ally, Leofric of Mercia, who shrugged. Neither wanted to stay longer than necessary at this council. In Siward's opinion, Stigand was naught but a backside licker, a secretive and ambitious cleric who served Emma. There was a rumour that the Queen wanted to place Magnus of Norway on the throne of England and Stigand was of Viking descent. Undoubtedly, Stigand supported Emma's scheming and whoever supported the Queen most assuredly also supported the Godwines. More arse washers! Between them, the Godwines held over-much power. And the lady presumed, too often, on the authority that she had once held in the past. Stigand, in Siward's mistrusting mind, was not the right man for a bishopric but perhaps it was wise to give the man enough rope to form himself a noose, one that could eventually loop around Emma's interfering neck also. Siward did not stand, he merely lifted his right hand, spread his fingers in a gesture of submission. "Godwine and Harold talk sense. Northumbria does not object."

Edward's pout intensified. If Siward and Leofric had put up more of a fight… oh, curse it, let the damn woman have her way! His head was pounding, he needed wine and the privacy of his chamber. The King flapped his hand at the cleric seated at a table below the dais. "Record the decision. Stigand is to be appointed Bishop of East Anglia." He brushed the cloak from his shoulders, made to stand, all others in the Hall instantly coming to their feet, save for Emma.

"Edward," she said, in the unconsciously supercilious tone that so irritated her son. "We are not yet concluded." She indicated that he ought to sit; he ignored her, remained pointedly standing, forcing her to rise also. None sat in the presence of a king who was standing, not even a queen, his mother.

She was a tall woman, Emma, thin of figure and face, her manner and voice austere, with little hint of laughter or gentleness about her features or character. Those qualities normally associated with the women's side of the hearth had been sapped from her, years past, by the succession of scandals and sorrows she had endured. Standing, erect and proud, her gold coronet reflected the flickering of the many torches set about the walls. The rubies in her necklace sparkled blood-red. "We have yet to discuss the matter of your marriage," she said. "A king must take a wife, A king must have sons."

"A king must rule his people and serve God," Edward retorted. "I do not wish for a wife."

Earl Godwine spoke, placating. "Lord, is it not your duty—"

Edward rounded on him with venom. "Do not remind me of duty sir! It is you, and the traitors you breed for sons, who need reminding of duty!"

Godwine, and Harold beside him, both reddened, both unintentionally glanced up at Emma.

Hurriedly Godwine said, "I am not responsible for my son Swegn. He is earl under your orders, Sire. He acts against Wales in your name."

"With an army of men paid for by my mother?" Edward strode towards Emma, his face contorted by rage. "And where will they march, I wonder, when Swegn has finished playing his game of shadow-chasing in the Welsh mist? To East Anglia? To join with this new bishop who is a lick-spit to you—to swell Norway's army when Magnus comes, at your invitation, to try the fit of my crown?"

Emma reacted immediately. "Do you seriously think I would prefer one who is not of my own blood as king? For all that our opinions differ, you are my son. Magnus is not." With practised skill she returned to safer ground. "Is it not wise," she said, her tone patronising, "to stem the menace that is repeatedly harrying our Welsh borders? Give the Celts free rein and there will be no end to their audacity."

Edward conceded the point, but added with a snarl, "I would have preferred to have been consulted." His mother was the taller by more than a hand-span, he needed to look up to stare into her eyes. "I will let your new-trained lapdog run on his leash, madam, but I warn you, and you, sir." He spun around to face Godwine, his slender finger pointing accusingly. "I warn you, if Swegn fails to subdue the Welsh, if he wastes the lives of English men and the coin of my treasury, then he and you will reimburse me for his incompetence."

Edward departed, stumbling down the dais steps in his haste to leave. Emma sank into her chair, a brief sigh escaping her lips. Her son tired her so. Swegn would not do well in Wales, he was too brash, too angry to plan properly, but she needed men such as he loyal to her, to be indebted to her. Swegn, unlike his father—or his brother Harold—would never be troubled by his conscience. And if Magnus should indeed consider securing England for himself, should cease his drunken boasting and act upon his rumoured threats…? Well, Emma would need the rash, the ambitious—and the indebted—to ensure her own safety. Could she perhaps retain her position of Queen Regent under Magnus? A pity it had to be Swegn who had agreed to be her sworn man at Wilton, not the more reliable and competent father, but Godwine might change his mind if the Vikings decided to come raiding next spring.

❧

Edward sank gratefully on to the embracing comfort of his bed, his arm shielding his face. "Fetch me wine, Robert," he ordered in a frail voice. "I need wine to swill the foul taste of my mother from my mouth."

Robert Champart was already pouring, for he well knew how tense Edward would be after yet another confrontation with that wretched woman. He disliked Emma, judged her guilty of the sins of murder, avarice, treachery and, although it had never been proven, adultery. She would be accountable for that, if not to the justice of this world, then most certainly to the final judgement of God.

For her part, Emma considered Robert, former Abbot of Jumièges, a zealously religious man of middle years, to be arrogant, conceited, hypocritical and re-pugnantly over-ambitious. There was something suspicious, she felt, about him. Why had he been so eager to leave behind the quiet contemplation of a Norman abbey to become chaplain and confessor to the King of England? Undoubtedly Champart had no intention of remaining in such a humble position for long, not when there was a chance of a bishopric to be filled.

Robert held the goblet against the king's dry lips, supporting his sagging body around the shoulders with his other arm. Edward sipped and swallowed, his hand resting lightly over Robert's, his long white fingers touching the firm strength of his chaplain's. Their eyes met.

"Where would I be without you, Robert?" Edward sighed. "You supported me during those long years of exile. Gave me succour and guidance while I was deprived of my rightful kingdom. And you are with me now, when I am in sore need of companionship."

Robert desperately wanted to ask who had been awarded the honour of East Anglia. Stigand, he assumed. That God-cursed, sour-faced, obnoxious man,

Stigand. Of course it would be he. Emma's grovelling little runt. Robert had no hope of advancement while she clung so obstinately to her title. She must be toppled; must fall from power! He stroked back the fine, pale hair that had flopped forward over Edward's pain-furrowed brow, his crooning voice making low, soothing noises.

Edward exaggerated, of course, but it was not Robert's position to correct an anointed king. If he cared to believe that Robert Champart had been his confidant and friend throughout his exile, then who was Robert to demur? In truth, they had known each other only eight short years, since Edward had left the household of his uncle, Duke Robert of Normandy. While the Duke had lived, Edward had been safe under his protection. An uncle had nothing to fear from an impoverished nephew, but the situation had changed under an only bastard-born son. A seven-year-old boy, with ducal responsibility thrust prematurely upon him, had everything to fear from men grown; men who could, so easily, relieve him of a duchy. Edward had not felt welcome under the patronage of the boy, William, and had removed himself to the sanctity of the abbey at Jumièges, where Robert was abbot. Their mutual liking was instantaneous, but Robert, an ambitious man, saw all too clearly how he could benefit from friendship with one who could claim the title of king. Robert, for all his dedication to God, had few scruples when it came to pursuing his own advancement.

A shy young man, Edward had fallen under Robert's quiet, contemplative spell; he had found, for the first time in his lonely life, sympathy and companionship. Edward, who had not known the love of a mother or the pride of a father, loved Robert.

Edward had been considering taking monastic vows but, unexpectedly, England had recalled her exiled heir to the throne and Robert had not hesitated to accept the request to accompany him home. Eight years, now, had Robert known Edward, and for eight years had he waited to rid the son of the vile influence of the mother.

It seemed that Edward slept, for he lay quiet, his chest slowly rising and falling. Carefully, Robert removed the King's boots, laid a fur over his resting body and murmured a prayer of protection—gasped with surprise as Edward, eyes closed, spoke. Yet it was not the suddenness of the voice that startled Robert, but the words.

"My mother wishes me to take a wife, but I do not care to be harangued by another woman's tongue."

Robert paled; sickness rose into his throat. Edward? Take a wife? A wife who would be constantly at Edward's side, who would influence him, divert his mind? A woman who would negate the necessity for him, Robert, to tend all Edward's needs? How could Robert tolerate the presence of another dictatorial harridan? Yet, as king, Edward must have his queen. A slow smile played around the corners of Robert's lips as the initial shock gave ground to sensible thinking. The blood returned to his pallid cheeks and his bouncing heartbeat steadied.

Had Emma considered this adequately? Had she, at last, made her fatal mistake? She probably had a scheme in mind, but what if Robert could out-manoeuvre her?

Until a king's wife was anointed as queen, the dowager retained the title, the power and influence—king's mothers in the past had taken great care that their daughters-in-law never received the church's official blessing of anointing. Was that Emma's intention? To marry Edward to some pale-faced, timid mouse of a girl who would never dare stand up to a woman who adamantly refused to relinquish the title of queen?

But what if Edward were to take a girl of different character? A girl of courage and ambition—or, if such a child did not exist, then one who had a father with power enough to enforce her rights?

Robert's eyes narrowed, a faint smile painted across his lips. It would be an-noying to share Edward's devotion with a woman, but Robert could endure that. The smile widened into an expression of reassurance as the King opened his eyes. "The right woman, my Lord King, could bring you much happiness."

Edward's mouth dropped into a childish pout. He detested women.

"A wife, Sire, could set you free. She must make certain vows to her husband." Robert tucked the bed fur more comfortably beneath Edward's chin. "She must vow to love and honour her lord." Added pointedly, "And, unlike a mother, must, without question, vow obedience."

6

⤙⤚

Bosham

Countess Gytha was well used to offering hospitality to the king, for his visits to her husband's Sussex estate were frequent, but on this occasion Edward's presence was proving difficult. The hunting would be poor, for an early frost lay heavy on the ground, with the stream beyond the manor wall already partially frozen. Ice had wallowed on the edge of the tide this morning, a rind of glistening white around the rim of the bay. Supervising the choice of preserves and joints of meat to provide respectable feasting, Gytha suppressed a churn of tempestuous anger. This embarrassment was Swegn's doing, damn the boy! When would he assume the responsibilities that ran with his age and position as eldest-born son? When would he recognise the consequences of these fool actions of his? It really was too bad of him to put the family in such an awkward situation!

Swegn's disastrous foray into Wales had caused nothing but problems for his father and brothers—and for her, for to the Countess fell the task of soothing a husband's and a brother's frayed temper. Edward was obviously deeply affronted by Swegn making alliance with Queen Emma—why else would he come south to Bosham at this time of year? He rarely hunted far from his own manor when the days were short and the weather so inclement. Was it possible to believe that this unexpected visit was nothing more than a whim? Of course not! By the middle of the October month, Swegn had been whipped out of Wales like a runt hound, barely escaping with his skin intact. Gryffydd son of Rhydderch had pissed his breeches laughing at the incompetence of the English, of Godwine's son, so rumour said. And to make an even greater fool of himself, Swegn had retained the men that Emma had allotted him—those few poor wretches who had made it back across the Severn in one piece, that is. A sensible man would have gone straight to his king, presented them into his service—but, oh no, not Swegn! Gytha, after years of denying it, finally conceded that her first-born had not an ounce of sense to his name.

"The pork," she said, pointing to a half-side of salted bacon hanging from one of the many rafters. The storage place of Godwine's Manor was rectangular, wattle-walled with a low shingle roof, the interior cellar-like, with several wooden steps descending two feet below ground level to a floor of laid slate: thick, hard-wearing slabs that repelled rodents and remained cool even on the warmest of days. An earl such as Godwine was expected to maintain a plentiful store of meat and grain for his household and guests. After the recent harvest— which had, for the sixth consecutive year, proven good throughout Wessex, the containers of preserved fruits and root vegetables were full; cheeses, wrapped in linen, were stacked to ripen and mature; meat of varying cuts was hung, smoked, from hooks, or packed into layers of salt within wooden barrels. "We will have that side of beef also," the Countess added, thoughtfully surveying the ample stocks, "and this one."

"What about these birds, my Lady? They are plump, and have hung an adequate time."

Absently Gytha nodded. Cedric was a capable steward who had served her and her husband from the time of their marriage. He did not require supervision— but she had welcomed an excuse to leave the Hall and the sullen-faced presence of King Edward. If he should openly accuse her husband of treachery because of Swegn's imbecility she would...Gytha sighed, wiped her hands on the square of rough linen that hung around her waist to protect her best gown from dirt and stains. What would she do? What could she do? Very little, apart from appease Edward by providing him with a sumptuous meal and bidding him welcome to Bosham Manor.

The steward sensed something of his mistress's apprehension, for he laid a hand on her arm and, smiling, offered reassurance. "Tonight there will be a banquet fit for the King, of that I can assure you."

She patted his hand. He was a good, loyal servant. The thought came, unbidden but strident: *loyal and faithful...unlike my son.*

All were welcome at Godwine's table, and the Manor was, as usual, almost full for the serving of the evening meal. Precedence of seating, below the immediate family and especial guests, went to the housecarls, Godwine's personal, elite body of fighting men: bodyguards, warriors and companions. Earl Godwine they served and no other man, until death released them from the oath of allegiance. In return, an earl undertook to house, feed and clothe these men and their families; it was for him to mount and arm them, to honour them with splendid gifts. When a lord, be he thegn, earl or king, provided generously for his followers' everyday needs, then he could be sure their courage would not fail when he needed it. A feast was an occasion for giving and receiving together—for getting drunk, an occasion to confirm the loyalty and unity of vassal and lord. This night Godwine's Hall, high-roofed, sixty feet long and thirty feet wide, was filled to capacity, the usual company swollen by the King and his retinue.

Godwine, like Gytha, had found it difficult to remain cheerful, but unlike his wife, found no means of escape. Even during the feasting, the atmosphere at the high table remained strained, with Edward as disgruntled as when he had arrived at mid-morning. Lamely, Godwine tried to think of a topic of discussion that would interest his King. "We will set the hounds tomorrow," he said cheerily, aware that he had already suggested hunting half an hour or so earlier. "The scent will be poor if this frost lies any heavier, but I have a new young bitch who is good: she may do us proud."

"No matter." Edward answered. He waved his hand, the shadow-flickering light from torch, candle and hearth fire glinting on the vibrant jewels in his finger rings. The gesture and his tone displayed his boredom. Then he turned his head and stared at his appointed earl. "I have a better quarry in mind. One that I have waited long enough to bring to bay."

"Indeed?" A beat of alarm jolted Godwine's pulse, but Edward had already turned his back and was talking animatedly to the man who sat, as ever, at his right hand: Robert Champart.

Countess Gytha caught the momentary look of alarm that swept across her husband's face and the smirk of triumph that sat, bold and brazen, on Champart's indulgent features. She took several deep breaths, fighting an urge to shriek her husband's loyalty. What good would that do? It was not a woman's place to meddle in the affairs of men.

The Hall grew hot and noisy as the feasting swung into the enjoyed consumption of good food and excellent wine. When stomachs were full, the trestle tables would be cleared and removed, benches shifted to the sides in preparation for the entertainment that always accompanied a feast.

Gytha, as head woman, poured wine for those seated at her husband's high table. As she served, there was much laughter and shouting from the lower Hall, and she looked up to see two men stepping into the central space to begin a friendly wrestling match. The cheering rose to the high rafters of the timber roof and hung there with the hearth smoke and the wood-carved spirit faces. This was a Christian household, but no man dare build without seeking the added protection of the Old Ones. The King, Gytha noticed, was talking again to Godwine; this time their conversation seemed light, even jovial. Perhaps, the Countess thought, their differences were settled, any misunderstanding caused by Swegn's foolishness set straight. Then she saw Edward lean slightly towards her husband, noticed a look of concern flash across Godwine's face. What now? She glanced again and relaxed as Godwine began to smile.

"I am thinking of taking a wife," Edward had stated blandly to the Earl.

Startled at this confidence, Godwine had momentarily found himself lost for words—but delight almost immediately suffused his features. "That is good news!" he enthused. "A wise choice could bring many an advantage to England." A king needed an heir to his throne and England needed secure alliance. A wife was the means to both. Godwine's alert political mind had already begun calculating, rapidly selecting and discarding suitable daughters, widows or sisters of emperors and kings.

A faint smile tipped the sides of Edward's mouth; he knew Godwine well enough to guess at those busy thoughts! "I have already made my choice," he stated. "I need to ensure that my back is shielded against treachery. With England secure from internal wrangling, we can outface anything Norway may throw at us." He paused. "I am going to choose a wife from the family of one of my earls." He watched, mischievously delighted as Godwine's brows dipped warily. A marriage with Northumbria or Mercia would bring extreme difficulties for Godwine—perhaps even ruin him.

Robert had indeed suggested one of Siward's kindred, or Leofric's youngest… ah, Edward had been sorely tempted to follow his friend's advice, to take the first step towards bringing Godwine to his knees!

"Siward's daughters and nieces are not so fair to look upon, yet there must be something good to be said of them, surely?" Edward was finally beginning to enjoy himself. Satisfied at the pale look of horror that flickered across Godwine's face, he added, "They may all have been bred in that uncivilised cesspit of the North, but one of them must have received an education, can read and write, and talk in an accent that is at least vaguely understandable."

His anger at Swegn Godwinesson's treachery, coupled with the impotence he felt in the face of his damned mother's interference, had decided him in favour of Robert's tentative suggestion. How disruptive to a king's routine and way of life would it be to take a wife? He only need bed her once or twice to impregnate her; see her only when public protocol dictated—she could have her own apartments, even her own palace. Once he had fulfilled his husband's duties he could hunt and pursue his reading and studies of God unhindered. And Robert, as his personal priest, would still be there to proffer comfort and understanding. Yes, the delight of putting a man such as Godwine back into place far outweighed the minor disadvantages of taking a wife.

"Alternatively, there is Leofric's only surviving daughter," Edward continued, immersed in his private enjoyment. "She is young, I grant, but that is no disadvantage to a man of modest years like myself. She will soon reach breeding age."

Godwine did not know how to answer. He could not appear churlish or fatuous, but, by God, he could not allow Edward to ally as son-in-law to Leofric or Siward! He swallowed, slid a pleasant smile across his mouth. "A woman fresh with the bloom of childhood is to be much desired, my Lord King, but to take such a young—and so often sickly—girl as wife would mean a long wait for a child of your own."

To his immense relief, Edward agreed. "My thoughts exactly, Godwine, I cannot look to Mercia. I have therefore made my choice, I will take your daughter Edith."

Godwine's heart pounded fast for several beats. Had he heard aright? God in His mercy, was this so? His daughter, his Edith, to be Queen? The mother of the next king! He had always hoped for it, of course, but had never dared suggest such a move. He looked up, saw Gytha; grinned broadly at her, saw her smile. She would be as pleased at this news as was he.

"There is of course dowry and such to be discussed." Edward said, offhanded, pausing to applaud a particularly excellent bout of the wrestling. "But it would be good for myself and Wessex to be bound together in alliance, would it not?"

Enthusiastically, Godwine agreed. What power and position a son born to Edith would give him!

As if reading those thoughts—indeed, they were all too plain—Edward then said, "For such a betrothal to be considered, I will naturally require unquestioning loyalty." Godwine made to reassure him, but Edward allowed him no chance to answer. "I ride on the morrow to Winchester, My Earls of Northumbria, Mercia and East Anglia have been summoned to meet me there, I would have Wessex with me also, when I have my mother arrested for treason."

⟪⟫

Harold's head ached, as did his limbs, his neck, his back. He gripped the reins, his fingers stiff and cramped—from the bite of the frosted air he assumed. He ought to push into a canter for he had only three days to reach Winchester, but it hurt to go faster than a walk and even that slow pace jarred his body with every step.

When the King's summons had come, Harold had been at Ely, settling some long-rumbling dispute over the ownership of church land. Bishop Stigand was not much liked or respected among the clergy, especially since he knew every trick of the law concerning what appeared to be his on paper. The written word, the monastery opposing him claimed, could be falsified, whereas the tradition of word of mouth could not. Ah, the Bishop had countered, but what was written and witnessed must be upheld in law…and so the thing had circled on. Harold had, in a way, been grateful to Edward for the timely distraction.

He was so tired! Why, he did not know; he had not overexerted himself these last few weeks. Was it the thought of the long ride ahead, the coldness of the air? The knowing that Edward was not over-pleased with any member of the Godwine family? If only he could stop, rest, close his eyes for a moment…his head drooped…and he was falling, slithering from his horse.

His servant was out of the saddle and squatting beside him within the space of two heartbeats, hands fluttering over his master's body. The skin was burning with fever, yet Harold was shivering.

Leofgar, Harold's chaplain, dismounted as rapidly and ran to join the anxious servant. He touched his own fingers to Harold's flushed face. "My Lord, you are not well. We must seek warmth and shelter for you."

"No, Leofgar, I thank you for your concern, but the King's summons…" It was difficult for Harold to speak. His chest felt as if it were bound by tight bands, his mouth was dry, face taut and stiff. He tried to uncurl his clenched fingers, but there was no movement in his left arm, no feeling beyond a heavy weight, as if it were encased in lead.

"…Can go to the devil," the chaplain interrupted. "The King will need do without your presence for the time being." Leofgar stood, surveyed the landscape, beckoned one of Harold's housecarls forward. "I am unfamiliar with much of this area," he said. "We need take my Lord Earl to a place of security, for I fear he is gravely ill. Where do you recommend?"

Scalpi rubbed his bearded chin with his calloused hand. Born not four miles from this very road, he knew their exact position. Either of the two villages lying ahead, Nazeing or Epping, would offer an inn. Or there was Waltham. He described all three, but added, "Eadric the thegn is as near a distance, if we take a track that follows south-west. There is no more trustworthy man, and his wife possesses much knowledge of healing."

Leofgar nodded. It was as suitable a place as any.

7

Winchester

Emma stood by the narrow window of her upper-floor room. She was cold, but did not move away from the draught. The wind, carrying a first early flurry of snow, buffeted relentlessly against the thick glass, finding small cracks and fissures in the wooden frame and around the lead that bound the small and expensive panes. The fingers of her right hand toyed with one of the rings that adorned her left, her gaze following the slow, hobbling gait of a lame beggar making his way up the street that ran the other side of her boundary wall. The High Street had been busy for much of the day, but with the November afternoon drawing in towards dusk and the onset of unwelcome snow, people had scurried for the warmth of their homes or the companionship of the taverns. The morrow, the seventeenth day of the month, was market day and then, whatever the vagaries of the weather, Winchester would become as bustling as a beehive at the height of summer. For now, the town appeared to be descending into winter hibernation.

Winchester was a royal and ancient city. The palace was of the Saxon style, said to have been built originally for the great King Alfred of Wessex himself. With timber and wattle walls, the domineering Hall, more than seventy-five feet in length and half that in width, boasted towering arched beams set beneath a high cruck roof, topped with overlapping wooden shingles. Only the numerous churches of Winchester and the imposing Minster, which rose majestic in all its glory a short walk up that same High Street, were constructed in stone—and then there was Emma's private residence; a rarity, one of the few non-ecclesiastical structures in all England to be partially stone-built and bear glass windows.

Emma's Queen's Hall had been erected during the first years of her marriage to the Dane, Cnut, a time when he, as a usurper king, had urgency to prove that he had shed the barbarian culture of his ancestors and had adopted the civilisation of a Christian. Upon her marriage Emma could have asked anything of him; she chose to have built upon her dower land a residence that befitted her status. Constructed in Norman stone in the French style, it was grand in design although modest in size. The boundary wall stood higher than a man astride a horse, its gateway leading through to an impressive square courtyard, edged by timbered buildings: kitchens, stables, storerooms. Opposite stood the two-storeyed building that had become Emma's favourite home. Solid. Secure. The ground floor was much as any noble-born's Hall, save that the walls and vaulting were of stone. This was the public place, where meals were served and audiences taken. A narrow wooden staircase at the rear led up to the first floor, to the privacy of the Queen's own rooms, which were comfortable and warm, richly furnished and hung with splendid tapestries. This had more traditional timber beams, and walls infilled with daub and plaster, with only the two crudely designed chimney alcoves built of fireproof stone.

There were three rooms: the solar, Emma's sitting room where she would read or sew or conduct private meetings that were not for the Hall's open-eared attention; her bed-chamber, with in one corner a chapel; and, beyond the bed-chamber, a third room, with a door of solid-carved oak. A small, windowless room without furniture or draperies, containing only several large and weighty chests. The royal treasury of England, which Emma, as was her right and duty as Queen, held in safe protection.

A horseman rode along the street, his head tucked in against the bite of wind, his face muffled by his thick-woven winter cloak. The Queen watched him, mildly interested. A well-bred horse, the rider dressed in garments declaring him to be of moderate status—was he a royal messenger? To her own annoyance, Emma held her breath...but he rode past the gateway, turned into the next lane and disappeared from view. He was not, then, come from the palace. She watched the street, waited. Her son was in Winchester, accompanied, so she had heard, by that awful man Champart and several earls, among them Godwine. That brought some cheer, for Godwine had shown himself to be a friend on more than the one occasion. Yet, Emma was forced to reflect to herself, he had not always kept his faith with her cause.

The King had ridden in yester afternoon, but no summons had come for her. He remained displeased with her, then, but when was he not? In frustration Emma rubbed away the breath that had steamed on the glass. She would not lower herself to send word to him, would not allow him to witness her niggling anxiety. Why did the product of her own flesh and blood not trust her to do what was best to govern England? Why could he not accept the advice born of her accumulated wisdom? Why? Because of a few harsh decisions that she had been forced to make in the past—decisions made to keep the peace and save

England. He had no conception of the reality of being a king—or queen. Did not understand the responsibilities that occasionally weighed heavy on the heart, conscience and soul. He would. One day he would have to make a choice that would be hard to explain to his Maker at the Last Judgement. And then, ah, then he would understand what it meant to be an effective and efficient ruler of a land as diverse and complex as England.

Daylight was fading. Emma snorted. Why was she fooling herself? Why did Edward not trust her—because there were too many rumours spitting from the lips of her enemies, that was why! Oh, she herself paid little mind to rumour, unless there was adequate proof to back the tattle, but Edward? Huh, he revelled in gossip!

This latest nonsense. He suspected her of sending written invitation to Magnus of Norway to come make a try for the English crown. Did Edward think her to be such a fool as to commit treason to parchment? Should Magnus turn his attention from the difficulties of annexing Denmark for himself and glance also in England's direction…well, she might then be interested in advocating his cause…but to invite him here? To play openly into Edward's hand? Madness!

Obviously Edward had no desire to see her. Let him sit and moulder in that damp and draught-riddled palace of his! By right, as Queen she had charge of the treasury, the jewels, the gold, silver and coin. The wealth of England was secured in those locked oak chests in the room beyond her bed-chamber. And while she held *that* security he was as tied to her as a new-born babe is bound to the necessity of the breast.

"Alysse," she commanded, turning suddenly from the window into the dimness of the chamber. "I would have the candles lit, this dismal day tires me." Emma suppressed an exasperated sigh as she folded the shutter across the window. What was she to do about Edward? What, in all practicality, could she do? I will dine here in privacy," she added as she settled herself into her chair. "I have no inclination to share the merriment of the Hall."

It was foolish and undignified to feel rejected. She had no wish to venture out into the cold evening to attend the banal company at a hypocritical court. All those self-important men, Leofric, Siward—what a vile stench emanated from the moth-addled wolf-skin cloak that man insisted on wearing! He was a Northerner, of course, with the poor manners and oafishness of that uncivilised area of England. Why could she not banish this dejection at not being summoned?

The girl lit the candles, bobbed a curtsey and left the room to see about food for her lady. Emma stretched her feet to the warmth of the hearth and laid her head against the high back of the chair. The chamber was still and quiet, with only the crackle of hearth flames, a shifting log, the occasional muffled sound filtering from the High Street. Her hands fell limp, her jaw slackened. She dozed, only to wake abruptly moments later, startled by sounds beyond the door. She stood, her brows dipping into a furrow of disapproval. How dare her men make disturbance beyond the privacy of her rooms! She moved angrily towards the door, her hand coming up to reach out for the latch; she stopped, the raised hand going instead, in a rush of unexpected fear, to her throat.

A voice she recognised sounded loud and insistent on the wooden stairs, accompanied by the scrape and stamp of men's boots. The door latch lifted and the door itself was flung open.

Edward walked into the room. His badger-fur hat and the shoulders of his cloak were pattered with melting snow crystals sparkling like miniature diamonds in the disturbed flicker-dance of frail yellow candlelight. "Mother," he said, acknowledging her shallow curtsey. He strode to the fire to warm the chill from his fingers, his back to her and the room.

Emma glanced at the men hesitating beyond the threshold. "Is it so intimidating to visit me, Sir," she remarked, her voice scathing, "that you dare not come unless escorted by three of your noblest and most brave earls?" She turned, composed and serene to the door. "My Lords, pray enter the lioness's den. The beast within has not eaten, but I assure you she is not unduly ravenous." Emma accompanied her words with a slight gesture of her hand, noting, with thin pressed lips, that her visitors were flanked by six of Edward's housecarls, ostentatiously bearing arms.

Edward, lifting his cloak so that he should not sit on its dampness, seated himself in Emma's chair. He did not lean back, but kept his chilled fingers to the warmth. His long and slender hands were so prone to the cold. He detested winter. November in particular depressed him; so many dull and dreary days stretching ahead.

Warmed, slightly more comfortable, the King nodded to his bodyguard, who moved with determined strides across the room, heading for the inner closed door. Emma walked swiftly to bar their way. "There is nothing beyond this door save my bed-chamber. My private room."

Edward barely looked at her as he replied. "I have no care for your bed-chamber, madam, nor for whom you may occasionally invite within it." He flickered a glance at Godwine, his insinuation quite open. Godwine's face tinged pink but he held his tongue. "It is the chamber beyond that interests me," he continued.

The Queen forced an easy, pleasant smile, realising it would do her no service to lose her temper. "I assure you," she insisted, "the chamber you refer to is adequately secure. It requires no additional scrutiny."

"Mayhap not," Edward answered, rising to his feet and dusting creases from his tunic. "But I feel a royal treasury ought be housed where a king can keep a close eye to it." He offered his mother a slight, informal bow. "However, I thank you for the good care that you have taken of England's wealth until now. Do let my men pass, Mother."

Emma had no choice but to comply. She stepped to one side and watched, helpless, as the men began removing the heavy chests from the strong-room, impotent fury blazing in her vivid blue eyes. No word passed anyone's lips as each chest was removed; the only sound being the laboured breath and grunts of the six men as they struggled to negotiate the steep wooden stairs down to the Hall below.

With the last box gone, Edward strolled to the outer door, where he paused and smiled mockingly. "I would suggest, madam, that you seek lodging at Wilton or, if you prefer, I can arrange a position somewhere as abbess. There must be a place in my realm that would be willing to take you. Or perhaps you would seek retirement in your homeland of Normandy?" His smile broadened, sickly sweet. "Mayhap Cnut left you some legacy in his land across the sea. Would Norway welcome you?"

Because of that vicious rumour she was to be packaged off, sent into obscurity, within a nunnery, Emma clenched her teeth, bit back a torrid retort. She would rather drain the lifeblood from her wrists first! "I am perfectly content here in Winchester, I thank you."

"But madam," Edward answered placidly, "this residence will be beyond your means to maintain, I would advise you to seek somewhere"—he paused for effect—"cheaper to reside."

Emma could no longer hold her anger. "You insult me! I have plenty wealth, enough to—"

Interrupting, Edward tossed his last jibe, enjoying every cruel and calculated moment. "Enough to what? To pay for soldiers to swell Swegn Godwinesson's pathetic little army? Enough to finance a fleet of ships for Magnus of Norway to attack England? No, madam, you *had* wealth. You *had* my treasury, I now have it, all of it, including your lands and movables. You will retire with grace, as befits a woman of your age, and you will no longer be allowed to commit further treason against the Crown."

"How dare you!" Emma hissed. "You cannot take my lands from me!"

"Ah," Edward retaliated, "for the charge of treason I can." He gestured to Siward who had remained with Godwine and Leofric on the far side of the door. "My Lord Earl carries the necessary papers. They are documented in a court of law, duly signed and witnessed."

Siward removed several rolled scrolls from beneath his cloak, held them so that she might clearly see the seals placed on each. He walked into the room and set them in a row atop a table near at hand.

Emma ignored the scrolls and glared at her son. As king, Edward had every right to confiscate property and goods from whoever he wished, if he had good cause. And any king could, with ease, find such cause if he so desired. "On what do you base your charge? Treason, you say. You have no proof."

"Should I find it necessary"—Edward raised a warning finger, held her attention—"I could find it."

The threat was clear, Emma had to accept his will, for now. There was one thing, however, that she would not relinquish. "You have no entitlement to my land and residence here in Winchester. It is my dower land and is outside the jurisdiction of the royal demesne. Beyond the touch of provost or shire reeve. It is land granted me by your father at the time of our marriage." Then she added bitterly, "Or will you take my dower also? Why not create total scandal and force me into exile?"

Why not indeed? Edward had considered it, but rumour was not enough to discredit his mother entirely. To exile a woman of her standing would be to invite his enemies to unite behind her. No, Edward would not banish her abroad. He needed to keep a close eye on her plotting.

"I have not your unyielding nature, Mother," he answered. "I have a sense of justice and forgiveness." Tongue in cheek, he continued, "I must have inherited that from my father." He moved to the table, sorted through the scrolls, selected one and, crossing the room, tossed it on to the fire. "You may retain your dower property here in Winchester, on condition that you live here quietly." Edward felt the blood pulsating in his veins; the sweet, sweet essence of victory! He had outmanoeuvred his mother! "Bear that condition in mind, Mother. I would prefer to have you permanently removed. I need only an excuse." Turning to the door he added a gloating afterthought: "You will hear soon, but I would be the one to tell you. I have ordered your choice of bishop removed from East Anglia. I do not consider Stigand's poor morals to be suitable." Dipping his head in farewell he strode from the room, his laughter echoing triumphantly up the staircase.

The three earls turned silently to follow him, but Emma halted Godwine, her voice scathing: "So this is how you treat me? How short-lived is your loyalty, sir."

"My loyalty must lie with my family, madam, with the future of my seed." He spread his hands. "I am sorry, but that is how it is."

"You put yourself first, then, above the love of your queen?"

Godwine was a proud man, he would not lie to one who had offered, and he hoped would continue to offer, patronage and friendship. "No, madam. My love for the queen comes above all else, but alas, you will soon no longer be the one to bear that title. My Lord Edward is to take a wife."

Emma's eyebrows shot upwards with startled surprise. Edward had actually agreed to take a woman to his bed? Gods! Would he know what to do with her? "So, with such ease you transfer your loyalty?" she mocked. "Did you then love me so poorly?"

Godwine, Earl of Wessex, faced Emma, Dowager Queen of England. "I love you as no man, who has already a Christian-blessed wife, ought love another woman. But there is to be one I must love the more. My future grandson. The next king."

For a long moment Emma stood, speechless, uncomprehending. Then threw back her head and laughed, great, breath-filled gasps—the laughter of finally accepting, outwitted, defeat.

8

⚹

Nazeing

Harold lay dazed and confused, aware he was abed. With so much that he ought to be doing he could not understand why. Nor could he understand why he could not move his arm to toss aside the covers that laid heavy over his aching body, as if he were being buried alive. Surely he was asleep? He would wake soon—but he could not open his eyes, could not surface from this threatening redness that engulfed his mind.

Voices—there were several—unclear and distant. He tried to tell them, whoever they were, to cease their mumbling, to speak up. No one listened; they just tucked those damned heavy covers tighter around his painful limbs. Sweat scrambled off his brow, down his face, yet there was no life in the iced blocks that were his feet and hands.

Once, when he did manage to open his eyes in this bizarre dream, he saw a man standing at the end of the bed, a man he knew not, with a black, cowled gown and a solemn, pale face. This man lifted his hand and made the sign of the cross, then shook his head and muttered something. A prayer? He had come, Harold was certain, to take him up to God's paradise. He must wake! Must make this man realise that he was only sleeping, that he was not ready to die, for there was so much to be done! He had been summoned to the King to meet him in Winchester.

A young woman spoke. "Rest, my Lord," she said. She held a drink to his lips. He swallowed, tasted the sweet sensation of honey and some other bitter substance. He saw her face bending close over him, saw the white skin of her neck, the haloed gold of her hair. So, it was too late, then, he was already with God. Harold closed his eyes, drifted into sleep.

Edyth, with her mass of fair hair and the lamplight glowing behind her, did indeed resemble one of God's angels. She looked up at her mother with wide anxious eyes, the red rims betraying that tears had been falling. "Is there nothing more we can do for him?" she pleaded. Her mother was so skilled with herbs and potions, yet this young man was suffering. "Surely there must be something more, Mama?"

Ælfthryth dipped a cloth into the bowl of cold water, soaked it and wrung the excess from its folds. She passed it to her daughter, shaking her head. What more could they do? She had tried everything she knew. "He is beyond our mortal care, child. If his own chaplain and our Father from the church at Waltham cannot between them bring healing with their prayers, what chance have we earth-bound women?"

It was a great pity that one as young and handsome should depart this life so soon. He had seemed to have the making of a fine earl, too. Why was it that the good were taken to God while the evil were left to pursue their wickedness in the world of men? Ælfthryth sighed. Of course, it was not for her to question God's will but was it not a cruel jest of His to send the Earl Harold here? How would she explain to his mother, when she arrived, that they had failed him? How would her husband be able to face Earl Godwine again, knowing that his son had died beneath this roof? And Edyth was troubled by the Earl's foundering, poor lass. She had barely recovered from the senseless death of that wretched dog; and now, here she was nursing the Earl, all the hours of the night and day, with a passion for him stirring within her.

With quick efficiency Ælfthryth straightened the crumpled bed-linen and tucked the bed fur tighter. With good fortune, Countess Gytha should arrive on the morrow. They had sent a messenger south to Bosham, asking her to come to Essex. Once she was here Earl Harold's illness would be out of their hands and Edyth's attention could be directed towards a more promising suitor. The Earl, should he survive this illness, might look at a thegn's daughter for a temporary companion to warm his bed, but he would most certainly be seeking a girl of higher breeding to become his wife.

"We have done our best for him," Ælfthryth declared aloud. That is all the God and Lady Gytha can ask of us."

Refolding the damp cloth, Edyth sponged the sweat from Harold's face. He had been mumbling again a moment or so ago, some deep trouble that must bother him greatly. He muttered often of the necessity to reach Winchester, where, so his companions said, they had been riding, Winchester! How she would enjoy seeing that city—or London, She had never travelled further than the village of Waltham, down in the valley. Her father, who had journeyed far as a young man, entertained them through the long and dark winters' evenings with the mysteries of distant places. Of Winchester, and London, and York, The empty north lands of Northumbria; the terrors of the Welsh borders; the soft-coloured rolling Downs of Wessex; the wild grandeur and splendour of the sea. The sea! Oh, how Edyth longed to smell the sea! "The sea, like the canopy of the sky, goes on, seemingly, for ever," her father had said. "It is wider than the broadest river or the largest lake."

Edyth found that hard to comprehend, for she could see with her own eyes where the sky met the earth not a few miles distant, but her father was a wise man who knew many things that she did not even begin to understand. Would she, one day, see the sea? Touch its restless tide with her fingers, delight in the spindrift of its surf, the swell of its life-beat? Perhaps, One day. Yet she was more likely to marry some near-by thegn, and settle in the next valley.

Harold had lost much weight; his cheeks were hollow and drawn, his hair matted and his eyes, when he had them open, burnt with the same fire that scorched his skin. She remembered his sparkling, laughter-filled eyes from that day when he had first come. It had been spring, soon after Easter. How she remembered his strength. His gentle, concerned sorrow.

The memory of that day, that awful day, lingered in her mind. The repulsive touch of Earl Swegn, his rough hands, his wet, dribbling lips. The brutal murder of her dog. Even now, at the thought of that vile man, her breath caught and bile would rise to her throat—but Earl Harold had been there also. Had been so kind. She ought to have thanked him for what he had done, to have been more concerned for the wound in his shoulder, the scar of which remained white and vivid against his skin. At least tending him now was a way of making amends for her neglect.

She touched her hand to his cheek, winced at the laboured breath that rattled in his chest. Her mother was certain that Harold would not remain overlong in this world, but she, Edyth, a mere maid, knew better. Harold was not going to die because she was not going to let him.

9

Rouen—January 1044

The cramp in William's knees and lower back was becoming unbearable. If he could only move slightly, stretch his shoulders…He squinted to his left. Difficult to see clearly without moving his head…Henry, King of France, knelt there, his eyes fixed firm on the crucifix upon the high altar of St. Ouen Abbey, its ornate, golden beauty bathed by the glow of candlelight. The King knelt with his back spear-straight, his chin high, palms flat together, lips moving in silent prayer; he, William thought, would not shuffle about because his knees were hurting him. Henry was a gaunt, serious-looking man with hair already brindled at his temples, although he was not far past his early years of manhood. During these cold January days the Frenchman wore an extravagantly cut ermine cloak, the black markings in startling contrast to the pure, bright white of the fur. Looking at that cloak as it draped in magnificent swathes about Henry's shoulders, William was reminded of a gyrfalcon that his father had once shown him, a gift from the King of Norway. It had been a splendid bird, pure white with flecks of black on its breast and wings. He remembered putting out his hand to touch the dazzling feathers, remembered marvelling at the softness beneath his fingers. Remembered also his father's laugh and rich, melodic voice. "You'd not have done that, lad, were she not safely hooded. Shed have had those fat, pink fingers of yours for her supper!"

Where had he been on that occasion? Surely, at Conteville with his mother's husband, the Vicomte Herluin? Yet he could not picture his two half-brothers with him, Odo and Robert, and it was rare that his father had visited Herleve there.

That his father had loved his mother, Herleve, was certain, but as the daughter of a tanner of Falaise, albeit a wealthy one, she could never have become Duke Robert's duchess. He had found for her instead Herluin, a vicomte, a man who desired sons of his own bred from a pretty wife, no matter whose mistress she had once been.

Ah, no, it was at Falaise where he saw his father, while he was staying with his maternal grandfather! When he eventually returned home to Conteville, his second half-brother had been born, so he would have been—William paused in his thoughts, clumsily worked out his age, stealthily using his fingers to count forward from the date of his birth, 1028—yes, five years old! And it was summer, for he remembered the heat of the day, the sun sparkling on the bells attached to the bird's legs and how, when he had looked up, his father's face had been hidden in dark shadow. It had frightened him, seeing the tall man without a face, and he had cried. Robert had given the bird to a servant and swung the distraught boy up into his arms, assuming it had been the jest about the bird pecking his fingers that had brought the tears. William frowned. As if he would cry at that!

They had not minded William then, the men of Robert's court, when the Duke had been alive. Robert had been seventeen years of age when he had sired William, Herleve also seventeen. They had expected Robert to enjoy his youth with pretty maids but, when the time came to take a nobleman's daughter as wife, produce legitimate sons. But he had died on pilgrimage, leaving a bastard-born seven-year-old as his only heir. There had been no wife, no other sons; only Herleve, a daughter, and William.

Tiring of surreptitiously studying Henry, the young Duke William rolled his eyes in the opposite direction, to observe his paternal uncle, Archbishop Maugar. He had his head bent, double chin resting on his clasped knuckles, eyes closed. He, William thought, would not mind this vigil, for he was well used to long nights of prayer. Even so, William could easily have assumed the Archbishop to be asleep.

Again, the boy focused his mind on the altar. He ought to be concentrating on inward reflection, on the glory that was God...on the significance of this night's event. Not dwelling on memories of the past or on the eddying draught that was slinking under the abbey door to find its way under his thin cloak. He was cold and he was stiff but in two more hours it would be dawn and he would no longer be a boy. For it would be his birthing day and he would be, at last, sixteen years of age. No longer would he be an unknighted child, the vulnerable only son of Robert, Duke of Normandy. William lifted his chin a little, straightened his back, contracted his eyes. No longer would they dare call him bastard to his face. And soon, very soon, neither would they dare insult him so behind his back!

William was to become a man this day. His overlord, the King of France himself, was to invest him with the regalia of the knight—armour, the emblem of virtue, a shield of faith, helmet of hope and a sword, the symbol of the word of God. William explored their meanings in his mind. Armour for excellence, quality and worth. Worthiness. Fine words that dispelled the slur—bastard born. Faith? *Oui*, faith that God intended him, and him alone, to rule this duchy with all the vigour of hope, while wielding a sword that carried the truth and might of God's power and his. *His* power. Once he was a knight, a man, just let them try to defy him...just let them!

Some had already suffered punishment for trying. Justifiable revenge, taken with swift finality by those few faithful followers of the boy Duke of Normandy, men who had been loyal to his father. Brutal punishment, meted out for the brutal murder of his various guardians. Comte Alan de Bretagne, the third of that title, who had set William upon the back of his first pony; Comte Gilbert de Brionne, swift to chide, but quick to laugh, who had taught William how to hurl a javelin; gentle, quiet-voiced Turchetil; and Osbern. Dear, loyal Osbern... he could not think of that night and Osbern.

William repressed a shudder, lest his two companions sharing this vigil assumed him to be shivering with the cold; he thought instead of his uncle, Walter, his mother's brother. Walter had saved his life when, not more than a few weeks after Robert's death, men had come to murder the boy. Snatching him from his bed, Walter had carried him through the night to a place of safety—had slept in the boy's bed after that, journeying with him from safe house to safe house, dressed him as if he were an ordinary man's son, not the child of a duke. They did not risk riding expensive horses, but used Walter's shaggy old pony instead; took shelter in poor men's bothies, sleeping on the floor beside a hearth fire or in a barn or cow byre. Men did not think of searching for a young duke among the swine. On fine nights they had slept beneath the stars, curled close together under Walter's cloak. Thinking of those days, full of fear yet tinged with excitement, William could hear distinctly the breath of a summer night, the call of an owl and the sound of the pony, grazing. The threat of death had been a constant companion through his childhood, walking always behind like a menacing shadow.

What had it served his enemies, that lust for murder? They had failed! He was alive, and he had reached manhood. Yet they had come close to achieving their goal a week past. A few miles south from here, at La Vaudreuil.

William stared fixedly at the ruby in the centre of the crucifix. Attempting to focus his mind on prayer, he closed his eyes, saw in the dancing patterns of light behind his eyelids Osbern's Viking-length flaxen hair, his vivid blue eyes, firm, determined jaw and heavily moustached mouth. Could almost hear his deep, powerful voice, smell the scent of horse and leather that always clung to his clothes. Osbern had been with him for so long. Had taught him how to handle a sword and to use a shield, how to ride a horse larger and stronger than the first little black mount given him by Comte Alan on his eighth birthday. Osbern ought to be here at William's knighting...

He swallowed hard. Blinked his eyes several times. Osbern could not be here, for a dagger had been thrust into his heart. A blade meant for William.

He had been abed, huddled beneath the furs, his feet and legs curled close against his belly to find what little warmth there was. It was cold, frost lay white outside, the water in the hand basin was frozen—even his piddle in the unemptied chamber pot had a rim of ice around it. His breath had come in great puffs of cloud from his mouth as he had removed his outer garments before scuttling into the bed. The brazier in that austere chamber had given off barely enough heat to warm the hands, let alone the entire room. Osbern was sitting at the edge of the hard, unyielding bed, removing leather over-tunic, cussing that his fingers were too ice-frozen to unlace the ties. The door had crashed open, William had shot upright, Osbern had shouted alarm, grabbed for his sword that lay sheathed on the bed. Two men were running into the chamber, weapons drawn, intent on spilling blood, William's blood, but Osbern got to one of them first. William had screamed, shrieked for help. He blushed at that thought now, as he knelt before the altar, blushed that he should have been so frightened at the hideous look of murder on the faces of those two men.

He released a sigh. It had not been the first attempt on his life, but it would be the last. At the age of seven, William had learnt that grown men rarely behave with honour. They harbour jealousies and greed for that which is not theirs. With the boy William gone, the door would be open for someone else to inherit Normandy, someone such as Grimoald de Plessis, Rannulf, Vicomte de la Bessin or Guy, Comte de Brionne, successor to Gilbert and that respected title, yet his very opposite in nature. All of them men who wanted the title of duke for their own; men who were prepared to risk much in order to get it. Including the attempted murder of a child.

William smiled, a slow, wide-spread smile of satisfaction. They had not succeeded. He was sixteen and he was still here, still very much alive. From now, he would rule as *he* wanted, as *he* wished. No more guardians or good-intentioned abbots, no more regents. And no more attempts at murder. The smile faded into an expression that bordered on the sinister. Those words, *no more attempts at murder*, rolled around his mind, as a good wine trickles around the palate. Come tomorrow—daybreak—those same men who were plotting to be rid of him would kneel and kiss his hand, would swear their homage and allegiance.

The ritual would all be pretence, of course, on both sides. From them, a public display of fealty; from him, a genial smile, a nod of greeting.

The capitulation of two in particular he was eager to witness, eager to watch the expression on their faces as they came to bend the knee before him. They would have received their gifts by then, Guy de Brionne and Rannulf de la Bessin. Osbern's son Will would have quietly and efficiently arranged it. Would they show fear and anxiety—or puzzlement and doubt? They would not be wholly certain that the gifts were from him, from their duke, from William, but they would wonder and tread with extreme care.

The pain in his knees and back had eased. Or had he found the way to ignore it? Soon light would come to the sky, dawn would stream through the three circular windows in the eastern wall of the abbey, illuminating the vibrant-coloured plastering and the gold-embroidered tapestries. King Henry would dress William in his armour and present him with arms, and then they would move to the abbey steps where the men who were to swear allegiance would submit in homage.

Kneeling there in the silence of the abbey of St. Ouen, a thought came to William, a passing, almost flippant thought, but one that would swell in its appeal throughout the years that were to follow. He, Duke William the bastard born, need kneel to none save God and Henry, King of France. And one day, perhaps one day, he need not even kneel to Henry.

◈

Guy, Comte de Brionne, grandson of Duke Richard II of Normandy, lay naked in bed, his arm tossed across the breast of his companion, the tavern keeper's nubile young daughter. She was pretty enough for his taste, but then his taste ran to any woman with red lips and a lingering smile. The tavern, the Rutting Boar, was a passable hostelry; Guy had spent one or two nights in this chamber before now, but not with the same girl. She had been a child on his last visit here to Rouen, what, three years before. On this occasion, as then, Guy had shared the jest of the tavern's name with his friends. "An appropriate place for us to spend this tedious night!" they had carolled as they stepped from the street into the noisy bustle of the inn, arms round each other's shoulders, eyes swiftly assessing the suitability of the serving girls. A few jars of wine and a belly full of stew confirmed their opinion that it was an agreeable place; it was not until late that Guy lurched up the staircase with the virgin girl to find a bed and sport for the night.

He had no especial desire to be here in Rouen, but the order to attend had come from King Henry himself and could not, without serious repercussions, be ignored. Would he have ignored the summons had it come from that poxed little boy who thought himself worthy of becoming a duke? From William the Bastard? They had laughed over that as they drank, he and Rannulf, each capping the other's lewd remarks about the boy's whore of a mother, eventually deciding that an invitation from Herleve would be readily accepted...but that a lengthy bowel-emptying session in the midden hut would be preferable to any from William.

They did not worry unduly about being overheard; few in Rouen held much fondness for William. Guy knew most would prefer to follow his own banner, should the time ever arise.

He was dreaming. His arm and leg twitched; his shoulder jerked. The girl slept, drunk from her father's wine, content with the handsome payment that the Comte had offered her. Guy was twenty-five years of age, held sway over a large rich domain, and his grandfather was the same man as the Bastard's grandfather. The difference was that Guy had been born to a daughter, William to a son. He regarded the issue of gender as irrelevant, for he was legitimate, not a by-blow of a whore. Normandy was his by blood, not William's...and he was damned if he was going to kneel in homage to that upstart come the morrow! New knighted or not. He grunted, angered, even in his sleep.

Outside the chamber a knuckle rapped on the closed door. Guy mumbled and turned over in his sleep. Again knocking, more urgent. The latch clicked downwards, the door opened. A young man, dressed only in hose and under-tunic, tripped across the doorstep and groped his way into the dimly lit chamber, his left hand holding a wildly flickering candle. Rannulf, Vicomte de la Bessin was four years Guy's junior and much influenced by the older man. He stumbled over to the bed and began to shake Guy's shoulder.

"What is it?" Guy complained, reluctantly opening his eyes. "Rannulf? What are you doing here? God's teeth, go find your own whore to lie with!" He began pulling the bed fur tighter around his chest, but Rannulf tugged it aside.

"My Lord! Guy! Something has happened—please, I beg of you, wake and listen to me!"

Guy pulled himself up to a sitting position and yawned extravagantly. The girl remained asleep, snoring gently. "Well?" de Brionne snapped. "Why are you here in my chamber, not amusing yourself in yours?"

Rannulf called forward a servant whose face was streaked as grey and fearful as his master's. He carried a wooden, lidded box, which he set on the nearest table, then scuttled out of the room.

"I found this in my room a few moments since, at the foot of my bed. I had got up to use the piss pot." Rannulf swallowed and took several breaths to calm himself. "I found this."

Guy sat forward, tucking the flea-ridden fur around his nakedness for warmth. "A box. How interesting," he said drily. Waited.

Again Rannulf swallowed, putting a hand over his mouth.

"And inside this box?" Guy drawled.

Without speaking Rannulf opened it, flicking the lid up quickly with one finger.

Shuffling from the bed, Guy peered inside. There were some red-stained, dirty pieces of something lying there. "What is it?" he asked, impatiently, his nose wrinkling from the putrid smell.

Rannulf worked his mouth but it took a while for the words to form. "Skin," he said, with a quick, gagging breath. "It is skin. Human skin."

Guy puckered his mouth in disgust and slammed the lid. "Some fool's idea of a jest," he said disdainfully. "I see no humour in it."

"I…I think." Rannulf was finding it difficult not to vomit. "I think it is to do with those body parts that they found at dawn yesterday. The parts nailed to the east gate? What was left of Robert, son of Roger de Montgomery, they think." Rannulf hastily crossed himself.

Guy flapped his right hand dismissively. Supposition! He crossed the chamber, poured himself a generous goblet of wine, drank it down and lit another candle. Robert fitz Montgomery had been implicated in the murder of Osbern, William's steward, a week or so ago. Damn fool had killed the steward, but not the Duke! So those gruesome pieces nailed to the gate—the bits that had been gelded and disembowelled—were rumoured to belong to Robert? That was fairly obvious. But to assume that the stuff in this box was from his body also? Nonsense!

He poured more wine, then thought to offer some to his friend. He turned and saw the younger man, open-mouthed in silent horror, pointing with a quivering finger at something beside Guy's bed.

Guy raised the candle, its light casting quick-moving, elongated shadows across the low-ceilinged room.

Rannulf recognised what it was first. He bolted from the room, his hand over his mouth, vomit spewing from between his fingers.

The item sat on a square of cloth. Red cloth, embroidered with a golden leopard. William's personal ducal emblem. On the cloth a severed head. The head of Robert fitz Montgomery. Robert, who had been well known to Guy and Rannulf, and all the others who plotted William the Bastard's death. Robert, who last week had slain the steward Osbern in William's bedchamber.

Guy stared at the eyeless, hacked and bloodied head. The meaning was plain. William knew who else was behind that blundered attempt at murder. And he could, if he so desired, punish them also.

Guy did not make it to the chamber pot. He spewed the contents of his stomach on to the timber floor at his feet.

10

Nazeing

Edyth stood at the edge of the small copse of trees, looking down into the valley. The river, swollen from winter snow-melt and recent rain, covered the flood plain, which glistened under the spring sunshine. Some of the fruit trees in the orchard were already breaking into leaf, their winter-bare branches bearing a distinct green bloom, and blossom was beginning to bud. A few more days of sunshine and the primroses would be clustered in their gay mass of yellow flowers under the elder and hawthorn hedgerows. The air was full of the sound of birds, exuberant in their courtship, busy with marking their territory and the building of nests. It would be nice to have the swifts, swallows and house martins back, raising their families under the eaves of the great barn, but it was too early, too cold, for them yet. Although today it was almost as warm as early summer.

She was dressed for riding, wearing loose-fitting, heavy-spun linen breeches, thigh-length tunic and a long cloak, her fair hair tied back in a tight single braid. She was waiting, as impatient as her fidgeting pony, for Harold to come from the Hall. After lying abed so very long, and with the sun so bright and cheerful, he had wanted to be outside. Had asked if she would care to ride to Waltham with him.

The Earl had been so much better this last week. He remained pale and painfully thin, but he felt well enough, at last, to sit a horse—although only a quiet gelding, not his own stallion. To ride rather than suffer the discomfort and indignity of a litter had very much cheered his spirits. Edyth was pleased that he was almost healed, but her joy was tempered by more than a little inward pain. For when well again he would leave Nazeing and return to his other life overseeing East Anglia. Once he was gone she would, like as not, never see him again. He would forget this farmsteading that crowned the high ground above the village of Nazeing. At court, he would be among the women of the nobility, would not remember her. That was how it must be, for he was an earl and she only the daughter of a thegn. How she wished he need not leave! And then she would chide herself for being selfish. That would be wanting for him a life riddled with illness and pain, of days abed and nights of sweating fever.

Edyth had a suspicion that it was more than the sun-bright day that had prompted Harold to ask her to ride with him. He had something to tell her—she had known it these past three nights, for several times he had begun to talk to her, only to stop himself. He was trying to tell her in the gentlest way he could that he would soon be gone. Would there ever be a kind way of saying goodbye? It would be easier for him at the church perhaps; she could find comfort there in the quiet company of Christ and His mother. Edyth was almost tempted to unsaddle her pony, turn her loose in the field and go find some task or other that required doing—but what point in delaying the moment? The pain would sear whenever she learnt of his going.

For almost a month, now, he had been carried down twice weekly to the modest little church of Waltham Holy Cross, to pray before its sacred stone crucifix. Perhaps the healing power of the Cross would help her, too? The story of the Cross was an old and much loved one. Edyth's father told it often and she in turn had related it to Harold as he lay ill in his bed. Mayhap it was her storytelling that had urged him to go to Waltham, when his strength had begun to return.

A carpenter of Somerset, so it was said, was once told in a dream to dig on the hill above his village. He ignored the dream at first, but each night it returned and so eventually he obeyed, and accompanied by the villagers went to the hill. After digging a great hole he found a marble slab broken in two and beneath it a stone crucifix, a book, a bell and a smaller cross. The lord of the village was a much loved man called Tovi the Proud, an official of King Cnut. Loading the treasures into a cart pulled by two oxen, Tovi decreed that the sacred items should be taken to a religious centre—but which one? The oxen refused to move until his modest estate at Waltham was mentioned, whereupon the cart began to trundle forward. And so the Cross was brought to the church in the hamlet of Waltham beside the Lea river in the shire of Essex. Tovi had the church rebuilt to house the relics and people came from far and near to see their wonder.

Earl Harold had benefited from his uncomfortable journeys to Waltham to pray—but although his strength was returning his left arm remained stiff and unusable, and that same side of his face drooped, the muscles slack and unresponsive, his mouth and lower lip twisting downward. The use of his arm, the apothecaries and doctors all agreed, would return in time, for he had feeling there in his fingertips. Time, however, was passing too slow.

Once Countess Gytha's second son had been safe from death, she had returned to her own home, leaving Harold in Ælfthryth's competent hands. And Edyth's. "Take care of my son, young lady," she had said to Edyth on the day she had left. "He has a fondness for you that will see him through his difficulty."

Edyth's pony, a chestnut roan of no more than twelve hands affectionately called Squirrel, nudged at her mistress's shoulder, snatching at the reins in an attempt to crop greedily the sweet spring grass. Edyth reprimanded her sharply, her voice carrying across the cobbled yard and through the open doorway of the Hall.

Harold stood inside, patiently allowing his body servant to adjust his cloak pin. He found it frustrating that so many tasks had to be done for him: his cloak fastened, his clothes laced, meat cut. He had not realised how essential the use of two hands were until he had lost the use of one of them. With the half of his mouth that worked efficiently he smiled at Ælfthryth. "I will take care of your daughter, Mistress Ælfthryth," he said. "For all her youth—or perhaps because of it—she is pleasant company. It is her laughter and agreeable chatter that has kept me from despair these past months."

"She is a daughter to be proud of. I would not have harm come to her." Ælfthryth's answer carried a hint of maternal warning, protective of childhood innocence.

Harold waved his servant aside, stepped closer to his hostess and took her fingers within his sound right hand. "Lady, you need have no fear for your daughter with me." He looked at the stiff fingers of his useless arm and shrugged. "I cannot personally defend her from wolves or thieves, but equally"—he grinned, making a jest of his misfortune—"I cannot take advantage of her!" He glanced at his feet, surprised to find that he felt a sudden rush of embarrassment. "I shall talk to your husband this evening but at this moment it is to you I speak, not him." Clearing his throat, Harold rushed on in one quick breath before courage should fail him. "I am aware that Edyth… admires me. At first I was too ill to notice or care, and then I began to find it flattering and amusing. But, Lady, these past weeks I have felt myself growing more fond of her." He sought Ælfthryth's eyes, held them to emphasise his sincerity. "I am almost healed of my illness and soon I must take my leave of your good care and kind hospitality. There is but one thing I regret. I am loath to leave behind your daughter."

Ælfthryth answered quickly and with concern. Too many men in positions of authority were eager to take advantage of a virgin maid. Ælfthryth had not judged Harold to be such a man, but what if she were wrong? "My Lord, for all that you are the second son of Godwine and earl in your own right, I would not have my child ill-used."

"Lady," Harold responded instantly, "you have my assurance that I would never ill-use Edyth." He kissed her fingers and took a step backwards. He had said enough; before he spoke more he ought go to Waltham and pray again before the Holy Cross. Be certain in his own mind that the path he was about to take was the right one.

◈

The church had been damp and cold inside, for the sun had not warmed through the split trunks and wattle that formed the walls. They had knelt together before the altar, Edyth and Harold, had prayed a while, then Harold had touched the stone cross reverently and sent one of his men to find Father Osbert.

"I am to leave for London in two days," Harold, emerging from the church, announced to Edyth as the elderly priest bustled forward to greet them. "But there are a few things I must attend to before I depart."

Edyth stood a pace or two behind Harold, shrouded in the deep shadows of the porch. She bit her lip to stem the tears that welled in her eyes. So soon? Was he to leave her so soon?

"I have found the quiet of your church a healing balm for my aching spirit these past weeks, Father," Harold said to the priest. "Yet I notice it is in grave need of repair, I intend to reward you and the good villagers of Waltham for your care and kind hearts and, in so doing, I will also give thanks to God for my recovery, which, while not yet complete, is almost so."

Osbert was unashamedly beaming. It had been an honour to tend a man such as Harold, but a reward, a gift to the church, had not been expected. What would he offer? Gold plate, silver candlesticks? The roof desperately needed mending and the timber of the north wall was mildewed and rotten. Heavy rain caused such problems…his mouth, however, dropped wide in astonishment as Harold continued.

"I intend to provide funding for a new and larger church to be built here, an abbey, in fact, with adequate grounds and lands for a monastery, complete with provision for the secular education of those wishing for a life devoted to God." Harold held out his hand to Osbert who had fallen to his knees, urging him back to his feet. "I will recommend to the King that you be named first abbot of Waltham Abbey, my good friend."

Osbert could not help himself: tears of joy slithered from his eyes. He had prayed for a miracle to repair his humble little church—and now it was to be rebuilt, enlarged…What a glory to God Waltham would become!

The inhabitants of the few dwellings that clustered around the church had crowded round; now their cheering turned to excited chatter as Harold mounted his gelding, A monastery would bring trade, travellers and pilgrims—before them, workmen, masons, builders, smiths, carpenters and craftsmen. Waltham was a poor village; the erection of a great abbey would transfer it into a town of wealth and worth. Hands reached out to touch Harold, cries of "Bless you!" echoed after him as he nudged his horse forward.

"That was well done, my Lord." Thorfinn, one of his housecarls, remarked. "An abbey here will be most fitting."

"What think you, Edyth?" Harold asked, twisting in his saddle to see the girl following on her roan pony. "There will be disruption to this peaceful spot, of course. Stone to be brought from abroad—Caen, in Normandy, I understand provides the best—there will be many people here for many years. An abbey, of the size I envisage, cannot be built in a matter of months."

"It will bring great joy to the villagers, my Lord," Edyth answered, attempting to put enthusiasm behind her words.

Harold reined in his gelding to keep pace with her. "Will it bring joy to you, my little one?" he asked quietly.

"Oh." Edyth attempted a smile. "Anew house of God can, surely, bring nothing but joy."

Chewing his lip, Harold nodded, then tactfully changed the subject. "It is such a fine day—I have no desire to ride homewards yet. Let us follow down river a while."

They rode companionably in silence along the lane, threading their way through an encroachment of new spring growth until Harold reined in beside a track that led off through the trees to their left. "To where does this lead?" he asked.

Controlling the unhappy tightness in her throat, Edyth answered with the brightest voice that she could raise, hoped that he would not hear its falseness: "This is Mott Street; it climbs up to a crest of high land that overlooks the valley."

Cocking his head to one side, Harold inspected the grassed track, just wide enough for a single horse to pass. There were several fresh-made deer slots in the mud. "I have noticed that the deer are plentiful in this forest of Waltham, perhaps I ought to consider building myself a suitable hunting lodge near my new abbey—but far enough to be distant from the noise and disruption of building, eh?" He deliberately put a question into his voice to make her look up and answer. She looked so sad, so lost.

"Aside from a few cottages scattered along the ridge, there is nothing up this lane." Edyth managed a pale smile. "It is a good place to ride if you seek the solitude of peace and privacy." She looked down at her hands curled around the reins. Looked up again to meet his eyes, her smile more confident. "I would be glad to share it with you."

It was, as she had said, a steep climb up through the crowding trees. The horses, hot in the remains of their winter coats, were puffing and sweating as they finally ducked through a canopy of branches and splashed through one of the numerous streams that tumbled down the hill. A panoramic view of the valley, lit by golden sunlight, was spread below, the grey trails of smoke from the houses at Waltham visible against the cloudless sky. Squatting at the centre of the village, the little church with its thatch roof and wattle walls was huddled amid its cluster of outbuildings. Many fields were already ploughed, on others grazed cattle, sheep and geese. The song of swans' wings whished overhead, causing Harold, Edyth and the two housecarls to look up. Three of the great white birds skimmed the treetops, heading for the river which meandered sedately through the lush green of the winter-flooded water meadows.

"Boats will come up there." Harold said, pointing to the wide ribbon of water. "Boats from London and the Thames river, laden with their cargo to build my abbey." He dismounted, tossed the reins to Thorfinn and went to lift Edyth from Squirrel. He found it awkward using only the one arm, but she put her hands on his shoulders, and she was so light that he needed only to put one arm around her waist to steady her as she kicked her feet free of the stirrups and jumped down from the saddle.

"Have you ever followed the river down to London?" he asked, guessing that she had not. "It is but a handful of miles, you know."

She shook her head. London? Would she ever see a wondrous place like London?

He kept his hand on her waist as he walked her away from the men towards the trees that ran behind them along the hump of the ridge. A deer trail rambled through the woods and although it was muddy, Harold suggested they follow it a while. "If we tread quietly we may see a doe, or perhaps an early-born fawn."

Edyth halted where the narrow track broadened among a swathe of silver-trunked birch. The trees, despite their height that reached to almost forty feet, were slender and dainty. She peeled away a layer of papery bark, marvelling at its softness, yet extreme strength.

"The silver-birch tree is often called the Lady of the Woods." Harold said, leaning his back against one of the nearest trees. "Did you know that?"

Edyth shook her head.

"It is the tree of the Norse goddess, Frigga. A woman's tree, the symbol of love and of new beginnings."

She had not known that either.

Harold reached up and broke off a length of supple twig, its small, spade-shaped leaves tightly curled. He pushed himself away from the trunk and gave her his simple offering. "It ought to be a garland, but..." He indicated his left arm.

Edyth took the twig and looped it around the fair skin of her neck, twisting its ends together to form a crude necklace. "There," she said, tucking her chin down to peer at her new finery, "it sits well."

Saying nothing, Harold took hold of her fingers, placed them within the cupped stiffness of his left hand, manipulated each stubbornly resistant digit to curl around hers. Her eyes lifted, questioning, to look into his face, then she dropped her gaze quickly, uncertain at what she had felt. She saw his fingers actually tighten, felt the pressure of his hand squeezing hers.

"You can use your hand!" she exclaimed with delight.

Harold grinned. "Aye, for a few days now I have felt tingling there, like the stab of pins and needles. I hope it will not be long before I have full use restored. I..." He paused, the grin fading to a more serious expression. "I wanted you to be the first to know."

Understanding the compliment, Edyth squeezed his hand back, whispering, "Thank you." She raised her other hand and touched the tip of her fingers to his cheek. "Your smile reached this side of your mouth, that is also healing."

Turning his head, Harold slid his lips beneath her touch, lightly kissed her fingers. Startled, she caught her breath and moved back half a pace, self-consciously twining her hands together behind her back.

"You have healed me," he said without trying to move after her, "with your captivating laughter and your sweet voice. And with the tears that you shed in secret during the hours of darkness. Edyth, I am to leave here, but I cannot bring myself to leave without you. If you can feel for me even a part of that which I feel for you, would you consider becoming my hand-fast woman?"

She made to answer, but he moved swiftly, touching his good hand to her lips, staying any hasty word.

"I am an earl, son to a man who, below the King, is the most powerful in all England. One day I will need to make a Christian-blessed marriage in order to forge an alliance for my family. Through such a marriage I may be able to put an end to the rivalry that has existed between Wessex and the Northumbrian or Mercian lands all these many years. That time is not yet, and until then I would follow the custom of our Danish ancestors by taking a first wife, a love-wife."

Edyth wanted to speak, yet the words would not pass the choking in her throat. So dearly had she not wanted this man to leave her, but she had never dreamt to hear what he was now saying. How could she answer him? Her joy was too great, too completely overwhelming.

A second time Harold asked, "Would you, my dearest, beloved Edyth, here among the silver trees, with none save God as witness, consent to take me as your hand-fast husband?"

Lifting her eyes, the diamond glitter of welling tears resting on her lashes, Edyth smiled up at him. "Yes," she answered, her voice so faint that he barely heard. Then she tipped her head higher, straightened her shoulders and said again, louder and with conviction, "Yes please, I would so consent."

Harold tossed his head back, laughed his delight and, threading his good arm round her waist, whirled her in a few dancing circles, guiding her between the upright silver trunks, her feet occasionally lifting from the damp soil. Breathless, he halted, and drew her to him, her body pressing against the firm strength of his chest. Then bent his head and kissed her, as a man who has found his love should kiss a woman.

Her arms went about his neck and as she returned the kiss he laid her gently down, taking her to him as his woman, giving in return his devotion. Giving it with care and tenderness, their union witnessed by God and the silver birch, the Lady of the Woods.

II

⤞⤝

London

London, Edyth realised, was larger, busier and noisier than ever she could have imagined. It also stank.

She had ridden the dozen or so miles from Nazeing in a state of bubbling euphoria. Her father had allowed her to borrow one of the farm's mares; Harold himself had presented her with a new saddle of exceptional quality, sent for some weeks previously as a thank-you gift and purchased, he told her, from the most skilled harness-maker in all London. "Soon, you will see where such things are made for yourself. And more besides."

They had left an hour after sunrise, thankful that the drizzling rain of the previous day had dried into a cloud-covered but pleasantly warm morning. Edyth wore a spring-green cloak, new-made riding apparel and a smile that Harold said was wider than the River Thames itself. She was also nervous, for she had never travelled so far from home, but Harold stayed always at her side, making conversation to put her at ease, although his enthusiasm for the journey was not as buoyant as he pretended.

The weeks at Nazeing had, once his illness began to abate, been a time of pleasure—not merely because of Edyth. Days of blissful abstention from responsibility; an opportunity to sit beside the river, quietly to observe the hypnotic current as it rippled and eddied. A rare chance to enjoy the spring flowers blooming, watch the wind scurry through the trees or the rain moving across the sky in banks of shape-changing cloud. He had rediscovered things from childhood that he had forgotten—fishing, riding for the pleasure of it, the marvel of new life on a farm: lambs, calves, chicks and piglets. The pace of a freeborn farmer directed by the cycle of nature had suddenly appealed, although Harold was aware that without adequate gold, such a living could be harsh. There was always work to be done—hard work—on the land, from dawn till dusk, through all weathers, all seasons. A peasant relied on a small patch of land, one pig, one goat, to provide his meagre existence; had no servant, no well-stocked barn or comfortable Hall. No fur-lined boots or cloak to keep out the cold of mid-winter. Harold knew all that, knew that the life he had been born to, of politics, leadership, warfare and government, to outwit an opponent, was the only one that he could follow. This pessimism that he was trying to hide from Edyth arose from a reluctance to return to the banal bickering of court and the tedium of pointless bureaucracy.

The office of earl was a demanding role, and there would be much for him to catch up with: legal matters to make judgment on, charters to witness and sign...he had reliable clerical secretaries who had kept him informed of the more important matters, but the first few days back in London would inevitably revolve around endless meetings, discussions and decision-making. Edward would expect his full attention too; would have much to discuss. Harold only hoped that most of it would be important, not a surfeit of information about church building or hunting. Though Harold was always willing to listen to a recounting of a good chase, Edward had a tedious habit of repeating particular anecdotes. And then there were his numerous Norman friends to be tolerated.

Naturally, Edward had brought his favoured companions with him when he returned to England and, naturally, some of them he had wanted to reward, but there were limits to the degree of honours presented to outsiders. Men like Robert Champart for example.

No doubt the matter of Queen Emma's removal would be high on the agenda also—his father's letters had seen Harold informed of that particular sour turn of events. He agreed with Godwine that to humiliate the Queen had been a mistake—all rumour of her involvement with Magnus had proven unfounded—but equally Harold had conceded his father's difficulty. If Swegn, damn him, had not been so foolishly implicated, then perhaps Godwine could have prevented the whole unfortunate business. Ah, but repercussions were bound to be swirling around court still...At least he had Edyth with him. She would be waiting for him at the end of the long days, with her happy smile and soft young body.

The road they followed was level and well gravelled, with only the occasional pothole. Behind them it ran northwards up into the ancient Saxon lands of the North and South Folk and the lonely windswept swathes of the East Anglian fenlands. Ahead, the distant smoke haze that hung in a ragged fug over the city of London was visible for most of their journey. Much of the land to the northeast of London, now that they had ridden away from the forested ridges above the Lea and Roding valleys, was flat marshland divided by rivers and streams, the reed beds and isolated clumps of alder or crack willow occupied by waders and water fowl. They had passed through hamlets such as Walhamstowe, Leaton

and Stokæ, where women and children had come from their houses to wave
and cheer; those working in the fields had halted their plough teams to watch
the cavalcade pass by.

The first thing that struck Edyth as they approached London itself was the
height of its walls. The Roman giants, Harold told her, had built them to defend
England's most important town from harm. "No one can attack London," he
informed her with pride. "Not without the prospect of a long siege and much
discomfort. London can only fall from within. When—if—the people decide
to surrender." And that, Edyth thought to herself, they would surely never do!

They followed the banks of the sluggish Walbrook river as it trundled towards
the Thames—and then they were at the Bishop's Gate, riding beneath its
echoing stone archway. Their escort, Harold's housecarls and servants, bunched
closer, their horses' shod hooves clattering on the road that was suddenly no
longer rough gravel but cobbled. The noise of the city was not immediately
apparent, for they rode down through the Corn Hill, where not so many years
past the wheat had been more dominant than the new-settled inhabitants. The
hovels were beginning to encroach further out on to the few acres of open
land, especially in the vicinity of All Hallows with its high-gabled, resplendently
thatched-reed roof. The Londoners affectionately called it Grass Church, visitors and foreigners, mistaking the common-used accent, knowing it as Grace
Church. The building squatted, serene, in the last oasis of peace before the bustle
of the market streets of East Cheap.

They turned their horses into the busy scramble—Edyth had never heard so
much noise, not even at the autumn slaughter. She thought the old bull last
year had bellowed loud, but this, this was incredible! Traders yodelled from
behind their heaped stalls, men and women bawling out the attractions of their
wares, haggling sharply and furiously with buyers, irritable with the slower
minded, quick to strike a bargain whenever they could. A barrage of voices,
high-pitched, gruff, cursing or laughing. Accents Edyth had not heard before,
languages she could not identify. The riders passed stacks of wooden, copper
and clay bowls; pewter ware; woven baskets of all shapes, sizes and forms. Stalls
bright with colourful bolts of cloth, fruit stalls, meat stalls, wine and ale sellers.
Leather and hides. Iron, wool…everything imaginable. She saw a black-haired
person with skin as dark as a bay pony's polished coat, another tall and fair with
a bright-bladed axe slotted through his belt. This was the part of London where
people headed, where trade flourished, where the gold and silver was made
and paid. They came to London from all over the world, the merchants and
the traders. From Denmark and Norway, Flanders and France and Normandy.

From further away than that: Rome and Greece and the Holy Land. From Africa and Spain!

Women carried bulging packages; men humped rolls of cloth, sacks or crates and barrels. Handcarts blocked the road, while ragged children darted in and out of it all. Barking dogs, squealing mules, lowing oxen. Above the noise rose the smell of unwashed people all crowded together. Muck and filth clogged the road. Debris and animal dung mixed with raw sewage. Yet no one seemed to notice either the raucous din or the appalling stench. It was all a part of what made London what it was—the busiest, almost the most important port in all the world.

Edyth did not know where to look first, what to see, what to hear. Her heart raced and thumped from the thrill of it all, her throat croaking a sudden cry of fear when her horse was thrust aside from Harold and the escort. The crowd closed into the sudden free space; a man, bent beneath heavy sheepskins, pushed in front of her. But instantly Harold reappeared at her side, his mouth grinning reassurance, his hand coming out to take the mare's reins, to lead her quietly forward.

They were through the press of the crowds and coming out on to Thames Street. More traders had set their stalls along the open embankment, fish sellers, pie makers—every culinary concoction imaginable. The river itself was no less crowded. Small boats and fishing boats. Merchant vessels with their high, swooping prows, flat-keeled boats with their single sails furled, moored against the oak timbers of the wharves or beached upon the clay reinforcement of the low-tide mud banks. Great sea-going beasts out of the water, some at anchor, others with oars out to manoeuvre against the water's flow before the flood tide should come in upon them.

Ahead towered the wooden structure of London Bridge sweeping across the river. Never had Edyth imagined that a mere bridge could be so wide or so long, nor that it could take the accumulated weight of so many. Surely, any minute it would creak and groan, and fall into the white-foamed water that was rushing beneath?

The mare faltered as her fore hoof touched the timber, but again Harold was there, coaxing her forward. "I can see I will have to buy you a mount more used to these crowds," he said. "As soon as I can, I will take you to the horse sales down on the Smoothfield market."

Curses and laughter emanated from the press ahead, a flurry, and a piglet, ears flat, tail bolt upright, ran squealing from between people's legs, heading for the street beyond the bridge. Several men made to clutch it, one woman tried to toss her shawl over it, but it dodged aside, hurtling between the hooves of Harold's horse. The animal merely snorted and sidestepped.

"There is every kind of mount imaginable at Smoothfield," Harold continued, as if nothing had happened. "Mares, geldings, ambling palfreys and high-stepping colts, destriers with quivering ears and proud hearts. Mind, there is many a rogue at the horse market—man and beast—but if you know what you are seeking you can find it, if you're prepared to haggle the price."

A boy, a barefoot, ragged-dressed lad of no more than seven years, darted in the piglet's trail, ripples of teasing and more than a few crude curses following in his wake. He dodged around the horses, leapt the last three strides from the timber bridge and scampered on up the lane to where astonished voices marked the animal's route.

Edyth had watched with growing horror as the pig narrowly missed her own mare's trampling hooves—what if she shied? She gasped as the boy almost collided with her mare's broad rump, hardly heard Harold's calm narrative of the horse market.

Staunchly, she concentrated on looking ahead, telling herself not to look down, not to think of that mass of water below. Her relief on reaching the other side was immense, quickly overshadowed by the realisation that they had arrived, were at Godwine's London estate, his Hall in Southwark.

It looked much the same as her father's steading, save that it was larger, with double the number of outbuildings—and that it was surrounded by a timber-built palisade fence that stood twice the height of a man. Guards stamped to attention as Harold rode through the open gateway; servants ran to take the horses and unload the pack ponies. Countess Gytha was suddenly there, coming quickly down the wooden steps from the Hall, her arms outstretched to welcome her son. Behind her came Godwine, rough-faced but wearing a beaming expression of pleasure, and beside him a fourteen-year-old boy, Gyrth, his fourth son, who strongly resembled his mother, with her high cheekbones and slender-shaped mouth and chin.

Others were clustering around, coming, it seemed, from every door and from around every corner. Family and kindred, servant and housecarl…so many people clustered into the confined space of the courtyard. So much noise and bustle!

Edyth sat her mare, uncertain whether to jump down or wait, embarrassed by the sudden realisation that she was in high company and had no idea of the correct thing to do. A tall blond-haired young man who had been vigorously pumping Harold's arm detached himself from the Earl and strode over to her. He thrust both his broad, strong hands around Edyth's waist and lifted her from the saddle as if she were as light as a single goose feather, proclaiming, "And who are you? Not attached to Harold, I trust? He has all the fortune when it comes to the finest-looking ladies!"

Embarrassed, Edyth blushed and looked at the toes of her boots, Harold rescued her, taking her hand and drawing her protectively close to his side.

"I am sorry, cousin, but my Lady here is spoken for." The pride in his voice was unmistakable. "She is Edyth Swannhæls, and she is my hand-fast wife. This, my dear-heart, is my mother's nephew from Denmark, Beorn Estrithson. He has an intelligent brain and a brave heart, but uses neither because he has discovered that his privy member has other uses than the necessity to piddle!"

Playfully Beorn protested. He made to punch Harold's shoulder; the older man, laughing, caught the fist and sent a mock blow in return. Two younger boys had darted into the assembly, their faces grimed, boots muddy, one carrying a fishing pole, the other three fresh-caught fish. From their colouring and appearance, and the way they launched themselves simultaneously on to Harold's back, feet kicking and hands clasping at his hair, they had to be his two youngest brothers, Leofwine and Wulfnoth, one eight, the other nine years old.

Edyth smiled shyly, aware that she was not one of the family. With Harold distracted by the boys, Countess Gytha stepped forward to embrace her, bidding a welcome with a genuine affection. Godwine, after half-heartedly admonishing his youngest two, patted Harold's shoulder and then turned to sweep his bear-muscled arms around her. "Delighted!" he boomed, holding Edyth at arm's length and looking at her approvingly. "I am delighted for you both. Every good fortune to you!"

When first she had met him, Edyth had been in awe of this bull-chested man, but had seen that beneath the ruthlessness of his public image he cherished his family. Edyth was a little frightened of his status, but liked him very much as a man. As her father-in-law, she had no hesitation in returning his embrace.

Two people remained within the shadows of the doorway, ambivalently watching the joyous reunion. "All this fuss!" Tostig snorted, folding his arms across his chest. "Our brother Harold is returned and the entire household behaves as if it is the Second Coming!"

"But he has been ill. Mother would not have ridden all that way up into Essex had he not been close to death." Edith, shocked at her brother's near blasphemy, was torn between the two loyalties for brother against brother.

"He looks to be in good enough health now," Tostig answered, acid contempt in his voice.

"You are just jealous because he is receiving all the attention." Edith pushed her arm through her favourite brother's, gave it a squeeze. "You'll be happy once you have an earldom settled upon you. Once I am wed, I shall see to it that Edward rewards you with some position of great authority. Perhaps something even higher than Harold? Would that please you?"

Tostig frowned. Even Emma, after her years of authority, had not managed half of what Edith was envisioning she would achieve once she was queen. And then he noticed Edyth.

"Well, well! He has brought the Nazeing whore called Edyth of the Swan's Neck with him! Swegn said our brother had eyes bulging in his breeches for her."

Edith looked, her expression hardening. She walked forward, her head high, her gown of expensive silk rustling as she moved. Tostig was not being fair. Harold ought to be welcomed with open hearts back into his proper place. A backwater steading somewhere along the Lea valley was all very well for a quiet convalescence, and temporary liaisons, but he was, after all, Earl of East Anglia and would soon be brother-in-law to the King of England. Strumpets might be acceptable to pass the time in the country, but Edward would most certainly not admit a common-born whore into his court.

Tostig watched, amused, as his sister swept down the steps to embrace Harold ostentatiously. He? Jealous of Harold? If Edith's performance down in that courtyard was not prompted by jealousy then he was the king of England! He snorted through his nostrils and stalked off towards the stables.

"Harold!" Arms outstretched, Edith joyfully launched herself at her brother. "I was so worried, so afraid that you would die—that you would not be well enough to attend my wedding! Have you heard of my marriage? I am sure you were told. I am to be Queen—think of that! You and Swegn boasting at becoming earls—and now I am to outshine you all, am I not? Papa included!" She tossed a coy look at her father, who guffawed, amused at her absurdity.

Linking her arms through Harold's, Edith drew him with her as she began to walk, chattering about her wedding plans, back towards the Hall. In midflow she suddenly asked, "Who is the wench, brother?" Without waiting for a reply, her high, clear voice sailed on: "I fully understand that you enjoy intimate company in your bed, but you are not thinking of presenting her at court, I trust? Edward has no liking for whores. Indeed, he respects only the Christian vows of marriage, has no patience with these archaic heathen customs."

As brother and sister entered the shadows of the Hall, any response that Harold might have made was muffled by the bustle of men and women returning to their duties, but Gytha had heard every word that her tactless daughter had spoken. From the tinge of pink on her cheeks, so had Edyth. Amiably the Countess offered to escort her to Harold's private quarters. "He has a chamber to the rear of the Hall," she explained. "It is modest but comfortable." Gytha indicated a narrow path that threaded beside the imposing timbered walls of the Mead Hall. "You can reach it from a passageway from within, but this is more secluded should you wish for privacy."

She halted before a rectangular dwelling set against the rear of the main building. Built of wattle and plaster, with sloping thatched roof and a single window with shutters open to the daylight, it seemed a house place that might be lived in by any man of moderate means. Gytha clicked the door-latch open, beckoned for Edyth to come inside. Within, the touches of comfort were undoubtedly Gytha's thoughtfulness—no unwed man would think to place such a sunny counterpane of yellow interwoven checks upon the bed, nor bother with the sumptuous bear- and wolf-skins spread across the oak-wood floor. Bright tapestries adorned the whitewashed walls; two chests and a table with an earthenware jar filled with spring flowers and a bowl of dried fruits upon it stood against one wall.

Edyth's eyes were drawn to the bed, curtained by swathes of saffron material. Large enough to accommodate a man and his bed-mate, it dominated the small room. She blushed as two servants entered carrying her clothes chest and personal belongings.

Countess Gytha caught her embarrassment, put her finger below Edyth's chin and tipped her young, innocent face upwards. "I ought not admit to having a favourite son, for I should value all my boys the same, yet Harold is special to me, perhaps because he is the most like his father. If you are able to make my son happy then I am most pleased."

She paused, wondering, not for the first time, what had happened to some of her children. Here was Harold, genial, good-natured and pleasant-mannered, a handsome man any woman would be proud to call son or husband. Her last-born sons also, Gyrth, almost into his manhood, Leofwine and Wulfnoth, boys full of mischief but with kind hearts. But Swegn, Tostig and Edith? Where had she made the mistake with those three? *Heaven help us*, she thought, *when Edith becomes the mother of a future king.*

She turned back to Edyth, her smile radiant and genuine, said honestly, "I am mistress of this house, not my daughter, and I am delighted to welcome you into my family."

12

⤖

Thorney Island

The King received Harold at court more effusively than even his family had. The cry of joy, the kiss to both cheeks, the embrace…all of it Harold shrewdly assessed to be false, an act. Godwine was not in favour with the King, and neither was Earl Siward of Northumbria or Leofric of Mercia. By openly displaying public favouritism or barbed sarcasm and displeasure as it suited his unpredictable whim, Edward could play one power holder off against the other.

Harold had brought his anointed king a present—bribery, some would call it—but it was always wise to keep Edward content. When he had become king, Earl Godwine had sought to curry his favour by presenting a sixty-oared, single-masted warship, complete with gilded prow, the best tackle and carrying eighty fully armed soldiers. Harold could not match that extravagance, but he had a gift of a similar nature to offer.

"Sire, your welcome is more than kind. I have greatly missed the pleasures of court and I praise God that I am now able to attend you." His words were in French, since Edward had recently, for reasons of his own, ordered that language to be spoken at court. It was the tongue of culture and achievement, Edward proclaimed. He was as capable of speaking and reading English as he was of using Latin, Greek or Danish, but whether he was missing his past in Normandy, or merely deliberately provoking his short-tempered earls, no one had yet decided. Leofric and Siward could understand few of the foreign words and could certainly not pronounce them. Another prod to deepen the rivalries of these powerful men. The Godwines, father, brothers and daughter, were fluent in many languages.

Modestly accepting a further embrace from Edward, Harold continued his re-hearsed greeting. "I have a gift for you, my Lord. It has not yet arrived but before Easter Monday comes there will be a modest craft awaiting you at Queenshythe Wharf. Bonny, sleek-built and swift of sail, she is being ferried down the Lea at this moment and will, I trust, be suitable for the boys' boat race on that day.

I would wager a gold purse that she can win that race, should you have a suggestion for someone to captain her."

The young man standing a single pace behind Edward widened his speedwell-blue eyes, almost hopping from foot to foot with sudden excitement. Turned fifteen, tall and fair of face, Ralf of Mantes was the son of Edward's sister. He looked from Harold to his uncle, like an overweight dog begging for a tit-bit. "Uncle," he asked tentatively, "I would be honoured to captain her for you."

Edward stroked his blond beard. "I have not yet seen this gift, my lad, yet already you ask to take it from me?" He shook his head slowly. "What if she is not all Harold says? The Godwine family are notorious for their exaggeration."

Neither Harold nor his father uttered a word. No reaction to the deliberate insult suggesting they were inveterate liars flickered on their faces. Harold merely firmed his lips slightly tighter; Godwine stored it away in his mind with the host of other collected ridicules and aspersions. One day, he just might be pushed into opening the lid to that store-box…

Edward continued talking to Ralf aware the jibe had wounded Godwine, satisfied that the man could not retaliate. A pity the mud should also spatter Harold on this occasion, but every opportunity to keep these precocious earls in check had to be made use of. "The race can be a dangerous affair. Ought I allow my beloved nephew to take such risks?"

Ralf chewed his lip. Edward looked at Harold, who stood, dressed in his finest apparel, his face schooled to detached stillness. Edward enjoyed his games of cat and mouse, but no one at court could be complacent about when or how the cat would pounce.

"You cannot captain her, uncle," Ralf persisted. "I know you prefer to cheer the competitors rather than sail yourself—you told me so, not many days past!" Wisely, he did not add that besides, Edward was too old to enter the Easter river tourney, which was for the boys of London, not the old men.

"Youngsters today, eh, Harold? It is all want, want, want, and take, take, take." Edward slapped his earl of East Anglia on the shoulder, becoming jovial again, the batting claws temporarily sheathed. "In my day we accepted what we were given and lived with it without mithering." Politely everyone nodded agreement. "You have commissioned this fine craft for me, Harold. Could my nephew captain her, win me the race?"

Harold allowed his expression to relax into a genuine smile. He liked Ralf, despite the Norman blood in his veins. "I would say this young man would represent England with honour, sir."

Delighted, Ralf leapt into the air, clapping his hands together. The King, Harold and Earl Godwine laughed appreciatively, yet other men scowled at this favouring of another foreigner. At least Edward, although come to manhood in Normandy, had been born in England with both father and mother committed to the English cause. Ralf's mother had been sent abroad as the child bride to a Norman nobleman; Ralf, born and raised across the sea, had come to England three months before Edward's coronation. He was a Norman receiving too many privileges from England and some feared that, as a kinsman of a king, he might have an eye on the throne itself.

The royal Hall was smoke-addled and stuffy despite air being drawn up through the smoke hole and the draughts riddling through and under walls and doors. Men of the Witan drifted into groups, debating the afternoon's prospective meeting of Council. Bishops and clerics huddled together; earls, shire reeves, aldermen and merchantmen sought the opinions of their own kind. Tomorrow would see the Easter Moot of the London Guilds, held in the city of London within the imposing Alderman's Hall. Erected in Aldermansbury Street, the place had, in the time of King Alfred, been a simple fortified Hall of timber and Roman stone, owned by a wealthy merchantman who had achieved the high and respected status of Alderman. During the settled years after Alfred, with trade flourishing and wealth growing, the merchants and tradesmen of London had begun to form themselves into guilds the better to serve their particular trade, setting agreed standards of workmanship, rates of price and pay, and authorising the number of apprentices. What better place than that same Alderman's Hall for the London goldsmiths guild to meet? The bakers, the tanners, potters and weavers to debate the selling of wares, limit the encroachment of foreign imports or complain against the high rate of taxation? Edward intensely disliked going to the Guilds' meeting house. In fact, setting foot inside the walls of London revolted him. It stank no more than other large cities—Winchester or York—nor was it any noisier or more crowded. No, London held too many sour memories for Edward. It was from London that his mother had yielded to that usurper's claim. And London's populace had not raised a single finger to protect him, his brother or their claim to the throne.

Edward, not wishing to be drawn into Guild or Council matters, took Harold to one side. "I hear you are to found a religious college at Waltham? It seems the fashion for all my earls at the moment. Siward founds a house, Leofric and his wife Countess Godgiva are to build an abbey at Coventry."

Harold could not understand Edward's scathing tone. It was not uncommon for wealthy men to become patrons of religious houses; if you could not earn

God's favour, then why not purchase it? To build a church was to acquire a meagre place in heaven. To build an abbey, a seat at God's side.

"I begin to feel," Edward continued peevishly, "that the men around me either have much explaining to do to God, or are taking the opportunity to parade their wealth and status. If that be the case, to whom? Each other? Me?"

A drink would have been welcome. To have taken a sip would have allowed Harold a moment to consider an answer. "I offer an abbey to Waltham," he said carefully—it was all too easy to offend Edward when he was teetering on one of his petulant moods. "Because my illness was cured there, a suitable way to give thanks for God's blessing, do you not think?"

"Indeed it is," Edward responded forthrightly, accepting the answer. "But that rogue, Earl Leofric, cannot claim the same."

There were two answers Harold could make. Aye, well, Leofric is a scheming, money-grabbing bastard who will buy support from whatever quarter he deems necessary. That response did not seem appropriate. Instead, Harold offered tact. "Why do you not consider building some monument to the glory of your reign? The greatest of kings ought always to leave some permanent reminder of their achievements."

The self-satisfaction that spread rapidly over Edward's face told Harold that he had hit the target dead centre. "A monastery at Islip in Oxfordshire, perhaps? The place of your birthing would be appropriate."

Scratching at his beard, Edward gazed upwards at the soot-blackened arched timbers of the sharply apexed roof. A damp, cold and dismal place, this Hall, with no pomp, nothing that impressed. The kitchens were on the far side of the courtyard—food arrived chilled and greasy; the stabling was suited only for mounts the size of shaggy ponies, not the warhorses that Edward had brought with him from Normandy. The kennels were overcrowded; two bitches had not whelped this year because of it. Edward liked his hunting and if hounds were not in fine fettle then the day's chase might as well not be bothered with.

The river fog and mists made this island so damp, of course. Now, if stone were used for building…Edward closed his eyes, saw in his mind the splendid citadels of Normandy that he had lived in as a child and young man. Duke Robert's palace at Rouen, the castles of Alan de Bretagne, Gilbert, comte de Brionne, the Counts of Eu and Burgundy. His sister, Ralf's mother, had lived until the death of her first husband in a stone-built fortification placed upon a man-made hill at Mantes. Her present husband, the Count, Eustace de Boulogne, lived in even grander style. Edward's eyes snapped open—and those men were nothing but counts! Here he was, a king, sovereign lord of all

England, standing shivering with cold feet and numbed hands in a timber shack, a wattle-built midden heap!

"Stone!" he proclaimed. "That is the material to use. I intend to erect something magnificent." He raised his voice so that those nearby might hear. "My council shall agree to have built, in my honour, a residence more fitting to my status. I will have a palace here on Thorney and, where the timber chapel of St. Peter's is frequently washed by the spring floods, the ground will be cleared and drained. There I shall rebuild that insignificant church. My offering to God will be an abbey, a minster of the finest stone, with windows of glass and a tower that stretches to the sky. It will be called the West Minster, and the aldermen of the guilds, when they have need to speak with me, will assemble here." He pointed at his feet. "Here in my new King's Hall within the Palace of West Minster!" He gazed at those present, eyes alight, and the bishops, clerics, merchants and aldermen put their hands together in polite applause. Siward and Leofric exchanged wry glances with Godwine and Harold, then joined the vociferous congratulating of Edward for his insight and wisdom. It was something they had overlooked in the enthusiasm of their own building: Edward would not want to be left out of the glory. His petty jealousies could reverberate for months.

Harold had no further speech with Edward until the preliminary meeting of the Council was due to commence. They were proceeding along the shadow-bound corridor that linked the Hall with the more secluded council chamber. Edward, wearing his royal regalia and his gold crown, led the file of men and instructed Harold to walk beside him. "Were you aware, Harold, that Baldwin of Flanders is again complaining about trade? He wails that our export tax is over high, our import restrictions too limiting. In particular he has been bellyaching about our wool exports. Yours, actually, from East Anglia."

Harold spread his hands, at a loss for the second time that day for a suitable answer. Baldwin of Flanders, although an occasional ally of England, was a pain in the backside when it came to complaining about the imbalances of trade.

"I have been ill, Sir, I regret that I have not kept abreast of the situation. Allow me a day or two to investigate and I shall report to you."

Impatiently Edward flapped his hand. "I have clerics who have seen to all that boring nonsense. No, it is for a more permanent solution that I have raised this issue with you. Baldwin has a brood of daughters, a few of them nearing marriageable age. I think it time you sought a Christian-vowed marriage, my lad. Ally with Flanders. That will sort the man's damned moaning."

Harold froze, pale with shock. Godwine, a few paces behind, cannoned into him. Harold was not short-tempered like his elder brother, nor was he a man of forthright views as was his father. He took his obligations seriously but equally, his private life was important.

How could he answer? "Begging your pardon, my Lord King, but I have recently taken a woman as hand-fast wife. I have no wish, as yet, to pursue marriage elsewhere. I am content with Edyth."

"But I am not." Edward fixed Harold with a brief stare of contemptuous disapproval, then turned to face Earl Godwine. "I am not content to take in marriage the daughter of a man who allows his son to sin against the laws of our Christian Church."

Harold caught his breath, as did other men, the muted sounds of shock tumbling loud in the quietness.

Godwine was an accomplished tactician, rarely lost for words. His quick mind was well able to deal with this new insult to his family. "By the laws of our land, my son is at liberty to take into his bed a legally acknowledged concubine. As do many men of your Council." Pointedly, Godwine glanced around at the men following. "More than a few of those who serve you have taken a mistress as well as wife. Even men of God are not reluctant to have their beds warmed by something softer than a fire-heated brick."

Godwine stood spear-straight, gazing without fear at Edward. "You, however, must take a Christian-blessed wife, for you must have a legitimate son. There must be no challenge to the next who may sit on the throne of England, as there has been between you and your half-sibling rivals, but Earl Harold here and Earl Siward, and Leofric and…" He paused. Many faces began to suffuse with red. "No." With a mocking bow of acknowledgement, he allowed his hands to drop. "No more names. Some here, for all that the custom is legal, do not wish their private liaisons made public. Let us just say that these men here, including my second-born son, will not become king and so they are free to follow the old laws if they so choose."

Edward's expression was turning petulant. Godwine stepped closer and added, so that only he could hear, "You would not want such eminent men to deny your request for a new palace, Sire? I remind you that the public purse is low and we may yet receive another invasion from across the North Sea this summer. There will be ships to provision, men to pay. The Guilds will not accept any rise in taxation…" He let the words falter, locked eyes with Edward. "You may need to fund the building from your own treasury." He said no more, allowed the words that would have followed to run as a silent but potent: *If you want your palace, leave the old laws be.*

Edward glared with what almost amounted to hatred at the silent men watching him, some with heads ducked, a few brazenly outstaring him as Harold and Godwine were doing. "It is a matter," Godwine concluded, "of liberal interpretation. We bow our heads to the laws of the church, so long as those laws allow us to follow the laws of our ancestors. And besides, it would be foolish, would it not, to ally with Baldwin of Flanders before we are certain whether he intends to go with, or against, Magnus of Norway?"

Edward scowled. *Damn Godwine* he thought. *Damn the bloody, arrogant, meddling man.* He turned his back and stalked alone to the council chamber with an expression of dark, rumbling thunder.

He had regretted the decision to take Edith Godwine's daughter as wife within twenty and four hours of announcing it. The arrogance of Godwine! Robert Champart's idea had been to restrain the insufferable Earl, to bind him neck, ankle and wrist. It had not occurred to either of them that betrothal to Edith might unlock the few chains of subordination that already existed and leave only a redoubled ambition for power. Oh, the plan had worked well at first—when Godwine had ridden into Winchester and so easily broken his alliance with the Queen—damn her meddling eyes. She was already prevailing upon notable men of the church to mount a plea of innocence on her behalf. It was only a matter of time before he would be forced to show public compassion to the manipulative old hag. Well, time wasting could be stretched two ways.

For their defiance this day, Godwine and Harold would be made to feel as much frustration as he did with them. Godwine would be made to wait! While this betrothal stood, Edith could not enter into agreement with anyone else. Godwine could seek no other alliance for her. If he required the help of other noble houses, well, let him force Harold into a Christian marriage.

Edward's contempt took in every face, every expression as the men of his Witan filed into the council chamber and took their seats.

Godwine and Harold—aye and all those other squirming toads—would pay dearly for this day's defiance. Edward grunted a bitter, hollow sound. *I do not forget. Never, do I forget*, he thought. *It is the one acceptable trait that I appear to have inherited, in full, from my mother.*

13

Southwark

"But Mother!" Tears of annoyed frustration were beginning to fall down Edith's cheeks. Irritably she brushed at her right eye; weeping, she knew of old, would not get her mother's sympathy. "Tears are for the tragedies of life, not the minor incidents," Gytha had often remarked.

A maidservant entered from the outer Hall carrying a basket containing hanks of spun red-dyed wool. Gytha pointed to the floor beside her loom. "Place it here, Fræda."

The girl bobbed a curtsey and left the chamber through the same door.

Edith, sitting hunched and dejected on a stool, was trembling with anger and frustration. "I am ashamed before the court, before all England. The King will not allow me to enter into his Hall. Will not allow me through the gates at Thorney…I was turned away, Mother! Not an hour since, turned away!"

Gytha was standing at her loom, threading stone weights upon the ends of the warp threads. This latest family crisis permitting, she intended to begin a new cloth today; the youngest boys were in desperate need of new tunics—how fast they grew! She dropped a weight, bent to retrieve it, inspecting the ring of stone with care to ensure no crack ran through it. With a sigh she answered her daughter. "Edward has been a bachelor for so many years, child. It must be difficult for him to adjust to the prospect of taking a wife into his bed."

A fresh cry rose from Edith's lips. "He will never take me to his bed, though, will he? Not now! He detests the sight of me, has set me aside. I am shamed. I may as well retire to a convent or drown myself in the Thames!"

Gytha was losing patience; she had much to do this afternoon. Perhaps it had been a mistake to bring Edith from Wilton? At the nunnery all this delaying on Edward's part would have passed her by. "Two rather extreme solutions, do you not think, daughter?" she responded with mild derision. "If Edward truly no longer wants you, then your father will simply find you an alternative husband."

"If there is any man desperate enough. Who would want me now—would take a king's cast-off as wife?"

Plenty of men, Gytha mused. *Men who would be only too pleased to ride on the back of Godwine's position and fortune, regardless of the status of the daughter.* But it was an unkind thought, she kept it to herself.

Edith had always been a capricious child, her moods changing as frequently as the direction of the wind. The Countess supposed that most of it was because she had been the only girl child among so many boys. There was no denying that the girl had been spoilt in compensation for having no sisters, for always being the one left out. The boys had pursued their interests in hunting, sailing, fishing, riding…male occupations. What had there been for Edith? Education, sewing, cooking, weaving. The use and lore of herbs. Just as the boys were expected to follow in their father's steps, Edith was destined to become a wife and mistress of some grand household. Young ladies did not hunt or sail, did not come home of an evening muddied and bloodied, as so frequently had the boys.

Edith leapt from her stool, toppling it to the rush-covered floor, her fists clenched, fair hair tossing. "This is all Father's fault! His and Harold's! Father has been deliberately antagonising Edward for weeks and now Harold has upset him by taking a common-born as his whore. I do not know how you permit it, Mother, he is your son, you ought have more care for his morals!"

"Your brother is a man grown, my dear. His morals are for his own conscience, not mine. Yours neither, for that matter, nor the King's."

As her rage grew, Edith missed the brusque note in her mother's tone. "Edward has denounced Father as contemptuous and defiant, Harold as un-Christian and immoral. Is it a wonder that he now does not want me as wife?"

With the first two statements Gytha had no occasion to disagree. She had heard the same complaints last night from her indignant husband as he prepared for bed. He had stamped around the bed chamber, hurling clothes to the floor as he removed them, cursing Edward's unreasonable peevishness the louder with each discarded garment. She answered her daughter as she had answered her husband: "Edward is finding his feet in the matter of government. He blows hot and cold, like the weather, because he is insecure. For too long was he left in Normandy. An unwanted boy, a man without home, country or place in society, neither follower nor leader. Suddenly he finds himself a king, with the incompetence of his father hanging over him and the interference of his mother to contend with. He has been released from the cage, but his wings remain stiff. One day soon he will realise that he can fly, independent of the demands of others."

Gytha was ever reluctant to see evil or weakness in any man or woman. Not everyone, she believed, found their strength, their talent or gift with ease.

"Edward is impulsive and inconstant because he is not yet sure of his own ability to make a correct decision. By next week he will be condemning some other inconsequential matter, my daughter. Leave this latest quarrel to burn itself out."

"Why has father not apologised to the King for so upsetting him at that first meeting of Council a few days past?" Edith demanded to know. "And would it be so difficult for Harold to appease the King and take a daughter of Baldwin of Flanders—to return his slut, bag and baggage, back to the Nazeing midden hut whence she came? Both of them, Father and Harold, are jeopardising my future for their own swollen-headed pride!"

When the serving girl, Fræda, had left the room she had pulled the door closed behind her, but the latch had not caught. A stray gust of wind trumpeting through the open Hall doors had buffeted against it and nudged it ajar, before running off to ruffle the wall tapestries.

Ordinarily, it would not have mattered; indeed, Gytha often left the door open. On this day, however, while Edith Godwinesdaughter was tormenting herself out of all proportion with the cruelties of fate, Harold's Edyth was seated not two yards from the chamber door in the public Hall, delightedly beating Gytha's nephew, Beorn, at a game of tæfl, a board game she had played often with her father. She was immensely enjoying this particular match because Harold had bought her the set for her own yesterday. The checkered squares were made from ivory and jet with the playing pieces carved from horses' teeth, the details on each "soldier" set with gold and minutely cut gems of sapphire and ruby. It was exquisite, while the game against Beorn, which she was winning, demanded all her skill.

Beorn's move. He sat well forward on his stool, concentration etched into his wrinkled frown. By Thor's Hammer, the girl had outmanoeuvred him! As far as he could see, he was surrounded on four sides and captured. He lifted his hands in surrender. "I have never lost to a woman before, but as you are so strikingly beautiful, I'll not hold that against you."

Edyth laughed and began setting the pieces in place for another game. "If it eases the pain of losing," she jested, "I have never claimed victory over so handsome a young man before."

"What?" a voice boomed from behind her shoulder, "do you say this upstart who has monopolised you this past hour is more handsome than me? Shame on you, woman!" Harold, returning from checking his lame stallion, affectionately kissed Edyth's cheek.

"You, my Lord," she answered, twisting her head to look at him, her eyes sparkling with merriment, "are over twenty years of age. You cannot claim to be a young man."

"Agh!" He clutched at his wounded heart. "Not only am I not handsome, I am also in my dotage!" He shooed Edyth off her stool, sat himself and pulled her down on to his knee.

"How is the horse?" Beorn asked, making the first move of another game.

"Oh, 'tis nothing serious, a swollen fetlock. Fool animal must have twisted it on the way home from Thorney yester-eve." Some of the gaiety left Harold as he remembered the previous day and yet another confrontation with a fault-finding Edward, But who cared about Edward's petty foibles when he had his dearest Edyth beside him?

The Hall had been full of activity: servants hammering a loose trestle-table plank back into position; a woman singing as she vigorously swept the timber floor of the raised dais on which stood Godwine's high table. But by a quirk of fate, a jest from the gods, for a moment the building fell quiet. The floor rushes whispered from a rustle of wind and from the private chamber shrilled Harold's sister's distressed voice: "And would it be so difficult for Harold to appease the King and take a daughter of Baldwin of Flanders—to return his slut, bag and baggage, back to the Nazeing midden hut whence she came?"

Edyth blanched, her teeth biting hard into her bottom lip to stem a ragged cry. This was too much to bear! She ought to have stayed at home where she belonged. Her coming to London had created nothing but difficulties. Edith disliked her. The King disapproved of her, was furious with Harold and his father. Harold must be feeling a prize fool for bringing her here, but was too kind-hearted to admit it. What was he doing with her, a mere thegn's daughter?

She would not weep in public, not before Harold's young cousin or the servants. They had all heard, of course, would be sneering behind her back, as Edith was. Nor would she weep in front of Harold. Edyth stood, brushing aside his hold. "I have a woman's matter to attend," she stated. She walked, with all the dignity she could summon, from the Hall, out into the blustering drizzle.

The wind caught at her veil. She tore the thing from her head. Were she at home in Nazeing she would have run to the woods or to the field to bury her head in her pony's mane. Edyth ran instead up to the walkway that strode along the top of the stronghold's outer timber walls. Only the watchguards stood up there, and they would mind their own business.

Harold took a few sharp, angry steps after her, then altered course and stormed into his mother's chamber, slamming the door hard against the timber and plaster wall. His mother and sister looked up, startled. Gytha guessed instantly what had occurred, but her daughter's ill temper only increased at the sight of her brother.

"You have ruined my prospects for marriage by being so inconsiderate—" but she got no further, for Harold was across the room, his hands gripping her shoulders.

"Since the day of your birth you have been cosseted and indulged. In this, I am as much to blame as my mother, father and brothers, but there will be no more of it from this quarter, my girl! Do you hear, no more!" As he shouted, his hands, none too gently, shook her. "I will tell you this. Listen well. I have no intention of allying with Baldwin of Flanders. I love and admire Edyth, and I intend to hold her as mine until the day of my death—and aye, even beyond. She is my chosen woman, will be the mother of my children, and neither you, the King, nor the damned Pope in Rome will force us apart. Do I make myself clear?" He shook her once more, thrust her down on a stool and turned to his mother. Muscles, jaw and fists clenched, he exhaled several shuddering breaths and, reining in his temper, apologised to the Countess. "Forgive the manner of my entrance and my harsh words, my Lady Mother. My woman heard what was said here this day and it has upset her, as it has upset me also. I think it is time that my sister learnt a lesson in humility."

Edith was outraged. She flew to her feet and ran to her mother. "Are you going to allow him to speak to me like this? Say something to him, Mother! Order him to apologise at once!"

Gytha had no hesitation. She would not tolerate fools or bullies; less still would she tolerate dishonour. Her hand came out and struck Edith across the cheek. "If anyone has brought shame on this house, then it is you by insulting a newcomer to our family who sleeps with my blessing beneath this roof. Perhaps it is your own arrogance that is turning the King against you, and nothing that my husband or your brother has done."

Edith, struck dumb, stared at her mother. She drew a breath, then turned on Harold. "You would not speak so were either of my brothers present! If Swegn or Tostig were here, they would have whipped you for your spitefully spoken words."

"But they are not here," Harold declared pointedly. "Tostig mislikes my company and has gone to join Swegn. To learn how to be defeated by the Welsh."

"At least two of my brothers are doing their duty for England, not wasting their days and nights whoring with a commoner!"

Harold folded his arms, his expression patronising, words acerbic. "Swegn," he answered, "could find a whorehouse with his eyes bound. He must know his way around every brothel in the land. Tostig wouldn't know what to do with either a whore or a Welshman."

Edith slapped him, hard, then fled the room.

"That," Harold reflected ruefully, as he rubbed his stinging jaw, "I did not do well."

"Which part?" Gytha asked neutrally.

Harold shrugged, then offered her a weak, apologetic grin. "All of it?"

Gytha touched her son's cheek. "Love is a precious thing. Hold it and guard it well, while you may." She sighed, closed her eyes briefly. "Marriage is no easy thing for a girl who has not the fortune of your Edyth, Harold. Where there is love a marriage is filled with spring blossom and happiness. Where the man takes with no intention of giving, there is naught but winter-bare branches and dark emptiness. Edward holds nothing for Edith, I suspect for no woman. He is using her in an attempt to control your father. As for love…" Gytha opened her hands, palms upward in a gesture of empty despair. "Edward has never known affection; where will my daughter fit into his insular life?" Gytha shrugged, unable to answer her own question. "Tolerate your sister's outbursts, Harold. They are wrong-footed, but her anger stems from fear of a lonely future without love or compassion."

Harold considered his mother's words. Nodded once. He too shrugged in resignation. "I must find Edyth. She has not, I think, much enjoyed London. I will return to my duties in East Anglia as soon as I can, find for us a house place where we can be independent of court and, with respect to your good heart, Mother, of the jealousies that surround your offspring." He bent forward, placed a light kiss on Gytha's cheek and left the room.

Gytha stood, twirling a loom weight between her fingers. Edith would be wed to Edward at some time in the future for he could not, no matter how much he wanted it, renege on this betrothal.

She sighed. Godwine had visited Denmark on behalf of Cnut; she had been in her first flush of womanhood, he a handsome, strong-minded, strong-bodied Englishman. The passion that had stirred between them had ignited into a fervent love that remained as potent now as it had been then. When Godwine had left Denmark he had taken Gytha with him as his wife.

She had been so fortunate with Godwine; few women were able to wed the man they loved. Betrothals, for women of noble birth, were for the political and financial uniting of two families. Love rarely came into it. A man could take a concubine as a love-wife, the woman could only pray to God for a kind husband and an easy time in childbirth. It was a fortunate girl whose father found for her a good husband. Those who chose their own men, as had Gytha—and Edyth Swannhæls—were rare breeds. As parents Gytha and Earl Godwine could not guarantee Edith a satisfactory marriage, although the chance to become Queen of England would make many a girl content to ignore the occasional beating, the straying to another bed—or the frustrating indecisions of an over-pious, captious, mid-aged man who would perhaps have been more suited to wearing a tonsure than a crown. And the faults would not be all on Edward's side. It was a hard thing for a mother to admit of her own and only daughter, but the child was disdainful and pretentious. "God in his Heaven help her keep hold on her sense," she said beneath her breath, "when Edith becomes queen and realises the full extent of her power."

14

Southwark

Emma—a lady who had perfected the art of exact timing—reached Earl Godwine's Southwark house as dusk was reluctantly giving way to the night. Her modest entourage drew to a weary halt in the courtyard, the riders as wind-blown as the horses, for the last few miles had been covered at a stout, bone-jarring trot.

A chill mist seeped up from the Thames. London Bridge was wraithed in the shape-shifting whiteness, the top of the two portal towers standing like disembodied heads above the shrouded supporting pillars. The sounds of the city settling for the night emanated from across the river, echoing with a hollow, muffled eeriness. A bell tolled from somewhere, its single, tinny clang monotonously dour in the fading light; a dog barked, voices called. Emma's hand-maiden shuddered as the horses turned in through the gateway, thankful that they were not to cross the river. She was tired, stiff and cold, wished she could be as strong in body and mind as her mistress. Very little flustered the Queen, she cared nothing for hidden shapes and evils that might lurk in the evening fog. Did not feel fear or cold, nothing disturbed her calm exterior—except perhaps having her possessions and land forcibly removed by her own son. Even then she had waited with patience through the long winter and the first few weeks of spring before beginning to rectify the matter.

Godwine's servants scrambled from various quarters, some wiping ale from their mouths, others hastily swallowing their supper; a man ran to take Emma's horse by the bridle, another slithered to a halt to stand, astounded, before hurtling back inside his master's Hall. A moment later Godwine himself appeared, fingers hastily tidying gravy residue from his moustache; he strode down the steps, professionally masking his own surprise; this visit had been unexpected, unannounced. Through his smile the Earl was rapidly deciding how to react—of course Emma was welcome, but what in Thor's name would Edward say of it? Silently, Godwine swore. The last thing he needed was to antagonise the King further by offering a welcome to his deposed mother, but what could he do— turn her away into the night? If nothing else, the laws of hospitality forbade it.

Emma had already dismounted. She smiled at Godwine with her eyes and mouth, a greeting that sprang from the heart. "My dear friend!" she exclaimed, coming forward with small, rapid strides to take his hands tight in her own. She kissed both his cheeks, her face suddenly looking tired and worried. "Forgive this intrusion—I had hoped to reach Westminster, but we have travelled slower than intended, and as you see it grows dark…" She vaguely waved her hand at the twilight. Godwine did not believe a word of the excuse, as she well knew. He only need look at the dark sweat on the horses' necks and flanks to see they had been urged far from slowly, but who was an earl to question the word of a queen?

Ah, will there ever again be such a fine and handsome woman? Godwine thought as he raised her hands to his lips.

"It is time to end my son's nonsense," she announced blithely, as if her quarrel with Edward had been some mild family scrap. "I have lived long enough as a displaced, penniless widow. The condition bores me."

Unfortunately it did not, yet, bore Edward.

Godwine was not sure how to answer her tactfully. He returned the genial smile, spread his hands and said candidly, "I am not entirely in favour with the King myself at this moment, my Lady. Perhaps I am not the best person to champion a cause?" He snorted amusement. "Indeed, if I knew how to do that I would not be in such a predicament myself!"

Laughing at the absurdity of their mutual situation, Emma slid her arm through Godwine's. "I will think of something that might aid the both of us," she said. "Now, escort me to Hall. I would rather discuss my ungrateful whelp with good food inside my belly and a cup of wine in my hand."

Seated at Godwine's high table, her hands cleansed, her gown changed and a meal inside her, Emma was already recovering from the weariness she had masked so carefully, a weariness that had overtaken her, these last months, in both body and mind. Although she never let her feelings become visible, the winter had taken a savage toll on her reserves of strength. While not in her dotage, at five and fifty she was no longer a young woman. Left by Edward's spite with no means of support or income, she had slimmed down her household to the barest essential servants—how many unfortunate souls had she been forced to dismiss! All the more for Edward's conscience to bear. Good people set to the streets for a king's whim, curse him! While she would have wintered at Winchester anyway, the thought of being nigh on a prisoner there haunted her. Oh, she was permitted to travel—but where would she have gone? Her wealth, her properties and estates had been withdrawn from her, all she had at her disposal was this modest entourage and virtually the clothes she stood in. No one who wished to retain the King's favour would offer her shelter or assist- ance—who would willingly support a woman with neither influence, wealth, land, nor status? Even if that woman was still, by law and by God's anointing, the legal Queen of England? Only Godwine, perhaps, would take that risk, yet he too was sailing up a shallow creek against the tide.

Being without income, property or power did not mean being without eyes and ears, however, and Emma, despite her need dramatically to reduce her daily expenditure, had maintained her informers. There were some things she counted as essential, a network of spies being one of them. She knew that Leofric of Mercia was currying Edward's approval by being robust in his collection of the taxes—and that his wife had quarrelled bitterly with him about it. That Siward had been squabbling, to the point of battle, with Scotland over the ill-defined border with Northumbria. Knew of Godwine's disfavour and that Harold had been close to death.

There were two new faces, unknown to her, at Godwine's table: Harold's hand-fast wife and a robust and cheerful young Danish man, Beorn, nephew of Godwine's wife. He appeared a good-natured lad, who had led the talk of the morrow's river tourney through most of the excellent meal, boasting that his craft would beat Edward's chosen crew. He and Harold had exchanged ribald jests on the topic until Harold had declared: "You give your best effort to win, cousin. To my mind, Edward does not deserve my gift of such a fine-built Lea craft."

Ah, Emma thought, *so the rumour of disagreement between Harold and my son is also true.* God's patience, was there anyone in this realm whom Edward had not recently insulted?

That the promise of marriage with Edith was faltering did not surprise Emma in the least. Had Edward wanted a wife he would have allied himself with some Norman family of worth years since. As far as Emma had discovered he was not interested in the intimate comforts offered by women. There had been a few doxies in his youth, when his body had first ripened into maturity, and he had shared a bed for three months with Alys, the daughter of a minor Norman count, until forced to leave the unsettled atmosphere of the new boy duke's court. Emma had no ideas—nor interest—in what had happened to the girl; the only thing that mattered was that she had not borne a child, living or dead. Either she was at fault or Edward was not master of his own manhood. The truth of that would be seen at some suitable date after his wedding night. If Edward ever managed to agree a wedding night.

She surveyed her prospective daughter-in-law surreptitiously. Edith was plain, but acceptable. Fair-haired with a clean, unpocked complexion. A pity that such a disgruntled scowl seemed so tightly etched there…Large hips, flat belly, a firm breast. A girl ripe for breeding. God's teeth, but Edward was a fool! If he reneged on this betrothal he would lose the respect of every nobleman in the kingdom. *Edward? King? Oh aye, king of oath-breakers!* And what was he intending to do about the small matter of acquiring an heir? Conjure a son from mid-air? Pray that a child would be conceived from a virgin's womb? She had assuredly bred a simpleton!

Had he listened to her advice, he would have been married with a whole brood of fledglings crawling around his royal chilblained feet by now…oh, this was pointless. Never would her fool son listen to her. Emma allowed herself a brief, self-satisfied smile except for this once, when she would meet with him on the morrow. The information she held could save England a long and costly war, but there was a price that he would need to pay in order to hear it.

The harper was taking his seat beside the hearth fire, his nimble fingers tuning the instrument for an evening of story and song. Later, after the men had over-partaken of wine and ale, these subdued pleasures would give way to wrestling matches and raucous singing and boasting. She would have quitted the Hall by then, along with the rest of the women, leaving the men to their excesses.

The Queen leant back in her chair and cupped her chin while she studied the young woman seated beside Harold Godwinesson. Godwine's daughter might be acceptable, but this creature was a rare gem, a beauty.

The pride in Harold's voice had been unmistakable when he had first introduced the girl to her, the shyness of the child as apparent. That there was a naïve infatuation shared between the two lovers was undeniable, but between the sister and this lass? Ah, storm clouds were brewing there!

"I hear the King would rather you took, with Christian blessing, a wife of higher status." Emma said to Harold, seated at her left hand. "Does the prospect of a grand alliance, and perhaps further power, not lure you? I understand your sister and my son both disapprove of your declaration of love for a woman bred of common land-folk. Would it not have been wiser to take her as your bed-mate until a daughter more suitable was offered you?" It was an impertinent remark. She had intended it to be, to gauge Harold's reaction.

He was a mild-tempered man who feared God, loved hunting, disliked over-indulgence and unnecessary fighting; enjoyed good wine, a warm fire, a companion in his bed. A man who fulfilled his responsibilities as best he was able. He loved Edyth. "My sister," Harold answered, giving Emma a full, unwavering stare, "is vexed that her own marriage is delayed. Her ill will towards my woman stems from frustration." He paused, took a sip of his wine. "The King," he continued blithely, "can go to the devil. I choose the woman who is to be my companion, not he." It was a bold—and potentially dangerous—reply. He had taken Edyth as hand-fast wife and hand-fast wife she was going to remain.

Rinsing her fingers in the bowl of rose water that a servant offered, Emma dried them fastidiously on the linen towel. Rarely did she say anything just for the sake of it. Harold's reaction had pleased her. Here was a man who would stand firm for his own beliefs, regardless of influence from others. Harold Godwinesson would make a good warlord, A pity the eldest son was not more like his brother. "Indeed, I intended no offence, Earl Harold, I wish you every happiness, at least for the length that your joining together may last."

As an apology it fell short of its target. Harold answered her politely, but with inflexible defiance: "This hand-fast marriage will last, my Lady Emma, for as long as I intend it to. And I intend it to last a very long time."

Seeking to soothe his ruffled feathers, Emma placed her hand on the stained tablecloth, a small, subtle extension to her apology. "I have had personal experience of concubine wives." She spread her fingers in a gesture of contrition, began absently toying with the rings that adorned them. Æthelred had avowed himself to a hand-fast wife prior to taking her in marriage, as had Cnut. Sons from both those bitches had caused Emma, as queen and mother of princes, no end of heartache. Had caused death and war for England.

She liked Harold, one of the few men she did like, possibly because he was the son most similar to her father. Few men—earls, thegns, freemen, hah! even kings—would put England before their personal greed, Harold, she thought, would prove to be one of the rare ones, one of the few.

For that, and for being honest, Emma would wish him and his shy, blushing maid no ill. She smiled at Harold, her face crinkling into lines of laughter that had rarely, through her entire life, been allowed a public airing. She lifted her goblet, clinked it against Harold's. "Then let you and me damn Edward together and drink to our prospective hanging for the crime of treason!"

Unlike Swegn, his elder brother, Harold seldom took offence and accepted apologies when given in faith. "Edyth is a sweet girl, madam, who makes me content." He grinned at Emma. "In bed and out of it!"

Edyth had overheard nigh on every word; her blush of embarrassment tinted from pink to crimson red as Harold leant across and smacked a kiss on her lips. Beneath the table his hand was rummaging under her gown. She flicked his exploring fingers aside, her eyes flashing a reprimand. He laughed and gave her a second kiss, firmer and more possessive. For all her self-consciousness at this public display of affection, her stomach gave a leap of anticipation. Not so long ago she had dreaded the first intimate touch from a man. How foolishly childish she had been—but then, she had not expected that man to be one such as Harold.

Emma, although she barely knew the girl, instinctively liked her. Cynically, though, she knew she liked her because Edward did not, would always go out of her way to oppose her son. What he liked, she detested. What he condemned, she endorsed. It was a habit she had acquired during those interminable years of marriage to Æthelred. All he had been interested in was the use of a young maid's untouched body. Was it any wonder that she hated Edward? Conceived through what had almost amounted to rape, birthed through two full days of an agonising labour that had come close to taking her life? Not until Cnut had shown her the meaning of love had she discovered the delight of the giving and taking of passion.

Love? Hah! Where it existed there was always a counterbalance of hatred or sadness lurking somewhere. A pity that before too many years passed this young woman, whom Harold professed to love so much, would have her heart broken when he left her for a Christian marriage of alliance.

And what of the other Edith? Godwine's daughter? Would she find love once Edward eventually made up his mind to complete this marriage? At least it was doubtful she would suffer from the same fear and pain that Æthelred had inflicted. More likely, she would have to tolerate an excess of prayers before she could settle to bed.

Would the marriage be suitable? If it were, more suitable for whom? Edward, Godwine—Emma herself?

Edward did not want a wife but he needed a son. He desired also to curb both Emma's interferences and Godwine's political power. Marriage to Edith, unfortunate child, was his solution to accomplish all three, while expending as little energy as possible.

Godwine wanted his daughter wed to a king. As father of a queen, grandfather of a first-bom heir, the ætheling, he would become the most powerful man in all England, especially if something untoward happened to the reigning king. Which was possible. Edward was not a young man; the position of regent was one well worth pursuing. As Emma well knew, for she had ruled as regent when Cnut had been king.

And, she mused, *what do I want for myself?*

She had been lady, wife, mother, queen, regent, widow and dowager. Each part she had played in the drama of her life had been a lead role. There had been no choice for her in the matter of marriage to Æthelred; years of disappointment and fear had followed. When Cnut offered her the choice of exile or marriage, what kind of fool would she have been to have chosen exile? To disappear abroad, to become a nothing instead of remaining Queen? No matter that this second marriage might have turned out harsh, without love or respect—she had endured all that with Æthelred. But fortune had blessed her. The choice had been a good one. Was that perhaps why Edward resented her so, because she had risen from the ashes of defeat like a sun on a beautiful summer's morning, while he had been left to moulder?

Emma sighed, swallowed her wine. The wife of kings, the mother of kings. Those months ago when Edward had so humiliated her she had wanted nothing more than ferocious revenge, would have waged war to redeem what was rightfully hers. But now? Now she was tired of it all. Weary to the bone of the continual struggle for survival. She cared not a dried grape for remaining the prima donna, was content to withdraw into the dignity of widowed dowager—but she would not do so at Edward's dictate. If she were to take a lesser part in this play, then she would write the lines of her exit. Power was not, now, so important; pride and dignity, the restoration of her independence and her wealth, had become paramount.

Let someone else wear the title queen, someone else battle for survival in the cruel world of politics. Edith would at least have an advantage, for unlike the young girl that Emma had once been, she had a father and brothers who would ensure her rights were respected. She would have also a mother-in-law who had every intention of taking a keen interest in the birth, upbringing and progress of her grandchildren.

15

∾

London

A river mist had lain late along the embankment of the Thames, but by mid-morning the sun had managed to burn away the creeping whiteness, leaving the river to sparkle beneath a cheerful blue sky. At Queen's Hythe the many little boats, moored alongside the larger sea-going keels, bobbed and buffeted each other as a slight breeze tickled the water. Spectators lined the bridge and riverside, those early comers who could not afford the luxury of the erected galleries setting down their stools and makeshift seats to secure a good view of the annual river tournament. Animated talk and the exchange of wagers on the entrants mingled with the cries of the street sellers and the excited chatter of the boys preparing their boats.

Accompanied by his court, Edward rode the two miles from Thorney Island at a leisurely pace and in good humour. The entertainment would begin with the river jousting—already the pole had been placed in mid-flow, its bright-painted shield set several feet above the height of the flood tide. Each boat, crewed by the young and skilled oarsmen of London, had chosen their marksman, a boy who with braced lance would attempt to strike the shield dead centre. If he did so, then the craft would pass by the pole amid cheers of praise, but all too many boys would miss the target and take a dunking in the river—to the laughter and delight of the watching crowd.

The King's servants had brought the royal throne downriver from Thorney and had garlanded it with spring blossoms, set it beneath a canopy erected on a raised platform, directly opposite the tilt pole. Edward dismounted and stood at the river edge, fluttering his hand at the cheering spectators. He so enjoyed these crown-wearing days when his people had a chance to see him in all his splendid regalia. Loved, too, the enthusiastic applause. This was what it was to be a king! To be seen, acknowledged. Admired and loved.

His good friend Robert Champart had advised him to dress sensibly in warm clothing today; even on a day of bright sunshine the river chill could penetrate a man's bones. Sensibly, but finely. A blue woollen mantle over a linen tunic drawn in at the waist; the softest of woollen cross-gaitered leggings, his feet comfortable in doe-hide shoes, dyed red. Both cloak and tunic were edged with broad bands of intricate design, gold thread woven among the silks of vivid reds and blues, the garments held together by splendid brooches that glittered in the light. Resting upon his head, his crown, with its exquisite jewels. The King, robed and crowned, preeminent in rank and law and dignity, with all under his authority and all paying him tribute. At least for Edward there came the cheers of a genuine affection. His father, Æthelred, had far too often had rotten eggs hurled at him.

Naturally, Edward had been informed of his mother's arrival at Godwine's Southwark house yester-eve. Godwine himself had sent the message, his man slipping quietly out of the gateway and running those few miles upriver. The Earl was no fool. Infinitely preferable to inform the King himself, rather than let others whisper it in his ear. The King, however, met with a surprise as Emma stepped forward from the knot of people around Godwine. She made no attempt to ascend the steps to the royal platform, but offered her son a deep curtsey that swept the puddled gravel of the pathway that ran beside the river. Edward was taken aback. He had expected a scene from her, a shrill demanding of her rights. Most certainly had not expected contrition.

Emma knelt and, with her head bowed, publicly pleaded her son's forgiveness, begged that he return her dignity. "The woman who bore such a beloved monarch should live as befits her position. I would not have the King ridiculed because his mother lives in poverty."

"Rest assured, madam," Edward countered witheringly, "I am not ridiculed now. On the contrary, I used to hear sniggers while your presence dominated my court. A man who cannot live beyond the clutch of his mother's grasping hand is not, I have discovered, much admired."

Raising her head, Emma stared at him, her eyes showing nothing but regret. "I wish only to serve you as best I may. That has ever been my wish. So, too, did I serve your father. To survive after his death, I took the only road offered me and served Cnut, in the hope that one day you, my first-born son, would find a way to return to England and take your rightful place at her helm." Nonsense, of course, but Edward had always enjoyed flattery.

When he, with the aid of his brother, had once attempted to take the throne from Harold Harefoot, Cnut's son by his concubine, he had been forcibly denied entry into the country—and his brother Alfred had been murdered. He did not mention that sorry episode as an indictment of his mother's failing him, however, for his own poor part in the affair deeply shamed him.

Instead, Edward asked tersely, "What of your son Harthacnut? What of those rumours of your support for Magnus? You preferred the first to become king above me." He strode down the wooden steps to stand authoritatively over her. "When have you given me your support? Eh? Answer me that?"

"You must allow for a mother's frailties, my Lord King," she answered quickly, her gaze steadfast. "Her youngest child is often her most dear, for it is the youngest who keeps her young. Alas, the eldest only reminds her of her ripening years. I supported your half-brother Harthacnut from vanity. From my fear of growing old. It was I, however, who urged him to recall you to England." She paused. Her knees were aching; the rough gravel was pressing into her skin through her gown, but she made no attempt to rise. As for Magnus of Norway…rumour would never outflank lack of evidence. She reached out and took Edward's left hand. "And on my life, I assure you that I have never been in league with that Norwegian whoreson, although I do admit to retaining contact with one or two men of influence within his court. I have been, in my time, a powerful woman, Edward. Across the seas I have friends in royal courts and thegns' homesteadings alike, and as they are loyal to me, so am I loyal to you." She placed her lips reverently to his signet ring. His face, which had at first puckered into a scowl, was now wrinkling into a frown of suspicion.

"As proof of my devotion I have information to offer, regarding Magnus's intentions towards this sacred realm of England." She spoke up now, playing to the spectators as well as Edward. She had not intended to reveal her spies' news until later but she shrewdly judged that Edward was succumbing to her performance of humble repentance, opening the doors to his guilt and conscience…

"I believe that Magnus himself intends to sail for these shores come the summer season," she announced. All those nearby drew breath. Too many remembered the fighting that came with Cnut's invasion, the cost in terms of blood and gold. "I give you this news, so that your ships may be made ready in time to set a blockade against him. No man, be he Viking seafarer, Norwegian or Dane, can match the superiority of our English keels!"

She declared the last with ringing voice, both her arms upraised. The listening crowd responded with a roar of approval. English ships were the best, English sailors without peer.

Edward was not quite the fool his mother thought. He knew the woman's humility to be a sham; guessed she had known of this news for many weeks—if not months—waiting for the right time to reveal it, a time to suit her own needs, not the needs of England. Huh, when did she ever care for others? There was only one person Emma cared for and that was Emma herself. But one of Edward's weaknesses was his emotion. He was not usually a deliberately cruel or hard man; he had been known to shed tears at a beautiful song, a heart-moving prayer. What chance had such sensitive feelings against a woman so plaintively begging forgiveness? And what choice had he? London held Emma in regard and high affection. Give him a few more years, some popular charters and favours granted, and he would be as heart-held as she...oh, she was clever, his mother! London would never allow him to dismiss her from his presence—how well had she chosen the occasion to outmanoeuvre him! To lose the support of Londoners could be to lose the crown. Cnut had known that—which was why Emma had remained in the city when he had invaded England. It was why he had eventually chosen a diplomatic course over one of prolonged siege and warfare.

For the benefit of the London public Edward bent down, embraced his mother, and invited her on to the platform to sit beside him. The Londoners cheered at his benevolence. Emma was delighted. Carefully laid tactics could so often avoid the spillage of a single drop of blood.

With the King seated, the signal was given for the tourney to begin. The wind, as Robert Champart, seated to Edward's right, had predicted, was indeed chill and he spread a woollen blanket over his king's knees. How carefully was he masking his anger.

Grateful for Robert's care, not noticing the tick of rage that stuttered at the corner of the eye, Edward smiled at him. "We shall have a fine afternoon's entertainment I think, Robert!"

Champart said nothing in return. Emma he hated. Emma had won.

The Thames river was calm, caught between the ebb and flood tides. The younger boys were to have their turn at the tilt before the tide turned to a seaward flow that would mulch the current into eddies and drifts, making it all the more difficult to handle a craft.

Emma had ignored Champart's presence. That he had instigated her son's maliciousness was probable—Edward, alone, would never have dared confront her on her own ground. Champart had surely suggested that Edward take Godwine's daughter in marriage, to divert Godwine from serving her, Emmæ Regina. A weasel of a man, Champart, intent only on his own gain.

Emma leant towards her son and confided, "To my surprise, I have actually enjoyed the peace of living away from the tedium of royal politics these last months."

The boys of the first crew were driving their oars into the water, their scrawny arms pumping, their faces grim with exertion. A red-haired lad stood proud at the bow, feet and legs apart, body swaying to maintain balance, his lance tucked against his ribs. He hit the shield square in the centre with a thump that bounded across the water, instantly drowned by the roaring cheer of spectators.

"I would wish to embrace fully the existence of the quieter life, but how can I?" Emma gave a long sigh of exhaustion. "When the crown was placed upon my head and those drops of holy oil anointed my brow, I vowed to serve my God and England. Alas, I cannot turn my back on duty because I no longer care for the demands of the role. I am, like it or not, an anointed queen. A queen must complement her king, sit at his right hand." She blinked slowly and pointedly at Champart who sat at Edward's right side with a smirk as bedevilled as a cat that has found his way into the dairy. "A queen," she continued, "must be trusted by her king to rule temporarily if, God forbid, he became incapacitated through illness or the need to lead his army into war."

"Trust and you, Mother," Edward commented drily, "are not words that ride easy side along side."

Her expression of wide-eyed innocence would have outclassed any roving actor's. "My Lord, you have me wrong! I do not speak for my own sake, but for the queen who is to come after me, I speak here for your future wife, for Edith, Godwinesdaughter!" The calculated indignation in her voice was lost as Edward stormed to his feet to shout home the next direct hit of lance against shield. He had heard her, however, for, reseating himself some moments later, he said with a growl of contempt, "I do not care for a wife who may turn out to be as much of a damned nuisance as you have been."

Emma genuinely laughed. "My dear son, you will never control a mother or a lover, but you can always control a wife!" She spoke true enough, for no woman would push her place beyond reason—not until her first son was born. Once a wife became a mother, ah, then all things altered.

Edward wanted a son. He enjoyed the company of children, wished dearly for a brood of his own. Could not stomach, though, the intimate details of taking a wife. At least, not one whose father wanted to take command of England, Godwine, damn him, was not going to!

Edward slumped in his chair, his lip thrusting forward, petulant. "I would have thought the last thing you wanted, Mother, was a chit of a girl to take your place at court. You might be content to allow her father to grasp me by the balls, but I am not!" He spoke sourly, the pleasure of the day fading. "What do you intend to get out of this pretence at meekness? The reinstatement of your land? Your wealth? Do you expect to have my treasury under your grubbing hands again merely for information that I could as easily have discovered for myself?" Edward furiously pummelled the cushion behind his back, snapping irritably at a servant who leapt forward to help. "I can do it, boy. I am not totally bloody useless! Though my lady mother would have you all think so!"

Emma repressed her irritation. Suddenly the thought of remaining secluded within her own sensible company at Winchester appealed in reality. "I want the lands that I am entitled to through both my marriages and the wealth that is personally mine. That is all. On the day that you take Edith as your queen, Edward, I intend to retire to Winchester. Leave you in peace."

Edward's laugh was sardonic. "Madam, you almost make me believe you!"

To his consternation, she answered with what was undoubtedly earnest truth: "I swear on Cnut's grave that I shall set aside my duties as Queen. I want nothing but the granting of my dignity, Edward. That is all I ask of you."

Edward's intention, throughout, had been to curtail his mother's power and to strip Godwine of his implacable pride, without upsetting the balance of law and order or giving either of them a dais from which to rally support. It had been done before, a king murdered by the uniting of his earls! *I initiated this wretched betrothal to shackle Godwine*, Edward thought, *yet he has done nothing but strut and pontificate since!* Another boat approached the target pole, her oars not pulling in unison. *I cannot trust my mother—but would I be a fool to squander what may be a genuine offer!*

Edward made his decision as the boy lancer missed the target and tumbled into the water, spray cascading in a spume over the despondent crew. *I will take Edith as wife, get a son from her and hold my mother to her vow.* His eyes narrowed, features hardening. He might not be a vindictive man, but there was a streak of spite within his character, a streak that was as capable of wounding as deeply as any war spear. *And once she is my wife, my exclusive property, I shall cast Godwine from court.*

Edward jeered and laughed at the sodden boy as, grinning, he hauled himself up the algae-slimed wooden steps to the sanctuary of the wharf. The King was uncertain how he would set about his plan, but Robert Champart would know. Robert knew everything. "I shall agree if you remove yourself to Winchester now. I shall wed Edith come Michaelmas."

Satisfied, victorious, Emma settled to enjoy the remainder of the afternoon. Michaelmas would do very well, give her time to begin the girl's instructions. She would take her home to Winchester—Edward could not very well refuse, for surely he would prefer his queen to be suitably tutored in all her future royal duties?

Over thirty boats, crewed by the boys of London, were entered for the race that would follow the jousting tourney; keels of all shapes and sizes, in varying degrees of river-worthiness. Expectant and excited, Edward leant forward as the shout came from upriver that they were away, the race begun. His boat, captained by Ralf, was all the Earl Harold had said she would be. A sleek, proud little craft that skimmed the water as if she were a swallow dipping for a drink on a hot afternoon. The King had high hopes of winning this race.

Nothing could be seen at first, for the contestants were around the bend of the river—only the shouting of the spectators—and then they burst into view. Oars flashing amid a churn of white foam, the crews using every ounce of strength, arms and muscles straining, expressions taut with concentration. In front, two craft, captained by Beorn and Ralf, raced hull to hull. Twice their blades clashed, the captains bellowing for the crews to pick up, dip deeper, pull harder. "Lift her! Lift her!"

Unable to contain his excitement any longer, Edward was on his feet, waving his arms, hopping from foot to foot. "He is going to do it, by God!" he shouted. "My nephew is going to win!"

Aware of the thorny path that he had been walking of late, Godwine seized the opportunity to reclaim lost ground. He stepped closer to the King, shouted above the tumult. "He is a fine young man, Sire. He will soon deserve higher command than that little boat."

Edward turned his head to glower at the Earl. His initial reaction was to answer with some scathing remark, but Robert Champart, standing at the King's shoulder, spoke briefly in his ear. Edward's scowl relaxed into a leering smile.

"You are right, Godwine, Ralf deserves reward. Champart suggests I grant him an earldom. It would be a good gift for my nephew, do you not agree?"

Godwine groaned. Damn Champart, that was not what he had meant…"That would be an excellent proposal, my Lord. In a few years' time, when Ralf reaches manhood and gains a little more experience, it would be a fitting honour for the lad." *God's breath*, Godwine thought as he mouthed the words, *how am I going to explain this to Tostig?* That was the difficulty in having so many grown sons. They all expected similar reward though it was not within their father's sole power to offer up vacant earldoms. That was for the King's giving with Council's approval.

Champart smirked to himself, knowing full well Godwine's predicament.

Ralf s crew was drawing ahead…the water churning, the boys' anguished breath gasping and catching in their throats, the sweat running down their naked backs…a few more yards, just a few more yards!

Harold had been standing to the forefront of the raised platform with his arm protectively around Edyth, sharing her excitement as she shouted for her chosen crew—Beorn's. She was enjoying this, but London, these last days, had become a disappointment.

His sister's unkindness had shaken Edyth deeper than she cared to admit. Her words hurt because at heart Edyth believed there was truth behind them. The King was disgruntled with Harold for bringing her here. Harold's mother and father, Beorn, had made her so welcome which, perhaps, had only served to heighten the petty jealousy. Edyth pitied Harold's sister, a girl expected to make a marriage of convenience to a man many years her senior. Harold squeezed her waist and she glanced up at him, the smile in her eyes matching the one on her mouth. How could she have been so fortunate to have found herself so fine a man?

The boats were nearing when something happened—two keels collided. There was a collective gasp as everyone craned forward to see the better. Who was it? Was anyone hurt or drowning? Harold, with a few other men, including his father and the King, moved nearer the river edge. Someone was coiling a rope, making ready to toss it to a boy splashing towards the bank.

Countess Gytha, frightened that in the mêlée of oars and keels Beorn's craft might have capsized, had run to the water's edge with her husband. Her daughter found herself standing behind Edyth Swannhæls.

The boys in the water had come to no harm, all were laughing, clinging to the side of one of the boats, exchanging ribald comments with spectators and fellow crew members alike. Taking advantage of the confusion, Ralf and Beorn forged ahead, their pace and steady rhythm of the oar beat unruffled by the excitement. The finishing line was so close…

Edith had only to take one stride, pretend to trip, thrust out her arm…

Edyth screamed as she fell. The river, rushing up towards her, deep and cold, took her under. The sunshine blueness on the surface was an illusion, for the water was muddied and dark, garbage and rubbish bobbed along its edge, raw sewage fouled it. She sank down, the surface closing over her head, her veil coming off, her gown cloying against her legs. Her boots, filled with water, becoming heavy, pulling her further towards the bottom. She tried to kick out but they held her—she was going to drown. God help her, the river was going to take her!

Then hands were reaching for her, grabbing at her, fingers clutching her clothing, twisting tight, refusing to let go. She kicked again and another hand had hold of her cloak, was pulling her upwards—her head broke through to precious air. She opened her mouth, found it hard to breathe; they held her firm, those strong hands, pulled and pushed at her, brought her up and into a boat, that was, once she was safe, being rowed towards the steps.

Ralf had seen her fall, had instantly ordered his crew to veer from their course, his keen eyes trained on the ripples where the woman had disappeared. He leant out from the bows, flailed with his hands, by some miracle caught hold of her before she sank too deep. The river was more than twelve feet here at high tide. Beorn had seen the fall at almost the same instant as his rival and steered his craft alongside Ralf's, helping to bring the woman up while the two crews held the boats steady. The other competitors flowed past them, the race open for anyone to take. For Ralf and Beorn it was over.

Harold was there, grey-faced. He had her, hauled her to him, half pushed, half carried her to firm ground. Everyone was clustering around, concerned, the race forgotten. Gytha, the Queen, Godwine. Her sodden hair tangled, tears falling, teeth chattering, hands shaking, Edyth clung to Harold, Countess Gytha removed her cloak and set it about the girl's shoulders. "We must get her home, see she is warmed and dried." Gytha's normal calm had disappeared for she had seen, as had Harold, that the girl could not swim. Knew as well as he, Ralf, Beorn, or any Londoner the treacherous currents that this river could hide.

Knew, as well as Harold, that she had not fallen by accident.

Edyth allowed herself to be swept into Harold's strong arms. She clung to his neck, her misery dark and pressing. He pushed through the crowd, his mother at his side.

"I will have her hide for this." Harold muttered.

Edyth heard, lifted her head. Harold's sister had pushed her, but she would not add to the feud that was already germinating between them. "I slipped," she said, her voice raw. "It was my fault, I stepped too close to the edge to see the race better."

Harold stopped, gazed down at her. Gods, but how his heart had thudded with fear as he watched her body sink under that water! He would never, for the rest of his life, forget the sound of her scream.

"Please, my lover," she said again. "Leave it, I slipped."

Taking a breath to steady the pounding in his chest, Harold touched his lips lightly against hers. He nodded, then looked hard at his sister, who had taken refuge beside Edward. The King had flounced back to his chair, pouting in his disappointment. It was no consolation that, though Ralf had not won, neither had Beorn.

Edith put her hand on to the carved high back of the throne, her movement declaring her immunity. *I am the future queen. Do you dare challenge me, brother?*

Harold stared at her, unimpressed by her bravado. "My wife slipped," he said aloud while his eyes conveyed to his sister, *but I know damned well that you pushed her.* Turning on his heel, he strode towards where the horses were tethered, his housecarls shouldering a path through the crowd, who were still intent on the excitement of the race.

Edith bit hard into her lip, her hands taking hold of her cloak, screwing the folds into tight-clenched bunches. What had she done? What had possessed her? She had only meant to…had not wanted to…had not realised that Edyth could not swim. Her family, all of them, born and raised beside the sea, were like otters in the water. But Edyth was of the land-folk, knew nothing of swimming.

She had been pleasant and kind too, had attempted to be friendly, to offer conversation, and what had Edith given in return? Snubs and insults. Rapidly she blinked away tears. She must not weep, not here in view of the whole of London. She turned to Edward for moral support, tentatively laying her hand upon his arm. This turmoil that eddied and churned in her stomach would disappear once they were married, once she was settled and happy.

Edward had not noticed her, or that brief, hostile exchange with her brother. He was busy demanding of the river master that the race be declared void. He shrugged Edith's hand from his arm as if she were of no more consequence to him than the irritation of a fly.

16

⤞

Winchester—January 1045

Emma thrust open the door to the bed-chamber and curtly dismissed the agitated maidservant. The girl who had fetched the King's mother here scuttled away with her, both relieved at having the burden of responsibility so easily removed.

Emma strode to the bed, tore aside the partially closed brocade curtaining with one hand and, with the other, ripped back the bed coverings of white-bear fur and best linen. Edith, merely curled even tighter into a foetal ball. She lay naked and cold, made no further movement, no response to Emma's sharp reprimand. "Get you from this bed, child! It is morning and the court will be awaiting their new anointed queen, I thought that fool of a girl to be exaggerating when she came in such a fluster, I see she was not." With less patience and more force, she added, "Have I wasted my time these last months instructing a lazy good-for-nothing slugabed?"

Receiving no reply, Emma turned away impatiently and began sorting through the garments laid ready across a wooden chest. The undergarments and hose were of imported silk, the gown of the finest spun blue wool, hemmed by gold embroidery, and the white veil was of a lightweight linen, edged with detailed gold stitching. "You have the Council to greet and your first charter as queen to witness and publish. As was agreed, it is to be a gift of land to the Minster here at Winchester and is to include, in gratitude for your ceremony of marriage yesterday, fifty shillings to aid the ill and poor of this city." With an audible exhalation of irritation, Emma returned to the bed, snatched at Edith's arm, attempting to pull her forcibly to her feet. "Get up!" she roared. "How dare you defy me!"

She was rewarded by the sound of an escaping desperate sob. "I am not queen, I will never be queen, nor wife!"

"Nonsense." Emma clamped her long fingers around Edith's bare arm and hauled her to sit upright. The girl's body was slight, the skin white and unblemished; broad-hipped, slim-waisted, her fair hair rippling loose down her back and over her shoulders, covering firm, rose-bud breasts. "Yester-afternoon on the steps of the Minster you were wed to my son in full view of the populace of Winchester. You were then taken to kneel before God's holy altar where you were crowned and anointed Queen of England." Emma made no attempt to conceal the note of triumph. That the marriage had taken place at all was little short of a miracle, what with Edward's constant excuses and his pathetic, delaying little illnesses. First the wedding was to have been at Michaelmas, then Advent. Postponed to Christmas, New Year—but yesterday, the twenty-third day of January, the last possible day before the earls and assembled nobility and men of importance made ready to return to their estates and supervisions, Edward had finally bowed to the inevitable and had taken Edith Godwinesdaughter as wife.

The months in between had not been wasted for, to Robert Champart's chagrin, Edith had spent them almost in their entirety with Emma. Now all the dowager waited for was the first son to be born. The role of doting grandmother appealed, suited her admirably. A quiet life spent in leisure and comfort, with the dear child playing at her feet and learning under her instruction. Queen by proxy. Most satisfactory.

Tossing the clothes draped across her arm on to the bed, Emma curtly ordered the girl to dress. "Since I have had to dismiss the servants, to minimise the gossip that will spread on the tongues of the idle, you must attire yourself—oh, for goodness' sake, child, stop that ridiculous snivelling! Do you think I took pleasure from my wedding night with Æthelred? Do you think many maids actually enjoy the rutting of the first night with their husband? So it was a painful and unpleasant experience, but you will become used to it. Most of us do."

It was too much. Edith's temper exploded. She propelled herself to her feet, her fists bunching as she spat her hurt and frustration in a torrent of venom. "Do you think that is why I have shed these tears?" she shouted. "Do you think that is why I am ashamed to leave this bed, this room? Because of the discomfort thrust upon my body by my husband? What discomfort, madam? Nothing happened in this bed last night. Your bloody son did nothing!"

It was rare for Emma to be struck speechless. She stood mute, lips parted, attempting to understand. The celebration after the lengthy religious ceremony had followed usual tradition: the sharing of the bride ale, feasting and drinking with entertainment by acrobats and harpers. Come evening, the couple had been undressed and set together side by side in the marriage bed. What did the girl mean, nothing had happened? Of course something had happened!

Frowning her puzzlement, Emma spread her hands, at a loss for what to say. "Child, your mother has surely explained all that is required of you as a wife?"

It was difficult for Edith to appear dignified while standing naked and vulnerable before this austere woman, but she drew herself straight and steadied her quivering breath. Her blue eyes flashed at Emma; she bent, tore the linen undersheet from the bed and wrapped it around her body. "I am not a child, do not call me such. I know the duties that are required of me, but I wonder, madam, does your son know of his?"

Edith swept away from the bed, went to a side table and opened a casket fashioned from elm and exquisitely inlaid with carved elephant ivory. From within she withdrew the queen's crown, Emma's crown—her crown—and swung round to face her mother-in-law, the royal regalia between her hands. "Your son," she said bitterly, "spent the first two hours of the night kneeling beside the bed, praying. He then fumbled at me a while with his cold hands before breaking into sobs of wretchedness and subsequently fleeing bed and bed-chamber. I am as virgin pure now as when I stood before that witnessing crowd yesterday in all my wedding finery."

Briefly, Emma closed her eyes. Was that all this was about? A bumbled wedding-night coupling? It would not be the first marriage that was not consummated until all the festivities had quietened down. In peace and privacy, nature would put itself to rights. She said with a patient smile, "Tonight, my dear, it will be different. You will both be more confident, more at ease with each other. Now come, dress; the court will soon be assembling." Emma retrieved the clothing that had tumbled to the floor and began again to lay it out on the bed.

"There will not be a tonight nor any other night, Edward made that plain to me." Edith made no attempt to move from where she stood. As Emma slowly turned to look at her, Edith lifted her hands, carefully placed the crown upon her own head, setting it there at a slight angle. "I have wept anguished tears at the prospect of wearing this trinket. I so wanted to be Queen, to be the Lady of all England, to be the mother of a king." The linen wrap slipped to the floor to lie in folds around Edith's feet. "Do you wish to know where your son spent his wedding night?" she asked, in a tone heat-scored with derision. "I think you ought. After he informed me that he had no desire within him for women, he told me that he was going to declare himself for God and remain chaste."

With disgust, Edith removed the crown from her head and flung it across the room. It hit the white-plastered wall, fell dented and spoiled on to the crushed rose petals that were strewn among the rushes. "He told me he intended to spend the night in prayer with Robert Champart." Her face contorted into nauseated rage. Spittle slurred her speech. "Do you think that is all they did, my Lady? Kneel together and pray!" Added bitterly, "There will not be an heir to the throne, because the bastard you spawned from your womb is incapable of setting a child within mine."

⁂

Emma sat on a stool beside the meagre warmth of the brazier, both hands nursing the thick stem of a silver goblet. How many difficulties and dramas had she confronted throughout these long years of her life? Too many to remember, too many to name.

For her own life, her fear had reached its height when she had been unable to flee London before the imminent arrival of Cnut and his army. She had needed to make a hasty decision that day, a decision that had to be correct or she would live in misery for the rest of her life. To commit London to the horror of prolonged siege and inevitable bloodshed or to sacrifice herself to a usurper king; lose just her sons already born or lose everything. She had chosen herself and Cnut, and the hope that there would be other sons. As she had now hoped for grandsons. She might have realised that Edward would disappoint her here too.

She drank three-quarters of the goblet, allowing the strength of the red grape to ease the tension in her chest. Her head thumped with a drummer's beat. This, again, would be a decision difficult to make, for it was not her life alone, her future, that she was about to tamper with.

One rule had Emma always adhered to, a rule taught her by her own mother. Weigh a decision as best you can, advantage against disadvantage, sense against folly. Once it is made, follow it through to its end with courage and conviction. What were the choices here, for Edith and for herself? Whimper like a whipped pup, curl up and be crushed? Or stand tall and fight? Godwine's daughter, although she was spoilt and full of jealousy, possessed spirit and determination. Surely something could be salvaged from this midden heap of a mess?

There was one simple question she need ask. "What is preferable—to be a childless queen, or a common mother?"

Edith had returned to the bed, hunching the expensive furs around her shoulders. She tilted up her head, her answer as direct as her gaze. "I would be queen."

Emma nodded, satisfied. "A good choice, made with the head not the heart. To be childless may well see you survive into middle age; too many women die during childbirth." She offered the girl a conspiratorial smile. "Do not forget, also, that youth is on your side. Your husband, my dear, has not that advantage. For you, as there was for me, there may be another husband. Other opportunities to bear sons."

A pity, after all this planning and expectation, that there would be no grandson—but then Edith might have borne only girl children, or the babes might not have survived birth or childhood. It was, perhaps, better to plan on what was, not on what might be.

Although Edith had implied it so, Emma was certain there was no indiscretion between Edward and Champart. Champart was too ambitious, Edward too God-fearing, yet it came as no surprise to discover the fool man had no particular passion for a woman's body. Did that make him a man who preferred intimacy with another man? If it did and others came to hear of it Edward would be finished as king and she would lose everything—everything that she had worked so hard to gain.

"All must seem as it should be," Emma said, rising to her feet and setting her goblet on a table. "It is imperative that you retain your dignity and position in the eyes of the household and the court. In public you act as though nothing untoward has happened, that your marriage is consummated." She swept her eyes around the room. The bed was rumpled, that was all to the good, it would be expected after a wedding night. Edith's crown lay on its side on the floor. Emma went to pick it up, her finger catching on a bent, sharp edge, an ooze of blood welling immediately from a thin and jagged cut. She made to suck the wound, smiled instead and, pinching it to bleed the more profusely, retrieved the linen sheet that lay on the floor. Finding the centre, she dabbed spots of blood on to it, then flung the sheet on to the heap of bed coverings.

"No one can deny the giving of your maidenhead, child. Your proof is that you were seen abed with your husband last night and blood stains the linen."

"What of Edward?" Edith asked, scornful defiance clenching her jaw. "He can most assuredly deny it!"

Emma shrugged. "Leave Edward to me. It will be his word against ours and I doubt even he will openly admit that he is incapable of rutting with his wife." She opened the bed-chamber door. "No thegn, noble or earl—especially an earl such as your father—would remain loyal to a man who preferred to take his chaplain to his bed. If Edward does not take care, he may find his wanting to become a monk a distinct possibility. In certain areas of his body as well as in spirit."

Emma smiled, well satisfied with herself as she walked along the draughty corridor of the royal palace at Winchester. Choices. A king, a queen, had always to face difficult choices. Edward's was perhaps not that hard. Honour Edith as his chosen queen—and herself as a respected dowager—or be gelded by his earls. Aye, the choice was not a difficult one.

17

Leominster

Swegn Godwinesson, resting his arm on the high cantle of his saddle, calmly surveyed the door, firmly closed before him. It was almost midnight and the rain of this cold May month was beginning to fall again with more persistence than the drizzle that had spattered intermittently for most of the day. Already not in the best of moods, Swegn was wet, tired, hungry and in need of a strong drink. He was also wounded, although not so seriously that he desperately required attention. He could probably manage to reach Hereford, but it was further to ride and he had not much inclination to return home. Home? If it was still his home! He would not be surprised to find that the King had decided to give the rest of his border earldom away to that spot-faced, upstart nephew of his, Ralf of Mantes. The damned bastard already had a decent-sized portion of it.

Stiffly, with pain lancing into his left thigh, Swegn dismounted and walked his stallion up to the door.

Ralf of sodding Mantes! Just like that, the boy had been awarded as a sixteenth birthing-day gift a quarter portion of Swegn's land! Land upon which that cock-sure little stripling had immediately built a bloody great Norman defence—a motte castle with stone keep, bailey, rampart and palisade. A castle that as yet neither of the warring princes of Wales, Gryffydd ap Rhydderch of Deheubarth or Gruffydd ap Llewelyn of Gwynedd, had succeeded in penetrating. Most of Herefordshire and the Marches had succumbed, at one month or another, to their raiding parties; slaughter and bloodletting had been common for years along these borders, increasing as the feuding between the two princes, vying for notoriety and superiority, had escalated. Swegn had been powerless to put a stop to it—until this last initiative. A masterpiece of strategic thinking: put an end to hostilities by pitting one prince against the other.

It had all been so easy! Ride into the northern Welsh lands under a token of truce, gain Gwynedd's trust and form an alliance with Gruffydd. Ride together into Deheubarth and hit the other Gryffydd hard. It had taken Swegn weeks to set the plan. The irony? It had been damned successful, but he had acted without consulting Edward, therefore Edward condemned the initiative. Swegn was furious. Returning, elated, from Gwynedd, he had been accosted by a group of the King's men, ordered to accompany them to court and forfeit all rights as earl! He was damned if he would!

Ralf of Mantes, meanwhile, had driven off another attack on his poxed castle, killed one of Gryffydd's younger brothers and taken a cousin prisoner. The King was delighted with his designated heir's loyal and prompt action, Ralf of bloody Mantes, as far as Swegn was concerned, could go boil his swollen head in oil.

Putting his hand to the bell-cord, Swegn tugged. How long before Edward heard of his refusal to attend court—of his fight and escape from the King's housecarls? Three, four days? Damn him! Damn Gryffydd and damn Wales also! Swegn kicked the door with his boot, pulled at the cord harder, again setting the bell swinging and clanging. "Open this sodding door," he bellowed, "before I torch the thing!" A useless threat. It had been tried before; the oak timbers still bore the blackened marks of Gryffydd's attempt to enter Leominster convent three seasons past.

A nun slid back the inspection window and peered through. "Who shouts so angrily at God's door?" she asked tetchily.

"Earl Swegn! Open up, I am in need of shelter and medical aid."

"It is past midnight, my Lord," the woman answered pedantically.

"I know it's past bloody midnight. I also know it is raining and that I am bleeding to death." That stirred results. The window snapped shut, bolts were withdrawn and the door creaked open wide enough to allow Swegn to lead his horse through.

The porteress eyed him warily, suspicious that a man claiming to be an earl rode with no escort, but he was wet through and the light of her spluttering torch did indeed show blood staining his hose. The man required hospitality and assistance. At her call, a yawning servant shambled from the stables to take the tired animal. She told Swegn to follow her to the guest quarters.

"No. I wish to see the Abbess."

The Abbess is abed."

"Wake her."

"That I cannot do."

"Then I will." Swegn snatched the torch from the nun's hand. If his leg wound was paining him, it made no difference to the way he strode across the courtyard and through a gate to the far left. The woman was already screaming her indignation and tugging frantically at the alarm bell. Nuns and servants were waking, coming at a run, dishevelled, frightened and confused. With the Welsh raiding so frequently and bloodily, their fears were justified.

This was a convent, however, not a fortified castle like the one that Ralf had built. No one stepped in front of Swegn with drawn sword to bar his way, no one challenged him. He ran along the narrow alleyways between buildings, across a smaller courtyard and through another door. A scantily furnished inner chamber, smelling of must and old books, lay in darkness. Swegn raised the torch, located the flight of wooden steps over to the left, took them three at a time. Shouting voices and running footsteps were following, but they were nuns and servants; had they caught up they would have been no match for Swegn. He remembered exactly where to go, though it had been more than five years since last he had been here. Nunneries changed little: a new roof on the chapel, new novices, occasionally a new abbess—but the woman who presided over the sisters at Leominster was not new. Eadgifu had been here for two months more than five years.

Swegn did not knock at her door. He opened it, walked through, banged it shut behind him and dropped the bar in place against intruders. She had already stirred from her bed, disturbed by the noise, had relit a small lamp and was standing in her night shift. Her hair hung loose, cascading down her back, hair that was by day braided tight and bound beneath her holy veil. Her eyes and mouth were wide with a mixture of surprise, anger and shock. Fear, however, was the emotion that thumped in her heart, but she dare not let it show, for this man would see and she could not let him know that she was still, after all these years, in love with him, yet so afraid of him.

Swegn dropped the torch into a sconce, looked around the room to locate drink and goblets, helped himself to the wafers left on a plate and poured a good measure of wine. There was no chair, only one stool. Taking both goblet and jug, Swegn seated himself as he drank thirstily. Stretching out his wounded leg he grimaced, then wiped residue from his mouth. "Well," he drawled. "Are you not going to welcome me as once you did?"

Eadgifu swung a cloak across her shoulders. "Once," she answered, "I was a young and impressionable girl. Now I have acquired more sense."

"You always did have fire in your tongue as well as your belly. Get rid of them. I wish to talk with you." The last was directed at the anxious shouting beyond the door.

"You may talk freely to me come morning. For now, you ought be in the guest chamber, or perhaps the infirmary." Eadgifu indicated the wound.

"It is nothing, more blood than anything. You are as capable of cleansing and bandaging it as any of the pox-free virgins locked away in this dungeon."

Haughtily Eadgifu answered, "I am Abbess, I do not undertake menial tasks." The best excuse she could think of.

The shouts of concern were growing louder, accompanied by a rhythmical hammering on the door, the bar juddering with each impact.

"You had best call off the pack before they break your door down," Swegn suggested lightly. He refilled his goblet, drank the contents. "A few words with you, that is all I ask, Eadgifu, then I will go meekly to your little infirmary."

Swegn, as Eadgifu well knew, had never done anything meekly.

A panel of wood splintered. It would be expensive to replace and the nunnery was already so short of funds. Eadgifu crossed to the door. Pulling it wide, she peered at the concerned assembly crowding the narrow stairwell, noting that several carried makeshift weapons of rakes, hoes—one ageing sister was holding a heavy gold candlestick. They would be cut down like hazel saplings to the hedger's knife were they to dare attack a man like Swegn.

"Everything is all right," she reassured them, grateful for their loyalty, yet fearing for their safety. "I am in no danger, this is Swegn Godwinesson who was once a friend of mine. You may leave us and return to your beds."

The servants and a few of the younger nuns turned away almost immediately, but the elder sisters remained, the one wielding the candlestick planting her legs wide, brandishing her weapon between both hands. Eadgifu inclined her head in gratitude, but commanded, "You may go. Even you, Hilteburge."

"It is not seemly to have a man in your chambers at this hour, lady. I will stay."

Swegn came up behind the Abbess, his sword held loose in his hand, as threatening to these ladies of peace as it would have been had he held it ready for use.

"Like she said, I am a friend. Get you gone, old crone."

Seeing a look of opposition setting on Hilteburge's stubborn, wrinkled old face, Eadgifu hastily intervened with a tactful compromise. "I will leave the door open, and you shall wait below."

The old nun glowered, but realised she had been outmanoeuvred. She descended the steps, frowning darkly as the door shut with a heavy thud behind her, as she had known it would. She grasped hold of one of the servants who had not been so quick about returning to his bed, ordered him to saddle a horse and ride hard for Leominster town.

"Fetch the Reeve, tell him we have a madman threatening our safety—no, tell him we have captured a Welshman, that will bring him all the quicker."

Swegn re-barred the door and ran a finger across Eadgifu's cheek. She tilted her head away from his touch. Impulse had brought him to the convent, and the need for aid and hospitality. Now that he was here, though, he remembered just how beautiful Eadgifu was and that he had once had the chance of having her for his own. "You are as beautiful now as you were five years ago. You were a fool to have agreed to this imprisonment. As my wife you could have worn the finest silk, and jewels."

"As your wife, I would have been treated no differently than when I was your mistress, forgotten about as soon as your eye turned elsewhere. I am content here as Abbess. I have no wish to be anyone's wife, least of all yours."

"You were a fool to have allowed yourself to be talked into coming to this wretched place, Eadgifu. You are a woman of the world, you need a man, and children to run around your skirts."

"I was a fool ever to have loved you," Eadgifu retorted, but he heard the wistfulness that told him she remembered.

Swegn took hold of her wrist, drawing her nearer so that their bodies almost touched. Her breasts rose and fell beneath the thinness of her linen shift, her lips were moist, slightly parted.

"Do you remember," he said, his voice low and husky, "when we made love in the woods beside the river? We were one, you and I, Eadgifu. One body, one love. We could be so again, were you only to consent to come with me."

Oh, Eadgifu remembered! She remembered the fear as she realised, after he had taken her maidenhood and then left her without a word, that he would not be coming back for her. Remembered the shame and anger of her father and mother; the pain inflicted by that peasant woman who had rid her of the child she had conceived.

Imprisoned, Swegn had said. Incarcerated. He had used those words five years ago, when finally he had decided to return for her. It was too late by then, she was already Abbess, a respectable position for the soiled daughter of a lord. And by then she had realised the true nature of a man like Swegn. A man who changed his mind on a whim, who was selfish and had no feeling for the women he took, then discarded.

"You will regret refusing me," he had shouted at her. "One day, when you are a lonely old woman, you will regret refusing all that you could have had from me!"

She had wept after he had gone that second time, galloping away with not a backward glance. Wept for what might have been, for what was—being shut away from the world in a nunnery. But the tranquillity of Leominster had seeped into her, easing her pain. Monastic life suited her quiet temperament; she found happiness. She would never have been happy with Swegn. Then, he had tried to change her mind by using charm and affection and, when that had failed, bribery and threats. Now, here he was these years later, trying once again to persuade her to go with him.

Swegn had no time for the niceties of subtle persuasion this time round; before long, Edward would learn that he had resisted arrest and send more men after him. Christ in His Heaven, he would not go to the King on bended knee, begging forgiveness! Was it not Edward's fault that Wales was yet again laughing at England—would he take the blame, though, the responsibility? Like hell he would! At court, Swegn would be reprimanded and ridiculed, verbally flogged; probably threatened with enforced exile now that he had also killed two of the King's men. Damn the King—and damn Wales. Damn the whole of bloody England!

Swegn tossed back the jug and gulped the wine down his throat. Much of it dribbled down his cheeks and moustache, dripped on to his cloak and tunic. He tossed the emptied jug aside, belched. "I will be plain with you," he said. "I want a woman to come with me to Denmark, where they appreciate good soldiers; where Svein Estrithson pays handsome reward for men of my ability. I was on the road, decided you would suit me well."

Eadgifu appeared quite calm, although her heartbeat was pulsing. Before, she had been infatuated by Swegn's handsome face and rugged manliness. Fascinated, too, by his quick laughter, his boasting and drunken bravado, the wild plans plucked at random from the wind that were, as she later discovered, as quickly tossed aside. Yet she knew also of his temper. He loved her, he had once said. Loved her so much that he had left her to face the torture of aborting her child? Ah no, Swegn loved no one but himself.

He bent to kiss her, but she stepped aside, put several paces between them.

"God's truth, you are as cold as ice!" Swegn snarled. "Do you now loathe me so much that my touch, the taste of my kiss, means nothing?"

"I do not hate you, Swegn Godwinesson, but nor do I love you. I will not come with you."

The drink on top of an empty belly was beginning to take hold of Swegn's senses. Wales had made the fool of him, so had the King...not this woman also. "So, that is your final word? You do not want me as husband."

Eadgifu shook her head. "I want you to go, to leave me in peace."

Swegn turned from her, stood head bowed, shoulders slumped. Finally he spread his hands in submission. "So be it." He laughed, crossed to the door, opened it and bellowed down the stairwell for someone to fetch his horse up to the gateway. To Eadgifu said, with a shrug and a smile. "You understand, I had to try."

Releasing her breath—she had not realised how tight she had held it—the Abbess gave him a single nod. She would not go with him, but aye, she understood.

"I have but one request before I go back out into the night," he said. "Pull a gown on over that night shift and a pair of shoes on to your feet. Come with me to the gate, bid me farewell for the last time."

Eadgifu hesitated, but what harm would come of it? She was in a nunnery, there were people all around...

His horse was a showy beast with an unpredictable temper, one to suit Swegn's nature. He mounted, curbing the animal as he danced forward, bent to cup Eadgifu's chin in his hand. She was shivering despite the thickness of her cloak wrapped tight around her body.

"It is a pity, madam, that you have decided against me, for I would have you as my own." With one hand tight around the reins, Swegn leant down, grasped Eadgifu's waist with the other and placed his mouth firm over hers. The kiss was lingering and intense, drawing gasps of horror and muttered rebuke from those several shocked nuns who watched, impatient for this brash intruder to leave. The protests turned to screams as Swegn lifted the Abbess off her feet and swung her in front of his saddle, across his stallion's neck.

Godwinesson's exultant guffaw of laughter drowned Eadgifu's own high, unending scream as he drove his spurs into his horse's flanks, sending the great stallion leaping forward into a gallop and out into the darkness beyond the gate.

18

Sandwich

Edith had walked for about two miles along the beach, deep in her own thoughts, when she heard the galloping of hooves coming from the direction of the village. She recognised the horse before the rider; her brother Tostig's chestnut was a distinctive animal.

She compressed her lips, irritated by the unwanted intrusion. For the past three days the rain-sodden gales blowing in off the sea had kept her and her family entombed within the King's residence here at Sandwich, the only apparent topic of conversation being Swegn's latest deplorable offence. Now that the wind was dropping, the fleet could set sail at last and her father and brothers would be gone. She would not be rid of Edward, though, for he would not be sailing with them to blockade the Kent coast. Edward disliked the sea, it made his stomach queasy and his head dizzy. He preferred to keep his feet firmly on dry land, and send only his good wishes and his heart out with those men defending his country and his crown against invasion by Magnus of Norway.

One disillusionment had followed another these months since Edith's wedding. She was a queen, with the finest jewels and gowns and servants, wealth and land of her own. Everyone in England, save for the King, deferred to her command or whim. Even Robert Champart was obliged to offer her the respect due to a king's wife, the Lady of England. Except Robert Champart knew that Edward was incapable of being a husband to her.

Emma had bought his silence, but Edith knew the thoughts were always there, manifested in that supercilious sneer. What exactly the Dowager Queen had negotiated with her son, Edith was uncertain—all Emma had told her was that Edward agreed to honour her as wife but had chosen to serve God by abstaining from carnal intimacy, a private decision, to be kept for their own knowledge. If the earls and nobles wondered or passed discreet conjecture between themselves of the peculiar relationship there was little they could do about it publicly—her father among them. Not even he could enquire of the king's personal capabilities.

Tostig was reining in his horse, sand and pebbles scattering as the beast skidded to a halt. He dismounted, his face grim with rage. She closed her eyes, sighed. What now? What new upset had occurred?

"That damned husband of yours, do you know what he has done? How he has further slighted me—us!"

"My husband," Edith responded tartly, "is the King. He may do as he pleases. I must remind you that although I am your sister, I am also the Queen. I expect to be greeted as such." She realised the words sounded haughty, but there were already too many disappointments in this sham of a marriage without losing her right to respect as well. She saw the flicker of annoyance in Tostig's eye, but he bowed—briefly. It would suffice.

"Edward has outlawed Swegn, has rescinded his earldom."

Edith swallowed the scream of annoyed frustration that lurched into her throat. Swegn! Swegn! Swegn! That was all she had heard from Edward, Tostig, her father—at court, in Council…Swegn. Damned, bloody Swegn! She rotated on her heel and stalked off. Another disappointment, another disillusion. She had always looked to Swegn as her hero and champion. The elder brother who throughout her childhood had comforted her tears; bandaged her grazed knees; taken her riding; told her stories. Swegn never chastised her, always found a way to smuggle her some hot pasty or sweet little apple if ever their mother had sent her to bed without supper. Swegn had always brought her the best presents, had taken interest in her poetry and music; had laughed and danced with her, coddled her. Tostig was also a favourite brother, but she had mothered him, whereas Swegn had cherished Edith.

"Heroes belong in the tale-teller's world, they do not exist in reality. They are made of naught but sand and moon-dust." She kicked her toe into the wet sand beneath her boot. Who had once said that to her? Ah, it had been Harold. She could not recall when, but the words remained with her because she had not believed him. She remembered shouting at him for saying it, screamed that he was mean-hearted to spoil her dreams.

All these years later, it came hard to realise that her dreams, along with the hero that she had thought her eldest brother to be, were nothing but shadow-flickered illusions.

"Well! Have you nothing to say, sister? Swegn has lost Hereford—and your husband is not going to give it to me in his stead."

Edith sucked the inside of her cheeks, continued walking, her hands clasped together against the barrenness of her womb.

"So you are not angered that Swegn has lost his lands, but that Edward has decided against favouring you."

"No, Swegn deserves every punishment the King can toss at him. He is being the biggest bloody idiot since the first fool was born into this world. I am the next brother, I deserve recognition. It is my right, it is my due. I asked Edward for the earldom—and he refused me. To my face, he refused me!"

Watching a seagull beating its way into the wind, its wings battling against the last rage of the gales that had blown in such fury these past few days, Edith was hardly aware of Tostig's final indignant words. The fleet should have set to sea long before now, for word had reached England that Magnus was about to make sail. Perhaps the raging winds had been too much for his ships also, for he had not yet come. The forty-five ships of the fleet were to make way as soon as the tide turned—in another two hours, to stand off the coast against any foreign ship that dared attempt to make landfall.

Emma had said yesterday that she doubted Magnus would come, that he was too aware of Svein Estrithson of Denmark treading on his heels. "Both of them want to re-create Cnut's empire. There is room for only one of them to succeed. To fight against England as well as each other would be a fool's mistake." She had spoken in confidence to Edith, as she often did, now that Edith was crowned and anointed. They had become allied friends, the older woman taking unexpected pleasure from the younger's keen mind, her enthusiasm and ability. In return, Edith was eager to learn from Emma's accumulated wisdom and experience.

"You will make a good queen," Emma had also said. "You have spirit and determination. And your pride is such that you will never submit to humiliation."

Emma, Edith had realised, welcomed the chance to take a step back from the incessant grumbling and whining of court. It was Emma's right to enjoy a peaceful retirement. Rights! Where were her rights though?

She bent, snatched up a stone and hurled it at the seagull. It missed by many yards, fell with a splash into the breakers. She had known of Edward's intention towards Swegn and the earldom—remarkably, he had told her last night as they shared supper in the privacy of the King's chamber.

Why, she was uncertain. To hurt her? To rub salt into the open wound? That had been her assumption, but she had soon set him right on her present feelings towards her brother.

She was only a head shorter than Tostig, now that she had matured into adulthood. She swung round to stand face to face with him and drew herself into a stance of royal dignity. She would repeat to him the exact words that she had used to Edward.

"Our brother has committed the foulest of crimes by abducting a holy abbess from her nunnery. For this abhorrence there can be no forgiveness. He was given the opportunity to return her, unharmed, within the fortnight of her abduction, but he has not complied. Instead, he has disappeared. For this loathsome act he is justifiably outlawed. The King has men searching for him. When found he will be punished with the sentence of exile."

Tostig stood impatient throughout the lecture. He interrupted as soon as he could. "I know all that. I agree. It is the earldom I want, not forgiveness for our brother."

Perhaps it was because her monthly time of bleeding was due, or because the wind and rain had kept them all close-cloistered that her temper was so frayed. "My husband is heart-felt sick of my brothers—as am I," she snapped. "You do nothing between you but bicker and squabble like unlearned children. Herefordshire will go to someone of calmer judgement and greater influence, who will, in addition, bring a useful alliance to the Crown."

Tostig frowned. "Then Edward has already decided?"

"He has. The earldom is to go to Beorn Estrithson, our mother's nephew. In this way England shows support to Magnus of Norway's declared enemy, Beorn's elder brother, Svein of Denmark."

"To Beorn?" Incredulous, Tostig bunched his fists, planted his feet wide. "Beorn? Who is all those years younger than I? Who is not of English birth? And you agree to this insult against me?" He swung away, stamped three or four paces, marched back to her. "By God, I wager Harold has had his oar in the water over this! Beorn always has been his close companion. It is a wonder they do not share that Nazeing whore, so dear is their friendship. Hah, perhaps they do, Beorn? God's teeth, I cannot believe you would so deny me my right in this, Edith!"

"Your right?" she screamed back at him. "You talk to me of your right? It is all I have heard these past days, your rights, your claims. The disgrace inflicted on you by our brother's crime. What of my rights? What of my disgrace—or do I count for naught?"

Stunned at the outburst, Tostig spread his hands wide, palms uppermost. "You? What have you to worry on? You are the Queen, You have everything."

He had no idea why his sister gave him such a look of loathing, nor why she snatched the reins of his horse from him, mounted and kicked the animal into a gallop onward up the beach.

Annoyed, Tostig considered running after her, but the tide would be turning soon and he had been given command of three ships. He trudged back along the beach, thumbs thrust through the baldric slung slantwise across his chest, Beorn? By God he would have words with Harold over this blatant presumption of favouritism!

Although he did not understand his sister's ill temper, he held no grudge against her. She always had been flighty and inconsistent. No doubt she had women's worries on her mind—probably did not fully appreciate the insult Edward had offered by overstepping the next brother in line for an earldom in favour of a mere cousin. He shrugged. Women simply did not understand the intricate politics of government.

19

Valognes—September 1046

The urgent knocking on his bed-chamber door roused William from a deep sleep. He groaned, rolled from the bed and, pulling a tunic over his nakedness, staggered, half asleep, across the bare timbered floor. He unbolted the door. Beyond stood Will fitz Osbern, son of that loyal friend so cruelly murdered before William's own eyes. He looked troubled, his hand hovering, William noticed, near his dagger. Beside him stood an elderly man whom the Duke did not know. A merchant of wealthy means, judging by his appearance.

"Sir," fitz Osbern said, "this man comes with information. I think there is trouble brewing."

William regarded the merchant a few long moments, taking in every feature, every line and wrinkle of his aged face. Clean-shaven, with whitened, short-cut hair, he was of about sixty years. "I do know you," William said thoughtfully. "You are—were—my father's wine merchant. I saw you once at Falaise, though I recall not your name."

"I am Henri de Brene, my Lord Duke, and *oui*, until my son took over the business I supplied your father with the best wine available in all Normandy."

"Rebellion, my Lord," fitz Osbern interrupted with an uneasy look over his shoulder as if the shadows behind him hid sinister murderers. "It seems your enemies may have settled the feuding that has divided them these past years. Have united in a common cause."

William grimaced. "Myself and Normandy being that common factor, I assume?" He invited the men to enter the chamber. A relative peace had reigned throughout Normandy since those early turbulent years of William's childhood. With Henry of France set on asserting the rights of his sworn vassal, the boy's rivals had been more inclined to fight among themselves for power, wealth and land, rather than combine against him. Yet it had been inevitable that the time would come when one man could build the strength to organise a revolt, the ultimate prize being Normandy itself. Every day, almost, William expected to hear that the new-emerging aristocracy of the duchy had stopped fighting among themselves to unite against the resident duke. That day seemed to have come.

He poured wine for himself and the two men. "So what has happened that required waking me less than two hours after I have retired to my bed?" he asked de Brene, cocking his head to one side.

De Brene glanced at fitz Osbern, to whom he had already briefly told his tale. He had no wish to be an alarmist, yet this young duke's father had been a good man and de Brene owed him a personal debt of gratitude that, until now, he had been unable to discharge. He did not know if the boy William was a man of courage and honour as Duke Robert had been; the lad was untried, yet if what he had surmised was true, then this young duke would have no chance to prove whether he was indeed worthy of his father's title. De Brene considered it his duty, in memory of the father, at least to give the lad fair opportunity.

"My Lord Duke, I once had occasion to thank your father for saving my life. He was a lad, then, no older than your own age of seventeen years. We were ambushed by brigands on the road to Rome. Several of our party were killed, guards and pilgrims alike. Your father ran through a murderer who was about to slit my throat. I vowed that one day I might find a way of thanking him in more than mere words. Alas, I was not able to do so."

William leant forward, did not trouble to hide his scepticism. "They must have been a particularly optimistic group of robbers if they were so bold as to attack my father's guards?" Pilgrims were often attacked, too many of the fools openly professed they carried wealth and possessions. It was becoming a materially rewarding business, pilgrim robbing. His father would not have ridden without adequate protection, however.

De Brene was nervous; his hands shook and beads of sweat pricked along his upper lip. "My Lord, if it is learnt that I have come here to warn you, then my life may well be forfeit. Those who attacked your father and our pilgrimage party were no ordinary ruffians. It is my belief they were professional men, paid to make an end of the Duke." He attempted a wan smile. "As I have reason to believe other men are also anxious to be rid of you."

"Go on." William said, his voice low and encouraging. He guessed already what de Brene was about to say.

The merchant spoke quickly, as if to say his piece faster would make it less dangerous. His fear of reprisal was genuine. "Sir, I have been a widower for many years. In recent months I have formed a liaison with the wife of a former client—forgive me but I cannot mention names. Last night I lay with her—in a house I rent, some miles south of here." He looked from fitz Osbern to the Duke. What if he had this wrong, what if he was being naught but a foolish old man? "Sir, there are men gathering to the east of the road that I followed home. Two hundred or so. Among them, I think I saw your enemy, Guy de Bourgogne—Guy of Burgundy."

The Duke audibly caught his breath. Bourgogne. No wonder de Brene was afraid. Guy had a reputation as vivid as the Duke's own for taking revenge on those who enraged him. "You are not certain?" William queried. "You may have been mistaken?"

The merchant chewed his lip. "I cannot swear that it was him, it was a glimpse only—but, even if it is not he, why are men with armour and weapons gathering secretively so near to where you presently reside?"

William stood. "Why indeed."

He moved to the slit window on the southern side of the chamber, peered out into the blackness of the night beyond. Banks of cloud driven by a vigorous wind galloped over a half-full moon, the courtyard below and the outer defence wall shadow-lit by its patterned light. Guy de Bourgogne wanted to make himself duke. Was, to William's certain knowledge, rallying men to his support. Men like Nigel de la Cotentin and Rannulf, vicomte de la Bessin, two of the most powerful magnates in the entire duchy. If they were to initiate rebellion, how many more lords from west and lower Normandy would be joining them? Ralph Tesson and Grimoald de Plessis? Since they had last attempted their bloody games of murder they had taken time to build up their strength.

Those men who would support Bourgogne in his claim were more experienced than William and, for all his determination, his personal authority over Normandy remained fragile. As Duke he was dependent upon the loyalty of those Norman lords who had favoured his father, but if outright rebellion reared its ugly head, for how long could a youth, untried in battle, keep their backing? If de Brene were right and Bourgogne was making a move against him, then he had no choice but to seek outside help from his overlord, the King of France.

William turned to face his friend and companion, fitz Osbern. "Did we not hear yesterday that there is rumour of an army collecting to the west near Lessay? Do we have confirmation?"

"No, my Lord, but if these things are true, then it seems your enemies are hoping to blockade you here in Valognes. If they should lay siege…" He had no need to continue; William knew the danger to his life were that to happen.

William slid a ring from his finger, held it out to de Brene. "I thank you for your information, it is comforting to know that there are some who are loyal to me."

De Brene did not take the ring. "*Monseigneur*, I seek no reward. It is enough to know I have been of some small help to Duke Robert's son."

And a ring from the present duke would draw attention, initiate questions. William replaced it on his finger, held out his hand instead. Then, if it will suffice, I offer you my gratitude alone." To fitz Osbern he said briskly, "We must assume that we have been timely warned of an attempt to overthrow me. See if you can ascertain any further information and send my uncle to me. Have horses saddled. Of a sudden, I feel no inclination to remain here."

The ride from Valognes was a waking nightmare. It galled William that he had to flee like a thief in the night, to have to ride for aid, not stand and fight. The time would come, though, one day soon, when the men at arms of Normandy would serve him without murmur. When a single command would strike fear into any who dared oppose him. For now, however, without alliance of a French army to put down insurrection, there would be no future for the Duke, for William the Bastard.

He had no alternative but to leave Valognes immediately and ride hard for France. Taking only a few loyal men—among them Will fitz Osbern and his maternal uncle, Walter—he galloped for the estuary of the Vire, risking crossing before the tide was at its safest low level.

Halfway across, his horse lost its footing, ducking them both under the ebb current. The escort of men shouted in alarm, but William kicked himself free of the stirrups and, clinging to his stallion's mane, swam across the channel to the far bank, and immediately shrugged off the concerned enquiries of his followers. "If Guy de Bourgogne cannot make so easy an end to me, do you think I fear a mere soaking in an estuary?"

Mid-morning saw them at Ryes. The horses were spent, their coats lathered, mouths and flanks bloodied. Refreshed, re-clothed and revived, the Duke and his men demanded remounts and galloped onwards, heading for the safety of William's birthplace of Falaise and from there to King Henry, who held court at Poissy.

All would whisper and mask smirks of derision when William eventually arrived, dishevelled and travel-grimed, but the Duke cared nothing for the arrogance of the French aristocracy. He had one concern only. To mobilise an army against those who dared oppose him.

20

Waltham Abbey

Looking down at the parchment spread wide between the hands of the master mason, Harold felt an immense surge of pride. The building of his collegiate abbey would soon commence—the first shipments of stone from Caen in Normandy were already being sorted down by the especially erected wharf. He liked the design that the French architect had finally decided upon. It would not be as grand as the King's construction at Westminster, but for a rural abbey it would be more than sufficient.

"We begin by building around the old church, then—adding a north to south transept across the present square apse at the eastern end?"

The architect nodded, his face alight with enthusiasm. "The present chapel will remain in use for some while. When we have completed the transept and its tower, we will remove these old timber walls and rebuild in stone, *non*?" His light French accent and quick speech were like a bubbling mountain stream, in contrast to the deep tones of the Wessex-born master of masons, whose accent was more like a somnolent stretch of a wide, ageing river.

The mason let the parchment roll up on itself. "'Tis not the way we usually do it, but I suppose it might work."

"It will work, believe me, *monsieur*! This will be a fine and glorious *abbaye*." The Frenchman almost skipped a few paces in his excitement, his arms spreading wide. "*Ici* shall be the transept that we talk about. Imagine the beauty of it! Its length and its height! The windows shall be narrow, double-splayed, rounded *en tête*, rounded heads. There shall be a chancel arch and the arcades shall also bear round-headed arches. The piers along the aisle shall reach up to the vaulting of the roof—a leaded roof bearing the tower and above that, a golden cross! It shall be *tout à fait magnifique, n'est-ce pas*?"

Harold smiled warmly at his delight, although he had very little idea of exactly how his abbey would eventually look. The mason was looking thoughtful. "We will need sound-based trusses, then, if you're planning on using lead." He shook his head doubtfully. That's a lot of weight-bearing you know."

"*Absolument*, I agree, but if we…"

Harold left them to it; their technical phrases meant nothing to him. It was like listening to men prattling in an unknown language.

He stood, hands on hips, trying again to picture how, several years ahead, all this would look. Over there, the cloister court and the chapter house, the dorter, frater and kitchens. The outer wall would remain the same, but perhaps the gatehouse could be enlarged? Fish ponds created down near the river and a herb garden somewhere. He sensed rather than heard the rustle of movement behind him, lifted one arm so that Edyth could slip hers through, entwining them together.

"Our friend from France is so happy with his work, is he not? This will be a beautiful place, Harold. I am so glad that you are building it." She smiled up at him, the shining light of her love dazzling in her eyes. For over four months had he been away, taking command of half the King's fleet. The days had passed quickly for her, for their manor house was now finished and furnished, but the long summer nights alone without him had dragged so slowly.

He placed a light kiss on the veil that covered the crown of her head. "As I am also. Edward is building Westminster with the prime intention of making it his mausoleum. He plans a grand and ostentatious tomb near the high altar. I was wondering whether I ought to incorporate plans for my resting place."

Edyth put her hand up to his mouth, her fingers pressing against his lips. "Please, do not talk of your death! I cannot bear to think of not having you with me!"

Harold laughed. "I'm not intending to make use of a tomb just yet, my lass! Although it occurred to me yesterday, as Edward insisted on taking us on a tour of his building work, that he had better pray for a long life. He is one and forty years old already and it could take anything up to thirty years to complete his abbey."

The construction of the abbey at Westminster was barely further advanced than this smaller one at Waltham, for prolonged and incessant rain had put it behind schedule. The Westminster foundations were thick with mud and flooding had always been a problem along that marshy stretch of the Thames. The periodic rise and fall of the river helped somewhat, though, for the gravel and alluvial soil brought down with the current were steadily silting up the tiny tributaries that separated the scatter of small islands. The spread-finger estuary of the Tyburn river was no longer as wide and Thorney Island itself had more than doubled its length of river bank since the time when Cnut had first enlarged the crude little chapel of Saint Peter into a monastery for twelve monks.

Edward had in mind nearer sixty monks and a building superior to anything yet known. His abbey was to be the finest, tallest, grandest complex of buildings in all England. Looking at the ooze squelching around their feet yesterday afternoon, Harold and his father had harboured strong doubts of the practicality of the dream.

Those three days spent in London had been frustrating for Harold. He had wanted nothing more than to return to Waltham, but Edward had insisted that those earls who had deployed with the fleet accompany him to London from Kent: Godwine and Harold, Beorn and Leofric of Mercia. Siward had not come south for the summer muster, for Scotland was pressing too close against the northern borders—over-much of Cumbria had already been appropriated by Scottish hands.

The King saw the summer's blockade as a great success, but then he had been safely ensconced in a dry and wind-proofed royal residence three miles west of Sandwich harbour. The rest of them had been alternately tossed, soaked or battered by the vagaries of the North Sea and its unpredictable weather. It had been a pointless exercise, the fleet sitting there at full strength supposedly safeguarding the coast against Magnus of Norway—who had, for certain knowledge, turned his attention away from England and was harassing Denmark instead.

Edward claimed that Magnus had changed his mind about England because of the fleet—what nonsense! All summer they had been pleading with him—Harold, his father, Beorn, even Leofric—to release their ships from the blockade and let them sail to aid the Danish King. Edward would have none of it, was determined to let Denmark look to her own protection—this despite an alliance made earlier in the year.

To join forces and be rid of Magnus made sense, but Edward maintained that to sting Norway in the tail might only serve to goad. In early July he had remarked, almost childishly, that Svein Estrithson was Godwine's nephew-in-law and England could not afford to favour the family any further. As a slight it had been a calculated and intentional one. Godwine had tactfully swallowed it down; Harold and Beorn—bitter that he could not take his men to help his elder brother—had returned to the fleet. Tostig had flounced away from court in a burst of resentment. Already his pride had been bruised by being overshadowed by Beorn and the Queen was making no effort to promote him. He saw himself as neglected and undervalued, was bored with the fruitless patrolling at sea and wanted some way to prove his worth—to his father and his king. Taking his portion of the family fortune, Tostig had bought passage on a merchant ship and sailed to Flanders in search of more obliging patronage and a potential bride from one of Count Baldwin's numerous sisters or daughters. This, despite the fact that Baldwin's coast was harbouring many of the pirates who were attempting to plunder English shipping; that Baldwin was possibly supporting Magnus; and that it was rumoured that their brother, Swegn, had fled to Bruges with his abbess.

Edward had railed about Tostig's departure for days. The sea conditions had been atrocious, the remaining Godwines had elected to remain with the fleet. Bad weather was infinitely preferable to the King's sour moods.

To add further insult, Tostig had almost immediately succeeded in his aim, for word had reached England last week that he had wed Judith, the Count's second-youngest daughter. Of Swegn, Tostig had sent no word. It was still not known where he had secreted himself and Eadgifu. For himself, Harold did not particularly care. The further away Swegn was, the better.

"My sister has granted yet more land to the estate of Westminster," Harold said, walking Edyth over to watch the Frenchman supervising the pegging out of lengths of thin rope, marking on the ground the dimensions of the transept. "I doubt my poor little Waltham will be able to compete—I shall have to find some relics or something to give the place more of an equal footing."

"What land has she donated?" Edyth asked out of courtesy; Queen or no, she had no interest in her sister-in-law.

"An estate in Hertfordshire. Father had given it to Swegn, but he reclaimed it when it became obvious that my dear brother had no intention of showing contrition. He passed it to Edith who has joined the ranks of those fawning upon Edward by giving enormous grants to Westminster." Harold laughed suddenly and tweaked the elegant folds of Edyth's gown.

"Edward traipsed us all around his building site yester-afternoon, Edith included. You ought to have been there, Willow-bud, the Queen in all her royal regalia stepping with such care among the puddles and sludge, her gowns lifted almost as high as her knees, displaying more than a modest amount of hose and garter!"

He guffawed again. "Edward was furious with her, he told her in no uncertain terms that if she spoiled her gown she would have to replace it from her own coffers. Edith snapped back at him that it already was her own gown and if it were not for her own wealth she would be touring the site clad only in her naked skin."

"If that were so"—Edyth chuckled—"then no workman would have eyes for laying one single stone atop another!" She had held the hem of her own gown away from the mud-rutted foundations, but as Harold steered her back on to the path, dropped the material from her hand, the gathered lacings at the waist allowing the soft wool of the dress to fall naturally into its sleek folds. She lifted her arms slightly to inspect the edging of the cuffs at the end of the long, drooping sleeves. Nothing had splashed on to the expensive material, only her shoes were dirtied, but as they were sturdy outdoor footwear, she ignored the slight damage.

She somewhat sympathised with Edith, for it must be difficult to maintain the dignity required of a queen. As a farm-born girl, she readily accepted that finery was for holy days and feasting, that shorter gowns with practical-length sleeves, plain-spun woollen hose and stout leather boots were more suited to muddy farmyards, cow byres and pigsties.

"What have you done with our little imp, by the way?" Harold asked, looking around for his son. Goddwin was almost two years old, a scamp of a boy always into mischief.

"He was here a moment ago." Edyth said anxiously, breaking free of Harold's hold, her head turning, searching for him.

"Over there!" Harold pointed, his laughter rumbling yet again. "And talking of mud, just look at the boy!"

The lad was busily stamping his feet in a deep puddle near the arched gateway that led out into the village high street.

"That boy is an urchin!" Edyth grumbled with a smile of maternal amusement as she ran to the child to rescue him and his boots before they were completely ruined.

Goddwin was a fair-haired, blue-eyed rascal. A son that any father would burst his heart with pride for. Harold had so missed them both. Edyth could have gone with him into Kent, but she had declined, preferring to oversee the completion of their manor, built up there on the hill overlooking the village of Waltham and the wide panorama of the river valley. It was a special place, steeped in memories for both of them. A place well suited as a home to their children.

Smiling, Harold followed her across the grass, took the protesting boy from her arms and tossed him high, making him squeal with delightful laughter.

"Nay, lad, your mother does not want you all wet and muddied. Come, let me take you across to the river—look there is another ship coming upstream. I expect she has come all the way from Normandy, carrying more stone to build Papa's church."

Settling Goddwin within one arm, Harold took hold of Edyth's hand with the other and breathed in the fresh, invigorating smell of the September afternoon.

All was peaceful in his earldom and he was home, back with his family, where he would remain, save for the brief visit to Edward's Christmas Court, until next spring should recall him to his duties as a soldier. But that was a long way ahead yet.

21

⌘

Bosham—March 1047

Save for Edith and the first- and third-born sons, Swegn and Tostig, Earl Godwine's family were gathered in their entirety at Bosham, his Sussex manor, prior to attending the Witan—the Council of Elders—at the King's Easter Court. There was much to discuss, much to plan. That Edward's grievances were mounting against Godwine was plainly evident, how to do something about it was not.

Gyrth, aged seventeen and the next brother after Tostig, skimmed a stone across the placid surface of the sea, pleased that he successfully made it bounce at least four times. "I do not want to attend court anyway, I would rather stay here at Bosham." He used the local traditional dialect to pronounce the village's name, Bozzum. "A lot of old men full of wind and their own importance, voicing opinionated bigotry. Who gives a damn?"

Both his father and brother Harold stared at him, for opposing reasons: Harold was amused, Godwine annoyed.

"Attending the King is a serious business, my boy," Godwine said gruffly. "As you will one day discover when you become earl. There are matters of state to discuss, laws to be made, charters to sign—" He broke off with a growl as Gyrth laughed.

"I was jesting, Father! I fully realise the importance. All the same, I am right about those who attend!"

"Only some of them," Harold retorted indignantly. "I'm not bigoted, nor is Father."

"Ah, but you don't enjoy attending court either, do you!" That was Beorn, standing a few yards further down, skimming his own stones. "And some of us, Uncle Godwine, although already made earl, have no land of significance to be an effective earl over. I agree with Gyrth, I would rather stay here and enjoy the fishing and hunting.

Selecting a handful of pebbles, Gyrth offered one to Harold's son, Goddwin,

It was the boy's first visit to Bosham and the sea. He was fascinated by the scurry of waves and the reflected patterns on the restless sway of water. Liked, too, the smooth feel of the stones and how his uncle could make them so magically skip and bounce. He tried throwing one for himself but it fell down with a disappointing plop into the little breakers washing at his boots. Beorn came to retrieve it for him, squatted next to the boy and showed him how to hold the missile between his fingers.

"He hasn't mastered the flick to his wrist yet," Gyrth decided, watching another unsuccessful attempt. He ruffled the boy's fair hair.

"Give him another year," Harold said with pride in his voice, "and he will beat both of you."

The natural harbour that created the inlet at Bosham had always been a favourite retreat for Harold, and he was delighted that his son seemed to have inherited his love of the place. When the tide washed out, the mud flats were criss-crossed by creeks and rivulets, the small boats left like landed fish, but with the tide in, especially on a sky-bright day such as this, the inlet appeared at its best.

Over on the far shore cattle grazed in the lush, fertile meadows, the surrounding woods creating shelter from northerly winds and a plentiful supply of timber. Several of the village fishing boats had up-anchored and set sail on the previous ebb tide; they would return come the next flood with, they hoped, a good catch. Harold's two youngest brothers, Leofwine and Wulfnoth, were busy with their own little boat inside the safety of Bosham Creek. Harold shifted the weight of his sleeping daughter to his other shoulder and waved at the two boys. Ah, to be like Leofwine, twelve again, with nothing more to worry about than the fitting of a new sail! The little girl snuffled but did not wake. Alfrytha had been born one year, almost to the day, after Goddwin, Unlike his robust and rosy health, she was a sickly child, prone to wheezing and coughs. Edyth thought the sea air might be of benefit to her, an acceptable excuse to come south into Sussex, though Edyth was close to her time of delivery of their third child.

"I am for keeping our heads down and noses clean," Godwine suggested, returning to the subject of attending court. "Edward will, sooner or later, be needing our support for something or other that those two farting bigots, Siward and Leofric, will oppose." He half grinned at Gyrth. "Neither of them can handle a ship as well as myself or you, Harold, and now that Magnus has taken half of Denmark from your brother, Beorn, perhaps the King will realise the importance of sending help."

Engaged in wiping dribble from his daughter's mouth, Harold was able to avoid making eye contact with Beorn and answering his father. Both he and his cousin fundamentally disagreed with Godwine. Edward would never change his mind and allow English ships to sail in aid of Denmark against Norway. It was too costly and too provocative. Edward jealously guarded his treasury and avoided any action that could provoke acts of hostility. Especially those that might endanger himself personally. No one, save perhaps his mother, would outright call the King a coward, but that was what his earls and nobles secretly thought. Edward preferred the safety and comfort of his palaces to the hazardous conditions of war.

Added to that, anyone related to the Earl of Wessex could be left to drown as far as Edward was concerned. Godwine was hoping that this current tide of unprovoked hostility would be turned at the Easter Court and agreeable relationships resumed. Harold considered his father to be unrealistically optimistic.

"Big boat. Look, Papa, big boat!" Young Goddwin tugged at his father's cloak to gain his attention, his chubby hand pointing excitedly seawards. There was indeed a sixty-oared sea-going keel making way in from the Chichester Channel, using the last of the incoming tide. She was a stranger, her sail was of pale blue, not the oxblood red of Godwine's own vessels, but from her course her master was familiar with Bosham Creek. Until one quarter of a mile from the village the creek ran at over a fathom deep; from there in it shallowed. With Chidham Hard almost submerged at high tide on the west bank and another similar though not so deep sandbank on the Bosham side, navigation was a matter of local knowledge and great skill.

"Are we expecting more company?" Gyrth asked unemotionally. "Bad enough having that fusty bishop staying with us uninvited these last two days." He was referring to Stigand who was desperately hustling support for his possible elevation to the bishopric of Winchester. He had arrived at Bosham unannounced and uninvited, irritating the younger members of the family whose natural exuberance was curtailed by his dour presence.

"We can be rid of Stigand," Beorn remarked, shading his eyes against the glare of sunlight to see the ship better. "All we need to say is that we categorically oppose his elevation. With Edward presently disagreeing with everything we even think, Stigand will be offered the position at once." They all joined in Beorn's laughter.

"Now that he has declared himself wholehearted for the King and turned his back on the Dowager Queen, without doubt he will get Winchester anyway," Godwine answered. He too narrowed his eyes to peer along the sea channel. His sight was not as sharp as it once had been. "There is no one else suitable; it is too rich a bishopric for Edward to risk putting in anyone who will not back him should Rome decide to poke her nose too far over our English Church boundary."

Referring to the ship: "Can any of you make out her standard? Edward has a poor stomach for the Pope's interferences, as much as the rest of us."

"Save for Champart," Beorn interjected quietly.

"He does not count," Gyrth said with certainty. "He's a Norman."

"He wants a bishopric for himself," Beorn answered. "Winchester would suit him nicely."

"Aye, but he does not suit the English. Even Leofric and Siward would object to his proposal."

"Which is why Stigand will get Winchester," Godwine concluded. "He must court the King's earls, however, because he is too modest a man to assert himself for such a prestigious promotion." They all chuckled. Stigand was even more opinionated and presumptuous than Robert Champart.

Harold, squinting, could make out a vague black shape across the square pendant fluttering from the head of the single mast. Was it a raven, or… "Bugger! It's a black boar. Swegn has come home."

Reaction was mixed. Gyrth grinned—the younger boys idolised Swegn's breathtaking rebelliousness and appreciated his bursts of ostentatious generosity. Godwine was relieved. They could sort out the unfortunate business of this wretched abbess woman at last, begin restoring the good name of the family. Beorn exchanged a wry look with Harold. Neither of them wanted to meet Swegn: Harold because he knew his brother would upset Edyth, Beorn because Swegn would argue over the land that Edward had confiscated and given him instead—that the King had done so deliberately, to set cousin against cousin, would be lost on Swegn.

Harold held his hand out to his son. "Come on, boy, we had better get you back to your mother, she will be wanting to wash that dirt from your face and knees." Edyth would not be pleased at Swegn's arrival. Her temper was understandably short these last few days, without the added frustration of being civil to a bastard like Swegn. Once the child was born she would feel better in her mind, spirit and body.

Goddwin's face puckered. "I want to see the big boat!" he screamed, throwing himself down on the ground, pummelling it with fists and feet.

"Not this boat, you don't." Beorn answered for his cousin, bending down to lift the boy bodily by the waist. "This is a pirate ship carrying a captain who eats little boys like you for his breakfast."

❧

By late afternoon, Godwine's manor house was suffused with an atmosphere of sharp, barely held tempers. The bright sun of the morning had given way to rain clouds and a blustering wind, driving everyone within doors. Swegn and Beorn, as the younger man had mentally predicted, had quarrelled viciously within the first hour. Godwine's patience had rapidly deteriorated once he realised his eldest son did not regret the embarrassment he had caused the family. Eadgifu herself was still attempting to stifle her tears at the hostility that now raged between Swegn and his father, and Gytha had sharply reprimanded her husband for upsetting the woman, which had enraged Godwine and embarrassed Eadgifu further. Matters were made worse by the baby that she carried in her arms.

No one had been expecting a child. Worse, the boy had colic. His knees drawn up to his chest, his tiny fists bunched and mouth open, he screamed his discomfort throughout the heated family row. To add to the difficulties, Alfrytha was running a fever and Edyth's baby had decided to initiate its entrance into the world.

Swegn sat, his boots stretched leisurely towards the hearth fire. He would have preferred the privacy of his father's chamber, but his mother had commandeered it for the birth of this wretched child. Every so often sounds emanated from that direction, or a woman bustled in or out for linen or water. He could not understand why there must be such a fuss. Animals just got on with it.

Beorn sat opposite, whittling a new dagger handle; Godwine was hunched over a scrolled parchment, his nose bent close to the writing. Harold prowled the Hall, fiddling with the tapestries and shields covering the walls, trimming a smoking candle.

His restless pacing irritated Swegn. "For the good Christ's sake, man, sit down!" he snapped as Harold passed within a few feet for the fourth time. "The woman's only in childbirth."

"Unlike you, Brother, I happen to think much of my lass. She has not carried this babe well, I fear for her safety during her confinement."

"So you think I don't care for Eadgifu?" Swegn retaliated, tossing his head towards the side of the Hall where she sat nursing the child. "You are not the only whoreson capable of loving a woman, you know."

"Love? Lust would be nearer the mark."

Beorn raised his eyebrow to the low ceiling. Another storm coming.

"Had you cared for Eadgifu," Harold continued, coming to a halt before Swegn and knocking his feet from the bricks of the hearth surround with his own foot, "you would never have abducted her, have subjected her to such humiliation."

Swegn rose lazily to stand before his brother. "She came willingly once she realised the warmth of my bed was preferable to the tight-arsed solemnity of that prison they call a nunnery. Before this damned babe came along Eadgifu was as full of lust as I." He turned away, murmured, "She's not ice frigid like your little bitch."

Harold heard. Lurching forward, he grabbed hold of Swegn's shoulder and hurled him backwards, his fist bunching ready to slam into his brother's sneering face. Godwine and Beorn moved as quickly, the one to take hold of his eldest son, the other to clutch at his cousin's arm. Others in the Hall looked up; several of Godwine's and Harold's housecarls getting to their feet, their hands going automatically to their dagger blades. Eadgifu, too, looked across at Swegn. Wondered, like so many times since last May, why she had agreed to stay with him.

"No fighting!" Beorn shouted. "Not at the birth of your child, Harold, it would bring bad luck."

"Aye," Harold breathed heavily. "Bad luck for my brother."

A scream came from above. Harold forced his hands and shoulders to relax, dragged his eyes from the door through which he so desperately wanted to go, to be with Edyth, helping her through her time of pain—but what could he do? She was about women's business, where there was no place for a man. He snatched up his cloak from where it lay across a bench, swung it about his shoulders. "I'll be in the stables should anyone want me."

The Hall settled again, the rapid flare of excitement over. Beorn collected up his whittling knife and the deer antler he was carving. "I have things I ought to do before the meal is served," he said, not having much care to stay in Swegn's ill-willed company if Harold was not there.

Setting his stool straight, Swegn sat, concentrating on the good taste of his wine. He had missed the pleasure of such fine stuff these past months. They had thought him to be in Flanders all this while, enjoying Count Baldwin's court, but in fact he had been in Ireland. Cold, wet, rain-misted Ireland. The place was almost as inhospitable as Wales. He had regretted the impulse to take Eadgifu within a few weeks; it had seemed a good idea at the time, but once her belly had started swelling with the child and she could no longer be a bed-mate, he had tired of her.

Godwine coughed, cleared his throat, almost as if he had read his thoughts. "What are you going to do with Eadgifu and the boy?"

Swegn shrugged. What could he do? "I had intended to marry her, you know," he said, "but I couldn't find a priest willing to join us."

Clearing his throat again Godwine made no comment. Marriage made little difference: the girl had taken her vows as a nun; Swegn had abducted her.

Nothing would alter the facts. In the eyes of the Church—and more important the King—he had committed the most dreadful of crimes. None too tactfully, Godwine reminded Swegn of it. "Edward has discharged your title and reclaimed your earldom, but has not declared you outlaw, ordered your exile. If you do not attend the Easter Court, you will also be stripped of all your personal land and wealth—I will be powerless to prevent it. Then what will you do? Live with them in poverty?"

Swegn drained his goblet of wine. He had known he would receive a lecture—and his father wondered why he had not, until now, cared to come to Bosham? "I fully intend to see the King when I am ready, but I will not go down on my knees to beg forgiveness for something I have not done." Emphasising his point, he leant forward. "I had intended to wed Eadgifu all those years ago, when first I knew her, but because her father detested you I was not deemed good enough for her. She was sent into a nunnery, to finish out her years—God, what a waste of a good-looking woman that was! I am being punished for giving her a choice of the nunnery, or me. She chose me."

"Did she have a choice after you had abducted and raped her?" Godwine snapped, adding, "The King is angry with you because you did not answer his summons to court—as for the other reason, it took you five years to decide you wanted her."

"I happened to be on the Leominster Road, it was an impulsive decision." Swegn had been watching Eadgifu attempting to suckle the child. Her milk-engorged breasts fascinated him. It had been weeks since he had lain with her. Those first few weeks had been idyllic, her slender, pliant body lying there next to him every night...The baby was crying again. Damn the thing. Everything had been all right before that baby was on its way. It was time she handed it over to a wet nurse.

Godwine must have seen the thought cross Swegn's mind, for he commented, "A mother needs time with her first babe. Give her a month or two and she will be your woman again."

Swegn stood up abruptly. "I expect a woman of my choosing to be with me all the time, not merely when it suits her."

⤶⤷

In the early hours before dawn a woman's screams woke the entire Hall. Godwine and Gytha were together on a pallet laid on the floor in their private living chamber, had slept for maybe an hour, for Edyth's baby girl had been a long time in its coming. Gytha started, looked up the narrow stairway to the chamber above. Harold ran down, a lamp held high, sword in his hand.

"What is it?" Gytha asked, sleep heavy in her head. "Is something amiss with Edyth?"

"No, that scream was not from us."

Godwine was crawling stiffly from his bed, reaching for a woollen cloak. Harold was at the door before him, several other men were on their feet, daggers in their hands, lamps and torches held high.

"Where is the watch guard?" Godwine commanded. "Are we under attack?"

Another scream, desperate and frightened, rose in a crescendo. It came from the direction of the guest places ranged as lean-to buildings along the north wall. Few of them were occupied—one had been offered, for privacy, to Bishop Stigand and one to Swegn and Eadgifu.

Men poured from the Hall, convinced the manor was in danger of attack. Countess Gytha, throwing a cloak round her shoulders, was running, her hand shielding a lamp, bare feet cold on the rain-muddied earth. She reached the doorway to her eldest son's quarters a moment before her husband and opened the door. "Swegn? What is happening, what is amiss?"

Then Gytha screamed too, her free hand coming to her mouth, the other almost dropping the lamp. Godwine pushed past her, Harold close at heel, both with weapons drawn. Beorn took the lamp from his aunt, stopped her from entering the small room.

Eadgifu was cowering on the floor, her night shirt torn, blood streaming from her nose and forehead. Swegn stood naked over his son's cradle, his hand covering the baby's face, pressing down, smothering the life from its six-week-old body. As his father crashed into the room Swegn abandoned his grasp on the baby, leapt for his sharp-bladed, double-handed axe. There was not enough room in the chamber to raise it—Godwine had hold of Swegn's arm, Harold, in almost the same instant, the other. Godwine's fingers dug into the flesh, forcing his son to leave go of that death-bringer weapon, drop it harmless to the floor.

Shrugging aside Beorn's grip, Gytha ran to the child and lifted him to her breast, tears of relief descending her cheeks as she felt the small being shudder a breath.

Stepping around the men, Beorn went to Eadgifu, wrapped his cloak around her shaking body. "What happened, lass?" he asked, although the answer was perhaps obvious. The child had been crying for most of the previous day and through the night. Fractious babies often did so, but that fact did not stop the irritation, the tightening of temper, the sudden, uncontrolled urge to stop the noise.

Godwine nodded to Harold, commanding he let go his brother, twisted

Swegn's arm up behind his back and shook the boy, bellowing his disgust. "This is beyond all belief! Attempting to murder your own son while under my roof? What ails you, boy? Are you moon-mad? Look at your woman, how dare you take your damned temper out on her?"

Swegn struggled, breathing hard. "What?" he shouted. "Have you never struck a woman? Never raised your hand to our mother?"

Harold answered for Godwine, the venom and repugnance blatant: "Our father has more respect for a woman, especially one not long from childbed! You have respect for nothing, Swegn. You care only for what is inside your breeches!"

Swegn twisted harder, almost escaped his father's hold, would have sprung at Harold had he been able. Godwine clenched his grip tighter. "I have never raised my fist to my wife."

Angry, tired from lack of sleep, his body aching for the release of a woman's touch, Swegn's temper was ablaze, like a fire-torch touched to oil. He thrust his rage-tormented face near his father's. "What, never? Not even when you discovered Cnut to be my father, not you?"

Silence slammed around the little room, echoing from wall to wall. Even the child ceased its whimpering. Godwine released his hold, stepped back a pace in a mixture of astonishment, blind, cold rage and abhorrence.

"He was here often, wasn't he, Mother?" Spittle bubbled on Swegn's lips. "All those long days hunting on our marshes and in our woods when Father was conveniently away on king's business? Spending all those long nights here at Bosham—but where, specifically, Mother?"

The rumour was an old one and untrue. Swegn knew full well it was one spread by Godwine's enemies to discredit the Earl when first he had begun his spectacular rise to authority. Knowing the truth made his vicious slander all the more hurtful.

The Countess handed the child to his silently weeping mother. She moved slowly, deliberately, her face expressionless, her hands by her side, stopped before Swegn her first-born son, who stood taller than her by almost a full head of height. The sound of her palm striking his cheek reverberated through the chamber. "Get out of my house," Gytha said, her voice quite steady. "Get you gone from my Lord Godwine's lands, from the earldom of Wessex and from England. Do not, ever, dare show me your vile, lying face again. I gave you life, and for the insult you have spread upon me this night, I claim the right to take back that life, should ever your shadow darken my hearth place again."

For a long, silent moment Swegn stared back at her, meeting her seething hatred head on, then he shrugged, turned and, snatching his discarded clothing from the floor, strode from the room, the men and women outside parting without a sound to let him through.

Suddenly gathering her stunned wits, Eadgifu ran after him. "Wait! What of me?" she cried. "Where am I to go, what am I to do?"

Ignoring her, Swegn walked down to the quay to where his ship was moored. The crew would have to wake, haul her out into the flood tide. No matter that they were probably drink-sodden, that their ale-filled stomachs would retch and heave from the exertion of pulling at the oars.

"Swegn, please!" Eadgifu shrieked. "What is to become of me?" He paused, but he did not turn round. "You have two choices," his voice hissed into the rain-spattered darkness. "Go back to your cursed nunnery or join the sluts in a brothel. It makes no difference to me where you go."

Bishop Stigand stood in the open doorway of his own small chamber, a bed fur pulled tight around his body. He caught Godwine's eye as his host stepped from the flickering lamplight into the circle of gathered people, shook his head. "The King, my Lord Earl," he said ruefully, "is not going to enjoy hearing of this."

22

Val-ès-Dunes

As king it was Henry's duty to provide support for his vassals in time of need. Although the degree of need and honour of duty was always a king's prerogative of choice.

Henry's army had marched into Normandy, advancing towards Caen via Mézidon, meeting with Duke William beside the Laizon. The King's host was far greater than the few sparse levies that William had managed to raise in Upper Normandy—were it not for Henry, William would have been lost. He might still be, for the rebels had crossed the river Orne and were waiting to join battle on the bleak and featureless plain of Val-ès-Dunes, a handful of miles south-west of the sprawling, rugged village of Caen.

The encounter was the young Duke's first experience of battle, his initiation into the bloodied, vicious world of the warlord and fighting men. He was enjoying every moment of it. This was what duke and overlord was all about, this was why he had learnt how to handle lance, shield, sword and horse. This was his first real chance to prove his worth and ability, to confirm to his many enemies and those who doubted him that his intention was to become the un-disputed master of this small territory within France.

Maybe the rebels were over-confident, or perhaps the lesser men were not as dedicated to their cause as were their ambitious lords. Fighting Duke William, an arrogant, untried young whelp, was one thing, going against the royal host and the King of France himself another matter entirely. Val-ès-Dunes became not a battle but a rout; isolated fighting between groups of cavalry, man against man. There were no archers employed, no infantry; no use of the supportive war machinery or the disciplined deployment of arms that was, later, to charac-terise William's renowned and ruthless fighting skill.

The disorganisation began before even the first drop of blood was shed. Ralph Tesson decided against further perjuring his oath of allegiance to King Henry, took his horses, men and arms, and rode over to Duke William's side.

The fighting that followed was haphazard, without formation or direction. In the early stages Henry found himself unhorsed, but the man who had felled him had no chance to finish the King, his conscience—or his cowardice—causing him to hesitate a second too long. He met instead his own death, his head ripped off his body by a single sword stroke from Duke William, a man fighting in earnest for the first time in his life.

As the macabre dance of battle swayed and turned, William found himself engulfed by a group of enemies. He had no time to experience fear, would not contemplate the possibility of defeat, but struck out at the nearest wild-eyed horse, his bloodied sword blade slicing into the animal's face, removing an ear and gouging out an eye. The bay stallion screamed and reared, toppling his rider beneath the thrashing hooves, his skull crushed as if it were a ripe grape set beneath a mallet.

The iron chain links of William's hauberk rang as, not raising his shield swift enough, someone else's sword struck against his shoulder. The jarring shudder that rattled his body dazed and winded him, but his stallion, resenting the close presence of another blood-heated animal, reared and, as he dropped down again, William was able to strike out with his own weapon. A lucky blow, aided by the momentum of the horse plunging forward. The honed edge of the blade ripped deep through the chain-mail of Hardez de Bayeux, slicing through his lungs and heart. The man was dead before his body tumbled from the saddle.

Horses suffering terrible wounds were running loose, screaming their fear and pain. Many dragged their riders, dead or dying, their feet caught in the wide, leather-bound wooden stirrups. The rebel army was beginning to disperse, the hearts and courage of the men faltering, failing.

Somewhere amid the confusion Guy de Bourgogne—or Guy de Brionne as he now styled himself, having claimed his inheritance of the strongholds of Vernon on the Seine and Brionne on the river Risle—fought as valiantly as any man could. His desire to see William gone and the ducal coronet on his own head had initiated this battle. How many long years had it taken to prepare? To pay, to bribe men to back him? How much gold had he spent and how many sweet words had he uttered to see this day's dreadful defeat? For defeat it was; victory was going to Henry of France. There was only one cheering thought: Duke William could never have managed this on his own.

A spear thrust under the guard of Guy's shield thudded into his belly. The pain was as if fire were consuming his body—but his life was not taken. If he could get away, reach safety, there might be another chance to fight for that coronet of gold, for a duchy that ought, he considered, by right be his. If Henry had not heeded William's plea for help, if he had only remained as indifferent as often he did…Guy wheeled his horse and galloped south, away from the bloodshed and carnage. If only Henry had not come; if only he could reach his stone-built, impregnable castle at Brionne…

Panic spread like wind-fanned fire among the rebels; there was no escape to the north or east. Men rode haphazardly, seeking a way off the battlefield, finding only the cruel thrust of a sword and spear to end their desperation. Escape to the Bessin was tempting, but the deep, muddied waters of the river Orne lay between Val-ès-Dunes and sanctuary. Few of those who drove their horses into the water, or those who attempted to swim, hastily discarding their heavy mail, reached the other side. The river ran red with blood and the mills of Borbillon downstream stopped turning, their paddled wheels clogged by the broken bodies of man and horse.

⤞⤝

The victory was William's but peace in Normandy was not yet to be. Many men paid heavily for their part in the rebellion, suffering exorbitant fines and public humiliation. Nigel de la Cotentin was forced into exile, Guy de Brionne, despite the severity of his wound, reached his castle and closed the gates to his duke who, within days, laid siege to its stout, high-built stone walls.

William, the man they called the Bastard, had, however, shown his indomitable strength and his unwavering determination. He was undisputed Duke of Normandy and, for a while, none would dare challenge his iron-willed rule of authority.

Some months after the battle at Val-ès-Dunes, when the spring rains had washed away the blood and the carrion crows had picked the flesh from the bones, leaving them to bleach through the days of hot summer sun, Duke William ordered the prelates of all Normandy to gather less than one mile from the site of his first great victory.

His defeated enemies were to swear an oath on the holy relics brought for this purpose from St. Ouen and a Truce of God declared. Its effectiveness depended on the Church's ability to enforce its code, but as ecclesiastical penalties consisted of excommunication and a denial of all spiritual comfort, the Truce seemed likely to hold, at least long enough to contain successfully the dissident families of Normandy, while William undertook his siege on the castle at Brionne and replenished his strength.

The terms? The making of war was prohibited from Wednesday evening until Monday morning; forbidden completely during the seasons of Advent, Lent, Easter and Pentecost.

To augment the Church's powers of enforcement, two men were excluded from swearing the pledge, were granted permission to maintain armed forces against any who might break their given oath to the agreed Truce. Only two men, therefore, could, without fear of excommunication, effectively make war on their fellow countrymen: Henry, King of France, and William, Duke of Normandy.

23

⁂

Bruges—April 1049

A sharp wind was blustering across the harbour, catching at cloaks and the wimples and gowns of the ladies. The ship was already fifty yards from the quay, the crew pulling the oars against a boisterous tide. As it lowered, her single, square sail rippled and cracked, flapped once then filled, releasing the ship forward as if it were a horse kicked into a gallop.

The girl, Mathilda, stood on toetip waving, the tears streaming down her face. "Goodbye!" she called. "Take care!" She doubted her sister had heard. Not that it mattered: they had said their sad farewells last night in the privacy of their mother's arboured herb garden and then again this morning, clinging to each other on the quayside while the servants loaded the last of the baggage aboard.

"Do not snivel, child," her mother reprimanded, catching hold of the girl's wrist and effectively putting an end to her frantic waving. "It will ruin your complexion and is not becoming. Whatever will Count Eustace think of you?"

We must pursue this child's own marriage, the Countess thought, frowning at her daughter. *She is running wayward of late; the firm hand of a husband ought set her mind to her expected duties.*

Mathilda did not much care what the fat and balding Comte de Boulogne thought of her. He had a wife and daughter, was of no interest to a bored young lady. The other man, Swegn Godwinesson, though, was a different matter. He was young, with thick, fair hair and deep, blue eyes. Was handsome, with a quick wit and a passion for laughter and dancing. Swegn was an adventurer who had sailed the seas, defied the King of England and fought alongside great men. Mathilda was convinced she loved him, although he was one year short of thirty and she a young-budded eleven.

The ship was almost out of the harbour, about to turn into the open sea. She was bound for England and the port that nestled beside the seven white cliffs at Dover, taking her two important passengers away from Bruges for ever. Mathilda had never imagined that she would be parted from her beloved sister, although Judith was three years her senior and wed to another Englishman, Swegn's younger brother, Tostig Godwinesson.

When he had first come to her father's court, openly seeking a wife in the year of Our Lord 1045, Mathilda had not seen him as a threat to her personal happiness. She had been seven years old, Judith ten, Tostig himself entering his third decade. Both girls knew of the importance of marriage, their elder sisters were the wives of noblemen, their unions bringing alliances to their father's domain of Flanders. They had been too young to worry when their father agreed that Judith should become Tostig's wife and life for the two girls had barely altered. Until eight weeks past, when Judith had turned fourteen and finally gone to her husband's bed.

Swegn settled his arm companionably around Mathilda's thin shoulders—although he had to stoop, for he was tall, she no higher than a hand-span above four feet.

"My brother may be a serious-faced, sententious bigot, but that may work in your sister's favour. She will be kindly treated and well respected. Added to that, unlike myself, Tostig is highly favoured by our sister Edith. I would wager Judith will spend much of her time as the Queen's companion."

Mathilda sniffed and attempted a pale smile; he was trying to cheer her and she was grateful for that. What she could not understand was why Tostig had so suddenly had to leave Flanders. He had appeared well settled here, with little inclination to return to his family or the service of the English King. It had, perhaps, something to do with politics and Swegn? An eleven-year-old child, a girl, did not bother her head with the see-sawing of government manoeuvrings—nor the petty squabbles of one man with another, although watching that ship take her sister away to England, Mathilda wondered whether she ought to. She could read and write, was intelligent, had just not bothered with such subjects before.

The group assembled on the quay began to disperse. Her father Baldwin, the fifth Count of Flanders to carry that name, was already mounted, his stentorian voice ringing out in loud conversation with his companion, Eustace de Boulogne. Now that was one reason why Mathilda ought take more note of the daily intrigues of court. Why was Eustace—brother-in-law to Edward of England and friend to Normandy—visiting her father here in Bruges?

"Would you care to walk with me, Mistress Mathilda?" Swegn asked with gentlemanly politeness.

Mathilda smiled, delighted that he should single her out, sought permission from her mother with a quick look of enquiry. The Countess nodded. The girl could come to no harm within such numerous company and she needed some distraction to wean her mind from Judith's going.

Having decided that politics might be an option to relieve the boredom that would afflict her now that Judith had left, Mathilda elected to pursue her new interest immediately by questioning Swegn in what she thought to be an adult manner. "I do not understand why your brother has decided to return to England, yet you did not wish to accompany him?"

Swegn laughed, a belly shout of mirth. Should he give her the truth—that his brother was embarrassed by his presence—or the polite version?

"Well, my inquisitive little mistress, aside from the fact that my brother and I fell out of friendship while on campaign together in that rain-sodden, Godless land of Wales, I am not welcome at King Edward's moralistic court."

Ah, yes, she remembered now, Judith had told her that Swegn was out of favour. Something to do with a woman and a child. She would try a different tack. "Do you have a wife and children, my Lord?"

"I have a son named Hakon. He is being reared in my father's house."

"And your wife?"

"Gone to God." As Swegn intended, Mathilda assumed the woman had died. He knew full well that Eadgifu had abandoned the boy and returned to her nunnery immediately after his own departure from Bosham. She could rot there as far as he was concerned.

Wondering what else to talk about, Mathilda searched her mind for further information gleaned from Judith. With a lot of giggling, they had spent much of a recent afternoon together discussing men's attributes. Some of Judith's comments Mathilda had not understood. She had found that one of her sister's more irritating habits now that she was married and suddenly so knowledgeable about adult matters. What was it Judith had remarked—that Swegn was a cock-planter? Whatever did that mean? She would like to ask him, but had a feeling the reference was crude. She opted for safer ground. "I have heard that you have been fighting with your cousin, Svein Estrithson of Denmark. It must have been a relief when Magnus of Norway so unexpectedly died."

Again Swegn laughed as he handed her up a flight of narrow wooden steps. They had turned away from the harbour now Baldwin's impressive-built fortress reared ahead, its guardian stone walls reflecting the wind-tossed shadow of the clouds that scuttled overhead.

"I have not fought with my cousin, little lady, but against him. I have been with Magnus's successor, Harald Sigurdsson, known as Hardrada, the Hard Bargainer."

Swegn had enjoyed those recent months looting along the northern coastline with the Norwegian fleet. Had earned for himself a chest of gold and seven ships; the Hardrada held him in high regard. Which was more than could be said of his own king. Moreover, piracy had been offensive to those back in England, which was one reason why Tostig had decided to distance himself from any mud that might cling, had left Bruges so soon after his brother had arrived.

The second reason was that, unlike Swegn, Tostig had no wish to find himself on the wrong side of a political upheaval. Europe's nobility could soon be at one another's throats again, for the localised rebellion against the German Emperor was escalating. Baldwin, with his accessible ports, was a central pivot to the affray. Naturally, the Count was backing his brother-in-law Henry of France, who expected support from his vassal, Duke William of Normandy. The Emperor was allied with Pope Leo IX, Geoffrey Martel, comte d'Anjou, and Svein of Denmark. That left Edward to decide between France and Germany. His predicament, that he had friendship—and kinship—with both sides of the grumbling disagreement.

None of this, Swegn conjectured, would be of interest to Mathilda. Instead, he smiled impishly at her. "I am a free man, willing to serve any lord who cares to pay me adequate gold. And if that lord happens also to have the prettiest of youngest daughters, then why should I leave?"

Mathilda blushed and smiled back coyly. She liked Swegn better than his dour brother Tostig.

If Swegn had been a more conscientious man, he would not have encouraged her, but Swegn had neither conscience nor sense of responsibility. She was unbetrothed, he had no wife: he saw no reason why, if Tostig had Judith, he could not perhaps have Mathilda.

He plucked a sprig of pink blossom off the nearest tree, handed it to her with a gracious bow. "Were I not in exile, I would follow my brother's example and seek for myself a suitable young lady as wife."

Mathilda's astute answer belied her innocence. "Any lord with sense, sir, would surely ignore the matter of exile and welcome a man of your capability, or at least your seven fine ships."

Thinking of Edward, Swegn chuckled as he kissed her hand a second time. "There lies the problem. Not all lords, my dear, though they be royal and wear a fine crown, possess the attribute of sense."

Had Mathilda been yet more astute, she might have applied that last criticism to Lord Swegn himself.

Three days later Mathilda was summoned before her parents. Her mother had subtly hinted that they were considering her marriage arrangements. Her maids and the other young girls of court all shared her excitement, helping her to dress hurriedly in her finest gown, the spring green one gathered tight at the waist, with long, trailing sleeves lined in a buttercup yellow and richly embroidered bands at cuff, hem and neckline. She pulled a comb through her fair hair and ran to their private chamber, full of hope and expectation. When had Swegn asked for her, she wondered? He had not been much at court these last days, had been busy elsewhere. But then, how long did it take to ask for a lady's hand?

She paused before the door to regain her breath and pinch a blush into her cheeks. Swegn would be there on the other side, waiting for her with laughter in his blue eyes and on his lips. She lifted the latch, stepped through the chamber.

Disappointed, her skin drained of colour and a lurch of despondency twisted in her stomach. There was no Swegn, only her mother, father and the obsequious Eustace de Boulogne. What was he doing here? What interest had he in taking a wife? He had married Edward of England's widowed sister some years past.

"My dear," her mother trilled, beckoning her to come in. "We have good news for you. With the Count as his ambassador, your father has arranged a most advantageous marriage for you."

Mathilda's misgivings grew. What had Lord Swegn to do with Count Eustace?

"Now that terms have finally been agreed, this marriage will make a fine alliance for me," Baldwin proclaimed, slapping his knee with pleasure at the sealing of the deal. "Between us, Eustace, the three of us will control nigh on most of the Channel Sea coast!"

Mathilda's heart lurched with sudden fear. "The three of us," her father had said. "Who?" she asked, tremulous. "Whom am I to wed?"

Her mother answered brightly. The match her husband had arranged was indeed a most fortuitous one. "William, the Duke of Normandy."

Disbelief flooded Mathilda, heart, body and soul; utter, complete, contemptuous horror. A child her age might not care for political squabbles, but she had heard of William of Normandy and what she had heard, she did not like. Never, never would she wed such a detestable man!

"Duke William? William the Bastard?" She spat her distaste at her father. "Do you so insult me? He is an illegitimate uneducated illiterate. A vassal lord with little chance of retaining hold over his lands for many more years. He is of common Viking blood—I am descended from the kings of all Europe, including the Great King, Alfred of England himself! You dare consider the Bastard fit to become my husband? His mother"—the words stuck like a grating fish bone in her throat—"his mother is the daughter of a tanner!"

Glaring at her father and mother, Mathilda turned on her heel and stalked, with the dignity of a grown woman who well knows her own mind, from the room. Beyond the closed door she lifted the hem of her gown and ran, tears of disappointment, rage and hopelessness coursing down her cheeks. She would not, she told herself, over and over, under any conceivable circumstances marry William the Bastard.

Her despair engulfed her as she threw herself face down on her bed. Would not marry him? What choice had she? None.

24

Sandwich

Ten ships of the King's fleet rested at anchor a reasonable distance from the coast of Kent. The cluster of buildings and moored ships that formed the harbour port of Sandwich nestled on the horizon, too far to distinguish any detail but close enough for comfort. Edward enjoyed the exhilaration of the sea air, especially on such a pleasantly warm day as this, but did not enjoy sailing too far from land when the threat of foreign raiders hovered on the other, seaward, horizon. The line of blockade out there, his commanders informed him, was holding well, the southern coast of England effectively sealed from pirates and unauthorised incoming trade: factors that would extensively damage the economy of Flanders and France.

During the few dark hours of night, however, ships did occasionally manage to slip past the patrolling fleet: at Bosham seven ships slid quietly into harbour, dropping anchor out in the Chichester Channel, their commander coming ashore alone as the August sun rose in the eastern sky, flooding the dawn with swathes of pink and gold-tinged cloud.

Swegn had decided to come home. Mercenary raiding was finally losing its appeal and the generous welcome that he had received in Flanders earlier in the year had been noticeably waning of late. Aimless roving, although attractive for its occasional excitement, was not conducive to homely comforts. He had amassed a substantial quantity of gold and intended to buy his way back into Edward's favour; offering his ships into Edward's service would guarantee the reinstatement of his title and lands. That had galled, hearing from Tostig that his entire estate had been divided between Harold, Beorn and Ralf of Mantes. What did Harold know of the Welsh? Had he struggled to form an alliance with Gruffydd of Gwynedd or suffered at the hands of that damned agitator, Gryffydd ap Rhydderch? Or Beorn—what did he know of border warfare? He was a seaman. Give him a ship and he could out-sail, out-flank, outfight any pirate raider. But avoid ambushes in the shape-shifting mist of the Welsh border hills?

Fend off attack from across those fast-flowing, turbulent border rivers? That was Swegn's speciality. Or so Swegn himself maintained.

There was only one difficulty with returning home to England. Not convincing the King—the gold would pay for that—nor reconciling his father. Godwine had always, eventually, forgiven his first-born's misdemeanours, no, Swegn's final hurdle would be to obtain the forgiveness of his mother. He had been wrong to insult her. It had been the drink, the accumulation of problems, the situation at the time. Surely Gytha realised that? Would be pleased to see him returned safe to England?

He was to be disappointed. Only the servants were at Bosham. His mother was residing with Edith at Sandwich in Kent, would not return until the autumn.

⤳

"My God, you've got a nerve!" Harold spoke for them all: for his mother, brother Tostig, cousin Beorn and the Queen. "You run the King's blockade, ride across country taking your time and pleasure, then walk in here as bold as a dog fox entering an unshuttered chicken coop and expect to be received with open arms! I assure you, brother Swegn, you will receive no such welcome!"

The atmosphere in Edith's chamber was deeply hostile. Semi-amused, Swegn thought that it might be easier to approach Gryffydd ap Rhydderch in his territories of Deheubarth, than face this glaring outrage from his own kindred. "I had hoped for an amicable reconciliation," he answered with sarcasm. "Not from you, of course, Harold. Now that you have got your grubby hands on my lands, I expected you to be too greedy to give them up." Swegn thrust his face closer to Harold's, jabbing at his brother's chest with his forefinger. "Well, let me remind you, brother, I am the eldest. When Father dies I inherit Wessex. Not you."

Tartly, Edith answered before Harold could deny his brother's jealous insinuations. "The decision who has Wessex will be the King's and Council's not yours." She was profoundly annoyed at Swegn's return, but for reasons different from those of Harold and Beorn.

It would be unrealistic to suppose that her marriage was happy, that she was fulfilled in her life. However, she lived in comfort and was respected by every man in the country, save for her husband and his wretched chaplain. But Emma had been right. With no fear of childbirth and no children sapping her energy—and figure—she could apply her mind to reading, the study of languages and politics. Edward was an ageing four and forty years to her youthful twenty, the probability that he would soon pass into God's kingdom high indeed. All she had to do was remain quietly at court, always in the background, always there, ready to step forward from the shadows when the right occasion presented itself. Groomed by Emma, Edith had slid neatly into the role of queen, making herself ready to rule when the time eventually arrived when Edward could not.

Swegn's arrogant homecoming would jeopardise all her hard work, for her father was bound to advocate his reinstatement. And yet another public clash between Godwine and Edward could reflect on herself.

She welcomed the support from her brothers Harold and Tostig, her cousin and her mother. Harold's vehemence surprised her, though, for he had never favoured Edith since that unfortunate episode at the boat race. She had been a child then, with immature reactions and feelings. Perhaps her brother realised that and had, when faced with a more serious threat from within the family, put the incident into perspective. Swegn, she realised now, was a man of greed and self-enhancement. Everything he did was for his own gain; his favours to her as a child had not been for her benefit, but to secure her devotion, to wean her from any affection she might show for his main rival, their brother Harold.

Annoyed at losing his temper so soon into the argument, Harold backed away from Swegn. He sat down in a corner of the room with one arm resting across his thigh, lips compressed, seething.

"It is not a matter of our forgiveness." Tostig tossed his own thoughts into the heated discussion. "It is God's. Abducting one of His holy daughters requires absolution from none less than the Pope himself."

Swegn sneered at him. "Oh, just what I would expect from you, Tostig. You always were a pain in my arse."

If the barb was intended to wound, it failed. Tostig had heard the same insult too often for it to affect him now. "I care nothing for your opinion of me, brother," he responded with a sardonic smile. "I think you may find the King agrees with me, however."

Beorn had been leaning against the wall, his broad shoulders brushing against one of the expensive tapestries that served the dual purpose of hiding the cracked plaster beneath and shielding out the more voracious draughts. "I have no intention of giving up my lands, at least not to you, a traitor to my brother in Denmark." His words were to the point, his tone bland. "If you want your earldom back, you will need to fight me for it."

Swegn snorted. Did this fine-clad coxcomb seriously believe he could beat him in a straight fight? He, Swegn, who had fought more border skirmishes than Beorn had dreamed of? He turned his back on the upstart. "And what of you, Mother?" he asked, looking directly at the woman seated with composed elegance beside his sister. "Are you content to allow your nephew to so threaten me? Your sons to bait me as if I am a bull chained to a post in the market square? I am the first son delivered from your womb. Surely I take first place in your heart?"

Countess Gytha stood, smoothing her gown straight. She was a just woman who would be willing to forgive anything if she thought repentance to be truly and humbly offered. But she knew that if there was contrition in Swegn's heart, purely selfish motives had set it there. "There are some wrongs," she said, moving away from Swegn towards the door, "that do not deserve forgiveness in this life or the next. You claimed before me that you were no son of my husband's. Well, I claim here, now, before you all, that this foul-mouthed, evil-smelling stench that passes himself as a man is no son of mine. I did not bear him, nor do I know him." She dipped her head to Edith by way of courtesy to her queen, and left the chamber, walking with quiet, upright dignity.

In the silence that followed Gytha's departure Edith looked from one to another of the men standing in the amply furnished room. There had been few occasions since her marriage when she had been able to exploit her rank. This was one of them. "You have insulted this family and disregarded our honour for your own gain. You come here, to my husband's court, expecting our delighted welcome? You will not get it. Do you understand me?"

Swegn carelessly shrugged one shoulder. He bowed low and as he returned upright, spread his hands in mocking submission. "I understand you, madam. In turn, you must understand this." He half bowed a second time to Harold, Tostig and Beorn. "As you stated, Wessex is not mine to claim from my father, but for the King to give." He smiled laconically as he moved with lazy ease towards the door. "Equally, the return of my title and lands is for Edward to decide, not you, my dear sister. We shall listen to his judgement. I have no doubt his opinion will differ somewhat from yours. Mayhap because his need of gold is greater, hm?"

Harold had unsheathed his dagger, was poking with its tip at some dirt uncomfortably lodged beneath his nail. In a flame of anger he hurled the weapon across the room, the blade singing through the air to embed itself in the doorpost, inches from Swegn's ear. "Then the King will need more than your Judas payment, Swegn. He will be confronted with a difficult choice—and we all know the King shies from having to make decisions." Harold strode across the room, took hold of his dagger and jerked it from its quivering resting place. Sheathed it. "If he as much as considers the return of your lands, he will face the strong possibility of rebellion from Earl Beorn and his Earl of East Anglia."

Slamming his boot against an empty barrel, Swegn sent it toppling and rolling across the darkness of the inn's squalid courtyard. He swore, vehemently and colourfully. He might have expected to get nowhere with his family! They were, all of them, utterly selfish.

After leaving his sister's solar, he had strolled to an inn for a hearty drink of ale and then wandered to the stables to await the King's return from hunting, hoping that his father's attempts to see him reprieved would have borne fruit. It would have, had Harold and Beorn not ridden out to meet with Edward on the road to persuade him otherwise.

Swegn kicked again, shattering the wood. No one, save for his father, had spoken for him, backed his claim or supported his cause. Not one damned other person. Nor was there opportunity to pursue it further, for enemy ships had been sighted prowling along the coast. To counter the threat, the full fleet of forty-two keels was to reset sail as soon as the tide turned, under the command of Godwine, Tostig and Beorn. Harold was to sail northward to intercept the raiders along the Essex coastline. There was nothing for Swegn to do. His ships were not wanted; his years of experience not required. He could have helped, but the King had dismissed him and his gold and his ships. Had given him four days to be gone from England.

He was damned if he was going to give up that easily, though. There must, surely, be some other way to influence the King into taking him back into favour?

25

Pevensey

News arrived at Sandwich, a matter of hours after the fleet had sailed, that not only the eastern counties of England were vulnerable to immediate attack. Whether by coincidence, or because he knew the King and his earls to be busy elsewhere, Gryffydd ap Rhydderch of South Wales had taken advantage of the periodic raiding by Irish Vikings by striking up an alliance. He and his new-acquired friends were making a thorough nuisance of themselves along the lower reaches of the rivers Severn and Wye, and into the Forest of Dean.

By chance, Swegn, who had tarried in Sandwich, vainly hoping to meet with the King, heard the news that his old Welsh enemy was rampaging on to English soil again. His first instinct was to leave it, let the King—and Earl Beorn who now held those lands—deal with it. He ordered himself a fifth tankard of ale, sat drinking it in the corner of a tavern. He would have liked to have dealt with Gryffydd himself, though, personally put a final end to the whoreson. Another two ales and he had convinced himself that he could do it. He had his ships waiting for him at Bosham, he could sail up the Severn and effectively cut off the attack. The Irish-Welsh alliance would not be expecting a counter raid, for the English fleet was occupied by the blockade—they certainly would not be expecting Swegn son of Godwine to appear!

By first light he was on the road, pushing his horse hard, his mind set on this way of proving his worth to Edward—and to his poxed sister, brothers and cousin. A few miles from Pevensey he learnt that part of the fleet had been driven ashore, was weather-bound. Swegn's smirk of confidence broadened as he rode beneath the gateway into the town, found stabling for his horse and tracked down the inn where his cousin, Earl Beorn, was apparently lodged.

Heads turned as a tall, well-dressed man strode into the tavern. In the way that it often does when unease stubbornly follows a man's character, silence settled, spreading in ripples from table to table. He was looking for someone, for his gaze darted across the room and fixed on the nobleman over in the corner.

"What do you want?" Beorn called. "If the King hears of this, he will hang you." The Earl stood slowly as Swegn stepped forward into the crowded room. Beorn resisted an impulse to curl his fingers around his dagger hilt as Swegn, spreading his hands to show he carried no weapon, pushed his way through the crowd of men.

"Forgive my intrusion, cousin, I am heading west for Bosham and heard you were in harbour." Swegn seated himself on the bench opposite. "That wind nigh-on swept me off my horse as I rode down the High Street, no wonder you sought cover."

Reluctantly, Beorn signalled for a second tankard and more ale. "So you were passing, and decided to seek my company?" he shook his head. "I think not, cousin."

Swegn shrugged, came direct to the point. "You must have heard that Gryffydd is raiding across the Wye into Herefordshire?"

Beorn nodded. He had heard. "The matter is being dealt with."

"Adequately? I doubt it! Gryffydd is looting your earldom, Beorn. It was once my earldom. I want it back—want something left to get back. I cannot sit by and see that heathen devil running loose, unchecked." Swegn leant his muscular arms on the grubby, stained boards of the table. "I shall soon be returning to Bruges, but before I do, I would like to ensure that murdering, thieving bastard is defeated and dead." He studied his hands a moment deep in thought, scarcely noticing the dirt beneath torn nails, the scar from an old wound across the knuckles of his left hand, the four expensive rings adorning his fingers. Then he looked up, locked eyes with his cousin. "It is an old feud that I would dearly like to settle. I could have ridden straight for Bosham, this wind will not be so fierce around the Island of Wight. I could have taken my ships and sailed up the Severn alone. Attacked and defeated those Welsh scum, and returned to court to claim all the glory for myself." He set both palms flat to the table. "But I did not do that. I came instead to seek you, to ask if you would come with me and take command of two of my ships. Two capable men will be more effective than one." Impulsively, Swegn reached forward, gripped his fingers around Beorn's wrist. Think on it! I doubt you can do anything here for the next, what, three, four days? We could be on our way to sort the Welsh once and for all. Think of the reward we will receive!"

"So you are doing this for reward? As you attacked Danish villages for reward from Hardrada?"

A scowl creased Swegn's beard-stubbled face. "Yes, I intend to do this for reward. Do you think I enjoy exile from my own country? Being shunned by my family, my king? I want forgiveness. I do not want to be away for another year and another after that. If I must leave England, I would rather leave exonerated, a free, untainted man."

Beorn knew how it felt to be a man in a country that was not one's own—but he had voluntarily left Denmark to join Godwine's family, for there had been nothing for him there. Uncertain whether to believe this sudden display of contrition, though, he said, "You should have thought of that before abducting a nun."

"Do you not think I have reprimanded myself on it? Oh God! Why did I act so stupid?"

Pity moved in Beorn's heart. In the past, he had committed deeds that he had regretted—who had not? And where a handsome woman was involved…He stood, walked around the table, laid his hand on Swegn's shoulder. "I will come with you. But I will take command of five ships, not two."

Swegn leapt to his feet, grinning with delight. "Three ships."

"Four."

Swegn hesitated. He had seven ships. Four for Beorn, three for himself? The men would not take kindly to orders from Beorn—ach, they could sort the details later at Bosham. "Four then. It is agreed!"

Their hands joined, palm to palm, fingers gripping. An alliance for adventure.

As Swegn had predicted, the easterly wind was not so strong further along the coast at Bosham, but that was the only thing he was right about. His men showed no disinclination to change allegiance to a new commander and Beorn had no intention of changing the agreement. Four ships he had asked for. Four ships he was going to have.

Swegn tried flattery; he offered bribes. Then, with temper rising, he turned to threats that escalated into angry abuse.

Beorn ignored all of it, placidly informing Swegn what he could do with his ships and his plans, and sent a man to saddle his horse. "Do what you like, Swegn. I am returning to Pevensey and the fleet. I will tell the King of your comments about my manhood and capabilities, shall I?"

They were on board Swegn's command ship, a sleek, clinker-built craft of Viking origin. Over fifty feet in length and thirteen wide, she towered above the quay, the fierce-eyed dragon-head at her bow glaring out to sea impatiently, awaiting that moment when she would be loosed from her mooring, allowed to skim the waves in freedom.

"Damn you, Beorn!" Swegn blocked him from stepping out on to the gang plank. "I'll not let you run tattle-tongue to Edward! You agreed to help me—or have you lost your stomach to face the Welsh? Too dangerous for you, are they?"

"I agreed to help in this thing for command of four ships. It is you who have gone back on your word, not me. But then you never were one for whistling the truth, were you, Swegn?" Beorn raised his arm, intending to push his cousin aside. Wrongly assuming he was about to be struck, Swegn reacted as any fighting man would, by instinct rather than thought. He hit first, a clenched-fist blow to the jaw.

Beorn went down like a felled tree. The tide was to turn within the half-hour; if they did not sail then this chance to intercept Gryffydd would be gone. Swegn knelt beside his cousin, slapped his cheek, shook his shoulder, but the man was unconscious. Several of the crew gathered round, offering unhelpful advice. The handful of men that Beorn had brought with him were ashore, awaiting orders. Beorn could not have brought more away from the fleet, not in this private venture, and Swegn had assured him that all seven ships were fully crewed.

Always one to act quickly, Swegn ordered Beorn's wrists and ankles bound, "Take word ashore that my cousin has decided to sail with me." Swegn grinned at his men. "We leave with the tide—and if Beorn does not agree with my tactics, well, all the more gain for us when we cut those Welsh throats!"

The men cheered, set about readying the ship. Most of them could not give a damn whom they served, or whether their betters quarrelled among themselves. As long as there was looting at the end of it, who cared if one lord toppled another?

The seven ships ran down the coast, hugging the land to avoid the worst of the winds, put in at Dartmouth to overnight. With the coming of the morning, only one ship remained, was left, solitary, beached upon the shore.

Beorn had taken exception to being bound like a common thief. The skin sore and bleeding, he had worked his wrists free of the shackles, intending to use the darkness to slide quietly over the side of the ship. Had Swegn expected him to try for an escape? He caught Beorn as he crept along the deck, threw him down, their fists pummelling, knees and feet kicking as they rolled together, fighting, trading blows, Swegn's temper was ever hot and easily spurred. He reached his hand for his dagger, the fingers closing around the hilt, drawing it from its sheath, the blade glinted...

Six of the ships took advantage of the night tide, deserted Swegn, left him to answer for the bloody murder of one of his own.

26

Waltham Abbey

Harold arrived home, dishevelled, begrimed and smelling of sweat, horse, blood and tiredness. The fighting along the marshland beside the Blackwater estuary had been short and fierce. Both sides had remembered the tales of another bigger battle of the past, told them around the hearth fires by their fathers: the great battle at Maldon, where the brave had fallen prey to the Viking kind. This summer's raiders were not warriors like their ancestors, these were mere opportunist pirates. Faced by the sword and axes wielded by the housecarls of the Earl of East Anglia, they ran, tails between their legs, to the safety of their ships—but the damage had already been done: villages burnt, women used or taken as slaves, men and cattle slaughtered.

Angry at the wanton destruction and needless taking of innocent life Harold, despite his best efforts, had found it difficult to keep the raiders at bay. Catch them along one headland, a brief flurry of fighting and they would move further up or down the coast, to a new location, a different village to plunder. They came for corn, cattle and slaves—and gold from the churches, though they professed to be Christian men.

Running the sea-wolves into the Blackwater estuary had been a stroke of luck, which Harold took full and successful advantage of. They would not be back, not this year, those who had escaped with their lives.

As he eased from the saddle, back, shoulders and knees aching, a boy ran from the cattle byre, feet pounding, arms pumping. He would be five years old, come Christmas, was short and chubby with a set, determined chin. He threw himself into Harold's outstretched arms, "Papa!" he shrieked. "My papa is home!"

Others had heard the horses, were coming out to greet the Earl and his men, Edyth herself, running from the Hall, joy on her face, Harold scooped the boy into one arm, clutched his wife to his chest with the other, kissing her passionately while the lad wound his arms tight about his neck. It was good to be home.

"You are growing tall, my lad." Harold said, releasing Edyth to lift his son high above his head with both hands. "I would say you are almost big enough to ride my stallion."

"I am big enough now!" Goddwin boasted with glowing pride. "I ride Mama's pony, I can ride on Squirrel!"

"What, that fat little turnip?" Harold winked at Edyth. "Your Mama used to ride her when she was a little girl. Would you like to sit on a real horse? Just this once?"

Goddwin was already wriggling, reaching out towards the destrier's saddle. "Be careful, dear," Edyth said, half to her son, half to Harold as he lifted the boy up. Stallions were noted for their unpredictable natures.

"Walk on!" Goddwin commanded, kicking with his heels—the big horse felt nothing, for the boy's legs were too short to reach his sides. Taking hold of the bridle and clicking his tongue, Harold led the animal forward, circling the courtyard twice, his son sitting proud and straight.

"My, you will make a fine earl one day!" Edyth declared, clapping her hands with approval.

"Oh, no," Goddwin answered. "I don't want to be an earl. I want to be a king. Kings stay at home while the earls do all the work."

"And who told you that, son?"

"Mama, yesterday."

Edyth blushed. "I meant no offence to the King..."

Harold swept his arm around her again. "Your mama is quite right," he said, laughing, to the boy. "But I am afraid you will not be a king, so you had best practise your riding and learn how to be an earl instead."

A servant led the stallion away; Harold's housecarls were greeting their own wives and families; Harold and Edyth stepped inside their manor house overlooking Waltham and the valley of the river Lea. The Earl was returned and it had become a complete home.

The Mead Hall itself was a rectangular, timber building fitting for Harold's status, but modest in size and structure, designed primarily as a home for a man and his growing family. The public area was large and airy, with central hearth and a vaulted, beamed roof. Swords and axes, animal skins and deer antlers, two aurochs' horns, gold-tipped, with carved patterns adorning them, decorated the walls. At one end, opposite the double, wide-flung entrance doors, was a raised dais where Harold, Edyth and any guest of importance would eat. By day the Hall was cleared of the trestle tables and mead benches, used instead for the routine of everyday farming life. As the sun drifted downwards, the benches and trestle tables were reset for the evening meal, when all were welcome to eat with their lord. In the northern corner beyond the dais, a doorway led to a wooden stairway.

Upstairs were the family rooms: Harold's and Edyth's private chambers, the solar and beyond, their bed-chamber, large rooms containing bed, tables, chairs, storage chests and Edyth's loom. Both chambers were decorated with a touch of pride and a handful of love. Richly embroidered tapestries concealed the plaster and timber walls, bright woven curtains kept the draught from the bed. The solar was comfortable and welcoming, the bed-chamber warm and cosseting. In Harold's humble opinion the best place to be in the entire kingdom.

They dined alone in the solar, Harold and Edyth, that first night, with only each other and the children for company. The two little girls were fair-haired and blue-eyed, looked much like their mother, with dimpled smiles and gurgling laughter, although Alfrytha was still pale-skinned and thin for her age. Harold had played with them for a while, giving the two eldest rides on his back and swinging them high in his arms until their laughter came in breathless gasps. Algytha, barely two years of age, took her share of being tossed to the ceiling and caught in her father's firm and confident grasp, her shrieks of laughter heard below in both courtyard and Hall.

They were tired when their nurse came to take them to their beds in the room against the eastern side of the Hall. The quiet in the solar after they had gone descended like a soft feather fluttering from a passing bird. Harold sat sprawled in his favourite chair. The brazier was unlit, the window shutters thrown open to the evening, the coolness of descending night a welcome relief from the summer heat. Harold sighed, partially closed his eyes, content. Edyth sat opposite, bent over her sewing, a relaxed smile curving her mouth. Surreptitiously, through his lashes, Harold watched her.

He could not quite believe his fortune at having her for his own. "You have produced some beautiful children for me," he said, without opening his eyes. "They are a credit to you." His expression suddenly broadened into a wicked grin. "Two girls, one boy. Would you be interested in trying for another son?"

Completing her stitch and pushing the needle in for the next, Edyth answered, pretending seriousness. "I have two boys already, one is just somewhat taller and more moustached than the other."

"One has the makings of becoming a fine warrior one day."

"I agree. Goddwin will as well, when he grows up."

Harold released a deep roar of amusement. He opened his eyes, stood and walked over to Edyth, put his arms around her waist. Her figure had thickened since childbearing, but he preferred some meat on her bones. "I love you, woman. You do not know how much I have missed you while I have been away these last months."

She tilted her head up at him. "Oh, I do. I know just how much, for I have missed you the same."

Resting his chin on her head, Harold said, very quietly and slowly, "Then why don't you put that damn sewing away and come to bed?"

⁓

The candles had burnt low. Edyth murmured in her sleep and Harold slid his arm further around her waist, drawing her supple nakedness nearer to his own flesh. He was drowsing in that half-awareness between sleep and waking, his mind and private parts remembering the lovemaking he had shared with Edyth before sleep had overcome them. He slid his hand over the roundness of her hip, along her thigh, the skin silk-smooth to his touch. Cursed aloud at the sudden thumping at the chamber door. "What is it?" he called, irritated. "Go away. Leave it 'til morning."

"My Lord! Urgent news."

Edyth stirred and rolled into the warm patch where Harold had been as he swung his legs from the bed, flung a cloak around his shoulders. He strode to the door, opening it wide.

"It had bloody better be urgent!" he cursed, glaring at the two men who stood beyond. One was the officer of the watch, the other a messenger, still catching his breath from hard riding. "Well? Tell me."

The messenger bowed, swallowed. "My Lord, I bring word from your good lady mother."

Bad news, that was obvious from the man's nervous licking of his lips. Harold's first thought was of his father. Had some illness overtaken him—or worse?

"Sir. Your cousin is dead. Slain by a dagger to his throat."

"Beorn? You mean Beorn, my mother's nephew? How? Did the fleet engage in combat then? Was the fighting bad?" The questions came in a tumble of bewilderment. Harold waved the messenger in. "What happened?"

Fully awake now, Edyth was sitting on the bed, the covers drawn close, her sun-gold hair cascading across her shoulders.

The messenger again ran his tongue over his dried lips. This news was not easy to tell. "My Lord. Earl Beorn was murdered. He was slain at the hands of your own brother. By Swegn Godwinesson."

Edyth screamed, thrust her fist into her mouth, tears cascading from her eyes. Harold stood quite still, too numbed to say anything, to move, to react. How was this possible? Was it some evil jest—a mistake perhaps? Yet tear marks streaked the messenger's face. Suddenly Harold recognised him—he had been one of Beorn's housecarls.

Then it was true. Beorn was murdered. Slaughtered in cold blood by one of his own kindred.

27

Caen—September 1049

Snatching the parchment from the trembling hands of his cleric and twisting it between his taut, white-knuckled fingers, William screwed the offensive letter into a ball and hurled it into the hearth fire with a bellow of rage. How dare he? How dare the Pope deny him permission to marry with Mathilda of Flanders!

Several men edged towards the open doorway leading from the great hall, those nearest managing a tactful unobserved escape. The Duke in a rage was not a man to keep company with. Yet, one man sat, unconcerned, sipping at his wine. He was dressed expensively, quality cloth covering his ample-proportioned frame, jewelled rings adorning his fingers, Comte Eustace de Boulogne had nothing to fear from William, whether in good temper or foul. At least, not while the Duke of Normandy relied on him—and should William turn nasty, as he had with others, there was always kindred by marriage to call upon for aid. Unlikely that William would, by choice, antagonise the King of England.

"Calm your passion, my dear Duke," Eustace drawled, patting the air with his free hand. "'Twill come to nothing. The Pope must trot out his impotent authority now and then, to convince himself he sustains some small power. We all know that he cannot even keep his piss in a pot."

"Calm myself? Are you a complete imbecile?" William lashed out with his foot, sent a stool skidding across the stone flooring, then, grasping a table in both hands, upended that as well, scattering bowls and tankards, fruit and dishes. A servant crouched down to retrieve the broken shards of a pot. William kicked him. "His Holiness declares that I cannot marry the youngest daughter of Baldwin because he has decided we are too closely related—that her fifth cousin is my aunt's nephew's daughter—or whatever it was." He kicked the servant again, harder. "All my plans, all my intentions ruined, and you say ignore it?"

He had several worries on his mind, without minor details of genealogy to bother with. His mother was ill, dying, the doctors said. Why could they not do anything? Give her some stronger potion, use more effective herbs? Pah, what did these cretinous idiots know? She looked so frail...God's truth, what was he to do when he lost her?

And there was the galling matter of Guy de Brionne. His castle had still not fallen to William's siege. How they were surviving inside those walls since the rebellion and battle at Val-ès-Dunes no one who wished to remain sane dared to consider. For more than two years had the castle been shuttered from the outside world. Surrender must—surely—come soon, before winter returned. Daily the Duke hoped for news that it was all ended, prayed that he would not need ride there again without a victory to his name.

That rebellion was the direct cause of his presence at Caen. Two years ago it had been a village of no worth; William's anger and determination for revenge had transformed it into an expanding town, a centre of importance. Rouen had always been regarded as Normandy's capital—until its citizens had supported and financed Guy de Brionne. William had punished the town, its citizens, economy and status with one simple blow, by moving his capital. Caen was rising like the glory of the spring sunshine after a snowbound winter. One day it would be the foremost town of Normandy, centre of law, government and trade, the seat of the Duke. When it was built, that was. Delays, delays! The castle was being given priority: turreted, stone-built, with curtain wall and strong, impenetrable defences, but the stone for the gatehouse had not been cut straight; heavy rain had flooded the foundations; men were ill from dysentery—malingering laziness, more like!

"My Lord Duke?" Eustace's wheedling voice roused William from his reverie. "No one with an ounce of sense in his brain, save for this particular Pope who possesses no sense whatsoever, would think anything of your minor kindred with this girl. The difficulty lies within the politics. I would consider that you are, in fact, to be congratulated."

Scowling, William slumped into his own chair. "And how, *mon ami*, do you work that one out?"

Eustace toasted his companion with his goblet. "The Pope sides with the Emperor of Germany, who vehemently opposes Baldwin and Henry of France. If his Holiness Leo, ninth of that name, believes your marriage too great a threat to the present balance of power—as he obviously does—then you are clearly considered a man of potential danger."

Narrowing his eyes into crinkled slits, William dissected the theory. He had a point. By God, he had a point! "The possibilities that might arise from such an alliance are ruffling a few feathers, then? *Bon*! I shall do more than ruffle.

Some plucking and roasting might be most pleasing." William rubbed his hands together, called for servants to bring fresh wine, to clear the mess strewn across the floor.

"I shall marry Mathilda, whatever Rome says. I am the duke here in Normandy, not the Pope. Let him see to his work, me to mine."

"And if he likes it not?" Eustace asked.

William tossed his wine down his throat, aimed the empty goblet at the rounded backside of a bending servant. "Then he can go to hell!"

They laughed, Count and Duke together, but then the Count, unlike William, could afford to. If he could no longer bask in the warmth of the Duke's reflected glory, there were always other stars to follow, his new-born grandson being one of them. Always best to collect eggs in more than the one basket. His wife was sister to Edward of England; that king had no son of his own, no heir, save for the feeble Ralf de Mantes, his wife's son by her first marriage. One boy was as good as another to be proclaimed heir...

Eustace de Boulogne sat drinking and discussing plans with Duke William late into the night. He had negotiated this marriage and was held in high esteem by both Normandy and Flanders. A clever man, he was already working out possibilities for the future.

Some would call his ability ambition. Other greed.

28

Canterbury—March 1051

Inconvenient, for Edward, that two men of the Church had died within two months of each other. Difficult to accept that Eadsige, Archbishop of Canterbury, had finally succumbed after his long illness but Alfric Puttoc, Archbishop of York, called to God also? What could be the Lord's meaning? If it was to cause as much trouble as possible regarding the appointment of two new archbishops, then the Almighty had achieved his aim. Too many people had too many candidates and opinions to proffer, and Edward was determined to hear none of it.

Harold left his lodgings to attend Council as late in the morning as he dared. Sleet was making the prospect of the day ahead more depressing, snow within the next few days seemed an inevitability. This mid-Lent calling of Council irritated everyone from cleric to earl, but archbishops for York and Canterbury had to be decided—although given that the King seemed determined to have his own way, discussion seemed pointless.

Edward was solving a succession of state problems with great economy, but whether his decisions were politically wise remained to be seen. Like his father, Harold was full of foreboding. He knew trouble for England was swelling beneath the horizon, as sensitive skin prickles when a summer storm threatens. Whether it broke out in thundering tempest or dispersed harmlessly on the wind, only the future would reveal.

Last year, at Easter, Leofric of Mercia and his supporters had argued that the naval fleet was unnecessarily large and had called for the disbandment of the Danish mercenary ships, all fourteen of them. The *Heregeld*, the tax levied to fund their upkeep, had been unpopular, and with their commander, Beorn, buried in Winchester at Harold's expense, there appeared no reason to retain the foreign ships. No reason, save for prudence, wisdom and the possibility of invasion, but Edward was under pressure to relieve taxes and he was inclined to listen too eagerly to poor advice.

That decision had been a direct insult to the House of Wessex, followed within a month by Edward's astonishing about-turn in allowing Swegn to return with full pardon. Mercy and forgiveness, he had professed, were the earthly tools of eternal salvation. Weakness, lenience and a lust for gold could be the downfall of kings, Harold had thought bitterly.

After that terrible murder, Beorn's Danish men and Harold with his brothers, sister and mother had vehemently declared Swegn *nithing*—nothing, a man outside existence. Godwine himself had been devastated, had remained silent and morose for many weeks after, his hair visibly greying, weight shedding from his cheeks and body. Swegn had fled abroad. He had not been missed.

That was all in the past, for once Swegn had succeeded in purchasing Edward's forgiveness, Godwine had with a father's love for a favoured son welcomed him back, leaving the family bitterly divided. It was a shrewd move on the part of the King to disunite the Godwines from within, to cleave son from father, wife from husband. Adamantly, Countess Gytha had refused to acknowledge Swegn; and Harold had barely exchanged word with his father since, not even to introduce his fourth-born child, a boy, Edmund.

Edyth was with child again, her time due towards the end of the summer. God gave with one hand, took away with the other. Tucking his chin against the cold, Harold walked the short distance from their lodging place to the Canterbury Guild Hall where the electorate council for the archbishopric was to meet. As he passed, he glanced up at the stone-built archway that led into the entrance courtyard of the cathedral of Christ Church, crossed himself and murmured a brief prayer. Their daughter was dying. Little Alfrytha was losing her battle with poor health. Harold closed his eyes. He had no stomach for this wretched meeting.

Laying his sword and dagger aside, and removing his sodden cloak, he entered the Guild Hall. The meeting was begun, verbal battle already joined.

"I will not be dictated to!" Edward cried, stamping a foot almost childishly in his building rage. "It has always been the prerogative of a king to appoint his bishops!"

"Of course, my Lord King, but we merely advise you to consider all options."

Harold recognised the weariness and exasperation in his father's voice, Godwine was wasting breath; the King's mind was set—the complacent expression on Robert Champart's face made that clear.

"Cleric!" Edward boomed, flagging his hand at the scribe sitting hunched over a desk, spread parchment to one side. "Make mark of this, Cynsige is to go to York, Spearhavoc removes from Abingdon to London."

Several gasps of disapproval from Council, Edward frowned at the noise. "I appoint my cousin Rothulf in his place."

Godwine, as senior earl present, was the only man with the courage to speak out, "Sire," he said, struggling to hold on to his composure, "do you not consider Spearhavoc to have inadequate experience for a position such as London? He is your goldsmith…"

Edward's hands clenched around the broad, curved arms of his chair, the knuckles whitening as he leant forward, his snarl adorned with affronted rage. "I consider him suitable. Do you doubt your king's wisdom, my Lord Earl?"

Spearhavoc is suited to the making of that precious new crown he has presented you with, and very little else, Harold thought sadly. *Ah, Edward, you go the way of your father; bribery and subornation are chiming the better of wise judgement.*

"And Canterbury, my lord? Whom are you to appoint as archbishop in Canterbury?" asked the Queen abruptly. She sat on her husband's right-hand side, her designated place within the Council of England, by the tradition and law of the Saxon peoples, Edith had contributed very little during the morning— indeed during the entirety of this two-day Council. Tired, lonely and bored, she trailed in Edward's wake as if she were his barely seen, faded shadow. He paid no heed to her attempts at conversation, sneered at her suggestions for the simplest of domestic decisions—furnishing for the royal palace being built at Westminster, the co-ordination of colours for cloak and tunic. Edward was incapable of dressing with taste—yet he listened to Champart, eagerly sought his advice and direction. If she could not be wife to Edward in these homely matters, what hope had she of being heard in her role as queen? On this morning, as with many others of late, Edith found herself envying her mother-in-law's retreat into retirement.

"The monks of Christ Church have expressed a desire for one of their own," she reminded her husband. "Their proposed candidate, Æthelric, is a good man."

"A choice you would naturally champion, Madam." Edward's reply was acerbic. "Æthelric is, after all, your father's half-brother." These persistent interferences from Edith were becoming more than annoying. She had not adopted the passive role that he had assumed a wife would take, nor had Godwine been subdued. The only advantage was that he did not have his earls pestering him to take a wife, as in those early days of his reign.

"I do not endorse him because of family connections, Sir!" Edith retorted. "I would remind you that I emphatically opposed your favouring of a certain member of my family."

Was that a reason, Harold secretly wondered, why Edward had decided in favour of Swegn? To spite Edith?

Edward's features wrinkled with displeasure as he regarded his wife. An interfering, sour-faced bitch, that's what she was. Influenced by her arrogant father who sought to control King and Council.

Council! Huh! What need had he of the mutterings of a group of old men? England needed young minds and spirits, eyes that looked to the future, not toothless old gums that regurgitated the past. Moribund men who were as tedious as his wretched wife.

Edward's confidence in government had increased as the years of kingship had passed. Apart from the occasional minor border or coastal raids, England had been at peace for eight years, a peace Edward was determined to see continued, if only the Council would allow him a free rein. He was King, damn it, and his word ought to be law! About time these humourless bigots realised that fact. All he need do was keep his nerve in the face of their opposition, make his decision and stick to it as firm as a spider keeps a fly caught on the web. He ruled this land, not his Council—and certainly not the family of Godwine.

"I have made my choice for archbishop." Edward stated, his scowl focusing on Edith. "Robert Champart, Abbot of Jumièges, is to go to Canterbury."

They had expected it, but still the clamour of outraged disapproval could have shaken the very walls of the building. All were on their feet, some shaking their fists, vociferously expressing horror that a Norman, a foreigner, should take such an exalted position. Only Edith and two men remained quietly seated: Robert himself, with an expression of self-congratulation idling across his mouth, and Harold, whose thoughts were with his daughter. Her breathing had been fragile when he had left, her skin damp. It did not seem right that God was soon to take one so young and innocent. What had she seen of the sun? To run and laugh, to find delight in the wonder that was His world

Edith sat stunned at her husband's sublime foolishness. Could he not see that England would never accept such an appointment? Unease was already rippling through the country that too many of Edward's Norman friends were receiving positions of high office: advisers, clerics, abbots, shire reeves and constables of law. If Edward wanted to ensure the loyalty of the land-folk he ought to promote the English-born, not the ambitious, greed-wasted friends of his exile. Champart especially would not be tolerated. Could Edward alone, among everyone within Council, court and country, not see his true character? That his fawning and grovelling was for naught but his own gain?

The protests clamoured in Edward's ears, jangling at his nerves and temper. How dare these imbeciles dispute his decision? What right had they to challenge the crowned and anointed?

"Champart is a foreigner!"

"A Norman!"

"This is not acceptable!"

"We must have an Englishman at Canterbury!" Godwine said and Edward unleashed his fury at the Earl, who in his mind was the instigator of all discontent and disorder. It was always Godwine who barred his way—Godwine who had supported Cnut, who had made no attempt to secure the safety of the two princes, himself and Alfred.

"My mother was a Norman foreigner!" Edward shouted at Godwine. "Yet you supported her without qualm. Nor is your wife of English blood. Is it, then, one law for you, Godwine, one for me? I owe much to those in Normandy who gave me succour when England cast me aside. I remember the kindness—aye, and the hatred that my mother and you held for me." Edward thrust himself from his seat, took three long strides to stand before Godwine. His spittle flecked the Earl's cheeks. "Nor have I forgotten the death of my brother."

Men had backed away, their shouts of dismay at Champart's appointment fading into whispers. The Earl of Wessex stood alone and vulnerable before the fury of the King. How Godwine wanted to thrust a dagger into Edward's uncompromising, shallow heart—but despite the occasional rumour and slander he was no murderer. He cared too much for his hard-won position, his wealth and family. Oppose Edward and he could lose everything.

The Earl breathed deeply, spread his hands, etched dismay and innocence into his voice and expression. "My Lord, your wisdom supersedes mine own. You are King, I am but an earl."

"Then remember it," Edward hissed. "You will begin by sanctioning my choice of archbishop."

Godwine retained a calm exterior. Inside, his rage was seething. One day Edward would push him too far. This came close—to capitulate to that scheming devil Champart…but what could he say? Do?

Godwine bowed his head. "Of course, my Lord King."

❧

The King's private residence at Canterbury was basic: practical for the necessity of government, but lacking in comfort. Several timbers of the high, arched roof beams were showing signs of woodworm and dry rot, the flooring was substantially patched. The Hall smoky, draught-riddled and stinking of damp.

Edward's guest, his brother-in-law comte Eustace de Boulogne, thought it more representative of a swine hovel than a royal building. "Duke William builds in stone. It is more enduring, and adequately expresses power, control and strength," he remarked casually to Godwine, as the two men strolled behind the King, inspecting his mews.

"Expresses the awareness of attack also. Protection is only required when there is vulnerability." Godwine observed, standing back so that Boulogne might admire a particularly handsome falcon. "I have no need of stone castles in Wessex because I am not likely to be attacked from within."

Boulogne haughtily cleared his throat. "Normandy is a young land; she perhaps has more troubles than do you." He turned to Edward. "You have some splendid birds here, Sir, I would be honoured to purchase a nestling or two from you."

Edward glowed at the praise; hawks and hunting dogs were his pride. "I shall arrange it—you must take something of worth back to the Duke too, in exchange for the generous gifts he sent. He is a young man of some renown, so I hear, a lad with promise."

"He is valiant in both battle and politics. Normandy is becoming an important duchy under his hand."

"A hand that spares not the lash, so I hear," Queen Edith said. She passed the kestrel that had been gripping her hand back to the master falconer, removed the stout leather gauntlet that had been protecting her skin against its talons. "It is said that his ambition is over-zealous and his kindness non-existent." She had no liking for Count Eustace, found him to be an obsequious lecher, who set his own worth above that of any other man—duke or king included—opinions not formed entirely by her own observations. Her sister-in-law Judith, Tostig's wife, had known him in Flanders. That he was here with some private motive, beyond his official representation of Duke William, was obvious. Edith could see his ambition as clearly as his puce-coloured nose. Edward saw naught but a man interested in hunting and hawking. The fact that Eustace had a grandson born to his only child, a daughter, added weight to Edith's suspicions. While Edward had no heir of his own seed, there would always be others coveting a crown.

Coming to the end of the row of birds, Edward indicated the door leading to the courtyard. They had inspected the hounds earlier—that bitch the Duke had sent was a superb example of a hunting dog—long, clean limbs, alert eyes and ears, slim head, muscular body and quarters. If William was as good a judge of people as he was of dogs, then aye, he should go far. Edward turned to Godwine as the group returned for refreshment within the King's Hall. "Eustace informs me that the Duke seeks alliance with England. I intend to agree his proposition."

"Council ought be consulted where any truce with a foreign power is suggested," Godwine stuttered. God's truth, why forge an alliance with an insignificant such as Normandy? What could that small duchy possibly offer England in return?

"On what terms, sir?" Harold asked. He had not wanted to join the royal party this afternoon, his thoughts still concentrated on his daughter, but after the disagreeable arguments of the morning he guessed it would not be politic to refuse the King's invitation. And what more could he do to alleviate her suffering? The physicians had done all they could, had told him it was only a matter of time before God took her to His heart. At least in heaven she would smile again, would be relieved of her pain. It all seemed so futile, though, standing here talking of hounds, hawks and allegiance with a poxed upstart who had no care for England, beyond what would be useful for himself.

Eustace de Boulogne answered for Edward confidently: "In return for England's affection and support, the Duke offers to censure all who use his harbours with the intention of prevailing upon your coast. He will attempt to forbid any piracy emanating from Normandy."

Edward nodded in enthusiastic approval. "We welcome such assurance. Is it not a fortuitous alliance, Earl Harold?"

Harold caught the gruff expression on his father's face, the scepticism that flooded Edith's. Could Edward not see that only empty air was on offer here? "Censuring and attempts at control are not binding conditions. We would require something more solid were we to ally ourselves with territory rife with rebellion and bloodshed."

Eustace, blustering, attempted to make a counter-remark, but Edward interrupted. "Nonsense, Duke William is my own kindred. I have every faith in his word. England is plagued by those who wantonly use his harbours for their own gain." Edward placed a light kiss on each of Eustace's cheeks. "On your return to Normandy you will take word that I welcome your duke's offer and that I warmly embrace him as my beloved kinsman and friend. Tell him that I have not forgotten the succour and kindness that Normandy gave me. So long as he looks to England's best interest, he will always be made welcome within my realm."

Boulogne beamed, delighted. It had been so easy to capture Edward's friendship and trust. Almost too easy.

Edward turned to his two earls and his wife, expecting approval; met instead, stony silence.

"It is prudent to close the Norman coast to our enemies," Godwine responded with patient tact. "I wonder if the Duke could also influence Flanders to do likewise?"

Edith had no such inclination to be tactful. Must she endure more of this sickening embarrassment? To be wife to this…imbecile. There was no other word for him. Well did she realise, now, what Queen Emma had suffered during those interminable years of marriage to this fool's father. It made her sick to her stomach to listen to the drivel that washed from his lips, the naïveté that swivelled in his empty-brained head. "Duke William," she announced, "seeks your alliance, Edward, not for England's well-being but because he is desperate to gain favour with influential friends of the Pope. He is threatened with excommunication for continuing his bid to wed Baldwin's youngest daughter. Once he has her, he will show no more interest in the safety of our coast. Indeed, he may well encourage those sea-wolves, for I have no doubt he shares in their booty."

Edward thrust his face at her, a scowling mask of hatred. What did this damned woman know of politics or government? How dare she interfere? "Go back to your loom, madam. I do not require to hear gossip from your tattle-telling lips."

Tartly Edith retaliated. "I am not a gossip. I am telling you the facts. The Duke is set on defying the Pope's ruling. It is not fitting for a man of your beliefs to ally with one who is soon to be excommunicated from the Church."

Edward was not alone in cursing Edith's interference.

"You may doubt my Lord William's intention," Boulogne said fiercely, his small eyes narrowing at Edith. "Let me assure you there is no duplicity." With deliberation he turned back to the King and bowed deeply. "If it pleases you to have assurance of our sincerity in this, I am willing, on my Duke's behalf, to place my young grandson into your personal keeping."

The giving of a hostage; a common strategy. How simply had Eustace's planning worked! "A child of your blood kindred"—Eustace smiled at Edward, his wheedling tone not lost on Edith—"would surely be most welcome within a childless court?"

Edith clenched the rage within her teeth. So she was right in this. That was indeed this odious man's aim. Unless a son was born to her and Edward—and that did not seem likely—at his death the nearest in blood kindred would stand good chance of gaining the crown. Ralf de Mantes, Edward's nephew, the son of Eustace's wife by her first marriage, was at this moment proclaimed ætheling, a man throne-worthy to be considered next for king. But why not Edward's great-nephew? A kingdom was a wondrous lure for an ambitious grandsire.

For his own part, Edward thought he had more sense than either his wife or earls credited him with. He had divined Eustace's intentions from the first day of the Count's ostentatious arrival two weeks past—why else would a man of his position travel abroad for an insignificant Duke, who would probably meet the wrong end of a dagger blade within the turn of a year or two? He had enjoyed Eustace's exaggerated flattery, however. Let the ass believe he had wooed and won the King of England, set his fledgling into the nest like a cuckoo. Here was a way to slam a door into the faces of both Godwine and Edith together, and neither could murmur a word against it.

"It is a good offer," he declared, with a delightful clap of his hands. "The child will come to my court and I shall nurture him as if he were my own son." Then he hurled his full spite at Edith: "After all, in that respect, my wife shall remain a disappointment to us all."

Edith's face flushed scarlet. How dare he put blame on her, make pretence that her childless condition was of her doing! Harold reached out to clamp his hand around his sister's wrist, shook his head with warning, advising her silence. The barb was deliberate, but now was not the time or place to pluck it from the wound.

She stared with contempt at Edward, ignoring her brother's warning. "From what I hear of Duke William," she said, "he is a strong-minded man, who possesses a remarkable sense of political ingenuity. He is a leader who knows how to fight for what is his. You may send your grandson to Edward's court, Lord Eustace, but I assure you he will learn nothing from the King of manliness. Here, he will learn naught but how to live as a monk and hunt game." Her insult was aimed direct at Edward and it hit its mark. She shook her arm free of Harold's restraining grasp and walked away, leaving Edward to splutter his indignation, and her father to placate him.

29

Dover

Self-satisfaction was a gratifying emotion. The pleasure of success radiated from Eustace de Boulogne as light flows from the sun. With his grandson entrenched in the royal household and written messages from the King to Duke William in his saddle bag, his future glowed rich with promise. Duke William would be delighted with the alliance that Eustace had established on his behalf, would undoubtedly reward him well. It had occurred to Eustace that perhaps his grandson's interests would be better served if he himself were to remain in England, but he could not bear to part with his lands and established station in life; and were he to alter allegiance from William to Edward, the Duke's anger against him would extend across the Channel Sea.

The road to Dover was dry and throat-choking with dust, the August heat shrivelling the crops, drying the streams and rivers. Unless rain fell in England soon the harvest would be a poor one this year, not that Eustace cared for the plight of English peasants.

His men, an escort of twelve Norman knights, rode sullen and sweating, their horses lathered and in need of water. The harbour town would offer a cool breeze from the sea and, hopefully, the ship that was to carry them back into Normandy would be awaiting their arrival. Now that he was going, Eustace was eager to return home, his men also, for they had not seen their families since the early months of spring.

Where the track crossed the river ford, a boy was allowing his father's small herd of milk-cows to drink. Eustace ordered his men to move the urchin on so that the horses might be watered. The lad, barefoot and dressed in a rough, home-spun tunic, ignored the approaching horsemen, not understanding their gruff French. The ford was wide and the water, although shallow from the drought, was there for all who travelled the road. One of the men rode his horse into the river, shouldering the cattle away, his hand gesticulating. The boy stared up at the man in his chain-mail armour, puzzled.

"Are you so insolent that you ignore my order? Move away, imbecile, before I take my sword to you!"

The boy stared at the knight's contorted, angry face. He had heard French before, for sailors who spoke that tongue often put into the harbour, but the words meant nothing to him. He shrugged, fear widening his eyes as the knight drew his sword and pointed the gleaming blade at his throat. Turning quickly, abandoning the cattle, the lad began to run. The Normans laughed, exchanging sneering remarks on the pathetic nature of these English as they allowed their animals to drink their fill.

To their disappointment, the ship was ready but the tide was not. Eustace was annoyed, but there was nothing to be gained by arguing. Ordering the baggage to be sent aboard and the horses loaded, he pointed to the White Horse tavern, straddling a corner of the narrow, sewage-strewn main street. With its candles and lamps just lit, the sound of talk, laughter and singing emanating from its open doors, it appeared welcoming.

Eustace and his men sat together at a table near the door, appreciating the evening breeze and fine English ale. Two of the knights had shoved aside the group of men who already sat there, using hands and swords; the Englishmen had moved, muttering angry curses. Merchantmen, sailors, men of the sea were welcome at the White Horse; rowdy, arrogant foreigners who thought them-selves superior to the local inhabitants were not.

All taverns harboured a whore who plied her trade around the ale-splashed tables. The girl at the White Horse was comely enough, although her hair was matted and greasy, her skin pock-marked and pitted with dirt. Well into their drink, two of the knights had made use of her services in the small, curtained back room. Eustace watched as a third from his party pulled back the shabby curtains and, reeling slightly, shambled across the room to join his comrades at the table, his hands fastening the lacings of his braies as he walked.

"By the virgin, that whore stinks!" he gasped, seating himself.

"She has all the necessary equipment in all the right places, though!" another cackled, simulating the shape of her bosom. "I will say one thing for Englishwomen, they are quick to lift their skirts for a proffered penny!"

"And we expect the penny to be paid!" The girl strode across to the Normans, her palm held out, flat and demanding. She spoke French well, if with an awkward accent. "I do not work for free, *monsieur*. I expect to be paid, even by a man with a pizzle as difficult to find inside your breeches as was yours."

"Get you gone, woman! You stink more than my prize sow. When I want to pay for gagging on such a foul stench, I'll visit the midden heap."

The girl stepped nearer, her fist raised to strike, but her opponent was a soldier and was quickly on his feet, one hand blocking her blow, the other grasping her hair, pulling her head back. His knee came up and crunched into her belly. She doubled up, fell to the floor, clutching at the pain that burst within her. The Norman lifted a jug of ale, poured its contents over her head. "There, you have been paid! I have given you a bath and a bellyache!"

The landlord of the White Horse was a small, squat man with balding hair and pale-blue eyes that crinkled often into a cheerful smile. There was no pleasure on his face this night. Wiping his hands, he bustled from behind his serving counter. The girl was a fool, but she was popular with his customers and these crude louts were annoying him. He crossed to the window and began closing the wooden shutters. "Good sirs," he said amiably, "I am closing, I would ask you to finish your drinks."

"Closing?" The man who had refused to pay the whore was refilling a tankard, oblivious to her body curled on the floor and the low groan hissing from her lips. "It is but early, nor have we drunk our fill!"

Count Eustace stretched. The place was shabby and smelt of decomposing cabbage, but it was near the harbour and he had no inclination to walk further than was necessary. "I am content with this slurry pit. You will stay open." He turned his full gaze on the innkeeper, daring him to contradict a count from Normandy. "Bring more ale."

Although small in stature, the taverner was of Viking blood. No foreign muckrake, however noble, was going to make such rude demands of him.

"I say again, sirs, I am about to close. Finish your ale and get you from my inn."

The whore managed to crawl out into the street. Men were making their way down to their fishing boats, preparing for the tide to turn, Englishmen of Dover who already disliked the Norman kind, who responded eagerly to the girl's screams for help. So the Norman scum were ill-treating the landlord of the White Horse?

What began as a scuffle rapidly turned ugly. Outnumbered, the Normans battled their way to the door, into the street; in the mêlée, a candle tipped against the whore's ragged curtain, flames engulfing it, taking hold of the dry timbers of wall and roof. Within moments the White Horse was ablaze. The innkeeper, dazed and bloodied from the savage beating the Normans had given him, staggered against an upturned table, fell. Was buried beneath the roof as it collapsed.

They ran for their lives, Count Eustace and his men, fighting off as best they could the anger of Dover. Two Normans were killed, one struck on the temple by a stone, the other, his skull split wide by the favoured English weapon, the axe.

Somehow, they reached their vessel, the Count bellowing for the crew to unship the oars and row. Anger thumped in rhythm with his pounding heart-beat; he cared naught for the several English dead, nor for the fire sending sparks into the night sky. No matter that his own people had begun the affray: the English peasants had murdered two of his men. The King must hear of it and the town made to pay compensation.

"We sail for Gloucester!" Eustace roared at the crew. "To where Edward resides with his court. I shall demand retribution for the insult paid me this night!"

30

Southwark

The port of Dover fell under Godwine's jurisdiction. The King, petitioned by an incensed comte Eustace de Boulogne at the gross public humiliation he had suffered, issued immediate orders that Wessex punish the town for murder and affray. Godwine categorically refused on the grounds that the Normans were as guilty of the same offences. Edward, adamantly listening only to Boulogne's account of events, retaliated by threatening to outlaw the Earl if he dared disobey his king's express command.

Finally, goaded too far by Edward's stubborn adherence to Norman influence, a war of words had ensued, with Godwine rallying his sons to his aid and the King summoning his Council and army to Gloucester. Godwine had halted his armed force fifteen miles from the town, at Beverstone on the Oxford-to-Bristol road.

Among the notables who rode to help their king, his nephew—stepson to Eustace—Ralf de Mantes, with an entourage of his French followers; the Earls Leofric and Siward, two men delighted to see their long-term rival publicly rebuked—and Robert Champart, the Norman-born Archbishop of Canterbury.

By skill and experience, Godwine had taken the initiative of the confrontation. With the strength of his sons' men at his back he was in a position to intimidate the King, but Edward had found reason, at last, to slice Godwine's feet from under him and, urged by his advisers and the Archbishop of Canterbury, was determined to move against Wessex. By the seventh day of September the exchange of anger was at red heat. Godwine demanded the surrender of Eustace's men, accompanied by an apology to the people of Dover from the Count himself. Champart voiced an implication of treason. While messengers carried accusations back and forth, the armies of England mobilised, Englishman preparing to fight against Englishman. Yet neither side wanted civil war. For his own part, Edward was eager to overthrow Godwine, but not with bloodshed, not if there was any other way to be rid of him.

To the relief of all, a trial before Council, to be held in Westminster on the twenty-first day of September, was agreed. King, companions, army and estranged Earl moved to London, Edward shutting himself within the security of his completed Westminster palace and Godwine entrenching into his Southwark manor. But before anyone left Gloucestershire the King demanded hostages. Godwine had mild reservation about surrendering two of his family into the King's care, but then his youngest son Wulfnoth and Swegn's son Hakon would also be under Edith's charge and no harm would come to boys who were protected by the Queen, their kinswoman.

"I say no, Father! If we agree to surrender our men to Edward, we will be left with nothing to outface him. We have an army ready to attack Westminster. Let us frighten the piss out of the King and his poxed Normans while we have the chance!" Swegn slammed the sword that he had been burnishing back into its scabbard, his expression that of thunderous anger—with good cause, for Edward had out of hand redeclared him outlaw, had given him two days to leave England.

Harold looked up sharply from the bridle harness he was mending. Swegn's arrogant stupidity again! Fortunately his mother was not there to witness it. "So at your urging we start a civil war? What with? We do not have adequate men. We have only the Wessex thegns loyal to our father, and our sworn housecarls. East Anglia has decided not to risk the accusation of treason and has declared for the King, not for me. Neither you nor Tostig have anyone to call on for support. Had you not been so stupid in the past, perhaps you would still have an earldom of your own. We would have had more strength behind us!"

"If you were more intent on your duties," Swegn hissed back, "rather than playing nursemaid to your whore and her brats, perhaps Anglia might have been more willing to back you!"

Harold stormed to his feet, flinging the harness aside, his hand groping for his dagger.

Godwine thrust between them, bellowing in anger. "Is it not enough that we quarrel with Edward? I do not need the pair of you at each other's throats as well!"

Harold backed down, apologising to his father. Swegn scowled and kicked at a hound sniffing for scraps of food among the dried reeds that covered the floor.

Godwine's head ached and his chest hurt, his breathing coming in shallow gasps. Could his eldest son not see the difficulty they were in? "With this safe conduct I will get to see the King. We must make a peaceful settlement. Unlike you, Swegn, I do not want a war."

"And you forget our sister, youngest brother and your own son." Tostig complained. "Are we to abandon them to Edward's mercy? If we commit ourselves to fighting, will they not be in mortal danger?"

"Father ought never have agreed for those boys to be taken. I said at the time that it was a stupid thing to do." No one contradicted Swegn that on the contrary, he had made no comment whatsoever regarding his child, Hakon.

"Edward is not a man who would harm children, surely?" Leofwine asked doubtfully. He was two months into manhood, had little expected to be facing so grim a crisis so early in adulthood. "Hakon is four years of age, Wulfnoth barely ten."

"That still leaves Edith." Gyrth, the fourth-born brother, added drily. What Edith was thinking, feeling, no one knew, for no word had been smuggled to her, nor a message received.

"Neither the boys nor Edith will come to harm," Godwine said with a quick, dismissive movement of his hand. "Edward is no murderer." That he firmly believed. His son, his daughter, his grandson were safe whatever the outcome of these next few hours here in London.

"Edward, no." Harold spoke softly, voicing the concern that drifted through their minds. "But what of the Archbishop and the King's other advisers?" There was no telling what Edward might be persuaded to do, so deeply was he under the influence of Champart.

The situation was escalating with the wild wind of a raging storm. Godwine needed to put his case rationally before the Council, explain the view of the people of Dover, what they had suffered at the drunken hands of those Normans. So far the earls and nobles had heard only Boulogne's version, had been influenced by Champart's deliberately twisted judgement. He could not believe, for all their antagonism and past disagreements, that Siward and Leofric, once they heard the truth, would willingly vote for war. Not once he had been offered a fair chance to set matters straight.

"I have to go to Edward—and will only be permitted to go if I give assurance of my peaceful intention. For that, we must surrender the men who would fight against the Crown at our command." What choice had he but to agree these latest conditions? He had to show that he had meant no harm in amassing these men who were unquestionably loyal to him. He had to disprove these outrageous charges of treason, to prove that he and his sons were, above all else, King's men, and that he, Godwine, had implicit trust in the word and just law of that king. Though, in his heart, he held little enthusiasm for such a declaration.

Godwine turned to Stigand, the Bishop of Winchester, who sat in Countess

Gytha's favourite chair to the far side of the hearth. "Deliver our men to the King," he said. "When I receive, in return, the surety of safe conduct and suitable hostages, then I will proceed, alone, to Westminster."

Relieved, Stigand nodded his head. He had never particularly liked Godwine, often in the past their opinions had differed, sometimes with more heat than intended, but in this thing he gave full support. Edward had listened to those who advised for their own gain, rather than for common sense.

"You have made a wise decision, my Lord." Stigand rose from his seat and left the chamber, calling for his cloak and horse within the same breath. He sighed as he mounted, set his bay gelding into a canter. It was drizzling again and the cold was blowing in off the grey, murky waters of the Thames. He did not much relish the ride to Westminster, nor the reception he feared he would get once he arrived. One as cold and wet as the weather, no doubt. Was he wasting both breath and time? What chance had he of turning ears that were as hard and as deaf as stone? But someone had to try and make the peace between King and Earl.

He returned to Southwark within a mere two hours. The Earl was not going to like this message that he bore from the King. Stigand did not much like it either.

⁂

"We are in a hopeless position, then." Godwine sat slumped, his head sinking deeper into his hands. His hair carried more silvered streaks than it once had, his cheeks were sagging, skin sallow. He was seven and fifty years of age, no longer a young man. Gytha crossed the room with quick and anxious strides, set her hands to her husband's shoulders, her paled face turning to Harold, her eyes betraying her fear.

Stigand's hands trembled as he took the ale offered him by young Leofwine. The words he had just spoken to this family, here in this warm and homely chamber, were among the most difficult ever to have passed his lips.

"The King bids me tell you, Godwine of Wessex, that this is your final summons to answer the charges of treason before him and his Council." Tears had trickled down Stigand's cheeks as he had spoken. No, he had rarely agreed with Godwine, had often doubted the Earl's intentions, but this was beyond all reason, all sense. Had the King lost his mind? Was he so very much influenced by the mischief that surrounded him at court? It seemed he was.

Stigand inhaled a slow, steadying breath. He had no desire to complete this obnoxious message, but it had to be done, and best get it done quickly for the sake of the lady. "Edward adds that he will be prepared to grant you full pardon, if…" Stigand faltered again, swallowed. Looked Godwine direct in the eye. "If you can restore to him his dead brother, Alfred."

Yes, Godwine had made mistakes in the past and yes, he wanted well for himself and his family—what man of courage and ambition did not? But beneath those human frailties he was a good man who had served king, queen, and country with a loyalty rarely observed among his kind. He did not deserve such a wicked dismissal of his integrity.

Godwine straightened his back. His sons were looking at him, silent, expressions and emotions blank. Swegn, Harold, Tostig, Leofwine and Gyrth. They would follow him into the bloody field of war against their king if he asked them, he and his sons alone, with not a single man at their backs. If he asked it. He exhaled a long and contemplative breath. "Then there is nothing for us," he said. "We are lost. We must seek exile." Godwine looked to the Bishop. "How long have we been granted?"

Stigand answered quietly, his voice tense with emotion. This ought not be happening—if Edward could be so implacable to a man as important and powerful as Godwine, then what hope was there for the rest of them left in the hands of these damn influential Normans? "Five days, my Lord. He gives you but five days to be gone from England."

31

Waltham Abbey

Edyth read the letter for a third time. The hurriedly scrawled words were unchanged, except the ink they were written in was becoming smudged by the tears that dribbled from her cheeks.

Harold was on his way to Ireland, taking ship from Bristol with his brother Leofwine.

"Edward will not harm you or the children," the letter read in its brief explanation.

> I, and the male members of the family, are declared outlaw. Our lands and entitlements are withdrawn from us and our lives endangered were we to remain here in England. My lord father and the others are to go from Bosham to Count Baldwin in Flanders, with as much of the family wealth as they can take on board ship. I know not when I may safely return. Kiss the children for me and God keep you, my most precious love.

The manor was safe, for Harold had transferred its ownership into Edyth's name at the birth of their first son, along with several other estates scattered throughout Anglia and southern England. In her own right Edyth Swannhæls, as an earl's lady, was numbered among the wealthiest of Englishwomen. What did she care for property and riches if she did not have Harold with her? She slumped forward, the letter fluttering from her fingers as her hands covered her face, sobs shuddering through her swollen body. She was eight months pregnant, the babe would be born with the coming of the autumn colours of russet and gold, and Harold might never see the child...

It seemed incongruous that the day was fine and warm, with a radiant sun and a playful breeze that trundled along the track opposite the manor, whispering among the sweep of the trees standing sentinel beside the cluster of streams that sprang from this highest part of the hill. A day that had started out so happily.

She had promised to walk with the children down to the Lea river, to see the swans. They had been watching the pair since spring, marvelling at how the pen sat so stubborn on her eggs, how the cob protected and nurtured his wife and the youngsters once they were hatched. "Swans stay paired and mated for life," Harold had once told her. "They choose each other and through no matter what, remain steadfast and loyal. As will I to you."

Edyth was certain her heart was to crack into two. Never had she expected this, that he would leave her, so hurriedly, without warning. That one day he would perhaps take a noble-born wife was always there as a possibility, but this? Surely it was all nonsense, a misunderstanding? Harold's letter confirmed otherwise. The King would not listen, would not entertain impartial justice for Godwine or the folk of Dover. She knelt beneath the copse of birch trees, the wind rippling the underside of the leaves into dancing waves of silver, closed her eyes, the tears slipping from beneath her wet lashes.

When Harold had left here less than twenty days past to answer his father's urgent appeal, he had assured her there was no need for undue concern. "It is all hissing steam from an over-boiling pot," he had said with an easy, confident laugh. "My father will sort things amicably, you will see."

"Mama?" A frightened voice quivered beside her. Edyth looked up, saw her eldest boy standing there, his face sombre, concern etched into his widened eyes. His grandmother had once said how much he resembled his father at that age of seven years; the same curl of fair hair, jutting chin and quick, exuberant laugh. "Mama?" he asked again, stretching out his hand to touch her cheek. "What is wrong? Are you ill? Shall I fetch someone?"

Attempting a smile of reassurance, Edyth gathered Goddwin to her. When would the boy see his father again? "No, my honey-sweet, I am not ill."

"Is it the babe, then?" Goddwin set his hand lightly on the bulge of his mother's stomach. "He kicks hard, I can feel him."

"He is kicking to tell me that he wants to be out in the beauty of the world, playing in the sunshine with his elder brother." Edyth kissed her son's forehead. He was a good boy, quick to learn, slow to cry or whine. Harold was so proud of him, of all their four children. Five, if you counted Alfrytha, who was with God, buried in her cold and lonely grave within the churchyard at Canterbury. Suddenly, afraid, she held the boy tight and close. She would never see her little girl again, as she might never see Harold...no she must not think like this. Must remain strong and calm. Harold had gone to Ireland to bargain for mercenary help, Godwine to do the same in Flanders. To buy aid in the form of men and arms, to return as soon they might to persuade the King to listen to reason. "Your father has had to leave England for a while," she explained to her son. "He will return when he can, as soon as he can, but that may not be some long while."

Goddwin chewed his lip, his young mind rummaging through the implications. "Why has he had to leave?"

"Because the King is angry with your grandfather." Best to answer simply and with the truth.

"But if the King is angry with Grandfather, why has my father had to go away?"

Placing a kiss on her fingertips, Edyth laid the caress on to the boy's lips and set him to his feet. "Because if a son loves his father, it is his duty to be with him in a time of great need."

The boy digested her words, then nodded. "My grandfather is lucky to have my father as a son, isn't he?"

"Aye. As your father is lucky to have you." Edyth pushed herself upright. The babe was heavy; she would be glad when this birthing was over. Goddwin bent and retrieved the piece of paper, squinting at the writing that he had not yet learnt to decipher well. With it, he picked up an unopened package. Gravely, he gave both to his mother. Rolling the parchment into a scroll, Edyth slid the precious letter into her waist purse, then unthreaded the knots of the string that bound the cloth of the package.

Inside lay a necklace made of threaded gold bullae and biconical gold beads; at the centre, a gold and garnet cross. It was exquisite. Edyth squatted down so that Goddwin could fasten it around her neck, emotion almost choking her as the tears once again welled up from her heart. A gift, sent with love from Harold. She cupped the crucifix in her hand, closed her eyes. "God protect him," she prayed, Please, God protect him." She could not know it, but Harold had sent the gift with the same prayer, aware that childbirth and all its possible difficulties would soon be upon her.

❦

Gytha also wept, but inwardly. At this moment there was too much to do, in too short a time, to indulge herself with grief. "No, not that chest, this one!" she called in agitation to servants removing items from the house place to the ship. The tide would be turning soon and they would sail to a new country, a new life. *Please God*, Gytha thought, *let us not be long from our home*. Bosham was where she had come as a young bride; where she had birthed her children and watched them grow…She drew breath. It was no good thinking like this. Better to do away with material things than the life of her husband and sons.

Harold and Leofwine were safe, would have sailed from Bristol. Wulfnoth?

Would he be all right with Edith? Godwine assured her he would. He had come unexpected, her last-born son—she had thought her childbearing years to be finished, her moon courses ended, thought nothing, initially, of the weight that had padded her belly. He had come so easy to birth, half of an hour from the first uncomfortable twinge in the hollow of her back...so unlike Swegn—two days had she laboured to bring him to life.

Swegn. Swegn ought to have gone with Harold into Ireland, but he was ailing, with giddy heads and blurring vision, his tempers the greater for the pain that stabbed at his brain. Gytha rarely allowed him to enter her thoughts, not after all the troubles he had brought to this family, but this, for once, was not his doing. This had been brought by those Normans who wanted her husband gone from court, from England.

She must remember the balm for Godwine's aching knee-joint. So much to pack, so much to leave. The finest table and bed linen were already stowed in chests and aboard ship, along with the six best wall hangings. Silver tableware and glasses had been set for safety in straw. Bolts of silks and brocades, linen and fine wool; fur robes, her finest gowns, Godwine's tunics and braies, his armour and weaponry. The Hall harp, of course, and the family's books. Her sewing box, jewellery and combs—nothing of value was to be left for Edward to confiscate. Besides, if they were to make a home in Flanders—however temporary—they would do so with honour and comfort. There would be no begging or casting for second best for the family of Godwine.

32

Westminster

Freedom tasted of fine wine and sweet, briar rose honey. This is what it was to be king: to have no one, no one at all, telling you what to do.

Edward propped his feet on the footstool and exhaled a contented sigh. Godwine was gone and, with him, all those damned annoying habits. The tactful cough, the patient sigh—oh, how Godwine had grated on his nerves! And now the Earls Siward and Leofric regarded him with wary apprehension, all he need do in the future, when one of them provoked him or overstepped his authority, was to reminisce how he had, single-handedly, brought down Godwine, Earl of Wessex? They would all think more carefully before voicing opposition, would agree with enthusiasm to his plans. Aye, Edward was well content.

Robert Champart, Archbishop of Canterbury, standing with his backside warming against the red glow of the brazier, cleared his throat, politely, reminding the King that there was business to be completed. Robert found it a difficult trial maintaining patience where the King was concerned. Edward's mind flitted from the essential to the frivolous within almost the same thought, was incapable of concentrating for any length of time on matters of government. The Archbishop had concluded that Edward had come to office too late in life, had never been taught the discipline of responsibility. That was his mother's fault. Had she taken care to ensure her son was nurtured for kingship, had she not abandoned him to exile, Edward might have learnt to take responsibility for himself and others.

"I am not persuaded about your proposition for East Anglia, my Lord." Champart said, his voice smooth, like silk gliding over unblemished skin. "Ælfgar, son of Leofric of Mercia, would be the better candidate for earl."

Edward ignored the suggestion, answering instead, "I think I shall hunt on the morrow. I'd like to see how those new young hounds fare—that brindle seems a splendid bitch, don't you think?"

"Sire. Anglia must have an earl." Robert's impatience showed. "Decision ought be made without further delay. Appointing Ælfgar will efficiently bind

Mercia to us. If he feels his son may lose control of a prestigious earldom Leofric will not tolerate any possibility of Godwine or any of his brood returning."

Edward's pleasure faded. He removed his feet from the stool, slumped forward and folded his arms. Why was this new palace of Westminster as cold as the old place? Scurries of wind danced around his ankles despite the thickness of the stone walls and panes of leaded glass in the windows. Querulous: "I do not much like Ælfgar."

"It is not a matter of liking, sir, it is a matter of appointing the most suitable man for the position. Ælfgar is, I assure you, the most suited."

"Nonsense." Edward hunched his shoulders and, to be awkward, added, "Harold was the best man, only he had the misfortune to be Godwine's son. I enjoyed many a good day's hunting with Harold. His forests of Epping and Hatfield hold especially fine deer."

Robert sighed. "The deer will remain in the forests under Ælfgar's prerogative, Sire. I believe he is a keen hawk-man."

"Hawking is all very well, Robert, but it is the chase that stimulates me, the chase!" To emphasise his enthusiasm Edward mimed the motions of holding the reins, circling his hands to imitate the speed and exhilaration of a gallop across country.

"East Anglia, my Lord—"

"Oh, to hell with bloody East Anglia! Let Ælfgar have the damned place." Edward lurched from his bench, swept his arm through the pile of neat scrolls on the nearby cleric's table, startling a squeak from the man as the ink pot toppled, scattering quills and black mess over parchment and floor. "Why can you not leave me in peace?" His stomach grumbled, he would need to visit the garde robe soon. These discussions of formalities either gave him thundering headaches or cramped bellyache. Decision-making, pah! He detested decision-making.

⁂

The third hour of the afternoon and already the candles and lamps were lit. Edith rubbed at the chill in her fingers but remained stubbornly sitting within the comparative privacy of the window recess in her solar, her eyes occasionally lifting from the Bible she was attempting to read, although she had not turned a single page this past quarter of an hour, A servant came to close the shutters, but she waved him away, did not, yet, want to lose what was left of this short November day. From where she sat she could not see the river along the eastern boundary of the palace. The Thames would be as bleak and grey as the louring cloud; the wind scuttling through the reeds like the path of an unseen predator. Snow would come soon.

The child was wailing again, its red face puckered and squashed like a wrinkled, dried grape. Eustace of Boulogne's wretched grandson. Edith detested the brat. If babes were this much of a nuisance then how glad she was that she would have none of her own! Edward adored him. He was attempting to rock him to sleep, while making crooning and clucking noises. Edith would have suggested he pass the child back to its nurse, but she dared not, for once already this dreary afternoon they had come close to quarrelling. She had merely suggested that perhaps the children ought to be removed to their own chamber. But Edward enjoyed games and merry-making with the children of the court, a variety of nieces, nephews, cousins and the like. To see a grown man playing with a toy sword, tossing a cloth ball or kneeling on the floor, marching carved wooden soldiers into battle…pressing her lips together, Edith again looked out of the window. Did he regret not having his own children, she occasionally wondered; no, Edward was nothing more than a child himself, had no sense of adult responsibility or duty; his moods and ill-judged, infantile humour were more suited to a lad in his early years of spot-faced youth.

Beyond the bailey and the height of the palisade wall Edward's abbey was growing upwards. This eastern end reached almost to its full height. The workmen had finished for the day, the sound of hammering, sawing, creaking ropes, curses and chattering had ceased…it was always so strange when quietness descended after the torrent of noise.

The private royal apartments and the armoury were situated here in this third, inner yard: the Great Hall, king and queen's bedchambers and ante-rooms, the chapels and the king's grand council chamber. Also guest apartments and the royal kitchens—Edward had ordered separate kitchens built near the Hall for he was tired of meals brought across the courtyard arriving cold and greasy, although the proximity had made little difference to the service and warmth of the food. The larger, middle bailey, adjoining to the north, was reached through an archway protected by a pair of tall, iron-studded oak doors. Oak was always used, for it was not an easy wood to burn should attack come from the outside, or fire take hold within. Would anyone dare attack the King while he resided in his new palace at Westminster? Still staring out of the window, Edith wondered if her father would so dare. Unlike Edward, she was not complacent over the consequences of Godwine's exile. Edward seemed to think he was safe, the thing settled. But Godwine would never leave it at that.

The outer, or first, courtyard, to the northern end of Thorney Island, accommodated the stabling, grain storage, bakery, brewery, dairy and forge, the barracks, kennels and the like. Westminster contained a whole town within this procession of courtyards, with their buildings strung together by walls, gates and archways, corridors and aisles. As impressive as anything he had seen in Normandy, so Edward claimed.

The baby's cries had withered to a moaning whimper; Edward gave the child to the nurse, beaming at his success. "You see! Patience and gentleness is all a child of that age requires. Patience and gentleness."

A no-nonsense firm hand would be more practical, Edith thought. At least the grandfather, Boulogne, had gone. Three blessed weeks now without his loud, boastful conversation and arrogant presumption. The pity that Champart and the other Normans who squirmed around Edward like piglets eager to drain the mother sow dry of her milk had not departed with him.

And now there were more coming! Next month, or so the messenger had said, Duke William himself was to make a brief visit to England to pay respect to his great-aunt and the King. Edward was delighted, not about the Duke meeting with his mother, but because he was eager to show the progress with his abbey and the splendour of this palace—to take the Duke hunting. Edith sighed, closed her Bible and indicated that the shutters could be closed. They had argued about that also, when Edith had politely suggested that perhaps the Duke would prefer to discuss important issues of alliance and trade. Edward had ordered her to keep her ignorant opinions to herself; of course the Duke would want to hunt—chancellors and clerics were there to deal with the mundane matters of state.

It had not occurred to Edward, who took no specific interest in politics, that this Duke of Normandy might be different, that he was not sailing to England during the vagaries of the winter weather merely to hunt deer or chase boar. Nor was he asking, as were his earls and Council, why, when so hard pressed by internal troubles within his duchy, the Duke should take time to visit England.

The answer was obvious to all except Edward. With Godwine gone, there was a power vacuum forming within the realm. Those of Norman blood were rising in status and William desperately sought favour, wherever he might find it, so that he could further his own ambition. He also, through Emma, had a chance to make a claim for the throne after Edward's death. That possibility had not escaped anyone's appraisal—save, it seemed, for Edward.

Edward was now seated beside the largest brazier, gathering the children around him. Her brother was there, Wulfnoth, innocence etched into his shining ten-year-old face. The younger children—her cousin Hakon and that wretched grandchild of Boulogne—had finally been taken from the room for their supper. At least some semblance of dignity was returning to the chamber.

"A riddle! A riddle!" they were shrieking, bouncing in excitement.

"A riddle?" Edward said. "I am not certain I know any riddles."

"You do! Oh, you do!"

Edith walked from her window seat to another of the braziers, stood, warming her hands.

"A creature came into my courtyard," Edward began. "It had one eye and two ears, two feet and twelve hundred heads, a back and a belly, two hands, arms and shoulders, one neck and two sides. Say, whichever one of you can, what was this creature?" He leant back, spread his hands on his thighs. They would never guess.

Edith's father had no fear for his boys, Edward would never, willingly, harm a child, but it was not Edward who held the reins of power in England at this moment. Godwine had kept a curb on the menace of rising Norman influence, until Count Eustace had—so common gossip said—ridden deliberately into Dover to stir up trouble. The boys would be safe, but would Edith? Except to cast barbed comments, Edward rarely spoke to her, barely concealed his distaste at her presence. They were lawfully bound in marriage and he had no just cause, without perjuring his soul, to set her aside as wife. Never would she contemplate taking a lover or allowing a male companion close without adequate escort, for she would not give Edward the opportunity to create lies against her dignity and innocence.

Edward wanted her gone, though, Edith knew that as well as she knew the answer to his fool-stupid riddle.

She glanced up, caught Robert Champart watching her from across the room. From Edward, she was, perhaps, safe, but what mischief was Champart and Duke William hatching between them?

"What is the answer?" the eldest daughter of Edward's personal silversmith asked. "I cannot think what it is!"

Edward clapped his hands. "A one-eyed onion seller!" His laughter joined with that of the children.

Pathetic and insane. Need she worry? What could Champart do to her? What could William offer or expect from England in return? Were he to have daughters who sought husbands then aye, she would be anxious. An alliance of marriage between England and Normandy...she shuddered, but the Duke was not yet married, had not solved his problem with the Pope, and his sister was safe married to Enguerrand, comte de Ponthieu.

Edith returned Champart's gaze, would not let him see that she feared him. All she need do was ride this storm and hope, pray, that her father intended to make a great fight for honour and earldom. And that Champart could not, before that time, invent too much of a plausible lie against her to whisper into the King's ear.

33

⁓

Bruges

Mathilda was aware that tears blotched the face and puffed the eyes, but she cared nothing for her looks or complexion. The uglier the better, then perhaps that hateful, uneducated man would not want her. She lay face down on her bed, arms over her head, sobbing. They would be coming soon, to take her down for her betrothal—she would not go, she would rather die than be forced into marriage with an illiterate bastard-born monster. Her mother had berated her foolishness, a variety of aunts and cousins too. No one seemed to care about her fate; all they were concerned for was how bad it would look if she continued to be so wilful.

She had at least expected her sister Judith to come to her aid, but she had changed since her own marriage, cared only for Tostig Godwinesson, had treated her younger sister almost with contempt. "We all need to marry, child. Take your fate and make the best of it. You may end up as happily settled as I." It was all right for Judith, her husband was as besotted with her as she was with him. Duke William did not care a tinker's dented begging bowl for his prospective bride.

He had arrived yester-eve, coming by sea direct from England where he had spent ten days with the king, Edward. Dishevelled, smelling of sweat and ship-board tar, he had not bathed or changed before demanding that she be brought to him for inspection—as if she were a horse or hawk that he had purchased unseen from a travelling merchant. The introductions had been frosty and reserved. He had not been over-pleased by her appearance—well, neither was she taken with him. She would never forget, or forgive, those first words that he had exclaimed as she had come down into her father's Hall.

"Is it likely that she will grow any taller? Or am I to wed a stunted shrub?"

Mathilda was dwarfed by his own comparative tallness. William of Normandy stood, stocky and broad-shouldered, at five feet and ten inches; she, slight and more than one whole foot shorter, had answered him with pert anger. "The smallest bush, sir, can bear the most perfect blooms."

"Then you had better bear a brood of strong sons and prove your worth to me, girl." With that the Duke had turned away from her to talk with his friend, another odious man who had resided at Flanders this past month, Eustace de Boulogne.

Mathilda tugged the pillow from beneath her head and hurled it across the room. She would not marry him. Was there no one else to lay claim to her—Swegn Godwinesson was here with his father and brothers, why could he not plead for her? Or the absent brothers who were in Ireland, Harold or Leofwine? Harold had no official wife, would it not grant the family higher strength by taking another of Baldwin's daughters? Yet perhaps that was being foolish. The Godwines, while not poverty-stricken, were in disgraced exile. Their vehemently proclaimed intention to regain everything the English king had unjustly taken might be nothing more than pride-injured boasting.

The situation was hopeless. Mathilda leapt from the bed and ran to a small side table, snatched up the fruit knife, short bladed but adequate to open a vein... she laid its edge over her wrist, steeling herself to slash the thing downward... gasped as the door was unexpectedly flung inwards with no warning. He stood there, alone, silhouetted against the smoking torches that illuminated the narrow corridor outside: William, Duke of Normandy.

"I am told that you refuse to come to your wedding."

Her throat ran dry and her hands shook. He had attended to his appearance, his hair shorn up the back of his head in the Norman manner, his chin clean-shaven. Had bathed, changed into clean and elegant robes. Was so much taller and more dominating now he was well groomed. Somewhat frightening, but alluring.

Mathilda found the courage to stand square before him, her head tilting upwards to meet his narrow stare. "I do not wish to wed you," she said with bold impertinence, although a high-pitched squeak entered into her voice halfway through the sentence. "I do not like you."

"I do not like you, but that makes no difference to me." William entered the small chamber, taking in its comfortable furnishings and the clutter of feminine trinkets with one hasty sweep of his assessing gaze. "You are insulting me with this childish behaviour. Were you a man, you would learn that I do not take insults lightly."

"Were I a man, I would have cut you down for the insult you offered me!"

William laughed at her audacity. Despite what he had said, he liked this girl, she showed courage and determination, qualities he admired. She was also, as they had promised, fair of face. A pity they had not told him of her limitations of stature, but of what consequence was small height? As long as she was capable of breeding him a son or two…He was not a man who was used to being defied, however. Once his mind was made up to something he would have it and he had decided to forge an alliance with Baldwin of Flanders, have Mathilda as his wife. Whether it was her wish or not, and whether the Pope gave or withheld his blessing.

"You will complete your dressing and accompany me to swear our wedding vows." William picked up the wimple that Mathilda had flung there and tossed it at her. "Dress yourself and come."

Mathilda stamped her foot. How dare this man enter her room when there was no chaperone or servant present? And then order her to do his bidding? "Get out of my chamber!" The fruit knife was in her hand; she raised it and awkwardly lunged for William's stomach. He merely side-stepped and, chopping with his hand, sent the little blade spinning across the room. She fell forward, wincing at the pain in her bruised wrist—and he was bending over her, pulling her to her feet, shaking her as if she were a rat caught by a dog. She tried to strike out, screaming defiance and a simultaneous plea for help. Dodging her flailing legs, he set his arm around her waist and hoisted her across his shoulder.

"I take it then, madam, that you are content to be wed as you are dressed. So be it. I care nothing for fripperies and niceties. I am here to take you as wife because I require an alliance with your father. And as I have stated, no one defies my will."

He marched from the room, descending the narrow stone stairwell two steps at a time. They were all there, gathered below in the Hall, ready to leave her father's house and walk in procession across the cobbles of the courtyard to the great doors of the cathedral that stood opposite.

There was laughter and much ribaldry as William threaded his way through the crowd. Her mother fluttered nervously among her women, but Baldwin ordered her to be still. The Duke knew what he was doing and the Count of Flanders approved wholeheartedly. In truth, he would be content to be rid of his most vexing daughter.

≪≫

William sipped his wine, his eyes roving the Hall, his ears monitoring the occasional overheard snatch of conversation. There were men here who did not care for him or his ambitions, papal supporters who would take every advantage of the interdict that would now be placed on his shoulders by Rome. Who was this Pope to say what a leader, a warlord, could or could not do in order to safeguard the security of his duchy? Normandy would be the better armed under Baldwin's friendship—would Rome send aid when that damned Geoffrey

Martel, comte d'Anjou, finally discovered the strength and courage to attack? Huh, the Pope was too busy defending the wealth and influence of his own friends, Germany and the like, to bother with Normandy. One day, however, one day, the Church would take note of William.

William's eyes rested on Godwine and his eldest son, his expression puckering with contempt. Had William found himself standing in Godwine's expensive red leather boots, he would not have run like a whipped dog, he would have gone to war. Would now be King of England, or have died in the attempt. To be a king, to wear a crown, sit on a cushioned throne, supreme above counts and dukes, equal to other kings. He liked the idea.

He had not much cared for England, the weather had been damp and foggy much of the time, and Edward profoundly irritating with his constant grumbling that he could not hunt in adverse conditions. Nor had he met his great-aunt, the Lady Emma. She would not come from Winchester to Westminster, Edward had explained, for she was unwell. As an excuse, William thought it a poor one. He had particularly wanted to speak with her, to reestablish their family connection for his own purposes. Perhaps it had not mattered? Edward had been ingratiating, professing his debt to Normandy for the years of shelter he had enjoyed beneath her protection. And he had admitted that as he had no expectation of his wife producing an heir, William was a cousin of potential worth.

A half-smile of amusement lifted William's mouth in memory of that particular afternoon. Fog had rolled, belligerent, across the murk of the river Thames, obscuring the far bank. Damp seeped into the walls of that idiotically sited palace—on a marsh-mired island? If the foundations did not sink, then the bordering rivers would undoubtedly flood it. And so opulent in its attempt at grandeur, useless for the purpose of defence. He would have built a castle nearer London, with high, stone outer walls, square, imposing towers to each corner, ramparts, ditch, drawbridge and iron-grilled gateway—not a feeble arch with wooden doors dividing track road from courtyard.

They had sat together before the hearth fire, sharing a jug of French wine. Somehow, William's sister Adelaide had come into the conversation—he could not recall how.

"Her husband is ailing," William had remarked. "He has almost reached his sixtieth year." He had leant forward, touched his goblet against Edward's. "Such is the frailty of our human existence. We are born, we grow, we die. Whether we can achieve all we hope within that short span of time depends on the will of God. We can but pray that our sons, and their sons, shall continue that which we began."

Edward had glowered, had drunk of his wine, made no answer.

"I shall seek a new husband for Adelaide immediately she is widowed." William had casually stretched his legs, pursed his lips as if in perplexity. "I shall need to find a man of integrity and honour, a man whom I can trust."

And Edward had answered as William had so hoped he would. "Were I not married, I would wed her myself."

During those few snatched days in England, William had studied Edward's queen, and found her a woman of modest looks and high intelligence. Edward and Champart had made a mistake there, in assuming they could bend Godwine to their will through her. Beneath his charm and pleasant banter, Godwine was arrogant, conceited and ambitious. Not that they were qualities William despised, but he disliked men who disguised their true motives. There was nothing wrong with ambition, but it was effete to conceal it.

William had lowered his voice so none other than Edward might hear. "Your father, I believe, set aside his wife in order to secure my aunt, Emma, your mother."

Edward had studied the last dregs of wine in the bottom of his goblet. The circumstances for that marriage were entirely different from his own and irrelevant. "Godwine would never permit it," he mumbled, not wishing to conduct a prolonged conversation on the technical variants of English marriage customs.

"Godwine," William had pointed out, with a laconic smile, "is in exile and could do nothing about it."

Remembering how Edward had looked up at him, eyes alight with eagerness, William's thoughtful self-indulgent smile increased.

Edward had hoped to be rid of Edith along with Godwine. As yet, Champart had not managed its legal doing. Did he seriously want another wife in her place? He disliked women, bossy, fussing creatures. They were all right as little girls, but girls grew up to become domineering matrons. It would drive the dagger deeper into Godwine were he to wed Adelaide of Normandy, though. He ought to have thought of it before—damn Champart, why had he not suggested it? The man was too preoccupied with his own affairs now that he was made Archbishop of Canterbury, had no care for Edward's problems and needs.

Watching the thoughts swirl and churn over the King's so readable face, William had dangled the bait, snared the catch and wound it in. "Normandy can help rid you of your boils." His voice had been low and comforting, so like his father's. "All I ask in return," he had added, "is that, as your close kinsman, you perhaps consider me as your heir."

Edward had shaken his head. "We do not follow the law of primogeniture here in England." Had added bitterly, "Although you would not think it so from my earls with their poxed sons. It is for Council to appoint the king, not me."

"Ah, but a kinsman is always considered, *n'est-ce pas*?"

"Not necessarily. The most suitable man is chosen."

William had frowned at the first part of Edward's answer, smiled at the second. "Then it is settled! I am your cousin—perhaps soon, even your brother—and I am, without doubt, the best man. I would be honoured to be chosen as your heir."

Later, Edward would puzzle how this young and vibrant duke had managed to proclaim himself as his heir, but did it matter? With the Godwines gone, there was a need for new alliances, for fresh blood to come into England, and Edward did owe much to Normandy, especially to the previous duke, William's father. Robert, Edward liked. He had been kind and attentive, had even attempted to help regain the throne from Cnut—although the attempt had failed, resulting in Alfred's death. Godwine had been responsible for that, and Emma, may God rot them both.

"I admired your father," Edward had said to William as they had clasped hands in friendship, "loved him, he was a good man. You have his eyes, and the same firm hand."

Jolting back to the present, William realised someone was addressing him—Godwine. Mentally he shook himself and acknowledged Godwine's congratulations.

"She is a handsome young woman," Godwine remarked. "I wish you good fortune and many sons."

"A man's fortune depends on his own determination, but for the sons I thank you. No man, if he is not to waste all he has achieved, ought be cursed with a woman who cannot provide him with the means to continue his line."

Godwine calmly returned this arrogant young pup's stare, eye to eye, as a group of dancers whirled past, feet stamping, heads tossing as the rhythm of drum and lute quickened the pace, their shrieks and laughter heightened by the headiness of the wine, cider and barley-ale that had poured so freely from jug and barrel throughout the afternoon. One, a Flanders man, knocked against Godwine's arm, sending his own wine splashing over the gold-embroidered thread of his tunic sleeve. The dancer called a quick, brief apology, but Godwine, laughing, waved him on his way. The distraction had given him a few seconds to think. What was this Norman whelp hinting at? "There are some women who are cursed with a husband who cannot—for whatever reason—sow ripe seed." Godwine said, a smile sitting easy on his lips. "Do you not breed horses, young sir? If mares do not produce foals, it is the stallion who is taken away to be gelded, not the mares slaughtered for meat."

Conceding, William nodded brusquely. "I agree, but if a stallion is removed, a replacement of equal breeding must be found, a younger, more virile colt."

So that was it! This Duke of Normandy was scenting out higher stakes for himself! Godwine allowed his shoulders to lift and fall. There was much that he could have said in answer, but he let the words lie silent. Cnut took England because Æthelred had proven an incompetent fool. A useless stallion replaced by the virile colt? All the more reason for Godwine to return to England, for Edward was too much like his father.

A knot of men and women obscuring the view of the high table parted momentarily, and William caught sight of Mathilda sitting there, her shoulders hunched, head dipped forward. All others were merry and enjoying the festivity. Damn her, why did the wretched girl appear so miserable?

"Your bride seems none too overjoyed at becoming Duchess of Normandy, my Lord Duke. Perhaps she is timid of the privy part of the ceremony?"

William swung his head towards the speaker who had approached to stand beside his father. Swegn Godwinesson, Godwine's eldest. A swaggering coxcomb, or so William had heard said. Flicking his eyes disdainfully up and down the man, the Duke could not reason why. Thin-boned, with dark bruising beneath his eyes, he looked pallid and ill, as if death shadowed his footsteps. Or was it that he had partaken of too much wine?

"Then her modesty becomes her." William answered with scorn. A man who allowed drink to override his senses was not a man to heed. "Unlike some men, I would not take a wanton to my bed as wife."

The Duke's thrust was direct, but Swegn, his skin grown too thick to feel such a harmless pinprick, ignored it. He was drunk because wine dulled the pain that was stifling his lungs, which spotted bloodied phlegm whenever the coughing fits came upon him. Drink took away the fear of knowing that unless his father attempted to return to England soon, he would not be going with him. Not unless it was within a coffin.

Disdainful of the company, William strode across the room, parting the jostling crowd of guests with his hands as if they were sapling branches overhanging his path. He reached the table, leant across and boldly lifted the girl up from her chair and over the table. She screamed her indignation and he laughed along with others in the Hall. "It is time we completed these nuptials," he announced. "We will away to our chamber!"

Mathilda beat her fists on William's back as he tossed her over his shoulder.

"I have never known such a willing maid!" he jested, masking his anger by making a pretence of humour.

Gathering tight-packed at the bed-chamber door the guests tossed their ribald advice at the groom. Within the chamber, the women were preparing the bed, scattering rose petals and setting out wine and wafers upon a side table. William roared at them to leave, sending them scurrying away, squeaking and twittering. Unceremoniously dumping Mathilda on to the bed, he turned to the door, slammed the wood shut in the faces of those outside and thrust the bolts home. He was alone with Mathilda and she would, whatever her objection, become his wife.

⁓

Lying in the middle of the great bed, Mathilda stifled her tears. It had hurt when he had taken her, forcing himself into her as she had struggled beneath him. If this was the pleasure Judith had spoken of, then Mathilda thought little of it. "Will it always be like this?" she asked into darkness. William had rolled from her, was settling into sleep. "Will it always be so uncomfortable?"

The Duke grunted. "A man faces pain and possible mutilation and death on the battlefield. Is it too much to ask a woman to suffer something for him in return?" He lay quiet, feeling the trickles of perspiration roll down his naked back. He had taken few women to his bed for he had rarely found any to be pleasing, either in looks or intelligence. Nor had there been much opportunity for dalliance when there were always daggers aimed at your back and traitors plotting to steal your duchy.

"It is possible," he said with detachment, "to gain some form of pleasure from the act of sexual union. It comes with the sharing of mutual trust, I should imagine."

Mathilda thought on that as she listened to his breathing slow and regulate into the calmer pace of sleep. Judith's ambiguous allusions to her intimacy with Tostig had given her quite a different impression of the delights of the marriage bed. She appeared to enjoy the experience. Mathilda had seen Tostig slide his arm around Judith's waist, whisper in her ear and kiss her cheek—had witnessed the coy flutter of lashes and blushing response of eager anticipation. There had been something wrong, then, this night. Did the problem lie with the fact that Judith wanted Tostig, while she, Mathilda, found William disagreeable?

She thought back to Judith's marriage. Surely she remembered hesitation and anxious fear? *Oui*! Had Judith not shed tears the night before going to a husband's bed? She had been pale and quiet those first few days after. Mathilda stretched. She was sore between her legs, but not badly so. If the privacy of marriage was to be endurable—was to become enjoyable—then there must be something missing from the experience. It did not take a Wise Woman to realise that the pleasure for William, too, had been minimal.

William was asleep. Mathilda moved her arm to encircle his body, felt him stir as her fingers brushed against his warm skin. He was a large man, well-muscled but not running to fat, his stomach was firm and solid beneath her light, explorative touch. Without intending to, her hand slid lower as he moved; she was surprised to feel that his manhood was rising beneath her fingertips.

"If we are to be man and wife," she said hesitantly, "ought our partnership not be one of shared trust?"

"You have altered your opinion of me, then?" he answered sardonically. "I am no longer disgusting to you?"

"You are an illiterate, illegitimate barbarian and your mother's breeding is wholly beneath my family, but if I must endure your presence in my bed for the rest of my life, I can at least determine to enjoy it as best I may."

William snorted his amusement. Few men spoke to him so frankly, let alone women. But how could he allow himself to trust this woman—this child? Dare he set aside the armour of self-protection that he had worn all these years, let someone through his defence? He had only felt comfort and ease with his mother—her alone, and perhaps her brother, his uncle Will, had he been able to trust implicitly. This girl, Mathilda, was a stranger, an unknown quantity.

He rolled over, kissed her mouth, his hand moving to fondle her breast. Was he capable, after surviving such violence, of allowing someone to unmask the inner, deliberately concealed person?

Mathilda had never seen him laugh or smile with genuine happiness. The skin around his eyes and mouth crinkled pleasantly, like the tracings of bird prints on fresh snow; his touch was light and gentle. There were two sides to this man, she realised suddenly. The outward hardness, the iron will, the indomitable persistence, and hidden on the inside, desperate need, vulnerability, insecurity. She was only thirteen years of age but astute. Duke William, she realised, that night of her marriage, was a man who had never felt or shown the raw nakedness of love. Harshness, death and blood had filled his upbringing, his life. He had never found opportunity to participate in the unguarded delight of pleasure and passion.

Their lovemaking was inexperienced and fumbled, with no great burst of giddy, shattering joy; but it was not painful this time, and if William turned from her immediately it was over to sleep, then perhaps that was what men always did. Providing he treated her with respect and offered her no further public humiliation, then she would be content with him. After all, she was now the Duchess of Normandy and William had told her, when they had been most intimate, that one day she might be more.

"How would the queen's crown of England suit you, madam?"

Well, she thought as sleep and contentment lulled through her body and mind, *it would suit most well.*

34

Winchester—March 1052

Death waited in the shadows of the hot and fugged bed-chamber. Emma could see it, feel its patient, waiting presence, yet it was not an unwelcome guest. She was tired of her bed and her life, of the fussing of her servants, the senseless weeping of her women. Death came for everyone, only those who feared it shunned its inevitability. Emma had never feared anything or anyone, except perhaps Cnut before she had met with him. Her only fear had been of dying before her ambitions had been accomplished. What had she to finish, now that she was old and frail, confined to her bed with the aching pain that was devouring her body from within? She would have liked a grandson for England. Ah, Harthacnut would have been the better king than Edward.

Emma drifted into sleep. She dozed often these last few days of life, because of age, illness and the bitter-tasting tinctures they made her swallow. She did not shun sleep, for she would often dream of riding across the heather moors with a wind blowing through her hair, her laugh soaring like an eagle in flight. Cnut rode beside her. She had loved Cnut, as he had undeniably loved her.

Waking, she watched the girl lighting the candles. Dusk was falling early; the day outside had been grey and rain-laden, the spatter of hail rattling against the tiny window panes. The girl went to close the wooden shutters, but Emma bade her leave them.

"I like watching the night turn its slow dance," she said, "and I welcome the lightening of the sky come morning." What else was there to do in this dreary, lonely room?

She sipped spoonfuls of the broth they had brought her, to please the servants more than sate her appetite. There were voices below, men talking, but Emma paid no heed. It was probably the good brother from the monastery come with more of his wretched herbs and potions. Footsteps on the stairs beyond the solar, the door of her bed-chamber creaking slowly open. Emma feigned sleep; she wanted no visitors.

"Mother?"

Harthacnut had looked so much like his father. Red-haired, strong-jawed. He had possessed the same quick laugh, the same passion for life, Emma was glad she would soon be reunited with them, with Cnut and his son, in heaven.

"Mother? Are you sleeping? It is I, Edward."

The pleasant illusion vanished, Emma opened her eyes, looked straight into the face of her first husband Æthelred, that limp-livered, mithering incompetent. If Cnut's son had been the image of his father, then so was Edward, even to the effeminate curl at the tip of his beard.

"So, have you come to gloat? To witness the end of the woman who has plagued you all these years? If you wish to know what piffling amount I have left you in my will, then you need wait only a few more days to discover it. The doctors say I have not long."

"You sent for me. Do you not recall? I was tempted to ignore you, but decided to pay my last respects, for though you never once offered me love or encouragement, you did give me life, for which I am grateful. Though, I suspect, had you choice in the matter, you would not have birthed me." Edward beckoned for a stool to be brought for him and sat at the top end of the bed where he could see his mother's withered face the clearer. His sight was not as sharp as once it had been, a matter that rarely troubled him, save when the chase was at full cry. Annoying not to be able to see clearly the glory of a pack of hounds running.

A blue tinge touched Emma's cracked lips as she formed a weak, amused smile. Yes, she had sent for him, knew he would come, for Edward was a man with a conscience. It was that which made him a poor king. Men who ruled well could not indulge in the luxury of listening to self-doubts. Of pandering to their guilt or curiosity.

He did not take her hand, nor was he alarmed or dismayed at the sunken hollows of her eyes and cheeks. She was three and sixty years of age; Edward reckoned that time had already been more than generous to her. Archbishop Robert had counselled against visiting her here in Winchester, but he was tiring of Champart's incessant interferences. He was turning out to be worse than his mother for nagging, poking and prying.

Edward had no fear of Emma: she was dying and he was full of life. How that must irritate her!

"I suppose I ought to ask where you wish to be buried," he said with callous mockery. "My abbey of Westminster is not yet half completed, but even were it finished it is to be my mausoleum. I would not share it with you. Perhaps you wish to be returned to Normandy?"

Not having the strength to raise her head, Emma turned her face to stare at him. Was he being deliberately obtuse? "I have already made arrangements," she stated. "The Bishop is to lay me beside my husband Cnut and our son, here in Winchester."

Edward laced his fingers. Of course Stigand would have been consulted, he and Emma had always been close. How close? There had been the rumour, once, that they had been lovers. What was she leaving Stigand in her will? How much of her estate was to go to her paid supporters…oh, let her bones rot here. Winchester would be of no significance once his Westminster Abbey was built.

Talking for any length of time was difficult, for her body burnt with the effort. But what she needed to say was essential. "You will soon have no more of me, a few days at the most, they say. I have achieved much with my life, Edward, most I am proud of, some of the things I have done shame me. A few I shall answer to my Maker for." She closed her eyes, was silent a long while.

Edward sat, fidgeting with his cloak pin, the laced ties of his tunic, his finger rings. Was she intending to confess to him? Admit all the tales? There were a few allegations he would dearly like to know the truth of. He thought she had fallen asleep, but Emma snapped her eyes open.

"I have never held much liking for you, Edward. That fact is not your fault, but your father's. It is difficult for a woman to show affection to the sons of such a brutal and worthless man. You have some traits that far improve on Æthelred's, however. Do not lose those few good qualities to the grubbing desires of mischief makers. Look to advisers who offer you wisdom for its own benefit, not for their own."

"To where is this lecture leading, Mother? I have no interest in all the things you had meant to achieve during your shabby life of murder and adultery."

Emma had expected no sympathy from Edward. She said blandly, "You and I were ever intolerant of each other. Of all the things I have disliked in you, I have never thought you to be deliberately cruel to those who have done you no wrong."

Edward shrugged his cloak tighter around his shoulders, drawing his head down, like a snail into its protective shell. "I pride myself on my justice," he mumbled, wounded.

"Just? You are punishing someone who has never wronged you or meant you harm. You have shut someone away who has committed no crime. You are weak and shallow. You allow others to tweak you by the nose and lead you where they may. You are as worthless as your father."

Edward's expression scrunched into an almost childish scowl.

"Release Edith from the despair that you have created for her. You have shut her away, for no reason save that you dislike her father, within the austerity of Wherwell in dismal loneliness, with no one to speak for her reprieve. It is not a convent for a young woman who cherishes life and learning."

Even with Godwine's family removed in their entirety, the repercussions of their exile were still rippling, like the wake of a distant, full-sailed ship slapping against the shore line. "She was unfaithful to me," Edward grumbled, his defiance muted.

Emma laughed, causing a racking catch of agony in her chest. "You ever were a poor liar! Did Champart obtain undeniable proof that Edith had a lover? Do you think the girl would be so foolish to place herself in a position where you could use such a potent weapon against her?" Emma breathed slowly, battling the rise of dizziness and nausea. "Above all else she wishes to be queen, she would not jeopardise that for any man—lover or kindred." Emma stared at Edward, forcing him to meet her eyes. "As did I. A crown, Edward, carries more weight to its wearer than gold and precious rubies." She sighed, closed her eyes, energy slipping from her. "More than the wasted pleasures of a bed. Wherwell is such a dour place. Set her free."

Rising, Edward shuffled towards the door. Robert had been right, he ought not have come. It had been Robert who had suggested Wherwell for Edith. Edward had objected to the choice, but had given in to the Archbishop's persuasion. He clamped his teeth together in annoyance. Archbishop Robert made many of the decisions that he would have preferred to make. There was always someone deciding for him, ordering him, pushing him. His mother, Godwine, Champart.

"I do not want her freed. I am to divorce her and intend, when the time is right, to take a new, more appropriate wife."

"Duke William's sister, Adelaide."

Edward gasped—how in hell's fire had she known?

Emma allowed herself a small, satisfied chuckle. Ah, the efficiency of amply paid spies!

"Are you as willing as my great-nephew William to become excommunicated? The Pope, Edward, will never allow such a marriage. Neither shall I, or Godwine."

"Godwine is removed and you," her son hissed maliciously, "will soon be dead."

"Godwine will be back—and my letter is already written to the Pope informing him of your intention, though you are not divorced and she is not yet widowed. I have suggested to his Holiness that he might care to investigate, with thorough regard, should anything untoward happen to either Edith or Duke William's elderly brother-in-law. The accusation of murder, no matter how much of a fabrication, can cling like mud, Edward. But you know that. A rumour of murder, deliberately spread, were it to be aimed at you, would not affect the sanctity of your mausoleum, I trust?"

"God's breath but you are a bitch!"

Emma did not waste effort in replying.

35

Alençon

The domination of the rudimentary Angevin empire had expanded east and south, at the expense of the comtes de Blois. A mere three years before Duke William's resounding victory at Val-ès-Dunes, King Henry had been forced to cede Anjou recognition over Touraine. By holding Tours, Geoffrey de Martel, comte d'Anjou, held a key route into the Loire valley and could blockade the road from Paris to Orleans. With his southern borders strongly contained, it was hardly surprising that a forceful, unprincipled man such as Geoffrey would soon begin to look northwards, and once secured in the region initially controlled by the family de Bellême itself, six roads were linked, crossed by the old Roman Way that passed through Alençon on its way to Falaise. With the approval of Henry of France, William moved his army to contest possession of the two main fortresses: Domfront and Alençon.

Fierce fighting at Domfront had not resolved the contentious issue and the long winter's blockade took its toll from both sides of the dispute. Geoffrey Martel himself had retired from Maine, but his captains and troops held firm in his name, despite the heavy falls of snow on the hills and Normandy's siege works of ditches and wooden towers. Men perished from lack of warmth and food, but William was determined to stand firm until the fortress fell into his hands. For three long years he had besieged Guy de Brionne in the same way. He was prepared to do it all over again at Domfront, if he had to.

At Easter, Mathilda was to come from her home in Flanders to join her husband at Eu, on the Normandy border. She had been outraged that William had left the day after their wedding to return to his blockade—not believing his excuse that for the present, Normandy was unsafe. He was obviously more interested in warfare than in his bride.

In fact, William had not lied. The scent of rebellion was in the air and Domfront was proving obstinate—he had too much on his mind to worry about settling his bride into her new home.

With Easter approaching, and no solution at Domfront materialising, he elected to alter tactics by withdrawing half his men to attack Alençon without warning. Mathilda was his duchess and he wanted her with him. What better way to prove to her that she had married a man of substance? The fortresses were going to fall before the spring snow-melt clogged the roads with mud and before she entered Normandy. He would give them to her as a wedding gift.

Under the cover of darkness, William moved up his engines of war, the mangonels that could reduce walls of stone to rubble, and the ballistas that fired javelins and spears with deadly accuracy at human targets, or brands of fire that set light to the thatch of buildings.

William sat on his horse, a handsome beast that was as black as a midwinter's night, silent, tight-lipped, watching the proceedings. The dry-ditch moat had been filled with cut timber and dead bracken—and the broken bodies of those who had already fallen from the battlements of Alençon. Dawn had come several hours ago, pink light that heralded a day of frosted pale-blue, cloud-patched sky. The fortress had panicked, their cries of alarm had risen with the strengthening light—but even William had to concede that the defenders were holding firm with spirit and fortitude.

The man next to him, William, comte d'Arques, pointed his sword arm at a group of men ranged along the eastern side of the battlements. The stone-work was crumbling in places where the siege engines had made their shattering marks; a trail of black smoke was spiralling into the sky behind the walls. "What are those men doing up there?" he asked, squinting into low sunlight. Then he snorted. "They're dancing! Look, they're capering about, waving their arms and leaping. What fools." Losing interest, he lifted a wineskin from his saddle and tipped the spout to his mouth. Wine dribbled as another of the group, Will fitz Osbern, also pointed with a sharp gasp of incredulity.

"They are not dancing, my lord, but taunting us! Look, their fists are raised."

"What are they hanging from the walls?"

Will narrowed his eyes, shielding them with his hand to his forehead.

The Duke had already seen. His lips pressed tighter and the knuckles of his hands gripped white around his reins.

They were hanging out hides. Cow, deer, pigskin. An array of animal skins taken from the tanner's within the walls. The noise of siege engine fire temporarily abated as a spirited wind sailed from the battlements of Alençon castle carrying the abusive calls of those mocking men with savage clarity: "Bastard by-blow of a tanner's whore!"

"Come get your hides, if you can, you bastard! Come get your inheritance!"

Men looked to their duke, their hands hesitant on the levers that would unleash the next onslaught of missiles. Will fitz Osbern licked his lips nervously, the comte d'Arques chewed at a split nail, suddenly preoccupied. They all understood the significance. A gross, appalling insult to their duke's honour. Many a man privately referred to William as the Bastard, few said it aloud.

The Duke had loved and honoured his mother, Lady Herleve, had wept openly at her death and had buried her with all honour in the new-founded abbey of Grestain. On the significant days, her birthing, name day, death day, he offered prayers for the soul of the gentle girl who had been seduced by a duke.

Ralph Tesson cleared his throat nervously. "They do it to goad you, my Lord. They hope to lure you into some act of folly. Ignore it."

Duke William ran his hand slowly along the crest of his stallion's neck, enjoying the warm feel of his coat. The winter growth would be shed soon, the summer sheen emerging from beneath. He wondered if his favourite mare had foaled yet, though it was a few weeks too early. He had put her to Sable, was hoping for a colt. Fillies were often born earlier than expected, colts late. Perhaps, then, he would be patient a few more weeks.

He pressed his spur against the black's side, putting him into a trot, heading for the next rise of land. "Will," he said to fitz Osbern, "see to it that all know of my command. I will offer handsome reward to the men who bring me those turds from the battlements. Alive, mark you. I want them alive."

❧

Alençon fell to William of Normandy within the month. Two days later he withdrew his army back to the siege at Domfront, where he made certain those snivelling behind the crumbling walls heard of the revenge that he had taken at Alençon. What was left standing there had been torched; those who had resisted him, killed without mercy. Unless Domfront surrendered, the besieged could expect the same fate. No one there dared taunt William, though. Not after what had happened at Alençon.

William, comte d'Arques, who had fought beside his duke at Val-ès-Dunes, was as sickened as the men and women of Domfront. Two days before the fortress finally surrendered, he withdrew his men and his support and rode back into his own lands.

Mathilda, waiting for her husband at Eu, received a letter William had dictated boasting of victory. She read it twice: the first time with innocent interest, the second because she could not believe the words written there.

"Is this true?" she asked of the courier who had brought it. "Is the Duke exaggerating either to impress or frighten me?"

The man nodded glumly. It was true, all of it. He knew because all at Alençon had been forced to watch. And three of those who had gleefully accepted William's reward of gold had, sickened, taken their own lives out of remorse.

Mathilda covered her mouth, fled to the privacy of her bedchamber, where she vomited profusely into the piss bowl. What manner of a man had she married? What kind of man was William?

The Duke had studied each captured man in turn, with a calm, impassive expression as they were dragged to kneel before him. They had protested with wild cries that they were not the men who had hurled those insults, knew nothing of hides. The Duke had ignored their pleas. At his command all five were staked to the ground, their hands removed at the wrists and then they were skinned, while life was still in them; their hides hung from the walls of Alençon.

36
❧

Porlock

They ran the flat-keeled ships on to the shingle, the first few men dropping instantly over the side to splash through the foaming waves, their axes and weapons at the ready, minds, eyes and ears alert, though no one had come running down across the marsh from the rising swathe of green hills to meet—or oppose—them.

Harold jumped over the bulwark and landed with a grunt of satisfaction on the shore. England. Home. After eleven months of exile as guest to King Diarmait in Dublin, it was good to be home, to reclaim what was his. He turned to grin at his brother, Leofwine, pointed with his sword to the moorland rising high on three sides of the three-mile stretch of bay. The reed beds of the Porlock marshes were silent, save for the cry of wading birds and the singing of the wind as it trailed, restless, over the emptiness.

"They are watching for us up there. On a day as clear as this, they would have seen our sails from far out. We'll give them something worth waiting for, shall we?"

The mix of Irish and Viking mercenaries that Harold had employed were already grouping into a tactical wedged formation, sharp-honed blades bristling from the outer ranks like the spines of a defensive hedgehog. Harold intended to approach the village and outlying farms peacefully, try to persuade them to support him, but he doubted he would be successful. Six months ago one of Edward's minor kinsmen, Odda of Deerhurst, had been made earl of this small coastal portion of Somerset that abutted the Devon border. He was not likely to give it up without a struggle.

Harold's lighthearted pleasure as he watched the high moorland reflecting the late summer colours of purple heather and golden gorse coalesced into something more serious as he looked across the sweep of the bay. With his father raiding along the eastern coast, from Kent down to Pevensey, this would be their only chance at reinstatement by force. They had their friends, but they needed to convince their opponents that it was futile to shut England's door to Godwine and his sons.

Nodding to his men, Harold ordered them to move out, up across the shingle. Primarily, they sought provisions—fresh food and water, arms and equipment. There was to be no taking of women against their will and no killing—unless for self-defence. Only if they were attacked would they retaliate. They were expecting a fight, for Porlock had never respected the Godwines. Swegn had been their earl for too many years to endear the family to the scattered population of this windswept Somerset coast.

Harold was gambling on the fact that Swegn had openly confessed his misdemeanours and was probably by now on the return journey from his pilgrimage to Jerusalem. Whether he could persuade wronged Englishmen that his eldest brother would be returning a repentant and chastened man remained to be seen. It would be difficult, for Harold barely believed it himself, although, according to his father's letter, Swegn had been sorely ill as he undertook the journey. How strange that men were all too eager to repent their sins when they realised they were not immortal. Aware that the thought was brutally cynical, Harold nonetheless mistrusted Swegn's motives.

Meeting only minor resistance that first day of landing, they made camp at the edge of the moors, where their lookouts could keep a sharp eye on the beached ships down in the bay below and for the approach of King's men, from whatever direction they chose to come. And they would come, Harold knew that. Odda himself was occupied in joint command of the fleet with Earl Ralf at Sandwich, attempting to head off Godwine, but thegns of repute had been left here in the West, with orders to repel any attempted landing. The information was reliable and up to date, for there were men sympathetic to Godwine's cause, willing to send messages.

Leofwine was nervous. At almost seventeen, he had not fought in anything more serious than a boy's wrestling contest. This would be the real thing; if they were intercepted, they would be facing death at the hands of experienced warriors. Harold, finishing his stew and setting his empty bowl on the grass, ruffled his brother's hair. "We have some good men with us," he said reassuringly. "Most of them have made fighting their lives."

Darkness settled. The men, almost five hundred of them, were arrayed around the scatter of campfires, some finishing their meal, others checking war gear, talking, exchanging laughter and tales of bravado. Many were already rolled into their cloaks and asleep, mindful that the morrow would be long and exhausting, save for the unfortunate who would not see the reds and golds of another setting sun. Leofwine was stroking his whetstone along the blade of his dagger, although it was already honed to deadly sharpness.

He held his counsel a long moment, then, in a rush, asked his brother, "Do you not feel fear? Are you not nervous of what we may face on the morrow?"

Setting his hand to his brother's arm, Harold laughed lightly. "Of course I am scared, lad! Most of us are. The man who goes into battle with no fear of death is the man who is likely to fall first. Contempt and confidence breed carelessness, my brother. The desire to stay alive and in one piece makes for quick thinking and fast feet." He tightened his fingers, nodded at Leofwine's blade. "Use that as you have been taught, keep your wits about you and you will be fine."

A rustle of movement beyond the light of the fires made Harold pause, his head going up, alert. Others had heard, hands going to sword, dagger or axe. A man materialised from the darkness, ducking low, his breathing heavy. A sigh rolled through those watching.

Throwing himself down before Harold's fire, the scout's head dipped in an unspoken acknowledgement. "Movement to the north. Maybe six hundred or so men."

"How far?"

"Six, seven miles. They will be in position come dawn." The scout indicated the direction with a pointing finger. "I reckon they will draw their ranks up on that rise behind us."

"Not so." Harold grinned. "We will occupy it first. I think we should be waiting for them. Come, Leofwine." He elbowed his brother with a gentle nudge. "Forget about sleep, we are moving ground."

With the ease of the warrior kind, the men stirred without fuss or noise, pulled on boots, fastened cloaks and began kicking out the hearth fires and collecting equipment together. By dawn they were holding the high ground waiting for the local militia to attack.

It seemed odd to be here, watching the first flutter of purple ease into a paler pink along the eastern horizon, knowing that the gentle peace of the moors would soon be shattered as the light flooded into the sky, and the enemy saw them, waiting, up here on the ridge. Harold had fought skirmishes and repelled sea raiders along his coast of East Anglia but, despite his bravado, he had not seen full battle either. And never had he stood as Englishman against Englishman, The first few birds were carolling their morning greeting. The rush and swish of the incoming tide, running up to meet the shore, was whispered on the wind. From somewhere distant, carried on the melting mist of the morning, a cow lowed and a dog barked. The fresh dawn smell was of the sea and heather.

A shout of alarm hurtled upwards to the sky from below, where the ridge mellowed into a scrub- and tree-dotted valley. The approaching men had seen the line of armed warriors, the glint of the first dapple of sun striking their swords and axe heads.

Stomach-churning fear catapulted through Harold as the first rush came into the attack, breath hot and panting as they ran up the slope, eyes wide with frenzied anger, weapons ready to strike. The purple heather and the gold gorse became trampled and spoilt, contaminated by blood, the dead and the dying. The lazy quiet of the calm August morning shrilled with the screams of men, the clash of weapons, the grunt and thrust of vicious fighting. Within an hour of the sun riding into the dawn-flushed sky it was over. Above forty warriors died, thirty of them Odda's men, only ten the hired Viking mercenaries from Dublin. The eight English thegns and their militia were no match for the sons of the sea-wolf and the black raven. Those English who could, trailed back down the hill to their homesteads and farms, their duty done. Harold let them go, for he was not his elder brother who would have had a point to prove. These were simple men of the fyrd, farmers and land-folk, obeying orders. They had come, fought, lost and gone. This stretch of coast would not now oppose Harold or Leofwine Godwinesson.

For that day and the next they rested, tending wounds, mending chain-mail and leather tunic, cleaning and resharpening blunted and dented weapons. Harold had sustained no injury; Leofwine merely a scratch across his cheek where he had tumbled over his own feet and caught his face against the snarl of a gorse bush. The men teased him mercilessly, Harold himself thumping his brother between the shoulder blades and saying casually, "You face several hundred fighting men and are wounded by a bush? Just as well the thing was rooted to the ground, I dread to think how it would have hurt you were it mobile!"

They returned to the ships, heaving the great, flat keels with their high, dragon-headed prows back across the shingle into the spindrift of foam that surged at their feet. Porlock was Harold's. As the heat of August began to soften into September's mellow heralding of autumn, much of Wessex, and all the men of Dover—grateful for Godwine's stand against Eustace de Boulogne—rallied without need of incentive. Verbal propaganda that promoted Godwine as the innocent victim, combined with the buying of alliance and the making of promises, increased aid threefold. From Pevensey to Sandwich, Godwine's influence spread, the rebellion expanding as each successive town offered support. Men who remembered Æthelred listened when Godwine or his sons declared that

Edward was too much like his father. Englishmen, especially those of Kent, were growing uneasy at the insidious authority that Robert of Jumièges, a Norman, was spreading from Canterbury.

As Godwine's fleet swung towards the estuary of the Thames, a few ships diverted to burn Edward's manor of Milton to the ground. As in all his raiding, Godwine commanded there was to be no unnecessary killing. He did not want to shed blood in order to achieve the reinstatement of his earldom, but to show that he was prepared to fight if he had to—and there was no doubting that Godwine would win. Those who would go against him had not the experience of command, nor the sheer guts to outface such an opponent. Earls Odda and Ralf, honest and sensible men, had tried to blockade Godwine's incoming ships at Sandwich. But what could two inexperienced men of the land achieve against those who knew the sea as well as a lover understood the whims and fancies of a wife or mistress?

37

London

By Monday, the fourteenth day of September, Godwine's ships were anchored before London Bridge at Southwark, awaiting the tide to carry them through to where Edward's army was massed on the northern banks of the river, awaiting them. The bridge was more than a means of crossing from one side of the river to another; it was as effective as any gateway, drawbridge or defensive bailey. Without consent from the elders and leading citizens his ships would not reach the far side; difficult enough navigating through those arched piers with the seething current slamming at the keel, without the addition of firebrands, rocks, arrows and spears hurling from above.

Godwine stood on the foredeck, called to the merchant guildsmen arrayed along the wooden rails of the towering bridge above him. Seagulls were swooping and calling, their raucous noise drowning his voice. He cupped his hands over his mouth and shouted louder, "Do you not fear for your established rights? Are your concerns being heard with sympathy by the King or turned aside with scorn and arrogance by his aide and confidant Robert Champart? Do you tell me that you are satisfied with the recent poor level of trade coming into London? That import taxation is not driving merchant of foreign lands to other ports, other towns?" His neck was aching from where his head was tipped backwards, his eyes watering from the glare of the sun, but he continued, for he had them almost on his side. Few up on that bridge were talking, most were leaning forward over the rails, listening intently, many beginning to nod with vigorous agreement. London remembered only too well the inadequate policies of Æthelred, and was displeased with Edward's regime.

"The King has allowed the export tax to be lowered, that is good—but customs duty has increased for imports. Who will come to buy if he has nothing to sell? A merchant ship cannot sail without ballast, and no ship will come to take out your wool or cloth if it cannot bring olive oil, or building stone, timber or silks and spices in exchange." He flung his arm towards the almost empty wharves of the Billing's Gate, where chickens, fish, dairy produce, timber and cloth were assessed for tax, among the more luxurious items of precious jewels, silks and fine-crafted embroideries.

"When I was earl, a London woman could buy the privilege to sell her cheese or butter here on the wharf for two pennies per year. By how much has Edward increased that tax to swell his own purse? Half a penny, a quarter?" Balancing himself against the movement of the ship as it jostled on the swell of the incoming tide, Godwine spread his arms wide to emphasise his point. "No, in his greed he has increased it by a full one penny!" Grumbles and murmurs of agreement rippled along the bridge. That did not happen while I advised the King. Were I back at his side, it would not happen again."

Godwine's assurances, of course, were dosed with a liberal scattering of salt. His promises were easily made, probably as easily broken or forgotten; but then, at least he was talking to the Londoners. The King talked only to Archbishop Robert, who had interfered too high-handedly with London's trade agreements.

A few of the men standing there, dressed in their elegant cloaks, tunics, and chains and badges of office, guessed that trade had fallen dramatically these last two months directly because of Godwine's ships' pirating, but who cared for the trivialities? Edward *had* increased taxation, *had* imposed unpopular new regulations. Edward and his archbishop were not liked; Godwine had always been a friend of London.

With the tide in full flood, and keeping to the southern bank of the river, Godwine advanced safely through the London defences and dropped anchor once more. The Thames, more than one quarter of a mile wide, flowed with sedate unconcern between the exiled earl and his aggrieved king.

Godwine's strength was greater than that of the royal command, his experience and ability superior, but he did not want to fight Edward, an anointed and crowned king. To do so would be dishonourable in the eyes of God, but it was his right to defend his own honour which had already been challenged. If he had to fight he would do so. The decisions of peaceful negotiation or bloodshed would be the King's. Godwine sent a messenger across the river, politely demanding restoration of everything of which he and his son Harold had been deprived.

Edward's reply was succinct.

No.

Godwine's response was prompt and professional. He swung his leading keels across the river and encircled Edward's fleet.

Edward sat at a table, slowly turning the pages of a book of gospels that he had recently acquired. It was a sumptuous thing, the illuminated lettering dazzling in gold leaf, vibrant reds and blues. So beautiful a thing was it that he felt reluctant to soil the corners of the parchment with his fingers. Robert was pacing the room, his hands clasped behind his back, pausing every so often to squint down into the courtyard below.

Monday evening. Edward had retired to his Westminster palace, leaving his nephew, Earl Ralf, and Odda presiding over the land forces encamped between the two army roads of Watling Street and Akeman Street. Perhaps they would be more efficient than at Sandwich when they had been forced to flee before Godwine's armada.

"Look at this page, Robert," Edward said with a gasp of awe. "Is it not magnificent? How wonderful that the frailties of the human eye and hand can produce such a splendid and holy work."

The Archbishop glanced at the page, murmured a mechanical answer. Was that horses arriving in the courtyard? He moved swiftly to the window, but could see nothing. To his annoyance, Bishop Stigand had been appointed by the Council as negotiator between the King and Godwine. He had been due half of an hour since. Not that Robert expected much of use from him; Stigand had made it no secret that he favoured the exiles and it was common knowledge that he wanted the position of Archbishop for himself—he would hardly be an unbiased envoy.

Robert snorted, unable to contain himself any longer. "You ought declare Godwine for the traitor he is and order his immediate execution." Added with vehemence, "He has pillaged and murdered, raided England for his own gain like a common pirate. Have done with him, I say, and this whole absurd situation will be settled."

Reverently, Edward closed the book. He did not want Godwine back, but nor was he content with Robert. The man had overstepped the border of late, had become more dogmatic and dictatorial than ever had Godwine. Besides, what choice had he? He was being undermined by a master tactician. Godwine had survived the rough storms of political manoeuvring for almost four decades and his experience was showing with a vengeance. Disposing of him was not a practical solution—Edward realised that now, doubted there was anyone with the strength to slaughter Godwine, save perhaps the devil himself.

Last year, the Earls Siward and Leofric had sided with the King against Godwine, hoping, no doubt, for a rise in their own fortune. They had expected public humiliation for their opponent, a heavy fine, a reduction in status, not exile. At the time it had delighted Edward, that feeling of ultimate power: if a king could so thoroughly remove Godwine, what hope had other men of England? He had refused to reward his earls, enjoying his pinnacle of dominance and authority, rubbing their noses in their inability to defy his will.

He had learnt much about being a king these past months. It took, he now realised, great skill to balance duty against self-preservation. Loyalty and respect were not to be commanded at will. It seemed incredible, to Edward's political naïveté, that men who had so very often been at each other's throats should now consider uniting in common cause. It seemed Siward and Leofric were contemplating agreeing terms with Godwine—at the least, if they were not thinking of committing their fighting men to the services of a rebellious exile, neither had they responded with any haste to Edward's orders to mobilise the fyrd when first Godwine had been sighted off the coast of Kent. It had taken them all these weeks to march south with a mere handful of men; indeed, they had still not reached London, but were lodged a full day's march away more than twenty miles to the north.

Robert's mind, too, was dwelling upon the Earls of Northumbria and Mercia. Edward had summoned them to court immediately, to explain their delay. Robert tapped a fingernail against his teeth, gazing out of the window. The light was fading. This failure to obey a direct royal command was worrying. Without their combined armies of the North to swell the paltry few who faced Godwine's able fleet, Edward would have no choice but to grant a pardon to the exile. If he were to fight he could be deprived of everything, crown and throne included. It had been done before, by lesser men than Godwine. And if Edward fell, then so, too, would he.

Leofric's son had answered the summons, of course, but then he had been given Harold's earldom, and had no care to lose East Anglia. The promotion of that boy had proven to be a disastrous move. He was an untrustworthy in-competent, no one liked or respected him, not even his father. Robert ought to have seen that before he had been so eager to take the lad's proffered gold. Was there nothing he could salvage? Turning his attention from the window, Robert spoke of Ælfgar.

"I have approached your Earl of East Anglia with a suggestion of alliance between the throne and himself. His daughter is a comely child, so I understand. Marriage to her would bring the security we desire."

Edward sniffed audible contempt. So Robert had said when he had taken Edith as wife. So Duke William of Normandy had promised. Both prospects had turned as sour as cream left to curdle in the midday sun. Attempts to curb Godwine had come to naught, and that poxed duke had married his sister to some peacock count of Normandy, not a month after her husband had died in a fracas during one of those interminable sieges that William seemed obsessed with.

"The girl is nine years of age and of no use as a wife," Edward grumbled, referring to Ælfgar's daughter. In Edward's opinion Robert was always arranging this or that matter of importance without consulting him or taking note of his objections. It was Robert who had insisted on Godwine's exile, he who had suggested placing Odda and Ralf in command of the fleet at Sandwich. As Archbishop, he might know his scriptures, law and history, but he knew nothing of war. Nor had he a keen eye for dress. Edith had occasionally, when Champart had not been around, been uncommonly useful, knowing the right clothes to wear for which occasion, matching colour and fabrics. A woman's touch, Edward supposed.

"Nine is a good young age." Robert forced a smile. "You can mould her to your liking."

"But Ælfgar would become my father-in-law!" Edward protested. "He is but thirty years of age and a pompous, self-opinionated pain in the arse!"

"Nevertheless, I think you ought consider the marriage. He has, after all, remained loyal to you throughout the upheavals of this past year around."

Aye, because his greed surpasses that of even the most devious of thieves, Edward thought, not bothering to argue further. He was tired of all this. Of Godwine, of Robert. All he wanted was peace and quiet.

Horses arriving. Robert started, caught his breath and strode to the door, bellowing orders that the arrivals were to attend the King without pause.

"Siward and Leofric are here," he explained to Edward, pronounced relief in his voice and expression. "At last we can make use of all our resources against those who would overthrow your kingdom." Rubbing his palms together, the Archbishop seated himself on a stool that faced the door, his pulsing heart slowing, rapid breathing easing. He had barely slept these past nights. If Godwine managed to claw his way back into power...Robert shuddered. It would be unfeasible for him to remain in England alongside that traitorous murderer.

Despite his orders, one quarter of an hour passed before the two earls entered the King's chamber. They had taken time to remove grime from their faces and boots, to partake of wine and food. Robert sat upright, arms folded, teeth clamped. Why was it that these belligerent English defied him, over and again?

"You have brought your men?" Robert said, before Edward had chance to speak. "We need them to flank the river Fleet. Set them between the chapels of Saint Andrew and Saint Brigid, to prevent Godwine occupying the London Marsh."

Siward made his obeisance to Edward, ignoring the Archbishop. His beard and hair were grizzled, grey-streaked as a badger's pelt, his hands and facial skin wrinkled with age like the rugged bark of an ancient oak tree. "I speak for both myself and the Earl of Mercia, my King, We have come because we have been summoned, but we have come with the intention of listening and talking within the laws of Council. We would hear what Godwine has to say." He turned his calm gaze to Robert and said with finality, "We have not brought our men to London, we have not come to fight, will not enter into a civil war. That may be how you Normans conduct your disagreements but we are English. It is more sensible to talk, not cut out each other's throats or balls."

Rage suffused red across Champart's cheeks and forehead. The insult had stung hard and the implications were clear. "Then you too commit treason!"

"On the contrary, my lord," Leofric said, "it is treason to seek to shed blood, not to talk of peaceful settlement."

"And what of your son, of Ælfgar?"

"He has developed a taste for an earldom," Leofric answered again candidly, "but he is an incompetent. I would counsel that he wait a while before being given such a privilege. If I can be assured of his being made earl in a year or two, than I am content."

Robert's fists clenched, the realisation slamming into his brain as if it were the blow of an axe. "By God," he exclaimed, his skin draining pale, "you have already spoken with Godwine and Harold! Have reached agreement with them!" He thundered his disgust and disappointment by sweeping his hand over a nearby table, sending Edward's precious book of gospels sprawling to the floor. With an exclamation of horror, Edward sank to his knees, scrabbling for the several pages that had fallen loose from the binding, tears of dismay pricking his eyes. Such a thing of beauty so wantonly damaged!

Siward lied without qualm or hesitation: "No, my Lord Archbishop, we have not. But we intend to. If those two worthy men will reach accommodation, we see no reason not to talk terms." Turning his back, Siward knelt before the King, retrieved another loose page and reverently handed it to him.

It is a wise man who decides that peace is the better path than a futile war. It is a wise king who makes the right decision for the needs of his people and his country. Godwine is a bull-headed, bluff-mannered bag of self-blown wind but, unlike some who have risen to advancement while he has been gone, he also possesses integrity, honour and knowledge. Cnut had good reason to make him Earl of Wessex. Those same reasons remain."

Siward and Leofric stared with calm certainty at the man who had, through his own efforts, been exalted into the highest office of the English Church. Much though both earls disliked Godwine, they despised these Norman interlopers more, especially Robert Champart, former Abbot of Jumièges.

He stood, looking down at the King, disgust rippling his nose and mouth. After all he had done for this snivelling little man. "And you, Edward?" Robert asked. "You agree with these imbeciles? Accept Godwine and you must accept his daughter. You will be forced to have Edith back as wife."

Edward remained kneeling, the book, spoilt and ruined, on his lap. No, he did not want Godwine or Edith, but nor did he want Ælfgar's daughter. What he did want was his solitude and privacy. And what was the saying? Better the known tricks of a devil, than the cunning of a fallen angel? Tenderly, he set the torn pages into their placings. Perhaps the book could be rebound by one who knew his craft well.

Robert left without further word. Within his own chambers he collected items of value, sent servants scuttling to pack what he needed. He had no choice but to flee England and go to Normandy, where Duke William would, he hoped, help him avenge this intolerable offence to his dignity.

Calling for his horse and guard to assemble in the courtyard, Robert ordered a further precaution to ensure his safety. He would take with him the hostages that Edward had demanded of Godwine, the two boys Wulfnoth and Hakon, as security in case these English tried to stop him leaving.

38

Waltham Abbey

Dawn had meandered over the horizon, cascading dew over the grass and overnight-spun cobwebs with a sparkle of fairy diamonds. Edyth stood at the edge of the manor courtyard, where the ground dropped away down towards the valley. In the pasture immediately below the cattle were grazing, their udders soft and empty after milking. She could hear young Stanwine whistling in the cow byre as he washed and swept away the detritus, and Mildred's high-pitched scolding. No doubt the children were under her feet again, but youngsters always did love the butter churn.

What ought she do today? There was employment to fill a day three times over, but she had no enthusiasm for chores. The remaining blackberries needed picking before Michaelmas, there would be this morning's crop of mushrooms to be threaded on string and hung for drying, the apples from the orchard to be stored in bran, the rose-hips to be boiled down and set in pottery crocks—and apart from the seasonal preserving, there was always wool to card and spin. She had started making a new gown, but had no inclination to finish the thing. What would be the point without Harold here to admire it?

There had been wild-running rumours since summer, tales of Harold and his father landing at various sites around the entire coast of England, from Northumbria down to the Isle of Wight. She knew of the success at Porlock from a letter penned by Harold himself—one of only three that he had managed to write since first he was exiled, or at least, that had been delivered into her hand. The rumours that their fleet had been heading towards Sandwich and from there to London were plausible, but where was Harold now? Had he indeed reached London? If he had, what had happened? Surely, oh surely, Edward must meet his senses and return their earldoms! Edyth shut her eyes to squeeze back the unexpected tears. For how much longer could she endure this separation?

If only she could open her eyes and see horses riding up the track, Harold's housecarls, his banner—Harold himself...a horse whinnied loud and clear against the early-morning mist. She jumped with astonishment, half convinced she had conjured the sound. It came again and she stood, straight, tense, hoping, hoping...but it was only Whiteface calling for her stable companion, protesting at being separated from her friend. Guthram could not ride both of them down into the village.

She would saddle her mare and ride to her mother's, take the two elder children with her on their ponies. Their grandmother would be delighted to see them, for she was so lonely since her father had died in the cold of last winter. At least Edyth knew she would, some day, see Harold again. For her mother there would never be another soft word or tender touch from her husband.

On the other hand her mother did not suffer this daily ritual of agonised hope and stomach-churning worry.

❦

By mid-afternoon the sweetness of the morning had disappeared into drizzle. Edyth, enjoying her visit to her childhood home, postponed returning to her own manor. She would leave before evening set in, but the children were invited to remain. Without them, she and her escort could travel faster. By the sixth hour, with the rain persisting and the clouds louring heavier, Edyth was tempted to stay the night herself, but on the morrow she really ought to oversee the fruit preserving. Those silly serving girls were inclined to chatter and giggle more than work when their mistress was not within earshot.

A mile along the muddied lane, Edyth's mare missed her footing and fell heavily on to her shoulder. Edyth, with a cry of surprise, was flung clear unharmed, but the rain had plastered the track, and her cloak and gown were sodden. Laughing to mask the shock of the unexpected tumble, Edyth scrambled to her feet as the first of the men reached her, anxious with concern. Assuring him that she had taken no hurt worse than bruised dignity, Edyth walked with him to inspect the mare. She too was mud-splashed, the fetlock of her near foreleg already swelling.

"A few weeks' rest for you, my lass, I think." Edyth said, patting the mare's neck. "We'll put a poultice of fresh dung and bran around it when we reach home, to bring out the heat."

One of the men was bringing his own horse forward for his lady to mount and continue homeward, but the animal stopped rock still, head up, listening. Horses were approaching, the thud of cantering hooves and the jingle of harness echoing beneath the rain-drip of the trees. A male voice called out—a voice which surely, surely, Edyth recognised...She stood motionless, quivering, as if she were a deer scenting danger on the wind, her hands poised on the reins, one foot lifted to be boosted into the saddle…and then she was running, heedless of the mud and the rain. Running, her fingers grasping her riding skirt, lifting it high above her stocking garters to run the faster.

Harold! Oh, Harold was here! Blessed Virgin, sweet Jesu! He had come home!

39

Wilton

Yesterday had been Edith's birthing day. No one of her family were there to celebrate with her, only the Abbess and the nuns of Wilton. Not that they were unwelcome, but she had not chosen their company. She was three and twenty, and had nothing to look forward to. Nothing save the loneliness of a discarded, unfairly discredited wife stretching ahead.

Talk about her father's and brother's raiding had lifted her spirits briefly, but since early September word from the lips of traders and pilgrims had dried silent. Dismally, she assumed their attempts had failed, for surely she would have heard something more by now?

She dipped her quill in the ink mixed from soot and honey and attempted to write more of her pleading letter to Edward. She had completed three sentences—oh, what was the use of writing again? Angry, she threw the goose-feather quill to the floor, the delicate shaft snapping as it hit the stone paving, and ripped the parchment to shreds. Wilton was a comfortable nunnery, she occupied the best guest room—but Edith wanted her palace at Westminster, her luxurious bed-chamber with its ante-rooms, the network of corridors, the rooms of state, the library with its musty smell of mystery and knowledge. The bustling kitchens where servants bickered and fussed to prepare royal feasts or a private tray of tempting dainties on those days when she had preferred her own company…the overflowing stores, the stables with the best-bred horses, the kennels with the wisest hounds—the fastest hawks, the fattest cattle…the list was endless. Oh! Edith wanted her crown back!

Why had her father and brothers been so stupid? Why had they not conceded defeat and bowed before Edward's will last summer? All this misery for the sake of that poxed town of Dover. A matter of principle, her father had said. The King had challenged his authority and credibility—his honour. Honour, bah!

Edith stalked around the room, fingering candle holders, picking up her Bible, setting it down; kicking the crumpled ball of parchment under the bed. Had her father and brothers considered her position when they had refused to meet Edward on his terms last year? No. Had they realised how dangerous their addle-brained rebellion would be for her personally, as the King's wife? Again, no.

No doubt her father had not thought Edward capable of setting her aside—but he had reckoned without the influence of that weasel Robert Champart? Archbishop? Huh! Bishop to the devil!

It had been he who had fabricated those vile lies against her, of course—how much gold had he paid into the purse-pouches of those men? They said she had taken a lover to her bed. Adultery? She was as virgin pure at the age of twenty-three as she had been at three—and she had told them so, those fusty, grey-haired old men Siward and Leofric, and the rest of Edward's Council.

"My maidenhood is intact!" she had screamed at them as they dragged her from the Council chamber at Westminster the day after Saint Stephen's day. "Let any physician examine me for the proof of it!"

She closed her eyes, swallowed tears. Never would she forget the fear and the humiliation of that dreadful, snow-grey day of winter!

Before the entire Council Champart had accused her, bringing in his vile minions to give testimony against her. She had laughed, denied it, stood before Edward and told them all how she could prove Champart was a liar, that this was a plot to be rid of her. Edward had sat with his head bowed, had said nothing as she told that his declaration of chastity was a falsehood, that he had no manhood in his loins.

Had they believed her? Probably, possibly, yet still she had been taken away, shut into a litter and removed from court to Wherwell Abbey, an austere and frigid nunnery where no one spoke or laughed, where the pleasure of reading or singing was forbidden. At least at Easter she had been brought from there, was now confined here at Wilton, where she had spent so many happier years as a child.

Confined. She had every comfort, every want or whim was granted, except for the ability to walk or ride through the gateway if she so chose.

Her letter was to have been another attempt to convince Edward her innocence. She had sent many similar entreaties; all had been returned, their seals unbroken.

Instead of writing, she would read. Taking a bundle of scrolled parchments from a wooden casket, she cast herself, stomach down, atop the bed and unrolled. Queen Emma's last communication, sent on the day it was written and dated the first day of March. It was not her own hand, for her health had been failing—she had died, having made her peace with God, in the late hours five days later. Edith read slowly, studying the words that she had read so many times over. Emma had been blunt and precise, her dictated sentences reading more as a list.

Do nothing to give ground for reproof.

Insist on your innocence with persistence, but with dignity. That which is repeated often is eventually believed.

The weakness of your enemy can be turned to your strength.

My dear, I have done all I can for you. You hold your future in your own hand.
My blessings. May God and His Lady be with you, always.

That had been all. No farewell or intimation that Edith's future was soon to look brighter—perhaps then, when the letter had been written, Emma had not known that Edward's conscience was pricking him. One week after Emma had been laid to rest within Winchester Cathedral, Edith had been escorted from Wherwell to Wilton. Why, she had not been told, except she was certain that Emma had had some hand in it.

A novice tapped warily at the door: Edith's blustering tempers were notorious. "Madam?" The girl's timid voice quavered. "The Abbess begs you attend her. There is a man to see you."

Edith rolled from the bed, abandoning her letters. "A man? Which man? Is he from the King?"

The girl shook her head. "I do not know him, Lady, but he is noble born."

Tempted to tell the girl to convey her refusal, Edith decided against the idea. What else had she to do with the rest of this dull-dreary day? If Champart had persuaded the Pope to annul her marriage and grant Edward a divorce, did it matter whether she heard now or later? What did anything matter? In her more rational moments Edith knew much of her melancholy was unnecessary, for she was welcomed and treated with respect and sympathy at Wilton. Whether the Abbess would stop her if she attempted to leave, Edith had not tried to find out, for she was fond of her and did not wish to compromise her. Besides, she had no wish to be returned to the dour oppression of Wherwell.

Fetching up her cloak, Edith followed the girl from the guest quarters to the private rooms of the Abbess.

Horses of quality snorted in the courtyard, the breath and steam from their coats showing that they had been ridden hard. News of some urgency, then? Edith gave the men holding the bridles a cursory glance as she swept up the steps into the Abbess's domain. There was nothing on saddlecloth or shield to identify them. Edward himself had not come, then, nor Champart.

She paused before entering and smoothed her gown. Gathering her breath and schooling her features blank, as Emma had taught her, she stepped, back straight, head high, into the room, A tall, fair-haired man sat with his back to the door, a goblet of wine in his hand. He rose as she entered, turned, and all Edith's pretence of calm vanished.

Tostig, In the flesh, in the being! Tostig! His face was full-fleshed, his eyes sparkled, his moustache and hair had recently been trimmed. Fur edged his cloak, his tunic of the finest spun wool was edged in gold brocade . , , here did not stand a man condemned as an outlaw.

"Well?" he said, resting his fist on the sword pommel slung across his left hip. "Have you no sisterly greeting for me? It is all over. The King agreed terms with our father over a week since, on the fifteenth day of September." He grinned, showing white, even teeth. "We are reinstated."

Edith remained motionless, her expression impassive, Tostig's words reeling in her brain. "And why then, may I ask," she finally responded with hauteur, "has it taken you so damned long to fetch me from here?"

40

Lycia, near Constantinople

Throughout the day the sun had thrust its spears of heat through the half-shuttered window, beating down on to the man lying on the floor, ragged, unshaven and in his own mess of vomit and excrement. His face was burning from the sun and fever, but he had been too ill to move into the shade, no more than three inches from his filthy bed. Someone, one of the few men who had remained loyal, had brought him water. It had tasted foul and he had vomited most of it straight up.

Dusk had come quickly, the noises in the street below rising as the heat went out of the day and people began to emerge from their shelter. Was this how it always was, he thought, closing his eyes against the pain that engulfed his body. At the end, when death came for you, was it always this lonely and desperate? If this was punishment for all the wrongs he had committed, then surely he would be purged of sin by the time he reached God's kingdom.

He heard laughter from the room below, the girl's high voice sounding clearly through the thin floorboards of this stinking room. A man's gruff answer. He could not distinguish the words. They had tended him at first, the innkeeper and his daughter, before the money had run out. His ring, cloak pin, sword and dagger, everything of value had long gone. His horse too, probably, with the fine leather harness and silk trappings. All the magnificent gifts he had bought in Jerusalem to take back home to England. The perfume for the women, the spices, the weaponry for his father and brothers. The casket of myrrh for the King, for Edward.

Swegn had no doubt that his father had redeemed the family name and fortune. He, Swegn, had pledged, before leaving on this long trek to the Holy City, that when he returned he would be a changed man. His family had never thought that he might not return. Nor had he.

He drowsed in and out of consciousness as the stars moved lazily across the dark foreign sky. At least now it was cool, but it did not matter for it was too late; his body was already growing cold. Swegn, the eldest son of Earl Godwine of Wessex in England, while returning from pilgrimage to Jerusalem to repent of his sins, was dead.

For three days Earl Godwine of Wessex lingered, unconscious of his pain, unaware that his wife sat, throughout, at his side without sleep or food or respite from grief. Harold and Edyth, Tostig and Judith, Leofwine and Gyrth watched and waited with her.

His daughter did not come, nor did the King, and only those men who had loved Godwine in life shed tears when, on the fifteenth day of April in the year 1053, the Earl was taken to God.

The Countess Gytha had him buried in the Minster at Winchester, within sight of the tombs of Cnut and his queen, Emma, whom Godwine had served without question. If any had been responsible for the wicked death of that young man Alfred, it had been she, not Godwine.

Unanimous support from the Council gave Godwine's son Harold responsibility of Wessex, while to balance the scales, Ælfgar, son of Leofric of Mercia, to his great pleasure, had East Anglia restored to him.

The King was indifferent to the decision-making. It had been Godwine he despised. Was it because the man had been so close in friendship with his mother and had shown no glimmer of affection for himself as boy or man grown? Or because of the rumours and implications of Alfred's death? Edward did not know the reason, did not care to analyse it.

Swegn too he had hated. The man had been a braggart and a liar. They were, both of them, gone to plead their case with God. Who would, most assuredly, judge them.

Harold was a Godwine, but a pleasant enough man, not arrogant or assuming like his father, nor brash and boastful as his brother. Edward had no objection to his promotion. As for Edith…well, it seemed he had to have a wife and it had been Champart who had so disliked her, he told himself.

Edward, always one to lay blame at the feet of another, could see only what he wanted to see.

arms caught him, whirled him around in dizzying circles. It was always the memories of the child, of the sun-filled summer days that lingered when death came calling. Harold, Edith, Tostig, the other boys seemed unconcerned that Swegn would not return to England. Gytha had said no word, shed not a tear. They were careful not to say so within their father's hearing, but Swegn's passing had been a God-blessed relief, for his quarrelling and indiscretions had been the main cause of Edward's contempt. With Swegn gone, the barrier could be, if not lifted, at least raised a little. Godwine knew all that, but still he missed and mourned his eldest son.

Easter and the holy festival of the Crucifixion and Resurrection. The King moved his court southwards, to Winchester, where his council and nobles were obliged to attend him. Lent had been as long and demanding as the bitter winter before it, the weather as dismal as the restrictions on food. The Easter feasting was always welcome, at least at the King's table where the shortages from poor harvests and a hard winter had little effect.

The King's Hall was not so grand as his new palace at Westminster. Seating at the trestle tables, set in their rows, was cramped and limited in elbow room. Table manners held good if men knew the eyes of the King were on them, but lower down the end of the Hall, where men of lesser rank were seated, the rules were not so rigorously obeyed. It was thought bad manners to eat if the hands were not cleansed in the proffered water bowls, for a platter was shared between two or four people, food served in communal dishes for each individual to select: flat loaves of bread, cheeses, pastries, joints of meat—a wing of chicken, pigeon or pheasant, cutlet of lamb or pork. To plunge an arm up to the elbow to search for a choice portion at the bottom of the bowl was considered distasteful; to scratch at fleas and lice, at sweating armpits and more personal parts and then take food frowned upon. But once the ale jugs had passed several times around the tables, who cared about the niceties?

Regard to good manners was the difference between the highborn and the low. There was no swearing or spitting at the King's table; finger bowls were fastidiously used. Better portions of the tastier, more appetising dishes were served. But Godwine ate and drank only sparingly. Indigestion niggled in his stomach, his appetite diminished by the King's determination to ignore him. On several occasions during the afternoon, Godwine had attempted to ask Edward again what could be done to negotiate the return of his two boys. The King had deliberately turned his back.

Harold was not particularly enjoying himself either. He had settled with ease back into the responsibilities of his earldom, but then Harold was younger than

his father, and had his wife and children to motivate him. For their future well-being, more than the politics, he had fought his way home from exile. The safety of the two boys was bothering Harold too, however, and, like Godwine, he had been unable to attract Edward's attention or concern.

"The King will not help us with Wulfnoth and Hakon," Harold said, leaning towards his father and selecting another portion of roasted chicken. "I am thinking that Edward wants them kept with Duke William for reasons of his own."

Edward's high-pitched laugh tumbled from the centre of the table. Godwine glanced in his direction, nibbling at a meat pastry. There was no pleasure in sitting here, being forced to listen, yet again, to Edward's repertoire of frivolous anecdotes.

"If William has set his mind on Edward's crown, then it would suit him well to hold English hostages—my son—for it would be Wessex who would protest most loudly against his insubstantial claim."

"It suits Edward too," Harold added, "for he has a new chain to bind us with."

Godwine sighed and set down the half-eaten pastry. Hostages, ah, hostages. So damned useful to those who would use their innocence to their own unscrupulous advantage.

"We will secure their release, Father, when the time and situation are right." Harold attempted reassurance. "Perhaps Edith can persuade him?" He flickered a glance along the laden table towards his sister. "She, out of us all, has come through the difficulties of the past month with equanimity." He had not intended any malice in the remark, but the disparagement was unmistakably there.

His father said nothing. Edith had chosen her position as queen over that of daughter. If Edward was ignoring Godwine, then Edith, too, had decided that her father no longer existed.

Riding away from confinement at Wilton, she had shrewdly assessed her tactics for securing her future. Emma had seen the potential in the child and Emma had rarely been proven wrong. The weakness of your enemy can be turned to your strength. The Dowager Queen had known Edith would make good use of her wisdom. To make certain she would never again be removed or humiliated, Edith realised that she must make herself indispensable, must ensure that Edward could not survive without her. She could never capture his affection through her body, but there were other ways to bind him. His weakness was his self-doubt, his frail conscience and a desperate need to be loved by all. Her Achilles heel was her husband's dislike of her father.

She began immediately upon her return to court by nurturing Edward's

vanity. She often admired his neatness of appearance, his self-restraint with eating and drinking, his depth of knowledge of scripture and history. She asked questions and listened to his answers with absorbed attention, soon discovering that it made him feel important to have her sitting rapt at his feet while he talked. As the new year ripened towards a late-come spring she had begun to discuss matters of interest with him, occasionally being mildly challenging. Lively debate was one of Edward's favourite indoor pastimes, provided he always won any argument. It proved to be a game Edith was most adept at playing.

For Edward himself, disillusionment with last September's events had been complete. He had never really wanted to be king, to have all this responsibility thrust upon him—oh, he enjoyed the pomp and respect that went with it, the sumptuous regalia, the authority, but where was the loyalty that did not need to be bought? The friendship that came without condition? He had thought Champart his friend. He had loved Robert, with a love that had perhaps not been suitable for one man to give to another, but Robert had never shied away from the closeness that had grown between them. Now he realised why, of course. It had not been for love of Edward that Champart had encouraged their bond, but for his own greed and ambition. The hurt speared deep. Edward felt battered and used. Like a drum beaten to keep the time and pace for the whirl of the dance and then tossed aside, forgotten and useless when the skin had lost its tautness. More than the hurt, Edward recognised that he had been played for a gullible fool; his pride was damaged, far more difficult a thing to heal.

Entertainment by jugglers and acrobats complemented the lavish feast, but once the bellies were full and the ale passed around, a cry went up for the songs. Hands thumped the tables with approval as the harper, smiling his acquiescence, settled beside the hearth to tune his instrument. He waited for silence before he began a narrative of the hero Beowulf and his fight with the lurid monster, Grendel.

> "And so the men led a carefree life and all was well,
> 'Til, with Hell in his mind,
> Grendel, grim and full with hate,
> Stalked the shadows: his malice made ripe for wickedness."

To the left hand of Edward's high table sat Leofric, with his wife and eldest son Ælfgar, a man nursing a grievance as black as any held by that hideous monster of

the harper's tale. Ælfgar sat hunched, goblet between his hands, scowling along the table at the guests who sat to the far side of the King. The Godwines.

> *"With the night came Grendel.*
> *In the Hall the nobles after feasting,*
> *Slept discharged from sorrow.*
> *Mad in rage Grendel struck quickly, a creature of evil and hate.*
> *Grim and greedy, unsparing and savage,*
> *He grasped thirty warriors and away he fled homeward,*
> *Glutted and bloody with the stain."*

Ælfgar sympathised with the monster. To be taunted by the laughter of men who flaunted what they had beneath the noses of those who had been stripped of wealth and position because of them. Ælfgar's fingers strayed to the hilt of his meat dagger. He had no other weapon, for it was forbidden to carry arms to table. Huh! He would need no weapon, he could do it as Grendel had, with his bare hands! His fingers could rip Harold's throat, choke the laughter from Godwine's age-withered windpipe...

East Anglia had been granted him when Harold and his kin had been driven from England. He had worn the title until the Godwines had returned, curse them and all their seed! Without pause, Edward had bowed before their every demand, presenting his backside for them to kick. Godwine reinstated as Earl of Wessex; to Harold, East Anglia rebestowed. To thrust the dagger further into his guts, his own father Leofric had agreed to it. No one at court had supported Ælfgar. All they had wanted was an amicable peace. Amicable? Well it was not amicable to Ælfgar! He did not want this merry carousing or the telling of heroic tales. He wanted an earldom—Harold's earldom.

"Grim and greedy"—how that phrase suited Godwine and his brood of thieves! Aye, magpies perched on a branch, waiting to take all they could for their own!

"Look at Wessex sitting there—it makes my flesh creep to watch him. Grendel himself would be more pleasant to behold than he squirming for favour." Ælfgar muttered the abuse beneath his breath, but his father heard.

"I have never personally liked Godwine," he rasped in return, "but I respect him. Holding a position of authority takes more than the ability to wield axe and sword. When a man becomes a leader he needs diplomacy and tact. And to know when to keep his mouth shut."

"That is why Godwine and Harold are so successful, is it?" Ælfgar sneered.

"Aye," his father answered curtly. "That is why."

"…Grendel waged war with Hrothgar, the wrongs he did the King!
He watched and waited,
Walked nightlong through moorland mist.
What man can know the mind of the demon and the damned?"

"Godwine would know of that." Ælfgar snapped disdainfully. "The wrongs he has done his king."

The harper had reached a pause in the narrative, laid his palm on the humming strings of his harp to still its voice, and the Hall was silent. Save for Ælfgar's ill-mannered remark.

Eyes turned to Leofric's son, who reddened, but stared back defiantly. The silence hung like an icicle suspended over an overhang of rock.

"And what mean you by that?" Earl Godwine asked placidly. Despite eating so little, the pain of indigestion had returned.

"I speak only what comes to mind. That you sit so at ease, without conscience, beside the brother of one you once had murdered."

Gasps, a bench scraped back, several of Godwine's personal housecarls coming ominously to their feet. Countess Gytha put her hand to her mouth; Harold's fists clenched. But for all those who were shocked and angered by Ælfgar's accusation, there were more than one or two who discreetly nodded their heads in agreement.

Godwine sipped his wine, letting the red warmness trickle down his throat, allowing his heartbeat to steady from the erratic lurching thud that seared through his chest. "I have said before and I say again, I am innocent of that ancient mischief. I took the boy Alfred prisoner, I agree. It was I who misguidedly placed him in the hands of Cnut's son—had I known how grievously he was there to be treated, I would not have done so."

"So you again insist that you had naught to do with his murder?"

"I do." The tightness in his chest was becoming worse; he would need ask Gytha for some mint leaves to chew.

Edward was becoming flustered, uncertain how to control this swift up-rush of anger. He did not want quarrelling at his table; Ælfgar ought be reprimanded, yet he had never been able to accept Godwine's denial of his part in that heinous death. He waved his hand at the harper, signalling him to begin the next part of the tale, but Ælfgar, wine muzzying his better judgement, retorted, "How easy it is to proclaim words of protest when there is no one to refute them. I wonder if the prince, Alfred, would agree with you, were his spirit here?"

"As God is my witness." Godwine declared with sudden impatience, "I am innocent of this lie!" He thumped the table with his palm, lurching upright—and

the pain tore through his chest, arms and jaw as if a spear had been thrust direct through him. He doubled over, clutching at the agony, his lips contorting, breath gasping.

Harold and Gytha were immediately on their feet, the woman's arms going about her husband's shoulders as he collapsed, dragging the linen cloth with him, bowls of nuts and dried fruits, goblets and tankards of wine and ale tumbling to the floor. A scream left her lips. Edward, his own heart racing with the suddenness of it all, shouted for his physician to be summoned; someone handed wine to Harold who put it to his father's lips, someone else kicked aside the debris and the dogs who had run in, hoping to scavenge for scraps.

"Does he live?" Edyth took Godwine's hand in her own, began trying to rub warmth into its creeping coldness. Harold had ripped open the lacings of his father's tunic. Tearing the cloth, he laid his ear against the scant grey hairs on the white skin, listened, then touched his fingers to the side of his father's throat, below the jaw. There was nothing—but then he felt a faint, irregular beat. "Yes," he said, with a quick breath. "Yes, he lives!"

Tears trickled over Gytha's cheeks as they carried Godwine away to the comfort of his bed, her eldest living son's strong arms supporting her as she followed. Her only daughter remained with the King; her face was white but she had chosen her path and on it she must remain.

The harper did not resume his tale of Beowulf. There was no place for songs, not now. The Hall was subdued; a few men took leave of their king and withdrew, others sat quiet or talked in hushed voice.

Edward sat erect in his high-backed chair, rigid and still. He felt sick, his head swam, his stomach churned. "As God is my witness, I am innocent," Godwine had said—and had been struck down no sooner had the words flown from his lips...*My God*, Edward thought, *Godwine lied; all these years, he has lied to me*. He looked at Ælfgar, saw the same thought resting on his face.

Edith caught the brief look of comprehension that passed between them. Had her father lied about the murder of Edward's younger brother? Had God issued swift punishment, or was it all a coincidence? Whatever, she could not risk losing her new-found stability; she must act, and act now, for her own security. For her own future. Whatever happened to her father, whether he died or lived, he was finished as a trusted earl of the King. Deliberately, she took Edward's hand within her own and spoke soft, so only he might hear. "Your brother lies in peace at last, my Lord. God has provided us with the truth."

Edward patted the cool hand that held his. "God will witness the truth. At the end, He will be the judge of all."

41

Winchester—April 1053

As the swallow or house martin would return to a familiar nesting place, Edith had returned to court as if she had hardly been away. Her father, however, had found it harder to adjust. He had never admitted—even to himself—the anxiety that exile had caused, the loss of dignity, coming so close to losing everything he had. He was no longer an adaptable young man. His hair was grizzled, his breathing more shallow. Twice since Christmas had the pains in his chest caught him off guard, so that he had groped for a chair arm, clutched at his breast, waiting for the agony that stabbed down his left arm to subside, the red dizziness in his head to clear.

Soon after the Christmas celebration at Westminster he had returned with Gytha and his two unmarried sons to Bosham. The winter cold of January and February bringing a despair with it, that wrapped around his heart like a rope, knotting and twisting tighter with each long, dark, melancholy day.

Edward had made no apology, no attempt to repair the damage that he and his Norman friends had caused. Had not sent after Champart to demand the return of Godwine's son and grandson. They were with William at Rouen, so rumour said, although the Duke had denied it. Champart himself, after whining to William, had ridden direct to Rome, to reiterate his complaints against England to the Pope, who would, no doubt, listen with sympathy, but was, for all that, impotent to do anything to help. England was a wealthy and strong-minded country; Rome could not afford to alienate her, and Normandy remained under an interdict of papal displeasure through William's determination to marry without Church approval.

News of Swegn's lonely death had been a further blow to Godwine's bruised spirit. The lad had had his faults and weaknesses, but he had been his father's first-born. Hard it was to set aside the memory of the child in arms, dimple-cheeked, pudgy-handed, reaching out to tug at his papa's moustache. Hard to forget tossing the boy as if to the sky, hearing his screech of delight as strong

42

Waltham Abbey

The chamber slumbered in quiet contentment after the children had been persuaded to their beds. Edyth bent to pick up their scattered toys, decided the servants could tidy away on the morrow, for now, all she wanted was to sit and take the weight off her aching feet, legs and back. Children were delightful, but Goddwin, Algytha, Edmund and even Magnus at nearly two years of age possessed more energy than both she and Harold combined. She put her hand to the seven-month bulge that was to be her sixth-born child, smiled.

"Is he kicking?" Harold asked. He lay full length along the bed, atop the furs and full dressed, save for his boots that were tossed, discarded, to the floor.

"No, but she is fidgeting," Edyth answered with a bright, homely smile. "Insisting on playing as boisterously as the others, I think."

Harold laughed, swung himself from the bed. He had joined in heartily with the children's games this past hour, crawling across the floor on hands and knees, giving them rides on his back or bouncing them on his shoulders. He ached!

"They are excited," he said. The nativity is always a time of adventure for children." He cast his eyes around the chamber at the hanging garlands of ivy and evergreens, the bright contrast of the red holly berries. The Hall below this, their private room, was decorated more magnificently still. The yule log was already in the hearth for its ceremonial lighting on the morrow; caskets and barrels of wine and ale brought in from the stores, the cooking pits prepared, the cattle, pigs and fowl slaughtered and butchered. He crossed the room on stockinged feet to circle his arms around Edyth, bring her as close as her bulk would allow. Birthing was a dangerous time for any woman. Harold never failed to worry when her labour came nearer, but as Edyth said, after that first birth, her children had all come out into the world without difficulty. "I have always welcomed the Christmas festival and the birthing of a new year. Putting the old behind, looking forward to new beginnings." And there was much to set aside from this last year, so many changes to accept in place.

"Christmas?" Edyth queried with a snort of impatience. "Christmas means winter. Short, dark, cold days and bitter winds. Chilled fingers and toes, rain and snow. Bellyache from overeating…and the pleasure of attending court."

"Aye, well, all that too." He darted a quick, boyish grin at her, his mouth slightly lopsided, the only residue of the illness that had stricken him so long ago. "I enjoy being with my family, Christmas or no." He kissed her forehead. "I enjoy being with you. Especially when we are alone," he added mischievously, kissing her again, more firmly.

She responded as always, her mouth parting. His smell of leather and horse and wine was familiar and comforting, his muscular body reassuring. Protective. Everything was so safe when Harold was nearby. His hands wandered from her enlarged waist to her breasts, caressing her neck and face, pulling her closer, his mouth more insistent.

"They say you must be gentle with a woman who is with child," Edyth reminded him as he began unlacing her gown.

"I am always gentle. With any woman," he answered with a hint of indignation.

She pulled back, her palms going to his chest. "Oh, yes? You have made love with many women then, have you?"

Harold bent and lifted her, swinging her up into his arms with ease. His body was lean and strong, his arms and shoulders well muscled, the skin still bearing a light tan from the summer sun and the autumn winds. He carried her to their bed, set her down and methodically began unlacing the remaining ties to her gown and the shift beneath.

"Only one or two women," he answered her at last, before removing his own clothing, discarding it haphazardly on the floor. "Only one in particular, though."

❦

Waking, with the pleasurable sensation of her naked body nestled warm and close to his own, Harold lay listening to the sounds of a stirring household. Someone was singing a carol, the girl's pleasing voice ruined by the old mule braying for his breakfast; clatter came from the kitchens as the cooks began preparing for the first meal of the day and the evening ahead of feasting. A robin sang from the oak tree where Harold had built the elder children a lookout platform—from up there, they could see along this whole stretch of the valley. The shining white newness of the rising walls of his abbey at Waltham, the meadows below the purple grey of the ridged hills and the wide, meandering ribbon that was the river. He would miss all this if they were to move into the manor at Bosham. A grander estate but the home of childhood. This manor belonged to his adult life, a testament to his own happiness. He had purchased the land, discussed the design, observed its building. Edyth had furnished it, made it their home. Bosham was for the harvesting of Gytha's memories, not for his.

Harold brushed his hand tenderly against Edyth's cheek as she stirred from sleep. "Willow-bud?" He touched her hair, allowing a strand of its sun-gold length to trickle through his fingers. "I am thinking that I do not want to leave here. That I do not welcome the thought of residing at Bosham."

Clinging to the last fragments of sleep, Edyth snuggled her head into his shoulder. So much had changed for him, for her, since Easter. To take up the mantle of the most powerful man in all England below the King was no easy task. Edyth knew Harold appreciated the honour of being made Earl of Wessex, for he was full of pride in his country and its people. He accepted those responsibilities that fell to him, but still he doubted his ability to mix diplomacy with authority as carefully as had his father. Edward was no easy man to contend with. Although he had mellowed since Godwine's death, his inattentiveness and distraction from government was markedly increased. Content to leave decisions to his earls and Council, the brunt of the work fell on Harold's overburdened shoulders.

"Do you not think that you ought be in Wessex?" she asked tactfully, while suppressing the jiggle of delight. The manor was her home, the place of her children's birth and growing, of her love with Harold. Bosham would be the place for his wife when one day he took one.

"I will need to spend some time there, but I am as much in London these days as I am in Wessex. Here, with you, I can forget the King and his inconsistencies, my sister and her brazen autocracy."

Edyth gave a non-committal sigh. The Queen's problem was a simple one to fathom, harder to solve. "She needs a child to care for."

Harold snorted. "Edith now panders to Edward's every whim. He behaves more like a child every day. He shows no care of interest in law or government, for matters of court or state. His only interests are how the scent is lying and how high are the walls of his damned abbey!" Harold's feelings for Edward were ambivalent. As a man—a neighbour perhaps—they could have shared the pleasures of the chase and a farmer's concern for the turn of the seasons. But as a king Edward was frustratingly simple-minded. He was a follower, not a leader. Had there been anyone else as choice of king, he would never have been crowned. Like it or not, however, he was an anointed king, blessed by the hand of God—outside murder, only God could remove him.

Edyth snuggled herself closer. "Perhaps Edward too needs a child."

Aye, or another Robert Champart to hold his hand.

The prospect of a pleasing morning withered. On the morrow, Harold would leave for London; this day, Christmas Eve, was to be his last day with his family for several weeks. Edyth would not be coming with him to Westminster for she disliked the clamour and smell of London. Even had she journeyed to Southwark, he would see little of her or the children, for there was a rising mountain of problems to be discussed during the coming days of Council. Gryffydd ap Rhydderch had begun a campaign of raiding across the Severn river—they would need to sort that annoying bastard with more than threats of reprisal before too many months passed—and King Macbeth in Scotland was posing a problem for Siward in Northumbria. Macbeth had been a boil waiting to be lanced since he had first usurped the throne from Duncan, he and Gruoch, his scheming wife. They were a troublesome lot, the Scots and Welsh.

And then there were the boys held in Normandy, Harold's brother and nephew. Negotiations for their release had ground to a halt. Duke William had no intention of surrendering such useful hostages. Short of declaring war on Normandy, there was little England could do to demand their return.

Above all else, the matter of Edward's succession must be decided—England could not be left vulnerable. With an empty throne a free-for-all would most certainly develop, whatever the present hindrances tying the hands of ambitious men. Edward was no longer a young man and death could creep in from the shadows with no sound or warning—no one had expected Godwine to be taken so quickly from them.

Who was there to follow Edward? Ralf de Mantes, as much a weakling as Edward. William of Normandy? Harold instantly dismissed that thought as absurd. One of the named earls? In an earlier time, perhaps, in those harsh, uncivilised days when the law was made by the sword and a man held no honour for his pledged word. Now no one person would receive the level of support required to overthrow Edward. If one earl decided to forcibly take a crown, then would the others not want also to try it for size? A bloody civil war would be the only end to that path.

What of other outsiders? Norway? Denmark? No, they were too preoccupied with their own fight for survival to glance elsewhere.

The possibilities drifted into Harold's mind, dancing there much as the dust particles were shimmering in the widening shaft of sunlight streaking in a narrow spear-shaft through the shutter and across the floor. Edith had ordered Boulogne's grandson back to Normandy, although Harold had thought to use him in exchange for Wulfnoth. Edith detested the child, and had used the general feeling against Norman blood as an excuse to be rid of him when Godwine had returned from exile. Fearing reprisal from his hand, most of the Normans had fled. What fools and cowards they were, imagining whetted blades drawn against them in every shadow! Champart, by fleeing so suddenly from London, had been responsible for starting the rumour; Edith, sending Boulogne's grandson hard on his heels, had not calmed the fears. Would his father have taken revenge on Edward's Norman friends? On Champart, probably, but for the rest, Harold doubted it. Godwine had not been a vindictive man, and Ralf de Mantes, with Norman blood in his veins from his father and maternal grandmother, had not been harmed or threatened, was indeed a trusted friend of Harold's.

Edyth was tracing a path through Harold's chest hair with her fingernail. "What of Edmund Ironside, Æthelred's son by his wife before Emma? Has there not yet been word of his sons' whereabouts? As grandsons of Æthelred, they are the closest kin to Edward. Is it not time they were found and brought home?"

The two infant sons of King Edmund, exiled from England after his death six and thirty years past. Tentative searches had been made for them when Edward had first claimed his crown, but no word of their whereabouts came back on traders' lips, despite the offer of generous reward. Hardly surprising, as it had been no secret that Cnut had wanted them dead. What assurance was there, when Edward had first become king, that he did not intend the same fate for them? The situation was different now that Edward had no son or brother. A son of the royal line of Alfred, Ædward the Exile or his brother, both sons of Edmund, grandsons of Æthelred. There would be no disputing that claim.

"Henry of Germany may know of something. Normandy and Flanders are shut to us, now that Edward's French friends have scuttled like beetles beneath the stones. Nor would it be of use asking Harald Hardrada of Norway or Svein of Denmark—either would as lief find the two for themselves and carry out Cnut's order of murder." Harold trickled his fingers across her breast and stomach. "Council though," he crooned, "will need find the solutions. For the immediate future, the Earl of Wessex has more personal matters to attend."

Part Two

Fight for Tears

I

Mortemar—February 1054

King Henry of France, realising he personally had little to gain and much to lose by continuing the war against Geoffrey Martel, comte d'Anjou, had ordered a reconciliation to be made. William of Normandy had flatly refused. Victory had been his at Alençon and Domfront, the power of the Bellême family had been incorporated into his vassalage, and Martel was on the verge of being broken, but Henry decided to dictate peace terms! William had poured scorn on the proposal and had stormed out of the French court without leave, in a vile temper. In furious retaliation, Henry of France turned about face and allied with Geoffrey against Normandy. William was not best pleased, but neither was he distraught. Henry had given an excuse for him to pursue, at last, his freedom and autonomy.

With the levies from the north-west of France mustered at Mantes Henry entered Normandy through the region of the Évreçin, while from the north-east, with troops under the command of William's brother Odo and Rainauld, comte de Cleremont, the Duke launched a formidable campaign of pillage, slaughter and destruction. The size of Normandy's immediate response was unexpected. Had Henry been hoping that the landowning nobility of upper Normandy would not, when it came to it, take that last step into treason? If he had then he was to be disappointed. William had mustered a force large enough to counterattack from both the eastern and western sides of the Seine. Normandy, as a whole, had decided to shed vassalage to France.

The February air was cold, frost whitening men's breath into steam clouds as they huddled beneath cloaks and blankets around fires that gave out little warmth. Tree, branch, fence, barn—whatever came to hand was torn down and burnt, the many spirals of dark smoke rising to blend with the melancholy grey of a low and brooding winter cloud. Daylight at this time of year was brief; a tiresome season for fighting.

Before Henry had so enraged him, William had no inclination to seek independence for Normandy from France, but his decision was forced. Capitulate to Henry's dictation or become his own lord? If he could keep his nerve and the loyalty of those who followed him…the notion flourished and, as he had hoped, not in his own mind alone. During the years of rebellion he had proven himself to those men who admired his resolute determination and courage. Normandy was a young country, planted and nurtured by Viking settlers a few generations beforehand. Autonomy and audacity were in the blood of her sons, as was respect for a man's success in battle. A man whose star was rising, bright and savage. Who showed, from the very first, a natural ability to rule and lead.

Such a man was William. Ruthless in revenge, compassionate in forgiveness. He calculated his response to every situation calmly, and deliberately combined leniency with ferocity. His temper was more dangerous than a mid-winter storm, but he was also fair in judgement and generous to those who served him loyally. The lords of Normandy had no respect for a man who altered allegiance on the whim of a cold-blowing wind, even if that man was the King of France Capable men such as Roger de Montgomery, Hugh de Gourney, Ralph de Tosny and Robert, comte d'Eu, elected to stand firm behind their duke. With them ranged Walter Gifford, William fitz Osbern, Roger de Mortemar and William de Warenne. Duke William they would serve and no other.

William's tent was little warmer than the winter air outside, despite several braziers and a scatter of furs on the floor. The Duke barely noticed the cold—what mattered chilled fingers and chilblained toes when tomorrow all of Normandy could be lost to him? He stood at the central table, hands spread over the map unrolled before him, concentrating on the inked lines that depicted Normandy, his mind on what was happening to the other side of that squiggled emblem that represented the river Seine, where Robert d'Eu was leading his troops against the approaching western attack under the French King's brother.

Murmuring quietly among themselves and rubbing surreptitiously at frozen hands, his noble lords and officers watched his intense stillness. They would have been surprised to have been privy to his thoughts at that moment.

A messenger had arrived an hour after dawn, bearing a letter from the Duchess Mathilda. At first William had been disappointed for he was desperately awaiting an encouraging word from d'Eu; however, a flicker of contentment had passed over his expression as his private clerk had read his wife's words to him. He had a daughter, of good weight and health, fair-haired and blue-eyed. Agatha, she was to be called.

He was thinking, not of battles and warfare, but of his daughter. He would enjoy having a little girl to curl her fingers around his and smile and gurgle at him. Who would grow to love and respect him as a daughter ought adore her father. He had a son, but he did not much like Robert. An ugly, loathsome child, continuously mewling and puking. Mathilda doted on the boy; perhaps now she also had a daughter he would not be so frivolously cosseted. William looked forward to watching her grow into a woman as beautiful as his own mother had been; counts or dukes or kings would seek her hand, a strategic alliance would be formed…but not if Normandy lost everything to Henry of France, if all was lost on the opposite side of the Seine, where the armies would be meeting somewhere near Mortemar.

If Normandy fell Mathilda would return to her father in Flanders. The children would be safe under his protection. No doubt she would find herself another husband…William's clenched fist thundered down on to the map. "I will not give ground to the whims of bloody France!" he roared. "Normandy is mine—as it is yours. Does Henry think we are feared of him? Does he think we are going to run squealing and whimpering from the poxed whoresons of his army?"

Enthusiastically they echoed his certainty, his courage, William fitz Osbern, Roger de Montgomery…the leather hanging covering the tent entrance flapped backwards as an officer of the guard stepped through, ushering a grime-faced messenger before him. The men within the tent turned as one to stare. The messenger bore the emblem of Robert d'Eu on his shoulder.

For a long moment no one spoke, moved, or barely drew breath.

William could feel his body trembling, a myriad diffuse thoughts tumbling and churning through his mind. He closed his eyes in a swift prayer, stepped forward, his hand stretching out to take the roll of parchment from the messenger's hand. If they noticed it shook, he did not care…he took it, gazed at the seal of Robert, comte d'Eu. His fingers snapped the wax seal. He stared at the dull black ink scrambling across the parchment in mystical loops, circles and lines. For this one moment William wished that he had been taught to read, to see for himself what had happened those few miles away across the river at Mortemar…

"Sir?" The cleric was there at his side, his hand reaching to take the letter. William gave it to him and turned abruptly on his heel, stalked to the far side of the tent, poured himself wine, drank it in one gulp.

The cleric read hurriedly, a smile touching the edge of his lips, broadening to a grin and a rousing shout of delight. "My Lord Duke! Sir! Mortemar is won! Henry's brother has fled, his troops slaughtered or dispersed. Guy de Ponthieu is captured."

"And that is not all!" Ralph de Tosny was ducking through the opening behind the messenger, the edge of his cloak glistening from frost, his breath coming fast as if he had been running. "Henry has received word of the defeat before us—he is withdrawing." Ralph crossed the tent in a few brief strides and knelt before his duke. "You have won victory over France, my Lord!"

A cheer erupted from those within the tent, except from William. He again closed his eyes in prayer, released the breath that he had not realised he had been holding. Opening his eyes, he allowed a smile of satisfaction to slide over his clean-shaven face. He would initiate a reconciliation with Henry, with terms advantageous to himself and those who had shown their loyalty.

He held out his hand to de Tosny, who touched his lips to the ducal ring. The fighting would not be over, for there would always be someone who wanted something from the Duke and no doubt Henry himself, once his wounds were licked, would try again to destroy Normandy's young duke.

William tossed back his head and laughed. He could try, but by God, he would not succeed!

2

York

In his earl's palace in York, the capital of the North, Siward, Earl of Northumbria, lay bed-bound, the curtaining pulled close on the side of the bed where the cold of a north-east wind persisted in breaching the shuttered windows. He had sustained a wound to his knee at the battle of Dunsinane fighting against that whore-poxed Macbeth of Scotland, a wound that had festered. He was dying, and had no son of age to follow him as earl, for his eldest had been slain at that same fight, an axe taking his head from his shoulders in one swift and terrible blow. Victory. Huh, what price victory? So Macbeth was defeated and fled into the northern isles, Malcolm, Duncan's son, was returned with England's aid as king of that cursed country, but for Siward Scotland was most certainly cursed.

There was no one to follow him now. Waltheof, son of his second wife, was too young, a four-year-old child. There was no one else of Siward's blood to take over the care of these desolate but beautiful moorlands of laughing rivers, swirling hill mist and singing wind.

York had been an important city long before the Vikings had taken it for their own. Roman armies had once lived here within its stone defences. The incoming English Saxons had used its waterways for sea trade several hundred years before the Norse adopted the city, named it Jorvik and expanded it into the second-largest settlement in all England.

To the head of the King's Highway in Conig Street, one of the few York roads to retain its Saxon name, Earl Siward had built his stronghold, from where he had ruled for almost forty years.

Of Viking birth, Cnut had appointed him as guardian of the volatile North—as Godwine had been selected for the South. He had been the right man, had bridged the gap between the established wealth of the South and the independent freedom of the North, a vast, rolling area of wild land that had once, not so long ago, been a kingdom in its own right, with its unique identity, where a dialect that was peppered with Scandinavian sound changes and meaning was unintelligible to many Southerners.

Siward breathed a long sigh. It would not be many more days before God sent his warrior angels to escort an old soldier up into heaven. His wife sat close beside the bed, her head bent over a tangle that had knotted the thread of her drop spindle. She looked up at the sound of his sigh and set her spinning aside. There was no disgust in her face at the smell of wasting flesh, no reluctance to be near or to touch her lord. She was a young woman in the full-blossomed beauty of youth and Siward she loved beyond life itself. She rinsed a linen cloth in a bowl of rose-petal water and wiped his face.

Catching her hand clumsily within his own, Siward stopped her. "You are to go with our son to Edward when I am gone. He will see you safe kept."

"Hush, husband, you may yet become well."

Movement was difficult for his body was swollen and contorted, but Siward lifted his hand to caress her cheek. "I am for God, my dear-heart. I will be happy to meet him when I am certain that you and Waltheof will come to no harm. Take care of the boy, for he must become earl one day when he is grown. Tell Edward this, that Siward, who has served with all faith, would see his son as protector of the North."

Who would be earl after him? Most likely Ælfgar would be moved from East Anglia, Leofric's sour-tempered son of a cur. One of Godwine's brood would be the only alternative—but as fair-minded as was Earl Harold, that clan held over-much ambition for England already. Ah, it was not his problem to worry on. The fate of Northumbria lay in the hand of God, as did his own.

"I would be dressed in my armour when the time draws near, and stood on my feet," he said. "I would meet my God as a warrior ought, not lying idle abed. And after, I would be taken to the church of my founding, at Saint Olafs to the north-west wall of this dear city. Perhaps there I shall be remembered for some short while."

"None shall forget you, my Lord."

Siward patted her hand. Let her believe it so if she chose. Few, save for those who had loved them, remembered the dead once they had passed on.

The woman struggled in vain to contain her tears. She could not face life without his gentleness, had already decided that Waltheof would indeed go to the King, but not she. She would be going with her lord, for it was too bitter a thing to remain without him. And it would be a bitter thing for this ancient kingdom of Northumbria to lose such a man.

Siward died as he had asked, dressed in his armour and standing on his feet, as the first snows of winter fell with a quiet hush over the night-darkened moors. Within a day his wife followed him, the blood let from her wrists after the four-year-old boy had been set within the arms of his nurse, surrounded by the protection of an armed escort and sent south, to Westminster.

Would peace have settled on Siward's departing soul had he known King Edward's choice for his successor?

With Champart gone Edward, in his boredom and despair, had sought entertainment and distraction and found both within an unexpected blossoming of friendship. Tostig and his wife were often at court, preferring the company of his sister, the queen, to that of his mother or brothers. Tostig was unlike the rest of his family. He frowned on an excess of drink or women, condemned ribaldry and foul language.

Edward began to like Tostig Godwinesson and his piety, and that liking, as once it had for Robert Champart, soon developed into something more like a dependancy. To Tostig, therefore, at the King's command, went the highest honour below Wessex. Tostig was given Northumbria.

3

Westminster—March 1055

Edith brushed a speck of fluff from the shoulder of her brother's cloak, stood back a pace to admire him. Tostig was a handsome man, full-faced, fair-haired and blue-eyed—as were all Godwine's offspring. His chin was firm and square, his shoulders broad above a strong chest with muscular arms. Of all her brothers, Edith loved Tostig the most.

"You look splendid!" she declared with pride, flicking her eye critically for a second time over the formality of his attire. "The apparel of an earl suits you well." She turned to smile at Tostig's wife. "You are fortunate to have such a fine man as husband, Judith. My one regret is that you will soon be leaving court now that Easter is upon us." Her happiness faded to a wail of dismay. "I doubt that I will come and visit you in that wilderness that is the North. They say that the wind blows all the time and that the populace is almost as uncivilised as the Welsh." Edith shuddered, rubbing her arms against the fearful thought of both evils.

Judith laughed, moving forward to cheerfully embrace her sister-in-law. They were devoted friends, these two childless women.

"Our winters we shall spend here with you—and for the summer, there is a fine residence at York, a city, I have been told, which boasts a minster and several churches."

"Oh, indeed," Edith agreed, admiring her sister-in-law's fortitude. "With also a rabble of foreign traders and an abominable stink from the poor quarter and the muck that clogs the waterways."

"So we will feel most at home." Tostig laughed. "'Twill be no different from the midden heap that is London. It is no use, my dear, I cannot put off going into my earldom any longer. Winter is not a time for riding northwards, but now that the catkins are dangling from the trees I must soon be away."

His pleasantry was to some degree faked, for he too had heard nothing good of the barbarian North—even the language was apparently unintelligible. But to counter his ill-ease, he was full of pride for his promotion—how long had he waited for such reward? And to get Northumbria for his own...! He would make a good earl, would rule with wisdom and a firmer hand than that old fool Siward. There was much to be done. Siward had turned too much of a blind eye to the blood feuds, murder, theft and highway robbery. That might be their way in the North, but it was not Tostig's. It would stop. Northumbria would, like it or not, become civilised, would benefit from the enforcement of the King's law. Siward had been old, set in the lawless ways of the past.

Settling his cloak more comfortably on his shoulder, Tostig touched his fingers to the diamond and ruby glitter of the cloak pin. Earl! He understood his brother Harold's pride in the title now—but equally, he puzzled over his brother's absurd leniency in matters of the law. Harold argued that to punish lesser crimes with harshness left little with which to punish those who deserved more severity. Remove a hand for stealing an apple from a tree—then what could be meted for stealing gold from a king? A whipping for the one, mutilation for the other, that would be Harold's choice. Tostig preferred to punish minor misdemeanours with a hard hand, so that fear would deter the more serious crime. Hah! Within the turn of the year he would most assuredly prove Harold wrong.

"So," he said, running his hand over the delicious feel of the marten fur. "For the first time I am to take my seat at Council as an earl. I confess that there has been occasion when I despaired of receiving such honour."

When Godwine had died and Ælfgar was installed as Earl of East Anglia, for instance. Tostig had felt that Harold ought to have remained there and he himself awarded Wessex. Although he was the younger, he was the more dedicated to duty and God, the more insistent on the letter of the law—and the harder-working of the two. Or if Harold must have been given Wessex, why had Anglia gone to Ælfgar, an idle, ineffective wastrel, more often than not drunk?

"It was only a matter of patience, brother," Edith said. "I have always wanted you as earl, but in the right place and position. Once Siward was gone..." She crossed herself, murmuring a brief prayer for the old man's departed soul. They never talked at court of the paganism that had surrounded his dying. To be dressed in his armour indeed! The old Viking way? Was it any wonder the North under Siward had remained so backward?

Brother and sister walked, arm linked through arm, along the echoing corridors to the Council chamber of Westminster Palace. Long and narrow, the chamber brooded beneath a high, vaulted roof of carved rafters that soared above plastered walls painted with scenes of past glory. The coming of Hengest and Horsa into Kent with their three keels; Saint Augustine at Canterbury;

King Alfred defeating the Danes; behind the King's raised dais, the hand of God stretching down to touch the emblazoned banner of England. The entirety of Westminster was designed to impress, occasionally at the expense of comfort, but Edith was as proud of her royal domain as was Edward. Lavish and ostentatious, it had become a place of absolute monarchy, where, beneath the King, Edith could now strut supreme. How things had changed since that terrible year of 1052!

Guards stamped to attention as she and Tostig, followed by their retinue of servants, passed by. As always the palace was busy, an administrative town in its own right, the length of maze-worked corridors always a-bustle with men about urgent business. Tostig, being a son of Godwine, had been used to respect, but now he was an earl, the bowed heads and nods of courtesy suffused him with pleasure. Aye, long had he waited for this day!

Meeting Earl Ælfgar face to face inside the open doorway to the chamber dampened his euphoria, as if iced water had been poured over his head. The man scowled a glower of hatred, looking Tostig up and down as if he were a swineherd. Dipping his head but slightly to the Queen, Ælfgar turned aside, pushed his way with surly rudeness through the crowd of men and disappeared out into the corridor beyond. Several eyebrows were raised, a few muttered comments exchanged. Tostig would not have been their first choice to become the warden of the North, but he was infinitely preferable to that bad-mannered churl Ælfgar.

Escorting his sister to her throne in the forefront, Tostig took his place on a bench, beside Earl Ralf de Mantes of Hereford, setting his cloak with care so he might not crush its fine making. Ralf noted the apparel and smiled to himself Tostig had a right to revel in this, his first taste of pomp and ceremony. All too soon the shine would tarnish.

Rapping the stone floor three times with his staff, a herald announced the coming of the King. All who were seated rose, speech rustled to a halt and Edward, escorted by eight of his housecarls, entered in full regalia. If the King's nephew assumed that Earl Tostig would soon tire of the panoply of ceremony, then Edward most certainly had not.

"Where are my Earls of Wessex and East Anglia?" the King asked, his voice echoing against the stone of the walls. "Did I not see your sour-tempered son striding away but moments past, Lord Leofric?"

Leofric was ageing, his joints ached and his sight and hearing were not so sharp as once they had been. Ah, age was a thing that crept up with more stealth than a huntsman pursuing a doe with fawn at foot. And his son was more of a disappointment now than he had ever been. Leofric sighed. "I know not where he has gone, Sire, nor why." Did not add that he did not much care.

Edward shrewdly regarded Tostig, then questioned Edith with his eyes. She told him what she wished to know. "Harold, Earl of Wessex, sends word that he has been delayed—that he will be here by noon on the morrow. As for the Earl of East Anglia, I conclude that he has no wish to be seated with our dear brother Earl Tostig. He is intent on pursuing this quarrel against your choice of promotion."

"Is he indeed!" Edward exclaimed. "Then he must think again." Turning to the captain of his guard, he ordered, "Fetch him here. I would have Lord Ælfgar attend my Council!" Then, seating himself, Edward granted permission for his lords and nobles to follow suit. With some coughing and talk, the men settled their backsides on the wooden benches; only those who had the foresight had brought cushions.

They waited ten minutes, fifteen.

Earl Leofric sat with shoulders slumped, anger beginning to override his embarrassment. At least God had spared his dear wife Godgiva this humiliation, for she had been taken to His bosom three months since. How her spirit must be weeping at the foolishness of their only surviving son!

The captain returned and spoke to Edward, who erupted from his chair in volcanic anger. "How dare he! How dare the cur disobey my order! Where is he now? Gone to his private room, you say? Well remove him! Remove him from my palace and from my kingdom. He is banished, I send him into exile, damn his insolence!"

The murmur of astonishment swelled to a clatter of approval. Few men present felt sympathy for the idiocy of the man. Ælfgar had precipitated his own sentence of exile by persisting with this hostile warfare against the Godwinessons. Good riddance to him. England would be the better without his stormy tempers, bad manners and foul language.

4

Bosham

The rain fell in a vertical curtain, so heavy that the view across the deserted
courtyard was almost obliterated. Edward closed the shutter with an exaggerated sigh of boredom. He had ridden south to Bosham for the purpose of
hunting, but until this rain—so unseasonable for May—ceased he would not set
foot outside. He sighed again as he turned away from the window and strolled
across the chamber, his lips puffing, arms folded. Everyone else was content, but
then, everyone else had something of interest to do.

This new upper chamber that Harold had built here at Bosham, Edward had
to concede, was a most pleasant room, A first-floor solar giving views—huh,
when there was a view—through four narrow windows of thick but small-
paned glass overlooking the sea. It seemed remarkable, he thought, as he glanced
about the recently completed chamber, that Godwine had never thought to
extend his manor upwards into this more elegant and fashionable residence. But
then Godwine always had been one for sticking like mud to the old, outdated
ways. It must have cost Harold much in gold to have the manor rebuilt to such
a fine standard. Bosham, Edward thought morosely, was more like a palace than
a manor.

"They say," Edward announced across the room to Harold, "that you are now
almost as wealthy as myself."

"Then 'they' are remarkably—but incorrectly—informed of private knowledge
that is not 'their' concern." Harold answered lightly, masking his annoyance. He
doubted that Edward intended to be rude quite so often, but the man expressed
himself so unfortunately, was so tactless, that he invariably set hackles rising.

Impervious to the signs of his host's irritation, Edward plunged on in his familiar querulous whine. "Your taxable assets reach almost two thousand pounds, I
believe. My own are scarcely more."

"Did you know a slave-woman is expected to feed herself through a harsh
winter on only three pennies?" Countess Gytha, seated on the opposite side of

the cheerfully glowing hearth fire, glanced up from her embroidery, aiming to turn the conversation to more general discussion.

"As much as that?" her daughter answered scathingly. "Half would be adequate, surely." She stood before the table by the wall surrounded by her clerk, two masons and an architect, the proposed plans for her rebuilding of Wilton Nunnery spread before them.

"Oh, do you think so, dear?" There were occasions when Gytha despaired of her daughter's lack of compassion for those less fortunate than herself. God knew she had tried to instil it into her throughout childhood, but the girl had always been wilful and selfish. Harold and Edyth kept rein on their only daughter who, at eight, understood her manners. Her son Gyrth's two young maids were also delightful children. With a grandmother's pride she smiled at the group of grandchildren playing a boisterous ball and skittle game at the far end of the chamber, and laid her embroidery on to her lap to applaud as Algytha scored full points by toppling all six "men." The girl's yell of triumph and the echoing cheer from her brothers filled the room.

Queen Edith glowered at them. She had a headache and was trying to concentrate on what this fool of an architect was blathering about. It was all very well for Harold's woman to allow the children in here, but their noise was becoming tedious.

"Did you see, Papa?" Algytha trotted to her father's side, raising her arms for him to lift her. "Am I not clever?"

"You certainly are, my sweeting, but look, your young cousin Alfgiva has knocked one over too!"

"One!"

"She is four years old, half your age, one is an achievement." Harold set his daughter down with a laugh and patted her backside as she went to rejoin her brothers and cousins. Gyrth's other daughter, Gunnhild, a year senior to her sister, took her turn with the ball, screamed in frustration as she missed the target.

"For the sake of God!" Edith snapped. "Can we not have some peace in here?"

Like Gytha, Harold's wife Edyth was enjoying watching the children. Considering the enforced confinement from the rain, they were all behaving well—but it wouldn't last. She tucked her needle into the woollen sock she had been darning and set her work into the basket by her feet. "I will take them below," she said, rising and ushering the youngsters to her side. "We can play better in the aisle of the storeroom." She held her hands out to the younger girls, asking Goddwin and Edmund to collect up the gaming pieces.

"Could we set the men as a real army?" Goddwin queried as he tucked the wooden skittle pegs beneath his arm, his brother Edmund, five, solemnly holding the wooden ball between his clasped hands.

"I should think so—battle formation, perhaps a defensive wedge or a cavalry square? What think you?" Edyth's voice drifted down the stairwell, the eager chatter of the children following in her wake like white-maned waves behind a full-sailed keel.

Gytha, too, set aside her sewing to go with her daughter-in-law. Edyth's presence among the family when Edward and Edith were guests was always fraught with embarrassment, for neither accorded her more than the minimum politeness. There was little their frosty reticence could achieve. Edyth was established as Harold's consort, and Gytha was never averse to showing, in subtle ways, her approval of the sweet-natured woman who, although she was reluctant to admit it, brought more joy than did her own daughter, for all she had achieved the acclaim of a queen's crown.

The chamber settled. A log hissed in the fire-grate, a blue-green flame dancing along the bark. Outside, and on the roof, the rain drummed, the occasional drip finding a way down through the two smoke holes in the apex.

Edward sat, his toes perched on the hearth, playing a simple finger game, matching each corresponding fingertip to its opposite partner, gaining speed with each round. When would it be time to eat? That would create some diversion, not that he was hungry and his stomach had been upset again these past few days. If only Tostig were here, there would be better conversation, Tostig was well gifted with the telling of amusing tales, was informed on so many subjects that Edward never tired of debating with him. He missed Tostig. A pure young man, fair of face and manner; had it really been a wise decision to send him north? If he had given it to Ælfgar or one of the others of the Godwine brood, then Tostig would be more often at court...Edward missed the mark with his fingers, tutted with frustration and refolded his arms, tucking the offending digits beneath his armpits. Ælfgar. Why had he thought of that wretched whelp?

"And how do we set our real army then, my Earl of Wessex? What of Wales and Ælfgar? May the devil take his hide and balls!"

Wales, a country of uncivilised, godless warmongers. Wales, a wretched land of mountains and fog; of rain and mud and lakes, goblins and hags and fire-breathing dragons. Few Englishmen held an unbiased picture of the Welsh, the King being no exception.

"The situation raises as many concerns now as when we discussed it at the

Easter Council, my Lord," Harold remarked, carefully choosing his words. Strange that he too had been pondering the difficult question of Wales.

In the early spring, Gruffydd ap Llewelyn, Prince of Gwynedd and Powys, had swept southwards into Deheubarth and, with apparent ease, killed his long-term opponent Gryffydd ap Rhydderch. Gwynedd now ruled all of Wales, a situation that posed a threat to the English border lands. Already Gruffydd had attempted a few minor raids on Shrewsbury and Hereford, and now that Ælfgar, exiled for his rudeness to the King, had allied himself with Wales...there was no under-standing the man. It surprised Harold to admit that he felt sympathy for Leofric, Ælfgar's father. He had always been a bitter opponent to the Godwines, but Harold knew the misery a traitorous son could cause a family. God's patience, but Gruffydd himself had slaughtered Leofric's own brother and his wife's father back in 1039! Ælfgar was fighting alongside the murderer of close kindred in these tediously repetitive raids across the Severn river.

"Would it be prudent to consider calling up the fyrd and marching on Wales in a counter raid?" Harold had tried suggesting this before, had already encoun-tered the prompt and curt answer.

"No. I cannot afford to pay for such an army, not at the moment." Edward was walking around the room again. "Would it not be better to pardon Ælfgar and allow him home? You ought never have quarrelled with him in the first place, Harold."

"He did not, husband," Edith interjected. Her headache, despite the children leaving, was worsening, her patience withering. "The quarrel was with Tostig, not Harold, because you sent our brother into Northumbria."

"Yes, yes," said Edward tetchily, knowing she was right. "I regret giving him that earldom now. If Tostig were not in the North, we would not be in this cursed awkward situation."

The Queen was as aghast at Edward's statement as was Harold, for differ-ent reasons. Edith needed the North kept within the family's control. With Harold overseeing the South, Wessex and parts of Herefordshire, Gyrth now proclaimed Earl of East Anglia in place of the disgraced Ælfgar and Tostig in Northumbria, only Mercia lay outside their influence...and Leofric was aged and ill. With Leofwine yet to come to an earldom, it was only a matter of time before all England came under the jurisdiction of the Godwine sons. Then let Edward ever try to set her aside! Not that he would, not now—but Edith was determined to ensure that he could never again publicly slight her.

She retorted, "With Tostig sorting out the disgraceful lawlessness that has been left to fester in the North by that old fool Siward, we at least have peace in that quarter. Had you given Northumbria to Ælfgar, who knows what chaos he and these Welsh friends of his would now be causing."

In that sense Harold agreed with her, but whether Tostig was actually bringing peace and prosperity to the northern moorlands…ah, but he was new to the career of earl, had yet to develop tact and diplomacy, and besides, there was Wales to consider at this moment. The North must look to itself for a while.

Edward sniffed, annoyed at Edith's censure. His throat was dry, beginning to ache, and his eyes were watering. All this atrocious wet weather was starting another head cold; no doubt he would be laid in bed for the next few weeks nursing a fever. What was the wager that the rain would then clear and the weather turn suitable for hunting?

"I did not mean that I did not want Tostig as earl," Edward grumbled. "I meant if Tostig were here, we would not be shuttered away bickering with each other. He amuses me. No one else bothers much with their king's entertainment. It's all war and fighting, tax and coinage." He waved an impatient hand at Harold who had been about to speak. "Yes, yes, I know I have to decide on a new minting of coin of the realm. I have not forgotten."

Edith closed her eyes in exasperation. Really, Edward was becoming more obtuse and perverse with each passing day. She selected a scroll of parchment from the table at random, spread it between her hands and, studying it briefly, nodded once, decisive. "This one," she said. "I will have this design for my renovation of Wilton."

Edward sauntered to stand beside her, inspecting the rough drawing. "Hmm, it seems appropriate. This window here, is it to be of glass?"

The architect scuttled to his side, eagerly answering, pointing with his fingers at the especial designs he had incorporated.

"If we do not act against Ælfgar and Wales soon," Harold said with quiet menace, "we may come to regret it."

No one was listening.

5

Hereford

When Harold had predicted an escalation of trouble along the Welsh border, he had spoken with the assurance of knowing the ill-tempered avarice of Ælfgar and the impetuous love of fighting of the Welsh. Gruffydd ap Llewelyn had no qualms about attacking the people whom his nation saw as foreign invaders, the Sassenach. The Saxon English had stolen the land of the British five centuries beforehand—and the Welsh had long memories. Even the term "Welsh" was anathema to Gruffydd and his people of the Cymry, an English word meaning foreigner. They needed no excuse to raid across the borders, but when one was so readily offered, why ignore it?

On 24 October in the year of Christ 1055, the King's nephew, Earl Ralf, had drawn his army into battle formation two miles from the border town of Hereford. Facing him, the combined forces of Ælfgar's mercenaries purchased from Ireland and the full ferocity of the Welsh. Before a single spear had been thrown, the Anglo-French cavalry that Ralf had taken so much pride in assembling had taken one horrified look at the mass of Celtic and Danish warriors, and fled. The Welsh that day had slaughtered almost five hundred of Hereford's remaining defenders, among them Ralf de Mantes, and then, before autumn darkness forced them to retreat homewards, had sacked the town with a glut lust of killing and looting.

Before the doors of the Cathedral of Saint Æthelberht the clergy were murdered, their throats cut as they vainly attempted to defend the sanctity of their church; the building was plundered, desecrated and set to the torch. Women and children who had not been able to flee were defiled and taken into slavery, the old men butchered. Such was Gruffydd's Welsh hatred and Ælfgar's English desire for revenge.

Beginning to rely on Harold as his second-in-command Edward summoned his Earl of Wessex to raise an immediate army. With the practised and organised expertise of the English administrative system, the fyrds of Gloucestershire, Devonshire, Somersetshire, Wiltshire, Hampshire, Sussex, Shropshire, Buckinghamshire and Oxfordshire joined the survivors of Herefordshire at Gloucester. As the burnished golds and flaming reds of autumn trees began to be tossed aside by the bluster of the first frost-tainted winter winds, Harold led the army across the river Severn and entered Wales. Only to find that the Welsh, with their accumulated booty of livestock, slaves and treasure, had faded into the rain-misted hills, the sole sign of their passing the trampled, winter-wet ground.

For three days Harold sat encamped with his men, scouts returning as dusk descended with dispirited, cheerless faces, cold and sodden to the bone. Nothing. No sign of occupied habitation or human life, only the track of hare, fox and deer, the plaintive cry of a solitary buzzard. Though eyes had been watching for certain.

Did they chance moving further into unknown territory and, undoubtedly, a laid trap? Or retreat? Harold did not much like the latter choice, but common sense was a powerful persuader. The army could advance, shambling around those cursed hills, become weaker from lack of food, dispirited by overtiredness, never seeing the ambushes until the death sting of an arrow or spear announced their hidden presence. How deep into Wales would Gruffydd dare lead them? For how long would he play his taunting waiting game?

No, Harold was not a man to fight in fruitless circumstances; the fyrd were only obliged to muster for so many consecutive days of a year, their commitment ought not be pointlessly wasted. Men's lives were too precious to squander on a face-saving disregard for practicality. Better to withdraw, attempt at suing for peace and wait for a more opportune moment to finish Gruffydd and his ally, the traitor Ælfgar.

Harold announced the order to break camp on the fourth morning. A heavy frost had hardened the ground overnight and the mature warmth of a late autumn was giving ground to winter's bite. With relief, the fighting men of the fyrd began to make their way home. Harold marched into Hereford with his housecarls and a few chosen regiments, leaving a suitable number to protect their rear should Gruffydd decide to come out from hiding. What they met in that devastated town sickened every man.

They rode in silence through the battered gates, which had been fired and rammed. The horses were uneasy, flicking their ears and snorting at the clinging scent. Fire had spread so quickly among the timber, thatch-roofed buildings which were close-built, wall touching wall. Where once the market streets ran in straight-laid patterns, charred beams and broken houses and shops lay in a higgle-piggle of debris, the acrid pall belligerently lingering over and through everything.

Some of those fortunate ones who had fled at the first alarm had returned in ragged groups. Women and children stood or sat dazed and silent, watching, almost aimlessly, as Harold and his men rode by. One man, his clothes torn and dirtied, stood before a heap of soot-blackened timber, head bowed. He lifted his head as Harold reined in.

"My wife was inside," he said. There was no emotion in his voice, his tone as blank as his eyes, "she was about the birthing of our fourth child. I had to leave her for the sake of the other children."

Harold nudged his stallion onwards, making no reply. What words could he offer? Words were futile—would they bring life back? Ease the horror, rebuild the devastation? As he rode, his fingers curled, tight, around the reins, his thoughts on Edyth and his own children. What choice would he have made? Abandon his woman to take the children to safety? Abandon them all to go, make a fight of it? Stay, and be killed with them? He swallowed hard to keep the vomit from rising higher into his throat, resisting the impulse to place his hand over nose and throat to mask the rancid smell of burnt flesh.

In the vicinity of the cathedral, virtually nothing was left standing. He dismounted slowly and stood, running his horse's reins through his fingers, trying not to look but seeing all too much.

What remained of the clergymen was blackened and twisted, unidentifiable save for a single sandalled foot and a charred, eyeless and flesh-peeled skull. To the left, what had been a coppersmith's shop—incongruous that, although fire-blistered and scorched, the painted sign of a copper jug still hung from a single standing post. Beneath, a pile of rubble. Harold turned away, closed his eyes, laid his forehead against his stallion's crested neck. A hand showed from beneath the charred beams, the fingers clutching at empty air. Somehow the flames had barely touched it.

A young child's pink and pudgy hand.

"My Lord? What do you wish us to do?" Brihtric Strongarm, Captain of Housecarls, spoke into Harold's ear, his voice tight. Older than his earl by almost fifteen years, he had witnessed many atrocities and seen much death in battle, but he too had seen that hand...

"He will answer for this, my friend," Harold vowed, clasping his fingers tight around Brihtric's muscular forearm. "By God, I swear that Gruffydd will one day pay for this day's work."

"And Ælfgar?" the Captain asked, the quietness of his words betraying the rage that quivered in his throat and belly. "Did he not play his part?"

Harold made no answer, but his hand moving to grip the pommel of his sword spoke eloquently enough.

Little could be done for Hereford. Town folk salvaged what they could as they drifted back from their places of hiding, setting temporary shelters among the rubble and soot, finding unburnt wood to kindle fires for cooking and warmth. Harold's men helped with the refortifying of the gates and the digging of a defensive ditch and earthworks. Some had wanted the cathedral cleared first, but Harold refused.

"God has compassion for His children. He knows we must offer hope and shelter to the living first. The needs of the spirit can be taken care of later."

He would see to it that corn and meal were sent to ease the immediate problem of hunger—from his own granaries if necessary. Word was sent also to the brothers from nearby monasteries to come and tend the sick and wounded. And, aye, do what they could for the shattered souls that needed to be cleansed of the horrors that had been witnessed.

6

Rouen—August 1056

Normandy was not at peace, but nearly so. While tempers rumbled over a miscellany of border quarrels, there was never any doubt now, after Val-ès-Dunes, Mortemar, Alençon and Domfront, that William's position and title of duke could not be challenged. The great families who controlled the estates of the duchy might still vie for land, but were almost all entwined into William's net of vassalage. He had not lost a single battle: to have the "luck of the Bastard" was already a common-used phrase. To share in that luck by being one of his sworn men was rapidly becoming the prerogative of many an aspiring noble.

One issue remained to irritate William, one that was beyond his control to rectify. No manner of siege or warfare was going to set it aright; this required diplomacy, patience and tact, three traits that were notably absent from William's authoritarian personality. Ralph de Tosny, while on a fashionable pilgrimage to Rome, had tried to help his lord, but he too had failed.

Duke William's marriage to Mathilda of Flanders had been emphatically forbidden by Pope Leo, ninth of that name. He had married her anyway, through sheer obstinacy. The Pope was interfering in politics for reasons of his own and William liked it not.

Negotiation to lift Rome's interdict moved with cumbersome slowness. De Tosny, a dutiful man of God, had attempted to contrive an interview with the Pope, but he had come from William and had not been granted audience.

With the toe of his boot, William kicked a log back on to the fire before it tumbled with a crackling belch of sparks and smoke from the edge. He had hoped that his new-found credibility after the victory at Mortemar might have influenced matters for the better. Apparently not.

"So," he asked of Ralph, "in all other respects, your pilgrimage was successful?"

"It was indeed, my Lord. Rome is a magnificent place. I could not begin to describe the splendours, the buildings, the history—"

"Yet no doubt you will!" Mathilda interrupted with a delightful laugh. "Your anecdotes will bore us grey-haired throughout the years to come. Whenever a wet day or deep snow keeps us confined to the hearth you will clear your throat and tell us of Rome."

Eighteen years of age and Mathilda had blossomed into a wife any man would be eager to take to his bed. Short and inclined to plumpness—caused by an enjoyment of foods sweetened with honey and a dislike of exercise—she was nevertheless a handsome woman, with straight white teeth, fair skin and hair, and a quick, pleasing wit that flashed as bright as her sparkling eyes. The bearing of three children and the carrying of a fourth had accentuated the thickening of her waistline, but William had often expressed, in the privacy of their bed, that he preferred a woman to be well-covered. "Give me an oak tree to build a sturdy barn, not an ash for flimsy fencing."

Some thought Mathilda to be haughty, others admired her for her fortitude, fairness and loyalty. That she was devoted to William, and he to her, was never doubted. Unusually William never strayed beyond the marriage bed, not in body, mind or eye. Some were adamant that such a ruthless man was incapable of any gentle emotion. A few jeered that his loyalty to the lady Mathilda was for her own ill-temper! Others made cruder references to his capabilities or inclinations…whatever the reason for his faithfulness, the marriage was successful and no damned Pope in Rome was going to rule otherwise!

William sipped thoughtfully at his wine. What more could he do to influence this implacable obstinacy? Already churches were being built, money pouring like wine from a cracked pot into the monasteries. The word of God was final in the law of the Church, and within Normandy William took care to ensure strict and direct control over the clergy.

Bishops—by coincidence, the Duke maintained—were appointed from the families of his more loyal vassals. His own half-brother Odo, though young, held Bayeux; Hugh, Bishop of Lisieux, was the son of the comte d'Eu; John, son of comte Rodulf, was Archbishop of Rouen; Bishop Geoffrey de Coutances was a Mowbray; and Yves, Bishop of Sees, stood at the head of the mighty de Bellême family. Patronage for founding religious houses had reached a new height of enthusiasm—Fontenay; the abbey of Lire; Saint Victor-en-Caux; the nunnery at Almenèches. All tactics designed to impress the Pope.

William glanced through the narrow windows of the great Hall of his castle at Rouen. The sky outside was clearing. Come the winter oiled linen would be placed over the openings, allowing in light but keeping out the worst of rain and wind. "The rain has ceased, I do believe," he said, the weight of depression lifting suddenly. "Come, de Tosny, I would see those horses you have brought me all the way from Rome!"

Sending a servant running ahead, de Tosny proudly conducted his duke, and the inquisitive company of men and women who had been thronging the Hall, to the stables, where waited three fine horses for William's inspection: two bay mares and a pale chestnut stallion with a mane and tail as golden as Mathilda's own hair. He was beautiful!

"They are from the desert land of Arabia," Ralph explained. "Such horses are prized more highly by the desert men than their women."

"They are not as much the unintelligent infidel as we think, then!" someone jested, causing laughter to swirl through the close-pressed company.

The handsome beasts, with their graceful head and tail carriage, exquisitely shaped faces and wide, bold eyes, pleased William immediately. He strode forward to run his hand down their legs, across shoulder and rump. The mares should breed some fine foals. He stood back, arms folded, to watch the stallion prance and preen; a horse as fine as any he had ever seen.

He pursed his lips, nodded approval. "I would ride him!" he announced, slapping his hands together, rubbing the palms. "Fetch saddle and bridle."

Mathilda stood to the forefront of the onlookers with her eldest son Robert settled in her arms, his legs straddling her hip. The girl Agatha and the baby Richard were within doors.

"*Regarde le cheval, comme il est beau,*" she said to the boy, pointing at William as he mounted. "Does Papa not look handsome?"

Robert ducked his face into her shoulder. A quiet, shy boy, he rarely strayed far from his mother or nurse. Strangers and tall men with their deep voices frightened him. Women with their fluttering wimples smothered him. Already upset by the thunder that had raged overhead this past half-hour, he did not want to watch his father, for he scared him almost as much as this enormous, breath-snorting, hoof-clattering dragon of a horse.

Applause rippled through the admiring spectators as William put the stallion through its paces. "He is superb." William dismounted and patted the animal's neck. "He is certainly a king among his kind—I shall call him Solomon I think."

"For a stallion he also possesses an agreeable temper." De Tosny beamed. "He is gentle enough for a child to ride."

"Indeed, he is!" On impulse William swung towards Mathilda, his arms outstretched to take his son from her. Robert yelped as his father lifted him, the sound rising into screams as he felt himself set on to the great beast's saddle.

"Take care, husband, he is a boy of delicate health." Mathilda's hand reached forward to reclaim the lad, but William brushed her aside. She did not care for this harshness in her husband, a side to him that was unpleasant and distasteful, but rarely did she personally witness his deliberate cruelties.

"He is delicate, madam, because you coddle him. Hush, boy! Do not make such a fuss."

From the day of his birth William had not much cared for his scrawny son. His daughter, though a mere two years of age, had more mettle than did the lad. Mathilda spoilt the boy.

The stallion snorted and began to prance at the unfamiliar noise. The terrified boy struggled, arms flailing and legs kicking. His foot caught William's mouth, sending his father staggering, blood bursting from a dislodged tooth. Robert, no longer supported, tumbled from the saddle as the horse skittered sidewards, the scream of fear rising as the ground rushed up to meet him.

Mathilda also screamed as she darted forward, distraught. She knelt on the puddled gravel, gathering him to her, stroking his hair as Robert flung his arms tight around her neck and clung to her? "*Mon petit*, my precious! Hush, hush."

"Damn the boy!" William cursed, dabbing at his mouth. "Is he hurt?"

Through her streaked tears, Mathilda shook her head. "I think not, my Lord."

"Then why in God's name does he squeal like a piglet about to have his throat cut? Has he no backbone in him, madam?"

Furious with her husband, Mathilda glowered up at William's great height from where she knelt. "He is but a child," she scolded, "a small child who is afraid of such a big horse. Do you not remember being afeared of anything as a boy?"

William was disappointed in his son and embarrassed at this contemptible performance. He needed a son with the heart of a lion, the strength of an ox. Not this mewling mother's-weed. "I was never afraid," he bragged. "I saw blood and faced death too often to offer heart-room to a woman's weakness of fear." He turned away from his wife and walked abruptly back to his Hall.

He had not met Mathilda's eyes. He had left her with the boy because she had looked at him and had known that he had lied.

7

⁓

Dives-sur-Mer

The morning had begun warm and fine, with the tinge of late summer touching trees bearing the faintest traits of approaching autumn. The day's hunting had been most enjoyable and rewarding for Duke William and his friends.

"I would have a hawk such as yours." William de Warenne said in open admiration as the bird perched on the Duke's wrist spread his wings in a flutter of annoyance. "My own bird is somewhat aged now. I have had her almost three years."

"Then you are fortunate—many good birds become lost or ensnared." William ran his finger down the bird's soft breast feathers to soothe her. "She hunted well for you—the way she took that wild coney was a superb example of breeding and training."

Will glowed at the praise. Some found the Duke difficult, but he had always found him congenial; quick-tempered, *bien sûr*, but what man of worth was not?

The second-born son, Will had soon realised that the family estate would pass to his elder brother and took the chance to improve his none-too-hopeful prospects by altering allegiance from his father direct to his duke. He was young, bold and daring, the sort of man that William was deliberately courting. Having distinguished himself in battle and shown especial loyalty, de Warenne had been rewarded with the castle of Mortemar and had become an especial friend to his namesake the Duke.

He beckoned for a servant to bring up a wineskin. The day had been long and hot. He offered the skin to William first, who shook his head. Will put the spout to his lips, drank, some of the liquid spilling down his tunic as his horse unexpectedly side-stepped.

Duke William bellowed with laughter. "By God, boy, are you so wet behind the ears that you cannot find your own mouth! It is the opening under your nose and above your chin. What a waste of a fine grape!"

Grinning, Will passed the skin back to his servant and brushed ineffectually at the spreading red stain. "No matter, my Lord." He chortled. "It will give me a good excuse to watch the laundress. They remove stains by covering them with sheep-fat soap and rubbing them against their bare thighs, did you know?"

William's next guffaw was louder than the first. "My friend, I am not in the habit of wasting my time beside the laundry tubs!"

"Oh, it is no waste of time, sir. I regard it as expanding my education."

The party drew their horses to a halt at the crest of the hill, looking down along the wide beach that stretched mile upon mile along the coast. The sea, a lazy, uninspiring steel grey, ruffled against the shore. A fishing boat was making way into the estuary of the river Dives, the silver flash of her catch quivering in the laden baskets on her deck.

Watching the boat, Will tried to imagine the feel of the deck as it rose and fell against the motion of the sea.

"What is it like, out on the sea?" he mused.

"Cold. Wet," the Duke answered. "Out there, the Channel Sea can be master or friend; frightening enough to scald the shit from your backside, or so exhilarating that you feel like shouting your immortality to the four winds."

Will nodded, watching the gulls wheeling and screaming in their intricate patterns behind the frothing wake of the boat. Would he enjoy taking a ship out into those churning waters? He thought not, for his stomach had once tumbled with fear when crossing the Seine in wild weather.

"England lies across there," the Duke said with precision. "A country rich in wealth but poor in ambition."

"What is it like?" Will again enquired with interest. He knew little of England. That the king was named Edward and William's aunt had been that same king's mother. Beyond that only gossip. "They say the men wear their hair long, as a woman would, and that they are rowdy and prone to profanities, murder and drunkenness."

William glanced away from the horizon where clouds were gathering. Rain? As well he had decided to hunt today, then. Mind, he would have ridden out anyway, whatever the weather. Mathilda was still in a disagreeable mood because of that damned boy's tumble. William had barely spoken to her this past week—he ruled all of Normandy yet had no authority in his own household. Ah let her coddle the boy as the poxed English did their weakling children!

"They wear their hair long, oui, and do not shave the upper lip. Prefer ale to fine wine, ride shaggy ponies and, more often than not, fight their battles on foot. They have no stone castles or fortresses, their churches and cathedrals are wooden built, but their forests are green and abundant with game, the land rich for the growing of corn and the grazing of livestock. English wool is of the best quality. Even for the poor, the wool trade can make a reasonable living." William stared out at that distant horizon. "England, Will, has much that I could put to a great deal of good use."

Without William the Bastard as its duke, Normandy's fledgling aristocracy would still have acquired status, land and wealth, but the duchy would have remained under the control of the French King. Under William's ambitious leadership Normandy was poised on the brink of autonomy. Opportunity was there for those who sought to win power and prestige by the use of the sword; all they need do was commit their loyalty to their duke and his ambitions.

Those who rebelled against him fell rapidly by the wayside, starved of favour. His friends were becoming the great and noted Houses of the future. The trick was to bind their fealty. A man was more likely to remain loyal if his accumulated wealth were to stay within his own family, passing from the one generation to the next. William had diplomatically extended the granting of titles and, simultaneously, created hereditary rights. It was always possible for a dog to turn and bite his master, but if the dog was fondled occasionally, allowed to sleep by the hearth and fed well...The structure of a feudal society that was still, as yet, in a state of development, was, under William's policy of securing loyalty, beginning to solidify. Serve William as sworn liegeman, receive in return his patronage and protection, and hold his land. The problem: Normandy was but a small corner of France and land was already in short supply. England's acreage would solve the problem.

England. "I will never forget the debt I owe Normandy for the shelter and kindliness she gave me," Edward had said. He had promised to consider William as his heir. Part of the agreement had been for Edward to wed his sister—but that was immaterial now, for the King had not, after all, set aside his wife. There was some nonsense that a new king had to be elected by agreement, the most worthy man being chosen...William had discarded that trifling detail. He would be the most worthy when the time came.

The Duke gathered up his stallion's reins, turned for home. The hunting had been good, now his belly announced that it was time for dinner and he fancied lying with his wife this night. She might be angry with him, but would not say no. No one said no to William once his mind was set.

He flipped his hand towards the English coast that lay somewhere beyond the cloud-grumbling horizon. "You may one day take that ship to England, Will, my friend. When Edward has gone to God and I am asked to take his throne."

8

Budapest

When the wind blew from the north the settlement froze with the cold. When it came from the south-west everything would dry and wither. This August had been hot, but the wind had stayed in the south-east and the occasional fall of refreshing rain had kept a greenness to the fields, the streams and rivers at a reasonable height. Last year, and the year before that, drought had scorched the thirsty crops and then torrential rain had washed away anything that had struggled to survive. Clouds were forming in heaped, lazy banks over towards the distant mountains. Ædward wondered if the summer storms were to come again this year, to destroy what little they had managed to grow in the spent soil.

One more year of bad harvest and the settlement would be finished. Already the old were weak and thin, the young malnourished. He rested his broad hands on the door lintel. What to do? What best to do?

Behind him within the house place, the sound of the loom weights clicking together distracted him a moment. Agatha enjoyed her weaving, but even the wool from the sheep had been of poor quality this shearing. Edgar was playing with the hound pups, evidently too close to his mother's feet, for Ædward heard her sudden scolding and then movement as the lad ran out through the doorway, ducking under his father's upheld arms, the pups tumbling in a litter of wagging tails and joyful barks along with him.

Ædward caught at his son's shoulder as his skidded past, his hand grasping his tunic.

"Now then, my mischievous lad, what have you been up to? Playing with your hounds near your mother's loom again eh? Tsk, she'll peel your backside one day!"

Edgar was four years old. He ought to be a chubby, well-grown, merry boy, but he was not. He was small and thin with a serious expression. His elder sisters, too, were both solemn-faced, slender girls. Slender? No, like their mother they were bone thin, lacking food to swell the flesh on arms, legs and face.

Ædward squatted before his son, staring into the boy's blurred face. His sight was dimming; soon, he would lose what little vision he had. What could he do for his family then? Already it was hard to grow the crops, to hunt for game; to be ready with spear and sword when the riders came thundering over the plains on their shaggy ponies to plunder and kill what little there was.

"Both my grandfather and father were kings, did you know that?" he asked his son, who stood with his thumb in his mouth, staring back, blankly, at his father.

It frightened the boy when his papa began to talk of when he had been a child of almost the same age. Of when he and his brother had been huddled into a big dark boat and taken down a river called the Ouse, from somewhere called York. He knew neither of them, assuming they were other names for the river that ran beside the place his mama called Budapest. He had been there once and had not liked it much, for there were too many people and too much noise.

"We had to escape, my brother and I, for the new king, Cnut, was intending to kill us. For many years we wandered from one place to another, seeking shelter where we could. Then we went to Kiev and found service for our spears beneath the grand prince—oh, I was almost a man grown then, no longer a lad, like you."

Edgar's eyes swivelled to the four hound pups who had found an old rag of some sort and were tearing and tossing it. He wanted to join in the game.

"My brother died fighting for the prince, but I was fortunate enough to meet with your mother, the daughter of another prince, the brother of the Emperor of Germany. I married her and by and by, when my fighting days were over because of my failing sight, we came to live here, to farm this fickle valley."

"Oh, for the sake of God, Ædward, look at those damned dogs!" Agatha had come from within doors and realised at once what it was the dogs were playing with. She ran forward, shooing with her hands, lunging for what had been her husband's only decent cloak. "You sit there repeating those endless old stories and let the whelps shred your only good cloak! Ædward, I despair of you and this wretched place!" Suddenly she was crumpled to the ground, her face buried in the chewed rag, sobbing.

Ædward went to her and set his arm around her heaving shoulders. "Your discontent has grown each day since that messenger arrived. I am thinking that perhaps we ought to pay heed to the offer he brought us."

Agatha looked up, wiping at her tears with the back of her hand. She was twenty-five years old and felt as if she were fifty. Her husband was not much her senior, thirty-six years, yet he too looked like an old man. The wind did that to you, of course, this persistent wind that weathered soil, tree and skin alike.

"I do not know if we should accept your kindred's offer of returning to England. We know nothing of Edward, of any of them. England shunned you. She lifted not a finger to help—until now. All of a sudden you are invited to return because there is no one else of the royal line? Can we believe that as the truth?" She lifted Ædward's hands, pressed her lips against his wrinkled knuckles. "What use would you be to them, husband? You have not fought in more than ten years, you cannot see the spear you hold in your hand, to make no mention of the target you aim for. For all it pains me to say it, they will never deem you worthy of anything once they meet with you."

Ædward turned his hands over to hold her fingers firm within his own. "Then you would rather stay here, in this wilderness, to die?"

She lowered her gaze, closed her eyes, shook her head. No.

"I have been thinking much on it. For me, no, there is nothing that I can give England, nor little that Edward can offer me in return, except for one thing. Hope. Hope for a better future for our two daughters and our son."

"He is a child, they will not want him." Agatha snatched her hands away and lunged to her feet, throwing the ruined cloak to the dogs who waited, tails wagging, a few yards away, Edgar squatting with them, his arms tight around the black and tan bitch.

Moving to grasp at Agatha's shadowy figure, Ædward missed his first attempt, caught hold of her arm at the second.

"Do you not see? They need to find a man to be king after Edward. He is not old, he may live for many years yet—long enough for our son to grow. They have indicated that they are willing to offer us any form of safe conduct that we request—all we need do is stand firm for what we need for ourselves: an agreement of noble marriage for Margaret our eldest and the title of ætheling to pass to my son. For Edgar, Agatha, we must go to England. For Edgar, not for me."

"But, fool of a man, they will not take him without you."

"Of course not, but they do not know what they are getting with me. Unless we tell them, how will they know?"

At last a smile wavered at the corners of Agatha's lips. She put her hand to Ædward's chest, patting her agreement. "Anything," she said, "would be better than remaining here."

Edgar buried his head into the soft fur of his favourite bitch. He did not understand much of what his father and mother had said this day, or during the past two, since that man had come with word from this town called England. It was bigger than Budapest, they had said. If he did not like Budapest, then he would not, he supposed, like England. Nor did he like this talk of going to see a king. This king in England had tried to kill his father and had set him in a dark boat that had been pushed out into a river. Edgar did not think he would like a king who tried to murder children.

9

Gloucestershire

The day was bright and warm, the air suffused with the scents and sounds of a drowsy summer: warm earth, the sweet, heady smell of hay, pollen and clover; lazy bees about their plundering of nectar; cattle lowing in the water meadows; ewes calling to their growing lambs.

An idyllic day, except the King was in a belligerent temper and everyone else was sick of being camped here beside the ferry at Aust on the bank of the river Severn.

Strolling along the horse lines, Harold tugged an alder twig from a tree and began idly stripping the leaves, playing that childish game: she loves me, she loves me not...From the far bank a fish leapt for a fly, leaving the spread of ripple rings. His eye caught the brief flurry of bright blue as a kingfisher darted through the darker shadow of trees.

She loves me not. He sighed, tossed the bare branch aside and went over to his own horse, a new and spirited dark dun stallion who, yesterday, had gashed his fetlock. With an hour or so to spare while Edward attended his toilet, Harold thought he might as well tend it. As good a way as any to pass this first half of the morning.

The Welsh problem had come to a head in June. When the Bishop of Hereford had died, he had been replaced by Leofgar, a man devoted to God but also a capable warrior. Many disapproved of his habit of wearing a moustache when it was generally accepted that clerics went clean-shaven, but for the nervous population of Hereford he appeared the ideal choice. A pity that his enthusiasm won the better of his judgement. Eleven weeks after his consecration, he led an army impetuously into Wales. Outnumbered, he and his men had been annihilated at Glasbury on Wye.

Campaigning against these damned Welsh provoked one disaster after another. Edward had not the treasury, or the men, to waste on pointless campaigns. Settlement was the only alternative.

Truce with Ælfgar was simple to conclude, for his father was mortally ill. Soon, another earl would be required for Mercia and the honour, unusually premature, was offered to Ælfgar. For now he was to have Anglia returned to him, Harold's brothers, Gyrth and Leofwine, being willing temporarily to step down from their award of joint custodianship, given them at Ælfgar's exile until the vacancy became available again. Gruffydd, too, could see the sense of accepting the offer of border lands and estates without the need to fight for them. Of course, he would renege on the agreement at some time or another, but such were peace treaties: give a little, take a little; smile and offer pleasantries; ignore what would happen a few more miles down the track. If peace could be claimed for a month or a year then something had been achieved. The problem came with the petty pride of a prince and a king, neither of whom would give ground. One of them had to step on to the ferry and go to the other to exchange the embrace of peace. Both of them were arguing that the other ought to be the one to cross.

Edward had decided to appear at his best when Gruffydd disembarked from the ferry on to this, the English side of the Severn. His earls agreed that trimming beards or shaving, having a haircut and wearing of fine apparel was indeed suitable, but going to the extent of bathing, even given that the weather was pleasantly hot, seemed a little excessive. Not that Harold was averse to submerging himself in a tub of hot water, but he preferred to do so within doors and preferably with Edyth there to scrub his back and share in the additional intimate delights. To bathe in a tub in a tent, with tepid water, did not seem worthwhile.

Harold had named the horse Beowulf, after the warrior of the saga. He stood just below fourteen and a half hands with a deep chest, a bold eye, quick intelligence and great stamina and speed: all the best characteristics of Harold's Wessex stud. Stroking the horse's velvet-soft muzzle, Harold fed him a titbit of a stale bread crust and picked up the injured hoof. Already the cut was scabbed over; it would be healed in no time. Satisfied, Harold turned to make his way back to the royal tent and saw a young woman leaning with casual curiosity against the trunk of an ash tree.

"He is a fine stallion," she said boldly, indicating the horse. "I would wager he has Welsh blood in him?"

Harold walked casually towards her, suddenly recognising her. "And how," he asked with a trickle of amusement, "would you know of the breeding of ponies, and the characteristics of the Welsh breed in particular? Do they teach such things to the daughters of English exiles, then, within Gruffydd's court?"

Ælfgar's daughter, Alditha, pushed herself from the tree. She was slender and tall, only a few inches shorter than Harold, with eyes as dark as a well's deep pool. She was fifteen years of age, balanced on the verge of womanhood.

"Prince Gruffydd had no need to teach me," she retorted with a toss of her black hair, the two braids, each as thick as Harold's wrist, bouncing against her shoulders and maturing breasts. The gesture reminded Harold of his stallion: alert and impatient. Beautiful.

She had emphasised the word prince, giving the lord of Wales his correct title, highlighting Harold's lack of respect.

"I know of Welsh ponies from my mother. I have had such ponies for my own since before I could walk." She tossed her head again and went to Beowulf, making her presence known by offering her hand for him to scent before touching him.

"He has the distinct dish to his face, a bold eye and a broad forehead, with small, well-set ears." She cupped her hand around one to prove her point, only the tip protruding from her lightly clasped fist. "A pony ought not resemble a mule. His neck ought to be of good length, the shoulder sloping to a good wither. Your stallion can carry weight over long distances, but with it, he is agile and light-footed." She ran her hand to his knee, indicating the strong joint, the flat bone. Then she cocked her head to one side to look at Earl Harold. "Well?"

Harold inclined his head. "He has half-Welsh blood in him, aye. His mother came from the mountains." He raised one eyebrow, indicating the land across the river. "As did yours."

Alditha returned Harold's assessing look boldly. He knew her breeding as well as he did that of the horse. "My mother was the daughter of Iago ap Idwal, son of the line of Hywel Dda and Rhodri Mawr, She died when I was a child of ten years old."

"Then you ought not have liking for Gruffydd. It was he who murdered your grandfather and took the title of prince from the dynasty of Gwynedd for himself, yet your father, her husband, would rather pledge his loyalty to the Welsh than those of us of his own kind?"

"I have no liking for Gruffydd, but he is at least a man who keeps his word. Unlike the English King."

Harold laughed outright, head back, hands going to his hips. "Forgive me," he said, spluttering, "but the innocence of the naïve is refreshing. Gruffydd? A man of his word? Ah no, my little lady, he keeps only those words that suit him."

"Can you say that Edward is any the better?" she retorted. "Has he respected my father or rewarded him?" Her dark eyes flashed diamond sparks of anger at Harold's mockery.

God's teeth, but she is going to be a beauty within a year or two, Harold thought. "The King has treated Ælfgar as he deserves, Mistress Alditha, And as for his merits? What merits would they be? None come immediately to mind."

Again that flash of anger in her eyes, that proud toss to her head. She turned on her heel, intending to stalk away. "You dislike my father, but you have him wrong. He is a man of courage and pride, a man who cherishes his family and who weeps, still, for the Welshwoman he once had as wife."

Her acerbic tone stung, but Harold was not one who took kindly to unjust accusations. He lunged forward and clutched her arm, answering her with the curt abruptness of the truth: "I do not dislike your father, girl, but neither do I respect him. He has the false courage of a fool and the pride of the vain. He thinks nothing of you nor your two younger brothers. He despises his second wife for her independent wealth and her good breeding. He has been disloyal to his own father. He may weep copiously for your mother, my dear, when under the eye of Gruffydd's court, but he did not show her affection when she was his wife. I am older than you, your father's temper has always been harsh. I never saw him treat your mother with kindness."

Alditha attempted to prise his fingers from her arm, her eyes glaring into his, contempt matching contempt. Her anger was made the worse for knowing he spoke the truth. "My father said that those of you from Wessex were the whelps of a cur! He was right!" she snarled, piercing the skin of his hand with her fingernails.

Harold yelped, but held on. "That he probably was," he retorted, "but it takes a cur to sniff out a cur."

The girl swung her free arm intending to slap Harold's face, but with the quick reaction of a fighting man he caught her wrist. Furious, she began struggling and kicking, her boot connecting several times with his shin. Harold held her body away from him so that her flying feet swiped ineffectually at empty air. Gods, but she was a firebrand! She had most certainly inherited the wild and dangerous nature of the Welsh from her mother. He did not know whether to tip her over his knee for a beating, or put his mouth to hers and kiss her. Were she not so young and vulnerable…by the Christ, perhaps it was time to return home to Edyth! He needed a woman.

"Your father cares only for the wealth and prestige of an earldom, naught else," he panted, parrying another of her kicks by sidestepping. "Why else would you now be back on English soil? Why else has he already bowed his knee in homage to Edward? Yes, Leofwine, you seek me?" Harold darted a look at the young man who was approaching at a trot, his arm waving frantically, calling Harold's name.

"Aye! The King is shouting for you, in a torrent of rage." Leofwine, Harold's younger brother, drew to a halt, panting slightly, his knowing grin admiring the girl struggling in Harold's grasp. "It seems," he continued, without taking his eyes from her, "that Edward is about to revoke the entire agreement that you and Earl Leofric have so painstakingly brokered. Gruffydd flatly refuses to cross the river, has sent a messenger to say that Edward must go to him. Our tactful king has threatened to slit that messenger's nose and return word that he will do the same to Gruffydd for his insolence."

Harold's attention being occupied, Alditha took her chance and sank her teeth into his hand. Yelling, he let her go; instantly, she darted away. "My father allies to Gruffydd because the Prince of Wales is not a weakling fool like Edward. Your king will never outmatch either of them." Then she was gone, with nothing but the call of an alarmed blackbird to mark that she had been there. And the teeth marks in Harold's hand.

He winced, inspected the wound. She had drawn blood. "I agree with you about our king, my pretty one," he said, then, louder, his hand cupped to his mouth, shouted after her, "but it will not be Edward who goes to war against Gruffydd! It will be me!"

"I thought you were going to kiss her," Leofwine said, desperately attempting to keep the grin from his cheeks.

"I was," Harold answered. "But the damn girl bit me instead."

Had Edward stamped his foot, or lain down on his belly and kicked the rush-matting floor, Harold would not have been surprised. More often than not, the King behaved absurdly like a child when he was outmanoeuvred.

"I have given orders to break camp!" he shouted.

"And I have countermanded them," Harold responded patiently.

"You cannot do that!"

"I can, I have. On your order, as your most able earl, I command the army, Sire. It is for me to judge what is prudent for the fyrd. It is not prudent to escalate a minor misunderstanding into a war."

Almost apoplectic, Edward spluttered his rage, "Minor misunderstanding? Good God, this is nothing of the sort—it is an outright insult, sir! Outright insult!"

God's truth, Harold thought, *I see why my father was so often out of temper when returning from Edward's court. I would rather face Gruffydd than try to persuade the King the meaning of diplomacy!*

"Sire," Earl Leofric interrupted, "it took Wessex and myself many wearisome days to bring about this peace. I have had to swallow my pride and forgive my son. In order to accommodate his reinstatement, Earl Harold's brothers Gyrth and Leofwine have willingly surrendered Oxfordshire and Anglia that was divided between them on my son's exile. We have all, in some way, had to concede something."

"So I must humble myself to that upstart heathen? Is that what you imply?"

Leofric sighed. "No, Sire, that is not my meaning." Brands of fire were twisting in his stomach. His wished his good lady Godiva were here with her cool hands and soothing potions. Ah, not long now and he would join her in heaven where pain did not exist. His contemporaries were all gone—Siward, Godwine, Emma—and he was so weary of this turbulent life.

"Sire." Harold took a step nearer to Edward, his hands spread. "Gruffydd is testing us. He is trying to establish how easy it would be to break this hard-won agreement, how deep he need poke with his stick. If we flounce away like blushing maidens whose modesty is compromised, what will he think of us? Will we not seem to him, to all the Welsh, as vulnerable as a nun in a brothel?"

The King did not reply. Eyeing a stool, Leofric wondered if he dare ask permission to be seated. He pressed his hand to the pain in his belly. "It will take a wise man to outmanoeuvre Gruffydd, my Lord King, and you, Sire, I am certain, possess that wisdom."

Harold flashed the Earl a brief, grateful smile. They all wanted this thing done and finished. "Sometimes," he said, on a wistful note, "it is the man who bends the knee first, who proves himself the stronger of mind and character, for it is he who can see the wisdom of preventing unnecessary bloodshed. Alas, such courage lives only in the hearts of the apostles and in Christ himself. No mortal man could willingly display such dignified humility."

He held his breath...Edward's brows had narrowed into a thoughtful frown. He moved to a small altar placed to the rear of his tent, knelt, joined his hands and bowed his head. Harold exchanged a hopeful, pleading look with Leofric...

Brusquely Edward finished his prayer, stood and commanded his cloak be brought, the ferry made ready. "I will not have it said that my pride created death and destruction. Let that epitaph fall on Gruffydd's god—cursed pagan soul."

⁓

Stunned that the King of England should so publicly discard his pride, the Welsh, on their side of the river, murmured their approval, their mutterings rising to open cheers as the ferryman poled the barge across the wide stretch of water, the King standing, benevolent and serene, in the bows.

Gruffydd's quick wit registered their sudden admiration and silently cursed the English for this subtle manoeuvre.

"My Lord?" The Welsh messenger sent to Edward had returned, shaken but unharmed, having been rowed in a quicker, more compact coracle. He had made his way direct to his prince, spoken quietly so that only Gruffydd might hear. "Sir, Lord Harold, Earl of Wessex bids me advise you in private that the wise leader takes advantage of a chance to appear the equal of his opponent. Were you to meet the English King halfway across the river…"

Gruffydd guffawed. He had heard much of Harold of Wessex—aye, and his father before him. Both were men of courage and diplomatic skill. Still laughing, he plunged down the river bank and leapt aboard his own boat, ordering that he be rowed to meet with England halfway.

Aye, he had heard much of this man, Harold. Would, no doubt, hear much more as the seasons turned.

10

⤜⤛

St. Omer—April 1057

Rome! Edyth could not fully believe that she had actually visited that magnificent city. Closing her eyes, she allowed her head to rest against the high back of her chair. Now that they were returned to St. Omer after their months of travelling and the children were settled into their beds, she could afford the luxury of a moment's idleness. Her body ached and her head swam, but it was not all from travel fatigue—excitement still tumbled in her heart and mind.

"If you allow that grin to spread any the wider." Harold said, bending down to place a lingering kiss on her lips, "your face will split in two."

Lazily, Edyth opened her eyes. "I am blissfully content," she answered. "I have accumulated so many wondrous memories that never again shall I want for something to think about." She linked her arms round Harold's neck, pulling him down closer to return his kiss. "I have not yet decided whether the best part was attending the lavish splendour of the court of the Holy Roman Empire in Cologne, spending Christmas at Regensburg with the Imperial party, or accompanying the Pope back to Rome." Her smile was a fixed sickle shape. Once, she had never expected to travel further than her own local villages along the river Lea, now she had seen the splendours of these great foreign cities. She stroked her finger across the stubble that was forming across Harold's chin, her smile fading, "stay with me and our children, Harold, We have such a great need of you."

Perplexed at this sudden change of mood, Harold set her on to his lap, his arms winding around her waist. She was with child again, had missed her second flux; an especial son or daughter this one would be, for its making had been in Rome, Was this perhaps a reason for the unexpected distress?

"I have no intention of leaving you. What sets you thinking as such?"

Edyth laid her head against his, her own arms going about his shoulders. He was strong and dependable, Harold. Oh, he strayed to other women occasionally, when matters of official business kept him away from her bed...what vigorous man did not? The passing use of a whore, however, was different from sharing the pleasures of love. She held him tight. "I am tired."

This would have nothing to do with that suggestion of marriage made to me by the Empress of Germany, would it? With her husband in his grave and a young son crowned in his stead, she perhaps has need of another man."

Edyth pouted. "I have always known that one day you must make a marriage of alliance…"

Harold laughed. "She is fat, fifty, and has the temper and character of a fishwife. I have no ambition to become her bed-mate or her son's tilting post." Setting her to her feet, Harold patted Edyth's backside. This guest room within the abbey was both comfortable and private, but it was Friday and the physical union of a man and woman on this fasting day was discouraged by the Church. Not that he was averse to bending the rules, but coming so recently from Rome, perhaps it was best not to flaunt his needs above those of God.

"Get you to bed," he said, trundling her in that direction. "I think I will go up to the castle, enquire whether any word has come from Ædward. When I confirmed his safe conduct on our outward journey last November, I gave him 'til the twelfth day of April to meet with us here in St. Omer. If he is coming, he has but the morrow to arrive. I would be back in England before Easter."

"Will he come, do you think?" Edyth asked, her hand going to unfasten her veil. She folded the linen neatly, placing hairpins safely in her jewel casket, began unbraiding her hair. "It has taken nigh on two years of searching throughout Hungary to find him—all that many more to remember him in the first place. Why would he want to bother with England now? England has not been bothered with him."

"He will come because Hungary is in the midst of new political upheaval. Where there is a change in leader, there is also a change of attitude towards those seeking asylum. Ædward was found, last summer, because King Andrew of Hungary wanted him to be found—and for that reason alone, Ædward the Exile must leave. If he cherishes his life and that of his family, that is."

Edyth was not convinced, but said nothing. "If he does not come, will you wait?"

"A few days only. Like you, my Willow-bud, I have taken much pleasure in our pilgrimage travels, but I now desire to return to my own home. That chestnut mare will be foaling soon, I am eager to see if she bears as good an offspring as did her mother."

Edyth flashed him a smile. She knew he would be content to remain here as an honoured guest, but he understood that her heart lay within the comfort of their manor, overlooking the green peace of the valley of the river Lea, that she wanted to go home.

≈

Harold lay abed, dozing, reluctant to be up and about the new day. Edyth was already up, and gone to see to the children's dressing and eating of breakfast. A rapping on the door startled Harold awake; he sat up quickly, rubbed at his nose and chin. Bleary-eyed and mildly disorientated, he stumbled towards the latch, swung the door open. Beyond stood a thin man of medium height, his hair and beard grey-grizzled, with eyes of a dark, slate grey. Beside him was a woman, younger, but also thin. Their dress, although not shabby, was more practical than ostentatious. Harold took them to be folk of a middle merchant rank.

Nervously, the man licked at his lips. There was sweat on his brow. He extended his hand, the palm up, and spoke in German. "You are the Earl Harold?"

The woman had already assessed Harold's appearance, taking in his stance, height and build, the weave of the tunic thrown hurriedly over his nakedness when he had come to answer the door. She nodded, once, as if satisfied with what she saw. "You are much as we expected you to be."

Harold raised an eyebrow and gestured with his hand for them to enter.

"It is a fine place, this abbey," the stranger said. "My wife and children are delighted with our accommodation, although it is somewhat close to the piggeries. We did not often see such fine building in Hungary."

The muzziness of sleep slipped from Harold's brain and a grin of delight slid across his face. He marched back to the man, took his hand and pumped it in vigorous welcome. "Ædward? You are Ædward the Exile? It is good to meet you, Sir! And you, my dear lady, must be Agatha! Come, sit, sit, make yourselves comfortable."

Harold served wine, then asked, candidly, "You will come to England, Sir? You must, for there is no one else suitable to follow on to the throne."

Ædward cast a tentative smile at his host. As he had expected from all that he had gleaned of this man during the long weeks of travelling from Hungary through Germany to St. Omer, the Earl of Wessex was a likeable man. "I have heard much of your courage and strength, Harold Godwinesson," he confided. "I understand that your patience and diplomacy is much admired and that you are well known and liked—whereas I…" He paused. "Whereas I am unknown beyond name and status. Ædward. An exile. What else do you know of me beyond those two limited facts, Earl Harold? Yes, I am prepared to go to England with you—else I would not have come all this way. I admit that I am flattered that the Council should have so much faith in me—but it has taken a long time for England to remember me." He looked up at Harold with wide, saddened eyes. "More than thirty years."

Harold took time to pour himself wine. Aye, England was adept at forgetting her born sons: this haggard man; Edward himself for all those years; his own brother and nephew still held hostage in Normandy with no diplomatic hope of securing their return. He seated himself opposite his two guests. When the Council had decided to try to find the Exile, they had never considered Ædward's attitude to it, assuming from the start that he would be all too eager to return to the land of his birth, would accept without question the hero's welcome and status of ætheling. Nor had they considered the toll that the passing of years might set upon a man's shoulders. Ædward was not old, but neither was he young. His shoulders stooped and his body, without doubt, was frail.

Seeing his furrowed brow and following the obvious thoughts, Agatha spoke up: "For the first few years of exile my husband was too young to understand anything except the urgent need to flee. It is hard for a small child to watch the shadows in case a dagger blade should be hidden there. He had no settled home, no security, but travelled from court to court, from one place of safety to another. Now England has sudden need of him. He has a wife and family now, contentment and security. Why should we give up all we have to return, on the whim of your Council and your childless king, to a land that neither of us knows or cares for and that speaks a tongue that we do not understand?"

Harold answered her just as bluntly, speaking also in German. "Because you will want for nothing in England. You and your children will live within the King's court. Your settlement beside the collection of hovels that is Budapest could never be as comfortable as that. Your children's future never as secure—"

"I have your word that Edgar will become ætheling after me?" Ædward interrupted. "And that suitable marriages for my daughters are guaranteed?"

Harold nodded.

"I must have proof," Ædward snapped.

Harold gestured agreement with his palm open. "It is agreed. I brought with me from England written documents signed by the King to contract it so. It is Edward's own wish that you follow him, that you are returned to your home and your family."

At that Ædward appeared satisfied.

"What if the Council of England decides against my husband?" Agatha asked. "A king must, after all, be elected by common agreement. When those

Englishmen of the Witan meet with Ædward they may decide they do not want him after all. What of my son then?"

Uncertain whether he liked this woman for her forthrightness, or whether she was just too blunt, Harold answered with a laugh, although there was a slight hesitancy in the sound. "We have gone to great expense and trouble to locate you, to bring you even this far. There is no one suitable to follow Edward. The agreement will not change."

Ædward had half finished his wine. A small round table stood beside the hearth bench; he leaned forward to set his goblet down, missed the edge and the thing tumbled, splashing wine over his legs and lap. Harold leapt to his feet, but Agatha was there before him, patting at the mess, Ædward profusely apologising.

"Forgive my clumsiness, I did not watch what I was doing."

"'Tis no matter," Harold responded. "Here, let me fetch you more wine." He retrieved the goblet, went to refill it. He was glad he had his back to the room when Agatha suddenly spoke again: Why do you support the seeking of my husband? Have you no ambition for a crown?" The question was candid and totally unexpected.

"Me? King?" Harold spluttered. "My grandfather was a thegn turned pirate! My connection with the royal line is at best dubious and only through the distaff line."

Ædward smiled at that, holding out his hand for the refilled goblet. "The Duke of Normandy's grandfather was a tanner, yet he appears to be doing well enough for himself."

"Normandy has different laws and customs from those of England." Harold's answer was terse. He? King? He had never thought on it. By God, if it were the duty and responsibility alone that counted for kingship, then he already possessed the title! It was he, Harold, as senior earl, who all but ruled England. He saw that the laws were made and obeyed; he led the army into war, not Edward. He shook his head, thrust that brief flicker of a potentially treasonous thought aside, said with conviction, "You are the man we want, Sir, for you are the son of Edmund Ironside. Not I."

"For my sins, Earl Harold, that, indeed, I am. But answer me this. What if I should die before Edward and he dies before my son comes of age? Who will become king of England then, eh?"

Harold could only shrug.

Agatha opened the door, threaded her arm through her husband's. "We shall be ready to leave for England as and when you wish."

Listening to the sound of their footsteps diminishing outside, Harold thoughtfully nursed the goblet between his hands. There had been something strange about Ædward, something that went beyond the unexpected ageing of a man who was only a matter of three or so years older than himself.

The Lady Agatha, too, was a puzzle. Forthright with her views, yet like a cat walking on hot bricks. Perhaps it was nothing more than their trepidation at returning after so long to England where, despite the assurances of agreement, nothing was, or ever could be, unbreakably guaranteed.

II

❧

Westminster

Tostig stripped off his gloves as he entered the Queen's chamber, unfastened his cloak and gave that, too, to a servant. Shivered and headed for the fire. April and the welcoming of spring? Sleet was falling and if the easterly wind were to shift more to the north there would be a return of the snow that had huddled most of England within doors since mid February.

"So he has arrived?" Edith asked, barely masking her indifference, only briefly glancing up from the writing of a letter to her mother. The Countess remained at Bosham for most of the year—and who could blame her? The roads were rutted and mired, the distance tedious and uncomfortable. Edith considered it her duty to write every so often, to enquire after her health and tell of Edward's and her own.

"London stinks," Tostig complained. The streets are running with sewage and there are drowned rats everywhere. Edward was wise to build this palace a few miles from the city. There will be plague before long, mark my word." He clicked his fingers at a servant to bring a chair nearer the hearth. "Aye, Ædward and his family are in London, comfortably accommodated in the house Edward has given them. Once they have rested and settled, they will come to the palace." He picked at some dirt beneath his fingernail. "If you think that is still a wise idea."

Setting her quill into its stand, Edith half turned to face him. "And why would I not?" she questioned, alert to what he was not saying.

The dirt removed, Tostig inspected the nails on his other hand. Cleanliness of the hands was essential. You could judge a man's quality by his nails. "Ædward, our returned exile," he casually informed his sister, "is blind—well, as near as may be."

Edith stared at him as if he had spoken in an incomprehensible language.

"Harold told me and then I witnessed it for myself." Tostig continued, re-crossing his legs and leaning back in the chair. Ædward's nails had been filthy;

Tostig had clasped his lower arm and wrist in greeting, had not fancied putting his palm against that clammy, dirtied one. "Our brother suspected something was wrong while in St. Omer—discovered it for certain during the sea crossing. Which means, of course, that we do have a problem. A man cannot be deemed kingworthy if he has no sight."

Edith digested the news, was silent for two whole minutes. "And why, then," she asked, "was this not mentioned before we went to all the bother of bringing him to England?"

"Why indeed? May I suggest, perhaps, because the Lady Agatha is desperate for better prospects than a Hungarian peasant's hovel for her son and two daughters?"

Edith rose, wandered around the room, her fingers linked, tapping against her lips as she thought, her astute mind calculating. "You imply that Agatha deliberately disguised her husband's affliction?"

Tostig nodded. "So Harold does believe. Would you have not done the same?"

Edith ceased her pacing and resettled herself at the writing desk. What would she have done? Proclaimed the truth and forsaken all hope of a secure future? A wry smile twisted one side of her mouth upwards. "Most certainly, had I a son with a good chance of becoming king." She fluttered her fingers at the two servants, bidding them be gone from the room, wrote another two sentences to her mother. She also knew what she would be willing to do next and was mildly surprised at discerning, for perhaps the first time in her life, the ruthless streak that pierced her. Surprised, but not shocked. The need for self-preservation had hardened her more with every passing year.

Alone with her brother, with no ear to overhear and therefore no mischievous tongue to wag, she said in a lowered, conspiring tone, "We must ensure that the lady's hopes for her son are not disappointed. The boy must be declared ætheling."

"Which he cannot if his father is denied the title." Tostig's reply was testy, stating the obvious.

Edith completed a last sentence, signed her name, *Ædith Reginae* with a flourish and sprinkled fine sand over the parchment to dry the ink.

"*Le roi est mort, vive le roi.* There is no one else. If there is no father to become ætheling, then the child will become kingworthy."

Pinching his moustache and upper lip between thumb and index finger, Tostig sat quiet for a long moment. Then he said guardedly, "But loss of sight is not life threatening, sister."

"Is it not, brother? You are wrong. In certain circumstances—if, say, a suggestion is whispered in the right ear, such an affliction can be deadly." She fingered the gold crucifix at her throat, wondering at her own calmness. "We must

ensure that Edward does not meet with his nephew. He has become a sentimen-
tal fool of late." Her words came slowly as the plan that had lodged in her mind
became clearer. "You said yourself there will be plague in London—Edward
can be easily persuaded to stay away and we can use the same excuse to keep
Ædward within the city walls. For as long as it takes."

Tostig frowned and slumped deeper into his chair, as if shrinking away from
the implications. "I am not sure that I like what I think you are suggesting."

Edith lifted her head, defiant as always when her mind was set. "Nor do
I much like the prospect of losing my crown after Edward has gone. Of not
having the security of a son." She walked to her brother's side, laid her hand
lightly on his shoulder. "Edgar is a child, too young to rule should Edward die
within the next few years." Her fingers gripped tighter. "Edward has become
most fond of you, Tostig. I would suggest that you nurture that friendship."

Tostig jerked his shoulder away from her touch. "He fawns over me, patting
and petting me like a favoured hound. I hate it."

"Hate Edward as much as you like, Tostig. But would the title of regent not
come as a good reward? A fair exchange for a little tolerance and the implanting
of a delicate suggestion to a desperate wife."

Tostig could hardly believe he had truly grasped his sister's meaning. Truth
and fear of God had always been his mainstay, but so far, where had that got
him? Always his elder brothers had received the accolades, the kudos. What was
there for him? Northumbria! That bloody, godforsaken wilderness! He could be
as good as—better than—Harold were he only given the chance to prove it. He
said quietly, afraid to put thoughts into words, lest once spoken they could not
be reclaimed, "You mean murder?"

Indulgently, Edith smiled. "No, my dear. I mean ensuring a fretful mother
sees to it that her son will be chosen as ætheling."

12

⤶

Falaise

Judith, helping to tidy away the mess that always accumulated with a birth, bundled soiled linen into the arms of a servant and glanced with a mixture of adoration and jealousy at her sister's new son. After all these years of marriage to Tostig Godwinesson, Judith's womb had never quickened. She was barren, A fact she could normally accept with equanimity, but at times like this, when the cry of the new-born tugged at her emotions, it was a fact that carried much pain. She was a good woman, Judith, would have made just as good a mother as her sister Mathilda, Duchess of Normandy, She sighed, gathered the last of the linen and piled it atop the servant's already cumbersome burden, giving instruction that it was to be taken immediately to be laundered, lest the stains became immovable.

The birthing had been an easy one, over within two hours, but then Mathilda, for all her lack of height, had wide hips and three previous children. Only by chance was Judith still here at Falaise to be of assistance, for a month already had she and Tostig been guests of her sister's husband at this castle where William had been born. Falaise was the town where his mother had lived with her father the tanner; where Duke Robert had first set eyes on her.

They would have returned to England—to Tostig's earldom of Northumbria— had travel to the northern coast of Normandy been safe. But William was once again at odds with Henry of France, the two men locked in bull-horned determination to be rid of each other, Henry had entered Normandy from the west, two weeks past, as a hot July smouldered into August and was busy making his presence known by ravaging and burning all in his path, pushing the destruction northwards towards Bayeux and Caen. William, intent on his wife's confinement, appeared unconcerned by the outrage. He contented himself with summoning his forces to muster at Falaise and waited for the birth of his son. And for Henry to make a mistake.

Mathilda thought her third son perfect—his father, peering at the infant sucking greedily at her breast, grunted that he was the ugliest thing he had ever seen. Laughing, she amiably dismissed his rudeness. "Ah William, you have said that of all our *nouveau-nés*. Children are often like shrivelled little grapes when they first come into the world!"

"I do not recall the other three having such puckered crimson faces. This crab-apple appears overripened."

Judith successfully masked her shock at her brother-in-law's insults. She would have been devastated had Tostig said anything so callous about a child, but Mathilda was unperturbed. She had long ago realised that her husband possessed no paternal feelings for her babies. It would be different when the boys were men grown, when they could fight at their father's side.

An uneasy silence had fallen among the group of men invited into the chamber to greet their duke's son. Judith noted their discomfort; they too were dismayed at William's apparent dislike of the boy. Someone had to say something.

"What are you to name him?" she asked, closing the door behind the last of the servants and casting a professional eye over the reconstructed order of the chamber. She expected her brother-in-law to answer, but it was Mathilda who commented.

"I think William would be suitable, do you not agree, husband?" She tipped her head at the Duke, who once more was bending over his son with an expression of acute repugnance. He straightened and shrugged with a gesture of indifference, replying that he was not certain he cared for the boy to be named after him.

"I am not suggesting we name him after you!" Mathilda responded indignantly. "Why, the poor mite will feel daunted enough as it is by your high expectations. *Non*, this is for our dear friend, William fitz Osbern." She regarded the man standing a pace or so behind her husband and held her hand out for him to kiss. With a polite bow, fitz Osbern raised her fingers to his lips.

"Do you not consider that Will deserves such reward?" Mathilda asked her husband. "This tiny man sucking so strongly at my teat might not have been blessed with the good fortune of having you as his father, were it not for Will's loyalty in protecting your back these past many years."

Judith was completely stunned at her sister's pert boldness, but then, Mathilda had always had a mind of her own. A woman's duty, Judith had often reminded her, was to be obedient first to her father and then to her lord husband. That lesson had obviously fallen on muffled ears. Judith, however, was measuring her sister's marriage against her own. Tostig was a strict, rigid, no-nonsense man who, although Judith would never openly admit it, was lacking in imagination and humour. Mathilda would have died of boredom were she wed to Tostig. He might offer stability but William offered the thing Mathilda had always yearned for and which Judith envied: excitement.

The Duke set a brief, chaste kiss on his wife's cheek. "I shall consider your suggestion," he said, a spark of amusement shining in his eyes. "Though Rufus—red face—would suit him the better."

Mathilda beamed at him. Perhaps she alone of all people, save for his mother, knew how William thought and why he acted as he did. To no other living person could he open the window into his heart and soul, for to the deceit and wickedness of the world he had to show unwavering strength. There was no room for weakness. None other save perhaps fitz Osbern could be permitted to witness any crack in his defences that could make him vulnerable. Too many in the past had turned against William, had traded trust and friendship for lies and hostility: guardians, uncles, vassals—Henry of France himself.

Despite the cruelty that she knew was within him, Mathilda had no fear of her husband, for she had given him her body and her heart. Whether he reciprocated with love, she was uncertain. If love meant treating her as his equal, not abusing her verbally or physically in public or private, sharing passion in the intimacy of their bed and never having need of another woman, then she was content.

"Come, my friends," the Duke said, clapping his hands together and rubbing the palms in a familiar gesture that signalled his desire to apply his mind to work not relaxation. "Let us leave the ladies to their women's business and be about our own." He clamped his broad hand on fitz Osbern's shoulder as they passed through the door. "Of course, I shall expect the compliment of naming my son after you to be returned when your own wife is safe delivered of her first child."

Fitz Osbern guffawed outright. "It is already decided so, my Lord! William be it a lad, Mathilda if a lass."

"Outright fawning will get you everywhere, my dear friend!" The Duke's laughter echoed back up the winding steps, amplified by the slabs of stone. This castle at Falaise was impregnable, one of his best-fortified.

"Do you not think me the most fortunate of men, Lord Tostig?" William went on. "Think on it, we might have each received the other sister in marriage—it could be you with a red-faced shrimp for a son and me saddled with the empty vessel! 'Tis just as well the fertile woman came to the better man, eh?"

Closing the door after the last of the men to leave, Judith reddened and bit her lip to stem the hurt. As well that she did not hear her husband's reply; Tostig was never one to put loyalty to kindred above the need to impress.

After patting the baby between his shoulders to bring up his wind, Mathilda handed the child to his nurse. She would feed him herself for a few days only, to give him the benefit of a mother's first nourishing milk. Then the wet nurse could have him. Motherhood suited Mathilda well, but not the inconvenience of swollen breasts, dripping milk and the constant demand of a baby's hungry belly. She watched with a critical eye while the nurse clothed the baby in clean linen and swaddled his body tight to prevent any risk of misshapen limbs, then laid him in his cradle. The child snuffled, grunting a mild protest at being taken from the security of his mother's warmth and smell, but within moments he slept.

For Judith, the tug of longing became almost unbearable. She would do anything, anything at all, to be blessed with the joy of her own child. The potions and charms that she had tried, the remedies and draughts...the hours on her knees before God's altar...nothing had worked.

"Perhaps a pilgrimage to Rome may help?" Had Mathilda guessed at the thoughts behind her sister's stricken expression? "I have heard that many women pray direct to God for the blessing of a child at the altar of Saint Peter." Her suggestion was well-intentioned, but her next was less tactful. "You are so thin, my dear. You ought to put more weight on your belly and buttocks, give your husband's seed something to feast upon."

Judith blinked rapidly, fighting the overwhelming desire to weep. She was behaving like some first-wed young maid. What with the birth of this child and her monthly flux just starting...two lonely tears trickled down her cheek.

"Come, sit beside me." Mathilda patted her bed. "Have you considered," she commented with a straightforwardness similar to that of her husband, "that your barrenness may not be of your doing? Tostig may be using a blunted spear?"

Aghast at the absurd suggestion, Judith would have leapt to her feet, were it not for Mathilda reaching out to take her hand. "There is no fault with my husband!" Judith declared, embarrassed. "He is a man of passion and strength. How dare you think otherwise of him? Why would he be any the different from his brothers?"

Soothing the unexpected ire, Mathilda responded with calm. "I meant only that there is perhaps another of his kin who cannot produce children. Queen Edith is also unblessed." Mathilda shook her head with genuine dismay. "If it is God's will for a woman to be barren, then so be it, but for a queen to fail in her duty? This is a dreadful thing."

It is a dreadful thing for any woman who desperately wants a child, queen or peasant, Judith thought swiftly and bitterly, but there was no point in saying so. Mathilda would not understand.

Her sister continued. "There was something, I believe, about Edward claiming to remain chaste. Do you not think that rumour to be nonsense? A ruse to hide the truth of her barrenness or his impotence, I would wager. William says that when the time comes and the English are seeking a strong man to succeed Edward, they will offer him the crown."

Judith sat quite still, her mouth open, no words coming from her astonished lips. Had she heard right? Could her sister be a little deranged from the trauma of the delivery? "He cannot become king of England," she said with bewildered hesitancy. "He is a Norman. He would never be chosen by the Council or accepted by the people."

"I fail to see of what relevance his nationality is," Mathilda said with derision. "Queen Emma was Norman. Cnut was Danish. My husband is the strongest, the most politically astute leader. On those criteria alone, he is the most suited. He has quite set his mind on becoming a king."

Judith lifted herself from the bed. Her sister had indeed changed since her marriage. She had studied her politics well—but they were Norman based, Norman biased. She had no concept of differing views or laws, no idea that English might not run parallel with Norman. "Your husband is a brave and valiant man," she responded with courtesy, "but he does not carry Wessex blood. Besides, the boy Edgar is named ætheling. He is more likely to be England's next king."

Mathilda regarded her elder sister with amusement. Poor woman, did she so little understand the drive of an ambitious man? Perhaps that was indeed the case. Tostig was a dullard when it came to the pursuit of power—and undoubtedly also in the passion of love. "Edgar?" she said with condescension. "He is of but tender years. My dear, even your staid husband would be more suited to wear the crown than such a child! William will be England's choice." Mathilda gave a single, sharp nod of her head; the matter was settled. She stretched. Her back and shoulders ached; so, too, did her head. "I think I shall sleep for a while, birthing is wearisome business. You are fortunate, you know, not to suffer all this tawdry mess and pain."

Hurt, tired, dispirited and still stomach-queasy from the beginning of her menstrual flow, Judith reacted to her sister's patronising with uncharacteristic outrage. "Why could Tostig not be considered? He is a much respected earl. He has brought law, order and justice to Northumbria. And I might remind you that, unlike your William, he carries some blood of the Wessex line in his veins."

Mathilda retorted sharply, "He also has an elder brother—or have you forgotten Harold? William considers that Ædward's death three days after arriving in

London was no jest of nature." She stared meaningfully at Judith. "To a man who has a secret ambition for a crown, Ædward's going to England would have been most inconvenient."

Malice suddenly flared into Judith's mind. How supercilious her wretched younger sister had become! She walked swiftly but with dignity towards the door, her rose-coloured wimple fluttering behind like a wind-filled sail "Except your hypothesis is fundamentally flawed. Neither my husband nor brother-in-law harbours such ambition. If anyone had a reason to arrange Ædward's murder, as you imply, madam, then it would be the man who would suffer most at his continuing existence. I would suggest that we look no further than your husband. It is he, after all, who lusts for a crown that will never be offered him while an English candidate lives." As a final parry she added, "Besides, he has Henry of France to deal with before he can look across the Channel Sea."

13

Varaville

Burdened with plunder and far inside William's territory, Henry of France made his way towards the Dives, reaching the wide tidal river at the ford near Varaville, north-west of Caen. His contempt for Duke William was complete. Did the man have no care for the well-being of his land or its people? To save his own hide, was he prepared to cower behind his castle walls and allow an invading army to lay waste all this western area of Normandy without making a single move to stop it? Not one arrow shot from a bow, not one spear sent with its bite of death. No barricade, nothing. That William was soon to concede that the power of France was too much for him was becoming more apparent as each day passed.

Once Henry had crossed this river, the whole of Normandy lay before him and William would have lost his chance to put up a fight against him.

The French army numbered in their thousands, their rapaciously collected loot an extra burden to carry on the supply carts together with all the necessary baggage and war machinery. Crossing a river took time, for the fording places were few and the logistics of transferring so many people and so much equipment in safety, and quickly, across deep water was a headache for any commander.

Only half the French army had successfully reached the far side when the tide turned and began to flood, making the ford impassable. It was then that Henry realised his mistake.

William was not afraid, nor had he been hiding. He had been waiting. Waiting for an opportunity to use his few resources against Henry's many. The King in his pride and greed had marched direct into the Duke of Normandy's trap.

With merciless ferocity, William attacked those who were left with inadequate defences on the western side of the river. Few escaped. The waters ran red, and when the tide turned once more, the dead and dying were swept out into the loneliness of the open sea.

Defeated and broken, Henry fled, and neither he nor his ally Geoffrey d'Anjou would dare bring an army so far into Norman territory again.

William was almost his own man. Now he could begin building his strength even further to a degree none expected. With no one to oppose him the Vexin, Mantes, Pontoise and the vast, wealthy territory of Maine could become his. He was undefeated—but not yet satisfied; ambition was a difficult lust to conquer.

14

Rhuddlan—January 1058

Alditha, only daughter of Ælfgar, the English Earl of Mercia, could not understand why she was here. Wales, the people, the beauty of the mountains, she loved. Prince Gruffydd ap Llewelyn, who had murdered her grandfather and taken Gwynedd—Wales—for his own greed, she detested. Why, then, had she pledged to him her marriage vows?

Gruffydd's Hall at Rhuddlan was crowded, mostly with Welsh, but there were fifty or so of her father's English followers present who, like him, had no qualms about taunting Edward. Ælfgar had disagreed with his king—again—not two months after Leofric his father had died last autumn. The old man had belligerently fought his debilitating illness, some said to make his son wait the longer to receive the earldom of Mercia—and like a charging boar, heedless of the consequences, Ælfgar had almost immediately quarrelled with Edward and been outlawed for treason. Without hesitation, knowing he would be welcomed by Prince Gruffydd, he had crossed into Wales, planning an ultimate gesture of defiance against England and Edward while assuring an alliance with the Welsh.

At Holy Well, before the doors of the reed-thatched chapel, Ælfgar, without consultation with her or more than a handful of hours of warning, gave his only daughter in marriage to Gruffydd of Wales. Through her the two men were to be linked as more than friends and allies, they were to be kin. Seated, arms linked around each other's shoulders, Ælfgar and Gruffydd shared yet another jug of barley ale and shouted their ribald comments that denigrated Edward and all his nobles. They were drunk, the pair of them, as were most men in the Hall and a good few of the women.

Alditha sat beside her husband at the Prince's table set upon the dais at the high end of the Hall, her head erect, hands folded in her lap. She had spoken barely a single word since Gruffydd had placed that wedding band on her finger. Her skin was pale, eyes fixed, unseeing. She felt nothing at the Holy Well as Gruffydd had lifted her up before his saddle bow and ridden off with her here to

Rhuddlan, his men and her father's galloping after them, whooping and yelling as if they were on the scent of the chase. Had lain rigid in Gruffydd's bed that first night and those following, not caring what he did to her body, thinking of nothing but the black, despairing scream that echoed silently round and round her mind.

She had adored her mother, a slender and serene woman who had told her of her homeland of Wales: of its soaring, dragon-breathed mountains, verdant valleys plunging with the white gush of waterfalls, its mood-changing skies. Told her too of its legends, its tales of heroes, magicians and poets. Alditha had cherished her part-Welsh blood, despite the other tales her mother had told, the more sombre stories of treachery and deceit, of lies, hatred and murder. Of the emptiness of an unhappy marriage and a life passed by without love.

She understood, now that her father had abandoned her into Gruffydd's iron-hard ownership. Understood how her mother had been traded to make an alliance. Understood how she too must once have fought the tears and the desperate wanting to take a dagger blade to her wrist...

Although often frightened of her father, Alditha had loved him as a daughter ought to love her parent. More—she had adored him with the unquestioning innocence of a child—until that hot summer's day when she had met and talked of horses with an Englishman called Harold beside the river Severn. She had scorned Earl Harold's disrespectful ridicule of her father, had defended his honour—how stupid she had been! How naïve and trusting—or had she been deluding herself? Not wanting to admit the truth that her mother had suffered the loneliness and despair of a forced marriage? Had borne children to an opinionated, deceitful and arrogant man?

In the hour before her marriage at the Holy Well, the deep pool of water sprung from the shed blood of Saint Winifred, Alditha had knelt and made her prayers to that blessed woman. But either she had not heard or had ignored the seventeen-year-old girl's desperate plea: Alditha had become wife to Gruffydd.

Her only hope, now that she could not escape, was that she might bear a son or daughter to whom she could pass on those tales of the heroes of Wales, of her mother's—her—ancestors. Of Hywel Dda—Hywel the Good and Rhodri Mawr—Rhodri the Great. Through a son of hers their blood would return to Wales. She would tell, too, of others from further into the past—of Cunedda who had come, exiled, from Scotland during the time of the ending of the Romans; and of King Arthur and Gwenhwyfar his wife. Only those thoughts kept the will to endure alive in her mind.

"Lady?"

She flinched, jerked her head to look quickly at the man who had come up behind her, looked into a weather-browned and wrinkled face. He smiled, apologising for startling her. Ednyved ap Davydd, seneschal to Gruffydd. They had met when first her father had come to Wales in exile and then again at that wedding ceremony four days past. Ednyved was an old man, as craggy and worn as the hills. The Snow Mountain carried a crest of white; so too did he.

"Lady, the hour grows late and I am too ancient a man for carousing into the small hours of the night. The heart is willing, but…" With a wry smile he indicated the staff he leant upon to aid his walking and rubbed at the joint-ache that swelled his knee. "Merry-making with wine and song is, alas, a pastime for those with a younger spirit. I am away to my bed, I bid you a good night." His crinkled smile reached into his speedwell-blue eyes as he took up her hand and placed a light, respectful kiss on her fingers. And then he said, so quiet that she barely heard. "I served under your grandfather. I, and many of my kind, loved him well. You have the look of your mother about you, but you have your grandfather's eyes too, lass. There are those of us who are hoping you have also his spirit and his courage." His solemn, insistent gaze met with hers as she realised his meaning. "We need one of his line to rid Wales of the traitor who killed him." He let go her hand, bowed and was gone, walking, despite his age and world-weary bones, with dignity from the Hall.

Gruffydd, sitting next to her, had not noticed Ednyved take his leave, nor had anyone else, for a new barrel of barley-ale had just been opened. The wise old seneschal had timed his exit well.

She rose from her seat, dipped a reverence at Gruffydd. "I am weary, my Lord, I shall await you in our bed."

He waved his hand at her without pausing from relating a lengthy tale of bravado to her father, barely noticed her leaving.

With fortune, Alditha thought, *he will be too drunk to find his way to the stairwell, let along the chamber above.*

A calm had settled over her, coupled with an iced hardness that had wreathed itself around her heart. There were others, then, who remembered and who despised Gruffydd for what and who he was. Who were waiting their opportunity for revenge, to be rid of him.

The emptiness of isolation evaporated. That opportunity, she vowed as she climbed the wooden stairs to her bed-chamber, would come. She would make it come.

15

Falaise—August 1060

On such a hot and humid day, Mathilda had elected to take herself and the children out beyond the castle walls and sit beneath the shade of the trees beside the river. The baby went too. Stripping her of her close-wrapped linen, Mathilda laid the three-month-old girl on her back on a blanket, let her kick and gurgle, her little fists waving at the glittering patterns of sunlight that flickered through the leaves. Cecily was perhaps the sweetest of all her children, but then the youngest always was. Three boys and two girls—if their next child were a girl also, that would balance the way of things so nicely.

Rufus—"red-face"—had remained as a family nickname for young William, three years old now and a sturdy lad, determined to help his two elder brothers catch the tiny fish that darted through the water reeds along the river edge. They already had plenty in their bucket, every so often carrying it over to their mother to show her their prowess.

Mathilda was a content woman. Beautiful children, a loyal husband—she rarely thought of his darker side, his ruthless streak. To crown her contentment, the silly squabble with the papacy about the legality of their marriage was at last ended. Mind, for the past few years the interdict on Normandy had paled into insignificance beside the backbiting in Rome itself over the election and reelection of a new pope.

"Mind you do not lean too far over, *chéri* Mathilda called to five-year-old Richard with an indulgent smile. "The river runs shallow here at the edge, but is deep to the centre." She turned her attention back to Agatha, kneeling beside her, the tip of her tongue peeping from between her lips as she sewed a few more stitches of embroidery along the two-inch-wide strip of braiding. The pattern was simple, but demanding for a six-year-old not yet dextrous with her fingers. For a second time Mathilda helped her daughter unravel a knot in the thread, and then the baby, Cecily, began to cry. Mathilda picked her up, cradling her in her arms, rocking her and crooning a lullaby.

Richard was the intrepid one of the three brothers, ever eager to explore, to seek adventure. It was he who would be found trailing in the wake of soldiers patrolling the castle walls or taking close interest in the men-at-arms' archery, sword and lance practice. Already he had demanded his own pony and a wooden sword. Bored with kneeling on the grass beside the river, Richard pulled off his shoes and stockings and, tucking his tunic high into his belt, slid into the water. He waded in a few feet and beckoned to his brother. "Come on, Rob, come on in. Look, the fish think my legs are reed stalks! No, not you, Rufus, you're too little."

Rufus, who had already begun to pull off his leather shoes, chewed his lip, a wail of protest hovering. "You stay there on guard." Richard advised hurriedly, "watch that no one steals our fish or well have nothing to eat for supper tonight."

It worked. Padding, one shoe on, one shoe off, over to the bucket, Rufus squatted down before it, intent on his important task. He was not certain that he could eat these wriggling fish for his supper, but if his elder brother wanted fish, then he would defend them valiantly against any thief.

The eldest boy, Robert, still sat on the bank. He shook his head. Mama had said the water was deep and he was not enthused by the thought of cold, clammy fish brushing against his skin. He shivered. What if there were other things in the river—eels, for instance? He was frightened of eels; they looked too much like snakes. At seven, and as the eldest, he thought perhaps he ought warn his brother of his foolishness. Rivers were dangerous places—Mama had told him so. "You come out, before Mama sees. She'll not be pleased that you are in the water, it's dirty."

"You're scared!" Richard taunted. "Frightened of getting wet, are you?" He scooped water into his hands and sent it splashing over his brother. Tunic, hair and legs soaked, Robert ran to Mathilda, thrust his arms around her stout waistline and buried his face in her skirt.

"What is the wretched boy weeping about now?"

Mathilda looked up at the sound of the voice approaching through the trees and squeaked her joy. Thrusting the baby into the nurse's hands while disentangling herself from Robert's distraught clutches, she ran to meet William, her arms outstretched, happiness lighting up her face.

"Oh, blessed Mary, you are returned! How long have you been back?" The questions came fast as she embraced him, her hands exploring his chest and arms—"You have come to no harm, there is no injury? Oh, but I have worried these months while you have been away at Thimert. Is the siege ended? Tell me it is and that Henry has ceded your rights to the castle!"

William took hold of both her hands to still their fluttering over his body, grinning boyishly at her. He was thirty-two years old, but felt and looked ten years younger.

"*Oui*, it is over, but more than that, this bickering between Normandy and France is ended. Completely and totally ended!"

Mathilda's eyes widened. "Then you have made peace? Oh, I am so delighted!"

William clamped his strong hands to her waist and twirled her around as if she were one of the children. "*Non, ma belle*, I have not had to make peace—Henry is dead. His boy son, Philip, is king. There will be no more fighting, Normandy is independent. A child could never threaten me!"

Her hands on his shoulders, her feet dangling several inches from the ground, Mathilda stared at her husband in disbelief. Could this be true? Was it all, really, over? "No more fighting? No more wars?" A smile of sunburst radiance spread across her face. "Oh, William, I need no longer fear for your life!"

Her husband set her down and scratched at his ear. It would not quite be like that; Geoffrey d'Anjou still prowled along the borders but, according to rumour, he was ailing. Brittany too was never a safe entity. He said nothing, though, allowed her the small pleasure of revelling in the thought of a peaceful future.

16

⚜

Gloucester—December 1062

On behalf of the King, Harold stepped out from the warmth of the Hall to speak to the messenger. Within, the Christmas revelries were under way, a chance for feasting, dance and song, trials of strength, games of wit or cunning. Out here, in the quietness of the courtyard three hours after dark, the frost was setting hard, the rim of ice in puddles and hollows cracking beneath Harold's boots as he ran down the steps and crossed the courtyard. The messenger was a Mercian man, wearing the badge of Ælfgar at his shoulder.

"Where is your lord?" Harold enquired brusquely, eyeing the heaving breath of the man's mount, the way it was not resting weight four-square on its offside foreleg. He bent down, lifted the hoof. No shoe, the nail holes torn, the wall of the foot ragged and the sole bruised. "Ælfgar ought to have arrived yester-evening. The King is vexed that his Earl of Mercia has not appeared at his Christmas Court." Ælfgar. That whore-poxed man was trouble. If he was contemplating running off into Wales yet again…

Since the summer of 1058, the peace had more or less lasted across the borders between Wales and England. Four years ago Ælfgar had turned traitor to England and joined with Gruffydd by marrying his daughter to him. Hah! But for how long had the two whoresons run together? Six months? Seven? They had not discovered, in England, exactly what had happened to break the union but they could guess. Ælfgar had quarrelled with his son-in-law—Gruffydd being overpossessive with spoils of war. Typically Ælfgar had jerked his fist in the air at Wales and returned to Edward's court pleading for another pardon. And, typically, Edward, soft-livered fool that he was, had granted it. Harold would have told Ælfgar to go sail a leaking ship. He sighed as he examined the horse's injured foot.

So peace, aside from minor raiding, had held. Mind, that was probably more because Gruffydd had been busy fighting among his own kind, trying to keep his head attached to his shoulders. Once he had sorted out the differences between those of the Celtic blood, he would be dipping his greedy paws into England's wealth again. And Ælfgar would again decide Wales offered him a better profit than did England.

"So?" Harold repeated, standing legs spread, arms folded. "What is Ælfgar's excuse for failing to attend the Christmas summons? I trust it is good enough to warrant laming a decent horse."

"My Lord Wessex," the messenger stammered. "Ælfgar is dead. Three days ago his horse stumbled and he fell. His neck was broken."

≈

King Edward's shocked cry of disbelief brought the boisterous game with the water-filled pig's bladder to an abrupt halt. Gyrth Godwinesson, in possession of the "pig," had been about to attempt to toss it through the willow hoop dangling from the central roof beam. He paused, his arm upstretched, his head, like everyone else's, swivelling towards the King.

A moment before Edward had been cheering and clapping, urging his chosen team, captained by Tostig and winning by four goals to three. Gyrth's opposing players had captured the trophy, had manoeuvred their way with ducked heads, shoving elbows and kicking feet through the rough jostle of players to the hoop, unaware of Harold bending to whisper in Edward's ear.

Something was wrong; silence ripped through the Hall to hang suspended and expectant, like that willow hoop. Unashamedly, tears began to flow down Edward's wrinkled cheeks, his fingers automatically reaching out for the comfort of Edith's hand as she sat, as often she did of late, on a stool at his feet. Harold was whispering to both of them; she shook her head, patted Edward's hand. The news was bad, that was plain.

Edward, too shocked to speak, motioned for Edith to break the news, A speculative rustle was creeping across the Hall like a spreading marsh mist. Edith stood, her eyes drawn to the two young men frozen in their stance marking Gyrth. Eadwine and Morkere, Earl Ælfgar's sons. A pair of most handsome lads, Eadwine the elder at fifteen, Morkere a year younger.

Edith stepped down from the dais and walked across to them. "News has come. Your father is dead." And she told them of how and when.

Stirred so easily by joy or sorrow, Edward had stumbled, weeping, after her. Unexpected death ever shocked him, particularly now he was nearing his fifty-third year on this earth. He caught hold of Eadwine's shoulders, embraced him. "My dear boy! I am devastated for you. It is such sudden, tragic news!"

How could Eadwine answer? With a lie, the truth?

Morkere, standing a step or so behind his brother, saved him the trouble of deciding. "Thank you for your condolence, but my father was a dog turd who ought to have been thrown on the dung heap at birth."

Edward's tears ceased; his mouth opened, appalled.

Glowering at his brother's tactlessness Eadwine hastily interrupted, "My father had no love for us, Sir, nor we for him. He was only concerned with furthering his own interests. We—myself, my brother Morkere and our sister Alditha— were nothing to him except useful stepping stones if he needed to cross a river." The lad looked around at the men and women of the English court: nobles, merchants, guildsmen and revered elders; the two Archbishops, Ealdred of York and Stigand of Canterbury; the lesser clergy of the Church. He snorted his contempt. "I doubt there is one man or woman present in this Hall who will grieve for his going." He indicated his brother who came forward to stand beside him. "At last we are free of him to serve you, my Lord King, as we wish, and as our grandfather wished. With honour and loyalty."

Spontaneous applause began to ripple, then spread like a bore-tide from hand to hand. Edward was weeping again—he truly had no control over his emotions— was, in a choking voice, ushering the two young men to come join him on the royal dais.

Tostig appeared at Harold's shoulder, "So Mercia's earldom falls vacant, I doubt Edward will give it to Leofwine or Gyrth."

Harold's low laugh was mocking. "That he will not. We already hold all else of England between us!" Through narrowed eyes he watched the King making a fuss of Ælfgar's sons, ensuring they had wine, were offered food. A moment before he had hardly noticed their existence. "No, my brother, Eadwine has just seen to it that he gets Mercia for himself. That was quick thinking neatly done. The eldest lad appears to have more of a brain in his head than his damned father ever had."

The disrupted game set aside, the occupants of the Hall turned to other entertainment. The mead barrels still contained much of their honey-sweetened amber liquid, the jugglers and acrobats began performing at the far end of the Hall. Gyrth and Leofwine Godwinesson pushed their way through the tumble of gossiping groups to join the two elder brothers. When Leofric had died and Ælfgar had claimed Mercia, Gyrth had been content with the giving of East Anglia and Essex, but Leofwine, who had been awarded Hertfordshire, Oxfordshire and Buckinghamshire, had always hoped for more.

"How ambitious is he, I wonder?" Leofwine asked Harold. "And what is there for Morkere? I am not prepared to give up land for his benefit, I hold next to nothing as it is."

Gyrth solemnly nodded his head. "We must not forget their sister. Ælfgar gave not a bent coin for her, but his offspring are close. I wonder what they think of alliance with Gruffydd, their brother-in-law?"

"Aye." Tostig agreed. "And what contemptible advantage will that poxed Welshman try to take of Ælfgar's death? Cheshire and Shropshire are temporarily without an earl to rally the fyrd. The simple-minded land-folk will be confused as to whom they are to follow. You cannot tell me that Gruffydd will miss any opportunity to make mischief."

Wetting his fingers with spittle, Harold smoothed the lay of his moustache. That trail of thought ran similar to his own—for how long had they been waiting for a God-given chance to strike at Gruffydd? "I wonder," he said ponderously, "if the daughter has yet been informed of her father's unfortunate accident? How long will it take Gruffydd to react to it? A few days? A week? Two?"

Gyrth allowed a slight lopsided grin to trip across his right cheek. "You are planning something, big brother. I recognise that gleam in your eye. You are hoping to go into Wales."

Leofwine's grin was broader. "Would this planning have anything to do with rescuing a fair-faced maiden from a Welsh dragon's lair by any chance?"

Harold slapped his younger brother between the shoulder blades. "Hah!" he chortled. "You remember the Lady Alditha also!"

"How could I forget such a beauty?" Leofwine answered.

Tostig took a moment to follow the ribald implication of his brother's remarks and dampened the jocularity by saying gruffly, "Alditha, the sister of those two lads, is wed to Gruffydd."

Harold patted Tostig's arm and began walking away towards the King. "Not so, brother. I intend to make her Gruffydd's widow."

17

Rhuddlan

This time, there was to be no waiting. Strike hard and fast. Unexpectedly. They left Gloucester soon after midnight, Harold riding north with those of his housecarls who had accompanied him to the Christmas Court, mounted on sturdy British ponies bred for their intelligence and endurance. Setting a steady rhythmic pace, they alternated a stout walk with a jogtrot that covered the miles easily as night lightened into approaching dawn. Once every hour the men—and Harold too—dismounted to lead the horses for ten minutes, reaching Shrewsbury, a distance of almost one hundred miles, by noon.

For one hour they rested the horses, watering them from the river Severn and feeding them corn dampened with ale. The animals rested, but not the men. A lame or sore-backed mount was of no use to anyone. Hooves needed tending, worn shoes must be replaced or clenches that had risen hammered in. Goose fat rubbed into any saddle or girth gall. The men ate their saddle-bag rations of cold meat and wheaten biscuits where they squatted beside their ponies. No time to waste on cooking.

Edward had been against a raid into Wales—Tostig had urged caution. Wait, they had both said. Spring would offer a better time for fighting—or summer, when troops could live the more easily off the land and daylight allowed for easy travelling. "Aye," Harold had answered with impatient anger, "if by summer Gruffydd has left us anything on the land."

Obstinately, the King had refused financial support, declaring, with what he had intended to be the final word on the matter, that if Harold wanted to waste his time and the lives of his men, then he could do so at his own expense.

Riding onwards from Shrewsbury, with a man who held a grudge against Gruffydd willing to guide them into Wales—the horses were tired but, brave, stout creatures that they were, had more miles in them yet—Harold recalled his terse answer to his king.

"Then it is agreed. Within four and twenty hours I shall be at Rhuddlan, outside the door of Gruffydd's stronghold. When his castle falls, all of value will be for myself and my men."

"Even my sister?" Eadwine had challenged.

"Aye, even your sister, were I not already married!" Harold had answered.

They doubted he could do it! Those poxed, cushion-using, courtly simpletons. Ride from Gloucester to North Wales within four and twenty hours? Your horses will be lamed, your men exhausted, they had jeered. Yet the Great King, Alfred, had once pursued the Danes one hundred and forty miles across land to Chester in such a time. Harold, his men and their horses, were muscle-fit and eager. Why could it not be done? All it required was determination and a worthy goal at the end of it all.

The English crossed into Clwyd and left behind the Saxon roadways, following instead rough, steep and twisting hill tracks that wound through closely wooded valleys. The pace slowed, the men dismounting often to lead their ponies in single file, their way, once darkness fell, lit by the wavering, tree-dappled light of a half-moon that sailed bright and clear in an unclouded, star-sprinkled sky.

Aleditha lay awake, watching the narrow strip of moonlight lancing through the gap in the window shutters. Beside her, Gruffydd lay on his back, snoring; at the end of the bed his favourite hound scratched at a flea. Aleditha disapproved of the dogs in their bedchamber, but Gruffydd always had his way and besides, at least the animal kept her feet warm. She could not sleep because she was cold and because her two-year-old daughter was ill.

Several times during the night she had gone to see Nest, padding in slippered feet down the wooden stairs, across the corner of the frost-frozen courtyard to the roundhouse outbuilding that was the place where the children slept, Gruffydd would not have the girl in their own chamber for fear of catching her fever, nor allow his wife to sleep curled with the children around the hearth fire because of his own needs. On her last visit, the girl's sweating had eased, thank the Holy Mother, the swelling to her throat not so pronounced. Aleditha had sat a while, the little girl cradled on her lap, while her nurse spooned more of the honey-sweetened mixture of feverfew, rue and coltsfoot into the child's mouth; had cuddled her close until she had fallen asleep.

So cold! Aleditha wriggled her toes beneath the weight of the dog, snuggled the bear fur tighter around her shoulders. From somewhere outside a wolf howled. There were not so many wolves wandering in the mountains as once there had been, nor bears. The fur for this bed had come from the wild highlands of Scotland. In the frozen islands out in the western seas there were great white bears, she had been told. Creatures that could knock a man's head from his shoulders with one swipe of a paw. Gruffydd turned over in his sleep, grunting. She wished a white bear would come to take off Gruffydd's head.

Sighing, sleep still refusing to come, Alditha slid from beneath the covers and, wrapping her thickest woollen cloak around her shoulders, went to the single narrow window, easing open the shutter to allow an inch or so of new-come daylight to peep through. As the pink and gold of dawn strengthened, the crisp silver-white rime of frost that clung to roof, wall and courtyard began to shimmer and sparkle. Tomorrow would be the first day of January. Another year gone, another mid-winter and yuletide festival finished and done with.

Looking out across the wooden rampart walls to the rise of the winter-bare, snow-topped mountains, Alditha could almost believe that spring would never return. Leafless branches of tree and bush, flowerless, frost-glimmered, bracken-dead grass. A smell of smoke on the air, a rustle of noise and movement from the wattle-built settlement clustered against the stronghold's outer wall.

A glint of light on something that shone…she did not realise what she was seeing…a standard lying limp at its pole in a breathless new morning, a man's helmet, horses…fire crackling along the thatch of a house place, a woman screaming…And the night watch were running along the walkway, the warning bell clamouring its alarm. Men tumbling from the Hall, sleep-blearied, half-dressed, hopping on one foot while pulling on boots. Gruffydd pushing her away from the window, flinging the shutter wide, leaning out, cursing virulently.

"Get my clothes, woman!" he bellowed, tugging leather gambeson on over his undertunic, cursing as he searched for his left boot. Ednyved his seneschal burst into the room. "Sir—the English have come upon us! Christ alone in His Heaven knows how the Earl of Wessex has managed it—he surely could not have heard of Ælfgar any length of time before us; we only heard the day before yesterday. I have ordered the men to the ramparts—"

"Curse the sodding men—get a crew on to my ship!"

"But we can make a fight of this! Harold appears to have only a few hundred men. If we can hold him off—"

"If? What if we cannot? Have you looked out of that window, man? The settlement is burning, the rampart walls will be next—or the gateway. A few hundred men? Jesu wept, what chance have we if Harold should get inside? What chance have I?" Gruffydd buckled on his baldric, slid his sword into its sheath. "I have no desire to dangle from a roof beam or be taken in chains to Edward." Brusquely he shouldered Ednyved from his path, ran through the door and started down the steps, Alditha behind him.

She caught hold of his arm, bringing him to an abrupt halt, her expression dark. "So you are to flee? Running like a hunted hare. What of us, my Lord? Of your men, of me and your daughter? Are you to leave us here to die?"

Gruffydd prised her fingers from his arm. "Only your modesty is in danger from Earl Harold, but once he discovers how ice-hard you are in bed he'll soon leave you be." He turned and ran on, out into the daylight, across the courtyard and through the water-door to Rhuddlan's river-wharf, Alditha's contempt ringing in his ears.

"You ball-less son of a heathen bitch! You cowardly dog turd!"

His own ship could not be made ready, too heavy in its ornamentation, too close moored to the river bank. He leapt for a trader's vessel, already making sail at the first warning of attack, stood in the bows as the craft was taken to safety by the current, which, by his great fortune, was at full ebb. He left behind his fleet and his fighting men. Barely an arrow or spear was hurled against Earl Harold's Englishmen; instead, the gates of Rhuddlan were opened to him.

Alditha waited, proud, on the highest of the Hall's timber steps. With her, Ednyved, leaning heavily on his staff. Behind her a woman coddled a whimpering child, wrapped well in blankets.

Harold dismounted, handed the reins of his stallion to his captain and stood a brief moment regarding the lady, his hand resting casually on the hilt of his sword.

The geese in their pen were cackling and honking; overhead, a rabble of seagulls squabbled. The people of Rhuddlan, fighting men and their women, servants, craftsmen, the entire community of a stronghold, stood in silence apart from a few muffled coughs and the monotonous tears of a child. In turn, they steadily regarded the tall Englishman.

Sweeping the lady a bow, Harold mounted the steps, took her hand and laid his lips to its smoothness, his eyes not leaving hers. "I offer you condolences for the death of your father," he said, "though if you cared for him as little as your brothers, you will not require sympathy." Added, "I would ask why it is that the Lady of Wales greets me, not her husband, Prince Gruffydd."

"The Lady greets you because her miserable husband is running like a whipped hound with his tail tucked behind his shrivelled manhood. Regrettably, you have missed the pleasure of his snivelling company."

Ednyved stepped forward, bowed, introduced himself. "I would ask for the safe keeping of those within this stronghold. We offered you no resistance, we ask for your guarantee of protection."

"You have it. No man, woman or child will be mistreated for I have no quarrel with the people of Wales, only with their coxcomb prince. I would have the place immediately cleared, however, for my men have orders to take what trophies they wish and fire everything remaining that will burn. Should Gruffydd return, all he will find of Rhuddlan is ash and smoke."

His housecarls, ranged on tired horses behind him, raised their war spears and axes with a shout of victory, then began to dismount and search through house place, bothy and barn for whatever there might be of value.

"And me?" Alditha asked as Harold's men pushed past her to ransack the Hall "What do you intend to do with me and my daughter? She is ill, would you leave us with no roof over our heads and the frost so cold in the ground?"

"I would wager there is suitable shelter within a day's walk of here, madam," Harold answered, "but you will have no fear of muddying your skirts. You will be mounted upon one of those fine horses that I see being led from your husband's stable and escorted with all courtesy back to England. King Edward and your brothers, I am sure, will welcome you."

Alditha stared at the Earl in defiance, said, hardly believing her own words, "I thank you for the offer of one of my own horses, but if these good Welsh people must walk, then I shall walk with them. I have no desire to return with you into England." What possessed her? She had no wish to remain with that coward of a husband a moment longer than necessary…yet she shared the heart of the people of Wales, could not turn her back on them.

Harold responded with a half-grin. "I am afraid it is not a choice I offer you. This is but a brief raid on Gruffydd's pride. I intend, soon, to take all of Wales from him. I cannot leave you for Gruffydd to use as hostage against those of us in England who care for you."

Alditha tossed her head. "Do you then care for me, my Lord? When last we met I was but a child. Now I am a woman grown with a child of my own." She was indeed a woman, one of beauty; was wasted here beneath these cloud-shadowed mountains. Needed a better man than Gruffydd to share her bed. Harold felt his manhood stir, his throat run dry…were it not for Edyth, or that this dark-haired siren still had a legal husband…

"I could serve you the better here in Wales," she said. "With my own hand I will cut out that bastard's heart if he should dare come within close range of my dagger blade."

Harold did not doubt her, but still he took her back to England.

18

North Wales—May 1063

Through the tedious grey of rain-laden winter months, Harold had set his mind to plan his conquest of Wales, strategy, options and tactics preoccupying his thoughts. That burning of Gruffydd's ships and property at Rhuddlan had only been a sting in the tail for the Welsh prince; this time, when Harold was ready to take an army across the border, the spear must bite mortally deep. For one or other of them, there would be no second chance.

Tactics. Strategy. Constant, restless thoughts that had isolated his waking hours and invaded his sleep. Sleep that soon became clogged by red-misted dreams of battle and death. Muddled dreams where Harold wandered alone and confused on high, snow-clad mountains or found himself trapped by men pushing and crushing, their faces ugly, voices screaming for blood to be spilt. Death was there in the blades of red-stained swords. And with death, the woman. Always, somewhere in each recurring dream, the woman had been there, sometimes with a child straddling her hips, more often alone, but ever silent, no gasp or cry leaving her lips as she watched him die at the hands of those men that crowded so close.

As the hedgerows blossomed with the white-frothed, heavy scent of the hawthorn, Harold was ready and eager to enter Wales. The King was equally enthusiastic, for this time there was no doubting that Gruffydd would be defeated. It would deplete his treasury to finance a war, but the reward at the end of it would surely outweigh the expense. Wales would be his to command as he willed, the first English king to bring the Welsh under total English rule. Aye, he well liked the idea.

And Edyth? Though she said nothing, Edyth knew the meaning of Harold's dreams. She knew that one way or another he would not be coming back to her. The stars wheeled in the sky, the sun chased the moon and the seasons turned. Babes were born and men died. Everything must evolve and grow. Nothing could ever remain static, for life—the world—would stagnate and begin to smell foul. For eighteen years had she been wife to Harold, her love for him never wavering, her need never diminishing. Six surviving children had she borne him: Goddwin, the eldest, nine months the younger than her marriage, now a man grown with a wife and soon-to-be-born babe of his own. Her last-born, Gunnhild, a girl of four years, Edmund and Magnus on the verge of growing up; Algytha, fifteen, ready to become a woman.

Wales had changed Harold; he had become single-minded. Determination to see an end to Gruffydd seared through him as if a dagger wound had penetrated his heart, stifling his good sense like a mould growing upon rotting fruit.

What would be harder to endure, Edyth wondered, as Harold mounted his stallion and rode out beneath the gate arch of their manor, a hand lifted in farewell: news that he had fallen in battle or that he had fulfilled his promise to that dark-eyed, half-Welsh woman?

Oh, Edyth knew who was the woman in those dreams. She had lain with Harold through those restless nights of winter, her arms clasped tight around him as he sweated and tossed through the night. Had heard the name that his sleep had whispered: Alditha.

⁓

Gruffydd ap Llewelyn had overreached himself. He had made the mistake of all who wanted too much for themselves and took it without regard for others. There were those in Deheubarth who resented the killing of his rival, Gryffydd ap Rhydderch, and not a few ambitious kindred, men pleased to accept the opportunity to be rid of him—even at the high price of bowing the knee to the representative of an English king. It had ever been a weakness of the Celtic peoples, their inclination to fight among themselves, rather than unite against a common enemy. Earl Harold of Wessex took full advantage of it as he sailed his fleet of ships along the rugged southern coast of Wales where he landed, encountering only token gestures of defiance from the Welsh who had no desire to shed blood for Gruffydd, a man who had fled with a sheathed sword from attack. The Welsh respected a warrior, scorned a man who pissed himself as he ran. Those who nursed a grudge against the North welcomed Harold as his longships beached on the shore; others needed convincing with sharpened blades. Harold made war in the time-honoured method of Saxon, Viking, Irish—and Welsh—alike. Ravage the land and plunder for valuables until the victim found it cheaper to agree to a treaty rather than be ruined. Treaties, after all, could always, when it suited, be broken. An economy was not so easily rebuilt.

Tactics. Strategy. Therein lay the vulnerability of the disunited Welsh. No tactics or strategy. Their warriors were brave and skilled, but their leaders did not look beyond the winning of each single battle. Harold did: he had planned throughout those long dark days of winter. This was what all those hours of training as a boy and young man had been for. This also was the blossoming of a natural talent as a commander of men.

With his own men raised from Wessex, augmented by those of his brothers Gyrth's and Leofwine's southern earldoms, he set Wales scurrying by campaigning from the sea, while Tostig marched over the border from Chester, driving the land-folk before him, leaving nothing but destruction in his wake. The Welsh, caught between the two brothers and the inhospitality of the mountains, had nowhere left to flee.

July was drawing to a close when, as planned, Harold joined with Tostig near the stronghold of Caer yn Arfon on the Gwynedd coast, with his army, several thousand strong, overlooked by the majestic sweep of the mountains of Eryri, the Snow Mountains. The Welsh had already decided their course. Tostig had come through the high passes and winding valleys, the sails of Harold's dragon-prowed warships filled the horizon. They did not want the English destroying their land, nor did they trust Gruffydd to stand and make a fight of things. A man who could show his spine to an enemy once could as easily bare his back again. The solution was simple.

On the fifth day of August, two months after Harold and his brother began their combined harrying of Wales, Gruffydd was slain by his own people and his head presented in surrender to the Earl of Wessex.

Whether Gruffydd's two half-brothers had a personal hand in his ending Harold did not ask. Better, perhaps, not to know. Both of them laid down their swords at Harold's feet and swore an oath to the Earl of Wessex, paying homage as vassals to the English King, surrendering hostages to ensure continued peace. Over and finished, as simply as that.

Harold ensured Wales would remain divided—and therefore impotent—by slicing her administration back into pieces, north divided from south, coast from mountain, split into small areas each with one leader who must kneel to Harold. The fighting would continue, the agreements would be broken—but not yet with England. For a while the Welsh would be too busy bickering among themselves, each clawing back what he thought was his above another's, to bother the English on the eastern banks of the river Severn.

Word was sent ahead and they were all there at Winchester to welcome the two brothers and the army home. In triumph they entered the town, parading their hostages and plunder before the cheering townsfolk. The King waited on the steps of his palace, his queen and clerics beside him, with the younger

Godwinessons and Eadwine and Morkere, sons of Ælfgar, to welcome home the warrior heroes.

Only one woman noticed the change in the Earl of Wessex. Edyth, waiting with his mother to the left of the King, knew that the man she had loved for what seemed all her life, her Harold, was not the same man who had ridden away from her at the manor that sun-dappled morning in late May. Acknowledging the crowd as they cheered and tossed rose petals before his side-stepping stallion, leaning down to kiss the young women who ran to touch his hand or knee, he was more self-assured, more ambitious, and, alarmingly, more ruthless in his determination to do what he felt was right, regardless of the opinion of others.

Only Edyth noticed how he had dismounted and walked, almost before acknowledging his king, straight to the Lady Alditha. He had taken her hand and removed Gruffydd's wedding band from her finger. Had lifted from its basket the head of a prince of Wales and presented it to her as gruesome fulfilment of his promise. Only Edyth had noticed how his eyes had lingered that moment too long on Alditha's.

Only Edyth, for no one else cared enough to notice, saw that more had happened to Harold, Earl of Wessex, than the mere conquering of Wales.

19

Westminster—June 1064

A restlessness that had been consuming Harold since his success in Wales spread and took root within him like a black canker.

England was at peace, Malcolm of Scotland had reneged on his treaty of homage, raiding over the borders into Northumbria, but Tostig had handled the situation with diplomatic negotiation, and had signed a new treaty. Mind, there were some in Northumbria, the older warriors, who grumbled that he ought have attacked in return, taught Scotland a lesson as Siward would have done. They were the men who held no liking for the King's favourite though, the ones who would stir trouble whenever excuse was offered them.

As Harold had intended, Wales was too occupied with internal wrangling between her fledgling princes to turn an eye towards England. Norway and Denmark were busy also, with their seesawing political arguments. Apart from seasonal pirate raids—an ongoing hazard for any coastal village or river-accessible settlement—peace had wafted over the whole country like a pleasant, hay-scented summer. Except there was no peace for Harold's spirit. The new-awakened lure of adventure, action and excitement bucked within him. He was bored by the routine inactivity of Edward's court.

Although a chill breeze was blowing off the river Thames—the wind often became more inclement with the flood tide—Edward insisted on personally inspecting the rising grandeur that was his abbey and expected those at court to accompany him.

Leofwine, Harold's younger brother, arriving at Westminster, had been invited to visit the building site almost before he had risen from his knee on greeting the King.

"But you must see my abbey!" Edward declared. In his enthusiasm, he leapt to his feet. "It is now more splendid than ever I had imagined it would be. Come, let me have my cloak fetched, I shall show you straightway!"

"We shall all go!" Edith trilled as she ensured Edward's cloak was tucked around his body and his cap fitted snug over his silvered hair, and, "Do you want your gloves, my dear? You know how your hands chap from the cold." Treating him more as an ageing father, Edith had found her niche as the dutiful wife who looked to his every daily need, tending his apparel, cutting his meat, warming hands and feet, rubbing salves into his aching knees.

Edward contentedly basked in her various attentions; it was all he had ever wanted, someone to mother him. He patted her arm, smiled an aimless, distant acknowledgement, talking all the while to Leofwine. "You will be most surprised at how far the work has progressed—why, it actually begins to look like an abbey at last! You younger ones, you must come also," Edward added, waving his arm at the children. "The fresh air will put colour in your faces." He threaded his arm companionably through Leofwine's. "We have been having problems with the labourers: every so often they decide to stop work for one trivial reason or another—the ramps are too steep and slippery, the conditions too wet. Yet I am paying them good wages, they get hot food once a day and I provide a Christian burial for those unfortunates who, through their own carelessness, meet with accidents. Only the other day a man stupidly stood right under a hoist—the rope had frayed and the stone that was being lifted…well, he was crushed instantly. Dear Leofwine, you should have heard the wailing from his widow! We told her it was his own fault for standing where he did; I gave her a penny from my own purse, that seemed to satisfy her." Edward, talking rapidly, stepped through the doorway and out into the sunlight.

Edith, her own cloak secured, ushered the younger children before her, smiling at the Lady Alditha who had made ready with the rest of the assembly. She was a quiet creature, obviously ill at ease at court, but then, few had made her welcome, unable to forget her father's outrageous acts of treason, or the fact that she had been married to a heathen Welshman. On several occasions Edith had overheard the women whispering between themselves about it—she refused to be drawn into ignorant conversations, but privately she did wonder if it was true what they said about a Welshman's manhood, that it was…Edith frowned, or was that a Jewish man…? She flushed. Whatever, she ought not be thinking of such details.

"My dear," she said, reaching her hand forward to take Alditha's within her own. "You are still so pale. Come! You will walk with my brother Harold, I am certain he can bring a smile to your cheeks."

With a single, almost careless nod of assent at his sister, Harold held out his arm for the lady, noting her dipped head and blush as she took it.

The two demure sisters, Margaret and Christine, walked, hands folded within their long sleeves, behind the Earl of Wessex. At seventeen and fifteen, these two daughters of Ædward the Exile had grown into pleasing young women, the youngest the image of her mother Agatha, who had passed into heaven less than a year after their father had so ill-fatedly died on arriving in London. Both had expressed a desire to dedicate themselves to God, although as their guardian Edward had made other plans for Margaret. A promise of considering giving her hand to Malcolm of Scotland had been a sure way for Earl Tostig to tame the Scots' lust for border warfare. Their twelve-year-old brother Edgar, the ætheling, once outside in the courtyard, made off at a run with Harold's sons Magnus and Edmund, whooping and hollering. The children loved to explore the building site—though they often annoyed the workmen, taking full advantage of the knowledge that no one would dare protest at their squawking nuisance.

The King took great pleasure in having the younger folk around his court, their laughter a contrast to the sombre faces of his councillors and lords. There would be over-much sobriety, he often declared, were it not for their gaiety. Edith would agree with him, though never did she forget that were it not for his own refusal of intimacy, her children would be among those who romped together like inexhaustible hound pups.

"So, my Lady," Harold said as he strolled with Alditha, "I am ordered by the Queen to make you laugh. What would you prefer? That I tumble a few acrobats or shall I recount an inane jest? I know several. I could perhaps sing. My cracked voice would raise a smile to the most solemn of faces."

"I thank you, but I am well content."

"The Queen does not think so."

The Queen, Alditha thought, *can go boil her arrogant, interfering head in oil.* Said aloud, "The Queen is most sweet. She has personally ensured that my every comfort has been attended to."

Harold guffawed. "It is entirely possible that you are the only living person to refer to my sister as 'sweet.' Our own mother would describe her more as sour vinegar; and if she is interested in your welfare then I assume it is because she has some private motive." Harold guided Alditha around a pile of horse dung. They could hear Edward ahead, his high-pitched voice berating those responsible for not sweeping the courtyard.

"Oh, she has a motive," Alditha answered, glancing sideways at the man beside her. "She is decided to find me a husband more suitable than the one I had before."

"That ought not be too difficult! Gruffydd was a toad. We can surely find you a frog or a tadpole."

When Alditha did not smile, Harold bent his head closer to hers and said with exaggerated seriousness, "It was a jest. You are supposed to laugh."

"Why? It was not amusing."

"No, but women are obliged to flatter the male ego by politely acknowledging our attempts at wit."

"We are more likely to laugh at your absurdities."

The quick retort came with a hint of a smile; Harold caught it, raised a finger. "There, you see, already I have pleased the Queen. You have smiled."

"I assure you it was not intentional."

"No matter whether 'twas or not. A smile well suits you."

A pinkness grazed Alditha's cheeks at the flattery. She had spoken only half the truth when she had told him that she was content. What was contentment for a young widow? She was of noble birth, with her own land and entitlement. Her brother Eadwine was Earl of Mercia, a county that had once been a kingdom in its own right. Marriage with her was of potential value to any man who sought a means to step on to the dais of power. Her future consisted of but two choices: marry a man she would probably despise, or enter a nunnery. Neither would be of her own, free-willed choosing, but a woman such as she did not have the luxury of free will or choice. She despaired of the shallowness of Edward's court, the gossip, the blatant pushing and shoving to reach a higher rung on the hierarchical ladder. The hypocrisy of it all!

An improvement on living as wife to Gruffydd ap Llewelyn, however.

"Truly, my Lord Earl," she said, "I am content, and if it pleases you and the Queen, than I shall smile more often."

Pleased at achieving his mission, Harold squeezed her cool fingers, his face shadowing into a frown as he caught a glimpse of his eldest son's glowering expression.

Goddwin stared with intense hostility at his father, his unblinking eyes challenging Harold to declare an interest in the half-Welsh woman. He could not see why his father was so drawn to her—huh, that was not true. No man whose pizzle was in working order could deny her beauty. Her dark hair, heart-shaped face, willow-thin figure and the way the light danced in her eyes...jealousy, an evil goblin that so easily wormed its way into the soul and mouldered there. He adored his mother, could not understand or accept what Edyth had always expected: that one day Harold would take another wife into his bed.

He had not wanted to come to court with his father; there was much to do on the estate that Harold had granted him as a wedding gift. That roan colt was ready for breaking to harness and the chestnut mare who had experienced difficulty with her first foaling needed careful watching. Goddwin preferred horses to people. People always expected too much of you: witty conversation, merry jigging to dance tunes, interest in their personal problems. Horses wanted only to please, to be fed, watered and groomed, to have their feet regularly trimmed; horses never held a grudge or made prejudiced judgement. You knew where you were with horses.

Harold met that jealous stare head on, lifted a questioning eyebrow, to which Goddwin ducked his head. They had quarrelled so often of late, father and son. Since Harold had brought this woman out of Wales, in fact. The Welshman's Whore, the court called her behind her back, save for two nights past when Goddwin had overheard an inebriated conversation conducted by two men of Edward's household. Harold's whore, they had said, cackling in that suggestive, crude way. Harold's whore.

Angry, Goddwin turned abruptly away from the gaggle of men and women around the King. Let them prattle about his damned abbey. Goddwin would have none of it. Fortunately, Edward did not see him go.

The ground ascended gently from the palace, slowing Edward's initial exuberant pace and bringing the breath puffing into his lungs. Perhaps it was his increasing age that made the slope seem the steeper? Next birthing day he would be sixty years of age and they told him often that he ought to take more rest. Piffling nonsense! He might be missing a few teeth and his sight be more blurred than once it had been, his hearing not so sharp, but he could still sit a horse and gallop with the rest of those young whelps when a stag was running. And his mind was alert, his bladder and bowels controlled; he was not yet the dotard they claimed him to be.

Ahead of the party, the east end of his abbey stood in all its splendour, a vast, soaring structure of Reigate stone, the sun's rays striking down through the wind-hustled clouds, highlighting the lantern tower as if God Himself were pointing out its wonder.

The square, lead-roofed tower stood six storeys high, rearing into the sky above the crossed section of north and south transepts, the army of surrounding roof turrets standing like a cluster of guardian sentries. The tiled roofing, above apse, transepts and upper part of the nave, had been set in place as soon as the walls had risen to keep the stone and timber structures below dry. Once the rain was kept out, work had progressed rapidly.

From this eastern approach the holy place looked almost complete, for as was traditional with cathedral and abbey constructions, building ranged from east to west. The height of the northern transept, immediately ahead of the royal party, successfully hid the slower progress to the western end—which consisted of the half-built northern wall of the nave, one tower flanking the western entrance completed but for its roof and its potential twin standing as a single storey of stonework. There was still much to be done.

They stood a moment, the group of onlookers, heads tipped back, gaping up at the great height of the tower, marvelling at the diminutive figures of men clambering over and along the higgle-piggle of scaffolding, not one of them seemingly concerned about the distance down to the ground. For many of those watching—save for those fortunate few who had made pilgrimage to Rome, or visited the grand new cathedrals that were springing up all over France and Italy—this was the tallest building they had ever seen. It was certainly impressive.

Edward entered through the cavern in the north transept that would, one day, be the northern entrance door and proudly led his audience into another world.

The square tower was borne over the crossing by an elaborate array of unobtrusive stone arches, like the branches of a gigantic oak supporting the canopy above. Spiralling stairs reached up inside, set in artistic symmetry against plain walls that rose to the carved beams of the roof. Windows, set at especial angles, allowed in wide shafts of sunlight that harboured a myriad of floating, dancing particles of dust.

It was a beautiful church. Uncluttered by unnecessary ornamentation, its clean lines gave an overpowering sense of length and height, a continuity of unbroken space stretching from one end to the other that, when finished, would cover more than 330 feet in length. The nave would support six double bays per side—two longer than the cathedral of Jumièges. Arches, each resting on plain cylindrical columns below a triforium stage with a gallery surrounding the vaulted aisles, and above that, the clerestory shadowed below the eaves. Further windows pierced the solidity of the lower walls, bringing light cascading down into the enclosed space. The abbey of Westminster was to be long and high, but there would be no gloom within. God's house, lit by God's hand.

Allowing sufficient pause for gasps and a crackle of admiring applause, Edward passed the raised steps that would lead to the main altar and thrust out his arm to indicate an open space. "Here," he said extravagantly, "is where I shall be laid to rest. Close to the bosom of God, where I shall sleep in peace within the sanctity of this glorious place."

His audience nodded; no one dared comment that the abbey of Westminster was, at this moment, anything but a place of peace.

So much movement and noise! All bustle and business. Men swarming like worker ants; carriers of wood, stone, water and lime, men recruited locally and paid by the day. Skilled craftsmen were as numerous as the labourers. Carpenters, masons, stonecutters; those who mixed the mortar, their essential task demanding huge concentration. A building was, after all, only as strong as the mortar that bound it together. Mixed poor, and a wall would crumble as the rain washed and seeped and the wind buffeted. Somewhere within the network of ladders, pulleys, ramps, cranes, hoisting gear and treadmills, the architects were overseeing the transferral of the design on paper into reality.

Hammering, sawing, the squeal of rope on wood as hoists took the enormous blocks of stone from ground level up to the heights of the roof; the indignant bellowing of oxen, the roar of the blacksmiths' bellows. Grunts and shouts, the overall swell of talk and laughter, grumbling and half-muttered swearing. The tramp of feet echoing on hollow ramp, the chink of chisel on stone, rumble of heavy-burdened wheels and the screech of metal against metal. The squeak of wheels as a man lumbered past with a laden handcart, sweat standing out on his face, biceps bulging.

And through it all, the swirl of grit, wood-chips and shavings. White stone dust on the floor, hanging in the air; layers deep along grooved edges of pillars and columns, of steps and crevices, on the sills of the windows. Dust that settled across the shoulders and in the hair of the working men.

Edward noticed a tall, stockily built man with a shock of flame-red hair standing in the centre of the nave, his back to the party, head bent over a sheaf of plans. The King called out as he hurried forward, ushering Leofwine with him: "Leofsi! Leofsi Duddesson! Come, Leofwine, you must talk with my master mason—Leofsi is a wonder with stone!"

Alditha had wandered away from Harold, was ambling down the aisled arcade of the semi-completed nave, looking up in awe at the row of arched window openings. The King had told her that every opening was to be filled with glass; some were to have small panes of coloured glass that would send ripples of colour over the stone floor when the sun shone through, like a rainbow dancing within doors. She did not see the abandoned coil of rope. Her foot caught, she tripped, falling forward on to her knees with a startled cry—and Harold was there at her side, too late to stop her fall, but quick enough to break its full impact. She glanced up, saw his concern, his smile. Smiled back. "How clumsy of me," she said, allowing him to help her to stand. "I was studying the windows. It will look so beautiful when it is all finished. Like I imagine heaven to be."

"Without the rubble and the noise, I trust? 'Tis difficult to imagine the monks singing among this shouting and banging. Are you hurt?"

"No, just a little shaken." Why was she being pleasant to him? Why was she smiling, her heart fluttering? Foolishness! She must not let herself fall in love with this rugged-featured, strong-muscled man with eyes as tranquil as a mountain pool washed by moonlight. But for the love of God, how could she bear being married instead to some fat-bellied old man, or an untried beardless youth?

She half turned her back and raised her skirt. Her stocking was torn and a dribble of blood trickled from a cut to her knee. She dropped the hem of her gown, busied herself with brushing off the dust and setting her veil straight. She was not a woman who dwelt on the unfairness of life. From birth the roll of the die was weighted against a woman, so why make the hardship worse? If the taste was bitter, swallow it down quickly and make the most of the honey whenever it happened along.

Gruffydd had been delighted to acquire Alditha for his own, but saw no deeper than her unblemished skin and the curves of her body. Beyond using her in his bed, he had barely noticed her. Few women expected ought else from a husband, but the hope, the dream that love might come, was always there.

Harold took her arm, bringing her back to the present with a startled jolt, and suggested they could take the opportunity to steal away. Edward was halfway along the length of the nave, would not see them leave.

"I suggest we seek your maid, get that knee cleansed and salved."

Alditha blushed. He had noticed, then, must have also seen her torn stocking. She had heard from the whispers at court—there were always whispers, some kindly, most not—that Harold rarely missed much detail concerning a maiden.

Goddwin Haroldsson was skulking in what would become the cloisters. He watched, angry, as his father escorted Alditha back towards the palace, their arms linked, his father's head bent attentive.

It was not right! Was not fair! His father already had one woman to love, what need had he of another? While he, Goddwin, was saddled with a sour-faced complaining sow! He walked with a quick, purposeful stride towards the stables, called for his horse, mounted and set off at a fast trot. Both his father and the King would be furious when they discovered that he had left Westminster without permission, but his stomach was full of court. He was going home.

❦

Linking his fingers and stretching his arms above his shoulders, Harold eased the ache of a long day from tired muscles. "My eldest son is, I think, somewhat annoyed with me."

"Lose a game, gain a game. Our sister is delighted. You have brought a glow into the face of the Welshman's widow." Leofwine lay on the bed, his long, lean body taking up the entire length. He still wore his boots. "Edith has plans for you, mark my meaning, big brother! She has never been content to let a man lie where it pleases him."

Harold scowled. "I have resisted her attempts to marry me off to some wealthy hag all these years." The scowl broke into a more amused expression. "She was so certain I would tire of Edyth Swannhæls, cannot forgive that I have disappointed her and would do anything to entice me into a marriage she approved of."

Leofwine folded his hands behind his head and grinned mischievously. "So you are not attracted to a certain dark-haired widow-woman then?"

"Of course I bloody am! I'd lay her tonight if I were not Earl of Wessex with my honour to uphold—and she were not the sister of Eadwine, Earl of Mercia!"

Reaching out for the tankard of ale that stood on the table beside the bed, Leofwine saluted his brother with it. "So Goddwin does have ground for jealousy!"

Harold conceded the point. "Why do you think I'm so damned embarrassed about what to do with his behaviour!" He was intrigued by Alditha, was attracted to her...perhaps if he did not have Edyth he would have courted her, but as it was, Goddwin's fears for his father making a fool of himself and his mother being hurt were unfounded. At this moment there was no one to challenge his status of authority as Earl of Wessex, second-in-command to the King; he had no need to seek new kin to assure his position. Tostig ruled in the North, outside Mercia, Gyrth and Leofwine controlled between them much of the rest of England. When Edward passed to God the situation might alter; then, to keep their place, the family Godwinesson might be forced to tie the loose ends, bind a few stubbornly independent hearts to them. All of which could depend on whom the Council chose as the next king—young Edgar was the attested ætheling and he had two as yet unmarried sisters. One of whom Harold might well need to use as security. Besides, he might have a man's natural desire for a comely woman, but he still loved Edyth.

"So what of Goddwin?" Leofwine asked, breaking into his brother's thoughts. "Are you going to ride after him?"

Harold rubbed his fingers over the stubble that was accumulating on his chin. He had no idea what he ought to do about his son. That he was resentful there was no doubting. He would talk to Edyth about it as soon as he returned to Waltham Abbey. Edyth possessed the wisdom of Solomon.

"Ah, he's young, leave him," Leofwine suggested when Harold made no answer. "He will soon realise the fool he has made of himself over this thing."

"And there speaks the accrued wisdom of one who is, what, nine and twenty?"

The two brothers laughed together, Leofwine hurling a pillow at Harold who caught it, tossed it back.

After a while, the younger man said thoughtfully, "Our sister means well. She has always been one to organise others—look how content she is mothering Edward. You would never have believed the pair could turn out to be so well suited. The one a clucking mother hen, the other an open-mouthed fledgling happy to have his dinner fed him."

Making no reply, Harold idly toured the chamber, his hand automatically fondling the ears of the two hounds stretched before the brazier as he stepped around them. As Earl of Wessex he was entitled to his own quarters within the complex of buildings that made up the royal palace at Westminster. Edyth had chosen the tapestries with especial care for their masculine content and strong colour—Harold particularly admired the one depicting a Viking long-ship. The waves were skittish, their white-topped caps splashing against the keel as the vessel ploughed her way ahead of a vigorous wind that filled and billowed her sail. The sea—there was always a thrilling excitement about the lure of the sea.

Leofwine had invited himself to share his brother's company and Harold had been pleased to take advantage of his good-humour. This restlessness was gnawing at his insides. He wanted to be doing something, to be away from the tedium of this faery world, this enchanted island where problems and political upheaval were held at bay by fixed smiles and prattled conversation.

"Diplomatic discussion can never fully compensate for the thrill of battle lust." His father, Godwine, had said that. When? Harold stood before the tapestry, his tankard of ale in his hand, staring at that spirited ship. Ah, yes, during their time of exile, when the family had reunited in that shallow bay on the Island of Wight before turning their attention—and their fleet—on London. Leofwine had been there, too. Tostig, Gyrth—Swegn was already dead, or was he dying at that time? Harold could not recall. Only their brother Wulfnoth and Swegn's son Hakon were missing. Taken as hostage into Normandy by that bastard Robert Champart. He was dead these many years now. A pity he had died of a natural cause; Harold would have liked to have slit his belly and let him die slowly and in agony for the trouble he had caused.

Wulfnoth and Hakon. Boys when they had been forcibly taken from England, men of twenty-three and seventeen now. How many petitions, pleas and offers of ransom had been sent to Duke William for their release throughout these years? Diplomacy? Hah! Would that he could take an armed force such as that which he had taken into Wales and demand their return!

Suddenly Harold turned, setting his tankard down with a decisive thud, startling the dogs awake. "I am going to Normandy. It is time we were united with our brother and nephew."

Leofwine lazily sat up, a frown creasing his forehead. "William always manages to find some plausible excuse to keep them with him. Our messengers report how charming and attentive he has been, how he has promised to review their plight as soon as opportunity presents itself."

"Opportunity that has not arisen for ten years, damn it! If he has reason to keep them hostage, then I think it time he explains it, personally to my face, not to some disinterested courier or in a letter that he can neither read nor write for himself."

Swinging his legs to the floor, attention aroused, Leofwine asked, "Have you some new strategy of assuring our uneasy English relationship with Normandy, then? If not, William the Bastard will not listen to you."

A slow grimace spread over one half of Harold's mouth. "No doubt I will think of something before I reach Normandy. If not, I'll rely on charming the stubble of hair off the back of his Norman-shaved head!" Harold's grin broadened. He leant forward, plucked the pillow from the bed and pounded his brother with it. "I could always negotiate a wife for you. William has two young daughters, I believe."

Protecting his head with his hands, doubled over and protesting loudly, Leofwine spluttered laughter through a sudden shower of feathers. "Ah, no, you take one of them, I've a mind for a Lady Alditha. You are not the only stallion with an itch to service a pretty filly you know!"

20

Bosham

Leofwine elected to ride south with Harold and his family; the June weather was sun-warmed and the court dull. He might as well enjoy the company of his brother's brood and visit his mother at the same time.

Of all her sons, the Countess Gytha considered Harold and Leofwine—eldest and second youngest—the nearest in looks, character and thinking to their father. Both reminded her so heart-wrenchingly of Godwine. In his younger days he had been as handsome as they, as quick to laugh; as restless and adventurous. From where Tostig had received his moral seriousness or Edith her capacity to make such a dramatic fuss Gytha had no clue. Certainly not from their father!

For all that his intentions were good, she was uncertain that Harold's impulsive expedition to Normandy was to be recommended. While she would welcome with open heart Wulfnoth's return, Gytha was uneasy at the venture. So many terrible rumours surrounded Duke William. All the more reason, Harold had pointed out with a quick laugh and fond hug for his mother, to deliver a hostage from the Norman's taloned clutches.

Leofwine seemed enthusiastic and the King had given his blessing, but then, with Tostig just returned to court from Northumbria, Edward was unlikely to take note of anything asked of him, preoccupied as he was with the new hawk Tostig had brought him.

By tomorrow, to Gytha's sorrow, Harold would be gone, sailing on the morning tide. This week had passed so swiftly. It seemed only yesterday that he, Edyth and their dear children had arrived, bringing a flaming spark of energy to the somnolent atmosphere of Bosham Manor. Not that Gytha minded the tranquillity. She would be sixty years of age come late summer and while she felt sprightly and energetic on such sun-filled days as today, the chill of winter sent an ache through her bones that had not been there in previous years. Today, it was pleasant sitting in the sun of her sheltered, walled garden finishing the hand-weaving of a border she had been working to edge a new cloak.

She lifted her head at the sound of a trotting pony's hoof beats, craned her neck to see over the wicker gate central to the west wall. Was that her granddaughter? Algytha had promised not to ride too far with the men as they set out to hunt after breaking their fast.

Within a few minutes a young woman opened the gate and ran through, her fair hair tossing and fluttering beneath the confines of a linen veil, a wide and attractively pleasant smile on her face. In her hand, a jug of her grandmother's medicinal drink. How like her to think of it without being asked.

"They have ridden out on to the marshes. I thought it too hot to ride far." Algytha flopped on to the grass, fanned herself with her hand a moment and said almost in the same breath, "Father says that if all is ready, he may well make sail on the evening tide and not wait for the morrow. I wish I were going with him. I love the open sea."

Countess Gytha tutted as her thread snagged. Harold was impatient to be off and doing, never had he been one—man or boy—to sit idle. "Have you told your mother so?" she asked.

"She is in the village still. I have left word in the Hall."

"Well, then," the Countess said, setting her wools safe, "we had best ensure a suitable feast is prepared for his departure. As well I have an adequately provisioned storeroom."

<hr />

The moon was high by eleven thirty and the tide calm, about to turn. With the ship loaded, all was ready. At the moment Leofwine regretted not agreeing to accompany Harold, but then, there was that young redhead he had discovered a while ago at the White Boar tavern. If he left her untended overlong, someone else with a keen eye for a shapely leg might pluck her away.

He had, however, accompanied Harold into Bosham church for evening mass. It had been a strange experience, that service, almost ethereal. Cnut himself had ordered the building of the church; his young daughter, drowned in the mill stream, was buried beneath the nave. Godwine was buried in Winchester, but there had been a strong sense of him also—so great, that at one point Leofwine had thought that if he were to turn round he would see him looking up the nave towards the altar. He had glanced at his brother to see if he had noticed anything untoward, but Harold stood, rapt in thought, staring at the chancel arch. Later, however, as they had walked the short distance between church and manor house in the fading light of evening, Harold had said something that had again prickled the nape hairs of Leofwine's neck.

"Father would, perhaps, rather have been laid to rest here at Bosham. He loved this place so. Winchester, for all its magnificence, does not have the quiet contentment that abounds here."

Leofwine had said nothing, walked on in silence, only his boots crunching on the gravel path.

"I have told Edyth that I would be buried at our manor if circumstances allow. My home is with her, whatever second wife I may one day take, whatever future track I may follow."

He had walked on, then, matching Leofwine stride for stride, and said nothing more until they had reached the open gateway of Bosham Manor. "Take good care of Edyth should anything happen to me, my brother. My heart has always, will always, rest with her."

Leofwine stood on the shore beside his sister-in-law, his hand poised in its rising, the other draped around Edyth's waist. Those few last things had been loaded as the tide flooded, bobbing the ship, anxious to break free of her mooring. Harold was to take gifts to Duke William: hunting hounds, a hawk. Gifts that would symbolise his intention of peace.

When Harold would be back again in England none of them on the shore at Bosham had the knowing. The three boys, Edmund, Magnus and Ulf, were off and running through the marsh grass to keep pace with the ship while they could. Little Gunnhild, six, was almost asleep in her mother's arms, her fair lashes sweeping down sleep-heavy over blue eyes. Edyth was biting her lip—Leofwine could see the blood oozing—trying not to weep out here where others could see her.

It must be so lonely, Leofwine thought, *being a woman so often left behind while we menfolk go off happily chasing our goblin-pot of ideas.*

"He will come home safe, won't he, grandmother?" Algytha asked, a tremor in her voice.

The Countess Gytha quietly took hold of her namesake's hand. "Of course he will, child. What harm can possibly come to the King's Earl of Wessex?"

21

Ponthieu

Had Harold possessed a soothsayer's foresight, then he would have turned his ship back a few hours into the sea crossing, waited at Bosham harbour another few days or abandoned all idea of the trip to Normandy. As it was, no one could have known that the sprightly wind would, in mid-Channel, turn malevolent and that the craft, as if she were a bolting horse, would not be turned those few essential degrees to the south-east.

Now, sitting chained, with body and ego distinctly bruised in a malodorous, damp and dim-lit cellar in the bowels of the fortress of Beaurain, the lure of Normandy and a mission to Duke William seemed suddenly not so appealing. At least he had the satisfaction of knowing that the imbeciles who had arrested him and his crew had suffered as many, if not more, injuries than their captives.

Unsure of the coastline ahead, but certain they were nearing Saint-Valéry-sur-Somme, too far to the north of their intended destination, they had reefed the sail and persuaded the ship into the mouth of the river to the nearer, northern embankment. Patting each other boisterously on the back in self-congratulation at avoiding certain shipwreck, they had waded ashore, to be met by what appeared to be a gang of cut-throat thieves.

"What? Is this how Normandy greets her visitors?" Harold had shouted in indignant French. "Is your duke so weak that he must welcome an envoy from England with such hostility?"

The reply was drawn daggers and "Ponthieu does not take kindly to pirates!"

The fighting was brief for the English were outnumbered and not prepared for such a ferocious reception. Harold's mission was peaceful; coming in armour and bristling with weapons would indeed have sent the wrong signals. It seemed this bevy of undisciplined ruffians were incapable of noticing the obvious, however.

Bound and tethered like slaves, Harold and his men were marched to Beaurain. Several times Harold attempted to convince their captors that their lord would have something to say at this gross misunderstanding, but no one listened.

On entering the fortress the reason why became clear. Guy de Ponthieu was not on the best of terms with Duke William and he was an astute opportunist. With the number and quality of merchantmen sailing between Flanders, Normandy and England, he found it was worth setting a patrol along his coast. Worth the easy pickings that bad weather provided. And occasionally there was a windfall: a rich mariner or passenger to be ransomed.

Harold's head throbbed. A cut above his right eye was oozing blood, his ribs ached. For three days had they been incarcerated here and the novelty was beginning to pall.

"I am Harold, Earl of Wessex, come as a peaceful emissary of Edward, King of England, to William, Duke of Normandy." What had been the point? Ponthieu had not listened, except to prick his ears and increase the price of the ransom he was anticipating. His only comment had been rude and officious: "Then you are unfortunate. I have a hatred of the English and I am not the Duke."

The insult was compounded by his arrogance in chaining Harold as if he were a common thief. Mind, that had partly been of Harold's own doing, for he had refused to give his *parole* not to attempt to escape. "I'm buggered if I'll give word that I'll sit idle and scratch my arse while you send to England for an extortionate ransom!"

Again, Harold tugged at the chains attaching his fetters to the wall; to no avail, the fastenings were secure. One of his men, needing to relieve his bladder, fumbled as well as he could at the lacings of his breeches, half turned to the wall, let his water stream to the floor. The smell of fresh urine made little difference to the already appalling stench. Eadric straightened his garments and reseated himself as far from the noxious puddle as his chains would allow. "I am not impressed by the accommodation here, my Lord. In fact"—Eadric's grin revealed more gum than teeth—"it stinks."

"Let us just hope Tofi managed to get clear," Harold answered with a sigh of frustrated boredom. There was little use in shouting, allowing full vent to his anger—he had already tried it—but once he was restored to freedom and status, then God help Guy de Ponthieu!

"He is a good housecarl, Tofi," another of Harold's men said, "one of our best. If anyone can reach Eu for help, he can."

"I am not so concerned about whether he can reach the cursed place," Eadric responded with a growl of frustration, "just when. What if those poxed Normans are as block-headed as this lot here? What if they'll not listen to Tofi? How long will we be sitting like surplus fowl, trussed ready for the pot?"

"You speak for yourself, Eadric!" someone else laughed. "You're plump enough, with that ale-belly of yours. Some of us have no dinner meat clinging to our bones."

"Aye, some of you would be better boiled down and used for toothpicks!"

"What would you know of such a nobleman's accessory, Eadric? You have no teeth to use one on!"

At least, Harold thought to himself, *though we may be in a damned awkward situation, we have our lives—and our humour.*

⟨≈⟩

Duke William was residing at Rouen. At Eu, Tofi, one of the most faithful and quick-thinking of Harold's housecarls, went straight to the fortress and demanded to speak with the man who held highest authority. The constable listened in silence to the Englishman, and acted promptly in response. Given a swift horse and an escort to Rouen, Tofi found himself attempting to explain to the Duke of Normandy in person that Earl Harold of England was in desperate and ignominious straits.

At first, William could not make sense of the garbled, breathless plea from the Englishman who spoke very little French very badly. Something about a strong wind and renegades? He did recognise the name Guy de Ponthieu. A creeping snail. An obnoxious, slime-trailed…

"*Est-ce qu'il y a quelqu'un qui parle anglais ici*?" he demanded, looking at the men clustered in curiosity around the visitor. "Does anyone here speak English?"

A man—Tofi took him to be a man, for he was heavily bearded and wore male apparel—stepped forward with a bow. This incongruous person stood barely the height of a large dog. "I am Turold," the dwarf said. "You must forgive my poor English, but it is better than your appalling French, *n'est-ce pas?*"

Tofi recognised, with relief, his own tongue and explained briefly but precisely the difficulty that his lord Harold had fallen into. Turold translated rapidly as he spoke.

William's face grew more clenched and venomous as this Englishman's meaning became plain. Before Turold had finished, William was on his feet, enraged, bellowing for horses to be saddled. "That upstart will not get away with such discourtesy! How dare he dishonour a man of rank who comes in peace to visit me? By God's Grace, Ponthieu will regret his greed and this personal insult to me!"

Tofi could barely believe that within the hour he was riding back along the same route, mounted on a fine stallion with the Duke's guard and the Duke himself. Two messengers had been sent ahead at the gallop, carrying dire warnings from Normandy. Ponthieu was to present himself and William's visitor, unharmed, at the fortress of Eu. William's curt message had carried an addendum. Explanation for embarrassing the Duke would be required.

If comte Guy de Ponthieu valued his land—and his head—he would be at Eu with Earl Harold, awaiting the Duke's pleasure.

22

⤞❦⤝

Rouen—September 1064

This was more palatable!

Eadric sat on a narrow bench before the immense heat of the cooking fire in the grand kitchens of Duke William's castle at Rouen, a blushing serving maid pulled firmly into his lap, a tankard brimming with golden cider in his hand. The smell of roasting pork on the spit and pies and pastries coming from the ovens filled his nostrils. The Normans, he had always been led to believe, were an uncouth, inhospitable, arrogant lot; that might be true of the nobility, but not of these buxom, cheerful-faced women of William's domestic buildings. Nor of the tantalising menu for dinner.

Being of the sea folk and having from the age of ten spent many a long month in a foreign port, Eadric had a basic knowledge of many languages: Danish, Flemish, a little Spanish and Arabic, and French. He was retelling, again, the story of Guy de Ponthieu's gross discomfort on coming face to face with Duke William and the consequent release of the English captives. His animated account had the kitchen in paroxysms of laughter.

"A mule, I tell you! De Ponthieu actually went to meet your noble duke riding a wag-eared mule, so desperate was he to show he had no intention of inciting war!" He set his fingers to the side of his head, imitating the beast's ears, and let out a remarkably convincing ass's bray. One of the cooks, rolling out pastry at the table, wiped her eyes with the back of her hand, spreading white flour over her cheeks. She could not remember a time when she had laughed so long. *Mais non*, the English were not the ragbag, dour-faced imbeciles that she had always assumed them to be.

Eadric was shaking his head. "I tell you, how we kept our faces straight as he, so very humbly, handed us into the Duke's care, I do not know. That man must have been pissing his breeches with fear at the fury on your William's face." He swigged a mouthful of cider. "And my Lord Harold—how he maintained his countenance I will never discover! He rides past the soddin' comte, his hawk—a gift from our King Edward to Duke William—perched on his wrist. He looks at Guy, smiles with that laconic twist of his mouth and says in perfect French, "*Merci beaucoup*. The hospitality offered by Ponthieu was most interesting. I would recommend airing the bed linen a little, however. The accommodation was somewhat damp.'" Eadric slapped his thigh with mirth. "The comte did not appreciate the jest, I think! His expression was sour as shit!"

Relaxing in grander surroundings than the kitchens, Harold, too, was relating the astonishing series of events of the past few days, although somewhat more sedately than his steersman, Eadric. The Duke listened gravely, for his anger at comte Guy remained acute, but Mathilda was laughing outright with the Englishman, enjoying his uninhibited portrayal of an amusing account at his own expense.

"I admit I would have been more concerned had de Ponthieu not been intent on making so much money out of me, but once it was clear that greed was his prime motive, all I and my men needed to worry about was the damned inconvenience of having to piss in a puddle. We discovered it is no easy matter to manage the laces of breeches with your wrists manacled! You ladies, madam, would have a definite advantage in such an indelicate situation!"

Mathilda clapped her hands and roared her delight. Harold's risqué storytelling was like a breath of spring air to her lively imagination—all too often her husband's court was preoccupied with such tediously serious matters.

"You would, of course, have had to endure the unpleasantness for some long while, had your man not brought word of your plight to me," William interrupted. He was not prone to extravagant mirth; there was so little in his past to have brought alive the frivolous side of his nature. "Did that fact not worry you, sir?"

Harold offered the Duke a slight and gracious bow. "I am most assuredly grateful for your prompt and gallant rescue. Had you not received word, our wait would have depended on how long it took for a ransom demand to be taken to England and fetched back to Ponthieu."

"And on whether my dear kinsman, Edward, would have been agreeable to paying it." The sarcasm in William's rejoinder was blatant. Harold chose to ignore it, uncertain whether the Duke had intended the insult. The King would not have been under any financial obligation, for Harold's own wealth would easily have paid the ransom. In the holding of land and entitlement, he was possibly wealthier than Edward, for the King squandered much of his income on books and trifles, and his Westminster abbey had drained much of his personal treasury.

The experience of imprisonment had been inconvenient and rough, but Harold was a soldier and a huntsman, used, when on campaign or tracking a beast, to sleeping huddled in his cloak on the ground, and making do with poor food and brackish water. He was not a leader who expected his men to endure something that he could not. It was this that brought him respect, loyalty and devotion from his men.

Unwittingly, too, Guy de Ponthieu had been of service to Harold, for through him William had welcomed the English into his court with arms open. Perhaps the Duke would have been as welcoming of any English envoy, but this hospitality ran deeper, for he needed to make amends. William had to prove to England that Normandy was no uncivilised backwater and that he, the Duke, had full, unequivocal control. Ponthieu had come close to revealing the opposite.

⤜⤛

For several weeks Harold and his men made use of the welcome offered them. Earl and Duke found they had much in common: a love of hunting, an interest in the new technologies of warfare and the intricacies of justice, law and politics, although with the latter their opinions differed greatly, giving rise to much eloquent and occasionally heated discussion.

Harold talked freely of the traditionally established English law and social structure, William listening intently to what he privately considered quaint and old-fashioned ideas. Laws and decisions ought to come from the holder of highest authority, not be decided by a rabble group of nobles, each out for his own gain. If he were king of England, the Witan would lose power, for he would take over the Council's authority. The organised system of tax collection appealed, however. England was well versed in the efficient raising of funds—all those years of paying Danegeld, the bribery of gold to keep the Viking raiders at bay, had seen to that. The organisation of the fyrd, the fighting men, was intriguing also. William learnt much of the Englishman's fighting ability from Earl Harold's proud descriptions of prowess on the battlefield.

Aware the Duke's interest might have an ulterior motive, Harold took care to talk only of what was common knowledge, of general ability and tactics, not of numbers or specific skills. His intention was to acquire William's trust. Anyone who knew of England could recount the number of days the fyrd would serve, the method of fighting, their style of weapons and armour. Anyone, from peasant to bishop, knew the extent and methods of taxation, the seats of power, the scatter of population. Which towns favoured the wealthier merchantmen, which harbours were safe in poor weather, which were rock-bound or pirate-patrolled. Oh, Harold talked freely to William, happy to have his wineglass refilled, the dishes of tempting pastries and fruits set at his side. It was easy to talk of those common things, for then the listener did not become aware of that which was not said.

His one disappointment: his brother and nephew were not at the Duke's court but residing as house-guests with noble families in the far south of Normandy. Harold had spoken of his hope to be reunited with his kindred on the very first day, couched within the tact of half-truth. "My mother, Countess Gytha," he had told the Duke, "is growing more elderly. It would delight an old lady's heart to see the face of her child and the son of her first-born, now dead, son." He had smiled at William, setting a simpleton's trusting expression on his face. "After all," he had added, "we as sons owe much to the love of our dearest mothers."

Ah, Harold had listened and read well of Normandy and her duke. A hard man, a man of cunning, a leader of renown, courage and stealth. But a man who respected his wife and honoured his mother.

William had answered Harold's hope of returning to England with the two boys with a nondescript shrug and aimless wave of his hand. "Of course, of course," he had replied amiably. "We shall talk of such matters soon, all in good time."

Harold had half smiled to himself. So Edward's ability to procrastinate on issues of import was not unique. A trait of a Norman, perhaps? Had Queen Emma had it? Harold had not known the great lady well enough, but from the little he remembered, aye, she too could dither and defer effectively as it suited her purpose.

Time, however, appeared to be yet another thing that was controlled and manipulated by the Duke. There was invariably opportunity for hunting and debate of his choosing, but always he became busy when Harold should mention, even in the obliquest of references, Wulfnoth and Hakon the hostages. Despite the gnawing frustration that began to build as the days passed, Harold admired William's vigorous hold on discipline throughout the province. Here was no soft-bellied vacillator, intent on glorifying himself simply by building churches.

Rapidly gathering impressions those first weeks, Harold partially liked the Duke—although there was something that he was uncertain of. There was as much that Duke William was not allowing Harold to discover of Normandy, as he himself was concealing from the Duke. But that was the excitement of the hunt: the careful stalking, the patient waiting.

William, short-cropped russet hair framing a full-fleshed face, was tall—the same height as Harold—and possessed abundant energy. His reputation was that of ruthlessness—but was that not a good thing in a commander? Peace could not be maintained by simpering words and pathetic hesitation—Edward would fail as king on the morrow were it not for the strength of his earls.

The Duke, Harold observed, ate and drank with moderation; his language was never foul or uncouth and he was faithful to his wife. But he also had a complex and enigmatic character. There was no looking direct into William's eyes. His duchess, Mathilda, was as different from her husband as day is from night. Harold found that he liked her. A woman of small stature but enormous heart, Mathilda was gracious and charming, a delight to engage in conversation, so unlike her sister Judith, who was shy and meek, reluctant to express any opinion that was not first endorsed by Tostig. How different this younger sister! No hesitation to express her view, a woman with a zest for life, excitement and passion. No wonder the Duke worshipped her. What man of sense would not welcome such a delightful creature into his bed?

Through those first few weeks as guest at court, Harold often found himself involved in conversation with the Duchess, in particular discussing the domestic issues of family life: the worries and treatments of childhood illness, the smile of a daughter, the hopes for a son. Mathilda was devoted to her children and, unable to express pride in them to William, who took little interest, she found immense satisfaction in sharing these eager conversations with a family-loving man. While Harold doubted William could ever enter into an unconditional friendship with any mortal soul, within a matter of days, such a friendship had become established between Duchess and Earl.

Playing with the children came naturally to Harold—an occupation that was anathema to William.

A favoured game was knights and dragons, played out on the grassed tilting yard. Harold had been elected as the dragon. Seven-year-old William Rufus, now growing into a robust, cherry-cheeked lad, used his flat wooden sword on the dragon's backside unmercifully while Richard and Cecily, four, caught hold of Harold's cloak and legs, and held him firm. Robert, eleven and un-willing to join fully in the game, yet reluctant to remain aloof from the fun, shouted orders and encouragement to his "men." Agatha, as the princess imprisoned in the castle—in this instance sitting happily atop the gate—fluttered her veil from her hand and called woefully for her gallant heroes to rescue her. Rapidly, the mild game collapsed into a free-for-all rough and tumble as the children toppled Harold over. Agatha leapt from her "prison" to join in with the immense hilarity of tickling the English Earl's ribs while Will sat heavily on his chest. Even Robert entered the mêlée, his laughter mingling with the delight of his siblings.

From the solar window Mathilda stood watching, chuckling at the merriment below. Distracted by the noise, her husband crossed the chamber to stand behind her, watching with a disapproving frown. Finally he snorted. "Is that boy not too old for playing childish games?" he commented gruffly as Robert pulled off Harold's boot and began tickling his foot. The Earl shrieked for mercy.

"Do you yield?" came Agatha's sweet but triumphant answer. "Do you yield to Normandy?"

"I yield! I yield! Pax, ah, please, pax!"

"Your son is but a boy," Mathilda chided. "Can he not enjoy the pleasures of childhood?" She tilted her head to look up into her husband's displeased face. "Through games do children learn; and it is rare for them all to join in such boisterous play together."

"Boisterous play I have no objection to, if they are learning the skills of a soldier along with it—but look at the boy, prancing about as if he were a girl! He is an embarrassment!"

Mathilda watched her eldest son prance around the perimeter of the grass as if he were a warhorse, saw him stop and scoop Cecily on to his shoulders. The girl yodelled with delight as he set off again at a high-stepping trot. "Nonsense, my dear, he is imagining himself to be a fine stallion, carrying the fair princess to meet her prince."

William snorted again. "He is almost a man. Such inane fancies are for infants."

"Yet the Earl plays the same," Mathilda said quietly but with insistence.

"The Earl is an Englishman. The English are known to be childish fools—look at that girl! Is Agatha not too old for such immodesty!"

William Rufus had begged Harold to take his arms and swing him round, in which Harold—thankfully replacing his boot—had duly obliged. With the lad's breathless turn finished, Harold had grasped Agatha's arms and was whirling her around, his legs moving faster and faster as she spun with him.

"Husband, she is ten years old! Allow her the freedom of youthful frivolity while she may enjoy it."

The Duke's response was gruff. "She is of an age to be betrothed. I think it time I decided on a husband for her." He strode back to the scatter of maps spread on his table, thoughts returning to more immediate matters. Conan de Bretagne was stirring up trouble again. He would need to be dealt with soon, before he outgrew the size of his boots.

Sighing at William's lack of a sense of fun, Mathilda followed him, peering with mild interest at a route of march that William had marked on one of the maps. She pointed to the river crossing. "Is it wise to cross the river Couesnon so low down? The tide can be unmerciful at the estuary."

"It is too far to travel inland," William answered, secretly pleased at her shrewd judgement.

A companionable silence fell between husband and wife. Around them the murmur of servants, two dogs growling; everyday sounds. The laughter from outdoors floated through the window opening; Harold's deep guffaw, the children's high-pitched squealing.

"I agree we ought soon consider a husband for Agatha," Mathilda said at length. "We must secure a useful alliance."

William nodded, unrolling another map of a different area of Brittany, but this one held too many scribbled words rather than easily interpreted signs and symbols.

In an intimately caressing voice, Mathilda said into her husband's ear, "An alliance with England could prove worthwhile when Edward dies, could it not? A kindred voice when the most suitable man must be considered for king?"

William allowed the map to roll up on itself, set it down and regarded his wife. "You have more political astuteness than I realised, woman. Such an alliance could serve me well."

Placing her lips lightly on his cheek before turning away from him, Mathilda walked back to the window. She watched as Harold, as "it," chased the children in an enthusiastic game of tag. When he caught hold of Agatha round the waist, Mathilda noted the girl's gleeful laughter. A husband of suitable status must be the priority, but how much better it would be to find one, also, whom Agatha liked.

"I intend to visit my army on Conan come the start of August," William said, joining her. "I wonder if our guest would enjoy a hunting trip with a more challenging quarry than a deer or a boar? The English, perhaps, could benefit from a Norman campaign."

"And that would give you time to consider a profitable marriage, would it not? I would be saddened to lose my daughter to England, but Agatha seems to like the Earl. It could be a good match, do you not think?"

William brushed his finger against the tip of her nose. *C'était vrai*, it could.

23

Mont Saint-Michel

Rising from the sea, as if it were some mystical island, the silhouette of the Mount of Saint Michael, dark against the fading sunset, was a breath-taking wonder. Harold had never seen such a sight—not even in Rome! The salt marshes stretched away into the sky and the distant sea, the mudflats ran between empty water channels and a hundred continuously bobbing and weaving birds waded.

The island, a granite citadel soaring 260 feet above the estuary, supported the most incredible buildings perched, as if by wizardry, on and intertwined with natural rock. The Benedictine abbey of Mont Saint-Michel rose with its stone and timber towers, pinnacles and colonnades into the August-blue sky. How it all remained standing, so precariously perched, Harold could not begin to understand. He stood, the demonic wind rushing over the mudflats, where the flood tide was already starting to return, whipping at his hair and cloak; stood and stared, transfixed. The island was like a ship, full-sailed, gliding over the shimmering, ripple-cast sand, would surely seem even more so once the sea returned to surround its towering beauty.

The sun was sinking gracefully to the horizon, a red, glowing orb that glinted for one last incredible moment of bursting joy against the two golden crosses adorning the shingled roof of the church. If this was Divinity made real among the squalor of life, then God was indeed immense and wonderful.

"You like it?" Duke William asked, coming to stand beside the English Earl. "The building of the monastery is not yet complete—there have been tremendous difficulties encountered, for all the rules of known architecture are having to be adapted. Almost daily some quandary is uncovered and a new technique must be explored." William looked with pride at the magnificent structure.

"My grandfather married my grandmother, Judith of Brittany, on the Mount, 'tis her kindred, Conan, the second of that name, we go to subdue. I will not allow ruffians such as he to terrorise my vassals. How dare he think he can lay

siege to Dol and be allowed to get away with it? Hah, he will soon realise he has
made a fatal mistake!"

"Is Dol far, once we cross this boundary river?" Harold turned his head
slightly, looking away from the marvel that was Saint Michel, and studied
the river.

The Couesnon was a wide stretch of slumbering water meandering through
the wind-rustling marsh and barren salt flats. Riding with his Englishmen in the
van, Harold had said little but listened well to the idle talk of the Normans—to
the cheerful boasts of the brave-hearted and the misgivings of the doubtful. The
river crossing had been the subject most discussed. Looking at its placid, shallow
width, there appeared nothing sinister. A river estuary, safe to ford as long as the
tide was low.

"*Pas du tout*," William answered. "Dol is not far, but first, as you say, we
must cross this river that makes the border between Normandy and Brittany."
He regarded Harold with half-closed shrewd eyes. What kind of man was this
Earl Harold from England, apart from a flatterer of women and a charmer of
children? What merit had he, William wondered, as a leader of men?

Instinctively, before this bold venture into Brittany had been suggested, Harold
had realised that his worth was being assessed and did not much appreciate it. He
had no need to prove himself to any man—duke, king, soldier or peasant—but
William was playing some secretive game. He had his suspicions of why, but was
not yet certain. For now, he was content to let this conceited duke watch him,
to play the amiable mild-mannered underling. For now.

Pulling at his moustache, Harold walked nearer the gently sloping river bank
and studied the ground beneath his boots. Firm here and solid, the grass short
and tough; he could taste salt on his lips. He stopped a few feet short of the
running water, gazing at its sandy blue calm. It did not appear deep and, with
the banks sloping on this and the far side, there would be no difficulty in taking
the horses and pack mules across. Would the baggage carts churn the river bed?
It appeared firm, able to take weight, but it was sand and mud, not gravel or
rock. No, this river would be soft and yielding, the worst kind of crossing for
heavy wagons.

Movement out in the bay caught Harold's attention. He frowned, squinting into
the gathering evening. What was it? A line of white, moving fast towards them.

"What is that, out on the flats?" he asked William, who stood with both
thumbs tucked through his sword belt, his piercing eyes never leaving Harold.

"*La mer*. The sea, returning."

Unconsciously, Harold found his hand gripping his sword pommel. This was indeed a strange, mystical place! Before his very eyes that faint line was becoming clearer, bolder. He could see that, aye, it was the foaming churn of breakers tumbling and swirling as the sea rushed in across that wide, flat bay. Moving so fast! Almost, Harold could fancy that those white-capped waves were the mythical horses of the sea, manes tossing, hooves drumming, galloping…galloping shoreward.

"The sea here at Mont Saint-Michel," William explained, his eyes, too, going to watch the rapid approach of the flood tide, "runs faster than the legs of a man. Within the span of a single minute the sea will travel more than one half of a mile. On days when the wind carries their sound, you can hear the desperate cries of the souls of those drowned by tide. Those who live by the shore keep watch for the white foam and listen well to the *chanson de la mer*—the song of the sea."

Harold watched, incredulous, as the bay flooded before his eyes. Soon the island of Saint Michel would, in very truth, became an island. Already, the water was beginning to encroach on either side, like two arms twining around. Within a few more minutes the river would be rising as the salt water overcame the fresh. The river water was clouding as the mud and sand and salt swirled and eddied.

"I am thinking," Harold said slowly, "that to the unwary, this river Couesnon appears unimposing. At first sight there seems no reason why I could not ride my horse straight across. It looks as though the water would come no higher than his hocks—that a man might easily wade from this side to the other."

William said nothing, merely raised one eyebrow. He had noted those words, the *unwary*, *appears* and *at first sight*. Was this English earl, then, more astute than William had given him credit for?

"I am thinking, however." Harold continued, "that this river is not the benign waterway it pretends to be. The banks are soft, as is the bed. This is a land of marsh and sea; it is hard to judge where one ends and the other begins." He took a breath, regarded the Duke with a long, calm gaze. "This river is deceptive. I would wager that if care is not taking in its crossing, men and horses could be lost either to the gallop of the flood or to unsuspected quicksands."

Duke William allowed a wry smile to curve one side of his mouth. Ah, *oui*, this earl did, then, know his business. He nodded, slowly. "We will cross quickly and with care when the light is good, on the morrow. If you notice, I have brought with me more pack mules than baggage carts. Lumbering wheels are not good in this devious river. An animal, or a man, can feel the shift of sand beneath the feet. A wagon cannot.

"Come, let us return to camp, the day has been long. Soon we will arrive unannounced at Dol and send that whoreson Conan running."

The infantry crossed first, wading with ease across the azure-blue river, and then half of the cavalry with scouts riding ahead of those first few who crossed over. Unlike Henry of France, William was not a leader to be caught with his army split and vulnerable on both sides of a dividing river.

With a cloudless sky and beaming sun beating on their backs there would be no difficulty in drying wet clothing. Harold crossed on his spirited grey stallion, then stood watching the gruelling task of bringing the wagons over. Mules were always so stubborn.

The entire army of several thousand men was crossing in disciplined formation, alert for enemy attack and, more uneasily, for the return of the sea. Soon the tide would be racing inwards again. No man would risk being in that river when *la mer traître* came to claim more bones to fill her deep grave.

A wagon was stuck, its wheels sinking in the softened sand bed. The mules were straining, with the assistance of an additional team, but the vehicle was as stubborn as the animals, was not going to move. Men pushed from behind, whipped the animals, hauled on ropes. Nothing, no movement, save for a precarious tilt to the high-piled, heavy cart. Other vehicles were having to skirt around it, which made their route that much longer, heightening the men's anxiety. Then the last was over, to be followed at a canter by the rest of the mounted men, a further three, four hundred. Agitation stuttered through the ranks still waiting to cross, echoed by their brethren on the far side. More men splashed into the water to help push and to dig at the firm-stuck wheels.

Bored of the performance, Harold turned for a final look at Saint Michel. Soon they would be making way again. He would have liked to have crossed the causeway, to pray within the chapel of Notre-Dame-sous-Terre. To have taken a quiet moment in the tranquillity of God's House to think of Edyth and the children back home in England.

All this—this openness—was beautiful, but it was also thought-provoking. The nothingness of the vaulted sky and the vast flat plain stirred the slumbering caverns of the soul and the mind. The Mont, rising so majestically, soared into the void like a shout of passion. Beyond the island the returning sea. And beyond the sea, England.

He would see this campaign through, for the sake of adventure and to gain valuable experience of the Duke's army. Then, after William had done with Brittany—and with luck and God's blessing gained an easy victory—he would try once again to raise the subject of the two boys and take ship for home. Normandy had its charms, but England held better. Norman women were fair, but not so handsome as Saxon lasses across that sea…the sea! God's mercy, the tide was almost upon them and that wagon remained caught fast in the mud.

Several men noticed that imminent danger at almost the same moment, for they rushed forward to add their weight to the frantic pushing and pulling. The last of them were beginning to cross now, the footing made all the more difficult by the churned bed and the heavier suck of the shifting undercurrents. Suddenly and with no warning the wagon lurched forward and lumbered up the shallow bank, the mules sweating and shaking with effort. One brayed, the noise intermingling with the back-slapping and shouts of triumph from the men.

The sudden burst of noise startled those horses still in mid-crossing; a grey squealed and lashed out with a hind leg, catching a bay square on the knee. The animal lurched violently to the right, crashing into a chestnut, sending it staggering off balance, pitching its rider into the water. The chestnut, legs thrashing, plunged to its feet and fled riderless after the other bolting horses; a hind hoof had slammed against the rider's head, leaving the man dazed and disorientated. Someone else nearby was crying out, the words indistinct, then a second hoof caught the unseated rider's shoulder and, screaming with pain, the soldier went down in an open-mouthed hand-grasping flurry beneath the water.

It all happened so quickly. On the bank, most of the men were looking towards the freed wagon, congratulating those who had rescued it; few heard the cries from the river or saw what was happening. The bay horse, its leg obviously broken, was struggling to rise. Its rider, with a foot wedged in the stirrup, was being dragged and trampled, his gurgling, water-choked voice calling desperately for help.

Harold had cheered along with the rest of them as the wagon had come free, but his attention had been more directed at the incoming tide and the level of the river—on those last horses to cross. He was one of the few to witness what had happened and he responded instinctively without thought for his own safety. He leapt down the bank and waded into the current, his arms pummelling his body forward. As he neared the terrified bay, he pulled out his dagger with one hand and with the other grasped the bridle. He brought the blade quick and deep through the animal's throat and the river ran red, the stain flooding upstream with the inrush of the tide. Then Harold was hacking at the leather of the stirrup, severed it and the man floated free, his face ashen, the pain of his own broken bones shuddering through his body as his chattering teeth attempted to thank his rescuer. Harold reached out a hand, grabbed at the man's shoulder and began towing him to where the second man floated, face down.

"Set your arms about my neck!" Harold urged the one with the broken leg. "I need my hands free!" The current was growing stronger, the swell and pull of mud and sucking sand around Harold's legs and feet making it so difficult to wade, to push forward, but he was nearly there...he reached out, caught hold of the second man's hair, dragged him nearer and managed to clamp his strong grip around the other's wrist, started back to shore... Three other hands grasped hold of the two almost drowned unfortunates, took their weight from Harold's aching shoulders, dragged them—and the gasping, spluttering earl—out from the water. Harold stumbled as his feet touched dry land; he sat, legs crumpled beneath him, air pumping into his lungs as he struggled to steady his breathing.

Conscious of a shadow across him, shielding the heat of the afternoon, Harold opened his eyes, lifted his gaze to stare up at William's tall, dominating height.

"That," Duke William said, "was either an act of bravery or wretched foolery."

Harold laughed, held out his hand for the Duke to haul him upright. "Well, I am not especially brave, so I must, then, be the fool."

William slapped his hand, once, in a gesture of respect on Harold's upper arm. "I think you are not the fool you masquerade to be, I think, my Lord Harold of Wessex, that perhaps you are a man who ought be courted as ally, rather than opposed as enemy?"

24

Dinan

The breaking of the Breton army besieging Dol was a disappointment to Harold. With siege warfare being an uncommon practice in England, he was eager to observe the strategy of dislodging an encamped force. Conan apparently held no similar interest, nor the stomach for a direct fight. With the might of the Norman army rapidly approaching, he fled west, leaving Dol to celebrate its liberation. Harold would have left things at that: Dol was secure and Conan taught the lesson that it was unwise to challenge his duke.

"In England, we would have offered a treaty." Harold observed as, after a single short day spent in Dol, William ordered pursuit of the rebels. Negotiation is preferable to bloodshed, surely?"

"Talk," William answered disparagingly, pausing before lifting his foot into the stirrup to mount, "is for women and monks."

Harold said nothing as he swung himself into the saddle. It did not particularly matter to him what path William took, but it seemed, to his mind, ludicrous to initiate a bloody confrontation if disagreement could be settled amicably. The insult to English manhood he ignored. Already he was learning that to take umbrage at every contemptuous remark aimed at the Saxon way of doing things would have left him in a state of permanent rage.

"I have no intention of ending it here at Dol," William announced gruffly to Harold's silence. "Conan must not be permitted to mock my authority. If he wishes to challenge me, then he can do so on the battlefield."

Harold half raised his hand in salute as acceptance of the Duke's explanation. He would be the first to concede that authority must be maintained, but was this determination to fight not an indication of a possible weakness? To subdue an enemy by agreeing peace terms required a superior strength of character rather than the raw muscle of conflict. Skill in oratory and diplomacy could be as powerful as the honed blade of a sword, especially when one was backed by the other. William's determination to fight at all costs showed Harold a crack in his defences. The Duke could only retain his command by strength of arms, but no man could fight for ever.

"Perhaps," William said scornfully to Harold as he nudged his stallion forward into a walk, "the king of your country would not have been so long in exile in mine, had there been more of an effort to fight against the invader Cnut when first he went into England."

"Or perhaps," Harold answered amiably, "had the royal household fought the harder against Cnut, our king would not have survived long enough to reach exile in the first place."

Duke William shrugged and kicked his horse into a canter, iron-shod hooves sending sparks flying from the rough-cobbled streets of Dol.

He marched after the rebels into Brittany, to Conan's own-held town of Dinan, encircling the city and threatening reprisal without quarter if Conan was not immediately handed into his charge. The citizens of Dinan, resenting the invasion of a Norman force, duly refused and Harold was at last to witness, first hand, Norman siege tactics.

William's army, entrenching their encampment beyond arrow range of the town's walls, began ransacking the surrounding countryside, looting what they could carry, destroying what they could not. Men were slaughtered—peasantry many of them, scratching a hand-to-mouth living from the soil. Cattle, crops, grain butchered or burnt. The younger women were useful for a soldier's pleasure, the elder ones and the babes were butchered along with their menfolk. For two weeks, black curls of smoke darkened the landscape, and the smell of burning flesh tainted the prevailing wind.

When everything within sight of the walls of Dinan was nothing but charred ruin, William began on the town itself. His terms were direct: surrender or burn. Dinan survived for a further three weeks, then surrendered—after letting Conan escape under cover of darkness. He left behind a minimum force which, as a token gesture of defiance, engaged the Normans in a small, insipid skirmish, in which two of William's men received minor wounds. The Duke's savage response was to let his men run riot within the town for four whole days. No one and nothing was left unscathed. Those killed outright in the first onrush proved to be the fortunate ones.

Listening to the rampage of unfettered vengeance, hearing the screams, watching the pall of smoke, smelling the blood-scent of death, Harold felt sickened. This was not warfare, a warrior matching his skill against an opponent of equal worth. Where was the battle honour in the slaughter of innocents?

While murder ran bloodily through the narrow streets of Dinan, Duke

William took his ease within his command tent, enjoying a meal of lamb delicately flavoured with herbs and garlic, roasted wildfowl, baked rabbit, fruits and strong goat's cheese. Rabbit was a dish Harold normally enjoyed, for the animal was barely known in England. Once or twice their meat had been served at Bosham, brought by incoming traders, but the English preferred the taste of their native hare. The animal had little potential value for the English, but for Normans living within fortified walls or facing the possibility of a prolonged siege, the coneys, so prolific in breeding and needing only the limited space of a warren, provided a ready supply of fresh meat.

Harold had half considered taking a breeding pair back with him to his Waltham Abbey manor—the younger children might enjoy making pets of them—but henceforth, they would always remind him of what was happening on the far side of those fortified walls. He would never eat rabbit again without hearing the screams of women and children.

"I will enter Dinan in full armour on the morrow," William announced as he cleansed his fingers in the silver bowl held out to him by a servant.

Could he hear the suffering? Harold wondered. Did it not stir his conscience?

"You too, my friend, Earl Harold, must dress in splendour. We shall show this scum our superiority."

Poking a strand of meat from his teeth with his fingernail, Harold could not immediately answer. One woman's frantic screams had risen above the other noises: "*Ne touche pas l'enfant! Ne lui fait pas mal!*" Then they stopped abruptly. *L'enfant est mort*, Harold thought despairingly, wondered how old the child had been. His stomach was retching, yet he dare not show weakness to the Duke. He reached forward for his wine goblet, to rinse the foul taste from his mouth. He was also mildly embarrassed. He had no chain armour of the quality of William's, nothing save for the iron-studded leather byrnie he wore. He flicked a glance at Will fitz Osbern, seated opposite, who, to give him his due, looked as green-sick as Harold himself must.

"My Lord," fitz Osbern said quickly, "Earl Harold came to Normandy in peace and joined our venture merely as an observer. I believe he is unarmed."

"What? Has my bold companion not yet been suited with mail?" William appeared genuinely taken aback that this had been overlooked. He thumped his fist on the table. "This will not do! My dear friend"—he stalked around the table to Harold and offered him a modest bow of apology—"forgive this insult to your integrity and honour—and after your bravery at Mont Saint Michel too!"

Further embarrassment overcame the Earl. While any man would covet the exquisitely made Norman armour, Harold possessed two full suits back home in

England. Graciously he waved the Duke's concern aside. "I have had no need of your fine workmanship, my Lord Duke," he answered with tact. "Besides, I am an Englishman, your guest, not a knight of your company."

William failed to catch the hint. "Well, sir, you ought to be!" he responded, gesticulating for Harold to stand. Fists on hips, the Duke assessed Harold's height, grunted approvingly.

"Will, fetch me my own spare mail. We are not much different in build or height, you and I, Earl Harold. I will give you a suit of my own, as reward for your loyal service and your bravery. And as for the other…" He drew his sword from the scabbard at his hip, commanded. "Kneel, sir, let me knight you!"

Harold spread his hands, at a loss for what to say. "I thank you for your generosity, but—"

The Duke thumped the table with his clenched fist. "*Non!* I have made up my mind to this!"

Harold let his hands drop and peered in consternation at fitz Osbern who had conveniently already turned away to open the wooden coffer at the rear of the tent.

Robert, comte de Mortain, Duke William's second half-brother, William de Warenne and Walter Gifford, all sprang up from the table, cheering the sudden announcement: "*Bravo!*"

Reluctantly, Harold accepted the Duke's enthusiastic embrace and knelt before him to receive the investiture of arms. What choice had he but to accept the honour with grace? To refuse outright would be an insult, yet Harold had a shrewd suspicion that this seemingly impromptu performance had been well rehearsed. Why should William be so determined to knight a man of foreign birth who had no intention of fighting under the ducal banner? What advantage would it bring to Normandy?

With foreboding, Harold placed his lips to the Duke's ring, aware that to receive a knighthood was to pledge loyalty in return, to be bound as a liege man. And he was also aware, because his men had overheard the whispers, that William still nurtured the hope of laying claim to the English crown when Edward no longer needed it.

In theory, as the Duke's sworn man, Harold would be obliged to support William in that absurd intention. A theory with implications that Harold did not care to dwell upon.

25

Bayeux

Promised a reunion with his kindred come the pre-Christmas gathering, Harold, who had begun to realise that Duke William's promises were no more solid than waves running upon the seashore, was not in the least surprised to discover that only one of the boys appeared at Advent. His nephew Hakon came to the cathedral town of Bayeux, but not his brother Wulfnoth.

"What of my brother and nephew?" he had asked William during the ride home to Normandy after that ragged victory in Brittany.

"Pardon?" William had answered the Earl, his expression quizzical. "I know not what you mean?"

Marvelling at his own patience, Harold had answered, "My brother and my nephew. Held hostage in Normandy this many a year. I wish to see them. It is, as I told you, the purpose of my visit."

Already he had tarried here in Normandy too long. The assault into Brittany, while interesting to observe, had achieved very little as far as Harold could see—and now this wearisome delay until the December Court.

Conan had fled deeper into his Breton lands, where it was too dangerous for William to pursue. He had achieved the restoration of Dol and the submission of Dinan, bringing a few miles of Brittany under Norman control, but for how long? Harold saw a parallel to the English war with Gruffydd of Wales, the incessant border conflict, tit-for-tat raiding, exasperating skirmishes. Conan remained free to taunt the Duke if it suited him; had William sued for agreement before chasing his opponent into a burrow too deep to dig out of…ah well, that was William's problem. Once Harold had secured the release of his two lads, he would head straight home for England, happily leaving the Duke to fend for his own future.

On that mid-September ride home from Dinan the frown had deepened across the Duke's brow as he had considered Harold's question. "Have they not yet been brought to court?" he had said with puzzlement to William fitz Osbern. "I surely issued orders soon after our guest arrived?"

Harold suppressed a sigh. Norman procrastination. He was damned sick of it!

Fitz Osbern had responded with his usual diplomacy: "You were about to, my Lord, but the matter of Conan suddenly arose. Many pressing matters were left untended, I believe."

"Ah, there you have it then, *mon brave*!" William had answered with a smooth smile. "Let us return into Normandy and announce my victory. Later I shall send for your kindred. You have my word."

Later? Aye, if empty Norman promises permitted it.

Bayeux was a rich, almost gold-gilded town dominated by the towering splendour of its elaborate cathedral—and equally elaborately attired bishop, Odo, Duke William's eldest half-brother. Yet Harold was not impressed: the outward sheen of wealth belied the underlying stink of bad drainage and peasant poverty. Nor did he care for the portly bishop, a pompous, odious man.

Odo was three years William's junior, born to their mother Herleve soon after her marriage to Herluin, vicomte de Conteville. The two half-brothers shared the same arrogance but nothing else of likeness, except perhaps a similarity of hair colouring. Where William was tall and muscular, Odo stood a mere inch above five and one half feet, his lack of manly height emphasised by his stout bulk. Whereas William at least had the right to unquestioned respect, Odo's haughty demand for deference stuck in Harold's throat like a scratching fish bone. Where was the humility of a man who served God? The caring for the poor and sick, the devotion to the teachings of Christ? Ah, no, Bishop Odo cherished nothing more than the rich pickings of this worldly life.

Without Harold being informed of his coming, Hakon arrived at Bayeux as another swirl of winter rain, heavier and more persistent, lashed across the courtyard. Duke William had not met Hakon before, for both hostages had been kept at various lodgings within the houses of lesser nobility. Harold had last seen him in England as a child of six years.

Although the solar was more comfortable than the public Hall below, Harold felt tense and restless. He wanted to be surrounded by his own family, relaxing within his own manor. Edyth's solar was so much more tastefully arranged than this rather carelessly furnished room. Harold could only conclude this was because the Bishop had no wife to make the place into a home. Although he did have a woman, a black-haired mistress, or so Harold's men had overheard. That was nothing unusual; only the most devout of clerics practised what they preached, and Odo, Harold reckoned, rarely even preached unless it were for his own gain.

The afternoon stretched ahead with no promise of relief. Harold was bored. He knew few of the men present and apart from the Duchess Mathilda,

Norman ladies rarely spoke to him. The silly rumours that Englishmen ate Frenchwomen for breakfast had affected what little manners these Norman noblewomen possessed.

A tall, slim-built young man with a tumble of fair hair worn in the English style entered and was escorted before William. The newcomer bowed, though not with the reverence usually shown to the Duke. There was something about him that attracted Harold's attention. His stance, his build…when William pointed in the Earl's direction and the lad turned to face him, Harold smiled and began immediately to move through the clustered groups of men and women, his hand reaching forward to greet his nephew. Seventeen years of age and the image of his father! Harold would have known the lad anywhere, so like Swegn was he, even down to the hauteur in his narrowed dark eyes and the pointed refusal to clasp hands in greeting.

"*Voilà!* Your nephew, my Earl Harold, as promised." The Duke looked smug as he indicated that the lad might go with the Earl, but added in a deliberately loud voice, "Though the lad seems none too pleased to be here!"

Hakon's disgruntled expression was evident to all who were watching. "So you have remembered my existence at last," he drawled, not caring for the interest he was stirring, looking Harold up and down as if he were judging whether an ox be suited for the plough or the cooking pit. "Why? What has brought you here to seek me out? Do you come to gloat at my predicament? Placate me with apologies and regrets for not coming ere now?" He stood two feet from Harold, arms folded, head raised high. Angry.

Aware of the intrigued audience, Harold nodded briefly in acknowledgement of the Duke's dismissal and forcibly steered the lad away into the relative privacy of a window recess. "Hush, man," he chided, matching Hakon's anger. "Do you want this court to hear every word? You do not want the Duke to misinterpret your behaviour."

"You tell me that?" Hakon retorted, his mouth twisting, fists clenched. "There is very little that I have not learnt of William these past years. Not least that once in his clutch the snare will never be sprung."

"It is not my fault you have been kept here for so long," Harold hissed. Through eleven years had he been pleading for Hakon's plight and now, when they were here, face to face, they were arguing. Christ's blood, how William must be enjoying the spectacle! At that, Harold glanced quickly over his shoulder at the Duke, saw that aye, he was watching with an amused smile. He took a breath and calmed his misplaced surge of anger. "We have repeatedly attempted to negotiate your return." He indicated Hakon's clothing, the fine leather of his boots and the gold brooch fastening his woollen cloak. "You do not appear too badly treated. You have not been left to rot in a dungeon as others less fortunate have."

"There are many forms of imprisonment; a dungeon is not obligatory. Being unable to ride where you will, write or receive letters without first having them read by the censoring eyes of others. Being shepherded day and night, aye, even to the privy or the flea-hopping bed of a tavern whore. That, my Lord Earl, is imprisonment."

Harold laid a placating hand on Hakon's arm and said, with sorrow. "It was not of my doing that you came to be a hostage Hakon. The events of 1053 were beyond our control. Everything was chaos, we were tossed hither and thither like autumn leaves torn from their branch by a gale, swirled high then abandoned once the storm was over."

"Aye," Hakon snorted, shrugging off Harold's touch, "and no one came to sweep the remains into a tidy pile. The household left the detritus to rot in the courtyard."

Fighting his inclination to walk away from the youth, Harold smothered his ire. The lad was hurting, confused and, aye, even though he had been well treated, angry at being abandoned to the mercy of Normandy. What else could Harold expect? It occurred to him that in this, too, Hakon was much like his father, who had been so given to unreasonable outbursts. But then, unlike his father, Hakon had just cause.

"You undervalue yourself, lad." Harold commented, calling on all his reserves of patience. "My mother, your grandmother, has one of the finest gardens that I have had the privilege to wander in. Her roses smell sweet in summer, the bees swarm to the herbs and flowers. To create such beauty she enriches the soil with compost made from fallen leaves. It is a fact, my lad, that what may be discarded by one is highly prized by another." Harold met Hakon's eyes. Had the lad understood his metaphor?

To his delight, Hakon relented; his shoulders sagged, his head with its jutting chin and blazing eyes lowered, the defiance gone.

Harold held out his hand as an offering of peace and friendship. "It was not my fault, Hakon, that you were sent here, but it is my fault that you have been left mouldering for so long. I am here to rectify that. For you, and for my brother." He glanced again at William, attracting Hakon's attention to the interest the Duke was taking in their contretemps. "I would not wish the Bastard to achieve his intention of alienating kindred from kindred."

Hakon immediately understood, regretted his churlishness. Slowly he took his uncle's hand. Found suddenly a burst of pleasure at having contact with someone on his own side, someone, alone in this entire duchy, on whom he could count. At last a friend for the sake of friendship alone. The lad attempted a tentative smile. He would never oblige William the Bastard. "Nor I, Uncle, most certainly, nor I." Was rewarded by Harold's wider grin and a sudden fond embrace.

Releasing Hakon, but keeping hold of his arms, Harold said solemnly, "You will be returning with me into England, that I promise."

"Returning? What, tired of us already?" the conceited voice boomed loud behind them, a plump hand descending on to Harold's shoulder, remaining clamped there, unwelcome but immovable. Odo, Bishop of Bayeux. Harold gritted his teeth.

With a guffaw that held more malice than jest, Odo announced scathingly, "You will not be returning anywhere these next few days I fancy, my dear Earl, not with this wind and rain. We're in for a storm, I reckon. Besides—the Duke expects you to make merry with us. I expect it." His small eyes—pig-like eyes, Harold thought—bored into Hakon's a moment, then flickered to Harold. His head nodded once to emphasise his point, then he walked away.

"As I said," Hakon remarked drily, "not all prisons have metal grilles and bolted doors."

"Ah, but I am no prisoner!" Harold objected.

Hakon shrugged. "Are you not? Try leaving."

⋙⋘

During the next few days Harold forced his nephew's warning from his mind, but the doubt had been planted. On how many occasions had Harold implied he was considering leaving Normandy? How many times, in return, had William— or Duchess Mathilda with her smiling eyes and fluttering lashes—persuaded him to stay a while longer? Unease lay heavy in Harold's stomach. On reflection, he realised the suspicion had been there from the very first, but had been lulled by the flattery and friendship of the Duke and his lady. Why had William been so intent on rescuing him, so urgently, from Guy de Ponthieu? Because, as he had indicated, he would tolerate no form of disobedience from his sworn vassals? Harold had believed the claim then, believed it, in part, still, for the Duke had, most assuredly, been angry at the humiliation Harold had suffered. It would not do for one country at will to imprison visiting dignitaries for ransom. No trade, no alliance—no outward semblance of trust—would coexist between one realm and another.

Yet, had William realised the potential of holding such a prestigious hostage for himself? If Guy de Ponthieu could exact ransom, then so, too, could the

Duke of Normandy. Perhaps not a monetary one, but something more valuable to an ambitious man. If holding a nephew and youngest brother had, for all these years, served a purpose for William, how much more useful would a king's most trusted earl be?

This visit of Harold's had no diplomatic motive, no treaty with England or Edward to discuss, yet William had welcomed Harold to court as if he were a long-lost brother. Why? Once roused, suspicion was difficult to eradicate, especially when the evidence began to emerge with sudden and startling clarity.

Friday, a day of obligatory fasting, was nearly completed. Once the final prayers of the Evening Mass had been intoned in the distinctly damp and cold cavern of Bayeux Cathedral, the deprivations of the day could be relaxed. Before making his way to the cathedral, Harold had tried something that he had hoped would send this gnawing fear scuttling back into the shadows. He had ordered a horse saddled and, riding alone save for one servant, had gone out beneath the gate of the Bishop's palace. No one had stopped him, no guard had barred his way. Through the narrow streets of Bayeux he had ridden at a sedate walk, the flare of the servant's torch flickering in the buffeting wind and with each hiss of rain that scorched the burning resin. The town's gates were, of course, barred once night had come. Harold had demanded they be opened for him. The watch had stamped to attention, but made no move to lift the heavy wooden bars.

"I need to leave immediately," Harold had said. "I demand you allow me exit."

The guard had looked uneasily from one man to another; relief appeared on their faces when an officer stepped from the guardroom.

"My Lord forgive me, but I cannot open these doors at this hour of the night without express command from my duke or his brother the Bishop."

"But I am Earl Harold of Wessex, England."

"I cannot, sir. Fetch word from the Duke, then I shall be glad to oblige."

Furious, Harold had returned to the cathedral, all the while telling himself that the watch were indeed being reasonable. Once the gates to a town were secured, rarely were they opened.

Duke William's family knelt in prayer to the fore of the congregation: the Duchess, surrounded by her brood of children—the boys, Robert, Richard and William, and the eldest daughter Agatha, her face rapt in the joy of prayer.

Harold watched her discreetly throughout the monotonous service. A child of ten years, round-faced like her father, short and plump like her mother, serious-minded with a shy smile and a delightful laugh. This very morning William had offered her as wife to Harold.

"You are among the bravest of my knights, I would have you for a much higher status, I would have you for son."

Why? had been Harold's immediate thought. *Why are you so eager to bind me to your side?*

"You honour me, Sir," he had answered, chiding himself for the uncharitable scepticism and attempting to think quickly of a suitable answer. "I have commitments to a hand-fast woman in England. A marriage such as you suggest must needs be considered with care, not answered on the spur of a moment."

"You have until Sunday," William had said, forcibly, which detracted somewhat from his air of good humour. Beneath the congeniality lay something darker, more sinister. Harold had not heard it then, but he could now. Now that he was certain he had confirmed Hakon's warning. Heard it as clear as the singing of the monks. He was held prisoner to William's whim.

What did he want from Harold? Not friendship alone, not from a man who was just an earl, albeit an earl who held the ear of a king. In truth, Harold was flattered by the unexpected—and uncourted—offer of marriage. To be united with the Duke of Normandy would bring much to the House of Godwine. Edith, Queen of England, Harold allied with Normandy—so much could be achieved…but at what price? Did Harold, the most powerful man in all England below the King, want to be chained to this arrogant Duke of Normandy? A man concerned with naught save the promotion of his own ambition? And then there was Edyth, dear, sweet, gentle Edyth, and the children, Gunnhild and Algytha, cherry-faced girls, bubbling with laughter like a brook gurgling beneath the summer sun; Edmund, Magnus, young Ulf and Goddwin. Ah, and Goddwin. Jealous, fiercely loving, loyal Goddwin, who adored his mother beyond all life and who mistrusted his father for what must, one day, occur.

How would my son, my heart, my pride, welcome the daughter of Duke William as stepmother? Harold almost laughed aloud at the thought of the obvious, none too complimentary answer.

By chance, he found himself beside Agatha as the royal party stepped from the cathedral into the incessant rain. Harold gallantly offered his arm and lifted the drape of his cloak around her shoulders. "Allow me to escort you, my Lady."

Agatha accepted Harold's huge, sheltering presence with relief. The roar of the wind as it shrieked through the narrow streets of the town, tearing at roof tiles and window shutters, toppling anything not properly secured, frightened her. It seemed as if the devil himself were riding across Normandy, crying out for the lost souls of the dead to join him. And Harold was a good, kindly man.

She could not imagine the Earl of Wessex erupting with uncontrolled bile at some inconsequential matter, as did her father all too frequently. Shy Agatha dreaded the approach of Christmas with its enforced frivolity, knowing full well that her father would soon be quarrelling with her eldest brother and vociferously berating men and women for their bawdy behaviour.

Often of late Agatha wished that she could remain for ever within the peaceful confines of a nunnery. Oh, the blessed joy of hearing naught but the voice of God for the rest of her days!

"In English." Harold said to her as they walked, his voice pitched loud to rise above the pummelling wind, "your naming would be Ælfgyva."

Politely, Agatha smiled at him, struggling with the strange pronunciation. English was a difficult language, uncultured, her father so often said, a tongue of simpletons. Harold was no simpleton, but Agatha knew instinctively how her father despised all but the noblest Normans.

"I think I had best remain Agatha," she answered after several failed attempts at Ælfgyva. "Your English is beyond me."

"You have no desire to learn my tongue, then?"

Agatha laughed at that. "Oh, no, my Lord. Of what use would English be to me?"

Perhaps you may marry an Englishman."

Agatha halted in mid-stride, so unexpected was his remark—so worrying. Her face paled. "No, Sir, I have no desire to marry, I wish to make my vows as a nun."

Harold stopped also. Suddenly he felt sorry for the girl. "I doubt that is what your father desires for you, lass. His decision is the one you must follow."

"My mother will speak for me, I am sure," Agatha raised her head, breathing courage and fortitude into her lungs, continued walking. Her mother would not marry her to a man against her will. Would not. Surely?

"Of course she will," Harold responded, and then, as if he were jesting, asked casually, "but would you not consider me as a potential husband?"

Her reply was immediate and, in its naïveté, answered the mud-stirred doubts that had chased Harold so doggedly these past few days. "I regret that my father would never consider a marriage with you, my Lord. You represent too much of a potential obstruction to his ambition."

Harold pressed his lips together. Had she realised what she had said? He doubted it. She was a child, had, in her innocence, repeated something that she had heard fall from either her mother's or father's own lips.

Entering Bishop Odo's imposing Hall, Harold stood aside, allowing the girl to go ahead of him. Blushing, she thanked him for his escort, then said, very quickly and in a whisper, "But if I had to marry, then I would surely choose you." And she was gone.

Harold watched her go, raindrops falling from her cloak as a scatter of diamonds. She was a child, only three years older than his own youngest daughter, Gunnhild. How could he contemplate marriage with one so young? Ah, but the political advantages could be so great, and the personal ones also. The more intimate formalities of union would have to wait, allowing time for Edyth to grow accustomed to the presence of a formal wife—perhaps she would even look upon the girl as another daughter? Watching Agatha scamper through a far door to the sanctuary of the women's quarters, how could he think of her as anything more?

If he had to marry for convenience—and one day he would have to—he could do worse than consider William's daughter, but something held him back: this growing sense of unease, like the current of a river trapped beneath the ice-bound freeze of winter. Temptingly placid on the surface, so dangerous below.

26

Bayeux

The Duchess Mathilda was certain that she was carrying another child. Her second flux had been due over a week past and her breasts were beginning to tingle. She shut her eyes. It had surely been an eternity since she had risen close after dawn! The luxury of bed and sleep beckoned.

With no knock or pause the door to the bed-chamber opened, William's overpowering presence dispelling the quiet atmosphere of the dim-lit chamber. He tossed his cloak on to the bed, sat, lifted his foot for his body servant to remove his boots, then gruffly told the boy to leave.

"And you." He indicated with a jerk of his head that his wife's three women were to go. They bobbed curtsies and hurried out, William slammed the door behind them.

Mathilda, disguising her exhaustion, formed a smile for her lord, rose gracefully from her stool and walked over to him, began unbuckling the leather straps of his tunic. At six and thirty years he remained a well-muscled man, his hair with only the merest hint of grey at his temples. In all the years of their marriage William had not once fallen ill, not to disease or injury. If his head ached, he but worked harder to drive it from him. If tiredness attempted to dull his mind, he concentrated more on whatever it was that required doing. He was not a man who would admit to frailties, or indulge in the more frivolous areas of life. Unlike Earl Harold, who enjoyed books, women's chatter, or the attention of over-excited children. He was six years older than William, but his equal in untapped energy. If silver flecked Harold's hair, then it did not show so clearly against his colouring. His mouth was fuller than William's, more likely to curve into a smile, break into outright laughter. His eyes, too. Where William's brooded, dark and ever watchful, Harold's sparkled bright with amusement and merrymaking.

Mathilda tried to concentrate on helping her husband undress. She knew she ought not think so much of Earl Harold; she fully realised the extent of her fortune. She loved William; he had given her all any woman could expect from marriage, especially the children. How she loved her children! Ought she tell him of her suspicions that she was breeding again? *Pas maintenant*, she would wait until later. For all that, why did she so often think of Harold?

"Has the Earl come to any decision regarding our daughter, my Lord?" she asked, kneeling down to remove his hose. Her chemise was of fine linen. Beneath, the silhouette of her breasts was clear and defined. William found himself looking at their enticing shape.

"He has not said, but *sans doute*, he will agree to take Agatha. He begins to grow impatient, is becoming suspicious of our generosity. I do not think I can delay his return to England much longer." He reached out a hand to cup Mathilda's breast, feeling his manhood quicken as the seductive heaviness settled into his palm.

Keeping Harold here in Normandy was becoming a problem, but perhaps it no longer mattered. William had learnt all he could of the man, or at least so he thought. That Harold was eloquent, easygoing and easily persuaded was evident. A fine horseman and huntsman, skilled in the use of arms, he possessed a flair for fighting. But he was complacently agreeable to other men's suggestions. Did not, William believed, have that especial quality of leadership that bound a soldier to his lord's battle standard. The Earl was too ready to discuss options and seek advice before making a decision. That was not the way to rule: a leader of worth must weigh the odds, certainly, but quickly and forthrightly, must never tolerate disobedience or question. Ah, but all these Englishmen were the same! Weak-willed, opting for the easy choice; more content to lie in the sun or play games with children than sweat on the battlefield.

"He attempted to leave Bayeux earlier. As ordered, the watch guard refused him politely." William bent to kiss his wife's lips, bringing her body nearer, feeling her against his naked chest. It did amaze him that this woman could so completely and easily disarm him, could make him forget that, maybe, beyond the bolted door stood a man with a dagger to thrust into his heart.

Mathilda slid the chemise from her shoulders and allowed him to lift her on to the bed. He kissed her throat, fondled her breast, moved his hand across her stomach, parted her legs. Always the same, he always did the same.

Her daughter would not take kindly to the prospect of marriage; she had her heart set on serving God. Well, she must be made to understand that the child of a duke such as William had no choice in the matter of her future. Perhaps Bishop Odo could help. As a man of the cloth he was in a position to persuade the girl that a nunnery was not a suitable destination for her. Odo, despite his pomposity, would be better than William in a rage, raving at the girl to enforce his decision. Force, as Mathilda knew well, was not the best way to begin a marriage—although, she supposed, it had worked for her in the end. She realised that her mind was wandering, that she was taking little notice of her husband's intimacy.

Would Harold's lovemaking be as forgettable as William's? Had his woman, this Edyth Swan—something-or-other, Mathilda could not pronounce the difficult English; Harold had translated it as "swan neck," implying her beauty— were her seven children conceived in a few minutes in indifferent boredom, or had she experienced this great enigma of pleasure that Mathilda had heard others boast of?

Her husband, she was certain, had underestimated Harold. The Earl had no need to mask fears or self-doubt to prove his domination or repeatedly enforce his will. That made him placid and calm, not vulnerable.

Spent, William rolled from her, fell almost immediately asleep.

If Agatha resented this marriage, then the girl was a fool. Mathilda would willingly welcome a man such as Harold to her bed…she gasped aloud at the adulterous thought.

"Mm? What was that?" William had heard!

"Nothing of import, my love. I spoke my thought, that be all."

"And what thought would that be?"

What could she say? She grasped at the first thing to come to mind. "Will you permit Harold to take this lad, Hakon, back to England?"

"Hakon? *Oui*. The boy is only a nephew with no living father, and a mother secured within a nunnery in disgrace. I shall allow the brother, Wulfnoth, to accompany Agatha into England when I think her of a suitable age to go to her husband's marriage bed."

"And when will that be?" Mathilda's hand moved across William's buttocks and down to his thigh, brushing against his incapacitated manhood. He had awakened her desire but not fulfilled it, but was frustratingly not ready for more lovemaking.

William's half-smile was composed and calculating. Harold could go home to England soon, for he had him where he wanted him. "When? When I am certain that he will do all he can to secure for me the throne of England."

The Duke rolled on top of his wife, his mouth bruising heavily against hers. There were ways of ensuring loyalty, some obvious, some subtle. He was using subtlety against Harold of England, luring him into friendship, tantalising him with the promise of an assured future. Binding his hands with invisible chains.

And tomorrow he would turn the key in the lock that would clamp those chains tight. Tomorrow, when the nobles and vassals of Normandy, and beyond, swore their annual oath of homage to their duke.

But that was for tomorrow. Tonight, he would ensure the fealty of his wife.

27

Bayeux

Agatha sat completely miserable, in a corner of her father's great Hall, as far from the glare of watching eyes as she could. She would have preferred to remain in her bed-chamber, but her mother had not allowed it. The exchange of heated words between them this morning had been almost as red-hot as the blaze of the yule log in the central hearth fire. She did not want to marry, could her parents not see that? She had a calling, her desire was to serve God. That was her duty, not the giving of her body to a man in marriage. Not that she disliked Earl Harold, he was kind and he made her laugh, but then, so did William de Warenne and Ralph de Tosny…many other men. And to go to England? Oh, she could not, could not! It was a country of heretics and pagans, where men worshipped beneath oak trees and took oath in the name of the gods, like Odin and Thunor. Where the women were all whores and their husbands adulterers…how could her father contemplate sending her to live in such a dark pit of iniquity?

As Bishop Odo's raucous laugh boomed across the crowded Hall, Agatha shrank deeper into her holly-green woollen mantle, clasping her fingers tighter together in her anxiety. Her uncle had been there this morning. Confronted by uncle, mother and father together, what chance had she, a ten-year-old girl, of making her voice heard? If she was frightened of her father, she feared Uncle Odo's chastisement more, for he brought the added wrath of God's word to his reproof. Agatha knew she could withstand any punishment, any beating, but not the condemnation of God. Surprising even herself, she had shouted and clenched her fists, declaring that she would not, would not, become betrothed to Earl Harold—and her uncle had slapped her, right there in front of her mother and father, slapped her so hard that the bruise would blacken her cheek for many days to come, in the name of God's displeasure at her discourtesy and refusal to accept her place as a woman and wife.

A tear dribbled down her cheek. Never before could she remember enduring such misery.

"Why the tears little mistress? What ails you?"

A man's shadow fell tall and broad across her. Her downward gaze saw only his boots. Doe hide, dyed blue. Earl Harold's boots.

He sat beside her on the bench, near enough to exchange private talk, distant enough not to compromise her honour. "I think we are all disenchanted this day," he said. "The rain and biting cold does sour our humour." He tried a small jest: "They say when this rain eases, that it will turn cold enough to freeze the feathers of a gander's backside."

No smile touched her mouth. Another tear dribbled; she brushed it aside.

Harold decided to try the direct approach. "Your father tells me that you have been informed of our intended betrothal." Still no response. He leant forward, cupped her chin with his hand and tilted her face upwards to look into his own. "Am I, then, so terrible a prospect? I am not so bad to look upon and at least my breath does not smell like that of your father's toothless old wolfhound. Nor do I scratch at fleas with my foot."

At last Agatha attempted a smile at his absurdity, then answered him with a choking stammer: "It is England I fear, not you."

Harold chuckled. "There is nothing especial to fear about England, sweet one. It is just as damned cold in winter as it is here in Normandy, just as wind-blustered by the northern breezes and flatulent men. Many of us in England are descended from the Viking race, as you are, and we all have as much passion for climbing the ladder of power, by whatever means, legal or murderous, as your father's fellow countrymen. The one difference between Normandy and England, Lady Agatha, is that we live in houses built of timber, not stone, and we prefer talking about fighting rather than risk smearing blood over our long hair and our trailing moustaches."

Agatha fiddled with her kerchief, drawing it fearfully backwards and forwards through her fingers. Whispered, "But I would know no one in England, I should be the only Norman."

Setting his large hand over the smallness of hers, Harold shook his head. "There are more than a few of Norman birth in England, child. Our King Edward, for one, is more Norman than English."

"But he is old and will soon die!"

"Aye, and then your father will try to enforce taking the English crown for his own. There'll be more than a few Normans attempting to come into England when that day occurs, I'm thinking!"

The girl's mouth had dropped open. "How did you know? Father has forbidden anyone to talk of his ambition for England!" Her mind raced. Had she inadvertently let it slip? God help her hide if she had!

Harold gently squeezed her fingers in reassurance. "You father, for all the love you rightfully bear him, is not as clever as he thinks. I have known all along, I am an important man in England; my word will carry much weight when the time comes to elect our next king. Your father has been courting me with as much energy as it seems I may need to employ should I make up my mind to take you as wife."

Agatha seized on those last words. He had not, then, yet agreed to have her? Oh, thank God! Mayhap he would not want her and she would be free of this. He seemed so unconcerned about being used by her father as a stepping stone to what nearly all men in Normandy privately said was an impossibility. Robert, her eldest brother, had said openly that their father was a fool if he thought he could ever persuade the English to accept him as their king. "Half of Normandy does not want him because of his tyranny and foul temper," he had told her not so long ago. "Why he thinks England would open her arms and joyfully welcome him, I know not. Not unless that country is indeed as moon-mad as our father often credits her to be."

Agatha had not been shocked by her brother's discourtesy; Robert detested their father with a vehemence that was becoming close to the hatred that existed between opposing armies. That was another whisper rustling quietly through the shadows of court: one day, when he eventually came into his own strength, Robert would be pushed too far by William's constant ridiculing and would retaliate by overthrowing his father. Except even Agatha could see that Robert, with his mood swings between spiteful bullying and effeminate parading, was not half the man her father was.

To Harold, she said, "Do you not mind that my father has been befriending you for purposes of his own? I should be most grieved to learn that I was only wanted as a friend because of my position, not because of who I am."

Harold suppressed another laugh. She was so young and naïve. How could he take her away from Normandy and subject her to the lonely life of an unwanted, unloved wife? Yet that was what probably awaited the poor lass anyway, whomsoever she might eventually marry. At least with him she would be getting a man who cared for her welfare. There were plenty of men—men four and five times her age—who would covet the pleasure of taking such a young maid to their bed and nothing else.

"Do I mind? *Non, mademoiselle*, not as long as the tactics your father is using suit my purpose also. I am willing to play the blind-eyed fool to his scheming if, at the end of the day, I can return home to England with my brother and nephew." At the seriousness of her expression, he added with an eye-wrinkling smile. "And warmed with the knowledge that I have had the honour of meeting the prettiest young lady in the whole of Normandy."

Agatha blushed. She envied her brothers. They would have some degree of choice in whom they married. It was so hard being born a girl. All the harder, she supposed, once the girl became a woman grown. "If I were to come to England," she said slowly, "there is the possibility that my father will become king and my mother queen. As your wife I would be at court often, would I not?"

"*Oui, certainement.*" What else could Harold reply? She would soon realise, as would her father, that Harold had no intention of promoting William's hopes before the English Council. Propose a bastard-born Norman for the throne of England? Had Harold heard William's eldest son's scorn, he would have cheered at his good sense!

Harold, glancing across the crowded Hall, saw William fitz Osbern frantically beckoning him. Now what did Duke William's attendant arse wiper want? "Excuse me, *mademoiselle.*" Harold stood. "I am being hailed and must go." He raised her hand to his lips. "I would ask that you keep our conversation private, for the reason that you may, one day soon, be my wife." He raised an eyebrow and stared his meaning fully at her for a long moment.

She nodded, the kerchief again threading in agitation through her fingers. He was telling her that if she betrayed his confidence she would regret the tale-telling as soon as he had her in England. "I shall say nothing. I expect Papa wishes you to witness the oath-taking of his lords and nobles. He always insists that all take some part in the ceremony."

Harold bowed to Agatha, then walked forward to meet an agitated fitz Osbern, who escorted him towards the raised dais to the east end of the Hall. There Mathilda sat, lavishly gowned, beside her husband; the eldest boy, Robert, scowled his displeasure from the front ranks of waiting noblemen. A few more years and he would be the first required to mount the dais, kneel before the Duke and pledge the annually renewed vow of fealty. If father and son had not succeeded in slitting each other's throats by then.

Harold found the prospect of this ceremony distasteful. In England a housecarl pledged loyalty to his lord out of respect and love for that man. They chose which lord they would serve and their faith maintained that lord's exalted position. If he did not keep faith with their loyalty in return then a lord would fall as swift as a mouldering fruit is plucked from the store barrel and flung to rot on the midden heap. These oaths of allegiance being sworn, monotonously repetitive as, one by one, William's knights came to kneel and kiss his ring, did not come from the heart. There was no pride in the step of each man who came forward, no sincerity in their muttered words. This oath was made under duress: serve me, be loyal to me, or lose all you have. That was the only choice available to these harnessed mules. Eustace, comte de Boulogne, came forward; Robert de Maine; le comte d'Evreux; le comte de Mortagne; Aimeri, vicomte de Thouars; Walter Gifford; Ralph de Tosny; Hugh de Montfort and Hugh de Grandmesnil; William de Warenne; William Malet; Roger, son of Turold; Turstein fitz Rollo; Richard fitz Gilbert; Alan Fergant de Bretagne, vassal of Normandy…so many more; Harold knew most of them by sight now. He stiffened as a man he had no desire ever to meet again knelt before Duke William. Guy, comte de Ponthieu. He caught Harold's displeased glower and returned it with a none too discreet gesture of lewdness.

And then eyes and bodies were swivelling towards Harold.

"My Lord Earl? Will you not also grant me the honour of declaring your intention of prospective kinship?"

The Hall had fallen almost silent. Harold stood, bewildered. William sat forward on his throne, one elbow resting on the naked sword blade that lay across his knee. His mouth smiled, but there was a glint of something else in his eyes. "Sir?" he repeated. "You are my knighted comrade. I myself put the armour about your shoulders, placed the sword in your hand, my kiss upon your cheek. You are, are you not, my declared vassal? Will soon, perhaps, become my son by marriage? I think it right you do swear the oath to me also. Do you not agree?"

This, Harold had not expected. The anger shuddered through him with the force of the bore tide that surged up the estuary of the Severn river. He licked his lips, trying to think what best to do, glanced at the watching faces hoping to spy a hint of help. No one met his eyes. Not one of William's whore-poxed lick-spits dared face him. How many had known of this trap? How many had privately laughed at the stupidity of this damned bloody fool of an Englishman? Some? All?

And then Harold saw Hakon standing at the back, his face drained of colour, the fear on it easy to read. Behind him stood two of William's guards, apparently positioned there by chance, but Harold could see their fingers hovering over their swords, their gazes firm-fixed on Hakon's back. Knew as well as the lad that were he to refuse to swear then both of them would be seeing the darker side of Duke William's damp and foul-smelling dungeon. And would be kept there until they died.

"You promised that you would take me from here!" The words leapt from Hakon's expressive, desperate eyes. "You promised!"

In these few short days Harold had come to know Hakon as a trusted and trusting friend. Something that ran deeper than the tie of kinship had sparked between them and the years of enforced separation had dwindled into nothing but a memory.

How binding was a promise? Ah, that depended on the nature of the oath and the amount of honour within the man. When a man offered his sword to his chosen lord he was bound to keep his word or lose his honour; the promise to set an afeared youth free of his shackles was equally binding. An English lord paid homage and loyalty by undertaking to do his best by the men who served him. To rule fairly, to protect the children and womenfolk, to lead bravely in battle. To take upon his shoulders the responsibility of caring for those men who had promised to serve without question. And in the Saxon tradition, above all else, a man could knowingly declare false oath and not be perjured for that swearing, if the safety or honour of another depended on it.

They were waiting expectantly, most of them hoping Earl Harold of England would show himself the greater fool by refusing outright the Duke's command. Harold must surely oblige them, for William had no right to demand he speak the word of faith and fidelity. It would be an oath taken against his will and better judgement. Yet had not most of the men here this day proclaimed their troth under the same harsh conditions? Swear, or lose your land and freedom. Or your life.

Duke William was holding his beringed hand out to Harold, the gloating smile broadening into triumph.

"We are allies, are we not?" he coaxed, his voice smooth with practised charm. "Soon, alas, we must set you on your way home to England, accompanied, no doubt, by your nephew. Soon, also, your brother—Wulfnoth be his name? Wulfnoth will honour me by escorting my eldest-born daughter to you. In return for the patronage of my kinship you will agree to represent my care and concern for the future of England's throne. You will remind King Edward that he did favour my claim. I shall expect him to honour that favour in the making of his will, and from you also, as my sworn vassal."

The fury choked in Harold's throat. Vomit rose in his gullet. So this was why he had been kept in Normandy, why he had been played for the simpleton! Once the annual day of oath-taking was past, once he had pledged this foul promise, he would be free to return to England. Aye, free, but bribed with the lure of the daughter of the duchy as wife, threatened with harm to his brother if he refused. Yet for the good of another an oath might be made and broken without loss of honour. For the good of Hakon, and more, for the safety of England...They were only words, after all.

Harold stepped forward, his throat and lips dry, his fists clenched. He stared with a hard dislike at William, then knelt, touched the sword and set his lips to the Duke's ring.

William nodded his acceptance, but before Harold could repeat the oath said quickly and with menace, "I think I may need some further assurance from you, my Lord Harold. Being that you do not reside here in Normandy." He clicked his fingers; two servants brought in two wooden caskets. "These contain the holy relics of Normandy's most precious saints. Swear your oath on them, Earl Harold, make your words truly binding."

Harold's rage almost boiled over the edge of restraint. It was one thing knowingly to break an oath made to a man, another to do so against God. Yet was not God, too, just and honourable in His wisdom? Did He not respect the time-cherished ways of the Saxon kind? Not bothering to mask the rage that was churning in his mind and stomach, Harold laid a finger on each casket, repeating aloud the words of fealty that Bishop Odo dictated to him: "I pledge to my Lord Duke William, son of Robert of Normandy, my fealty and my loyalty. Do offer my duty as Earl of England to your honour. To speak your words, as if spoken from your mouth, to the noblemen of England's realm. To provide for you, when Edward is at the end of his noble life and called unto God, the crown, the sceptre and the throne of England, so that you may rule in the way of Edward's wisdom." It was done. With gorge in his mouth, but done.

Duke William nodded, satisfied. He took and held Harold's hand between his own palms a moment. Met, as he rose to his feet, Harold's blazing eyes.

In them there was no calm of spirit, no come-what-may frivolity. Nor was there any hint whatsoever of fear. In that one brief passing instant William realised he had made a vast error of judgement. All these long months observing Harold, assessing him, deciding his worth, moving each piece of the game, square by square, slowly, surely; calculating the ultimate goal. Again and again William had won his private tournament against this English Earl Harold.

Looking direct into Harold's eyes, that mid-December afternoon, William belatedly understood, with stomach-churning dread, that Harold, too, had been playing a game. His foolery, his complacence, his mild manners had lulled his opponent with blithe ease into a false appraisal.

Harold said nothing more as he turned without bowing and walked away from the dais. He made his way through the low murmuring of the crowd to the doorway, Hakon following at his heel. He left the Hall and went direct to the quarters where his men lounged.

"We are leaving," he announced curtly. "Now, as soon as horses may be saddled and our belongings packed."

He turned away, realised Hakon had followed.

The younger man's expression was grim, his skin grey and pale. "Now do you believe me about William?" he asked.

"I never doubted you, lad. I only misjudged the depth of how much of a bastard he is."

Hakon headed straight to the stables. "I have nothing that I care to take with me from this cursed place. I shall await you by the gates."

Harold made no comment, was barely listening. Over the spilt blood of death would William become king of England, and never with help from Harold's hand. That was a second, silent oath that Harold had made as he had spoken aloud those obscene words. That never, never, would he allow William on to English soil.

If the need came, if there was no one worthy or suitable to follow Edward, then he, Harold Godwinesson himself, would take up the crown and do his best, unless death prevented it, to protect England from Norman ambition.

Part Three

❦

The Anger...

I

❧

York—December 1064

The five men leant their arms on the worn and stained table, each close-cradling a pewter tankard of ale, each carefully watching who else might be coming, or leaving the tavern. They had deliberately chosen this corner table, tucked well into the shadows, in an inn not often frequented by men they might know.

"Even if we are espied," Gamalbearn had gruffly pointed out, "we are but five acquaintances quenching our thirst together." The others had agreed, but not wholeheartedly.

"Aldanhamel was slain by Earl Tostig's orders before the steps of the chancel at St. Cuthbert's in Durham." Ulf Dolfinsson said to his companions in a low, contemptuous voice.

"Aye, after he had pleaded sanctuary."

"And all for refusing to pay in tax what he had not got."

"A thegn such as Aldanhamel! Outlawed and slain in so vile a manner!"

The men shook their heads in sorrowing agreement with the last speaker, Gluniarn, all of them equally appalled at the profanity of what had amounted to murder within the sanctity of the cathedral.

"The King's friend will stop at nothing to accumulate more wealth."

"And it is us, mud-caked foot-stools beneath his feet, who are helping him achieve it." Dunstan slammed his tankard back on to the table in disgust. Tostig Godwinesson: the name was becoming a curse on the lips of men suffering under his regime of discipline.

Some thought Earl Tostig's ambition had grown worse since Gruffydd ap Llewelyn's downfall. Until then, Tostig had concentrated on enforcing the haphazard and neglected laws, over-industriously some had said, but if a man committed a crime then he should be suitably punished. If too many men were beheaded for murder and rape, or had hands removed or noses slit for robbery, then perhaps there had been over-much crime in the first place. Not one of the thegns within Tostig's jurisdiction had complained at his establishing the right to walk the roads without attack, but no thegn would tolerate this excessive demand for taxes. The North was so much poorer than the South by way of population, trade and sheer practicality of the rough, moorland terrain, and for that Tostig cursed and pined. Had he been made Earl of Mercia or Anglia, Kent or Oxfordshire...but no, he had the undowered North. He could not, in all reason, raise the level of taxation to match that of the richer South. Yet within a few weeks of his brother's sailing for Normandy he had done just that, to the rage and disgust of those forced, by decree of the King, to pay homage to him.

The thegns agreed that it was the Welsh campaign, for all that it had been fought under Harold's command, which made Tostig overconfident. It had given him the experience of the battlefield and the kudos of a victory. Since Wales, it had seemed that there was nothing beyond Tostig's increasingly corrupt capabilities. The problem was compounded by the King's unrestricted favour, for in Edward's eyes Tostig could do nothing wrong; he would hear no word of criticism or grievance against him. The five men knew this for certain, for they had, by subtle means, tried. Had Earl Harold been in England these last months when the problems of the North had suddenly escalated, then things would have been different; he had the knack of holding both the King and his brother in check.

They were meeting, these five thegns, to discuss what they could do next. Dunstan voiced the frustration of them all. "I have eight and forty hides of land, for which I have paid sixteen shillings in taxation. I now must pay twenty-four. 'Tis too much, I cannot afford such an outrageous amount."

Gamalbearn, the eldest of them, chewed his lip angrily. His father had been thegn before him and, aye, his father before that. They had fought loyally for England; he personally had sworn fealty to the old earl, Siward, who lay cold in his grave beneath the slate floor of St. Olafs church here in York. Siward had never been so grasping; Siward understood the ways and difficulties of those of the North; their steadfast traditions and their wary mistrust of the affluent, uncompromising South.

Nursing his ale, Ulf took up the complaint. "'Twas two shillings for every six hides, now it's two shillings for four hides only. A goddamned increase of nigh on half as much again."

The December afternoon was drawing to an end; dark came so early during winter. The open-fronted shops would soon be sliding their shutters closed, market stalls packing their wares. Micklagata, the main street, would be crowded with those who lived outside the city making their way home to steadings and farms, and this tavern was filling as folk, their work finished for the day, passed by on their way down the street of the shield makers, Skeldergata.

Gamal Ormsson jerked his head over his shoulder, indicating the growing press of customers. "We had best finish our business here."

Reluctantly the others agreed. If Tostig received word that five of his thegns were talking together in the Black Bear down Skeldergata...aye, well, let him hear of it and speculate on the nature of their conversation!

"Then we agree." Gamalbearn said, "that we must put our case to Tostig? Two of us shall go to the Earl's palace and ask leave to see him. We must do it this night before he leaves for Edward's Christmas Court." He paused, looking from one man to another. All wore doubtful expressions, for they privately wagered that Tostig would not listen to one word spoken.

Dunstan selected five rushes from the floor, sliced with his dagger to make them all equal, then carefully cut two the shorter by half. Gathering the pieces into his fist so that all appeared the same length, he held his hand gravely to each man. One by one they chose. Gamalbearn, long. Gluniarn, long. Gamal, short. Ulf, short, leaving the last for himself. He could barely conceal his relief. Long.

"Then you go, Gamal Ormsson and Ulf Dolfinsson. Luck and common sense be your companions."

Ruefully, the two men rose from the bench, finished their ale and shouldered their way through the tavern to the door. The light was fading outside as they made their way, cloak hoods thrown over their heads, towards Conig Street and the Earl's palace.

Perhaps they would not have gone had they known Tostig had no liking for thegns who decided to challenge his rule of law. He was later to claim they had attacked him in a frenzied attempt at assassination.

Their three companions knew nothing of their fate until the next morning, when the heads of Gamal Ormsson and Ulf Dolfinsson swayed on spears, decorating in grisly warning the gatehouse above Micklagata.

2

Gloucester

Throughout the previous day the last of the noblemen and their families had been arriving for the annual winter gathering of Edward's Council The royal buildings at Gloucester, never wholly suitable as a king's palace, were crowded almost to capacity with the number of men and women housed beneath the rush-thatched roofs of guest chambers or sleeping crammed together on straw pallets in the Hall. Litters, wagons and carts were set, higgle-piggle, in the pasture beyond the gate, and the rain-flooded pathways were churned into deeper mud with the tread of so many hooves and feet. Over it all hung a smell of cooking that barely masked that of human body odour, wet horses and dogs, the mustiness of wet thatch and fungi-smeared walls and of drying clothing.

The rain had eased during the early evening of the previous day, although louring grey clouds threatened more of this wretched weather. Even so, Edward, bored with being within-doors, had decided to hunt. On Christmas Eve, four fattened geese had been slaughtered in broad daylight by a fox; Edward required no second misdemeanour to track down the thief come the earliest opportunity. Foxes were considered the creatures of the devil, their colour and stink being the very essence of hell. The King ordered all earths to be stopped with faggots and two peeled sticks set in a crucifix to warn the creature, should it attempt to return, that the wicked evil of gluttony and theft would be punished.

The throng that set out through the low archway of Gloucester Palace was in merry mood: about thirty or so men and six women mounted on fine horses that pranced and snorted, excited by the eager, yodelling voices of the hounds. The copse where the ground began to rise upwards to meet the thicker beech woods, where that pest of a torn-eared, grey-muzzled dog-fox often prowled, was to be their first draw. A vixen had also raised her cubs there last season.

"That be the beggar you are after." Edward's constable had informed Edward as together they had studied the paw prints by the goose pen on the day of the killing. "A cunning brute, who sets his brush close to Lucifer's shadow, I'd wager."

Trotting along the lane, Edith closed her eyes, breathed in deeply, enjoying the uncluttered openness of the outdoors and the fresh, clean aroma that assaulted her senses. There had been a catastrophe yesterday—the wind had lifted the shingle tiles almost clean off the solar roof, leaving the chamber below open to the weather. Her tapestries and furnishings were quite ruined; it was as if the wind had picked everything up, swilled it around and dumped it down again. The room would be unusable for days. Disaster would happen while they were in residence—why not while they were at Winchester or Westminster? So damned inconvenient! Apart from her bed-chamber there was nowhere to be private. Never over-fond of company not of her own choosing, Edith disliked the bustle of the Hall—the inane chatter and laughter, the nearness of so many unwashed people. She detested Edward's palace here at Gloucester at the best of times. Why they always had to come here at this gloom-skied season she knew not. It would be so much better to spend Christmas at Winchester, but Edward insisted that tradition must be maintained. Tightening her fingers around the reins, as she rode along the slippery track, Edith vowed that when he was gone she would see about altering poxed tradition. She and Tostig together would have the opportunity to change many things once the Council declared them joint regents of England.

She glanced ahead at her husband. Edward was talking animatedly to Tostig on his right-hand side; on his left rode the boy, Edgar, joining in, chatting about their shared love of hunting, no doubt. She smiled. They made a most appealing trio: king, earl and ætheling.

Edgar would reach his teen years on his next birthing day; a dutiful lad, attentive to his studies of history, languages, numbers, reading and writing, but just as eager in his lessons at archery and weapon practice. Polite and devoted to the King, there were few who doubted that, as a man grown, Edgar would be unanimously chosen as the successor—but unless Edward should live for many a year more, the boy was still too young to rule. Would yet need a guiding hand on his shoulder. And Edith had every intention of ensuring that hand would be her own entwined with Tostig's.

Edward doted on her brother, constantly sought his companionship; moped and mithered like a disconsolate child throughout the interminable months when Tostig had to be in his earldom. On occasion it nauseated Edith, this reliance that her husband placed on Tostig's company—and if she felt sickness rising into her throat when Edward simpered over him, then how did Tostig himself contend with it? Her brother loathed Edward's attentions but, like herself, knew the reward that might lie at the end of it all. What were a few smiles and platitudes in exchange for a kingdom?

They reached the copse and spread out, waiting for the huntsmen to unleash two couple of hounds and send them into the undergrowth.

Recently, other more ambitious thoughts had been preoccupying Edith's mind. Edward was getting old, almost three score years. His skin was wrinkled and pocked with brown age freckles. His white hair, short-sighted eyes and befuddled memory did not belie his age. Despite his insistence on hunting, he tired easily, but slept less at night, frequently dozing wherever he sat—more often than not while in Council or in judgement at law. He would sit on his throne, propped by cushions, and his eyes would cloud, head would nod, a snore emit from his occasionally dribbling mouth. He was not a dotard, or feeble, just old. They would leave him when he slept, Edith and whoever was assisting at whatever government function was under discussion. The King rarely made any relevant contribution anyway.

Since Edward's last bout of illness had taken him to his bed for several weeks, Edith had begun to wonder if it were possible to play for an even higher reward than that of a regency. Even if Edward lived another year, or two, or three, there might be those who could be persuaded that Edgar was too young. The most suitable candidate would be chosen to take up the crown—and could the Witan of England, in all conscience, however much they admired the boy's eagerness, regard him as suitable?

Within the copse a single hound spoke, then another. They had found the trail. Edith observed the winter undergrowth for any flicker of russet. For the chosen king not to be of full royal Wessex blood was unusual, but not unknown—Cnut had not even carried a shred of English blood in his foreign veins. Tostig was trusted, favoured by Edward, had proven his ability to govern. Northumbria had been a barbarian place until Tostig had set about imposing law and order. And had he not campaigned with success in Wales, distinguished himself in various skirmishes with rabbles from across the Scots border?

Hounds were speaking, singing their music in unison; the red rogue would be breaking cover shortly. What if Edward were to die soon? Next week, next month? It was possible. He could fall, or succumb to some dreadful illness. She refused to entertain the possibility of the opposite, of Edward living for many more years…no, he was an old man.

Someone a few yards along shouted. Gospatric, a thegn from Northumbria, but no friend of Tostig's. He raised a horn to his lips, sounding a burst of quick notes. A flurry of blurred movement and a dog-fox shouldered, with an air of disdain, from the shelter of the bushes and loped away across an open ploughed field. The pack of hounds slipped quickly off their leashes, streaked away after him. Edward waved his arm, hollered and blew his own horn to sound the gone away. He kicked his horse into a gallop, Edgar and Tostig close at heel, with the rest of the hunting party in rapid pursuit.

Edith gave her plunging mare her head, forgetting all thoughts of intrigue, coronations and kings as the wind from her gallop whisked through her firm-secured veil, and her eyes watered and stung with tears, nothing but the reckless thrill of speed and freedom filling her exultant mind.

The fox was running easily, aware of his territory and the escape routes, all the shadows and sheltered places. He slipped into a smaller copse, trotting towards where he knew a deep-excavated earth to be, stopped, confused, as he found its entrance blocked with piled sticks and stamped-down earth, the intrusive unpleasant stench of man wrinkling his sensitive nostrils. He trotted on, heading uphill. The hounds had checked where he had entered the copse, were not able to slink so efficiently through brier and draping holly bush.

Gospatric Uhtredsson, thegn of Bamburgh, had only one thing in common with his overlord Earl Tostig, and that was a delight in hunting, although on his own manor, vermin such as foxes were poisoned or trapped, the thrill of the chase being preserved for more worthy game. However, he had to admit, as his horse plunged down the steep bank of a tumbling water course and through the swollen, white-foamed current, this red-coated beast was giving them a fine run. He kicked his bay up the far bank, swung him right, ducking low beneath the bare, low-sweeping branches of beech trees. A thin, whip-like branch caught his face as it swished backward; he cursed and put up his hand to feel blood oozing from a cut that jagged from nose to jawbone. Hauling his horse to a halt, Gospatric dismounted and, looping the reins through his arm, bent down to the stream, scooping cold water to dab at the cut.

The sounds of the others crashing on through the woods faded quickly as the chant of the horn told that the fox was once again streaking out into open country. Gospatric could catch up: it would be easy to follow the trail left by so many.

The horse was not so content to be left behind. The animal was snorting and stamping, neighing anxiously. Irritated, Gospatric tugged at the reins, but upset and excited the horse tossed its head with a sudden jerk and simultaneously backed away. The leather reins broke with a snap and the horse was gone, whirling around in a flurry of legs, dead wood, beechmast and swirled leaves from the autumn fall. The Northumbrian man leapt quickly but was not fast enough. He stood, fuming, as the god-damned animal galloped away after his companions.

Sour-faced, Gospatric slithered down the bank and waded into the rain-heavy rush of stream water. No good chasing after the beast, he would never catch the damned thing. Better to head for home. Huh, more than a five-mile walk! The water came to mid-calf, fortunately no higher, but the opposite bank was steeper and mud-churned. By the time he had pulled himself up to solid ground, he was thoroughly wet and grimed, and in poor temper. He called out, hoping some servant or peasant might be near at hand. Nothing. No sound save the raucous cawing from a nearby rookery and the toss of branches clattering against each other as the wind grubbed through the bare tree canopy.

As he stumbled on, his temper increased. Twice he slipped on wet grass as the woods began to drop sharply down; added to that, his boots, new a few days since, were already rubbing. He vaguely remembered urging his horse upwards through these trees—aye, there was the trail. Holding on to a low branch he wondered whether it would be safer, on this steep slope, to sit on his backside and slither down. A long, ditch-like gully ran off to his left—aye, he remembered someone shouting "ware the hollow." He turned left slightly, then stopped abruptly. A mounded shape lay in the bottom of the chasm, protruding from the gush of sluicing rain water. A horse, a dead horse.

Minding his footing, Gospatric tentatively made his way over to the dead animal. Its neck was broken, he could tell. He thought he recognised the dark chestnut—a wry grin of smug satisfaction tilted the corner of his mouth upwards. Tostig's horse. He edged around the body and stopped, folded his arms and stood looking down, the smug grin etching deeper.

Always thought he knew it all. Always the clever one who would never take advice from anyone…that was Tostig, Earl of Northumbria. Tostig, who lay, eyes closed, groaning, among the blackened, mud-crusted leaves, his leg caught beneath the bulk of his dead horse.

Gospatric loathed Tostig. Would, without qualm, wish him dead. Tostig was not from the North, had no right to bully those, like Gospatric, who were descended from the ancient noble families of Northumbria. Did this jumped-up whoreson think they would forget the brutishness with which he meted out punishment on the poor and the innocent? The viciousness of his oppression of freeman, thegn and noble alike? The arrogance of his demand for respect that he had in no way earned. His greed, his avarice. The murder of those two men at York—men Gospatric had known and liked.

Aye, Gospatric, the last surviving son of Uhtred of Bamburgh, whose family had once ruled in their own right, had no shred of compassion for Tostig. They had all been warned to beware of the gully, had ridden carefully around it, but not Tostig it seemed. Gospatric looked to the far side, where the top of the bank was pocked and distorted. Aye, the braggart fool had attempted to jump his horse over—well the man deserved all he got.

Tostig pleaded for someone to help. The fingers of his hand clutched helplessly at the soft earth, sweat stood out on his forehead. His eyes flickered, attempting to focus on the vague, misted shape of a man who stood above him.

"Please, help me! My leg is trapped."

Gospatric said nothing. He pushed himself away from the dead horse, scrambled up out of the gully and swung on downwards, emerging out of the wood on to the grass common land that ran towards the town of Gloucester.

All colour had drained from the landscape, the sun blotted out by the thickening winter cloud. The wind, blowing from the northeast, drove a drenching rain across the hills. Gospatric shrugged his cloak tighter about his shoulders; he would be sodden to the bone before he reached home—but rain or no rain, he had no intention of hurrying. How could they prove that he had found him? None of them could. None of them would know. Serve them right for not realising he was missing from the hunt!

Christ's truth, Gospatric thought, *if a favourite's presence cannot be missed, God help those Edward may dislike!*

He walked on, keeping an eye to the approaching rain. Below, a big dog-fox, the colour of dead bracken, flowed along the line of a ploughed furrow, three fields ahead of the hunt. The cunning animal was doubling back on his tracks. The pack was closing, heads down, firm on the rank scent. Gospatric watched, fascinated, as the fox, out on common land now, swerved several times through a flock of panicked sheep then, leaping a stone-built wall, trotted direct through the centre of a farmyard, into the pigpen, disturbing the old sow, and out again on to the midden heap, where he took the opportunity to roll. Gospatric laughed. Hounds would never trail his scent through those rich odours.

3

Gloucester

Queen Edith's fear for Tostig had been near-hysterical. Thank all the gods that he was not seriously hurt beyond a bruised and torn ankle and calf! Jesu Christ, he could have been killed in that fall this morning! Or died unfound, completely alone, beneath the weight of that horse, soaked by the rain, chilled by the wind...

Edith was supposedly listening to Wilton's Abbess giving a report on the progress of the rebuilding of the nunnery. Too late, she realised she had not heard a word, but had no heart to ask for repetition. All she wanted was to go to her brother, see how he fared. She had not noticed that Tostig was not with them on the hunt, had assumed that he was up at the front with the King. She had been too preoccupied with that beastly mare—wretched creature had pulled at her arm sockets, blistering her hands. And Edward—huh, Edward who professed to being so fond of Tostig but had not realised that his favourite was not beside him? How could her husband not have noticed, for heaven's sake!

"There are several caskets of relics here, madam, for you to choose from, though I am not certain 'tis right that we ought take from one holy shrine to place in another..."

Edith's eyes narrowed as she gazed at the Abbess, her attention drawn back to the matter in hand.

All important holy places were enhanced by the possession of relics, the remains of saints. A finger, a lock of hair, a fragile collection of bones. Occasionally something of greater value: a sliver of wood from the true cross or a few worn threads from the Blessed Virgin's mantle. To Edith, it was inconceivable that lesser shrines should parade their sacred possessions while she had nothing for the glory of Wilton. As Queen, she had no chance to make a pilgrimage to Rome or the Holy Land to acquire something for herself and equally, as Queen, saw no reason why those who already had such things should not offer their treasured artefacts for her use.

That the abbots attending this Christmas Council took exception to the Queen's view had not been missed by Wilton's good Abbess, but had been steadfastly ignored by Edith. Evesham in particular was grumbling. Saint Egwin, Bishop of Worcester and founder of Evesham, was its principal patron; the loss of his relics, should the Queen decide to take them for herself, would be a severe blow to the credibility of the abbey...and so a compromise had been quietly agreed between the monks. The Abbot took to Gloucester, instead, the lesser-valued relics of Saint Odulf, The Queen could have them and gladly. Few bothered with Saint Odulf when they had the holy Saint Egwin to pray to.

"Yes, yes." Edith rose to her feet, waving the Abbess aside and beckoning for the boy, Edgar, to join her, Edward was weeping in his chamber, bewailing the fate of his dear friend Tostig. You would think her brother had died, the fuss he was making. When they had been unable to find the scent beyond that mud hole of a farmyard it had been agreed to end the day's sport and ride for home—and then it had become apparent that no one had seen Tostig since the start of that last uphill gallop more than two miles back. Several were certain he had entered the beech woods; retracing their trail they had found him, about an hour later, as the rain had cascaded down in a torrent. Tostig had rambled something about seeing a man standing over him as they had heaved the carcass from him. Said that he thought it was Death come for him. No, Death had left him to live, but would come to the one who had abandoned her brother there. Oh, most assuredly it would!

Edgar had found them, the boot marks in the soft earth beyond the dead horse. Someone had been there, had gazed down upon Tostig, Some bastard had deliberately walked away from him—an earl of the realm, the Queen's brother, left him there to...and that was the fear that trembled in her heart. Without Tostig, what chance had she of achieving her hopes for her future? She would not be made regent on her own; without Tostig she would be forgotten as all those other queens of the past had been as soon as the crown was placed on the next head.

Edith steered Edgar down the steps from the dais to where several caskets were arrayed on a trestle table. Well, she would not be unremembered! She and Tostig would rule—for Edgar—when the time came and she would be made a saint along with her husband. Saint Edith: it had a good ring. For this, she was rebuilding Wilton, had commissioned a Life to be written, ostensibly of Edward, but centred on herself, and she was to bestow relics of holy value that would be forever associated with her name. Saint Edith.

To Edgar she said, "Let us inspect these reliquaries together, my dear. You will help me choose. I suggest we seek something modest but significant for my nunnery." Of the nearest abbot Edith asked, "Are there any women's relics among the collection, do you know? The bones of a female saint would be most suitable."

The Abbot shook his head. "With regret, madam, I think not."

The Queen tossed a scathing look at him. Why had the fools not thought to bring something more connected to a nunnery? She commanded her goldsmith to break open the seal of the first casket, standing close behind him, her head tilted so she might see clearer inside as each successive lid was lifted.

By the third one Edgar was rapidly losing interest. He was not sure what he had expected, certainly not a shrivelled piece of something that they said was skin, that for all its holy worth looked and smelt disgusting, A broken toe bone and some faded and frayed ragged old cloth. He would rather be with the other boys, playing knuckle bones or teasing the girls—there was a wager on that no one dare sneak close enough to proud-nose Margaret, his pious sister, and tweak her braid.

At Edith's nod the goldsmith lifted the next casket. Evesham's contribution: the relics of Saint Odulf. He took his chisel, with care, to the wax-sealed lock. The casket itself was a beautiful thing, a box three hand-spans high, five long, one wide, exquisitely carved from walrus ivory, inlaid with bronze and gold. Eagerly Edith craned forward; this, she felt, was the one. Something that would enhance the prestige of Wilton. Something that encapsulated profound holiness and would enhance the memory of her own name.

She glanced up at the Abbess, intending to smile, but caught the woman's unguarded expression of worry. The Abbess, Edith remembered, was not enthralled by this idea. That the deliberate removal of an article of value from one holy place for the benefit of another might not be acceptable in God's eyes had not occurred to Edith. Below Edward's new Westminster, Wilton was to be the next most prestigious abbey. To achieve that status, it must house relics of worth, wherever they might come from.

Behind the Abbess she caught a glimpse of more faces, all those who were crowded into the King's Hall waiting for the serving of supper. Her eye lingered on Gospatric. Something would have to be done about that man. She neither liked nor trusted him. He had registered surprise and concern when he had eventually reached the palace and heard of Tostig's accident, an hour or so after they had returned. Protested that if only he had known he would not have made his way back on foot across country, but would have remained to assist in the search. Liar! What cared he for Tostig? It was well known they detested each other, that Gospatric took every opportunity to undermine Tostig's authority. Aye, a troublemaker, a friend with those others who whispered of defiance and insurrection.

As the goldsmith put his hand to the lid, Edith turned her mind from the foul man and leant further forward. It lifted…and a cloud of dust billowed from inside the casket, puffing upwards into the air.

Gasps, a few hastily muffled screams as everyone took a rapid step backward, fearing the devil himself might be released among them. The emanating stench was putrid. The goldsmith ducked aside, instinctively closing his eyes and raising an arm to shield his head, but Edith was not so astute. The particles wafted into her face, grit entering her mouth, settling on her lashes, in her eyes. She reeled, putting her fingers to the burn of daggers seemingly piercing at her sight.

"I cannot see!" she screamed, terrified, her arms flailing. "I cannot see! I am blinded!"

Among the immediate flurry of alarmed movement, the monks of Evesham exchanged brief, knowing glances. Most within the Hall automatically crossed themselves, one or two even sinking to their knees in prayer. Wilton's Abbess rushed to comfort the distraught Edith, ordering the Queen's physician to be summoned.

Only Evesham's Abbot remained still and calm. "It is a sign from God," he announced with solemnity. "A sign that you are not to remove any relics of His saints from a place where He has commanded they rest. God, my Lady Queen, is showing you His displeasure by removing your sight."

Pitiably, Edith sank to her knees, her eyes closed tightly from the agony, tears slithering from beneath the tight-shut lids. She ordered the goldsmith immediately to cease his work, to reseal each casket.

"I vow that never again shall I violate the resting place of a saint, of any holy shrine—oh, if only my sight will be restored. By blessed Saint Odulf, I do so swear it!"

The Abbot rested his hand upon her forehead, gave her his blessing. Wilton's Abbess, who had hastily beckoned for a servant to bring a bowl of water, began bathing the Queen's red, sore eyes.

The tears streamed, the cold water felt refreshing and cool. The intense pain started to ease. Hesitantly Edith opened her eyes. Blurred, watery, she blinked rapidly…she could see. Oh, God's blessed grace, her sight was restored!

With joy, she raised her hands to heaven and praised God. Wilton, she decided, would have to manage without relics.

4

Gloucester

Edward was not attending council this 28th day of December. His head ached, his chest was tight with a cold. Caught in all that rain yesterday. And the anxiety of Tostig's accident had tired him. Edward had retired to his bed and now refused to leave it. Edith, therefore, was presiding over this final day's meeting of the Christmas Council.

Men now looked to her with respect for her wisdom as much as her position but how long had it taken her to earn that veneration! All these years of patient waiting! At Council, in court of law, when interviewing petitioners or messengers, whatever duty the King had been required to attend Edith had been there with him, occasionally seated beside him on her throne, more often charmingly arrayed on a stool at his feet. He would hold her hand or fondle her hair, worn loose beneath her veil as was her right as Queen. With each passing Council he had sought more of her opinion—did this man deserve leniency, this one punishment? Was this official speaking the truth or was he fawning for favour? While surprised and flattered at first, she had soon realised that, in fact, Edward was merely taking an easy option for himself.

Edward had never liked governmental duties, finding concentration tedious and decision-making difficult. How much easier to rely on his wife's discreet nod of confirmation or make a slight shake to her head in disagreement? He would sit as if rapt while some haggard old crone rambled on about the injustice of her land being taken from her because her husband had been careless enough to die intestate. Had become adept at giving the impression that he was avidly listening, while all the while he mused over some parable from the Bible or an uplifting poem or song he had heard the previous night.

From her view, she had little care as to why Edward began to trust and rely on her. It was the results that mattered. Edith had worked hard to gain experience and respect; she had learnt to recognise the catch in a voice that was attempting to conceal half truths, to recognise the subtle body signs of outright lies.

A furtive look, partially downcast eyes, nervous licking of lips or fidgeting hands and feet. Sweat beading a brow.

Gospatric had displayed nearly all of these a few minutes past when Tostig had accused him of leaving his liege lord to die beneath a dead horse in a rain-swept beech wood.

Council had gasped at the accusation. Gospatric had angrily protested his innocence. Another sign. How vigorously men bluster when they know themselves to be in the wrong!

"It is but circumstantial," Gospatric cried, his neck and face suffused with red. "I was thrown from my horse and trudged home through that damned rain—head down. How was I to know you too had suffered a fall? What, do I possess a witch's second sight?"

"Circumstantial? No proof? No, Gospatric, that it is not!" Tostig was bellowing. "I saw you. I opened my eyes and through my pain I saw you, as bold as you stand there now, gloating and grinning—"

"I protest!" Gospatric shouted in response. "You admit yourself you were in grievous pain—'twas but an illusion, I never entered the wood!"

The two then began to exchange insults, others of the Council coming to their feet to side with one or the other, abbots and bishops pleading for restraint.

Edith sat patiently on her queen's throne, her hands folded neatly in her lap. Technically, she could make no judgement without the King's endorsement, merely preside over this meeting as an impartial curb on any over-exuberant discussion. As, most assuredly, was this heated exchange. She had no intention of observing the technicalities, however.

"As I see it," she said, raising her hand, palm out to order silence, "the Earl of Northumbria either saw a vision, or you, Thegn Gospatric Uhtredsson, lie. All we need do to settle this distasteful matter is prove who speaks wrong."

Edith beckoned her brother and the thegn to approach the dais, while instructing the scribe to ensure he made accurate note of all that was said. The man nodded; he was attempting to do so, if only these men would talk slower and not use such blasphemous words. Words he scrupulously refused to record.

The Queen linked her hands, raised and tilted her head to the left, sucked at the insides of her cheeks. It was a pose that Edward's mother, Emma, had often adopted, one that, unconsciously, Edith had copied since almost the beginning of her marriage. "My brother, you claim to have seen the figure of a man standing over you? This is correct?"

"I did. A red-haired man, tall, stout of build."

"Did this image of a man that you saw say ought?"

"No, He turned from me and clambered up the far bank out of the gully. Disappeared over the top. I called out for help; he ignored me."

"And you, Gospatric, deny that this man was yourself, you say that you did not enter the beech wood?" Edith was enjoying herself, glorying in the surge of power coursing through her, preening, almost, in the sublime knowledge that her word, her decision, was law.

"I certainly do!" Gospatric hissed, belatedly aware that he ought to have curbed his anger.

Edith tapped her thumbs together, debating one accusation against the other. She knew Gospatric's reputation, had discussed his menacing presence more than once with Tostig—as she had discussed this very situation with her brother last night as he lay abed, fuming with the pain coursing down his leg and with wrath directed at Gospatric.

"Yet..." Edith spoke slowly, unfolding her hands and setting them elegantly on the carved wood of her chair arms. "Yet your horse was found at the far side of the wood with its reins broken. And boot marks, of a similar shape to those boots you wore for hunting, are clearly visible on the side of the gully where Earl Tostig lay."

"And," a supporter of Tostig's called from the back, "several of us recall seeing you ride into the wood. That in itself you lie about."

Gospatric's face paled. He had been in the rear; no one, surely, could have seen?

"I think you lie, Gospatric," Edith said languidly. "I think you must face trial." She flicked her hand at the King's guard, four housecarls who stood to attention behind her throne. "Arrest him."

Trial would have been the better option for Gospatric. To have asked for the King's personal judgement through ordeal would have been endurable—to plunge his hand into boiling water, grasp the stone, and carry it those few yards, and then, later, show that there was no blistering or burning. He could have taken the opportunity to prove himself innocent, but Gospatric came from a hot-blooded family. The last surviving son out of a brood who had all died violent deaths, Gospatric was no different from any of those of his kindred who held an ulcerating grudge against the South, and Wessex in particular. His father, Uhtred, had hated Godwine, as Gospatric loathed Tostig.

As the guards came to stand around him, Gospatric lost hold of his senses. "Aye, I left you!" he admitted. "Left you to rot in the muck of your own making! All of you bred from Godwine's loins are vipers, crawling with black gloating greed. Your father was a liar and murderer, grabbing at all he could to line his own coffers; you, Tostig Godwinesson, are little better—and your sister too"—he flicked a contemptuous glance at Edith—"you glory in the delusion of your sovereignty. There are those of us"—he was shouting now, hurling his words at the stunned Council—"those of us who have the sense to oppose the greed of the Godwines. To ensure none of them survives Edward's death!"

It was enough. He had condemned himself before all eyes and ears.

Edith, her hands now clenched tight around the chair arms, glared at the four housecarls. "Remove this scum from my presence," she demanded, her words slurred with rage, "and hang him."

5

Wilton Abbey—January 1065

Tostig was seated beside Edward, a sheaf of parchment pages on his lap; the Queen sat, as usual, attentive at her husband's feet. Tostig was reading from the work that Edith had commissioned from the Flemish monk Goscelin of St. Bertin, an account of her husband's life. Well, in truth it was her own biography, but her mother-in-law had been so condemned for the vanity of her *Encomium Emmae Reginae* that she, Edith, had decided not to make the same mistake. The *Vita Ædwardi Regis* would be sufficient for her purpose—providing that self-congratulating fool of a monk kept his wits about him and wrote a sensibly balanced history.

> *Et ut statum siue formam…on his appearance and attitude the King, Edward,*
> *is a fine figure of a man—of outstanding height, distinguished by his milk-white*
> *hair and beard…*

Edward beamed at the praise, his fingers proudly and fastidiously touching his hair and beard.

> *…Always dignified but pleasant he is affable to all. To petitioners he will grant*
> *graciously or graciously deny, so that his denial appears as the highest generosity.*

Delighted, Edward clapped his hands, those slender hands that Goscelin had so well described. 'Tis an excellently written work." He beckoned the monk forward. "A brave work, sir. My wife did well to find so accomplished an author for her commission. This is but the first chapter you say? How many do you plan?" Edward's enthusiasm was reassuring; the monk had been on edge for most of the day, anxious that the King might not like this first draft—or worse, that the Queen would not. It was she who was paying for the thing, after all, and she who had decreed that just the right balance of her own family's history was to be interspersed with that of the King.

The monk bowed appreciatively. "For this, the first book, I have six chapters in mind, my Lord King, being the history of yourself and the Queen. A second book will concern your attention to religious devotions."

Edward took the loose pages from Tostig and peered at the rounded, minute Latin hand. He could barely decipher one word, so poor was his sight now. Handing it back to Tostig, he said with a smile at the monk, "I shall enjoy hearing further instalments, though I trust you will not dwell on my mother's part in my life?"

Goscelin flushed. The problem of the King's dislike of his mother had been almost impossible to overcome. At Edith's suggestion, he had eventually decided to begin at the inception of Edward's reign, glossing over his childhood and involvement with his mother, except where unavoidable, and then only reporting the more pleasing anecdotes.

"Your mother, my Lord King, had the wisdom to produce her account of her courtly life—it is not my pleasure to retell that which is already written."

Edward nodded. Just so.

"Shall I have a part in the story?" the boy Edgar asked, tipping his face up to squint at the tall monk. "I am the ætheling, after all, I ought to be mentioned."

Goscelin coughed, discreetly hiding a rise of embarrassment. Of course the prince would have a place in the book, but not until Edward was dead! Thankfully, the Queen answered for him. "Of course you shall be spoken of, my child, and your father, mother—God rest their souls—and your sisters. But not until the appropriate place." She smiled. "Perhaps, when one day you are king, you shall have your own life written down."

"Oh, when I am king," Edgar scoffed. "I shall be too busy to bother with musty old books." He wrinkled his nose. "Why do they always smell of mould so?"

No one answered him, for there came a discreet knock at the chamber door and a novice nun entered, followed close at heel by a tall, heavily cloaked man. Snow was spattered on his shoulders and hood and stuck to his boots. He tossed back the hood and was greeted by a gasp of surprise.

"Earl Harold!"

"Brother?"

Edgar's and Edith's exclamations sounded together, only one was with delight, the other mild annoyance. Edward smiled, the blurred figure identified, and he rose, holding his hands out in welcome.

Harold looking tired and saddle-sore, crossed the room, knelt before his king and kissed the royal ring, acknowledged Edith in the same manner, but not with as much enthusiasm. "Aye, 'tis me! Despite all the foul weather that the Narrow

Sea and this damned country of ours could toss at me these past weeks, I am here. Although I wasted some time travelling first to Gloucester!"

Noting the ice coldness of his earl's skin, Edward invited Harold to sit before the fire, calling for mulled wine and hot broth. "You must be warmed both inside and out, else you take a chill and fall ill. I myself have not been well for most the Christmas—we only left Gloucester at Epiphany, three days past."

Harold nodded. So he had discovered.

His heart would have sent him straight home to Waltham Abbey, but protocol dictated that first he must see his king. Add to that, these disquietening rumours that he had heard in Gloucester…What in all hell had been happening in England while he had been away?

Goscelin the monk carried a stool to the fire for the newcomer, then discreetly withdrew from the room, realising that there would be no more praise for his work this night.

"So, what of Normandy?" Edward asked with interest as he seated himself. "Has my cousin the Duke sent me any gifts? A new couple of hounds would not come amiss—those we used at Christmas were useless, you know. I ordered their throats cut. Lost the scent of a fox—a stinking fox, mind you—in a farmyard. Useless."

Harold muffled an exasperated sigh. Edward and his petty interests! God help us if William did ever decide to come! He said nothing, though, for he had already heard in detail the sorry tale of Tostig's accident and Gospatric's execution. Except they were calling it murder in Gloucester. Gospatric's men, disgusted, had deliberately lingered to spread their version of events; no doubt the telling would be double-tarred with inaccuracies by the time the tale-tellers reached the wilderness settlements of the north. If Harold were Tostig, he would have returned home to his earldom immediately to quiet rumour and any unrest that might—most assuredly would—arise from that ill-handled business. Oh, Lord, what had he come home to?

"Duke William has sent you four couple of the most finely bred hounds, my Lord King—and further substantial gifts besides. Though I fear he is expecting more by way of recompense in the future."

Edward frowned. "Meaning, my Lord Earl?"

"Meaning that Duke William has his heart set on obtaining for himself a crown. Your crown."

Edward barked amused laughter. He ruffled young Edgar's blond mop of unruly hair. "Edgar here is the ætheling, it shall be he who follows me when the far-off time comes. Eh, lad?"

Edgar smiled up at Edward from his stool, although he was not all that certain he actually wanted to be king. It seemed a dull occupation, all this arguing in Council. And others before him had met worse fates. His grandfather had died fighting for his crown, as had many another king. He did not much relish the thought of fighting. It was the smell and sight of blood—it did so easily turn his stomach queasy.

Harold shrugged, in no mood to go into detail. He was tired; the ride had been long and weary, made all the more difficult by the swirl of snow that was settling deeper. As much as he wanted it, he might not be able to make his way to his manor for several days yet. Tomorrow would be a better occasion to tell Edward of all that had happened in Normandy, of the mess of dung that he had managed to step into. Aye, tomorrow, for the King's hearing, not Edith's and Tostig's. "Suffice to say," he said, "that Duke William has overreached himself with dreams."

"And the reason for your going? Our brother and nephew?" Edith asked, Edward squirmed to one side, peering at the door, expecting to see two more blurred outlines arrive. "Have you brought them with you?"

Harold held his hands to the hearth fire. He was thawing slowly, the sharp prickling needle stabs of pain tingling in his near-frozen toes and fingertips. "I took ship to Bosham. Hakon, our nephew, left with our mother. I did not have the heart in me to take him so soon from her company."

"And Wulfnoth?" Tostig said, a sneer in his voice to match the scowl on his face. "Did you leave him also at Bosham?"

Like his father before him, Harold, as with Edith, could read others well. Edith's greeting had been no more cordial, but then, their mutual regard had for some years grown further apart. Tostig blew hot and cold as it suited him. This day was distinctly chill. Harold had the sudden uncomfortable feeling that his return home to England was unwelcome. Why, he would have to discover, but not yet; it could wait. He had to report to the King and catch up on affairs of state, but beyond that, his priority was to ride home. Nigh on seven months had he been away from Edyth and the children, seven months too long.

"Wulfnoth was not permitted to leave Normandy," he said succinctly. "The Duke continues to hold him as hostage." The words came out more bitterly than he had intended.

Tostig snorted his derision. He had known this fool idea of Harold's was but an empty gesture. In truth he was piqued that Harold had gone on this family mission. His mother, Edith, no one in the family had said it, but he knew they all silently reproached him for not making more effective attempts at securing the boys' freedom when he had, in the past, been a guest of Normandy. Judith had mentioned the two lads to her sister on more than one occasion, had been promised that the matter would be looked into. It never had, but that was hardly Tostig's fault.

He was becoming tetchy, sour-tempered. His leg was aching abominably. The ride to Wilton had not helped and soon, after the consecration of Edith's abbey, they would be returning to Winchester: more long days in the saddle.

Gospatric's vehement outburst had shocked Tostig—frightened him. That there was dissent in Northumbria he well knew, but he thought it nothing more than a storm in a village duck pond. Ignore it and it would bluster itself out. But knowing that a man could so cruelly and deliberately leave another to die was playing on his mind; nightmares visited him: he was lying trapped, smothered, and a man stood over him, laughing…he had not realised his enemies were so embittered. Scornfully, he took his insecurity out on Harold, who had always been so well liked by everyone; so successful in all he did. "So you have failed. While you were so concerned with a brother neither of us knows or remembers, and with the bastard-born brat of Swegn's whore, I have had to deal with great difficulties here in England. How like you not to be here when I needed you! There is dissent and grumbling against me in Northumbria. I could have done with your support, but no, you were off, pursuing your own interests."

Harold laconically folded his arms. "Would these grumbles have anything to do with the murder of two men who were invited into your own chamber in your palace in York? Or with the disposal of Gospatric?"

Edward's head was turning from one brother to the other, attempting to follow the bewildering conversation. How had he missed the cause of this sudden rise in temper? All he had asked was if Harold had brought the lads with him. Not that he cared, he had no recollection of either of them.

Tostig made to snarl an answer, but his sister interrupted. "They were, all three, traitors to the crown. The two in York were plotting outright to murder Tostig—would you have let them harm our brother? And Gospatric openly admitted his guilt. His execution was lawful and by my command."

"Aye," Harold remarked, belatedly realising that because of tiredness his temper was getting the better of him, "at your command, but most ill advised. The North will make much of it for its own purpose."

Perhaps it was despondency over his failure in Normandy that made Harold feel drained; he suddenly did not give a broken pisspot about anything. Or perhaps it was because of this stark reminder, so early upon his return, of all that was different between him and his brother and sister. The pair of them were scheming and plotting for naught but their own gain, with no care for whom or what they dragged into the mire as they passed.

He thought, inexplicably, of the parable of the good Samaritan. His brother, unless there was some gain for himself, would not have paused to help a man lying injured on the road. His moralistic hauteur had always been for show, deliberately paraded to goad Swegn's temper, or to set one brother against another. Tostig always reminded Harold of the pretty shells that his children collected from the beach: beautiful on the outside, but when opened, containing nothing except black mud. There was no genuine goodness inside Tostig, he was too full of jealousy, greed and self-importance.

"You have brought the dissatisfaction that is swelling in your earldom upon yourself, brother, by ruling too ruthlessly. The law is better served by a degree of leniency, and high taxation is only justifiable if it is necessary for the common good, not for private gain. You are attempting to enforce the structure of Wessex on to a people who have lived by different ways. Northumbria is a fiercely independent land. You do not quieten a nervous horse by beating it into submission, but by offering it kind words, care and comfort."

"You always were a soft-hearted fool." Tostig thrust at him. "Treat peasants and imbeciles with honeyed words? The North understands only the lash of the whip. They are unmannered, vulgar, primitive barbarians."

"And this is a land that nourished the Christian centres of Durham, Whitby and Lindisfarne? Venerable men like the saints Cuthbert and Bede?" Harold retorted mockingly.

"I retract what I said." Tostig sneered. He bowed briefly to Edward, then headed for the door. "You would be of no help to me—go back to Normandy, you and William are well matched, both pathetic dreamers!"

Provoked beyond endurance Harold moved with two long strides to catch his brother's arm. He thrust his face close, said with vehemence, "If you assume Duke William to be inadequate, then you are the fool He is a man to be reckoned with. If Edward should die before Edgar reaches a suitable age, England will be dragged into a war similar to—or worse—than that against the Danes. The Normans are descended from those same Vikings who produced Cnut—but I tell you this William is not, by any short measure, comparable to that noble man."

Tostig brushed his brother's grip from his arm, answered with contempt, "You may fear this illiterate, illegitimate foreign bastard, brother Harold, but I do not. He is husband to my wife's sister, I know him well and do not fear his ambition. Nor do I fear the consequences of Edward dying within the next month or year. The King is to name our sister as protector of the child. She will guide the boy when England elects him king; there will be no possibility of William querying his crowning. We will be quite safe from both hobgoblins and aspiring Norman sea-wolves."

Harold was sickened. His throat constricted. He looked at Edward, who was sitting fiddle-fiddling with embarrassment at the embroidered hem of his tunic. "So when was this decided?" he asked incredulously of the King. "Was it made without the agreement of Council—as you made a similar decision all those years past to offer your crown to Duke William and so put this greedy notion into his ambitious head?"

Edward licked his lips and put out his hand to Edgar to help him rise. "It is time I sought my bed, I think. I often take a nap of the mid-afternoon. Come, lad, escort me to my chamber."

Edgar leapt to his feet and took hold of the old man's arm. Harold bit back further remonstrations. There was no point in arguing with Edward, he was too blind to the consequences of his fool promises.

Edgar glanced up at the Earl as he escorted the King past, saying, "No one has asked what I want. I do not much like the sound of this foreign duke, nor the wearing of the crown."

Harold made no answer. Stood in stony silence as Edward left the room. In some weird way he almost wished he had stayed in Normandy. Then he looked towards Tostig, who had moved to stand behind Edith, his hands resting lightly on her shoulders, said, "A woman cannot rule. Edward's successor must be deemed kingworthy. Edgar may yet be of a suitable age when we need consider it, but has he the ability? Admittedly he is a boy still but he displays no interest in what ought become his. England will be in desperate need of a man of courage and strength to hold back this tyrant from Normandy, should he decide to come. I do not think Edgar will be that man."

Tostig squeezed his sister's shoulder and lifted his chin proudly. "Aye, brother, I agree we need someone suitable. You are looking at him."

Harold's jaw clenched, but Edith forestalled any scathing retort. "Neither of you need have any fear for England. Ædwardus Rex reliably informed me but two days past that he intends to solve the problem of his succession simply by living for ever."

6

&

Waltham Abbey—I January 1065

Last night it had been intensely cold and snow had fallen again. Come
morning, the air was as brittle as glass and an ice-clad wind ploughed across
the valley and into the nostrils of Harold's children. The bare branches of birch
and willow waved forlorn against the frigid sky. The meadow below the manor
was a carpet of white, touched only by the prints of birds and the track of a
fox. Gunnhild, turned seven years as January dawned, and Ulf, rising eleven,
being the two youngest and most excitable, had been the first outside for an
energetic session of snowball-tossing. The temptation to join them in the snow
had been too much for their brothers Magnus and Edmund, though they would
see fourteen and fifteen their next birthing days, and when Goddwin strode
up the hill known as Mott Street from his own farmsteading at Sigurdstun, the
game became a wild snow fight in earnest. Even Algytha, eighteen next week,
came to watch, leaning on the gate and laughing at the antics of Goddwin's two
brindled wolf hounds, Dane and Weyland, barking and leaping in excitement
at the flying snow. The game became ever more unruly until Goddwin called
a breathless halt. Their cheeks red-rosy, breath blowing from their mouths like
steam from a boiling pot, they all leant against the rails of the meadow gate, the
two dogs lying, panting, their tongues lolling.

"I trust none of you has a mountain of snow worked inside your boots!"
Edyth called jovially, appearing at the door of the house place. Her hair was
tied back in a tight braid, a kerchief was bound around her head and a sacking
apron covered her gown. In her hand a birch broom. Today, snow or no,
was cleaning day when the shields and weapons were taken from the walls
and dusted, the cobwebs banged and thumped from the hanging tapestries
and the timber floors cleared of old rushes, thoroughly swept and spread
afresh with a new layer. "As you all have so much energy, you can come help
within doors…" At the unanimous groan of protest she added, "Or you can
take food up to old Granny Gnarl-hand. She has none to fend for her now

her son is dead; it is our duty to keep an eye on her, especially during these winter months."

The younger children glowered, for neither chore appealed. Algytha brushed snow from the hem of her gown, offering to help her mother, Gunnhild too, for she enjoyed a closer look at the magnificent weapons that hung on the walls. The boys were reluctant to walk to the widow's cottage that sheltered below the high ground where the oak, birch and alder gave way to stately beech, especially as the letter Mother had received yesterday had reported that their father would soon be home. What if he came today? "As soon as may be possible, with gifts for you all," his curved, polished writing had declared.

"I will go with the boys, Mother," Goddwin offered and whistled the dogs to heel. "There is little to do at my own steading and my wife is also elbow-deep in cleaning." He grinned at his family. "Would you believe, I came up here to escape being dust-mired! Perhaps the dogs will put up something suitable for the supper pot."

Magnus and Ulf whooped their pleasure at the prospect, Edmund shouting that he would catch up with them after he had fetched his new hunting spear.

Edyth smiled to herself as she watched the boys set off across the snow-thick field, Edmund soon racing after them, stopping to collect a handful of snow to toss at his eldest brother's back. The two of them were almost of the same height; Edmund had shot up since last autumn—Magnus, too, promised to be a tall young man. They were all fair-haired as Harold and herself; Goddwin, perhaps, being the most like his father, sharing a similar shape of eyes, chin and mouth. Edyth sighed. Goddwin did not possess Harold's easygoing temper, though. He had not forgiven his father for what he saw as an insult to her, his mother. It was all so senseless! They were two fool-brained march hares boxing at each other.

"But don't you mind?" Goddwin had raged when he had come galloping home from London. "Don't you mind that he may be bedding with another instead of you!"

What had she been supposed to answer? That aye, of course she minded that Harold did occasionally look for his needs elsewhere; that aye, she cared that one day he might take another wife? Instead, she had regarded her first-born son with a direct, steadfast look, and told him of the truth.

"A man may bed a woman he admires or lusts after, but he need not love her. It is to the woman he loves that he will always return."

She picked up the birch broom from where she had leant it against the wall, returned inside the Hall in time to reprimand Gunnhild from getting in the way of the servants lifting down Harold's war axes from the wall for cleaning. "If one should fall on you girl, it could take your head from your shoulders!"

With a squeak of alarm, Gunnhild stepped back hastily. Could an axe do that? She resolved to ask Papa when he came home.

Beneath the trees the snow had not fallen so thickly, the debris of last autumn covered only by an uneven shawl, pocked here and there by deeper drifts. Along the track, every hoofprint that had churned the mud before the snow fell bore a fragile film of ice that cracked as the boys deliberately stamped their boots. All lay still and silent, hushed as if set under an enchanted sleep—and then a dog-fox suddenly appeared, his coat winter-thick, a rich, chestnut red. Unconcerned at the yelping leashed dogs, he stood, one fore-paw raised, his amber eyes contemptuously staring, and then he turned and streaked off, leaving only the pungent whiff of his rank scent. Goddwin released the dogs, but the creature had gone and the dogs were eager for more enticing scents to follow.

The wind bit into their exposed skin as they stepped from the shelter of the trees to cross the open plain that topped the ridge, before plunging downwards again through the scattered army of bare-branched beech. At the bottom of the hill a grey column of smoke rose in a lazy spiral from the smoke hole in Granny Gnarl-hand's roof. The barking of the dogs had alerted her, for the woman stood waiting on her door hearth, her smile gap-toothed, her aged shoulders bent. She beckoned her visitors to come inside, warm themselves by her fire, grateful for their company as much as the welcome gift of provisions from their good-hearted mother.

She had lived in this wattle-walled cottage with her husband since the day she had come to him as bride, nigh on forty and six years past when she had been a fair-haired girl of fifteen years, but no one remembered her at that young age. To this small community she had always been grey-haired, shrunken and aged. It was to Granny Gnarl-hand that children came in summer to ask for the telling of tales, from Granny that the young girls sought love-potions and charms. To her mothers brought their ailing children, their women's problems, their doubts and fears of approaching childbirth.

When her son had been killed two years past, she had feared for her own survival. She was fortunate, though, for Lord Harold was a good landowner; he would not see an old woman turned out of her home to await death in the clutch of winter.

She ladled herb and root broth into wooden bowls to warm their insides. "Be there news of your father yet?" she asked. "He has been so long absent these past months." Concealing the pain that whined in her chilled old bones, she lowered herself into her wicker chair beside the hearth fire. Magnus, always one to chatter, answered her, "Mother tells us that our father will be home soon. He has had great adventures while with Duke William—has ridden to battle with him and been given gifts. He is bringing us a pair of rabbits—creatures that are like hares but smaller and with not such long ears. He says in his letter that they make good eating, but that our little sister Gunnhild will delight in their soft fur and comical actions."

Goddwin scowled, said nothing, concentrated on supping the watery broth into his belly.

Granny Gnarl-hand rubbed at the knobbed, pain-wracked twist of her knuckles that gave her the name. "Rabbits, you say? Never 'eard of such critters!" Her eyes sparkled at Magnus's rapid talk, nodded at Edmund that he might refill their bowls. "If you'll be so good as to replenish the wood beneath the pot, first." She regarded the silent eldest born with her sharp blue eyes, said, "Do you not welcome your father's return then, Master Goddwin? Why be that, eh? Be there some silly quarrel atween you?"

"You ask too many questions, Old Mother," Goddwin answered, with a polite but curt gesture of dismissal.

"He is angry with our father because there was talk at court of him taking a well-born woman as wife," Magnus said carelessly. "Mother says it is a thing that our father must one day be expected to do. If she does not mind this thing happening, then why should my brother?" Magnus set his bowl upside down on the floor to show he had finished and wiped the back of his hand over his lips. "Edmund and me, though, we think he's cross because he'd rather have a pretty blossom for himself than that stinging nettle he already has." His elder brother's scowl furrowed deeper.

"You'm be careful not to let that wronged look sit for long on your face, my lad," Granny Gnarl-hand chuckled at him as if he were a child. "Lest the wind change and set it there for good."

Goddwin silently cursed. "With respect, Old Granny, I am one and twenty years old. I do not need lecturing as if I am but Ulf's age."

"Nursing moon-fool jealousies like a child leads others to treat you as such. I expect your mother has told you so often enough."

The three younger boys grinned at each other. They would wager as much as a shilling each that Granny would get the better of Goddwin!

"My woman is a dutiful wife. I have no complaint against her and Mother is hiding behind a brave smile and a stout heart, but I have seen her eyes red-rimmed from the tears she has wept whenever my father is long away from home." Angry at himself for being so easily riled, Goddwin slammed out through the door.

"He has been like a boar with a headache for months," Edmund confided by way of apology. "It has been his ill temper that has upset our mother on occasion, not our father being away." Added as an afterthought, "Though that does sadden her greatly."

Granny nodded, said cryptically, "Loyalty be a difficult thing to set straight in a fuddled mind."

Magnus was not quite certain what she meant. Loyalty was to trust without question, as he trusted his mother and father. Either Goddwin did trust their father's judgement and was therefore loyal—or did not, which made him an enemy. Ah, it was all beyond a boy's reasoning!

Edmund too wondered about his father's relationship with his mother. They all knew that they were not church wed, that the marriage could be easily dissolved should both parties agree, but their mother would never agree to divorce, so why all this fuss?

Ulf, the youngest, was perhaps the most confused, for during the Holy Days of Christmas he had overheard Goddwin quarrelling with their mother. "Goddwin said that Father no longer loves our mother or us, that is why he has been away so long in Normandy and why he seeks a new wife." He looked sharply at Granny, desperate for her to deny it, so afraid that she might nod and say aye, it was so.

"Then your brother," Granny said firmly, "be talking out his arse, lad. Lord Harold has always, and will ever, give love first to your fair mother and the ones born of his seed set in her womb."

She pushed herself out of her chair and shuffled to the doorway, and looked at Goddwin's solitary tracks plunging away through the snow. "You be a fool unto yoursel' to rage so. You'm be wed to a Christian-taken wife; it be no good lusting after someone different," Granny mumbled. "And if ever your father took another as wife, it would not be your mam to lay abed alone at night, knowing he took his need elsewhere. It would be the other wife to be a-wonderin' that, for your da'll not ever be giving up his Edyth Swan-neck."

❧

Goddwin's temper cooled before he had gone a few hundred yards. Why was he so damned touchy these days? Perhaps because of the sourness of his wife's mood? Frytha was a disappointment to him. He had married her because it had been expected of him since his childhood; her father was a respected thegn and she came with a substantial steading as dowry. Moreover, she could cook and weave, and manage a Hall as efficiently as any woman. But she was sullen, endlessly grumbling. Worse than that, there was something missing in his marriage, something that his father had with his mother. A little thing called love. What he could not understand was why his father could so easily think of ending his marriage with the woman he adored when he, Goddwin, had no mortal chance of unshackling himself from Frytha in favour of someone as beautiful as Alditha, the Widow of Wales.

7

Waltham Abbey

After the snows, flooding threatened the vulnerable lowlands of England where, even during the driest summers, marsh could remain oozing among the alder and willow, reed and rush. Almost overnight the water meadows turned from a spread blanket of white to the ripple-shifting shimmer of lake-like water. The wide flat spread of the Lea valley could not escape the inrush of melt-water. Already over-fed, a series of high tides pulsing up the Thames and into its tributaries pushed the banks of the river beyond the limit of endurance. Like an invading army, the flood marched onwards, unstoppable, mercilessly invading the tranquil host valley.

This morning, Edyth stood at the unshuttered, narrow window of her first-floor bed-chamber, her fingers automatically plaiting her loose hair. It had rained again in the night, only a drizzle but even that might be enough to raise the Lea a vital half-inch more.

Please God, she thought as she reached for a ribbon to tie the end of her braid, *that the sea-tide, downriver, does not come high again today.*

"The water has risen, I swear," she said.

"Need you stand with the shutters wide? 'Tis cold in here."

Edyth twisted her head to observe what was visible of Harold above the heap of bed furs. For six days had he been home, days during which he had immersed himself in the needs of the steading, local business, his family and friends. In Edyth's comfort and warmth. None of which was yet sufficient to drive aside the worry that hung like a rain-sodden mantle around his shoulders. Normandy. Tostig. The succession. An endless round of disquiet that disturbed his sleep and offset his happiness at being home.

"If it rains again, I fear for the village. Will the crypt flood if the waters break through the abbey walls?" Edyth mused aloud.

Harold sat up, yawned and wrapped a fur around his nakedness to join his woman at the window. Leaning his hands on the sill, he peered out. Cattle, sheep, swine had all been moved these last few days to higher ground, were grazing uneasy in more cramped conditions. A few families, those with house places close by the river, had taken what possessions they could and moved to safer havens. Others, belligerently, intended to stay. His son, Goddwin, among them.

"There is a story," he said, encircling Edyth with his arms, bringing her close under his fur, "that Cnut once proved he was only a mere mortal by attempting— and failing—to turn back the tide. We need God's hand to help stem this rise of water, for I fear, like Cnut, no man can stop it." He kissed the tip of her nose. How he had missed her these last months—and only these next two or three to be with her before Edward wanted him to go off again? Dissension was reheating in southern Wales, but at least Wales could be quashed. Normandy and Tostig were not going to be so easily controlled. Sodding Normandy and bloody Tostig! What was to be done with the both of them—what *could* be done? And even if there was anything, would Edward do it? Harold doubted it.

As long as the King lived for three, four more years. As long as Edgar was allowed by God to come to manhood. His eyes searched the water glistening along the valley. The river banks needed shoring up with turfs, mud, stones, anything that might hold the water at bay. As did England. A tide of danger was rising to the north and across the Channel Sea. Either it would recede and the danger would pass, or the defences would break and the flood tide pour in to engulf them.

"I do not know what to do about this ambitious greed of my brother and the Duke," Harold admitted to Edyth. "I feel like I am stuck, holding everything at bay as best I may, while the water gushes between my feet."

"Tostig will find his own course, surely? You have warned him to tread with care; beyond that, what can you do? This thing is for him and the North to settle, is it not?" She was uncertain if that was so, for if it was, why would Harold be so anxious? Would an uprising in the North adversely affect the South? As far as she could see, these grumbles were the same as the troubles in Wales. A diplomatic intervention, a show of disciplined strength and the dissent would be smoothed. At least for a while.

"Mayhap Tostig will see that he is pushing men's patience over-far. We can only hope he does, but Normandy..." Harold released a lengthy sigh. "I fear that Duke William does not possess a half-ounce of sense in his smallest finger, let alone his worm-addled brain."

Something caught Harold's attention; he leant forward, squinted out of the window. A rider was coming, fast, from the direction of Goddwin's steading, "Someone comes, I think there's trouble."

They dressed rapidly and went to meet the rider, one of Goddwin's retainers, as he pulled a sweating horse to a standstill.

"My Lord," he panted, "my master bids that you come with all available men. The river is about to break its bank. If it cannot be held, the steading will be lost."

Within ten minutes, Harold was riding at a fast canter down the hill with fifty of the manor's men, all of them knowing that there was little to be done but that they had to try.

Edyth's instinct shouted at her to ride with them, to help bale and build, but her practical self knew otherwise. She would take down food and ale, then fetch back those who, for their own safety, could no longer reside in the valley. Among them Frytha. Goddwin's wife would have to leave her home, although she would protest and grumble as was her tedious way, but with their second child due within six weeks, she would have no choice. Edyth sighed, resigned. Not that she welcomed Frytha's dour company, but it seemed she too had no choice.

The water was sloshing over the river bank, running into the meadow. Twenty yards beyond stood the steading courtyard and its buildings, the winter-stocked barn, house place, sty, kennel and stable. Goddwin himself was standing in the river, stripped to the waist, taking his turn at heaving the cut slabs of turf into a secondary bank. If they could only shore up this stretch so that the water would break through lower down into the western fields, then perhaps the farm would be safer. An inch or two of river water would cause little harm. Let this portion of the bank give way, though, and the flood would do untold damage.

Leaving the horses tethered on higher ground, Harold and his men ran to join Goddwin's, who were already mud-spattered, sodden and weary.

Seeing his father, Goddwin stood a moment, fists at his hips, catching his breath. They had spoken once only since Harold's return, and that a curt exchange. Now Goddwin still said nothing, but words were no longer necessary. He held out his broad hand as his father came up to the bank to take his proffered clasp, readily acknowledging his son's unspoken gesture of thanks. Quickly, Harold removed his cloak and tunic, lowered himself into the water alongside Goddwin and the line of desperate men, and took hold of a clod of turf to pack it into the makeshift wall. Then another and another. The river reached to mid-thigh, the slippery mud beneath his boots uncertain, the water cold. Once, his footing gave way and he fell, tumbling backwards into the mud-swirl current. Goddwin, with a cry of alarm, lurched to grab at him, help him regain his balance.

Harold grinned, wet hair dripping into his eyes. "I'm trying to decide," he said amicably, grasping his son's arm and allowing his quickened breathing to settle, "whether 'tis better to do battle with this damned river, or pluck up the courage to inform Duke William that I want to chain myself to him as much as I'd welcome a constipated turd in my bowels."

"Which is the greater threat?" Goddwin asked, heaving another turf to the top of the reinforced bank. So far they were winning, the thing was holding, but the tide would have been rushing up the Thames by now and would be sweeping up the tributary of the Lea.

"That is what makes decisions hard, lad," Harold panted, scooping mud to fill the cracks. "Which takes precedence, danger to yourself and your immediate family, or to the wider spread of the people you hold responsibility for? You or your country?"

Goddwin was about to answer that family must come first, but he had no chance to form the words, for the river suddenly swirled and lifted. Water seeped through the wall they had just laboured so hard to build, finding cracks, areas of softer mud, lighter turfs not so well clamped down. A trickle or two became three and four, more, became a gush of water. Frantically Goddwin attempted to stem the flow, cover the widening holes; men, shouting with fear, were scrabbling from the river, running from the crumbling bank. Harold heaved himself from the water, leant down to grasp his son's arm, angrily pulling him out. "Leave it!" he bellowed. "Leave it, it's going to go!"

As the turf and the natural bank collapsed in a seething torrent of overspilling water, Harold clasped his son's arm; together they waded and battled their way through the flood. Already water was swirling at the walls of barn and Hall, creeping under doors, sucking at the timbers.

They stumbled to the rising land of the north pasture and stood, panting and defeated. Nothing now would stop the river as it cascaded over the bank and into Goddwin's home.

A chicken, squawking with terror, wings flapping, sailed by, clinging desperately to a floating log. A basket full of sodden wool bobbed past; a cooking pot. The steading was lost. Harold stood, one hand resting in offered comfort on his son's shoulder, looking out over it all. Trees, buildings, all so rapidly half submerged. The mud and silt and debris that would lie foul and stinking, when the water receded.

At least this building could be cleared and rebuilt. How much damage would his brother's thirst for power cause? A mere trickle, a full flood—or annihilation? And Duke William? How much of a threat was he to England? If Edward lived and Edgar came of age, then none at all. But what if Edward fell ill, or met with an accident while hunting? What then for England, should William rise and batter at the cracking, insubstantial banks?

There was nothing more to be done in this part of the valley, save wait for the water to go down. Perhaps if they had been better prepared, if the banks had been strengthened earlier…perhaps.

There is little I can do to divert Tostig from his track of madness, Harold thought as he and his son walked to where the horses waited. *But I can keep an eye to Normandy. Wait and see whether the tide rises.*

◈

That night, with the thick curtaining pulled close around the bed and with an iced wind beginning to moan through the thatch and rafters, Harold lay with Edyth, their bodies entwined after the giving and taking of shared love.

"There will never be another woman that I love as much as you, Edyth," Harold said into the darkness.

Edyth snuggled herself closer to his firm solidity. "Love," she said, her breath brushing his chest, "has little to do with marriage."

"Nothing at all," he answered. A pause, a minute, two. *Which takes precedence,* he thought, echoing his words to Goddwin earlier in the day, *danger to yourself and your immediate family, or…your country?*

The selfish choice of his family's need was the obvious one to make, but he was responsible for a wider family, for Wessex and, perhaps, if God was not prepared to give them time, for all England. If Edward were to die before Edgar was old enough then, without doubt, William would make a bid for the throne. That Harold could not allow. Nor could he allow Tostig to unleash a civil war.

With surprising calm, he said, "I do not intend, for the foreseeable future at least, to annul this betrothal with William's daughter. He backed me into a corner, but that does not mean I am defeated. If I escape his trap by allying with him as son-in-law, then that is what I shall do. Although I intend to secure my position before any formal wedding may take place."

Edyth made no comment.

"There is a chance," he added, his words coming slowly as the thoughts formed more clearly in his mind, his hand gently stroking the softness of her chamomile-scented, unbound hair, "that I may decide to proffer myself to the Council as ætheling, should there be no suitable successor. I cannot let England stand vulnerable."

Edyth made no answer, no movement. Her only thought was that Harold had taken a damned long while to see the only possible path open to him.

8

❧

Britford

As the summer green had mellowed to autumn reds and golds, rebellion in Northumbria flared from a few feeble sparks into a full, wind-fanned blaze. Individual grievances varied but amounted, in the end, to much the same thing—a hatred of Tostig.

Once too often had he used the law to claim land for himself from those who opposed him—it was not only the estates of Gamal Ormsson and Ulf Dolfinsson, of Gospatric Uhtredsson, that had been taken into the Earl's private keeping. Settlements, farm-steadings, a few hides here, two or three more there…gradually Tostig was building his holding of land and wealth by taking what he could in forfeit of alleged crimes and supposedly unpaid debts, while more and more families found themselves destitute or outlawed.

Taxes were to be collected at the end of the summer, the joyous time of harvest, but this year of the Lord 1065, there was little celebration north of the Humber river. By decree of Earl Tostig, the tax demand was, once again, to rise. The North, mistrustful of ambitious magpies from the South and already crippled beneath the financial burden, finally broke and refused to pay.

Tostig Godwinesson's heavy hand had become too much for it. The Earl cared as little for the northern land-folk as he did for the desolate land itself. He had no patience with the local dialects, which he found unintelligible and coarse; he sneered at the poverty; found no reason to endanger the lives of his housecarls in pointless reprisal against Scots raiders. As long as the troubles did not come uncomfortably close to his palace at York, Tostig reckoned there was little worth fighting over. If Malcolm of Scotland wanted a few more mangy sheep, had nothing better to do than burn a few peasants' crofts, then let the fool waste his time and energy.

Tostig rarely travelled further north than York—occasionally he visited Durham, where he was received well, but then he and his lady, Countess Judith, had always supported the cathedral with lavish gifts and donations—nor did he remain in his earldom any longer than he deemed necessary. Late spring to autumn sufficed. By mid-September he was riding south to join King Edward in Wiltshire, where the hunting was especially fine. Coincidence, of course, that his leaving occurred just as his tax gatherers set out with their neatly written documents, oxen-hauled wagons and swords hung loose at their sides in case of trouble.

The rebellion began on an estate where a sudden skirmish led to the accidental slaying of a tax collector, and escalated rapidly. A few disgruntled thegns joined with aggrieved freemen—ah, it did not take long for one flame to become fire. They marched south, the band swelling into an army as with each mile more men—young, old, rich and poor, armed with axe, sword, hoe and pitchfork—gathered together in protest against southern tyranny. Their destination, York, Earl Tostig's capital.

He had misjudged the smouldering anger. Through the rain-wet summer his spies and scouts had not informed him of the growing discontent, for they too had northern blood. On the third day of October the rebel army reached their destination. The city threw open its gates in welcome, and all who supported the absent Earl were slaughtered without mercy, housecarls, retainers and servants. The heads of tax collectors were hoisted to feed the carrion crows above Micklagata, where criminals and rogues were ignominiously displayed—where, not so long past, Tostig had ordered the heads of Gamal Ormsson and Ulf Dolfinsson be put.

The northern aristocracy of elders, thegns and nobles took possession of Tostig's considerable arsenal and treasury and, seizing the opportunity to be permanently rid of the damned man, declared him outlaw and elected to continue south to take their grievances direct to the King.

Northumbria had successfully risen against degradation and oppression, and in consequence a lord of high influence decided not to stand in the way of this flood-tide of anger. Eadwine of Mercia stepped quietly aside as the Northumbrians swept southward, making no attempt to bar the men from swathing a path through his earldom.

But then, Eadwine had his own reason for supporting the rise of the North against Tostig of Wessex. Astutely, the noble-born who had raised the rebellion had invited Eadwine's landless younger brother, Morkere, to lead them. Morkere, son of Ælfgar, grandson of Leofric of Mercia, the North had unanimously declared, would be the more suitable and acceptable earl.

Edward, when he heard, was furious. Rarely did he concern himself with things that interrupted his hunting, but this, this would not be tolerated. That they were not rebelling against him, their king, made no difference. The North had insulted and condemned Tostig, his most favoured friend; the insult was as deeply thrust at himself. At his integrity, judgement and word of law.

Clench-jawed, the King sat on his throne within the small timber-built Hall at his manor of Britford, a few miles from Salisbury. Before him stood two messengers sent by the Council of the North, as that rabble called itself. At his side was Tostig, his fingers clenched around his sword hilt; face suffused with rage. Twice, Edward had to restrain his earl's arm, else the lad would have been down off the dais and slitting those two ignorant imbeciles' traitorous throats.

How they had the gall to stand there and make demands, Edward could not conceive. To reinstate the law-code of Cnut, that Tostig had reneged upon; to remove him from office forthwith, replace him with Earl Morkere, duly elected by themselves. Effectively, the Anglo-Scandinavian population of Northumbria had reasserted its ancient right to independent authority, had demanded self-government.

Enraged, Edward had the messengers stripped of their clothing and thrown out of the gates of Britford. Let them ride naked back to Northampton where their scum friends waited. He sent no reply with them, his action taking the place of words.

Harold ran his hand through his hair, exasperated. For several hours now had they talked around the same circle: Tostig being openly accused by the King's hastily summoned Council of bringing the trouble on himself by his hard-fisted misgovernment; Tostig angrily countering by dismissing the rebellion as organised dissent by the Earl of Mercia and his cock-poxed brother.

"They are the sons of Ælfgar!" he shouted, hammering his clenched fist on to the table. "And we all remember what a traitorous whoreson he was!"

Nursing the remnants of a head-cold, Harold was bone-tired and resented being summoned from the comfort of his manor—and Edyth's bed—by an accursed, imbecile brother.

"Eadwine and Morkere are not like their father," he interjected. "Eadwine has more sense in his little finger than Ælfgar possessed in his entire brain."

Tostig, his pride wounded, his confidence shaken, rounded on him. "Oh, aye, you would defend Eadwine! You were hunting with him not a month since—and more than your eyes have shown an interest in the sister, Alditha. You have always been sniffling round her Welsh-soiled skirts like a panting dog in search of a gutter bitch."

Controlling his temper with efficiency—but great difficulty—Harold considered allowing the absurd accusation to pass. His brother seemed incapable of listening to any voice that urged sense, but the untruth was too damning to let lie.

"I remind you that I am already betrothed to Duke William's daughter, Agatha. One such betrothal is sufficient. I do not especially want a wife of alliance, being content with the woman I already have; I most certainly do not want to court *two* of them!" He leant back in his chair, swallowing the burn of a sore throat and stuffed nose. The tankard of warm honey and wild garlic that he had sipped was empty. He could do with some more. "I was with Eadwine a month or so back, aye, but then so were our brothers, Earls Leofwine and Gyrth." Harold indicated the two men sitting together on the opposite side of the table. "Do you accuse them of the same as you do me? And what exactly, brother Tostig, do you accuse me of?"

He had seen the girl, Alditha, during the summer. Did admire her pretty face and enticing, slender body—perhaps more than a man his age, with a wife he loved and another official betrothal, ought, but then there was nothing wrong with looking.

Displaying good sense, Tostig held his peace, although thoughts of alliance or treachery tumbled in his mind. He suspected that Harold had discussed the possibility of a northern rebellion with Eadwine and his turd of a brother. Hah, it stood to reason! Harold was green-sick jealous, envious of his close friendship with the King, of Edward's indication that he, Tostig, would be put forward as regent or successor, not Harold. How it must stick in an elder brother's throat that the younger might stand a good chance of wearing a crown! Was it not already obvious that Harold was plotting against Edward? Courting the prospect of alliance with William of Normandy? Now this with Eadwine and Morkere, and openly taking side against his own brother!

"I say we ought to ride for Northampton, confront this rebel mob, hang the leaders and send the rest home after a birch thrashing."

Gratefully Harold took a replenished tankard from the servant, savoured its soothing effect as the liquid eased down his throat. What he would really like was a warmed bed and a cold compress over his throbbing forehead. "And with what men do you intend to enforce this hanging and thrashing? You'll not have the use of my housecarls for such foolishness, nor, I doubt, those of our brothers." He glanced at Leofwine and Gyrth for confirmation, Leofwine readily shaking his head, Gyrth, perhaps a little more reluctant, but all the same agreeing that nay, their men would not fight. "Nor will you, my Lord King, commit men into what could, so easily, be misconstrued as a declaration of war?" Harold looked at Edward with an eyebrow raised.

Edward, in his extremity of rage, would have been quite happy to concur with Tostig's suggestion, so it was as well Harold had spoken. He most certainly did not want—could not afford—a civil war. Reluctant to disagree with his favourite, Edward shook his head, laid a hand over Tostig's. "I would not endanger your safety, my dear friend. A rabble can so easily turn ugly—those brutal deaths in York proved that." Edward shuddered. Butchered, they said they had been. Tostig's loyal men, his supporters and followers—Tostig's men, King's men. He twined his fingers in Tostig's, squeezed them briefly in a gesture of comfort and relief. "I just thank God that you were not there."

Harold drained his tankard. Said nothing. If Tostig had been in York, had been there all these past months, paid more attention to his earldom, his people's needs and grievances, his duties, then this whole damn mess might have been averted.

Edward announced his decision: "Harold shall go, discuss the matter. Sort things for us."

Tostig scrabbled to his feet, protesting. "My Lord King, no, Harold is in league."

"Now, now, Tostig, my mind is made up. Earl Harold is very capable of smoothing ruffled feathers. He can negotiate a settlement and we can get back to normal." Edward stood, indicated that the meeting was ended. "Come," he said, setting his arm around Tostig's shoulders and steering him towards the door, "my growling belly tells me that it is time for our supper." He tossed a look back over his shoulder at Harold. "You will leave at first daylight, my Lord Earl? We shall await your return here at Britford."

Harold, as had the rest of this small Council, had risen to his feet when the King stood. He bowed, ducking his head so that Edward might not see the expression on his face. The very last thing he wanted to do was leave his bed at dawn and ride to Northampton.

It was a waste of time anyway, as he had guessed it would be. The Northumbrians were adamant. They refused to take Tostig back and rejected the King's command to lay down their arms and air their grievances through the royal courts. Offered, instead, their own ultimatum: eject Tostig from the earldom and England, or war would be brought against the King also.

Almost apoplectic at Harold's nonchalantly delivered message, Tostig urged Edward to summon out the fyrd immediately.

And the rebels, in retaliation, advanced to Oxford.

9

Oxford

By the twenty-seventh day of the month of October Edward had removed his court to Oxford, intending to block the advance of the rebellion with the summoning of the fyrd. He had already his personal guard of 800 housecarls and with them the 300 or so of his Earls Harold, Leofwine, Gyrth and Tostig. But the English fyrd did not come. It was a freeman's duty to serve an agreed number of days at arms, called out by the overlord to whom he paid rent or tax, summoned by the boom of the war horns. Earls Harold, Leofwine and Gyrth, flanked by lesser nobles, thegns and elders, however, refused to entertain what could, so easily, become the nightmare bloodbath of a civil war. The war horns had remained silent. No one, besides Edward and Tostig, cared to set South against North like cocks in the pit.

That it had been Earl Harold who first refused to comply with Edward's demand to call out the armies of the South was not lost in Tostig's vitriolic condemnation of his brother. Mistakenly convinced that he was sympathetic to Morkere, Tostig accused him of blatant treason before the assembled Council of southern lords.

"You plot with Eadwine and Morkere—why? To secure their armies at your own back when the time comes to take England's crown for yourself? Is that what you plan, Harold?"

There were audible gasps of horror at such a vehement accusation. Edward himself cried out, shock on his thin face. Edith too gave a gasp, covered her mouth with her hand, stared, round-eyed and fearful. "Tostig!" she breathed. "Hold your silence, I beg you!"

Tostig did not see, hear or care. Harold had been instructed to negotiate with that plague-tainted rabble and what had he achieved for his own brother? Nothing! That's what, bloody nothing, aside from allowing them to gather more strength. They were a mile from Oxford, 400 short of 3,000 men against the King's pathetic few hundred A few hundred that would have been multiplied by five or six times had Harold not countermanded Edward's order to the fyrd. Aye, Harold had done that—Harold. Was it not obvious why?

"What did you say to those peasants from the North?" he sneered. "Well done? Good work? Well soon have Tostig gone and the King down on his knees. How long, brother, before you lay claim to the crown?" Then, as an afterthought he added, "Is it for yourself you have encouraged this rebellion, or are you securing a future by working in league with Normandy?"

Harold's face had also drained chalk pale from disbelief and a profound rage at his brother's foolishness. He had been trying to warn them about Normandy these past months—yet arrogant fools like Tostig and their sister, and those complacent like Edward, had refused to listen. He had no wish to become king unless there came no alternative choice—that honour was for Edgar, the lad who carried the true blood of Wessex. He was not insensitive to the prestige a crown would bring, but he loved his family and his freedom. A king, even one as incompetent as Edward or his father Æthelred, had no independence or respite from responsibility. Royal power was an attractive cloak to wear, but it was one that weighted a man's shoulders; privately he would be prepared to carry that burden if God decreed it must be so, but publicly he had wholeheartedly declared his support for young Edgar—and had made it abundantly clear that Edgar must rule as his own man, that there would be no toleration of either the Queen or Tostig acting as regent. Could Tostig not realise that it was precisely because of his contemptible rages and poor judgement that Harold could never back him for such a role? Christ Jesu, he had made a midden mess of Northumbria...to let him loose on England with a man such as Duke William watching like a hawk from across the Channel Sea! Harold eased his clenched fists, struggled to retain composure.

"I would remind you, brother, that the matter of the succession is not what concerns us here. We face civil war—brought about by your greed and crass stupidity. I suggest that the subject of who next wears the crown be set aside until God decrees that our present king has no more requirement of it."

"Set it aside? Ah, no, brother, 'tis top of my agenda." Tostig stalked around the table, his finger pointing at Harold. All the grievances, the jealousies and petty hatreds that had niggled at his vitals since childhood exploded in his senses, sending judgement and reason into oblivion. Harold had always been the favoured one. The clever one, the successful. Harold had Wessex and wealth, respect and friendship. Why should it all go to him? He, Tostig, was just as capable. Was it his fault that others were not so enthusiastic about suitable punishment of outlaws and thieves? Aye, they all fell on their knees for Harold, the fools. Never looked beyond his charming smile and affable manners. What good was that in a leader? You needed courage and conviction. Morals and purpose. Was it his fault that men were so stupid that they could not see that these lazy good-for-nothing Northerners needed their backsides kicking?

He stepped closer to Harold, his finger poking at his brother's chest. "You are so like our father, taking and taking, never considering how the rest of us may feel. How we are shoved aside and belittled." He stabbed his finger again, harder. "Well, I am as good as you, brother, and when Council elects me king instead of this old fool we are saddled with, I shall prove it!"

The entire Council, save for Edward, were on their feet shouting, condemning, their anger unleashed. Harold too. He raised his arm, blocking that stabbing finger and thrusting it aside, clutched at the folds of Tostig's tunic; gathering them tight around the throat he savagely rammed his brother's head up and back. "Because of your contempt you have misruled an entire carldom. Have provoked rebellion and now you are advocating a war, a blood-bath of vengeance, for no reason but to salvage your injured pride. Yet you accuse me of treachery?" Harold shook him as a terrier would a captured rat.

Edith cried out with fear for her favourite brother, ran from her chair and began beating at Harold's back with her fists. "Let him go! Let him go, Harold! Oh, you have always poured scorn on his achievements!"

Without releasing Tostig, Harold turned his head to stare in contempt at his sister. The accumulated years of bitterness had aged her, she was no more than six and thirty years, but appeared ten years older. Harold should have felt pity for her loss of youth, but he felt nothing for her. Nothing except an overwhelming loathing. She and Tostig had always run as a couple, wanting and whining for more and more. He would not, ordinarily, be cruel to any woman, but these self-centred, self-seeking, nest-feathering cuckoos had pushed him too far. "Tostig's achievements? What achievements would they be, Edith? To insult and offend? To grab and grasp at all he can lay hands on?"

"Enough! Enough! Control yourselves or must I summon in the guard!" Edward was ineffectively fluttering his hands, making calming motions, his face anguished, uncertain what to do. Tostig's words reverberated in his mind: "when Council elects me king instead of this old fool we are saddled with." Had Tostig truly said that? Did he mean it? The Devil was surely at work here! He crossed himself, looked pleadingly from one contorted face to the other.

Leofwine and Gyrth came forward; each grasped at a brother, pulling them forcibly apart, Leofwine neatly fielding his sister's batting hand with his raised arm; Tostig remonstrating furiously with Gyrth who, besides their sister, had always been the closest to him in opinion.

Gyrth released his brother and shook his head. In this, he could not agree with Tostig. "I am sorry, but Harold is right. We cannot start a war over what amounts to personal pride and gain."

Tostig let his hands fall to his sides, the fight abruptly going out of him. But his anger had not died; took instead a different, more menacing twist. "So, you too are against me. And you, Leofwine?"

Leofwine looked down at his boots before glancing up again, direct into Tostig's face. "I too. Our father and Harold never treated us with anything but respect and equal love. It swells in your own mind, this twisted hatred. Harold would lay his life down for you, but not at the expense of England and her people."

A weird grimace distorted Tostig's mouth. He turned to the King. The room had fallen silent, those present aware that the mood had subtly changed. "And you, my king, what do you say? This man here"—Tostig flicked a disdainful glance at Harold—"has refused to obey your command to call out the fyrd. What do you intend to do about it?"

Edward was trembling, his heart pounding, head thundering. Do? He had no idea what he ought to do.

No one moved or said anything; finally, Edward looked up from studying the rings that sparkled on his fingers. "What can I do Tostig? How can I order any man to war when we are so outnumbered by the opinion of my Council?"

Edith moved to her husband's side, knelt, clutched his arm. "If you love my brother, Edward, you must help him recover his earldom! It is Harold who disobeys you—remove him from office, give command of your army to Tostig and again summon the fyrd." She glanced up, swiftly, deliberately, at Harold, her meaning plain. "Either men obey you, Edward, or commit treason."

Tostig saw her reasoning, moved also to the King's chair, knelt, his eyes pleading. "I can lead the fyrd, my Lord. I can march against this rabble that is daring to defy you. Every one of them shall be strung from the highest trees! Grant me the authority, find me the men, I shall so do it."

"Except," Harold interrupted with cold and precise pronunciation, "that this rabble, as you call them, has not taken arms against their king. They have made that explicitly clear. They seek only justice and their legal rights. Northumbria bends its knee to the King—it but defies you, not Edward."

Tostig glared at his brother then returned his gaze to Edward, his angry eyes staring into bewilderment. "If you do not do this for me, then how can you love me?"

Edward took Tostig's hand, held it between his palms. "I regretted you having Northumbria, my dear friend, for you must be gone so long from court. Perhaps"—his breath caught with eagerness, a sudden pounce of hope; his hand tightened around Tostig's. "Perhaps we can agree some compromise? Let Morkere have the earldom and I can give you something else, something better...something where you could be more often here as my companion."

Tostig interrupted: "Wessex? Would you give me Wessex?"

There were sharp intakes of breath, an audible hiss of fury from Harold.

Wessex, the richest, most powerful earldom. By the very nature of his wealth, status and given responsibilities, whoever was appointed to rule Wessex could, theoretically at least, become a prime candidate to rule all of England.

For perhaps the first time in his life Edward was forced to admit the truth to himself: that he was a weak and easily influenced king; that it was only through the combined wisdom of his Council, not his own management, that peace had been maintained within this realm; that Harold Godwinesson was a sensible, practical man who cared for England above all else, and wore honour and integrity openly as his badge of office; that Tostig was but a shadow to his brother's light, with a priority for his own selfish gain.

Despair twisted around Edward's heart. Was this how his father had felt when he eventually realised how hopeless had been his rule? Or had his mother spoken the truth when she had so callously told him that Æthelred had never recognised contempt, not even when the people of England had hurled it at him in the form of cow dung and pig-shit?

He looked at Tostig, slowly shook his head. "I cannot."

Tostig erupted into a blaze of anger. He snatched his hand from the King's touch, his lip curling in repugnance. "So you do not care for me? Will not defend my reputation, nor give me the honour I am entitled to?"

Tears glistened behind Edward's lashes, his shoulders slumped, his hands fell limp into his lap. "I never wanted to be a king. I was content with exile in Normandy, where I had friends for the sake of friendship alone, not for who or what I was. Where the days were full of peace and the nights sighed quiet. I have tried, once or twice, to be the king you all expect me to be, but have not succeeded. Council does the thing so much better than I." He stretched out his hand, imploring Tostig to understand. "Even were I to give Wessex to you, I doubt Council or your brother Harold would let you keep it."

Tostig snatched his hand away, took a long step backward. "You pathetic old fool! This one thing I ask of you, after all these years of suffering your attention, your foul-odoured breath, your pawing and simpering. Of overcoming the disgust that rises like bile within me whenever I am forced to sit beside you?" Tostig shuddered with fury, longing to hit someone, something; to release his disappointment and hurt by flinging it back. "I hope you rot in hell, Edward, with the rest of these ball-less arse-lickers!"

Tostig Godwinesson turned on his heel and stalked from the chamber. Outside, he bellowed for someone to fetch his wife, to bid her take what she could within a saddlebag and for their horses to be saddled. Bewildered, tear-blotched and fearful, Judith left Oxford riding beside her husband with no idea of why, to where they were going, or if ever they would return.

No word, no outcry followed Tostig's outburst. Men stood, shocked and stunned, staring open-mouthed at the closed door through which he had stormed.

Edith sat slumped among the rushes of the floor, her arms curled around herself, rocking backwards and forwards, tears coursing down her cheeks. Her hopes, her plans all ruined. All shredded into nothing. How would she survive as Queen without Tostig?

No one immediately noticed the King, forlorn, silent and so alone.

Harold went to him, hunkered to his heels before him. "My Lord? My Lord, be you ill?" He took the cold hands within his own, attempted to rub some warmth into them.

Broken and devastated, the pain cramped tighter around Edward's heart, seared into his chest and shuddered down his left arm.

10

⁓

Westminster

Some whispered that if Tostig Godwinesson had elected to go quietly into exile, prepared to wait for the things said about him to fade from memory and for his elder brother's anger to calm, then perhaps the King might have found a reason to struggle against the illness that struck at his body and mind. Or perhaps if Tostig had not been so cruel or proud.

That he had ridden straight for Bristol and made sail in a flurry of outraged pique for Flanders did not, at first, cause concern to anyone of the Council except Edith and her husband. By November, they all privately thought either that England was well rid of him, or that he would soon see sense, would settle his bruised feathers—or at least his wife's father would insist he do so—and would humbly return home begging forgiveness. Count Baldwin, however, was in Paris, had not the opportunity or the inclination to waste time on a son-in-law whom he thought a pompous fool. Tostig himself, too easily influenced by his dignity, was determined to regain his earldom, whatever the cost or consequences. He had endured and defeated exile once before, admittedly with the burden shared by his brothers and father—but who needed the support of deceitful kindred out for their own gain? There would be others he could approach for help. Svein of Denmark, Malcolm of Scotland, Harald Hardrada, King of Norway, and even William of Normandy. As short-sighted as Edward when events tumbled out of control, Tostig was blinded by his indignation, never wondering why, and for what advantage, any prospective ally might agree to support his claim.

The seizure that had gripped Edward at Oxford had left him feeble and ailing. As a wind-driven November rattled into the frosted winter month of December, Edith had him taken by litter to Westminster, for her own convenience more than his spiritual comfort. He was soon nothing but skin-covered bone. His mind wandered, his fingers shook and his body could often not control the natural functions of bladder and bowel.

Christmas Eve fell on the Saturday, but there was to be no merriment in the celebrating of Christ's birth this year, Edward was ill in the evening, retching profusely, his bowels loose and stinking. He groped his way through Christmas Day, the holy service in the chapel and the banquet in his King's Hall. Not that he ate, or remembered much of what happened around him. By the Monday he was too weak to leave his bed. As the day progressed he slid from awareness to wandering confusion. He was dying.

For himself, he had no fear of death, for the Kingdom of Heaven was a joyful prospect, but the place he had chosen for burial that he had cherished into being from a wattle-built shack to stone-built glory, was not yet consecrated. Lying helpless, empty and defeated, drifting between consciousness and sleep, the worry tottered in and out of his mind. Until his abbey at Westminster was dedicated to God he could not be laid to rest within its walls—and that he must have! He tried to tell them that he wanted the ceremony to be completed, but none of them would listen. None took a moment to sit patiently and wait for him to form those wretched sounds in the slurred mouth that would not obey his will. How could he be at peace before his abbey was dedicated to God and Saint Peter?

Throughout the Monday and Tuesday, they came and stood at his bedside, tutting and shaking their heads or weeping and wringing their hands. The men of his Council, of his court. He recognised their blurred faces, could hear their words as if they spoke from a great distance—but could not, could not, make them understand!

There was his doctor, Abbot Baldwin of Bury St. Edmunds, who came daily to bleed him, to smell his breath and inspect the waste evacuated from his body. Edward endured the purges and tinctures, took comfort from the prayers and blessings muttered over him by the Abbot and the Archbishops Stigand and Ealdred.

They had all come: abbots, bishops, thegns and shire reeves. His Earls Eadwine and Morkere he did not so easily recognise; Leofwine and Gyrth took his hand, kissed the ring that hung too large on his wasted finger, Harold: his Earl of Wessex sat a long while beside the bed through most of one night, although Edward did not know which. Why did Tostig not come? There was a reason, but he could not remember it. Perhaps he was hunting. They had often hunted together. Once Edward thought he heard the pack, the music of their voices as they found a scent. What would happen to his hounds he wondered, when he was gone? To Hawise, that little brindle bitch who could flush a hare from any meadow, to Shadow, the black and tan with that amazing turn of speed? He so hoped Tostig would look after his hounds.

Edith was attempting to spoon some foul-tasting broth into his puckered mouth. Edith was always there, sitting next to his bed. He wished she would go away, or at least cease her weeping. He was dying; there was nothing they could do about it, for it was God's will. She ought to accept it. If he did not fear its coming, why should she? He tried to bat the spoon away, succeeded in knocking her arm, sending the stuff splashing over the bed furs. Edith thrust the spoon into the bowl, impatiently handed it to a servant.

"God's breath, Edward," she chided as the broth spilt. "You are more exasperating than a child. All I ask is that you eat something. You will never regain your strength unless you do. Then where shall I be once I am alone? Answer me that!"

A slurred mumble left Edward's lips, trying to say that it was not his strength he wanted but his abbey consecrated. Edith did not pause to listen. "What am I to do when you die? How shall I retain respect and dignity? Who will listen to me, seek my opinion? I am not yet an old woman, I do not want to be shut away in a dreary nunnery or a secluded apartment somewhere as a grieving widow. I want my court and courtiers. My position." A wail of despair cracked her thin voice. "I want to keep my crown!"

Her world was crumbling around her ears and she had no idea of what to do to stop it. A king, once anointed, was always a king, but a queen remained so only while her husband reigned, or her son as successor took his own wife. She knew now why Emma all those years ago had so desperately clung to her crown. She covered her face with her hands and wept.

Edward closed his eyes, shut out the annoying noise of her sobbing and filled his mind with pictures of his completed abbey. Saw angels flanking the gold altar, light streaming from the heavens through the windows...

The door to the fuggy bedchamber opened and the Countess Gytha quietly slipped through, wrinkling her nose at the stench. Nearing the close of her sixtieth year, she felt of a sudden her full age. Rarely did she leave Bosham, for journeying wearied her and court life held no interest, but how could she have not come to Westminster this Christmastide when so much of importance was occurring, and her offspring, one way or another, at the very heart of it?

She pursed her lips. Would this daughter of hers never pull her senses together and cease this futile weeping? Tears would do nothing except blotch her face and give her an aching head. She crossed the room, peered at Edward and said to Edith in a sharper tone than she had intended, "How fares the King? Does your sniffling not upset him?"

Edith glowered. Who cared if it did. His refusal to stand by Tostig had upset her, yet he had not been concerned by that. "He is being awkward, will not eat. When he dies what is to become of me?"

Gytha said nothing, for she had realised Edward was awake, listening. Taking the broth, she sat on the edge of the bed, scooping a little of the stuff on to the spoon and encouraging him to swallow. "You must eat, my Lord King, we are all so afeared for your well-being."

Again he tried to speak. The Countess leaned forward, her head cocked, and caught one feeble word.

Edith was paying no attention, she was walking to and fro, twisting a linen square between her fingers, bemoaning a dismal future.

"What is it you are trying to say?" Gytha dipped her ear close to Edward's lips, ignoring the foulness of his breath. "Edith, do be silent, he is trying to speak. I think it is important."

Edith's breath caught in her throat. The succession—was he trying to tell them who should come after him? The Council had asked her several times, had been discussing it discreetly between themselves since Christmas Eve—hah! Before then also! Like scavengers they had descended on Westminster, ghoulish and curious, anxious to curry favour with whomever they were to elect as the next king. Edith closed her eyes. Oh, Tostig ought to be here! He ought to be promoting his cause, demonstrating his worth, his ability, not sitting across the sea somewhere buying ships and planning a war against the very people who could, if persuaded, give her what she wanted.

"Abbey?" Gytha queried, unaware of her daughter's anguish. "You are concerned about your abbey?"

Edith swore under her breath, a word that her mother would have been shocked to hear had she spoken it aloud. His abbey? Was that all the old dotard could think of?

Tears were beginning to trickle from Edward's sunken and bruised eyes. His abbey. He had so wanted to be buried in his abbey.

The memories of her own husband dying were all too vivid in Gytha's mind. How she missed him, even after all these years. It was not loneliness, for she had good-hearted people around her—servants, friends, family. No, it was the little things that she missed: the exchange of a glance that only they understood; the sharing of laughter or tears, of secrets, hopes and fears; the comfort of his strong arms around her; his occasional bursts of flurried temper, and the sheepish appeal for forgiveness.

Edith, poor child, would not miss Edward for any of those things. Without love, what was there to miss? There would be nothing, only the emptiness of what might have been.

"I think, my dear," she said to her daughter, "that he is concerned for his abbey."

At first when Gytha had arrived at Westminster, halfway through the month, Edith had been delighted. She so desperately wanted someone to empathise with her bounding fear of the future as a widow. Gytha had sat with her, wept for Tostig's exile, agreed that Harold ought to have fought harder to help him, but that had only been on the first day and had, Edith soon discovered, been to calm her down. None of those words had been true, not after Gytha had spoken to Harold and heard his power-grubbing version of those disastrous events at Oxford. She might have known that their mother would take his side. Harold had always been Gytha's favourite. These weeks on, she wished her mother would take her meddling interferences and go home.

"What of the damned place? Is my future not more important?"

Gytha bit back an impatient retort, reminding herself, yet again, that distress did so play tricks upon the common sense. "Of course it is, my dear, but has no one thought to reassure him that the consecration is to take place on the morrow?"

Edith hesitated. Had he been told? She tossed her head, irritable; of course he had. The ceremony had been arranged days ago, before Christmas Eve, it was one of the first things Harold had done on reaching Westminster from his manor at Waltham. She remembered, unbidden, her brother's scathing words: "Could you not take a moment from your own selfish preoccupations to organise the service of consecration for him?"

She had been too busy sorting out her approaching widowhood. There was so much to do and no one reliable to help her! Documents to be read and signed, letters to be written, plans to be made—part of the royal treasury to be discreetly removed to Winchester. Oh, everything had changed from how she had expected it to be! Edward was to have died gloriously and bravely. Swiftly, with none of this lingering that gave men time to conjecture. And Tostig was to have been by his side, to receive the King's blessing.

Much had angered Harold that day, she now recalled. He had arrived at Westminster in a temper, had imperiously taken command. By what right had he censured any further removal of gold from the treasury? She was Queen, she had every right to do so.

Edith shut her eyes. How her head drummed. Harold had taken control over almost everything, from what was served by the kitchens to what was written on a royal charter. Acting as if he were king in Edward's place. He was second-in-command, it was true, but second beneath the sovereign. She was Queen, she was sovereign, yet had he consulted her? Damn him, damn his efficiency, his authority, his ability! Damn the fact that he had been right over the matter of the abbey.

To justify her negligence she said, "Edward will not be well enough to attend the service, so I do not see how it matters."

Sharply Gytha retorted, "It matters a great much to your husband." Really, the child was insufferable! Gytha again tempted Edward with a small spoonful of broth. He swallowed, a lopsided smile crimping his lips in a grotesque expression of gratitude. Tomorrow she had said. He could manage until tomorrow.

Countess Gytha patted his hand, realising he was trying to thank her. *The pity of old age*, she thought. *Are the ones who die quickly in battle more fortunate than those of us who must wait and endure?*

The abbey of Westminster was far from completed. The two western towers stood at half-height and at that end of the nave the roof needed tiling, the windows glazing. The unfinished work, however, was distant from the sanctuary and altar beyond the transept and could be screened. They would have to carry Edward by litter and ensure the ceremony was as brief as possible.

Edward's head had drooped. A snore reverberated in his nose. Gytha gave the bowl to the servant and bade him take it away. It was cold, anyway, unappetising.

"Have you heard from Tostig?" she asked Edith, automatically wiping the incessant trickle of spittle from Edward's chin with a linen cloth. The thing was soiled; she tossed it to the floor, demanding something clean be fetched.

"Why would I have heard from Tostig?" her daughter answered with a false bravado that immediately proved that she lied.

"I wondered merely if Judith was well. It must be hard for her, this worry."

"What has *she* got to worry about?" Edith retorted with indignation. "She is not about to be widowed! She isn't about to lose everything she has worked for, for twenty years!"

The callousness struck Gytha with almost a physical force. Was there no compassion in her daughter? Could she truly not see beyond the effect for her own self? "Judith has as much to lose as you, Edith—in fact, I would say more. The uncertainty of exile can be far worse than anything you will ever encounter."

"My husband is dying and I shall lose my crown. Judith has a husband and hope for the future. Once Tostig returns to claim what is rightfully his with the ships he is commissioning, Judith will be reinstated as a countess—I can never again be Queen!"

"So, you have received word from Tostig. He plans to invade?"

"Yes!" Edith snapped her confirmation. "Did Father merely shrug and accept his earldom being wrongfully stolen from him? Was he content to accept exile?

I think not, Madam! Tostig wants what is his and will fight to his last breath to get it, as our father did."

Countess Gytha walked swiftly to stand before her daughter, her irritation giving way to quickened anger. "Your father went into exile to avoid bloodshed, came back with the intention of, as far as he was able, securing his earldom peacefully. He did not want to fight against his king, nor, daughter, was he a man of dishonour." She nodded her head once, curtly, and left the room.

Why had sense, she wondered, been so poorly distributed between the children she had birthed?

II

⤞⤝

Westminster

Before the last of the light faded from the wet December day, the twenty-seventh of that month, a tiler had managed to climb up the height of the scaffolding to place a golden weathercock in position upon the roof of Edward's proud Westminster Abbey. Only from the west, from below the choir and from the outside, did the place resemble a building site. On the morrow, they would enter through the north door, see only the splendoured newness of the eastern end.

Harold stood alone facing the cloth-draped, bare altar. No candlestick, no salver or crucifix, nothing would adorn this holiest of places until the consecration and blessing. There was no sanctity within this wondrous building, nothing save the emptiness of space, height, of soaring walls, pillars and arches. With night beyond the tiers of narrow windows, the darkness crowded close, only the lantern in his hand and the few candles that burnt in wall sconces creating dim islanded pools of cheerful yellow brightness.

Yet there was a presence here. What, who, Harold could not decide. Nothing sinister, not a feeling of being spied upon, no, just a comfortable awareness of not being alone. Something, some faint-echoed shadow of expectancy of waiting. God perhaps? Harold wondered. Was He already here, waiting to be formally welcomed into His house?

The Earl of Wessex walked slowly towards the first in a row of wooden benches placed across the nave in readiness for the morrow. Tomorrow, there would be people here, many people. Tomorrow, too, the articles of Holy Church would be blessed and placed upon the altar, the choir filled with song, prayers offered and accepted by God—and God himself would no longer be a distant tingle of breath, a whispered promise, a sigh upon the wind. Harold's footsteps echoed on the stone floor. Left. Right. Tap. Tap. The sound reverberated through the chancel arches, down into the nave, through the enclosure of the choir. Bouncing off the walls, flying up to those rafters that soared high, as high as heaven.

Wine and water would be sprinkled over the altar while blessings were intoned and the chanting of the Benedictine monks echoed clear and sweet beneath the high vaulted roof. The perfume of incense would permeate through the odour of new-cut stone, timber, mortar and sawdust. As the Christian is baptised and confirmed by water and oil, so the altar of Saint Peter would, on the morrow, be dedicated to the Lord by anointing.

The hand of God would touch Edward's abbey, but the King himself would not be there to witness the final glory. Edward was too ill to leave his bed, was, beyond doubt, nearing death. Outside in the darkness, the drizzle of rain beat its tedious rhythm on roof and rutted mud alike, Harold sat, wearily leant his forearms across his knees. The quiet, he had thought, might help to sort out his wild-running thoughts. He chewed his lip, tapped the pads of his thumbs together. His idea was not working.

A side door opened and a novice monk, unaware of Harold's presence, entered and began dowsing the candles. The hour was late and until God dwelt here in His house, economy ordained the saving of tallow. The lad started as he noticed the Earl sitting there, and stammered an apology.

Harold smiled and rose to his feet. "Nay, 'tis I who must beg forgiveness, I ought not to be tarrying here, I came but to see for myself that all was ready. The morrow will be a day long remembered."

The boy nodded that aye, it would.

Walking back to the north door, Harold paused, staring out at the rain. He would have to cross to the palace soon, seek his chamber, the warmth of his bed. Edyth was awaiting him, but he was unwilling to go to her, to ask for her quiet love, her gentle comfort. This one night, out of all those they had shared together, he did not know how he could face her. She would probably be already sleeping, for the hour was late. Most in the palace would have sought their beds, save those few of importance—the two Earls Eadwine and Morkere and Archbishops Stigand and Ealdred, who would perhaps have remained discussing matters of state between themselves, finishing the jugs of wine and tankards of ale that half an hour or so ago Harold had been sampling with them. He looked across the winter darkness to the palace complex. A crack of light showed through one of the closed shutters of the King's upper-floor chamber, then flickered as a shadow moved beyond. His doctor, perhaps?

It would not be the Queen, for she had gone to bed to nurse her angry tears almost as evening had fallen. She had spoken few words to Harold this Christmas—all of them harsh and uncompromising accusation. He snorted disdain. Did she care about Edward? Had she ever cared? Edyth had said this morning that his sister was hiding behind her fear, that were she to think about the King, then the reality of her coming loss would be too much to bear. Instead, she was wallowing in grief for their brother Tostig. Harold had not disillusioned Edyth by telling her that he knew his sister better. She grieved for the impending loss of her sovereign status, for the fact that Tostig had let her down—and she blamed everyone for their joint downfall save herself and Tostig. He sympathised with her, but Edith could not remain Queen. Her calculated greed, placed so implacably above the good of England and its peoples, had made that an impossibility.

◈

Edyth was not asleep. She sat on a cushion before the floor brazier, her feet and legs curled beneath her, a bed fur thrown over her shoulders to give extra warmth. She had been combing her hair, but she had ceased, was sitting, staring into the red glow of the charcoal, her mind miles distant.

From the first she had expected that one day she would lose Harold to another wife. Yet as the years of happiness had rolled by and their love had solidified, she had, despite chiding herself for it, become half convinced that perhaps her assumption had been wrong. That he did not require a noble-born woman to consolidate his position. But that depended on Edgar becoming king after Edward.

Strange that although they had known Edward was old, that death would come upon him sooner rather than later, now that it was here, how much had they all been taken by surprise. The court was numbed and shocked, finding the inevitable difficult to comprehend.

Would she now grow old with Harold? Would they become grey-haired together, sitting reminiscing beside the fire in the winter years? Or was that for this other woman, the one he must take as wife?

Cold, Edyth bundled the fur tighter. Edgar could not be king, he was only thirteen, too young. She closed her eyes, shunned the thoughts that crowded her brain so insistently. Perhaps it would not be so bad if she could share Harold? If he did not entirely set her aside?

A tear, part sadness, tiredness and hopelessness, slithered down her cheek. She did not want to share him, but then, neither could she bear to lose him completely.

Alerted by a sound at the door, she hastily scrubbed at the trail of moisture, set a welcoming smile to her lips, and turned to watch Harold enter their chamber. She scrabbled to her feet, her hands helping to remove his cloak. "Look at you, man, you are wet through! Get those boots and garments off before you catch your death of cold. The bed's been aired with hot bricks. Get you between the covers. Tsk! What have you been doing—dancing in the puddles?"

"If I had known you were so keen to get me undressed and into bed, I would not have lingered so long." Harold laughed. He stopped her fingers tugging at a rain-soaked knot in the lacings of his tunic and enfolded them within his own. That small laugh faded. He studied her face, her eyes, her hair. He so loved everything about her. Her fair hair was beginning to streak with lines of silver, but her eyes sparked as intensely blue as they had that first day he had seen her, flush-faced, embarrassed but defiant, within her father's Hall. He set his hands to either side of her face, tilted her mouth up to his own and put his lips tenderly against hers, his kiss lingering only a moment.

A lamp glowed from the table, the brazier showed red-fired charcoal from within its grate. The heavy, draped wool curtains were drawn three sides around the bed, the wooden shutters tight closed across the windows.

It had to be said. He could put this thing from him for another hour, for the duration of the night, but to what end? It would still be there, come morning, and somehow he did not want to say this thing in the cold impersonal light of day. This was for them to share in private. There would be enough doing in public these next days, weeks, to satisfy a lifetime.

He said matter-of-factly, "I have been asked whether I would be willing to be considered for election as king." He drew in a steadying breath. Was it then so easy, after all, to make a decision? These thoughts that had rolled and battered in his mind since he had talked with—listened to—those four men in Archbishop Ealdred's chamber. The indecision, the uncertainty—the rush of excitement. And now his answer had come, without him realising it. The accepting of what he must, what he wanted to, do. "I am willing. After Edward, if the full Council agree to elect me, I will be king."

The wick of the lamp was burning low, it would gutter soon; more charcoal was needed on the fire. The rain pattered outside, cascading from overflowing gutters, spattering against the closed shutters, drumming on the roof shingles. Ordinary things, ordinary sounds. Nothing in the room had altered, moved or changed shape, yet for Edyth the whole world had just leapt upwards and come down again, subtly, indistinctly, shadow-shifted different.

She licked her lips, lifted her eyes to look into his. Of all the ways to lose him—to a woman, to battle—it was to happen because of a crown. She was to lose him to a more demanding companion than ever a wife would have been. Was to lose him to England.

Her chin tilted, her shoulders set straight, she said, wondering at her composure, "The Council will be fools if they cannot see the worth of such a man as you. I give you my blessing and my loyalty and ask only the one thing of you."

She paused momentarily, a mere heartbeat, to steady her pounding, breaking heart. "I ask that you choose a woman worthy to be your queen."

Harold made to speak, to protest, but she silenced his words by putting her fingertips to his lips. "Nay, do not deny the truth of what will be. There will be debate, perhaps argument and disagreement, but the Council will elect you, for as all of us in England know, there is no one else to follow Edward at this moment. You will need a queen, a woman with kindred with whom a new-crowned king must ally." Again she paused, looked briefly down at the wisps of acrid smoke that trailed from the lamp. Then she stretched up and kissed him. "I ask only that you and she be happy, and that you rule well."

With a small moan, Harold pulled her to him, enfolded her in his arms. He felt as if he were two separate people. One, a man who had been offered the greatest power, the highest accolade. He could not deny that he wanted it. To be in supreme command, to answer to no man, to have his every aye or nay instantly obeyed…but then there was his other self, the man who loved this woman who was so desperately trying to hide her tears…A man who wanted only the laughter of his family, the comfort of his home, the pleasure of being a part of the turn of the seasons on his estate. Ploughing, sowing, harvest. The endless renewal of life. There would be no more of his manor at Waltham Abbey, for he would reside at Westminster, Gloucester, Oxford or Winchester—any and all of the royal manors in between. There would be no more of Edyth.

"I would that I could have both!" he groaned, burying his face in her hair, breathing in her perfume, her life, her being. Lifting her, he carried her to the bed. This night, perhaps this very last night, he would allow his damned fool inner self free rein. Tomorrow or the next day, when time ran out for Edward, he would need to be the other man, the one who would be king.

For this night, he would be nothing more than a husband to the woman he loved.

Part Four

The Fear

I

❦

Westminster—January 1066

The fifth day of January. For the first occasion in many a week, the sky had cleared and brightened from the misery of rain into the vivid blue of clear winter sky. There was a nip of frost to the air, the sun was low, eye-dazzling, glittering through the diamond-bright grass and reeds.

Throughout the short hours of daylight Edward's breath rattled in his chest, incoherent words flowing from his blue-tinged lips. As the sun set, burning gold over the Thames marshes, the temperature dropped to below freezing. Come morning, there would be a white crust riming the edge of the river, the courtyards would be a film of treacherous ice.

Edith was at his feet, attempting to rub some feeling of heat into them. Earl Harold stood, wrapped in his own thoughts, beside the brazier, absently adding more charcoal. By Edward's bedside stood the King's personal priest, Robert fitz Wimarch, the Archbishops Stigand and Ealdred and his doctor, Abbot Baldwin.

"I like not this dishumour," Baldwin muttered, laying his fingers on his king's feverish temple and shaking his head in resignation. There was nothing more he could do for the dying man.

Stigand bent over the bed, shaking Edward's shoulder with anxious temerity. "My Lord King, wake up. My Lord, please rouse yourself!"

Edward's eyelids fluttered, then, for a long moment, he lay still, quite silent, the breath caught in his throat. Suddenly his eyes flashed open and he recognised Stigand leaning over him. His eyes wide and fevered, within a skeleton-like, translucent face, Edward stared into the startled face of the Archbishop.

"I am for God," the King croaked. "I have no fear of meeting Him, I look forward to sitting at His feet. Bury me within my mausoleum, now that it is made ready for my coming."

Stigand nodded. "There is no need to fear death, for you have served God well and you go to an everlasting life from this transitory one."

"The succession." Edith hissed. "Quickly man! While he is lucid, ask him of my brother and the succession!"

Harold, remaining beside the brazier with arms folded, had to admit his sister was resolute.

Either Stigand deliberately misunderstood his queen, or had no intention of mentioning Tostig's enforced exile from England, a subject that could upset the King mortally. Whichever the Archbishop held the monarch's bone-thin fingers and said, "We are here, my Lord Edward. Your beloved wife Edith and Earl Harold be at your side."

"No, no. Tostig, remind him of Tostig!" Edith brushed Stigand aside and took her husband's hand earnestly within her own.

Irritated but unable to retaliate, Stigand curtly beckoned Harold to come to the bedside. With reluctance, Harold complied. It did not seem possible that Edward was actually dying, that so much was going to change from this day forward. As a king he had fallen short of expectation, was, Harold had to admit, almost as useless as Æthelred had been, yet unlike his father, the people loved Edward. For his unstinting care and concern for the well-being of the common folk he could not be faulted. In affection, Harold had never felt anything but amicable indifference—neither liking nor disliking him. There were things he admired about Edward, others he despised, but that was so of any man. None save Christ himself was perfect.

Edith glowered at Harold, furious that he had not demanded Edward reinstate their brother as earl, or, in protest at the gross insult to the Godwinessons, gone into exile with him. As they had all those years past when their father stood accused of treason.

Harold had tried explaining to her the difference between the charge against Godwine and that against Tostig but she had adamantly refused to listen to sense and reason, too wrapped in her own fears and disappointment to recognise the truth. Perhaps a more astute king would have made a move against the trouble brewing in the North before it came to the boil, would have urged caution or removed Tostig from office before it had been too late—but Edward was not a wise man. What was woven could not be unravelled.

Harold sighed with regret for what might have been. He supposed there was room inside the hearts of some men for one area of excellence only. For Edward, it had been in his worship of God and the building of so splendid an abbey. He stared at the sunken face beneath the white, silken beard, the blue eyes that sparkled, not with a zest for life, but from the heat of fever, *ðæt wæs gód cyning*—he was a good king. Harold sighed again. He could not deny Edward that epitaph, though it was not the full truth. It was not of his fault that he had made errors of judgement along his way, that he had been weak where he ought to have been strong. Edward had not wanted the weighty responsibility of a crown. He should have been an abbot, an archbishop; in that sphere he would have warranted ðæt wæs göd.

"There is much I need say!" Edward rasped. "I would have my household around me." He glanced fretfully at those few occupants of the room. Harold nodded to fitz Wimarch who went immediately to the door.

They were waiting below, the members of the Council and other men of importance who had served the King. Were waiting for a summons, or to hear that their king was no more.

In silence, save for the noise of their boots treading upon the stone stair and brushing through the fresh-spread rushes, they filed in one behind the other to encircle the King's bed. He had asked to sit up and Robert fitz Wimarch stood behind him, tears blurring his eyes, supporting the frail old man.

"I had a dream," Edward said, his voice clearer than it had been for many a day. "I saw two monks whom I knew well while I was in Normandy and who passed into God's safe hands many years ago. They told me of the evils of the men around me, of my earls, my bishops and my clerics. They told me in this dream, that unless I warned you to repent and bow your heads in shame before God there would come evil to my kingdom, that the land would be ravaged and torn asunder by the wrath of God."

"That is indeed a vision of warning, my Lord King." Stigand said with grave concern, making the sign of the cross as he spoke.

Agreeing, Ealdred of York nodded his head. "There is evil intent in all mankind and unless we humble ourselves before God we shall all face His anger." He glanced meaningfully at Edith. "Men and women must serve God, and the chosen king, as they are commanded."

Satisfied that his archbishops could be trusted to do their best to save the tormented souls of men, Edward spoke, with a dignified clarity, the words of the verba novissima, the will declared aloud on the deathbed, naming lands and gifts that were to go to those who had served him well. He spoke of the loyalty that his wife had shown him and said that like a daughter had he loved her. He smiled up at her, begging her not to weep. "I go to God. May He bless and protect you."

In vain, Edith had attempted to sniffle back the flood of tears, but now gave in to her despair. She had not thought that she had felt anything for Edward, had simply endured his presence, his whining and pathetic weaknesses, but suddenly, now that she was to lose him, Edith realised that she looked upon him, this man who was three and twenty years her senior, as a father. Did she love him? She did not know, but she would, without doubt, miss him. She let the tears fall.

Similar tears were pricking in the eyes of them all. Some fell to their knees, others bowed their heads. Nearly all murmured the prayer of the Lord.

"Sir," Stigand said softly, again leaning nearer to Edward, who had closed his eyes. "We would know your last wish. Would know who it is you would commend to follow you."

Edward's eyes opened. He attempted a weak smile at his Archbishop of Canterbury, fluttered his left hand towards Harold, who took it, absently rubbing his thumb over the taut surface of the proud-standing knuckles.

"My Earl of Wessex." Tiredness was creeping over Edward; his words came with difficulty. He allowed his eyes to droop closed once more, his hand fall limp within Harold's. "I commend my wife's protection to you."

Energy drained, his body slumped against the supporting arms of fitz Wimarch, the breath catching with an indrawn choke in his chest. The effort of putting thought and speech together had taken everything from him. "Leave, me," he gasped. "I would make my confession."

They left Edward's chamber, quiet and subdued. Another death was a sober reminder that an end must come, eventually, for all who were born and breathed.

Only the King's doctor and priest remained, and Edith. She knew the rest would go to the Council chamber to discuss the practicalities of her husband's death—the funeral, the succession. Tears and breath juddered from her. All of it had been so pointless, so utterly and completely pointless! Oh, if only Tostig had not been so damned stupid. If only Harold had supported him. If only Edward were not to die…if only, if only. Where did those pathetically useless words end? If only Edward had been a husband to her, if only she had borne a child…

The murmur of conversation was low within the Council chamber, flickering in unison with the dance of the candle flames. All but a few of the Witan were present. Nine and thirty men. Two Archbishops: Stigand of Canterbury and Ealdred of York. The bishops of London, Hereford, Exeter, Wells, Lichfield and Durham; among the abbots, the houses of Peterborough, Bath and Evesham. Shire reeves and thegns—Ralf, Esgar, Eadnoth, Bondi, Wigod and Æthelnoth among others; the royal clerics, Osbern, Peter and Robert; Regenbald the King's chancellor…and the five earls of England: Harold, his brothers Leofwine and Gyrth, and Eadwine and Morkere. They talked of the morrow's expected weather, the succulence of the meat served for dinner, the ship that had so unexpectedly sunk in mid-river that very morning. Anything and everything unrelated to the difficulties that lay ahead in these next few hours and days.

Archbishop Ealdred exchanged a glance with Stigand, who nodded agreement. He stood and cleared his throat. "My lords, gentlemen, we must, however hard it be for us, discuss what we most fervently would have hoped not yet to have to."

The light talk faded, grim faces turned to him, men settled themselves on benches or stools, a few remained standing.

"It is doubted that Edward will survive this night. It is our duty, our responsibility, to choose the man who is to take up his crown. I put it to you, the Council of England, to decide our next king." Then Ealdred folded his robes around him and sat.

Those present were suddenly animated; opinions rose and fell like a stick of wood bobbing about on an incoming tide. Only two names were on their lips: Edgar the boy ætheling, and Harold.

The two in question sat quiet, on opposite sides of the chamber: one still asking himself if this was what he wanted; the other, bewildered and blear-eyed from the lateness of the hour. He had never before been summoned to attend the Council. It was not a thing for a boy, this was the world of men, of warlords and leaders. He was not much impressed by it.

Edgar looked from one to another, listened to snatches of the talk. He had been immersed in a game of *taefl* with his best friend—had been winning. One more move…and they had come, fetched him away, curse it! Sigurd always won at *taefl*; it had been Edgar's big moment, his one chance to get even…

For an hour they debated, the hour-candle burning lower as the discussion ebbed and flowed. Occasionally someone would toss out a sharp question to the boy or Harold, seeking opinions, assurance. Edgar answered as well he could, Harold with patient politeness.

Midnight was approaching; servants had come and replaced the hour candle with a new one. The same words passed around and around.

"As I see things." Archbishop Stigand said, his voice pitched to drown the rattle of debate, "we have talked of but the two contenders. Edgar?" He beckoned the lad forward. He came hesitantly, not much caring for this direct focus of attention for he was a shy lad.

Stigand continued, not noticing the boy's reluctance. If Edgar were elected king it would make no difference that the lad did not want the title. To be king was a thing ordained and sanctioned by God, personal preference did not come into it. "He is of the blood, but not of age. Second, Harold of Wessex." Again the Archbishop paused to motion the man forward. "He has ruled England on Edward's behalf these past many years and has proven himself a wise and capable man. But there is a third possibility. Duke William may claim the crown through the Lady, Queen Emma, and through some misguided impression that Edward once offered him the title."

Immediately there were mutterings, shaking of heads, tutting. Uneducated foreigners, especially Norman dukes, it seemed, were unanimously declared as not understanding the civilised ways of the English.

Stigand half smiled, said, "I take it, then, that William is excluded from the voting?"

"Aye."

"That he is!"

"Damned impudence, if you ask me."

"Does he think we would stoop so low as to elect a king who could not sign his own name?"

The clerk at his table to one side was scribbling hastily, attempting to write down as many of the comments as he could; the records would be rewritten later in neat script, the irrelevancies deleted, the gist of the proceedings tailored to fit the Church-kept—and censored—chronicle.

"Duke William cannot be so easily dismissed," Harold interrupted. He waited for the babble of voices to quieten. "The Duke will not heed anything said in this room. If he has set his mind on wearing a crown then he will come and attempt to take it, I have no doubt of that. If he is rejected here in this Council, the question, my lords, will not be if or how or can he attack us, but when."

"But he may be satisfied knowing a grandson of his was to hold England." The Chancellor, Regenbald, spoke up, "You are to wed his daughter, does that not adequately relieve the situation?"

Aye, they were all agreed, it did. All except Harold.

He stood beside Stigand, saying nothing more. It was not his place to influence Council, but it was difficult to keep his tongue silent with some of these more inane remarks. Duke William looked at things as if through thick-blown glass, his view distorted to match his own expectations. Besides, to placate William with an alliance of marriage presupposed that Harold would be elected king, and they had not, yet, done so.

The door to the chamber opened, eyes turned, speech faded. Abbot Baldwin entered. He had no need to say anything, his expression told his message.

Archbishop Ealdred murmured a few words of prayer, joined by Stigand and other holy men. "Amen," he said. Then he looked up, his eyes sweeping across the room.

"We are agreed then? The King commended his wife, our good Lady Edith, into the care of the Earl of Wessex. It is in my mind that by this he intended for Earl Harold to protect and reign over England."

There came but one murmur of disapproval: from Morkere, new-made Earl of Northumbria.

"It is in *my* mind that Earl Harold, once crowned king, may go back on his word and restore his brother to favour. I have no intention of relinquishing my earldom." He spoke plainly, but firmly. His brother, Eadwine, close at his side, nodded. Several thegns and nobles from the northern earldoms agreed also. A bishop too, Harold noticed. The representative of Durham, was frowning. No doubt once Morkere had chance to donate as many gifts as Tostig had, opinion there would dramatically change.

Harold stepped forward, offering his hand to Morkere. "My brother has become a jealous fool. I make no secret of the fact that I would rather have him back in England, where I can keep eye on him, but he will never return to Northumbria. You have my sworn word."

Morkere did not take the proffered hand. "Is your word good, my Lord Earl? Did you not grant your word—your oath—that you would support William of Normandy in his claim for England?"

An uneasy silence. Harold smiled laconically. Morkere showed signs of becoming a good earl, a worthy man to hold Northumbria.

"That oath," Harold said, "was taken under duress. I am under no obligation to keep it. I was given the choice of losing my honour or my life and freedom, and that of my men. There are oaths, and oaths, my friend." He nudged his hand further forward, inviting Morkere to take it, still smiling. "I made that vow to William knowing full well that it was more dishonourable for a lord to endanger the lives of others than to pledge an oath with no intention of keeping it. I make this one to you with a view to the opposite." Aware he had to give some other insurance to convince this rightfully suspicious young man, he added, "Within our traditional law there is no dishonour in breaking a promise to a man who is himself dishonourable. To those who are worthy 'tis different." For a third time he offered his hand. "Take my word, Morkere, Tostig will not have Northumbria while I am able to prevent it. I give that unbreakable vow to a man I would call worthy to receive it."

Morkere was tempted to look at his brother, seek his opinion, but did not.

He was his own man, earl in his own right, with his own decisions to make—be they right or wrong.

Decisively, with a single, abrupt nod of his head, gazing steadily into Harold's eyes, he set his broad hand into the other man's. "I accept your pledge, my Lord of Wessex." Corrected himself. "My Lord King."

There was no need for Morkere to add anything further, for Harold understood the look that accompanied that acceptance from steady, unblinking eyes: *God protect you, though, should you break it.*

2

⁂

Westminster

Standing flanked by the Archbishops Ealdred of York and Stigand of Canterbury, Harold struggled to retain his concentration. A combination of tiredness, excitement and unexpected nerves was getting the better of him. To his left, a slab of marble lay new-mortared into the floor before the altar. Harold stared down at it as the abbey echoed from the singing of the *Te deum laudamus*, the ceremony of acclamation. Beneath the slab rested Edward's coffin and the shrouded body of the dead king.

But he is no longer king, Harold thought, incredulously. *The people have been asked if they will accept me as their sovereign and they have acclaimed me so.* Ealdred's explicit words reverberated in Harold's mind: "The King, elected by the clergy and the people."

The abbey of Saint Peter of Westminster, this sixth day of January in the year 1066, was as crowded now as it had been earlier in the day for Edward's funeral—some of the populace who had trooped from London and neighbouring villages and hamlets, unwilling to give up a prized position on a bench, had remained stubbornly in their seats, drinking their skins of ale and chewing goat's cheese and bread. A cold easterly wind raged outside, another reason to stay warm and dry within.

Reading in English from a schedule given him by the Archbishop, Harold solemnly declared the triple oath, his mind flirting with incongruous personal thoughts as Ealdred proceeded to give instruction and admonishment for his own good and for that of his people. Soon, he would ask Harold to make the promises to keep true peace within the Church of God and the whole dominion of his Christian people, to forbid rape and wrongful acts in every degree, and to ordain that justice and mercy should be observed in all legal judgments: the traditional preliminaries to the ceremony proper.

Several times Harold felt the urge to run from the abbey, flee before it was too late. He was to be king, the first to be crowned in this abbey—by God's good mercy could he do this thing? Edgar, the boy, was the heir and ætheling—but if he, a man grown, was filled with these doubts and anxieties, how would a lad of his age grapple with the enormity of the task ahead? Those doubts had almost overcome Harold in the early hours of yesterday morning as news came that Edward was dead. "Do I deserve to be elected king?" he had said to the Council. "I am a statesman, a warlord, but am I the stuff of kingship?"

"What is it you shirk from?" his brother Gyrth had asked. "Or do you fear those who will, undoubtedly, oppose you? The commitment to God and country? The responsibility?"

"I fear all those!" Harold had retorted emphatically. "I would be the greater fool were I not to."

"Which is why you will make a good king," Eadwine of Mercia had countered, offering his hand in friendship as Harold had to Morkere.

In the abbey, Harold jerked his attention back to the ceremony. Ealdred was again standing before him, anointing his head with chrism, the holiest oil known to the Church, and the anthem "They Anointed Solomon" lifted from the sweet, clear voices of the choir.

Trouble would come from Normandy over this. Could there be any doubting that unofficial word was already speeding on its way southwards? Officially, a letter would be sent by courier on the morrow, duly endorsed by the newly crowned and anointed king, greeting William and asking that the marriage arrangement be upheld, to unite Normandy and England in the union of kinship. Kinship? What stability or loyalty did kinship bring?

A brother. Tostig. How was he going to react to this day's crowning? Harold could guess only too well. And his sister Edith, where did her loyalty lie? With a brother, certainly, but not with the one declared by the Council as king. She had refused to attend this ceremony, claiming it was too soon after Edward's death. Harold admitted she was right there, for he too had protested, yesterday, against a kingmaking coming on the same day as a king's burial. Edward had died in the early hours of the fifth day of January, was put into his grave on the morning of the sixth and his crown placed on the head of his successor that same afternoon.

"We wait until the next calling of the Council, then, do we?" the Council had responded with unanimous scorn. "Let England flounder like a beached whale, inviting our enemies to come through the wide open door to sample our ale and women?"

For too long already had earls been absent from their manors, thegns from their farm holdings, bishops and abbots from congregation and monastery. Council ought to have disbanded three days past, for the weather was turning bitter with cold. Snow would be coming soon.

Archbishop Ealdred had said boldly, "We must all of us leave Westminster on the morning after Edward is buried. We cannot wait until the next Council for a coronation. It would be better for you to claim your crown now. By Easter, who knows who else may come to try for the fit of it."

Morkere had added, with his own brand of dry, Mercian-bred humorous pessimism, "Besides, we may not have time to think about a crowning later in the year, when we are busy fighting to keep your unanimously elected backside on the throne."

To combine the laws of land and God together, the Church had created a liturgy for the investiture of the Regalia of Kingship. There were five items of holy symbolism: the ring, sword, crown, the sceptre and rod, given to the King with the blessings of the Mother of God, Saint Peter, prince of apostles and Saint Gregory the apostle of the English and all the saints.

"May God make you victorious and conqueror over your enemies; may He grant you peace and with the palm of victory lead you to His eternal kingdom. May God bless this, our chosen king, that he may rule like David and govern with the mildness of Solomon."

And the abbey, which smelt of sawdust and mortar, incense and male sweat, was filled with the answering roar of acclaim, shouted from every lip and every heart as men came to their feet, three times lifting their arms in salute and their voices in endorsement: *Vivat Rex! Vivat Rex! Vivat Rex in aeternum!*

Harold sat, enthroned, enrobed, his expression a look of almost childlike wonder. He saw a sea, an ocean of faces, all with their right arms raised, mouths open acclaiming him. Long live the King! His brothers Leofwine and Gyrth— his nephew, Hakon, so delighted to be home in England among his kindred. The Earls Eadwine and Morkere; ealdormen of the Council; men of the Holy Church. His friends, housecarls, thegns. To one side, his mother Countess Gytha, sated with pride and pleasure. Beside her, his sons, his daughters. Goddwin, Edmund, Magnus, Ulf, Algytha and Gunnhild. The boys with great moon-full grins, hands raised, chins jutting, shouting *Vivat Rex!*

And Edyth. His heart ached to run forward, gather her to him, wipe from her cheek that glistening tear that he could see, trailing silver. She was smiling, shouting as loud as the rest of them, shutting out the pain within her as the door closed, finally, on the years, those good, loving years, that they had shared as man and wife.

3

Rouen

The messenger refused to hand the letter sent from England to the Duke personally. Instead, he sought fitz Osbern.

"But this is for Duke William. Why have you brought it to me, man?" Fitz Osbern was irritated. Naught had gone right this day—before leaving his bed he had quarrelled with his wife, then he had discovered his favourite hound had been in a fight during the night, sustaining a torn ear and tooth-gouged neck. Added to that, indigestion was burning in his chest and now this fool was standing there hopping from foot to foot, proffering a parchment that was meant for the Duke. As if he did not have enough of his own correspondence to see to this day!

At least the messenger was honest in his reply. "Sir, I bring it to you because it contains bad news. I have no intention of being on the receiving end of his temper."

William fitz Osbern sat at his table, maps and letters spread before him, a quill pen leaning from the ink well, shavings from other trimmed quills brushed into a neat pile. He had stared at the scrolled parchment in his hand. It was from William, Bishop of London. He sighed. There was so much to do and so little time in which to accomplish it. Norman administration would be easier were the Duke able to attend to the reading of charters and letters himself, and if the whole system were not so complicated. The recording of taxable land in England, for example, was much more organised, with everything meticulously written down and recorded in one set book within each shire.

"If it is about King Edward's health, then we are already aware that he is failing. The Duke is expecting to hear that he is dead." Will handed the scroll back to the messenger. "You have my assurance that he will not bark at you for that." Mint leaves would be good for his bubbling stomach. Perhaps he ought to send a servant to fetch some.

The messenger took a step backwards, emphatically refusing to take the document. "'Tis not the bark that concerns me, my Lord. 'Tis the sharp-toothed bite!"

Fitz Osbern suppressed a belch. "For the sake of God, man, you have been paid to deliver a message to Duke William. Do so." Fitz Osbern tossed the scroll at the man, who made no attempt to catch it.

"Nay, sir, 'tis not my place to disagree with you, but I were commissioned to fetch this to Normandy as soon as might be possible. That, sir, I have done. No one said anything about taking it direct to the Duke himself."

Exasperated, Will heaved himself from his stool and fumbled for the scroll which lay among the floor rushes. "I assume that this great reluctance of yours is connected with the knowing of what is contained in this scroll?"

"*Oui.*"

"Which is…?" Fitz Osbern's fingers clasped the letter.

The messenger, a bearded, middle-aged man who, Fitz Osbern discerned, was in desperate need of a bath, scratched his nose. "Which is that, aye, the King of England is dead, and that Earl Harold of Wessex is crowned and anointed in his place."

Fitz Osbern's grip tightened rigid around the parchment. Slowly, very slowly, he straightened. "Repeat that."

The messenger did so.

Fitz Osbern, mouth open, breath stopped, walked back to his stool, feeling as if he were ploughing through knee-deep mud. He could almost imagine the words written on the scroll burning through. Someone would have to read them aloud to William. His indigestion paled into insignificance as a different kind of sickness rose into his throat.

He nodded, once, very slowly at the messenger. "You may go. See my steward for payment."

Relieved, the man fled.

⁓

Duke William sat very still. Only the slow, systematic rubbing of his thumb passing backwards and forwards across the back of his hand and the tight clench of his jaw indicated his fury. "Read it again," he snapped.

Fitz Osbern reluctantly complied. Duke William's lips parted slightly, his nostrils flared. The thumb stopped moving.

The chamber was not crowded, but all within exchanged furtive glances of apprehension. Both servant and knight alike knew to beware of their duke when a rage threatened.

Duchess Mathilda, seated beside her husband, flicked a glance from the pale-faced Will fitz Osbern to her husband and moved to rest her hand on his arm. With irritation, he jerked away. The abrupt movement broke the stillness. He lurched to his feet. William was a tall man—in anger, his stature seemingly heightened.

His words however, were low: "I knighted him. He swore homage as my vassal."

"*Oui*, my Lord." Fitz Osbern allowed the scroll to roll upon itself.

"He swore to speak for me to convince the English of my claim."

Again, fitz Osbern answered simply, "*Oui.*"

William clenched his fists, the nails digging into the palms. "He swore. He took an oath before me." The words were becoming slurred, spoken through that rigid jaw. He turned his head with a jerk, gazed at fitz Osbern. "He made no effort on my behalf? No attempt to speak for me?"

"It seems not, my Lord. William of London has always proved to be reliable and accurate in his information."

Mathilda rose and put her hand over her husband's fist, persuading the fingers to relax. Was surprised to find William's hand was shaking.

She too could not believe that what was written in that letter was the truth. Harold had seemed such a pleasant man, so benign—so honourable. She felt a blush tingle her face as she remembered him close to her, his laugh, those startling, vivacious blue eyes…Ashamed at that flurried erotic memory, Mathilda stifled the lurch that had knotted her stomach and peered up at her husband. "My Lord, you are a greater man than ever Harold will be—and is it not as well that we have discovered his true nature before committing our daughter further into his care?"

Had William heard? He made no sign that he had. His anger was swamping him, penetrating his senses, thundering in his brain. He had been betrayed before, other men had sworn allegiance and reneged upon their oath. And other men had paid the price of their duplicity.

"So. This is how an earl of England repays my kindness?" Resentment spewed from William's mouth. "I could have left him to rot in Ponthieu, could have taken him for ransom for myself, but no! I welcomed him as a guest, I treated him as if he were one of my allies, offered him my confidence and my friendship—God's breath…" William marched ten paces, turned and glared at the silent group of men and women. "I offered him the honour of becoming my son by marriage!" He lunged forward, scattering goblets, jugs and food bowls from a table, tipped the table itself. Struck out at a servant, clawed at a tapestry and ripped it from the wall. A few of the women screamed, men drew back, several dogs in the Hall began to bark.

Knowing no one else would attempt to calm him, Mathilda intervened, her hands grasping his flailing arms. She was so small against him, her head barely reached his chest. She gripped tighter, shaking him. There were more than a few in that Hall who secretly admired the woman's bravery. "It is done. The thing is finished. Forget him, forget England."

William stared down at his wife, his expression a vice of hatred.

"Forget him? Forget England?" he said ominously. "On the day I wed you, I promised that you would not think of me as an illiterate barbarian, I promised that I would prove to you my worth and my strength, that I would give you a crown."

Interrupting him, Mathilda declared, "There is no need to prove anything to me, I have all I could wish for. A husband who is loyal to me, who has given me handsome sons and beautiful daughters."

Her words did not penetrate his mind. "I vowed that I would make you my queen. And queen, madam, you will be." He pulled away from her, swung towards fitz Osbern. "So, this English whoreson wishes to challenge my intention, does he? Then let it be so. We shall see who is more determined, I will not be made to look the fool. I want England and I shall have it."

❦

A long-legged, lank-bodied, spot-faced youth entered the solar, seeking the Duchess, his mother. Robert's tunic had a jagged tear down the front, ripped by a blunted sword while practising on the tourney field with other boys of the court. He wanted her to mend it immediately. There were serving girls a-plenty who could have stitched it for him, but he wished to boast to her that he had toppled the boy responsible and given him a sound thrashing. That the lad had been three years his junior and considerably shorter, Robert would not be mentioning. William's eldest had no sense of fair play, even less of honour. Why would he require either? He was the Duke's heir, at thirteen he could do as he pleased.

To his annoyance, he found no one in the upper-floor room apart from Agatha, his sister. The emptiness was unusual for this hour of the afternoon.

"Where is Mama?" he asked tersely.

"Cloistered with our father and Will fitz Osbern. Papa is in a rage and Mama has been weeping." Agatha closed the Bible that she had been attempting to read. Her mother had tried to teach her the shapes of the alphabet, but it was such hard work remembering how they were all to sound when strung together into the written word. She wondered whether learning to read English would be as difficult as Latin. Not that she would have the chance, not now.

"Are we at war again, then?" Robert asked, without great interest. He strolled to his father's chair beside the hearth fire, seated himself cross-legged upon its padded cushion, Agatha frowned. Their father would be cross were he to discover Robert sitting there.

"Has some bugger of a comte reneged against our bloody father?" he continued. "I suppose he will be leaving Rouen with the army soon. I hope so—but Mama is always so unhappy when Papa is away." The boy could not understand why this should be, for he was delighted whenever his father was absent. When he was at court, Mathilda had little time for her children—for Robert. With William gone, he would have her more to himself again. He reached out for the bowl of dried fruit beside the chair.

"A messenger came from *Angleterre*," Agatha said. "Papa is most angry."

Robert tossed a raisin in the air, caught it in his mouth. Chewed, swallowed. When was he not? William was always angry, most often at something his eldest son had, or had not, done. Robert hated him. Would, on the day that William did not come back from making war, be delighted. "So what has happened?" he asked, only half curious.

"King Edward has died." Agatha said, matter-of-factly. "Earl Harold has been anointed king in his stead."

"What?" Robert untwined his legs, lurched from the chair. "You mean that innocuous Englishman has defied our father outright?"

Astonished at her brother's whoop of excitement, Agatha frowned. "'Tis nothing to celebrate! There will be far-reaching complications." That was word for word what her mother had said not half an hour since, when Agatha's own face had lit up on hearing the news. "Father is considering war with England, Mama is distraught, the court is in disarray—did you not notice the bustle on your way up here?"

"Well, well! So all the while Harold was playing his own private game of constable and thief. While our father was thinking he had cornered all the playing pieces, Harold had a second army in reserve." Robert's delighted grin broadened. How wonderful, someone had bested his father! "I always thought Harold had more sense than Papa credited him with."

"Oh, you did, did you? Then you must be a better judge of men than I have given you credit for."

Robert spun round, his face blanching. His father stood in the doorway, his great size filling the space. William strode over to his son, Robert resisting the temptation to step back a pace although he would have done so had the wall not been so close behind.

"As you seem to know so much more than I, perhaps you had best talk with my vassals into pledging their support for a war against England. Do you think you could do that? Hah, boy!" William spat the last, jabbing his face forward into Robert's own, his hands coming out to fasten on the lad's tunic neck-band.

Whimpering, Robert, of a sudden, desperately needed to empty his bladder.

William shook him roughly, then tossed him aside as if he were a rat with a broken neck. "Get out!"

Robert ran, fear cramping in his throat, tears stinging his eyes. He fled to the kennels, where he knew he would be left alone. God's teeth, he hated his father!

Agatha pressed herself into a window recess. She had liked Harold, with his quiet calming voice, his gentle teasing. He had been kind to her. She would not be wife to him now, Mama had said, in a curiously taut, angered voice. Listening to the rise and fall of conversation—the frequent outbursts of blasphemous oaths from her father—Agatha had tried to understand what was happening.

A letter was to be sent immediately to England, demanding that Harold relinquish the crown; a similar missive was to go to the Pope in Rome, protesting at Harold's usurpation; and then Papa was to order ships to be built, and for all his vassals to pledge their support of an invasion of England. Agatha was not much the wiser. She thought her father had liked Harold, that was why he had pledged her to him. What difference did it make if the kind Englishman wore a crown and not he?

Agatha breathed on the rough texture of the window parchment, watching the droplets of moisture form and trickle downwards. No doubt things would happen as they usually did: her father would besiege a few castles in England and kill any man who persisted in opposing him. She wondered whether her father would allow Harold to remain king once he had defeated England. If she could not be a nun she would have quite liked to have been a queen and worn a crown.

But what did a twelve-year-old girl know of the intricacies of war and invasion? Of victory and conquest?

4

York

There were, it seemed to Harold in those first tentative weeks of kingship, not sufficient hours in a day to complete all that was so suddenly and urgently expected of him. He thought that under Edward he had acquired a grasp of government and administrative decision-making—but he soon discovered that his expertise was minimal. So much to be done. So much to learn! Rarely did he seek his bed before midnight—to be up and about again by the sixth hour of the morning. Throughout January and into the early days of February, Harold could almost believe that England as a whole—and beyond—was queuing at the gateway of Westminster Palace to speak to the new king.

Exhaustion was creeping up on him; and as ever when his body was overtaxed, the signs of his old illness surreptitiously re-emerged. His fingers would stiffen, his jaw sag, slurring his speech as the hour grew late and tiredness increased. He longed for the chance to hunt, to fish, to relax, but there was never a respite.

Writs, grants, appointments. All lands held in trust in the King's name to be scrutinised, confirmed or withdrawn at his discretion—from a single-held hide of farmland to the vast acreages of the earldoms. So soon into his reign there was little he wanted to alter. Nobles and lords—and a few women—who had loyally served Edward were confirmed in their landlordship. There was no cause to doubt their constancy, at least not yet. In those few, very few, cases where questions were raised the landholding was passed to another of Harold's choice. For the earls he made no change except in one area. Northampton and Huntingdonshire had been held by Tostig, but had not been transferred by Edward to Morkere. To reinforce his directive that Tostig would not be reinstated, Harold passed that small portion as a new, separate earldom and awarded it to Waltheof, the young son of Earl Siward, to be held in trust for him by Morkere until he came of age. He hoped that would please the Northerners—and it did, but it was not so easy to convince them of his long-term intent.

Northumbria, it soon became apparent, was not over-anxious to embrace another son of Godwine. Had it not already been shown that Wessex had no consideration for the North? How many southern kings had put the interests and concerns of the people of the North as their priority? What would make this new-crowned king any different—and aye, him a Godwine along with it. He had taken their side against Tostig when outright rebellion had threatened—but for whose benefit? For the North's? Nay, 'twas only to prevent a costly war for the South. Earl Morkere was liked and welcomed, but he was more than likely soon to be proved the fool in trusting a southern Godwinesson to look to the North's interests.

Rumour was a powerful tool for the stirring of mistrust. How long, men asked each other over a jug of ale in the taverns, or while haggling for a bargain in the marketplace, before this king waits for us to drop our guard? How long before we again find that bastard, Tostig, strutting his arrogance through the streets of York?

Verbal reassurance from Harold, spread by messengers chosen to infiltrate those areas where the whisperings were loudest and harshest, failed. As mid-February approached the discordant rumblings grew more persistent; a strong wind of blustering opinion was blowing up into a gale.

Once the administrative details at Westminster had been tended as well as he could, Harold took the decision to visit York. Better to get out and do rather than brood, wait and hope.

Without doubt Tostig would soon raise a following from somewhere abroad; an attempted invasion would come. In Tostig's place, Harold would do no different. The justifiably wary Northerners needed his reassurance. Before he left London, Harold signed the charter proclaiming the provost of Abingdon to be promoted as abbot and issued orders that all else of importance was to be forwarded to York. He had ideas a-plenty for reform but they could wait. The North, the stability and safety of the kingdom, held priority. Also, riding northwards held another advantage personal to Harold: it gave him a chance to draw breath and to think—a luxury that, since Edward's death, he had not been able to entertain.

Although cold, the weather was dry and Harold's party of mounted men made good progress, for the road—where once the red-crested Roman armies had marched—was well maintained. They had been on the road northwards from Peterborough for no more than an hour, and their mounts were fresh and eager. Lincoln was to be their next major stop, where they would rest two or three days, Harold taking opportunity to receive homage and hear local appeals for justice, as he had at Royston, Huntingdon and Peterborough. He deliberately travelled with a small entourage to demonstrate his peaceful intent. A few housecarls only accompanied him, with his clerks and court officials. Beside him rode Bishop Wulfstan of Worcester, a respected man suited as a mediator, should, as was likely, one be necessary.

"There are those who are natural leaders, and those who are more fitted to following." His father had told him that on the day he had been appointed Earl of East Anglia. A lifetime ago!

What else had he advised, that Easter day twenty-three years ago? Words that had been applicable as earl, but were become more poignant now, in this unanticipated high position. "In a position of power," his father had said, "you very soon discover who are your friends and whom you can trust—or not. It is unfortunate that it is the "nots" who cause the most pain, come slower to the fore and are harder to unmask." As earl, Harold had eventually discovered the men who had courted favour with him for their own gain; as king, more were slithering from beneath the stones, like worms and slugs on a rain-damp day.

And the most meaningful advice? Harold checked his stallion as the animal stumbled over uneven ground, ran his hand soothingly down the arched crest. Nothing could totally prepare an honest man for power until the responsibility of it came. Harold was grateful for the wisdom, but regretted his father not being with him. How does a man who thought he had already reached the limits of his ability prepare for the ultimate test of kingship? The people of England— accepting and cheering him as his entourage passed by their farmsteadings and hamlets—would be the ones to suffer if he should get things wrong.

The uncertainties had been there at the outset, when Council had asked this thing of him, but they had been overtaken by a quick breath of excitement, a gleam of wonderment, the gathering speed of unreality. It was too late to undo what had been done, but the doubts were crowding back, pushing and shoving from every direction. Again Harold stroked his hand along his stallion's neck. Aye, he had found the chance to think, but were there not too many thoughts that he had deliberately set to one safe side? Could he carry the burden of this crown? Why had he not taken an easier option, agreed to be regent over Edgar? The accountability, the blame would then soon pass to the boy—nay, that was fool's thinking! He had become king because the armies of England would not follow a boy into battle. Because Edgar could never outface Tostig when he tried for his earldom, nor William when he eventually tried for the throne.

Huh, Duke William! Harold signalled that they increase the pace to a jogtrot, nudging his horse's flanks with his spurs. To invade England would take no small amount of expense and organisation, practical factors that Harold assessed

William would automatically dismiss as irrelevant. He would never consider that there might not be a suitable number of boats, that tides and winds could go against him—that men might not be eager to support him. Harold had learnt that much of William while in Normandy. He rubbed at his moustache, smiling in enigmatic self-mockery. Duke William would never doubt, as Harold was doing at this moment, his personal ability, his aptitude, his right. Perhaps that was why he doubted himself, for he could concede an area where the Duke of Normandy was the stronger of the two.

Then other worries swept over him. Who was to say that England would remain loyal to Harold Godwinesson? Approval for him was widespread and apparently unanimous—at least, south of Lincoln it was—but who was to say how long it would last? A year, two, three ahead, would these same people who lined the roadways as he passed by cheer and wave, and give their blessings?

"You look pensive, my friend. What troubles you?" Bishop Wulfstan jolted the King from his reverie. "If you are concerned about the loyalty of the North, it is only that they fear for their own well-being. Once we have allayed those fears, all will be well"

Harold smiled at his old friend and travelling companion. "Nay, it is my own fears that concern me, my own self-questioning."

"It is no bad thing for a man in authority now and then to examine his conscience. Doubt, my Lord King, balances aggression and a greed for power. So what troubles you? I possess a good ear for listening, and occasionally can find a sensible answer."

Harold shook his head. "You of all men carry a fathomless well of wisdom. No other is so apt to say the right thing at the right time as you."

Wulfstan snorted. "Nonsense, I am older than most men and have therefore fallen into more difficulties—and found my way out of them again, that is all."

Declining to argue, for the Bishop was, above all else, a modest man, Harold admitted, "I have a weight of doubts and troubles rattling in my head, but it is for me to sort them."

Beneath the shelter of the hedgerows, nestling in deep rifts and pockets of undergrowth, lay a carpet of white flowers, looking almost as if fresh snow had fallen in a haphazard scatter overnight. Yet few of the men took notice as their horses trampled by, for the snowdrops had been in bloom for several days and were no longer greeted with pleasure as the heralds of spring.

Ahead stood a mill set beside the race of the river. Folk were coming from within wiping floured hands on sacking aprons, faces eager and curious, expressions turning into excited delight as the banners were recognised. A woman sent a boy running up the road, to summon out the villagers; a little girl stooped to pluck a fistful of new-budding celandines, their opening, even more than the snowdrops, signalling the last flourish of winter. Gravely, she held them up to Harold as he passed. He smiled, leant from the saddle and accepted the posy, tucking the ragged stems through the pin of his cloak brooch. She reminded him of Algytha, as she had been as a child of six or seven. Blue, wide-amazed eyes, pert little mouth, cherry-coloured cheeks. And Algytha reminded him of Edyth. As if he needed reminding! Christ God, but everything reminded him of her. A blue sky, A thrush's song, a bank of snowdrops...Edyth? Would he ever, ever see Edyth again?

They rode on past the mill and through the village, accepting the gifts and good will of the land-folk. Several boys ran with them a way, keeping pace and chattering with the last men of the phalanx of riders. On into the woods, the deeper shadows of oak and ash and beech. No birch. Harold was glad of that. Of all trees, the silver bark of the birch brought Edyth's dear, sweet face too close to mind.

"I have made up my mind as to the problem of satisfying the North," he said after a while to Wulfstan. "There is one way I can convince those northern nobles that I intend to remain true to my word. I shall forge an alliance with their earl, one that cannot easily be broken." Turning his head, Harold met the wrinkle-lidded gaze of the Bishop with his keen, clear-sighted eyes. "I shall offer to wed with Morkere's sister Alditha."

Wulfstan pursed his lips, nodded approval. "And you doubt your wisdom? Ah, no, my king, 'tis excellent thinking."

Harold returned his eyeline to the front, studied a bone-thin goose girl herding a gaggle of hissing geese to new grazing on common land. He ordered that someone toss her a coin. A new-minted penny, which bore not the head of Edward but the new king, of Harold, second of that name.

"It was not of my thinking," he admitted to Wulfstan. "Edyth, when last I saw her, suggested it."

Holding his peace for a few paces, the Bishop observed, "It takes a brave woman to suggest a suitable new wife for her own husband."

Harold made no answer. It took a braver man not to break down and weep as he had clung to such a woman. And Harold had realised, at that instant of saying goodbye to his love, that he was not a brave man.

❧

Alditha stood with her two brothers on the entrance steps to the Earl's palace in York. She dipped a deep curtsey as Harold, stiff and cramped after the long hours of riding, dismounted. The townsfolk had waited at the London gate and lined the narrow streets to see their king ride in. Some had cheered his coming but many more stood silent. A few had dared to jeer, cursing the name of Tostig Godwinesson. The housecarls had made moves to reprimand them for the hostile welcome but, with a sharp word, Harold had forbidden any retaliation.

"It is not me they show disrespect to, but my brother. I know him better than they and have every sympathy for their ill feeling."

"My Lord King." Earl Morkere stepped forward, bowed and greeted Harold with an embrace. "It pleases me to welcome you to York."

Harold returned the embrace, then said, without a qualm, his hand flicking to the sullen crowd. "It seems not all the folk hereabouts share your enthusiasm for my arrival." Seeing Morkere's unease, he added with a broad smile, "I must, then, make an effort to ensure that when I leave, they regret my going." Gallantly, Harold then turned to the Lady Alditha, kissed her hand and offered her his arm to escort her within doors.

Morkere exchanged a wry glance with his brother Eadwine before gesturing for the Bishop Wulfstan to proceed after Harold. Neither man had missed the radiant smile with which their sister had appraised the King, nor his answering expression of delight.

"You are as thin as a peasant goose girl we encountered on the journey here." Harold remarked to her as they walked together. "Shall I cheer you by tossing you a penny with my portrait stamped upon it?"

"I have no need for pennies or portraits, my Lord."

"No, indeed, not when you have the man in his very flesh beside you. I do believe I am not as hard or round as coin though. Somewhat of a higher value too, I would say."

She smiled at his absurdity. She had, she must secretively admit, missed his company.

"I was surprised not to find you at court when I returned from Normandy," he said. "Was Edward not kind to you after I had gone? Or were you pining for your brother's company—or for Wales, perhaps?"

Since his questioning had been candid, Alditha answered in a similar vein: "I doubt King Edward could have been deliberately unkind to anyone. The ladies were somewhat tedious, and my brother Eadwine's household suited me better. As for Wales, I have always admired the scenery. 'Tis but a shame the temperament of the people cannot always be as beautiful."

"I think you will find that the new king will be as kind, and that the ladies of his court will not be so glib with their remarks." Harold halted, placed his finger beneath her chin and tipped her face upwards. "As for Wales, no scenery could match in beauty that which I see before me."

She blushed crimson and moved her head away, but almost immediately found her courage and stared back at him. "Kind words, my Lord, but words come easy. Sustained kindness that issues from the heart is far harder."

Harold laid his fingers lightly over hers. In what was almost a whisper for her hearing alone, he said, "That depends, does it not, on who speaks the words and who owns the heart?"

5

Waltham Abbey

"Mother? Why not come with me to see the foals? It is a beautiful evening, a pity to waste what promises to be the first fine sunset of spring." Algytha slid her arm around her mother's waist and kissed her cheek, noting the pale thinness of her face, the tiredness of her eyes. Grief, the loss of a loved one. Would it have been easier for her mother to have accepted Harold's leaving if he had died? Algytha caught her breath—no, not that. Do not, ever, think that!

Edyth peeped at a small pot of water simmering over the cooking fire, grasped a handful of yellow flowers from the basket on the table and dropped them in. "I am making cusloppe tea for Gunnhild. With a little honey added, the poor child may sleep sounder this night. She has been so restless of late."

"She is excited about those pups coming soon; Silk has only a few days to go before her whelping."

"Aye, and the young lass does love that bitch so!" Edyth smiled as a memory flooded her mind. "I once cared for a dog as much as she. We were inseparable, he and I." Hastily she gathered more flower heads, stirred them into the infusion, banished the memory of Thor from her mind. Her dog, her friend. His violent death…Harold.

Algytha selected one of the leaves from the plant and nibbled at it. The cowslips and primroses had bloomed in abundance this spring, their flowers bringing a burst of yellow sunshine to hedgerow and meadow edge—an alternative sunshine to that which had been lacking in the sky these past cloud-dulled April days.

Algytha put her hand under her mother's elbow and eased her away from the fire. "Someone else can keep an eye on that infusion, Mother. You haven't slept soundly either; a walk to the top of High Meadow will relax you. There are four foals; you know you enjoy watching them prance."

Undecided, Edyth looked from the steaming pot to the open doorway. The trill of evening birdsong filtered in, and the sweeping rays of golden sunlight highlighted the swirl and dance of floating dust. The evening outside beckoned, rich with pleasure.

Removing the old square of patched linen from around her waist, Edyth smiled and nodded. Beside the door, she slipped her soft house-shoes from her feet and donned stouter hide boots. There would be puddles a-plenty, and mud between the gateways, but if this sun and boisterous drying wind continued for a few days the ground would soon lose its winter weariness.

They passed through the huddle of trees in the apple orchard, scattering the chickens scratching for the last of the day's grubs among the blossom that flecked the grass. The sun, a low ball of fire-red, was sinking towards the purple-dark ridge on the far side of the valley, the sky behind, the vivid, clear blue of early evening. With the wind fresh in their faces the two women, arm linked through arm, walked up the gentle sloping hill. Laughter rippled from the spinney ahead. The boys, Magnus and Ulf presumably, for Edmund had waved to his mother from the lower meadow, where the last of the bulge-bellied ewes were to lamb.

As they passed through the new growth of rich, spring grass, their feet left a double silvered trail, for the dew was already descending. Reaching the haw-thorn hedge, which showed a trace of white from the blossom that would soon be smothering it, Algytha pointed to a blackbird's nest. The mother bird crouch-ing on her eggs peeped out at them with her bright black eyes but never stirred.

"Brave little bird!" Algytha said. "How many mothers would sit so determined in the face of such a threat?"

"I suppose it depends on the nature of the mother—look at the cuckoo bird, she abandons her children the instant the egg is laid."

Algytha gave her mother a loving squeeze. "Glad I am, then, that you are the hen blackbird, not the cuckoo."

Algytha lifted the latch of the gate, allowing her mother to pass through. The mares were grazing beneath the oak trees. They lifted their heads as the women approached, scenting whether there was cause for alarm. Algytha held out her palm, a shrivelled crab-apple from last autumn balanced there. The nearest mare, a pretty, black-maned dun, took a tentative step forward and daintily took the morsel, her foal sheltering close to her offside, peering warily beneath her dam's neck. Eager for titbits, the other three mares crowded in, one setting back her ears and squealing, kicking out at her neighbour's dark-coated colt.

"No apples if you are going to squabble!" Edyth admonished, rubbing a chestnut mare's white-starred forehead. The dun mare's filly put her nose forward, sniffing delicately at Edyth's unfamiliar smell—and then, without warning, skittered away, head ducking as she bucked and cavorted. That set the other foals into a whirl of similar antics, the four of them hurtling into a gallop across the meadow.

When the titbits were finished, Edyth suggested they walk on to the crest of the hill. The sun had dipped almost beneath the horizon, and the sky was flooding with streaks of gold and purple, its glory reflected on the gold cross atop the nest of Waltham Abbey and in the meandering expanse of the river, its winter-risen depth still covering the meadow plains to either side. At least this year the floods had not come as they had last. As they watched, a hawk hung, poised, against the gold-painted sky, stationary except for quivering wings. He plunged, suddenly, and was gone.

With a curious frown, her finger pointing to the purpling sky, Algytha said, "What is that? Look, there, that star! How bright it is—it looks as if it is trailing a stream of hair behind it, blowing loose in the wind!"

Squinting to see more clearly, Edyth looked to where her daughter pointed. "I have seen such trailing stars before," she said, "but never one as wonderful as this—it is like a dragon crossing the sky!"

"Where has it come from? Do you think it carries a meaning?"

Edyth gestured a hand motion of uncertainty. "Your father always said that a star falling to earth was the track of Our Lady Mother's tears, weeping for a departed soul, but this is not such a star. It is not tumbling, but riding the sky-wind."

"Perhaps it is for a birth, then? Something like the star that sailed the heavens when our Lord Christ came to be born on earth?" There was a questioning note in Algytha's voice, and a slight hesitancy. The star, brightening as the sky darkened behind it, was beautiful, but mysterious and a little frightening.

Perhaps it is sent for the coming of a king." Edyth's answer was almost a whisper. The strange star shone yet brighter, more brilliant, hanging low in the south-western quarter of the sky, above where London clustered beside the Thames river. London and Westminster.

He was there, at Westminster Palace, had returned for the Easter Council. The first Easter that he had been in England and not with her. Was his new wife with him, Edyth wondered? Was she yet with child? She stared at the shining star, blinked away tears that misted her vision. A star for a new king. For Harold, King of England. Or for a child that the woman, his taken wife Alditha, might be carrying for him?

The first tear shimmered down her cheek, followed by another and another. She had tried to set aside these feelings of jealousy and anguish, tried so very hard. But how did you begin to forget a man who had been there through most of your life, as friend, husband and lover? Forget the father of your children?

Begin to accept that now he lay through each night beside the warmth of another woman?

Algytha, nineteen years old, a woman herself, although one who had not yet been touched by the intimacy of love, settled her embracing arms around her mother, her cheek, also damp with tears, resting against hers. And above, as the sky faded from a darkening blue to night black, the comet blazed in a glory of radiant silver, seen by all who looked up to the spatter of stars, dimmed against its magnificence.

6

Westminster

Queen Edith might have been content with the dull colours and the crucifixion theme of the tapestries covering her chamber walls within the palace at Westminster, but Alditha hated them. They were morbid and depressing, like so much of this dark-shadowed palace. Perhaps it was the lingering memory of Edward's death or her own lethargy that made the place so melancholy? Whatever, she felt alone and miserable. Her daughter, Nest, had been mithering all day, intermittent tears between bouts of rage—by late afternoon Alditha had had enough of her, had slapped her legs and ordered the seven-year-old girl's nurse to put her to bed. And now she felt guilty, for the child was running a fever, her face and back covered in the white-spotted blisters of a childhood illness. The poor lass must have been unwell for most of the morning and no one had listened to her discomfort. As her mother she ought to have realised.

Alditha rubbed at her forehead; a headache was starting. She wanted to scream, shout—weep with despair. Instead, she sat before the hearth fire, her legs tucked beneath her. They were all sniggering at her; behind her back she could imagine their clucking words.

"Calls herself a mother, didn't even realise the wee lass was carryin' the spots."

"Aye, an' 'er with all 'er airs an' graces!"

She should not care what the serving women said of her—nor the wives of nobles and lords, but God help her, she did! Cared so much that the pain of their dislike hurt like a knife twisting into her heart.

She ought to go to her bed, for she was tired, but she wanted to take one last look at Nest before retiring, and Harold might come. Doubtful, but he might. He had been in London all day, for it was the folkmoot,when the people met at the hustings beside the Cathedral of Saint Paul to discuss the business and laws of the city. He had ridden in, not an hour since, as dusk was falling over the river Thames, would need to eat, then finish the government tasks of the day; he would be tired. Too tired to come to her bedchamber.

She fingered the gold brooch that clasped her tunic at the shoulder, a pretty thing, patterned with flower-petal shapes and four lion-like beasts. She unpinned it and read aloud the inscription engraved to its underside:

Aldgyð me ag: *ag hyo Drihten*
Drihten hine awerie   *ðe me hire ætferie*
Bvton hyo me selle   *hire agenes willes*

Alditha owns me, may the Lord own her. May the Lord curse him who takes me from her, unless she but gives me by her own choice. Harold had presented it to her on the dawn of their first day together, as his own personal morning gift.

Their wedding. A cold, bright-skied frosted day. She had walked beside Harold, flanked by her two brothers, to the Minster, the streets lined by the people of York. They had been pleased, shouting their greetings and blessings, showering the couple with snowdrops and yellow-dusted catkins, there being no other flower petals to strew in their path late in February. Her dress had been of yellow silk, her veil a pale blue, her shoes a darker hue. An expensive garment: it had been her mother's wedding dress, had fitted as if made for her.

She had been certain her mother had been beside her during the service, was sure she had smelt her flower-scented perfume. How pleased she would have been that her daughter, as soon as the marriage vows were exchanged, was to be crowned and anointed as Queen of England. Her father would have been pleased too, although his would have been the gloating of arrogance, of enjoying the prospect of a grandson becoming the next king. York—all the North, so they said—was equally delighted by the match. Her brothers had grinned throughout like inane barley-drunk peasants, and Harold had taken her hand and smiled gently upon her. Herself? She sighed, stretching her foot for it was beginning to tingle with pin-and-needle stabs. How had she felt that day, seven weeks ago in York? Happy? Content? She supposed, aye, she had, but in truth, she had felt very little. She liked Harold, he was a good and kind man, but she did not know him, and the memory of her first husband had still numbed her mind.

They had not asked her whether she wanted to be Harold's wife, his queen, had assumed she would agree to their proposals for alliance. As had her father when he had arranged her marriage to Gruffydd. At least Westminster was not so far to travel to as had been Wales! But then she had, despite the fear for her husband, much liked Wales, the place and the people. Did not much like Westminster.

She had been nervous that night, after their marriage ceremony and feasting; she had thought then how foolish she was to be quaking with fear. A woman grown, mother of a child, bedded and used by Gruffydd of Wales. Yet she had gone to her marriage bed with Harold as if she were a shy and innocent maid. Gruffydd had taken his pleasure on her and fallen instantly asleep; she had felt nothing but discomfort when he had used her.

Harold had been different, gentle and considerate, ensuring she received as well as gave pleasure. Before that wedding night, she had been unaware that a woman, too, could experience an exhilaration from the act of coupling. Gruffydd had been a man with a constant need to prove something, be it his ability and strength in battle or bed. Harold had nothing to prove, not to her or anyone else, unless you included his need to prove that he no longer thought of Edyth Swannhaels. Except he did think of her. Often. Especially now, when they were here at Westminster and she was so close, but a short ride away.

Her family, Eadwine and Morkere, basked in the reflected glory of her being England's crowned queen. The North had settled, accepting Harold and his promise to them, because of her. Even Nest was content—before she had fallen so ill this day. Alditha allowed herself a mother's indulgent smile. On that wedding day Nest, too, had been dressed in her finest, the little girl's excited delight infecting them all in the chamber where her mother had been dressing for the occasion.

"Are you to wear a crown, Mama? Queens wear crowns, do they not?"

"Aye, *merched fach*, Mam is to wear a crown."

"Am I to wear a crown too? I should like a crown. A silver one."

Alditha had told Harold of the exchange later, as they lay together, entwined, drifting between the throb of lovemaking and the tranquillity of sleep. He had laughed, a father's appreciative chuckle at the innocence of children.

"She shall have her crown, a silver circlet. I shall order one made, especially for her."

Harold kept his word, something Gruffydd had never done, giving it to her a week and a day after the wedding, two days before they rode south, here to Westminster.

There was a noise from down in the forecourt, people calling beyond the closed wooden shutters that covered the windows. She had thrown them open during the day, taken down the oiled parchment that had been stretched over the openings, to allow in the fresh air and small amount of sunshine. This chamber faced east, though, so the sun only lit the room through the morning. Harold's chamber, the King's room, set to the south, was far more pleasant, but Alditha was never summoned there, by day or night. She had a suspicion that Harold himself spent little time in the chamber that had once, not so long since, been Edward's.

She sat looking at the wall, thinking of nothing in particular, fleeting images of her childhood, her mother, father, brothers passing through her mind. Her hopes, fears. Her loneliness. The tapestry hanging within her direct line of sight was embroidered with dark, sombre colours, reds and browns: Christ suffering on the cross; the clouds of a brewing storm; behind, women weeping at His feet, Edith had chosen the decoration for this, the Queen's chamber; her taste was very different from Alditha's. Alditha would have chosen the parables, perhaps, or Christ's entry into Jerusalem, joyous images, filled with light and vivid colour. The blueness of the Galilean sea, the green of palm leaves. Yellows, oranges…On impulse, she lunged to her feet, took hold of the tapestry with both hands and pulled, her frustration and years of disappointments funnelling into fury at the ugliness of the thing. The bound edge ripped and the tapestry fell, the broken hanging-frame knocking her down, the torn material covering her as if it were a tossed mantle. Her ensuing oath was passionate and explicit, though fortunately in Welsh.

"I have no idea what you just bellowed, but I assume it meant something significant." An amused smile wrinkling his lips, Harold bent and lifted the remnant, then held his hand out to assist his wife to her feet. "I did knock, but you can't have heard," he said as, her face blushing red, Alditha brushed dust and frayed threads from her gown. "Then I heard you shout." He reached his hand forward, removed a cobweb from her hair. "Thought perhaps you were being attacked." He raised his other hand, showed the dagger he held, slid it into the sheath at his waist. "Though I reckon your oath would be enough to scare away the fiercest of tapestries."

Embarrassed, Alditha mumbled an apology for ruining the wall hanging. "I merely wished to pull it down…"

"You must be stronger than you thought—you are not descended from that mythical demigod Heracles, are you?"

"I did not intend to tear it." She risked a glance up at him, fearing that he would be angry with her, as Gruffydd would have been. He would have beaten her, most probably.

To her wonder, Harold was laughing. "Shred all of them if you wish," he said, waving his arm vaguely at the walls. "I always thought my sister's taste rather too morbid. She was never like that as a child." He walked towards another tapestry, peered at it, his expression puckering with distaste. He flicked a finger and a cloud of dust billowed out. "Does no one take these things down and beat them? Gods, there are more spiders and fleas in this horrendous thing than there are stitches!" Turning back to Alditha, he said, "Give orders to your women on the morrow that these are to be removed and burnt. Choose something that you like to replace them." When a smile spread on her face, he added, "You ought to smile more often, it suits you better than that sombre frown that sits there most the while."

For a moment, neither of them spoke, both uncertain what to say next, then words tumbled out together.

"I came to see if you..."

"I was about to go and..."

They stopped, laughed together.

"I am sorry, my Lord, I interrupted."

"No matter. I, er..." Harold felt stupid, as if he were a lad again, talking to the first woman he had taken to bed. How embarrassed he had been as he fumbled and fiddled, how patient she had been with him, and all for the price of a penny! "I came to ask if you would like to come and see the bearded star that has appeared in the sky." He spoke quickly, words gushing in a torrent, but he slowed as he stepped towards her, his hand reaching out to touch her cheek and hair. "It is almost as bright as your eyes, but not, I think, as beautiful."

Flustered, uncertain, Alditha half pulled away from him, glancing around the room for her cloak. "I was about to go and see my daughter. She is unwell. She is running a fever, has itching spots on her body."

Harold nodded. "I was told. I have already been to see her. Her nurse gave her a mild sleeping draught and she is sound asleep. She is healthy, and with good nursing should soon recover. All of my children suffered a dosing of the white spots."

Puzzled, Alditha stopped, her cloak half tossed around her shoulders. "You have seen her? But why, my Lord? She is not your child but the daughter of a Welshman."

Taking the cloak, Harold fastened it about her, then rested his hands on her shoulders. "She is also the daughter of my wife and my queen." He dipped his head, his lips close to hers, pausing to find the right words. "I will not mistreat you, as Gruffydd did, nor will I intentionally hurt you. You are my wife and—" Again he paused. He ought say, "and I love you," but he could not insult her with a lie—he thought too much of her for that. "I am heart-fond of you."

She wanted to ask, "Fond? What of Edyth? What of the woman you do love?" But she said nothing, for Alditha was no fool. If a woman had a husband who treated her with kindness and respect, what more could she ask? Few women possessed even that. To hold a man's love for as long as Edyth Swannhæls had was a rarity.

Harold read her silence, was aware she must think often of that other woman of his. That night when he had lain first with her—and felt the intensity of pleasure as her lithe and supple body had responded to his caress—he had murmured a name into her hair. It had not been Alditha that he had whispered though, but Edyth.

"I cannot say that I will not, ever, go to Waltham Manor again, but this I will promise. I will not visit Edyth while you are resident here at Westminster. I will not embarrass, or compromise, either of you in that way."

Alditha touched the tips of her fingers to his lips. His hair was beginning to silver at the temples and the moustache that drooped to either side of his mouth bore the first grizzle of age. Yet his eyes were as blue as speedwells, and his smile did not just touch the corners of his lips, but came through those eyes, direct from his heart. It was that, above all else, that made him so different from her first husband, from so many men. His smile was genuine.

"I expect no promises of you, my Lord. No woman can of her husband, but I would ask you one thing." Her heart was starting to pound. Dare she ask? Would he think ill of her? Think her wanton and immoral?

He lifted his hand, palm open. "Ask."

"I was sitting here earlier, thinking that you must have a special love for Edyth, as you have been with her so long."

He answered quietly, with the truth. "Aye, that I have."

She looked deep into his eyes, wondered at her own daring as she said, quickly before her courage failed her, "I know you will never love me with your heart, as you do her, but could you, would you…" She turned away abruptly, so that he would not see the flush of red crimson her cheeks. "Would you teach me how I may love you, with the intimacy of my body?"

Harold walked around her, lifted her face and set his lips light against hers. "You do not need teaching, sweetheart, you have it there already. It needs liberating from its cage, that is all."

"But can you unlock the door?"

"I have the key, right here."

They forgot about the comet that was racing across the heavens. For that night, at least, Harold also forgot about the news he had received that his brother Tostig was waiting to attack England. Forgot William of Normandy, riding furious to each of his apathetic lords and nobles to persuade them to join his cause. Almost forgot, for that one moment during the height of their passion, Edyth.

7

Dives-sur-Mer

Shells scrunched beneath William's boots as he crossed the wide, flat stretch of sand, his long stride taking him rapidly nearer the group of men standing, hands shading their eyes, watching as the ship was manhandled towards the sea. The vessel was slowly lumbering along a series of wooden rollers laid beneath its keel; a few more yards and its bow would be touching the first shallow ripples of the Channel Sea. Another ship completed. One more to add to the Duke's impressive fleet.

One of the men watching turned at the sound of his footsteps, William fitz Osbern's expression breaking into a welcoming smile as he recognised his duke. "Good day, my Lord!" he called. "Is she not a beauty? And there are almost one hundred like her, moored in safety along the river."

"Only one hundred?" William snapped gruffly. "There ought be double that. Treble. What are these imbecile shipwrights doing? Make them work harder."

Fitz Osbern repressed a sigh as William stalked on past, heading for the ponderously moving ship. The intensity of this moon-mad venture was playing heavy upon the Duke's temper and everyone else's patience. Not an even-tempered man at the best of times, William was daily becoming ever more impossible to tolerate with equanimity. The sheer logistics of this enterprise were already overwhelming—and as yet, they had not mustered sufficient to invade a kingdom across the sea.

Will gazed along the almost infinite length of sand. The estuary ran across golden sandbanks, the land low here but rising to a modest headland, beneath which a fishing village huddled, before sweeping into the wide bay of Honfleur. Duke William had chosen this river and stretch of coast because it was sheltered from persistent sea winds and conveniently close to Caen, so he could keep an eye on progress.

Within a single handful of weeks, these beaches would begin to fill with tents and men; soon they would be swamped by latrine detritus and smoke curls from hearth fires would stain the blue sky. The coast would be denuded of game and timber. *En outre* a glut of bastard-born children would appear in nine months' time. Sufficient grain was already being laboriously transferred to the huge temporary barns, but men always liked their meat if they could get it. Both of the four- and two-legged kind.

The first of the horses had already been turned loose to graze in the Dives valley; at least they would not require feeding, not while the spring grass was lush and fresh. The ships were arriving too, sent with their cargoes of timber—to build more ships—of grain, other supplies, weapons, armour. Delivered early by those few barons and nobles who unswervingly supported William in this venture. Bishop Odo of Bayeux had fulfilled his quota of one hundred seaworthy vessels, William d'Everux eighty, Robert d'Eu sixty, Robert, comte de Mortain one hundred and twenty. Will fitz Osbern's own submission of sixty deep-draughted craft, each capable of transporting ten horses...and more would be coming. Clinker-built sea-going cargo and trade ships designed for sturdiness and stability rather than speed and manoeuvrability, powered by sail, not oar. Ships from wealthy men like Walter Gifford, Hugh d'Avranches, Hugh de Montfort. Eight hundred such craft were, they estimated, needed. Eight hundred. Will ran his hand through his short-cropped hair, whistling silently. Eight hundred. Half accounted for through the muster, the rest to be built. Already the seasoned timber was almost all used, they would be needing to cut and use green wood, unsuitable for building for it would warp and twist...but then, they would not be requiring the ships after they had reached England. The sailing, for most of them, would be one way.

"Where is this poxed Englishman you say you have caught last evening?" Duke William's abrupt question roused Will from his thoughts. They had captured an English cur-son, spying on the number of these vessels, on the preparations for invasion.

"We have him safely chained, over in one of the smith's forges. He will not give his name or his business here, though he has been thoroughly questioned."

Changing direction, Duke William strode purposefully towards the clutter of shacks and bothies, from where came the rhythmic sound of hammering. The master shipwright oversaw the cutting and fitting of the timbers for each ship. But so many others, with their different skills were crucial to the construction. Blacksmiths, carpenters, the prowwright, who performed the most difficult and vital task—connecting the lines fore and aft, taking especial care where keel and strakes met stem and stern. Four masters and the manual labourers...twelve men for each ship.

Fitz Osbern indicated the back of one of the bothies where a man, chained at wrists and ankles, squatted. He looked up as the Duke approached and kicked his thigh. Blood had dried above his left eye and cheek, where bruising was already darkening to purple and black. His lips were swollen, his long hair matted, his tunic ripped and stained with more blood.

"So you will not tell us your name?" William stood with legs wide, seemingly relaxed and uninterested. "Well, I have no desire to hear it. It's enough to know you are English scum. But I do wish to know what you have learnt from spying on my shipbuilders. What you were going to tell Earl Harold when you returned to England."

The captive regarded the man standing before him with a blank expression. That he was the Duke was obvious by his stance, dress and air of authority; that the Englishman understood no word of French as apparently obvious.

William narrowed his eyes, glaring at the chained man—and then, with unexpected speed, lashed out with his fist, striking hard at the Englishman's stomach, sending his breath woofing in pain from between bruised lips. "Do you think I am a fool, English turd? I know that you understand my language. You would not be here to spy on my movements if you did not."

William hunkered down. With one hand he gripped the man's cheeks, squeezing the battered flesh. "Your oath-breaking lord wishes to know how many ships I have, *n'est-ce pas*? How many men I will be mustering—how soon I will be ready to sail for England and remove the whoreson from Edward's throne? You wish to know? I will tell you! Tell you all, because I want you to return to England. I want that bastard liar to know that I am making ready, that I will be coming for him, and for England."

For a long while, William squatted there, his eyes boring into the Englishman, recounting his proposed number of ships and men. The man listened, stored the information in his memory, wondering, at the same time, how much of what William boasted was fact, and how much exaggeration. This he did know, however, that many ships were being built, that a vast fleet was being assembled. That William's intent, however fanciful, however impossible, was becoming real.

Stooping to pass below the low entrance to the bothy, William went back out into the sunlight, lifted his head and took a deep breath of salt air. The day was warm and pleasant, the wind fresh. "I shall inspect the moored vessels, I think," he announced, beckoning fitz Osbern to walk with him in the direction of the river. "Ensure that worthless rag in there is taken to England on the next tide. I want him left somewhere where he can reach London with ease.

Harold is to hear what I am doing as soon as may be. I want him to worry, to lose sleep at night, knowing that I am making ready." Abruptly the Duke's eyebrows creased into a frown of anger. "Have you heard news of that idiot husband of my wife's sister?"

Fitz Osbern nodded, bracing himself mentally for another torrent of vehement outrage. Earl Tostig of Northumbria, another accursed, double-dealing Englishman—but then, it seemed all the English were scum, not to be trusted.

Word had come that he had reneged on his agreement with Baldwin of Flanders, his father-in-law—William's father-in-law. Through the winter the exiled Englishman, with his handful of followers and his wife, had sheltered beneath Baldwin's protective roof. They were brothers by law, William and Tostig, and William had sent sympathetic messages, promising to help Tostig in his plight, had endorsed Count Baldwin's supply of almost fifty ships for Tostig to command.

"Help me fight Harold," William had said, "and I will restore Northumbria to you when England is mine." Brothers by law, united by marriage.

Huh! If a man could go against the brother of his blood, then why expect him to remain loyal to a brother by marriage? Tostig had readily taken his ships from Flanders and sailed, not for Normandy and the muster point at Dives, but direct for England.

Tostig, as much a cheating toad-spawn as Harold. Tostig, whose own grubby hands were stretching for that same crown.

"He plundered the Island of Wight, sailed eastwards, harrying the coast and there met with Danish allies." Duke William spat into the sand, growled, "He has now amassed a fleet of sixty ships. Ships that he agreed to bring to my invasion fleet!" All these difficulties that were twining round his ankles like rampant tangling weeds. Ships, so slowly built; weaponry to be crafted; men to muster; horses to obtain. The majority of the aristocracy and elite yet to persuade into supporting him.

Fitz Osbern had done all he could since the winter—riding in person from one estate to another, persuading, cajoling, threatening where necessary. Ah, there were more than one or two debts that had been called in these past months! And as many more reminders of misdemeanours that had conveniently been re-remembered.

So, they thought their duke a fool, a dream-chaser, did they? These hearth-gazing, barrel-bellied Norman cowards! An invasion of England to claim a crown was an impossibility, was it? What did they know! Their Viking ancestors had almost overrun all England once, had claimed a good portion for their own—would have taken all of it, had their leaders possessed the military genius of their present duke. Did his barons and nobles not realise that they could not disagree with his decisions? That they had no choice in this undertaking—that it was not advisable to say no to William?

He was going to England with an army, and he was going to claim his right, no matter how long it took, how much blood was shed. Or how many bastards shrugged and pretended to become suddenly deaf, ailing or poor of purse.

"Mayhap Tostig will slay Harold of England? Have you considered that possibility, my Lord?" Fitz Osbern said, almost trotting to keep pace with his duke's impatient stride.

"I doubt it," William retorted. "Tostig Godwinesson likes to boast that he can afford quality breeches, but has no potency in the balls concealed beneath." Abruptly, William stopped, watching as the new-launched ship made her way around the estuary and into the shelter of the river. She handled well, a good craft.

"Summon my barons to a third Council. Caen, early June. I think we must finalise the details of my conquest. They must all attend, excuses will not be accepted—my wife's cathedral of la Trinité will be ready for consecration, we shall incorporate that into the occasion." He stalked off to intercept one of the master shipwrights. "See to it, Will. I'll leave the arrangements to you. Anyone not attending will be tried for treason."

Will fitz Osbern massaged his salt-rimed chin and cheeks with his hand. See to it! Had he not enough to see to? If this cursed obsession of William's ever came to anything more than craftsmen hammering at planks of wood and strips of metal, then the credit should go to himself for the organisation of it all. Will shook his head. It would not, though. Those who did all the work and worrying were never recognised once the fighting was over. He snorted disdainfully. The credit? Huh, the ones who deserved the credit were normally the first to die.

8

Caen

The service of dedication in mid-June of the convent abbey of la Trinité, Caen, was beautiful, moving enough to bring tears to Duchess Mathilda's eyes. At least, she told herself that her tears were for joy at the completion of her abbey—a splendid contribution to the city her husband was creating here at Caen, a building to equal his own monastery of Saint-Etienne. Her abbey, though, she thought, was more beautiful, being built of lighter-coloured stone, with higher and wider windows and situated in a more elevated position. Saint-Etienne, she considered, was too masculine a place, sombre in both construction and atmosphere, a place for the warrior, the nobleman, the administrator. Her feminine abbey made you feel gay and light of spirit, made you want to lift your voice in the singing of hymns. Except, today, she did not feel any of these things.

As another tear wound a path down her cheek she brushed it aside, tried, yet again, to restrain her attention from wandering towards the little girl sitting beside the Abbess. Cecily. Six years old, a cherub of a child with fair, curling hair and wide, summer-blue eyes. Dimple-cheeked...her dearest daughter, little Cecily.

Mathilda studied the words of her Bible, open on her lap. It was an honour to give the child to the nunnery, to the service of God. An honour for herself and the girl. One day, Cecily would, perhaps, become Abbess of la Trinité—what more could a mother pledge to God as an offering of dedication and love? As a plea for His protection?

She stole a furtive glance at William, sitting straight-backed and serious on the men's side of the aisle. He would not notice if all their children were sent to live within abbeys. She sighed. But then, he had noticed nothing these last months, not if it were night or day, wet or warm. Nothing concerned him save this damned obsession with England.

They all said that the planning of this invasion was close to the ravings of a madman. They being the nobles—her own father one among them. None had said as much in public, of course, but private whispers had a habit of leaking out.

Damn the fools! Perhaps, had they amicably trotted after him along this insane path William would have dropped the idea, but no, because they opposed him, he now had an even greater point to prove. To Harold of England and to those who doubted his integrity and ability, Jesu Christ, if he but knew that Mathilda agreed with those nobles…she filled her lungs, straightened her back, lifted her chin to listen with more attention to the intonation of the blessing. Humour him, agree, enthuse…hope he would change his mind. The surest way to drive William into a forthright gallop was to stamp your foot and say *non*.

He could not force any one of them to join in a venture outside his own territory; support in this must come voluntarily or from mercenary payment. During February and March she had dared to hope that William might be forced to abandon his plan, to satisfy himself with piling every curse under God's heaven on Harold and England. No one wanted to waste his life or livelihood on a project that did not have a bent spear against a leather shield's chance of being successful.

Why could he not be content with what they had already achieved? Normandy was, after all these years of wars and discontent, a settled, thriving duchy, expanding in her territory, wealth and importance. There was no one, at this moment, liable to or capable of declaring war within or on the edge of their borders. Philip of France was an untried boy, Conan of Brittany was recently dead, with many of his magnates declared for Normandy. Why must William seek bloodshed—court death—when there was no reason for it save to heal his hurt pride?

Mathilda crossed herself and whispered a plea to the Mother Mary. Few men, outside of those dedicated loyalists who would follow him to hell and back if asked—or England, much the same thing to her mind—expected Duke William to succeed in this madness, few had initially thought he would raise the necessary fleet, let alone manage to sail across the sea to England in one piece. If he did, he would be cut down by the English fyrd. He must know all this himself, must doubt and query and worry—yet he said no word of it, showed nothing beyond this racing determination, despite all advice to the contrary, all sense, practicality, logistics and cost. It was indeed as if some devil-driven madness had taken hold of his senses.

Muttering the familiar words of response to the Abbot Lanfranc, Mathilda's mind again drifted. A madness engulfing her husband? No one had dared, ever, to swear allegiance to William and then, with outright taunting, scud the harvest gleanings into his face. That William had underestimated Harold—and that the Earl had almost certainly deliberately played him for a fool—consolidated this determination for revenge. No one embarrassed or threatened William without paying the penalty. Mathilda closed her Bible, held it close against her bosom. Only, what if it were William—and Normandy—who paid the price for this foolishness in the end?

Guilty at her inattentiveness, she reopened her Bible and shuffled through the pages of minute script. For a while she concentrated hard on the Abbot, staring only at his thin, impassioned face, his articulate hands, his richly embroidered robes. Lanfranc had been of no help in dissuading William from this folly—had actively encouraged him. England, he had said, had fallen away from the Church of Rome. Too many of the prelates of the English Church were corrupt—Archbishop Stigand for one. It was Lanfranc who had persuaded William that the claiming of England was a crusade, had agreed that Harold was a perjurer and oath breaker. Lanfranc insisted Earl Harold—earl, they all called him earl, none would say king—had tricked the English nobles into crowning him—as he had tricked William. He had placed the crown on his head in indecent haste to ensure no one had time to object—the very afternoon of Edward's burial!

Lanfranc himself had travelled to Rome to seek papal blessing for this holy invasion. The Pope's answer had echoed Mathilda's private thoughts. Why would Rome support a small duchy against a wealthy, ancient, Christian kingdom? Why support a duke against an anointed king, chosen and crowned by the people of England? Rome, it seemed, while deploring England's persistent arrogance and neglect of the laws and wishes of the Pope, and agreeing with Lanfranc's personal dislike of Stigand, would not go as far as proclaiming war on a Christian sovereign state. But Pope Alexander II had not forbidden it though. He would think on it, he had said. Consider the matter. Or to look at it another way, William's and Lanfranc's way, he would wait and see who won before bestowing his blessing on the victory.

Mathilda had been there, in the chamber with her husband and Will fitz Osbern, when Lanfranc had returned with that answer. Had listened, and doubted, her stomach churning with fear. No one else knew of Pope Alexander's actual words. And if the words passed on to others were not strictly accurate, who was to know? When it was all over—one way or the other—who would care?

At Council on the morrow, William intended to tell only the partial truth— that Rome did not object. That God was on their side.

Closing her eyes, Mathilda murmured another prayer. If William were slain— by God's grace, let him not come to harm! Already her body was shaking with the fear at the thought of his going to what was almost certain death. Fear of the burden of responsibility that he had placed on her shoulders while he was to be gone.

Later in the week in a service at Saint-Etienne, their eldest, Robert, was to be formally designated as heir. If William did not come back she would rule Normandy as regent until he came of age. She would rule! Mathilda found the prospect exciting and challenging. All her listening and learning of politics and law would finally be of benefit...but that would mean William would have to die.

Robert wanted that. For all she loved and treasured her son he upset her in that. She wished there had been some spark of love between father and boy. Robert was headstrong and eager, a fledgling bird stretching its wings at the very edge of the branch, making ready to fly. Agatha, too, had been delighted at the acrimony between Normandy and England for she had never wanted the betrothal. Foolish child, did she not realise her father would find her some other husband? If he came home in one piece from England.

Lifting her Bible to her lips, she kissed the page that was open before her. "Sweet Lord," she prayed silently, "send me some sign that this venture of my husband's is just. That he will not come to harm!"

There had been the star, of course, the tailed star that had burnt with such brightness for over a week in the evening heavens. It was an omen of good fortune, they said. But for whom? For Harold or William?

Mathilda glanced across again at Cecily her daughter. The child was sitting with a rapt expression on her face, marvelling at the beauty of the sunlight filtering through the small panes of glass and dancing across the marble floor. She was happy. The serenity of the abbey had touched the child's spirit and bound her to the perfection of life within a community of nuns. For an instant Mathilda envied the girl, as she knew Agatha did also. Wished she, too, could remain safe and protected here within the secure walls of la Trinité.

⁂

The heat of the sweltering afternoon hit them as they left the abbey by the western door, their chatter and laughter as bright as the colours of their garments. All had come to Caen and this dedication service showing off their finest dress and most expensive jewels. William himself wore purple and his ducal crown; Mathilda, a summer green and her circlet of entwined gold and silver. She and William walked at the head of the procession winding down through the town back to the castle. The people of Caen lined the route, cheering and shouting, waving pennants and flags, calling blessings on their proud and brave duke and his serene, beautiful duchess.

They had barely reached the lower slope of the hill when a man, grimed and dishevelled, sprang out from the crowd to drop to his knees at William's feet. The guards lunged forward and pulled him roughly aside; but the man cried out, begging for his duke to hear him.

"My Lord! I am come from England! I must speak with you!"

William's head shot up as if he had been hit by a physical blow. He dropped Mathilda's hand, thrust his guards aside and squatted before the man, hands gripping his shoulders. "Where in England? What is it you must tell me?"

Duke William's heart was thundering, his mouth had run dry. News of Harold? Had something happened?

"I come from the estate of Steyning in Sussex. It is land held by the Norman abbey of Fécamp. I was steward there until several days since. I was a good and loyal steward, my Lord Duke, they had no right to treat us as they did, to turn us out with no food for our bellies, no cloak for our backs!"

"Who, man? What is it!"

"Harold's men. The fyrd, his housecarls. Vicious, blood-crazed thugs, they are. They have occupied the estate of Steyning, for it is on the southern coast, overlooking the sea. Taken it for their king, they said!" The man spat to one side in disgust. "They were heavily armed, preparing for war. They beat us, then threw us out, every one of us who insisted on remaining loyal to you and our masters of Fécamp."

Abbot Remigius from Fécamp itself strode forward from the processional line, his face grim, his anger great. "I recognise this man, my Lord Duke, he is indeed who he says, A most trusted servant—how dare this oath-breaking tyrant steal land that is entrusted to my keeping!"

William regained his feet and held out his hand to the man kneeling on the roadway, helping him up to his feet. "You have no need to fear, my good friend, you are now in the company of men who keep their word and their vows." He turned to Abbot Remigius. "You will have that estate of Steyning returned to your abbey." He stumbled over the unfamiliar English place name. "If God sees it fitting that I win the victory over Harold of England, then it will be so. You have my pledge."

Mathilda briefly lifted her eyes to heaven and sent up a prayer of thanks. Was this the sign that she had sought, a message sent from God through His servant on earth? Fécamp Abbey, he was saying, would have its stolen land returned through the courage and strength of her beloved husband. She was satisfied, would not doubt William's resolve again.

9

Isle of Wight

On the last day of August, the rain stopped and the wind-squalled clouds parted into flowing mares' tails, the sun valiantly attempting to warm the wet and dripping world below. All was new-washed and laid out to dry, gently steaming in the unexpected heat.

The gales of the past few weeks had largely abated, but up here on the headland seemed as demon-strong as ever. With his cloak streaming out like a banner, the weight of its billowing straining at the brooch at his right shoulder, Harold walked to the top of the rise, his collar-length fair hair writhing into a knotted tangle the instant he stepped up by the cliff edge. This was the highest point of the island, where the wind buffeted straight in off the sea, seven hundred, almost sheer, feet below. Shielding his eyes, Harold could discern three ships ploughing through the wave crash of the tide, their earth-red sails tightly reefed, the oar thresh of the sea foam frothing to either side of their sleek keels. Headway was slow, for although the tide was carrying them, they were beating against the wind. Harold could almost feel his own muscles pull and strain with the rowers.' He had taken his turn at the oars as a young man, knew the pain of calloused palms and aching back, the pull of the grabbing current on the blade, the buck of the ship as she plunged against a heavy swell. In his mind, he heard the steersman's call as he shouted the beat that kept the oar time: "Lift her! Lift her!" He closed his eyes, smelt the sharp, saline tang of the sea, felt the rasp of the wind and the stinging kiss of spindrift on his lips and cheeks. The rise and dip of the waves…

The August weather had seemed more fitting for autumn chill or winter misery. The harvest would be poor again this year: what had escaped the lashing rain had been flattened by the high winds. Trees were down; roof, barn and house place were wrecked as if a rampaging giant had trampled a swathe across the landscape. The sea had been no less disturbed, a-churn with spume, and sea trade had fallen slack; few except the most experienced—or foolhardy—had dared to risk setting sail to cross devil-whipped open seas. Land and sea folk alike had begun to wonder whether the summer would ever appear. But for Harold and the safety of England, the squalid weather had come as a blessing.

In mid-June, Tostig's invasion plans had been blown into disarray. He had attempted to make landfall on the northern shore of the Humber estuary; Eadwine and Morkere had seen him off, sending him running, yelping, with his tail tucked tight atween his legs. The westerly gales had finished the job, scattering his ships, snapping masts and oars as if they were dead twigs. Those mercenary sailors from the south coast, who had been offered the adventure of a fight for a handful of gold, deserted him with as much eagerness as they had joined.

The threat from Normandy, too, was eased, for no grand fleet of ships could voyage in convoy across the Channel Sea and hope to remain together—but Harold was not complacent. Word had come with those few traders who braved the crossing that Duke William's shipbuilding was almost completed and that the muster to arms, whatever the weather conditions, had been set for the second week in August. It was now the end of that month and, although the damp permeated through woollen cloak, reed roof thatch and strained temper alike, the winds were no longer gusting. All it needed was a shift from west to south and the Duke would be here.

There was no doubting that he would be coming, for William had made an inescapable commitment to this thing: gold promised to the mercenaries of Flanders and Brittany; an escalating sea current of debt, bolstered by his own bravado. He was too far in, now; to turn tail would mean the loss of his own duchy. No man would follow William again if this attempt at England failed.

From Harold's perspective, this aggressive lust for warfare at all cost was a failing of William's character. He was not a man to sheathe a drawn sword or swallow his pride; apology was not a word contained in his Norman vocabulary. Fight, not talk, was his way. An effective English king would aim, ultimately, to use as little force as possible, trusting peaceful solution over military might. The threat of the muster of the fyrd was often enough to entertain a settlement. In England, pitched battle was avoided unless of absolute defensive necessity.

But oh aye, Harold knew William would come—what he did not know, could only guess at, was the when of it.

One of those three ships was the *Dolphin*, Eadric the Steersman's craft. She was the goddess of longships, the Cleopatra, Helen of Troy, of craft. Eadric was in command of the scyp fyrd, the sea warriors, for he was the most capable of Harold's men. If William were to put to sea and attempt to run the coastal blockade, Eadric and his sea hounds could be relied upon to fight as only those who had not forgotten their Viking blood could fight.

Did the Duke, Harold wondered, as he stood on the high headland watching those three craft, realise what awaited him on this northern side of the Narrow Sea? The Normans had become a land army, used to besieging stone-built fortresses or fighting in ground-force formation on foot or horseback. They relied on their machinery of war—the mangonels, ballistas, siege towers and crossbows—and on their heavy coats of mail to ward off a sword blow. Mail kept the body safe, but it also restricted movement where instant agility and speed were an advantage. At sea, for instance. The ships Duke William had requisitioned were merchantmen, deep-wallowing sailing craft without the oar space—or trained oarsmen—to manoeuvre them swiftly. When William came, unless he understood how to run the gauntlet of the waiting scyp fyrd, few of his followers would make landfall.

Harold breathed in a lungful of sea air. The question in his mind: had William made plans to avoid the English blockade? Had he set aside his own self-importance and heeded the advice of those experienced in the ways of the sea?

Beside the King, his brother Leofwine squatted on his haunches, also looking towards the three gallant ships. There were others out there, of course, beyond eye vision, oar-riding the waves or, where the waters were not so deep, at anchor. A shield wall of ships, each in view or hailing distance of the other, lined from here on the Island of Wight to the seven cliffs of Dover. And beyond them, the outrunners, the swiftest and lightest of craft that could be pulled by the oar into any wind, against any sea. It was towards these ships that Eadric was steering, to hear of latest news, of sighting and of feelings that itched below an experienced sailor's skin.

Waiting, all of them, English and Norman, waiting for the wind to back.

Leofwine had unsheathed his sword and laid it across his knees, his fingertips resting, with the lightest of touches, against its bright, deadly gleam. "Raven's Wing," he called it, for the dark streaks of interlocking patterning within the blade, formed beneath the hammer in its making. Up near the pommel there was a shape that resembled the outstretched wing of the raven, the bird of the battlefield. A fitting pattern, and a fitting name for the weapon given him as a present by his eldest brother when he had become earl.

"I am thinking," he said into the wind, "that Eadric may have a good fight some day soon."

"I am thinking you may have the right of it. Soon now, surely, the war horns will boom and the sea riders will set their oars to the ocean, their daggers loose at their belts."

"It may be a fight that we will regret not being a part of," Leofwine answered with a wistful sigh.

Harold laughed. "You will have fighting enough, have no worry of that. Eadric and those men, for all their ability, will not stop every ship of Duke William's. Some will land along our coast. We will have our fight against them then."

One of the few housecarls who had ridden with Harold to this high and lonely point saw riders approaching at a fast gallop. He called out in warning to his King. Alerted, Harold studied the four swift-coming horsemen. "It seems someone else is anxious to join the fight—or has brought us news of one, perhaps," he said. "Come, Leofwine, let us see who so urgently seeks me."

"God sail with you, Eadric," Leofwine murmured as he pushed himself upright and strode back down the hillside in the wake of his brother.

Leofwine was as surprised as Harold to recognise one of the riders as their own brother Gyrth, and with him, their nephew Hakon.

"Well met, Gyrth! Hakon! What brings you here?" Harold greeted them as the young men reined in their sweating horses.

"You bring me, my Lord—and our other brother!" Gyrth held out his hand, Harold clasping it, palm to palm, in greeting. "I have been a-visiting our mother at Bosham Manor—she is well and sends her love." Gyrth explained. "I heard that you were here, keeping watch for our Norman friend. I thought I would see if you had heard tell of the latest news of Tostig? Our nephew decided to ride with me."

Hakon spat. "That bastard of Normandy is no friend of mine. I would be here when he comes, to run my sword personally through his black heart."

"Aye, we know you like not Duke William." Leowfine laughed. "But your opinion of him is somewhat personally biased. We"—he gestured to himself and Gyrth—"have never had an opportunity to meet the man and judge his nature for ourselves."

Hakon snorted displeasure; Leofwine laughed the louder. "I am jesting, lad, I'm sure your assessment of the man is accurate."

Ignoring the byplay, Harold was frowning, his eyes creasing into narrowed slits at the mention of his brother Tostig's name. He guided Gyrth some few steps from earshot of the men, beckoning Leofwine and Hakon to walk with them. With hardness in his voice, he said, "I would that I could say I never cared to hear of Tostig again, yet I must, for I need to know what the cur is plotting."

Gyrth scratched at the fair beard new growing around his chin. "It is not news you will like to hear. But first you must hear something from my own lips, lest someone else tells you and makes a fat goose out of a sparrow's breast."

This sounded ominous. Harold stopped walking, waiting for his brother to speak.

"During the early summer months," Gyrth said, "Tostig asked that I join his fleet, take up arms against you—but this you know, for I sent word to you immediately that I had refused him."

Harold nodded. This he knew.

"I received further word, not a few days since while at Bosham with our mother. A letter, begging me again to join him, written in Tostig's own hand." Gyrth lowered his head. "I had no choice but to hang the messenger who brought me it. I could not risk you thinking that I was not loyal to you. Tostig may be my brother, as are you, but you are also my King. And that makes a difference in this thing."

Setting his hand to Gyrth's shoulder, Harold indicated his grateful understanding. This was no easy thing for Gyrth, no easy thing for any man of honour and conscience. "I am grateful to you, Gyrth, as king, aye, but more as your brother."

"Tostig and I always ran together as litter mates. You and Leofwine"—Gyrth glanced at his other brother—"are joined in spirit, as Tostig and I once were. It saddens my heart that my favourite brother has turned against you so foolishly. I had hoped that, once you were anointed king, a negotiation could be made atween you."

"As had I." Harold agreed. "I had no intention of making war on my own kindred." He snorted a brief guffaw. "I have enough outside of my blood to occupy me in that!"

Gyrth smiled appreciatively. "You sent embassies and messengers, even a letter in your own hand, but Tostig neither heard nor read any of them. Our mother's letters could instil no sense into him, nor could any word from our sister."

To that, Harold made no reply. Edith had made no attempt to avert this quarrel between her brothers. Although he had no proof, it seemed likely that her communications had, in fact, urged the opposite.

What price and value a crown? Harold thought. Gyrth would have been aware of Edith's letters, probably of the contents, but no sense rubbing a nose in the dung.

"There is more," Hakon added gruffly. "Tell him everything that was set down in the letter, Uncle." He nudged Gyrth none too gently with his elbow.

Again Harold waited, resisting the sudden urge to put his hand to his sword pommel. He was not going to like this.

"After the mess he made of landing along the Humber our brother went north to seek Malcolm of Scotland's aid, which was promised—not that his promise is worth the shit it is written in. Then Tostig sailed to the islands of Orkney. Islands that are under the protection of Harald Hardrada of Norway. It seems…" Gyrth swallowed; he lowered his head, his eyes, finding a need to stare at his boots, the grass, anywhere but at Harold. Then he continued quickly, spitting the sour-tasting words from his mouth. "My King, he confirms in his own words, that he has agreed to fight against you with the Hardrada under the banner of Norway. It is to that alliance he urged me to join with him." Falling silent, Gyrth opened a leather pouch at his waist, pulled from it a crumpled piece of parchment. Handed it to Harold.

The King took Tostig's letter, unfolded it slowly and read, taking in every word. When he had finished, he tore it in half and scrunched the pieces into a ball. He looked out to the sun-sparkle on the sea; clouds were louring in again from the west. The warmth of the sun, then, had been for a short visit only.

Hardrada, King of Norway, who had also decided to take the opportunity to expand his territory. In the vein of Cnut before him and the aspirations of Magnus, his predecessor, Hardrada had decided to try for an additional crown.

So, Harold thought, *from the south I am to face William of Normandy, and from the north-east, my own brother, united in war with the Hardrada.* He clenched his fingers around the damning parchment, brusquely jerked back his arm and hurled the thing from him with a wordless cry of pain. "God grant me blessing," he shouted aloud to the wind-driven sea, "that I shall not need to fight both the devil-spawn scum of brother and duke at once!"

10

The Channel Sea

When the wind shifted further to the south, they knew things might, at last, begin to happen. There was a new uprush of expectation among the Englishmen of the scyp fyrd. Daggers were eased loose; hands gripped tighter on the oars of the warships, the sturdy thirty-two- and forty-oared Dragon Craft, and all eyes were keening southwards. Towards Normandy.

Across the Channel Sea, Duke William would be waiting and watching, cursing the poor sea conditions. The English spies had worked well, had a very good idea how many ships he had mustered, how many—how few—would be under oar. Showing that he was no sea warrior. The majority of William's fleet relied on sail, requiring a fair-set southern wind to accompany them across the ninety-odd miles between Dives and…and where? That, the English spies could not discover, only conjecture, and that too, might depend on the fickleness of the wind. William, once he set sail, could beach anywhere along the southern or eastern coast.

Eadric the Steersman stood, eyes squinting into the brightness, balancing with the lift and fall of *Dolphin*'s foredeck, his head up, nostrils scenting the sea wind as if he were a wolf seeking prey. They were all one of the pack, these English ships, waiting to be loosed for the hunt. All they needed was a sight of that prey to start the run. The King was relying heavily on his fleet commander's instinct and great knowledge. The movements of tide and wind were family to Eadric, being mother, daughter, wife and mistress. He knew all its moods, its tempers, cunning and subtleties. His senses told him now that William's fleet was coming. He could not see sail or wave thresh, but they were there, heading north. Had anyone asked, he would have answered that he could smell them. As an animal would smell an approaching storm. His bones felt them. Or at least, if William had not ordered his men to sea, then he was a fool, for this was ideal weather. If it held.

Eadric bit his lower lip, deep in thought, turning his mind from the south. There was no cloud, no breeze, but would this wind hold? Or would she, capricious as she had been all summer long, swing back to her previous hunting run across the Great Sea to the west? If Eadric could not decide the mood of the wind, then neither, he doubted, would William's sailors. Had the Duke committed himself to action, or was he dithering? Was the pricking of Eadric's skin, the tingling behind his neck, playing him for the fool instead? Happen they had all been on edge too long during this frustrating summer.

The Norman army was growing restless, this much England knew as fact; supplies were diminishing, the eagerness for adventure dwindling into exasperation. Waiting for the wind was a desperate occupation. Hah! He ought to have used oar, not sail. With oar the Duke would already be here—but then with oar, he would have needed to find the men to row them, or the time to teach such men the skill. That was a thing the King, Harold, had also discovered of William's nature. He was not a man to bide his time, to be patient, to wait and wait again until the thing clicked, right, into place.

A voice, distant but clear, sounded from the steerboard side; Eadric swung his head round, questioning, then raised his hand in acknowledgement to Bjarni Redbeard from the *Sea Star*, a craft that matched the length and speed of the *Dolphin*. Eadric cupped his hands around his mouth and shouted back, "Nay! I see nothing—but they are there, mark you. I know they are there!"

"Aye, we all feel it! He would be a fool, I am thinking, to pass by this opportunity—" Bjarni was about to say more, but his shout was abruptly silenced, for the horn sounded, distant, from the south, from where *Wave Dancer* was patrolling. All the men lifted their heads, alert, breath held, listening. Again, the long, mournful cry of the war horn…and a third time. Eadric himself was the first to break the enchantment. He leapt, in four strides, from stern to mast, took up *Dolphin*'s own horn—the long and curving aurochs' horn—and blew three blasts in response, the sound scudding over the creaming waves, caught by the wind and lifted to the high clouds. In that instant, the men, too, had come alive, racing for the rowing benches, hands tight-gripping the oars, heads turned, expectant, to Eadric their master for his signal. For a long moment he stood there amidships, fists bunched against his hips, legs spread, feeling the eager roll of his tight-held ship, the salt taste of the sea stinging his lips, the song of the wind springing past his ears.

His eyes snatched to a white wake that folded around the keel—and another, and another, a silver glistening back, afin…he tossed his head and laughed. "Look, my brothers!" he crowed. "We have our friends to accompany us as we go to meet this bastard Duke of Normandy! Look! The dolphins have come to run with their sister!"

A shout of exultation was tossed to the height of the mast, the strain was taken up by arm muscles and Eadric shouted the command they so eagerly awaited: "Lift her! Lift her!"

Dolphin and *Sea Star*. From the west, the answering boom and boom of the war horns from *Moon-Crest* and *Sun Singer*. From the east, *Cloud Chaser* and *Gull*. The wolf pack was loose, and running fast on the trail of its prey.

Like most of them crammed tight into the ships, Duke William was no sailor, but at least the strong wine he had swallowed before embarkation was keeping his belly where it ought be—unlike many of them who were hanging over the sides, spewing up their guts. How the horses were faring he could only guess, but at least the sea had calmed its heaving once they had cleared the leeward coast of Cap d'Antifer. That had been one of the most terrifying ordeals of his entire life—and he had seen plenty. The wind was not blowing from as far south as they would have liked, but the decision to risk embarkation had to be made. They had already waited over long and the opportunity, so William had been advised by his seafarers, might not come again.

"What are our chances?" the Duke had asked them as they gathered together in a solemn group outside his command tent. Some, not willing to commit themselves, had scratched at neck and cheek, fiddled with ear lobes. Others had slowly shaken their heads, but most had agreed that the wind was unlikely to prove kinder this side of autumn. Clearing that lee shore was the dilemma. If only the wind would back a little more. Dives, the majority confirmed, was not the most favourable place from which to launch a sailing fleet. This prevailing wind was too westward, the lee shore too hazardous, with not enough experienced oarsmen to row them off, should need arise. Further along the coast would have been better—Eu, perhaps? Closer, too, to England.

This particular argument had swung, blade about hilt, throughout the year, but William had been adamant. His muster point was Dives. Closer to Caen. Mile upon mile of sand suitable for the initial building of ships and the encampment of men. Beyond, sufficient grazing for horses. Add to that, an ideal embarkation point. Higher up the coast would mean a shorter, quicker voyage, but what was nearer for William was nearer for Harold too. His English fleet was more capable at sea, his spies were efficient. Dives was more protected because of its distance. When Harold learnt of Norman manoeuvring, the invasion fleet would be almost upon him.

The captains had been right about that lee shore, however.

William stood at the prow of his command ship, the *Mora*, his nails digging into the wood of the curving rail. He closed his eyes, saw again the spew of wave foam against rock and cliff, heard in his ears the rush of the sea as it beat against that coast, too close to the steerboard side of the fleet. The ships' masters had known what they were doing and the wind had held. All but three ships of the convoy had slipped past the danger zone and headed out into the open sea.

∽

They were almost halfway across, so the *Mora*'s commander had said. So far all had gone to plan, even allowing for those few difficult horses who had been abandoned at Dives or had their throats cut, their carcasses heaved overboard. The mood of the men was buoyant and eager after these weeks within the confines of the camp. A few more weeks and William would not have been certain of holding their loyalty. Loading the supplies had taken much of their attention, but once that had been completed there was nothing to do save wait...no matter, now, they were under way, the thresh of spindrift frothing the water into a white churn of spray, curving beneath the bows of more than seven hundred ships.

William gazed with pride at the array: large, sturdy traders' craft, smaller fishing boats, a handful of warships, all held in tight check so as not to outrun the slower vessels. So many of them! Patterned sails, plain, striped, patched; red and blue, white, green, brown and saffron. Some men in the next ship saw the Duke watching them, raised their arms in salute and cheered his presence. Content, he waved back.

His own was superb, a Flemish warship given as a present from his wife, built and paid for from her own purse. He gazed up at the wide billow of her striped red and saffron square sail, the bronze crucifix at the masthead glinting in the late-afternoon sunlight. Come nightfall, a lantern would be raised, as there would on all the boats to enable them to keep together—at least until any damned English ships were sighted. To avoid them, he was relying on the skill of his own Norman warships, riding ahead. They must discover the waiting English, signal word so that lanterns could be covered, sails reefed, course altered...over seven hundred vessels to be brought through a blockade under the secrecy of darkness. They had assured him it could be done, his captains and sea commanders. If they kept their nerve and their wit, they had said.

The Duke raised his head, sniffed at the salt wind. The sun was dipping towards the western horizon. An hour until dusk. One more hour. Come dawn, they should be seeing the grey outline of England's southern coast...

∽

They heard the hollow boom of the war horns before they saw the indistinct shadow-shape of ships. The white of oar stroke and bow wave, the gleam of bronze and glint of gold reflecting the sinking sun from the carved, grinning heads of the curving prows. Dragons, wing-stretched ravens, sea monsters. At their head, a craft with a prow shaped as a leaping dolphin. The English scyp fyrd, the sea warriors.

Duke William watched in morbid fascination as they approached, racing through the creaming waves. So fast did they fly—even against the wind, but then, they were powered by thirty, forty, oars and were carried by the run of the tide. Eight knots or so could they speed across the open sea under the power of those oars, he had been told—by whom and when he could not remember. He could see the bank of oars to either side of the dolphin ship; could hear, now, the shouts echoing across the expanse of water between them, an expanse that was rapidly narrowing. Could hear, but not understand the meaning.

"What is it they shout?"

"It is the steersman, sir, calling the beat of the oar."

Unaware that he had spoken aloud, William stared at the man behind him who had spoken, a Fleming sailor. "And what ought we do about them?" William asked caustically.

The sailor shrugged, pointed vaguely at the sails of the Norman fleet. "We do as the others are already doing, my Lord. We turn about and run. Else we drop to our knees and pray."

The blood streamed to William's face, his breathing came in rasping gasps from his throat. "I run from nothing and no one!" The words burst from his mouth as he swung down from the foredeck, his strides taking him aft, to where his captain stood, issuing a burst of orders to the crew.

"We fight!" William bellowed. "Give the order on the horn—set ready the archers. We fight!"

"No, sir!" the *Mora*'s captain countermanded. "Your warships that were ahead must surely have already been destroyed. Your fleet is made of merchant vessels; when such encounter pirates, they run. It is not prudent to fight one of those dragon ships—and besides, our luck is turning against us twice over. See our sail, my Lord Duke? It is flapping. The wind has cast against us. She is veering to the west."

The Duke's proud and glorious fleet began to scatter in disarray. Each ship, careless now of keeping within the discipline of the convoy, broke free and fled before the westering wind. Better, the seamen all agreed, to run for Normandy than meet the fire arrows of the English, all except the Duke, who stood rigid at the stern of his ship, with no choice but to watch. As well the words that ran through his mind were not voiced, for his oaths would have shocked even sea-tainted sailors.

II

⤟⤞

Westminster

Alditha sat upon the window seat, lost in her own thoughts, watching the intricate shadow patterns of the late-afternoon sunshine dancing through the wind-tossed foliage of the orchard's fruit trees. A small orchard, only ten apple trees, but the grass beneath was lush and green, and the geese appreciated the freedom to graze there.

Harold had returned to London yesterday, his face grey, eyes dark bruised, body-weary from the long summer of worry. At least for this year, it seemed the danger was ended. Duke William had seen his invasion fleet scattered, had lost more than forty of his slower, clumsier transports to the fire arrows of the English scyp fyrd; lost men to the grappling irons and savage hand-to-hand fighting that had followed.

Eadric had accompanied the King to Westminster, the man's joy at victory self-evident, his story of the fighting listened to in awe by all within the King's Hall of Westminster, A tale, surely, to be told at the hearth side over and again on many a winter's night. Harold himself had swept his wife into an immediate embrace as he had dismounted, kissed her full on the mouth and led her, arm linked through arm, into the palace, among the crowding throng, all anxious to hear the true version of what had happened along the southern coast and upon the sea. To her surprise, he had been attentive to her throughout the evening, had sat by her side, occasionally taking her hand or sliding his arm around her waist. His look had been unmistakable. That of wanting. She had told herself that his consideration was for the child swelling within her belly—this would be her sixth month. He had never concealed his delight in children, and for her to produce an heir so early in this marriage must be pleasing to himself and his court. It was, most certainly, to her brothers.

Come the night, their first bedding together since the bloom of early summer, they had lain together, his lovemaking careful, mindful of her pregnancy. A blush slipped on to her face as she remembered the quiver-feel of his touch upon her.

Gruffydd would never have absented himself from a celebration to lie with his wife. He would have staggered to bed, drunk and incapable.

She half listened to the voices of the men: Harold, his two brothers, his nephew Hakon and the commanders of his housecarls, gathered around the high table. She must cease thinking of that damned man. Gruffydd was dead. Harold was her lord now. Harold, who cared for her, who had shown her how to enjoy the passion shared by a man and a woman. Gruffydd was gone—and, thank God, William too was gone, though she would not rest easy until his bones were also being picked by the worms. If Harold had not returned, if she had lost him so soon after she had found this wonderful feeling that was called love...

The fyrd, that mighty force of men who protected England, had been disbanded yesterday, sent home to gather what they could of a poor harvest. The King's brothers and his commanders would also be leaving soon. Everything was returning to normality, as if there had not been a summer-long run of fear, as if nothing from before Edward had died had altered, save that Harold was now king and she was queen. Queen of England, the Lady.

Alditha could barely comprehend the implications. Naturally shy, she found it startling to have all eyes upon her, men bowing, women curtseying, to have her every word noted and obeyed. Were she to order a peasant to jump, head first, into the midden pit, would he do her bidding? She was Queen. Emma had been admired and feared for her knowledge and authority, Edith rapidly becoming cherished for her long devotion to Edward. What was there for herself? She did not ask much; all she wanted was to be appreciated and loved.

She looked towards Harold. He sat at the table, listening to the flow of talk, not entering the conversation himself. He had slept ill, despite his weariness, his body twitching and restless. Several times he had spoken out in his sleep, most of his words unintelligible. A few clear and unmistakable.

Once, when she had stretched out her hand to soothe him, he had been hot and fevered, his face, even in sleep, haggard, with cheeks hollowed and eyes sunken. His jaw hung slack and she had noticed, as he had prepared for bed, that the fingers of his left hand were stiff and clumsy. His illness of long past, he had said, plaguing him whenever he felt excessive tiredness aching in his bones.

The need to be ever alert had played heavy on his mind, the weighty responsibility of ensuring England's coast, to south, east and north, had been adequately guarded. It was one thing to be a king, as had Edward, with nothing more than the level of taxation, the making of laws and passing of judgements to contemplate, another matter entirely to be a war lord. Edward had little more to worry on, once his decision of where and when to hunt had been made. Perhaps, Alditha thought, that was unfair, but Harold had not met his first few months of kingship with the same ease as had Edward. Facing imminent invasion from two quarters had taken its toll of his strength, both mental and physical. Discreetly watching him and the men sitting with him, Alditha privately defied any of them to match the courage that her husband had displayed these last months.

He ought to be elated, though, that William had been sent running, that Tostig, too, would probably not be seen again until next spring. But was it the strain alone that brought this deep, bone-aching weariness to his expression and body? Not his age, certainly, for he was only into his four and fortieth year, a young man by comparison with his father and Edward. Alditha watched him as he stared vacantly out of the windows to the north-east.

From where he sat he would be able to see little except the blue sky overhead, but was it the sky he was seeing, or was his mind elsewhere, at Waltham Abbey and the manor house that stood on the high land above the valley? Those words, during the night? They had been Edyth's name, called with longing.

There was much to be dealt with at court, things that had had to be set aside: an accumulation of petitions and charters, a bishop to be appointed, letters of greeting to be acknowledged, sent by kings and princes of foreign lands. The clerks and administrators had attended to what they could, but to some things only the King could put his signature and seal. There were others, however, that even for a king were difficult to deal with: two women in particular. One he loved with all his soul; the other he was growing, daily, more fond of.

Harold had been pleased to see Alditha waiting there to greet him, yesterday, in the courtyard. How loving had been her smile of welcome, her delight at having him home. She was pretty and sweet-natured, was undemanding and so innocent. He regretted the marriage, not because of her, but because of his own knot-tied feelings. How could he hurt her, bring her sorrow? But in God's good name, how could he stop loving his Edyth? He sat at the table, the voices of his companions rising and falling in an indistinct *sshh* of sound, like the swell of the sea heard when a shell was put against the ear. He was not listening to a single word. All morning had he been busy—but at least the duties of government had kept his mind from wandering to this other thing. Was it because he was tired and dispirited that this heavy cloak of blackness was clamped so tightly down on his shoulders?

He had tried, yesterday, to offer Alditha the respect that she deserved. And he had been pleased to see her, had enjoyed their lovemaking—she had learnt well and quickly during those brief weeks when they had been first together. That

Welsh prince had been a fool, had missed the chance of having a good, loving and loyal woman bound close to his side. Was he, too, then, behaving the fool?

He stared out of the window at the scudding clouds. His head ached; his arm felt stiff. A flock of starlings wheeled into view, swirling and screeching. He wanted to offer her his love, his attention. Was eager for this child to be born—but wanted it to be girl born, did not want another son, for it should be Goddwin to come after him, or Magnus or Edmund or Ulf. It should be Edyth sitting over there by the window…he groaned inwardly, a sound in his head, his heart. He would not let it reach his throat, would not, could not let Alditha become aware of the aching that throbbed inside for the need to see, to touch, to be with his Edyth.

❧

Two hours before dawn, Alditha woke, startled and disorientated. She had been dreaming of war. Of dragon ships and bright-bladed axes. She turned to Harold, expecting to curl up beside the firm security of his body, but found that he was hot with fever. Trembling for fear that he was mortally ill, she struck a flint and lit the bedside lamp, set her palm to his damp forehead. He was drowsy, but awake, his fevered eyes glazed in the dim light.

"What can I do to help?" she said, leaving the bed to rinse a linen towel in the hand basin of water, running back to lay it over his hot, sweat-damp skin. "I must send for your physician!"

He caught her hand. "No! I beg you, word must not reach the ears of others that I am ill. I know not how many spies there are at court. Enough, I would guess, to pounce as quick as a hunting cat on a cornered mouse."

"But you are ill! I cannot let you suffer like this, I must fetch someone, must do something!"

Attempting to sit, but realising he had only the strength of a new-born child, Harold managed a lop-sided smile, intending to comfort her anxiety. "Leave me to rest. 'Tis only tiredness. Edyth knew that sleep was the best for me."

Biting back an un-Christian word, Alditha wiped at frustrated tears that were threatening. Edyth? Damn, bloody Edyth! She would have noticed Harold's illness before this, would not have allowed him to stay up so late talking with his brothers' friends, would have brewed him herbs and tinctures. Oh, all the gods curse this wretched situation! Why in hell's name had she met Harold that day beside the Severn river, when she was still but a girl? Why had her heart, from then, always lurched with a thrill of excitement whenever someone had mentioned his name? And then he had come into Wales and liberated her from that bastard tyrant she had been forced to call husband and lord, had taken her into

England, where so often, after, she had seen him, watched him, A girl's fancy she had thought. But it had proven more than that. When he had come to York as king, had taken her in marriage? She had not realised that such happiness existed.

She again wrung cold water into the linen, laid it across his forehead. What in Thor's fury was she to do? Edyth would know. Alditha squeezed her eyes tight shut, took several deep, calming breaths. Aye, Edyth would know, but Edyth was not here and was no longer his common wife.

Quickly, before she changed her mind, she said, "I shall summon a litter and you shall be taken to Waltham. Edyth Swannhæls will know how to care for you. We shall say that you are journeying to your abbey to give thanks to God."

Harold stared at her, trying to read her thoughts. Had she really said that? Did she think so much of him that she was willing to send him to Edyth? It was going to be hard, the future, but he had to outface the difficulties. He could not, must not, allow himself to hurt this lass.

"I promised I would not see her again, now that I am wed to you." He attempted a laugh, the sound slurred by his stiffening jaw. "Despite the propaganda Normandy has attempted to spread about me, I am no oath breaker."

Putting a fingertip to his lips to silence him, Alditha answered him forthrightly. "I am your queen and wife, but Edyth remains your love. I have ever known that as the daughter of Ælfgar I would only be used as a means of securing an alliance. It was why I was married to Gruffydd. Why I am married to you. I at least know you are fond of me, and you offer me kindness and respect. Which is more than *he* ever did." She took a shuddering breath, ploughed on. "I cannot, and do not, expect more from you. All I ask is that you do me no public dishonour, that whenever you go to Edyth, it will be with discretion."

With an effort—he was so damned tired—Harold patted the bed covers, gesturing for her to sit. He eased his arm around her, brought her body against his own. "That asking I will honour. I cannot deny that I shall always love Edyth, but I am growing to love you." He brushed his fingertips against her cheek. "Let me sleep. Don't wake me for a week and I shall be fine." His smile was lopsided, his eyes drooping. At that moment, the weariness was so intense that he hardly cared if he never woke.

He closed his eyes. Ah, by the God of mercy, this situation with these two women was not what he had wanted. The old king, Cnut, had had it the better, for he had ruled over two kingdoms separated by the entire North Sea, so could easily separate his first common-taken wife from the second legal one. One had been settled across the sea, the other, Emma, in England. A wise and fortunate man, Cnut.

What if he were to attempt something similar? Eadwine and Morkere would welcome a tangible reminder that they were connected by blood and kinship to the crown—would most assuredly welcome a child born of their sister and the King within either of their earldoms. What if Alditha were to reside at York, for instance, rule the North in his name? He would be free to visit Edyth whenever he was in the South—autumn and winter, say—and reside at York for spring and summer. That way, too, he would have more control over the uncertainties of the North—and would reinforce his intention that Tostig was not, under any circumstances, going to have it given back. It was an idea worth pursuing—but after he had slept. He would think on it. Later.

12

⚜

Waltham Abbey

Edyth Swannhæls sat within the September shadows of her husband's abbey at Waltham. She was alone. Here at Waltham you could hear the silence of heaven if you discounted the noise of voices, rumbling carts and the braying and lowing of ass or ox filtering in from beyond the abbey wall. Earthly sounds, balancing this holy place.

She gazed at the altar cloth, the fine silver psalter and candlesticks, the golden crucifix; then across to the carved, walrus-ivory reliquary caskets. All Harold's generous donations. He had, by their giving, been assured of a place by God's side, the Abbot had told him. Edyth smiled at the memory of Harold's answer, that if eternal salvation was so easily bought, then heaven must be filled by arrogant and pompous aristocrats and rich merchantmen. Many of whom he despised intensely.

The Church was so happy to receive expensive gifts. What, she wondered, had happened to the principle of poverty and humility? It was most certainly not a requisite for those who resided in Rome. Surely it could not be right that a wealthy man could do wrong but still be blessed, while a man of humble means, but with a clear conscience, had no chance of seeing heaven? Rome. She regretted thinking of Rome. The Pope, Alexander, was saying that a man ought only to have one, Christian-taken wife and that a husband must remain faithful to that one woman alone. She tilted her head, staring up at the vaulted beams spanning the high roof. The ideals of Rome were all very well, but England had always gone her own way—Rome was too far distant in mileage and awareness to control how things were done in England.

Rome. Duke William had sent his eloquent liegeman Lanfranc to Rome to plead the case for his domination of England. She counted the Norman exaggerations on her fingers. One, pleading holy crusade to mask ambitious greed; two, declaring that her Harold had broken a sworn oath; and three, that Stigand of Canterbury, who had crowned Harold, was guilty of simony, having received his archbishop's pallium from the hands of a now disgraced Pope, making the coronation invalid. All inaccurate. The oath Harold had over and again declared not binding, because it had been exacted from him by intimidation. Stigand had been blessed by a pope who, although later replaced, had at the time been considered as holy as this present wealth collector, Alexander, who had not thought it behoved him to discredit or remove Stigand before now—and besides, it had been Ealdred who had crowned Harold, not Stigand. Politics of convenience. Half-truths and manipulations.

Harold ought to send a representative to Rome to rebut the false charges made by Normandy. Not that Alexander would listen. Not unless the messenger was accompanied by a chest of gold, double in weight to the one Lanfranc had, no doubt, taken with him. Nor would she have a chance to suggest it to the King.

The King. Her feelings for Harold were so confused. Sad that they would no longer share their lives together. Fearful that she would endure old age alone. Envious of Alditha. Resentful. Proud, so very, fiercely, proud that he had been acclaimed as the most throneworthy of all men in England. Incongruously, she found it interesting that there could be so many emotions all tumbling at once within her head.

The door at the western transept opened, creaking on its hinges. Footsteps: a man's. She turned to see who had entered. Her son, Goddwin, was walking down the central aisle. He was so much like his father. Even down to the slight roll in his gait. His expression was serious as he genuflected to the altar, then sat beside her.

"A messenger from Westminster has come to the manor. My brothers sent word to find you."

Edyth's mouth ran suddenly dry, her body froze. What was wrong? Oh, God's good grace, what had happened? "What, what is it?" she stammered.

Goddwin did not answer at once. He stared, as his mother had, at the altar... "My father's brother, Tostig, and the Hardrada from Norway have together entered the Humber; were, when urgent word was sent south from Earl Eadwine, running with the tide up the Ouse river."

Tostig. Determined to take back Northumbria.

"So," she breathed, her initial panic that something else had happened, something terrible, fading. Yet once the reaction had eased she realised the implications. This news was, perhaps, worse than Harold falling ill or having an accident. It is war, then," she said. "Your father will be going north to meet him." She crossed herself, a prayer for his safety darting through her mind.

Were she a man she would be running for her horse, making ready to go with him. She looked at her son, at the way he sat beside her, so quiet, his hands resting in his lap, head erect, staring in front of him.

He cleared his throat. "I..." He released his breath in a rush of uncertainty. "I have decided that I shall be riding with him." He spoke quickly, stopping his mother saying anything, objecting, attempting to make him change his mind. "I have been a fool these past years, nurturing childish passions of envy and jealousy. There is no room for such stupidity within a family." He turned his head to regard Edyth, who had made no attempt to speak. "Tostig has shown me that. I will not allow my father to go to war against his own kindred without the support of his son."

She slid her hand over his, squeezed it, once. "You will be taking Edmund with you?" How could she say that so calmly, she wondered?

Goddwin nodded. His eldest brother had been insistent upon it. "And Magnus," he admitted. "We shall all three go north." At Edyth's stifled gasp he added, "Magnus is but fifteen. He will not fight, but I cannot stop him from riding with us."

Tightening her grip on his hand, Edyth fought down the rise of nausea that was cloying her throat and the scream that was there with it. No, that he could not, no more than could she.

13

Westminster

Alditha could understand none of it. "He is your brother."

"Your father went against your grandfather—'tis not much different."

"But that was a family quarrel. My father rode into Wales in a temper because he could not get his own way. A temper that soon cooled once he realised his action was leading him nowhere except along a stonier path."

Holding hard to his patience, for there was much to do, Harold glanced up from the map he was studying and looked at his wife. Her eyes seemed bigger, her mouth wider, for despite carrying the child she had lost weight. Worry and stress. These months had not been easy for her. Harold snorted to himself: these years. She had been trundled from pillar to post, never treated with the devotion that she deserved.

When he came back, when all this was sorted out, he would have the time to put that right. He would indeed send her to rule the North—a double chance to prove to Morkere and his brother, to the northern land-folk, that he was determined to fight his own brother in order to keep the peace and the laws of his kingdom. That a king's sworn word would not be broken.

"This, too, my love, is a family quarrel, one that has spread wider than the boundaries of normal sense. Jealousy is a dangerous weapon if allowed to grow out of proportion."

Crossing the bed-chamber—Harold was in her room, for it seemed the only place where he could find the blessed sanctuary of peace this busy day—she gazed at the map spread over her small dressing table. He had cleared it of the pots and phials, the brushes and combs, the precious silvered mirror. They all lay in a discarded heap atop the bed covers.

"This is your intended route? The North Road, direct to York?" she asked, tracing the inked line of the road with her fingernail. It did not seem so long, two hundred or so miles, drawn thus on a parchment map. When she had travelled south from York as Harold's new wife, it had taken the royal entourage almost four weeks to reach London. Admittedly, their progress had been slowed by the crowds that had come to greet them, and they had rested for several days at Nottingham and Leicester. Nor had that been the more direct route, but even so, an army marching could take all of two weeks to reach York.

Reading the thoughts by the expression crinkling over her face, Harold explained, "We shall all be mounted. I take no infantry." He pointed from London to York. "I hope to traverse the distance in seven or eight days at the most."

Her eyes widened. Could that be done? She opened her mouth to ask it, remembered Harold's swift attack on Wales after her father had died and closed it again. Observed instead, "Tostig will not be expecting that." As Gruffydd had not expected it.

He leant forward and brushed his lips briefly against hers. "No, he will not." He paused, studied the map again, before adding, "The messengers have given me an estimate of almost three hundred ships." He resolutely turned his thoughts from the niggling horror that he might have to order his own brother hanged if he was not killed in battle. Too much to hope that he would see sense and turn aside from this venture. "We may face several thousand men. Hardrada will undoubtedly leave a rearguard for the fleet." Harold wondered whether Alditha was interested in the details—Edyth would have been—and to his pleasure found that aye, she was.

"My brothers have raised a defence, I assume?" she asked. "Have called out the fyrds of Northumbria and Mercia?"

"That they have. Let us pray to God that they have already sent these seascum running back to their ships, as they did at their first attempt."

He lifted the map and rolled it. This day was the eighteenth of September. They were to leave London at dawn on the morrow. He was impatient to be mounted and going. If only they knew what was happening up there, how things were going—had gone.

It would be much easier to learn that Tostig had already surrendered? Or been killed. Ducking the responsibility and shuffling around the consequences, aye, but so much damned easier!

∽◈∾

They left London, under the protection of Earl Leofwine and the boy Edgar, in the early hours of the morning. Others joined the King's housecarls, the warrior elite, as they rode north. The experienced and the battle-scarred; the young with their swords new-oiled, spears new-shafted. Earl Gyrth came from East Anglia with his fyrd; Evesham Abbey and the Abbot Ælfwine of Ramsey readily sent the fighting men of their estates. Godric, thegn of Pagelsham in Essex, added forty of his best men to the column of horsemen...and Harold's own three sons, Goddwin, Edmund and Magnus. Harold had openly admonished young Magnus's determination, but had then ruffled the lad's unruly fair hair and sent him to ride with the baggage boys. "Mind you earn your keep, lad," he had ordered sternly. "No one comes along for the joy of the ride. You can groom my horses and clean the mud from my boots."

Magnus had grinned back at him. "Most willingly, Sir!"

"And for me? What do you wish for me to do, Father?"

It had been the first evening, camp had been set—a makeshift one; they stopped only for a few hours to give the horses a chance to graze and doze. There would be little sleep for the men. There had been no opportunity to talk before then, for the pace Harold set was a steady jogtrot and, as they rode, messengers had been continually clustered around the King, coming and going at a gallop.

Goddwin asked his question, staring direct at Harold across the blaze of the campfire, one man to another. The shadowlight of the flames illuminated his father's face: the high forehead, the straight nose, jutting chin. Goddwin was almost as tall as his father, but not as broad-shouldered; his eyes were a shade darker. He sat, resting his hand on the sword Harold had given him for his six- teenth birthing day. A fine weapon, well-crafted, with a clean blade that could bite the wind. He had not yet had the chance to use it beyond the practice field.

Considering how to answer, Harold chose to tell the truth of it. "As your father I would ask you to mount your horse and go home before we smell and taste the salt of spilt blood, our own and theirs. To take your brothers with you." He raised an eyebrow and began to stretch out his hand above the smoke scutter of the fire. "But as your King, I ask you to ride beside me, to fight"—he paused, grinned—"where I can keep a damned watchful eye over you!"

He thrust his hand further forward, clasped it, palm to wrist, with his eldest, first-born son.

"Strange," Goddwin said, his own white-toothed grin matching that of his father, "but that is exactly what my mother ordered me to do for you!"

Word of foreign ships in the Humber river had spread throughout the Middle Lands of England with the speed of a rushing wind. Men waited for the sound of the war horns: alert, ready, weapons set beside the doorplace, hauberks, war caps and byrnies checked for damage. Horses shod, bridle and saddle to hand. When the summons came, they rode out in ones and twos, met with others on the war trail, becoming four, eight, ten, twenty...came to swell the great army of men on their sturdy war ponies, heads and manes tossing, bridles jingling.

Miles passed beneath their shod hooves. Rest for an hour during the noon of the day and then on again. Halt at dusk, the mounts watered and fed on a ration of good corn, allowed to graze; a few hours of snatched sleep for their riders, on again before the midnight hour came. And all the while, more and more men came up on to the North Road that had first been built by the red-crested legions of Rome.

In places the surface was worn, potholes needed tending, the occasional collapsed bank or choked drainage ditch causing ankle-deep muck, but the English system of maintenance was long established and efficiently organised. Each town, each village was responsible for the upkeep of a designated section of the King's highway, with heavy fines to pay if the work was not attended to.

There was one blessing: the fyrd of Middle England had not been called for duty most of the summer, as they had in the South, where the patrols had been set in case William had come. Many a man, in addition to Harold himself, considered the irony of it. Ready and waiting for William to land in the South, only to march northwards, in the end, to meet Tostig and Hardrada.

As the host travelled further north, the numbers joining Harold's army dwindled and rumour became louder. On the fourth day of marching, the twenty-second day of September, a grimed, exhausted messenger galloped down past the column of mounted men—riding twelve abreast where the width of the road permitted—his eyes fixed on two standards, the Red Dragon of Wessex and the King's personal standard, the white figure of the Fighting Man. He reined in, pulling his lathered horse back on to its hocks so sharply that the floundering animal almost fell. He dispensed with any formalities of royal acknowledgement: "My Lord! Eadwine and Morkere have fought and lost in battle two days past, on the twentieth day, at Gate Fulford. York has surrendered to the Norwegian, to Harald Hardrada!"

Harold had halted, the men around him reining in also, the column easing to a stand. Word whipped forwards and backwards along the line, a murmur of appalled disbelief rippling in its wake.

"My two earls live?" Harold asked.

"Aye, but both have suffered wounds that will take some weeks to heal. Casualties were heavy—on both sides."

"Are they captured?" Harold barely dared ask it.

"No, my Lord. We managed to get them away. They are safe in a manor out on the moors. They say they wish to come, to fight beside you."

"No. Not if they have wounds. They would serve the North better by healing surely and quickly." Harold ran his thumb and forefinger down each side of his nose, smoothed his moustache. Did not much want to ask this next thing. "My brother?"

"Fought as Hardrada's second-in-command. When I was sent south, it was he who had entered York on the Hardrada's behalf."

Harold looked ahead. It would be dusk in another two hours. They ought to be seeking a camping ground.

"He had best enjoy his victory while he may, then, for it will be of short duration." The King stood in his stirrups, calling out in a loud and positive voice, "We do not make camp this night. We shall rest as soon as may be for two hours, no more, then march on to York. This day is Friday, if we double our pace, we can be within striking distance of York by the Lord's Day!"

The pace would be gruelling, but the animals were fit, the men all eager for a fight. The anticipation of unsheathing their swords had been humming like lightning electricity all summer, and now that their blood was up, the song of the battleblades was vibrating through the static-charged air.

14

Stamford Bridge

They reached Tadcaster an hour before noon on the Sunday, hot, tired, dusty, but confident. Some of the mounts were lame, and men nursed blisters to heel and backside: minor injuries, nothing that goose grease, a rest and a meal of wheat-baked biscuits and nourishing barley broth would not cure.

The news was grim, but information plentiful and readily given. Tostig had entered York, putting to the sword without mercy men who had played a part in removing him from his earldom. Had retrieved tribute and sworn homage from York's leading citizens. Hardrada himself had returned to his army encampment at Riccall, on the northern bank of the River Ouse. Now was the time when Harold must make good his promise to Morkere and Eadwine—that he would not allow Tostig to take vengeance. York had capitulated to the invaders through lack of choice, but York was only too willing to declare for their king—if that king was willing to fight for them in return. And he was. More than willing.

At Tadcaster they paused, letting the sweating ponies gain their breath and the men take their ease for an hour or so. Harold and his commanders were gathered beneath the shade of an oak, thankful for this short respite from the heat of the day. At least these last three hot, dry days had ensured no mud-deep roads and miserable tempers from wet and damp—although the heat of early autumn had its own annoyances. The ponies' coats were already thickening, thirst increased for mount and man, the road wore harder on ponies' hooves and raised a dust cloud that choked throats and irritated nose and eye, flies were a nuisance.

But these discomforts meant little to a fighting man whose thoughts were focused on an invading army and an approaching battle.

Harold pointed a sharpened stick at the map scrawled in the dirt at his feet. "Hardrada and Tostig are removed to Stamford Bridge, eight miles east of York, where four roads meet." He looked for confirmation at the fourteen-year-old lad who had brought the information. "They await the arrival of hostages and further tribute, I assume?"

Waltheof, the young son of Siward, had judged it prudent not to surrender and plead homage to Tostig. As with many another, he had fled leaving hurriedly through the north gate as Tostig had ridden in through the south. Morkere was his guardian and because of that Waltheof had been in no doubt as to his fate had he decided to stay. He nodded slowly at Harold, answering for all those who had fought so valiantly. "Stamford is most suited for meeting with those who have no choice but to capitulate—good to march to or from in all directions."

"They know of our coming?" That was Gyrth, Harold's brother, his voice eager.

A laconic smile spread across Waltheof's face, which was, as yet, unshaded by beard growth.

"They must know of that, my Lord Earl, only a fool would not expect the King of a land such as this to sit idle in London while usurpers attempt to wrench the crown from his head. But they cannot know how fast you have come, nor how near you are. For if they knew this, would they be resting easy with their wine, their stolen meat and their captured women? Would they not, instead, be preparing to come to meet you or defend themselves against you?"

"Would they not, indeed!" Harold answered, delighted, slapping his thighs with the palms of his hands. "We shall ensure that this whoreson Hardrada who dares to violate my kingdom, and my brother, the traitor who lopes at his heel, receive more than they are expecting on the morrow, at this meeting place of Stamford Bridge."

He returned the boy Waltheof's gaze, matching his earnest stare with one as determined. "We march at first light, pass straight through York and surprise the bastards. We shall catch them while they sit on their backsides, expecting only the defeated." His expression hardened. "Instead, they shall meet their own bloody defeat."

⟨⁂⟩

Monday dawned with a covering of white-wraithed mist that, come an hour after sunrise, had burnt away in the rising temperature. By nine of the morning it was already hot and, as their mission to the bridge at Stamford was solely to bring to a peaceful conclusion the treaties previously agreed in York, many of the Norwegian army left their heavy leather-studded byrnies within camp at Riccall.

They were in holiday mood as Hardrada marched 5000 of his men along the old Roman road. Tostig, glowing with pleasure at the ease of their taking of York, was reciting accounts of successful hunts in the area. "I brought down a boar over to the left there, by that hillock. An ugly great brute it was, gave me one hell of a fight. And over there, by that copse, my favourite hound caught a hare—what a magnificent chase that was!"

Harald Hardrada was not listening, his mind occupied by the more important matter of what should be his next move. Wait here, near York, for Harold Godwinesson or cross the Ouse and meet him while he rode north? Best to await his arrival, let the English be the tired ones, the footsore and weary. Especially in this late September heat. The fighting at Fulford had been a close thing—too many of his men were wounded. As he rode, his experienced eyes automatically scanned the countryside—over there would be a good place for an ambush. The grass away to the right, bright green and lush, indicated boggy ground, ideal for drawing any attacking force towards. He wished Tostig would stop prattling— he was a man over-stuffed with his own importance. When he had claimed the crown for himself, would he be able to abide this fool as Earl of the Middle Lands and the North as they had agreed? Hardrada shifted weight in the saddle, scratched at a discomfort in his crotch. Once he was king, Tostig could be disposed of easily. He allowed a wry grimace to curl at the corner of his mouth. As they had agreed—hah! How binding were agreements? That this invidiously resentful younger brother coveted the English crown for himself had not been lost on Hardrada's intelligence. Each of them had agreed to the alliance because they needed the other's help—fully aware that once Harold Godwinesson was out of the way, their own warring for the owning of a sovereign's trinkets would spit like sparks from a smith's hammer on iron.

Tostig boasted he knew the country around York well, but Harald had his doubts, for it seemed to him that this Englishman had spent more of his time pursuing his leisure at the old king's court than taking notice of the lie of the land. No matter. He had scouts who could recognise a suitable place to meet this English king in battle. There was no word yet from the men Tostig had sent out from York to keep watch on the road—that was becoming another niggling worry. He had advised against sending Northumbrian-bred men, for all that they were men who had remained loyal to Tostig throughout the troubles of this last year. To Harald's mind a man would be as pleased to serve any lord if the reward were high enough…ah, well, that was for Tostig to sort out. For now, these northern moorlands must be secured, homage paid and hostages given, otherwise they would be watching their backs while defeating this King Harold in battle.

The noblemen of Northumbria were not due at the rendezvous until late afternoon, giving the Norwegians time to make camp. The men caught up on sleep or played dice and started on the ale barrels they had with them. Someone had brought along two cockerels and a noisy cockfight was in progress to the edge of camp, near the sluggish water of the Derwent river. Tostig, weary of idling within his stuffy command tent, was strolling through the makeshift village of tents and bracken bothies, exchanging a word here and there with faces he recognised, commenting with swaggering pride on their success at Fulford, on their future victory.

Drawn to the excited shouting, he paused to watch the two cockerels. The larger of the two, a solid bird with green plumage round its neck, seemed to be gaining the advantage over the lighter, younger bird. "I wager a silver coin on the younger!" Tostig declared, slamming his coin down on the betting barrel. "He may have less experience, but I reckon he has more stamina." He pushed his way to the forefront of the yelling circle of men. "Come on, my son! Fight him!" The younger against the elder—aye, as it would be for him and his poxed brother!

It was soon over. As Tostig had predicted, the younger bird possessed greater strength. His spurs, long and sharp, raked through the older bird's chest and it was done, finished, in a splatter of gore.

Gloating, Tostig collected his winnings and strolled the last few yards to the river to rinse his hands. Oh, for a hot day like this earlier in the summer! More men in the mood for a fight might have rallied to him had the weather been more pleasant. Had that happened, this thing between him and Harold would have been finished by now, with the ease and finality of that cockfight. He would not have had to go begging for help from Hardrada—nor would he then have to dispose of the foreign bastard. Once the crown was on his head, Normandy would have no claim on England. Duke William's contest was with Harold, for the breaking of a sworn oath. The Duke had no cause for disagreement with either him or Edith.

The river reeds grew in thick clumps along this, the eastern bank. He knelt, bent forward and dipped his head into the water, savouring the coolness as it swirled through his sweat-greased hair. He was almost tempted to wade in for a quick swim. When these essential concessions had been wrung from the poxed Northerners, he would return to York, to the comfort of his palace. Enjoy the luxury of a bath. He tilted his head back, eyes closed, trickled water down his throat and under the sweat-stained collar of his leather tunic.

Something made him open his eyes, some sound, some inner sense of alarm. He was looking across the sky-reflected blue water towards York. At the rising incline of land. A glint of something metallic along the brow of the hill, the sunshine reflecting on...on...

Tostig screamed. He scrabbled to his feet, began running. The war horns from the sentries were sounding the alarm. Men, confused and startled, stared around, uncertain what was happening, saw, with dawning horror, the shuffle of movement no more than one mile distant, their shouts drowning Tostig's own cries as he ran. Waking from sleep; board games tipped and scattered; women with their skirts dragged up, breasts exposed, abandoned. Hardrada's army lurched for their weapons and armour. Cursed their stupidity at leaving most of it behind at Riccall.

"Harold!" Tostig gasped as he burst into Hardrada's tent. "My brother Harold is here!"

Hardrada had already been roused by the activity and noise from his own quick-snatched sleep. He frowned with aggressive annoyance at Tostig. What nonsense was this Englishman raving now? Hardrada was a giant in stature and reputation, had the strength of a bear and shoulders of an ox, a chest as deep as a whale's and stood a full two hand-spans more than six feet. With his bushed beard and mass of curled red hair, he epitomised the warrior Viking king, who certainly did not panic at such nonsense. "Do not be an imbecile! Your brother could not have come so swiftly from London."

Angrily, Tostig crossed the space between them in two strides and confronted Harald, his fist clutched around the pommel of his sword, his legs planted wide, the effect subdued by having to glare up at the formidable face towering above. "Come look for yourself, then! Harold's army is massing on the hill beyond the river—then think of calling me an imbecile!"

<hr>

A man, alone, carrying a green branch in his left hand, rode within an arrow's distance of the wooden bridge that spanned the twenty or so yards of somnolent, deep-running river. He halted his stallion and hailed the man who stood beneath the Norwegian banners that fluttered in the light breeze on the far side of the water. "Tostig Godwinesson!" he called, using the English tongue. "There is no need for this insanity between us. Englishman ought not to fight Englishman. We will offer you a return from exile, the land you own in your own right and a guarantee of peace, if you but furl that banner of war and lay down your sword."

"What will there be for my ally? For Harald Hardrada?" Tostig shouted back. "He looks for English land also—and what of my earldom? Will Northumbria in its entirety be once again my earldom?"

"No, not your earldom. That is held by Morkere."

Tostig sneered. "But I have already taken it from him! Have you not heard of Fulford? It is mine by right of victory, since Morkere ran away with shit sculling down his backside!"

The man sitting relaxed on the stallion on the eastern bank shrugged. "Then it will be taken back from you. As for Hardrada, he will be granted only enough land to cover his body in a grave."

Tostig made a dismissive cutting motion with his hand. "Then I see no point in our talking." He drew his sword to emphasise his statement. "It seems we fight."

The stallion's rider let the branch slide from his fingers, raised his sword hand to his war cap in a salute of acceptance and wheeled his horse round, setting it with his spurs from a stand to a gallop. As it plunged, the animal's hooves mangled the leaves of the peace branch.

Tostig translated the exchange to Hardrada who, watching the horseman gallop back to the ranks of the mounted English army, nodded his head in approval. "And who was the messenger?" he enquired. "You know him?"

"Oh, I know him," Tostig answered derisively. "That was my brother, Harold, King of England."

Absently Hardrada ran his thumb along the blade of his two-handed axe, his gaze remaining on the horseman. "That is a fine stallion. He rides well, your brother the King."

"Who gives a damn how well he rides?" Tostig barked with annoyance. "It is how he fights that is of consequence!"

Raising the axe head into his line of vision, Hardrada squinted along the wicked-looking edge, taking pleasure from its perfection. "And how well does he fight, then, my friend? As well as he rides perhaps? Better than you?"

Tostig scowled. Harold could do everything well. Always had done, damn him. Then he remembered, suddenly, the cockfight. The elder is often the slower. And it is not I alone whom he opposes. Harold may be good on a horse and in a fight, but he is wrong if he thinks he is a greater warrior than Harald of Norway!"

Hardrada let the axe head fall through its own weight down to the grass. "Then we had best set about showing him his mistake, had we not?"

Although he would not let Tostig see, Hardrada was angry. Harold Godwinesson had made a fool of him—but then who would have expected the cursed man to march so quickly from the south? How had he done it? God's justice, but that had taken some doing! Angry, also, that he had not heeded his own instincts. What had happened to Tostig's "loyal" Northumbrian men? Those men who were supposedly so keen to serve him once again? Either dead or had altered allegiance to Harold—not one had ridden with news of the English.

This was not a good situation: caught unawares, poorly armed and with only half his full strength. As he issued orders to deploy the men he had, Hardrada sent two riders, at the gallop, to fetch up those from Riccall; all who could run and hold a sword. "Tell them Harold of the English holds the route from Gate Helmsley—they are to ford the river at Kexby." It was a longer route, rougher going, but there was no choice. "And for your love of me and your God," Hardrada called as they mounted, "tell them to hurry!"

The English were advancing, mounted men in the centre, the infantry—formed of the fyrd of Northumbria and Humberside, those who had survived that first battle—to right and left. Harold had decided not to dismount, but to make use of cavalry in this open country, presuming correctly that Hardrada would employ the obvious tactics of the solid line of a shield wall. The most important thing was to delay. The longer the English could be held, the more chance of their reinforcements coming to their aid. The best course was to keep Harold on the far side of the river; he would not be able to swim either man or horse across without casualties. Hardrada's first priority was, therefore, the bridge.

His men were brave and strong warriors; those dispatched to hold the wooden structure of the bridge fought long and well, but the English force of numbers was overwhelming and, within the hour, Harold was across, his housecarls thundering over the planking on their sturdy warhorses, man and beast as fresh as if they had been out on naught but a summer stroll, rather than a forced march of more than 200 miles in six days.

The Viking line was drawn up 300 or so yards behind the river, on rising ground, a wall of shields, glinting axes and death-bearing swords. Banners flew proud, voices bellowed the war cry—and the clash of battle joined rang through the valley. Determined, their bloodlust raised, the English hammered forward at the gallop time after time,the mane-tossing, foam-flecked, sweat-drenched horses charging and reining away to re-form and return, again and yet again. The infantry, fighting for their own land, for their personal freedom, struck with savage vehemence at right and left flank, archers sending their flights of arrows singing into the ranks to maim and kill, to make the shields drop.

Hardrada bellowed at his men, cheering them on, bullying, entreating and intimidating. He urged those in the rear forward as men in the front fell or dropped back from exhaustion—and then his booming voice fell suddenly silent. Nothing but a choking gurgle issued from his mouth as he staggered backwards, his hands clawing at Tostig, who stood, open-mouthed in horror. The arrow shaft thrusting from the giant's throat quivered, dark blood oozed, Hardrada sank, slow and ponderous, to his knees. Fell on to his back, eyes open. Dead.

The noise continued, swooping and tumbling: horses screaming in anger and pain; the crash of metal upon metal or wooden shield; the sobs of the mortally wounded, the exultant cheering of the successful. Tostig heard none of it. Saw none of it. Stood in disbelief, staring at the body of Harald Hardrada at his feet. Exiled by Cnut from Norway, he had sought service as a mercenary in Bulgaria and Sicily, become the champion of the Varangian bodyguard of the Eastern Emperor, been rewarded with titles and rank, had accumulated a wealth of booty and experience in battle. After the death of Magnus of Norway he had fought and bullied and bribed his way to becoming king in his place. Harald Hardrada, the Thunderbolt of the North. Dead. Killed by an English arrow lodged in his throat.

Word was spreading. "Hardrada is dead!" The solid line began to waver— several horses burst through, their riders screaming triumph, swords cutting, axes splitting through bone and sinew…Tostig came to life. He would not admit defeat, would not lose his earldom! He sprang across Hardrada's stiffening body, seized the Norwegian banner and ran forward, his own housecarls and those of Hardrada running with him.

"To me!" he shouted. "All men to me! We shall avenge his death! We shall avenge!" He thrust the banner into the standard-bearer's hands, lifted his sword and joined the mêlée of warriors hacking at the cavalry riders who had broken through the line, beating them back, stabbing, slaying and wounding. Horses fell to their knees, hamstrung, blood rushing from opened veins, slashed bellies or cut throats. Dead men, dying horses. Where there had been grass and a scattering of late summer flowers, there was now nothing except churned, bloodied mud and death.

A stir on the left flank, a flurry of activity. Renewed, fiercer savagery of fighting. Word running from mouth to mouth…

"Eystein Orre has come! The men from Riccall are here!"

It was a brave attempt, but most of those men had been left behind in camp at Riccall because they were not fit for fighting: had received injuries at that other day's battle, were exhausted from their frenzied march to help their beleaguered comrades. "Orre's Storm" the final onslaught was later to be called, but it was no use to Tostig Godwinesson, for it came too late.

Tostig never felt the axe blade that took his head from his shoulders.

15

Saint-Valéry-sur-Somme

Mathilda stood at the river edge, heedless of the mud that was sliming her boots, and the cold of the evening penetrating her thin cloak and dress. With the dawning of this day, the twenty-seventh of September, the wind had swung lazily to the south and the rainclouds had miraculously evaporated. The sun shone with warm strength.

Embarkation of men and horses had been swift and organised; stores and weaponry, armour and the timber for the construction of wooden fortifications were already aboard. Before the evening tide turned and the ebb began to empty the Somme estuary, leaving the sandbanks exposed, the fleet was assembled off-shore, making ready to sail. The Duchess watched the oars of her husband's ship swing out and dip into the red-gold sunset-reflecting water. The sail would not be unfurled, not until the rest of the flotilla were at sea.

With that last disaster, she had come to hope that this year of madness was ended. Morning and night had she prayed that her husband would abandon this cursed attempt at crossing the sea to invade England. But these last weeks he had pursued it with a frenzy of determination; had alternately raged like a bull or wept like a child; pleaded, cajoled, threatened and sworn at the men who had tried to dissuade him from pursuing this obsession. He would have none of it.

Somehow—in God's good name from where did he find the strength?— William had marshalled the scattered ships, the disappointed and disillusioned men, to the estuary of the Somme river, to here at Saint-Valéry. Had revived their enthusiasm, had convinced them that they could succeed, that England could become Normandy.

The lantern suddenly blazed yellow from the masthead of her husband's ship. The *Mora*. Mathilda had been proud to present him with that gift, but resented her generosity now. *Merde*, but that was childish! With or without that ship, William would be going across the sea this night. With or without his wife's blessing.

Winding her fingers together, the Duchess strained her eyes to see the figures on board, but could make out nothing, for the distance was too great. Men had died on that first unsuccessful crossing. Ships had sunk, been rammed and burnt at the hands of the English scyp fyrd. And that was just at sea. What would happen when—if—they reached the English coast in one piece? Perhaps the menfolk, because of their stupid pride, would not admit it, but Mathilda knew! *Assurément*, Duke William's wife knew all too well. The English fyrd, with Harold as their king, would cut the Normans to pieces, would slaughter them as they struggled over the shingle and the sand.

She had said nothing of her fears to William. Had hidden her trembling under pretended enthusiasm, had given her support as, in a matter of days, not more than a week, he and his advisers had assessed the damage from that encounter at sea, made repairs to the ships that had come into the harbour and rekindled the affection and determination of his men. Those drowned bodies that were washed ashore were buried in secret along the beaches; the loss of ship—either wrecked, burnt, sunk or deserted—accounted for by the unpredictable nature of the wind. A wind that William had waited, with such uncharacteristic patience, to change. He had pretended that all was well—and got away with it.

With the sun set, the vibrant colours began to fade. Many lights were bobbing at stern, bow or mast; the sea was turning blacker than the panorama of the sky. Mathilda gasped as the trumpets suddenly sounded. Voices, every word clear, drifted in with the lazy lap of the waves, the creak and groan of rope and oar, the flap and crackle of sail.

They moved slowly at first, so many of them that it was difficult to see how they could all make way together. Only when she realised she could no longer distinguish the distinctive shape of the *Mora*'s prow, or the lantern at the mast, did she understand that William had gone and that this time, this time, unless he conquered England he would not be coming back.

⟨✦⟩

At the first misting of daylight William found himself alone out on the sea. *Mora*, unladen by cargo, troops or horses, had outpaced the fleet during the night. Around the Duke was nothing to be seen except mist, sea and sky, and a lone gull, gliding solitary on the wind. Unperturbed, putting his trust in God, William ordered his breakfast brought to him, and sat on the afterdeck, enjoying a meal of cheese, bread, honey and fine wine.

Like ghosts, the foremost keels slid from the blanketing mist, ship after ship emerging into the daylight one mile from the coast of England. Together as a fleet and unopposed, the Normans beached at the place called Pevensey, running their flat-bottomed keels into the shallows. William stumbled as he leapt from his craft, going down on to his knees in the white churn of surf, his hand stretching out to break his fall. He winced as a stone cut into his palm. From those on board the ships nearby a disconcerted murmur rippled—a bad omen? The murmuring swelled into a babble; soon word would run from ship to ship, panic spreading among those whose nerves were already jumping as if riddled by fleas.

William fitz Osbern ran to his Duke's side, dropped to his own knees and raised his hands in prayer. "May God be our witness! My Lord Duke William grasps hold of England with his hand—is it not ours for the taking?"

A cheer swept up. William hauled himself to his feet, using his good friend as a support. Grinned. That was quick thinking, Will. I thank you and vow that you shall be well rewarded—soon. As soon as may be."

Fitz Osbern inclined his head. He wished that he could answer that he sought no reward, but it would not be the truth. If they had not come to take land and riches, then why had they come at all?

Pevensey, however, was not where William had intended to make landfall. They were too far west, but no matter. Scouts secured their immediate safety; the masts were unstepped, horses unloaded and a portable fortress erected in a matter of hours within the compound of the old Roman defences. On the following day, as dawn crested the eastern sky, the Norman army moved, by ship and land, to the more suitable harbour of Hastings.

One thing concerned them. Where were the English? The men of the fyrd?

16

⟨❦⟩

York

They buried Tostig within the York Minster, his coffin laid a discreet distance from the altar, a granite slab covering his resting place. Some grumbled at the honour granted him, murmuring that he was a traitor and a murderer, but most were filled with the exultation of victory and paid little heed to those less benevolent. In death, the man could do no further harm and he was, after all, brother to the King.

The victory had been great—worthy of a tale-teller's saga. The march north to surprise the unsuspecting enemies; Hardrada and Tostig killed; substantial casualties for their luckless army. Among the English, a few noble and good men were killed, others wounded, but a mere handful only in comparison. Among them, though, were Harold's own sons: Goddwin had received a sword slash to his right arm, which would most assuredly ache on a winter's night, and Edmund had a fractured leg, but a clean break that would mend with rest and time.

Swinging with confident strides back along the road to York, yodelling their victory songs, the English proclaimed Harold a great warlord and a worthy king. Harold accepted the flattery with good grace, but nonetheless remembered the truth of Stamford Bridge.

Hardrada had been careless. He ought never have marched with so few men in hostile country, and certainly not without taking armour or proper precautions. Tostig too was responsible. Undoubtedly, a part of their failure had been due to his arrogant assumption that Northumbria would bend its humbled knee to him without question and that men who had professed loyalty to him would prefer a Norwegian foreigner over an anointed, English-born king.

The rout that had followed Tostig's death had been complete. Those who had not died trying to swim the river had been slaughtered or captured. Three hundred longships had made their hostile way up the Ouse; only enough men to sail four and twenty of them survived to return to Norway. Fewer than one thousand men. The keening of the widows would darken the coming winter with the song of sorrow. The rest of the fleet, Harold kept for himself as spoils of victory.

Magnanimously, he allowed those men captured to leave England with their comrades, Olaf, son of Hardrada, among them. Eadwine and Morkere, come from their place of safety, were all for beheading him, but Harold was wiser. It was unlikely that Norway would try for England again; Olaf was no Hardrada. Better to receive his homage and agreement of peace, and allow him to return home—he would be fully occupied these next few years with consolidating his own inherited kingship.

Come the fourth day of the October month, the feasting and merry-making was ended, the men of the fyrd returning to their homes, the noblemen picking up the abruptly severed threads of government. Wounds were healing, life returning to normality. Winter would soon be coming, and there was always much for a man to be doing to ensure the well-being of house place and livestock before the first snows fell.

For himself, Harold had felt little joy in the victory. How could he take pleasure in the slaying of his own brother? A brother who had been fighting in fury against him? He stood in the quiet solitude of the minster, looking down at the tomb. Aye, he was pleased at the splendid achievement of the men who had marched north so quickly, who had fought with exceptional bravery—what king would not be justifiably proud of such heroes? But the fight, for his own heart, was tainted by too much sorrow.

"I trust you are satisfied. Now that you have no one to stand against you."

Harold raised his head. His sister Edith was standing on the opposite side of the graveplace, her expression one of cool contempt. Her face had thinned, these last months; she looked pinched and hag-bound, like a frustrated, mean-spirited spinster. An unfulfilled woman who had never found happiness, nor was ever likely to. He ought to feel sorrow for her, but there was no room left within him for anything beyond loathing.

He had not seen Edith since the funeral day—his coronation day—when she had swept from Westminster, taking all she could carry with her to Winchester, the Queen's city. By right, Winchester ought be Alditha's, but Harold had not had the opportunity to claim it from his sister. And he knew, were he to do so, he would have another spiteful fight on his hands, the possible spilling of yet more English blood. Edith would never, willingly, give up her dower land to the woman who had replaced her. Regarding her sour, condemning expression, Harold realised, all these years later, why Edward had so hated his mother for her refusal to give up and retire quietly.

"There is no point in my saying that this saddens me," he answered, gesturing to the grave. "You would not believe me."

Edith had arrived two days previously, her entourage of 500 men sweeping into York, demanding hospitality for the lady within the palace. Morkere, his wounds paining him, his mind occupied with settling the trouble Tostig had stirred, would rather have kicked her backside over the sea with those humiliated Norwegians, but she had been queen to King Edward, and therefore required respect.

She must have been on the road well before the twenty-fifth, the day of battle. Prudently—in case she answered with something he would prefer not to hear—Harold had not asked how she came to be riding to where she expected their brother to be residing. And with her so many men bearing arms and armour. That she had come to aid Tostig did not need to be asked. She had been about to commit treason, but it mattered for naught now. Tostig was dead and she had no champion. Her cause was ended and already beginning to moulder beneath this granite slab.

"He was never a favourite brother, Edith, but for all that, he was my brother. Our mother's son. I had no wish for this. It was not of my doing. His own greed caused it. Not me."

Edith's response was to step around the grave and slap Harold's cheek, the sharp, bare sound ricocheting from the stone walls, echoing across the nave and chancel. Monks gathered in a western chapel glanced up, concerned.

"You did nothing for him!" she spat. "You betrayed him by making no attempt to regain his earldom, to help him salvage his dignity! And then you pushed him down to his knees by setting Edward's crown upon your own head—and still you made no effort to help him!" Again she slapped him, the force of her anger and grief thrusting behind the blow. Harold's head reeled, a bruise instantly reddening from eye to jaw, but he did not move, said only, with such great sorrow, "He could have had anything he wanted, Edith, had he only asked. Anything, except for Northumbria."

She spat at him, a globule of saliva that landed on his cheek and dribbled into the trail of his moustache. Turning on her heel, she stalked from the minster, her boot heels tap-tapping in her haste. Outside, the sun was shining as if it were midsummer; the weather was most assuredly turned inside out this year. Irritably she called for her mare and was preparing to be boosted into the saddle when the clatter of hooves, coming fast along the road that ran towards the London gate, halted her movement. Edith's guard, monks, the minster folk, men and women of York, housecarls and soldiers all turned to watch the rider come galloping through the wide-flung gateway, sparks flying from the shoes of his horse as he hauled at the reins. The lathered, sweat-dripping animal came down on one knee; blood oozed from his flanks where the spurs had driven him. The rider flung himself from the saddle and, pausing merely to ask the whereabouts of the King, took the steps in one stride and ran into the minster.

Curious, Edith followed him into the shadowed coolness. She watched him run the length of the aisle and stumble to his knees in front of Harold, his lips moving before the King had barely registered his presence. Standing within the doorway, her back to the sunlight, Edith saw Harold's face drain chalk pale, his hand go to his sword, the fingers clutch, tight, around it. He asked a few brief questions, which were answered with equal despatch.

The King nodded his head, once, and headed for the doorway. He brushed past Edith without seeing her, shouting for his horse. He mounted by vaulting into the saddle and heeled straight into a canter, giving simultaneous command that the officers of his housecarls were to be summoned.

"What is it?" men were asking, perplexed, a little fearful. "What is wrong?"

Ealdred, Archbishop of York, came hurrying, his vestments gathered into his fists so that he might run the faster. He put his hand out to signal Harold to stop. "What has happened, my Lord? What tragedy? What is wrong?"

"We are in dire need of your prayers, my Lord Archbishop," Harold said quickly, as he hauled the beast to halt. "I must ride south immediately. Duke William has landed his fleet at Pevensey."

17

London

Harold reached London late in the evening of the ninth of October. The news was bad. His brother Leofwine awaited him at Westminster, was first down the Hall steps into the torch-lit courtyard as the King rode in.

"Well?" Harold demanded as Leofwine ran up.

"He has fortified himself within that area of marsh-edged land known as the Hastings Peninsula. It would be difficult to take our army in there—boundaries of marsh and river are as effective as any palisade wall. For the moment he has no lack of supplies, is living off the land, looting all he can and destroying what remains."

Harold tossed the reins of his stallion to the nearest servant, unbuckled and removed his war cap as he strode up the wooden steps leading into his Hall. Alditha stood at the top, the cup of welcome in her hand. She offered it to him, he took a quick gulp and passed it back, pressing a light but inattentive kiss to her cheek. "I have no time for formal welcome, lass, but would appreciate a tankard of ale and something to eat—cheese will do." He kissed her a second time, more fondly. "You look tired," he added. "Does the child bring discomfort?"

"No, my Lord, the child is well," Alditha answered him, but he did not hear, for he was talking again to Leofwine and others of his command who were gathering around the table set beside the eastern wall, already cluttered with maps and parchments. His queen, for want of something to do to help, went to fetch ale.

"I have been studying the route south, and the entire Hastings area," Leofwine said, indicating one map unrolled and spread, a salt box, tankard, ink pot and wooden fruit bowl anchoring the four persistently curling corners. "From what we have already learned, these villages"—he indicated three—"have been burnt, razed to the ground."

"Casualties?" the King snapped.

Leofwine cleared his throat, glanced at his own captain of housecarls, knowing Harold would not be pleased at the answer, "Several."

"Aye, I would expect the Bastard to butcher the menfolk."

"'Tis not just the men. There are bodies of women and children—bairns, some of them, still at the breast." Leofwine swallowed hard, reluctant to continue. The brutality of the battlefield was no stranger to any of the warrior kind, but this, this was sickening. Quietly, his voice hoarse, he said, "Many are only charred remains—they burnt with their houses. Nothing has been left standing. No one left alive. It seems he has not come merely to conquer England, but to destroy everyone and everything in the process."

Harold was standing with his palms resting flat on either side of the map, looking at the markings of river, coast, settlement and hill. He set his jaw, said nothing. He dared not. The words that were sticking in his throat would have erupted into fury had he released them. He swallowed down his anger with a gulp of ale from the tankard that Alditha fetched him, his mind turning to campaigning in Brittany...

William's determination to succeed, whatever the cost in human life or suffering. His manic obsession with winning. Too clearly could Harold see in his mind that smouldering ruin of Dinan. The senseless killing of the innocent. Of women and babes. Heard in his ears the screaming as women and their daughters, innocent of men, were violated. Now it was happening to his own, to English people. People he knew—and knew well, for he held estates in that coastal area, had hunted there often as boy and man grown. He had a stud of fine breeding horses at Whatlington, and Crowhurst held a mews with some of the best hawks in the country. His hawksman there was a loyal and good-humoured man, his wife and four daughters all exceptionally pretty. Crowhurst had been one of the places Leofwine had pointed to.

After a while, when his breathing had calmed, Harold asked, "Do we know the extent of his supplies? The Hastings land will not feed him for ever."

"With the number of ships he has brought with him, I would say he is capable of withstanding a siege through the winter at least."

William could devastate the area in that time, and aye, it would be difficult to flush him out. The Hastings Peninsula might be no stone-built fortress, but it mattered not. A siege was a siege, whatever the defensive circumstances, and Duke William was well versed in siege warfare. Nor, Harold reflected grimly, was he likely to make foolish mistakes through arrogance, as had Hardrada.

"I say leave him to rot!" That was Gyrth, who had just entered the Hall, stripping off his riding gloves as he did so. Like Harold, his beard-stubbled face was grimed with white dust, his clothes sweat-stained, eyes tired. Twice, in a matter of weeks, had they made the journey between London and York in six days.

Once in itself was feat enough for any man, but twice? Surely this king deserved the respect and loyalty of his subjects!

"We shall ensure he cannot get reinforcements; therefore he will run out of food eventually—perhaps his men will not stand firm if we starve them out," Leofwine added.

Harold pushed his weight from the table, hooked a stool forward, sat. He was so weary. His body felt a dead, limp weight, but he could not afford the luxury of paying mind to it. "We need to consider this carefully," he said. "I know Duke William. Know some of his vile tactics—he made damned sure I did. I see why, now. He hopes to goad me into hasty action through what he has ordered done to my people in Sussex."

"He intends to draw us into the arena, do you think?" Leofwine spoke his thoughts out loud. "Is waiting for us to go in after him, lure us into an ambush?"

"Or, once he has burnt and plundered everything in sight, will he march out towards the Weald?" a housecarl captain asked, indicating a possible route with a grimed nail. "Could he have designs on Winchester, or Dover?"

"That we must wait and see." Harold selected a chunk of soft goat's cheese and bit into it, not tasting its tangy saltiness. "I do not care to let him run riot in the Weald. With only one narrow road in through dense woodland and impass-able marsh he is safe from any land-based attack, but equally, that makes only the one route out. Within Hastings, we have him contained, can choose our own time to attack." He ruffled his hair, then brought his hand down over his nose, across his chin. "It is easier to spear a boar while it is trapped. Only a fool would prod such a creature out into the open."

"How long do we wait?" Leofwine queried. "A few days, weeks?"

Harold answered him with a vague shrug. His mind was too tired to think, to make decisions...He forced the drowsiness aside. "We wait as long as we can. We are all tired, many of the men are wounded and are still straggling south—we were too short of horses for us all to ride with haste.

"My poxed brother's treachery has placed us at a disadvantage. Let us just hope William is as uncertain what to do next himself—he cannot have made plans, for he would not have expected us to be occupied in the North."

Not for the first time during the dash south did Harold wonder at that, though. Had William known? What if Tostig had made an ally of Normandy also? There was no reason, save that of family honour, to have prevented him. And honour was a quality Tostig had been grotesquely lacking.

"The fyrd, I assume, is alerted?" he asked of Leofwine.

His brother nodded. "The war horns await your orders for their blowing."

All summer had the fyrds of the south and eastern counties been on alert, alternating their patrolling of the coastline. Now they were to be called out again. They were not obliged to come, for already they had served their compulsory time. Before Stamford Bridge, Harold might have doubted their eagerness, but not now. They would join together under his banner, for no warrior would miss the chance of a good fight, a good victory.

⁓

"Will you not come to bed? You need to sleep," Alditha stood beside her husband, laid her hand over his. Midnight had passed; she had been abed, asleep, but had awoken to find Harold sitting brooding before a brazier that was only feebly glowing.

He began to rub warmth into her fingers. "I have too many thoughts tangling in my mind. Sleep would not come."

She knelt and laid her head in his lap. He stroked his hand over her loose hair. She always smelt of chamomile. So did Edyth.

"Can you defeat Duke William?" she asked.

"I defeated Hardrada." But that was different. He slid his palm along her cheek, down the nape of her neck. "The fight with Normandy will depend on how long I can delay. If I can delay."

She looked up at him, her solemn eyes questioning. "If? Surely you will wait until all can reach you? You will not march with only half an army?" Even Alditha, a woman, could see the potential for disaster in that.

"I have lost men and many horses. If your brothers and the fyrds of Northumbria and Mercia could have come south with me, then Duke William, for all he believes he is superior, would not have stood a chance against us. As it is, the North has fought twice with great bravery already, has taken a hard toll of casualties. Both your brothers were wounded at Gate Fulford. Eadwine, like my son Goddwin, has an arm wound that lost him much blood. Morkere took a spear deep into his thigh. They will heal, but not fast enough to be of immediate help. How long will William wait before pressing for an advantage? Once he learns that my armies are not at full strength he will spare no mercy for me or England."

Digesting his answer, Alditha buried her face within the folds of Harold's cloak, but the sob that she tried to suppress escaped her lips.

"What is it, sweetheart?" Harold tipped up her face with his finger and wiped away the trail of a tear.

She made several attempts to pluck up the courage to speak and at last blurted out her fear. "What if you were to lose to him? What will become of me and my daughter, of this one, in here?" She clutched her swollen belly. She had not liked to ask. It was taboo to mention defeat, but she had to know. Had to!

Harold wished he could comfort her by saying that William would not harm a woman. Would he hurt a queen? Would he dare? But if he got to Alditha, it would be because he, Harold, was dead—and who then would be able to protect her? And the child. What would he do to a boy child? No, he could not pledge that she or the babe would be safe in William's bloodstained hands.

Cradling her to him, arms around her, he rocked her as if she too were a child. "I shall not give up my kingdom easily. I intend to win, dear heart. He may well take victory at a first battle if we are drawn into a fight too early, but the winning of one battle does not always mean the end of a war. Look at our Great King, at Alfred—at the numerous battles he fought against the Danish invaders."

Aye, Alditha thought in answer, *and look at other kings who have failed, who have been slaughtered in the fighting.*

Harold did sleep, for an hour or so, before dawn crept in with the bright promise of another sun-filled day. The chattering birds beyond the window woke him. As he stirred, Alditha groaned, snuggling closer to his warmth, reluctant to wake.

He would send her north, he had decided, where she would be safe from William. Her brothers could be trusted to see to her security—for the child, if not for herself. And if the worst happened and William succeeded, from York she could ride with ease to Chester and from there reach the safety of the Welsh, her mother's people.

He closed his eyes, drifted into another doze. And that would solve another problem also. What to do with his three sons. Goddwin, Edmund and Magnus had remained in York, unable to ride although they had begged to accompany him. It would not surprise him if they limped and crawled their way down the North Road—but if he sent word that they were, between them, to protect the Queen and the unborn child...

Goddwin did not like Alditha, but neither would he like what William might do to the boy or girl that was destined to be his half-brother or -sister. Especially not if Harold ensured his eldest son knew all that had been happening in Sussex.

Word had reached London of what had been found at Crowhurst. Farms, buildings, the chapel, all burnt to the ground. The land-folk of the settlements and farmsteadings—including those of his manor, his hawksman and servants— all of them, young and old, fearing Duke William and his men, had sought the sanctuary of the church.

And William had ordered its firing, heedless of these Christian folk sheltered within.

18

Waltham Abbey

Algytha had ordered the trestle tables brought outside for a good scrubbing while the weather held so fine. She paused, puffing with exertion; why did men make such a mess with their ale and meat? Could they not keep at least some of it within the tankard and in the bowl? A horse's neigh attracted her attention and she glanced across the courtyard, expecting to see one of the farm folk, or someone from the village. It was too soon for it to be one of the boys home and her father would not have the opportunity to leave London. Not with this latest news of William.

Edyth heard it also. Her cheeks red from the effort of beating dust from a tapestry, she rested her fist on her hip and, breathing hard, watched the gateway for the visitor to arrive. She too doubted it would be Harold…even if he were not so busy with the Norman landing, why would he come here? Westminster, Winchester, wherever his court resided was now his home, not the manor. She wished someone would come from the palace, though, for she was anxious to hear how her two eldest sons fared—they had been wounded but would live, that she knew. Anxious, too, to hear what was happening in Sussex; how Harold was and what he intended to do.

Her smile of pleasure was exaggerated by the surprise of her wish being granted, for she recognised that distinctive bay—it was ridden by one of Harold's most trusted captains. Laying down the beating broom, Edyth made to walk forward to greet the newcomer, but stopped short, her expression crumbling into horrified dismay. Harold was come—but he was not alone. He rode beside an open-sided litter; inside lay a heavily pregnant woman. The Queen Alditha.

Edyth had seen her briefly at court, during those months when she had first been brought out of Wales, but had never spoken to her. Seeing her again, she was reminded of how pretty she was.

Harold dismounted, hugged Algytha who had run to greet him, then handed the woman from the litter and led her towards Edyth, who stood, conscious of her musty, old and very patched working gown and the kerchief covering her hair. Why, of all days, had he chose this one to bring her here? On the very day Edyth, for want of something to occupy her mind, had decided to clean out the Hall thoroughly before winter? Everywhere was chaos and confusion. Oh, why today?

Edyth dipped a curtsey to the Queen and bade her welcome to the manor, then flashed Harold a glare of anger. "My apologies that we are in disarray, my Lady. You are welcome to the privacy of my own chamber, which is not so disordered." Harold, she noted, wore the marks of tiredness. Was it any wonder?

Looking about her with interest, Alditha followed Edyth within doors and up a short flight of timber steps to the spacious room above the southern end of the Hall. The room was light and airy, with south- and west-facing window shutters thrown wide to allow in the sunlight. Tapestries of hunting scenes decorated the lime-washed walls, a bright patch-worked cover lay over the wooden box bed in one corner, its red-dyed curtaining swathed back with embroidered ties. There were comfortable chairs; several carved chests for clothing, linen and such; glass goblets; silver platters. A vase of autumn flowers stood in the centre of a table, at which a boy sat, legs dangling from a high-legged stool, a book lying open before him. He looked up as they entered, yelled with delight as he saw his father and ran to him, arms outstretched.

"My youngest son," Harold explained to Alditha as the lad jumped into his father's embrace, legs and arms clinging around his waist and neck. "This is Ulf, who at twelve years of age is becoming too big for leaping on me as if I were a pony!" With fond love, Harold ruffled the lad's hair, then pointed to the book. "What are you reading, boy?"

"'Tis one of your falconry books, Papa. Thorkeld says I may help him in your mews, if I am prepared to learn all I can."

"Learn from Thorkeld also, there is little he does not know of hawking. You may tell him, when he thinks you have learned enough to take care of her, that you may have Freya. She is one of my best goshawks. Fly her well, lad."

Ulf whooped his pleasure.

"Do you not already have a hawk of your own?" Alditha asked politely of the lad. He was a good-looking boy, with the features and mannerisms of his father.

"Aye, Lady, I have a merlin, I call her Beauty. Papa gave her to me on my tenth birthing day—but a merlin cannot be compared to a goshawk."

"It most certainly cannot! I had a merlin when I lived in Wales. She was so fast when she flew that it was difficult to keep your eye on her, and when the sun dazzled on her feathers I thought her the most beautiful thing I had ever seen. Your choice of name is a good one."

Pleased that his wife was attempting to make friends with the lad—it was no easy thing for her to come here—Harold was reluctant to intervene, but there was so little time and so many things that required attention.

"Ulf, put the book away where it belongs and get you gone to tell Thorkeld your news. I would speak with your mother." As the boy ran from the room, his tread loud on the stairs—with the unmistakable thud as he jumped the last four—Harold thought bitterly that his son's love of hawking might, for a while, be disrupted.

Offering wine and a seat, Edyth discreetly brushed at her unbecoming gown, patted her loose-braided, wisping hair. Alditha, despite her pregnancy, was elegant and well-groomed. Edyth smiled, played the dutiful hostess, but was inwardly seething with a rage directed at Harold. Pointedly, she was ignoring him. How dare he bring this woman here without giving her adequate warning! How dare he humiliate her so!

Algytha entered, bearing a dish of sweetmeats and pastries; her mother noticed that she had found a moment to remove her apron and kerchief, and to slip on a clean over-tunic.

"I would have word with you, Edyth," Harold said, motioning for Algytha to sit. "Will you be kind enough to entertain the Queen a moment, my daughter?" Taking Edyth's elbow, Harold steered her from the room, not waiting for a reply from either of the women.

Once down the stairs, Edyth exploded, "How could you do this to me, Harold? To bring her here with no word? Look at the place—look at me! What must she be thinking?"

Withstanding the tirade, for he recognised it was justified, Harold let her have her say. Then when she paused, apologised. "I appreciate the inconvenience, but blame it on Duke William, lass, not me. I do not have time for niceties. Edyth, I can but stay the hour, I must be back at Westminster by the afternoon. The call to arms has gone out. The fyrd is to muster on the thirteenth day of October at that old apple tree on Caldbec Hill."

Edyth bit her lip, ashamed of her churlishness. She knew the tree, had seen it on numerous occasions whenever they stayed at his Sussex manor. An ancient, grey-bearded old man of a tree, of a curious twisting shape, it thrust from the ground like a hand with misshapen fingers, two of them making the distinctive pagan horned sign to ward off evil. An appropriate augury.

"It would be prudent to wait him out, hope for a poor winter to starve him into submission—but how can I abandon those people, my people, who are suffering? Do I abandon them to his mercy until the spring?" Harold could not, of course, which was William's whole strategy. They, the two men, had studied each other well, knew each other's limitations. William had no conscience; Harold cared. It was a defect which William considered to be a liability.

As with most of an incredulous southern England, Edyth was struggling to accept the reality that William had landed, to understand the implications. The politics of it did not interest her, all she knew was that Harold eventually would have to fight this Norman duke. And that fighting could lead to pitiable wounds. Or death.

"And your queen?" she asked. She could not bring herself to use the woman's given name, that would be too much like accepting her, liking her.

"I am sending Alditha north. She is only here because I am setting her on the road, and…" Harold paused. He did not know how to go on.

They were standing apart. He wanted to hold her, touch her. Dare not, but… he lurched forward, put his hands on her upper arms, gripped them tight, with urgency. "And I want you to go with her. At least follow in a day or two."

As she started to shake her head, Harold shook her again, lighter but no less determined. "I have sent word ahead that Goddwin is to await her at York. Edmund will not be leaving until his broken leg has healed. Magnus is looking to his needs. I have asked Goddwin to stay with Alditha."

"He will not like it." Edyth observed.

Harold released her, and said quietly and with despondent honesty, "Nay, he will not. But it seemed the most convenient way, without offending his pride, of keeping him from straying over-close to William's clutches, should things not go well in Sussex." Reaching for her hand, he added, "I want you and our children safe also. I had no choice but to lose you as wife, but I can do my utmost to protect your life. If I am not here to—"

"No!" Edyth almost screamed the word, then covered her mouth with her hands. *Dear Lord God, do not tempt providence!* "Do you think I could go north, suffer the agony of waiting all those days to hear what is happening to England, to you? I have had to endure torment these last weeks. I cannot, shall not, suffer the not knowing again!" She pulled her hand free of his hold, folded her arms, stood straight and defiant. How often had he seen that same determination once she had set her mind to something. "You may send your queen north, Harold, but you will not send me! The housecarl's women will be on the heels of the army, to cook the food and tend the wounded. I shall be with them."

"As would I, Lady Edyth, were I not so heavy with child."

Both Edyth and Harold spun round, startled.

Alditha was coming down the stairs, her skirts held high to forestall any risk of falling. She stepped down the last and released her garments. "Your lady, my husband, has the advantage twice over. Duke William will pay her scant attention. To him, she is merely a discarded mistress. Should Normandy see victory, you would do well to play on it, my Lady Edyth, for your own and your daughters' safety. You are also not heavy with child. Sons, whether legitimate born or no, William will not permit to enjoy their freedom." She put her hand to the bulge of her stomach. "I cannot risk remaining in the South to bear a son born of an anointed king. Not until we know that king is secure upon his throne."

Alditha was frightened but hid it well. So recently to have found contentment and happiness, to have stumbled on the edge of what could become a deep and trusting love...and to have it all, perhaps, snatched away by an obdurate Norman madman..."Until this child is born, and is safe from William, I would have Edyth with you, my Lord. You are tired, you will become more so yet, before this thing can be finished. You need one of us with you to ensure you do not fall ill. That one must be Edyth."

Easy, it was, to suggest something if you only looked at it from the practical side.

19

The Hoar-Apple Tree, Sussex

Evening descended with one of those soft ripples that is barely noticed. The sky had darkened gradually, so that it was only when night actually fell that it was realised the day had ended. Evening ushered in the autumnal chill, the grass dew wet, the air nipping at fingers and face. Before many nights passed, frost would be sprinkling the bronzed leaves and dying bracken.

There was no doubting that Duke William was aware of the English muster. Normandy had scouts who knew their job—had been observed by King Harold's own scouts. Word would have travelled before the marching army as it left London, two days and sixty-odd miles away, over the northern Weald beyond the densely thicketed forest of Andredsweald. They had marched on foot, most of them—the housecarls, the fyrd—for there were no adequate sound horses, but it did not matter. The walk was not so long from London into Sussex, and surprise and speed were not essential for this coming battle.

By the late afternoon of the thirteenth day of October several thousand men were adding their rough-made encampments to those already gathered on the wind-riddled slope of Caldbec Hill. More were coming: in small groups, pairs, ones and twos. Esegar and Godric, both Shire Reeves, settled their men at campfires after dark; Leofric, Abbot of Peterborough, joined his freemen of the fyrd with those of Abbot Ælfurg of Winchester. The men of Thurkill of Kingston and Eadric the Deacon sank wearily into the huddle of their cloaks, hardly caring that the women were offering them food, such was their weariness. Through the night men came, expecting to have a wait of a day or two, perhaps more, before their weapons and skill would be wanted. Scattered over the hill, a hundred and a hundred campfires mirrored the sparkle of the stars wheeling across the heavens: Orion the Hunter, the Bull, the Bear.

The King's own tent was pitched within yards of the old tree, which had proved its worth as an easily recognised rallying point. Outside, his two banners fluttered, toyed with by the restless southern wind: the Dragon of Wessex beside the Fighting Man. Nearby stood the command tent of Earls Gyrth and Leofwine with their own banners. Within Harold's tent, the lamps lit, they were arguing.

"It is senseless for you to fight, brother. If you are killed, what will happen to England? Let me take your place." Leofwine was vehement, his obstinate stance backed by many of those leaders also present—captains, bishops, thegns…

"And what will happen to England if I did that?" Harold roared back at them, slamming his fist on the table top in front of him, making tankards and goblets, maps and the paraphernalia of war bounce. "I was elected king, as Harold the second of that name, elected as the man most worthy to lead our armies. Do I, then, abandon my responsibility at this first hint of danger?"

"But you fought at Stamford Bridge—you have adequately proved your worth…" That was a captain of his housecarls.

"And I shall fight here at Hastings!"

Leofwine swung away from the table, his hands raised. "Is there no reasoning with the man?"

"Happen you could try it more successfully with Duke William?" Gyrth said drily. "Our messenger got nowhere. You might be more persuasive."

Leofwine tossed a lewd, dismissive gesture at his brother. The offer of negotiation sent this afternoon had fallen on closed ears; William had refused even to consider the possibility of talking. A monk from Harold's own abbey of Waltham had ridden those eight miles to the coast, carrying the green branch of peace high. "My Lord King Harold bids you peace," he had said, "and offers you the freedom of withdrawal, with no reprisal or savagery against the destruction that has been committed here in his kingdom. Our King was legally elected by the Council of the Witan and the people of England. He has been anointed and acclaimed by the same."

The terse reply had been as ever it had. Earl Harold, as the Normans persisted in calling him, had sworn oath to become vassal of Normandy, had broken his pledge. As duke and rightful king, William had the support of the Church of Rome and the hand of God within his own. He had then laid down his own terms: "Let Harold surrender to me now, before blood is shed and the killing commences. I shall grant him adequate land for himself and his kindred."

The Waltham Abbey monk had shaken his head. "King Harold already has adequate land. He has England."

Countess Gytha, collecting empty broth bowls from the finished meal and handing them to a servant, added her own impassioned pleading to that of the men. "There is no one to lead if you should fall Harold. England can fight a second, third, or fourth time. William has but this one chance. He must win, for if he does not, how can he try again? He will not have the men. He must win or die—you do not."

"No! I have but the one chance also! Do you all not see?" Harold whirled away from them, his fingers raking through his hair. "I am new to kingship and I am not of the royal blood. I have to prove my ability—Stamford Bridge was a start, but 'tis not enough! Will the North stay loyal if I sit idle and let you, Leofwine, do all the fighting on my behalf?" He lowered his hands, a desperate plea for understanding contorting his face. "Duke William is a warrior lord. He will see naught but weakness if I flinch from facing him—that in itself may win him the day. Have no doubt that if I do not take the field, William will crow of my reluctance to prove the truth of this thing."

He crossed the tent, placed a hand on Leofwine's shoulder, glanced at each man present, at his mother. "I quarrel with William, but do not wish to do so with all of you also. I have come this far and will lead my men into battle. As for the rest"—he spread his hands, let them fall to his side—"that is in God's hands." With a sudden display of affection, Harold pulled Leofwine to him in an embrace, patting his hand on the younger man's back. Leofwine returned the gesture of peace.

Then, grinning, Harold shuffled through the maps spread on the table and selected the one he required. "Now that matter is settled, let us make our plans. William is encamped here, by the Hastings shore. He will be wondering whether we are to attack him where he sits, or whether he will need come to us." He looked at the men present: his two brothers, the commanders of his own housecarls and those of Gyrth and Leofwine, at the shire reeves, the more important thegns. "He has sufficient spies watching our every movement, as we are keeping close eye on him. Come dawn, we shall both know how many of each other's men carry the cock-pox!"

Gyrth laughed with the rest, then ran to the tent flap. "So you are watching us, eh, Bastard Born? Well, see this and take notice!" He unlaced his braies and thrust his bare backside out into the darkness to appreciative applause.

"You had better not do that when we meet in battle," someone guffawed. "I hear the Normans are skilled with the bow and arrow—that fine rounded bum of yours would make a most suited target."

"It is a broad one, that's for certain!"

Harold joined in the merriment, letting it swirl a while. Laughter was a good tonic. "What we need," he said as the chuckling subsided, "is time. Another day, two, and all those men summoned will be here. Eadric ought to have the fleet in position—seventy of our craft are blockading the sea lanes. Within a few days the Normans will not be able to get in or out."

"Do we wait here, Sir? See what he intends?"

"That is what I propose. I have no wish to go down into the peninsula. We have successfully cut William off from moving further out into England. He can either wait out the winter, or fight us. And if he decides to fight, we shall be here." He stabbed his finger at a charcoal line drawn on the map. "On the hill above the Sand Lake, on Sendlach Ridge."

⟢⟣

Countess Gytha left the men to their planning. She could not bear to listen to the talk of death and killing. Outside, she closed her eyes, breathed in the dampness of the earth, the lingering smell of woodsmoke and cooking—the aroma of stewing and sizzling meat, the acrid stench of a part that had scorched. Someone, she mused, had not watched and turned the spit. What would Godwine have thought and said of all this? Of Harold he would, without doubt, have been proud; of Leofwine and Gyrth also. But of their other son? Of Tostig?

She walked through the groups of men, some sitting, talking and laughing, others curled up, trying for sleep. Many of them had their weapons laid across their knees, or cradled within their arms as if the axe or spear or sword were a woman. Where the path was narrow, they shuffled to allow her passage, doffing their hats, bringing their hand to their left shoulder in salute. They all recognised the Countess. Had not many and many of them served her dead lord before this one?

What were they thinking, she wondered, of her son Tostig? Of his betrayal, of his utter stupidity? Two sons had she lost to the grave. Swegn she had never forgiven. Would she, in the years to come, think as bitterly of Tostig?

At the edge of the slope stood a copse of trees, the canopy rustling as the wind played chasing games with the autumn-tinted leaves. In a week or two, if the weather turned and the wind strengthened, the leaves would fall and the trees stand unclothed, for all the world dead and finished. But unlike men slaughtered in battle, the shoots would bud in the spring and the trees would come alive again. Two sons dead and a third, not seen all these long years, held captive in Normandy. Did he still live, or had William had Wulfnoth hanged, or his throat cut?

She sat on a fallen log, dimly illuminated by the flickering light of a campfire. If Wulfnoth had died at the Duke's hand, then let God have seen to it that it had been quick and painless. Oh, she knew what William was capable of, how he could butcher and torture, how he could order a man—and his wife, so she had heard—shut within a dungeon and left to starve. All for defying their duke.

She gazed out at the stars, hearing the eerie call of a hunting owl, the quick scream as it caught its prey. A mouse, perhaps, or a vole. Two, three sons lost to her, and a daughter.

Edith she had tried to see in Winchester, wanting to talk sense into her, to make the fool girl realise the consequences of what was happening all around her. But Edith had refused her mother an audience, said she was too deep in mourning for her brother to welcome visitors. The rebuff had been as sharp as it had been poignant, implying her mother had no feeling for Tostig.

Oh, she was wrong in that! Very wrong. Gytha had many feelings for Tostig, feelings that were not suited to a woman, to a mother.

The message she sent back to Edith, as she left her house in Winchester, had been as succinct: "Had I known the future as I lay birthing the son who came to be called Tostig, I would have taken the cord and tightened it around his neck myself. For this one act that I did not do, I may well lose three more of my sons, and a grandson with them!"

20

Hastings

Before sunset, Duke William had the relics upon which Harold had sworn his oath paraded before the men. Archbishop Odo of Bayeux walked at the head of the procession, laying his hand on those soldiers who knelt before him, offering prayers and blessings. The exercise imbued the men with renewed strength; they were restless and uneasy for they were in a strange land, penned in with no way forward, no way back. The English ships had been sighted during the late afternoon and word had already spread that Harold had come...There was no getting out of this now. Either death or victory awaited. There could be no losing, for there was nothing to lose, save life itself.

William had decided no definite plans or tactics when the fleet had sailed from Saint Valéry—too much had depended on the wind and sea and on their reception upon landing—if they managed to get that far. God had been with them for voyage and landing. A few peasants had attempted to make a fight of it as the Normans entrenched themselves in the village of Hastings, but they had been cut down. As the English army would be, when they met on the battlefield.

His men were experienced, war-hardened soldiers—there was not a man here who had not at least one battle scar etched on his body. And he had the horses, the skilled and powerful cavalry, Harold did not. William's scouts had told him that the English were mostly on foot or mounted on shaggier riding ponies, not war mounts.

It was well known that infantry fared ill against cavalry. The English stood little chance if they elected open battle. The Duke only wished he knew of Harold's intentions. The hill where Harold had mustered his men formed an effective gateway, lying across the road that led out from this narrow strip of marsh-locked land. Were the English intending to hold that barrier, entrusting that their ships could retain an effective position seawards? Or would Harold approach the coast, provoke a fight nearer Hastings? *Non.* Any sensible general would entrench at the narrowest point through which the enemy must march to gain new ground. Cage his opponent, create an effective siege. Ah, but was Harold an effective general? Was he or not?

Duke William poured himself wine and sipped. In Normandy he had taken the English Earl to be a cock-crowing, uninspiring sort of man. A family man, a woman's man. Look how Mathilda had admired him! Pah, she'd claimed she had no liking for him, that she had merely been attempting to find out what she could from him. Did she think her husband so naive? What was it she had said? That there was more to Harold on the layers beneath than on those that were visible to the eye? She had certainly been right where his devious double-dealing had been concerned! But what did a woman know of what made a good leader or no, of the making of battle plans?

As she had come to mind, William briefly considered how Mathilda would fare in Normandy if he were to not return. Could she hold the duchy together until their son reached maturity? He had left sound men to assist her; Robert de Montgomery he could trust implicitly, for the firm promise of a lion's portion of English land as a reward for his loyalty, if for nothing else. Nor would her father, Count Baldwin, allow Normandy to fall to anyone other than his grandson.

He tossed back the wine, savouring its mellow fruit. No point in brooding over what may be, not when the now must first be considered. He doubted any man could hold the duchy together as effectively as had he, had no particular care of what happened after his death. He was not doing all this for the reward of others, this was for himself, for his own satisfaction. As for Robert, he had no real feeling for that irritating boy who was—God knew how—his son. Let him see to the muddle if there came one. If he could muster the manhood to do so.

"What would you do, fitz Osbern?" William asked, repeating his previous thoughts aloud, kicking his second-in-command's boot from where it was stretched before a dying brazier.

Fitz Osbern started, grunted. He had been dozing; the day had been long and wearisome. His scouting venture with the Duke earlier in the day, covering those few miles to observe the English position, had depressed him. There were so many of the English, and they would be fighting on their own soil—they would dictate the when and where. In addition, the day had been hot and humid, the return walk to Hastings seeming twice as long as the outward trek. Fitz Osbern had felt dizzy and unwell—his stomach had the runs. This brackish-tasting English water was upsetting many of them.

They had taken their hauberks as a matter of course, but had not worn them. Once, stumbling, Will had fallen to his knees, the weight of the mail in his arms dragging him down. He was sweating, exhausted—but not Duke William. He had put a hand under Will's elbow, lifted him up and carried his armour for him along with his own. Did nothing hamper or deter this duke? He had the courage of a lion, the heart of a stag and the strength of an ox—ah, but there were so many of those English!

Will fitz Osbern tried to formulate a helpful and suitable answer. "Were I in Harold's position," he opined with slow deliberation. "I would build a timber blockade and fortifications where I sit. Starve us out."

"And that, my friend," William said, "we cannot allow." Decision made, he strode to the tent opening, calling for his captains and commanders. Then he swung round to grin confidently at his companion and friend. "We cannot afford to be penned up like herded cattle awaiting the autumn slaughter, nor can we allow this man who calls himself 'king' the chance to catch his breath."

Men began arriving at a jogtrot: Comte Brian de Bretagne, Eustace de Boulogne, Robert de Beaumont…both the Duke's half-brothers, Bishop Odo and Robert, comte de Mortain. D'Evreux, de Mortagne, vicomte Thours, Walter Gifford, Ralph de Tosny. Mont-fort, de Warenne, Malet, Guy de Ponthieu and more, the blood in their veins rising with the excitement of approaching battle.

"Call in the foraging parties." William barked as his first order. His next was: "We march at dawn."

❦

First light, an hour before sunrise, on a dew-damp Saturday morning, the fourteenth day of October. A pale, laundered blue spread like an incoming tide from the east. The sky swung high and clear, decorated by skimped wisps of cloud that would tinge pink once the sun rose.

Harold had lain awake, staring into the darkness, his arm cradling Edyth, her head nestled into the familiar, comfortable hollow of his shoulder. She slept, her eyes flickering, body twitching, from a visiting dream. A smile was on her face, so it must be a good dream. They had made love twice during these few short hours of privacy, the first time with the frantic desire of need, the second for the sharing, the giving and taking, of love. He had come to bed late, close to the midnight hour, for there had been much to see to: the briefing of his commanders; a tour of the camp, talking to the men, exchanging conversation with those he knew, enquiring after family—a marriage, a birth, a death—asking after the healing of wounds received, in honour, at Stamford Bridge, exchanging anecdotes of that day's victorious fighting. With those he knew not, asking their name, their home, kindred. All the while making it seem that each man was the important one, their king's friend and companion. It was the way of a good commander to talk on equal terms with his men, to listen, to be together as brothers. As they would be, come the day of fighting.

As the tent lightened with the dawn, he slid from the bed, settling Edyth's head gently on the pillow. He dressed in tunic and hose, unlaced the entrance flap and stood in the opening, looking out on to the new-born day. Men were awakening, he could hear the sounds of stirring: stretching, coughing and yawning; from the nearer tents, the cruder body functions. So many thoughts in his mind. Alditha and the coming child. Goddwin. His daughters—they at least ought to be safe. Gunnhild was receiving her education at Wilton; he had sent Algytha to join her there. Ulf he had taken to London, to be with Edgar and the remainder of the court. Edgar had wanted to come to Sussex, but Harold had forbidden it, for the same reasons that he had seen his own sons safe, and for the sake of England should things go wrong here in the South. He would rather his own son, should Alditha bear him one, follow him as king, but if William should by chance win his way out of this enclosed peninsula and he, Harold, was unable to take the fight to him again…Edgar remained ætheling. It would be for Edgar to rally the North, to fetch Eadwine and Morkere to London…He must not think pessimistically. William was the one who was caught like a rat in a trap. Not he.

He would like good marriages for his girls—it was by far time Algytha were wed. Perhaps as a wife for Edgar? It was worth considering. He must mention it to Edyth…ah, Edyth. He had not wanted her to come, not where there was to be fighting. Battle was no pretty thing. All the stories, the sagas and songs told of the glory and the pleasure in victory; you never heard the truth from the taletellers' lips: the cries of the wounded, the screams of the horses, the stench, the spilling of gore and blood.

He was on the very edge of pulling back, of agreeing terms with William. The man could not rule both countries with the efficiency he would crave, would have to appoint some lord to rule as regent. *Would it*, Harold thought, *damage my own pride so severely if I were to abdicate? To save the slaughter, the widowing of too many wives, the slaying of children's fathers? Earl of Wessex is no mean title—do I need to be king?*

Movement behind interrupted his thoughts, a hand on his back, an arm slipping round his waist, the summer-flower scent of Edyth. He lifted his own arm, brought her closer to his side so that she too might see the glory of this autumn morning. No, he had not wanted his beloved Edyth to come, yet he was glad that she had: something beautiful to see and touch, to ward away the ugliness of conflict.

He looked southwards, towards Hastings. Was William standing, questing northwards with his mind and instinct to help him decide what to do? Or did he already know?

Small in the distance, a man was galloping down the incline of Telham Hill. An English scout. Harold's arm tightened around Edyth's waist. He dipped his head, lightly placed his lips on the crown of her hair, guessed the news the runner was bringing. They had known, last night when he had walked through the camp, they had all really known. He had known when he had lain and loved with his Edyth, that William would not wait.

❧

At dawn, Bishop Geoffrey de Coutances had taken mass and offered Communion to Normandy's commanders and to her duke. Had blessed them and prayed for God's deliverance on this most especial day.

By the half-hour past six, Duke William's army was on the move. Bretons, with Poitou, Anjou and Maine, headed the column led by comte Brian. Next the Franco-Flemish—the fierce fighting men of Picardy, Boulogne and Flanders with comte Eustace de Boulogne, Robert de Beaumont and William fitz Osbern. And then came the Normans, the infantry, together with the cavalry on foot, leading their horses so the animals would be fresh for the hardship ahead. Across the saddles lay their hauberks, the chain-mail armour, ready to be donned when the time came to form the battle lines.

Duke William himself rode his black stallion, the Andalusian charger, a gift from King Alfonso of Aragon. He was a good horse, coming from a man who could prove useful to Normandy. He would make a suitable husband for Agatha, when this business in England was satisfactorily completed. Snorting and prancing, the magnificent, long-maned beast paced beside the column of men. William, clad in leather under-tunic and braies, the mail leggings and sleeves laced and tied, rode from the rear forward, so that he might have a chance to speak to every one of them as he passed. Again and again he repeated his words as he trotted past rank upon rank—close on 18,000 men.

"Our hearts and spirits fly high this bright morning! Fight well, this day, my brothers, and your reward will be great—and for those of you who do fall, die well, knowing you enter God's Kingdom with the honour of a warrior. The sons of your begotten sons, or the children of your brothers and nephews, will say with pride: my kinsman fought, that day, in England at the place they called Hastings!"

He was there to watch them, as the long, long column of men dispersed upon the hill that by the afternoon would be called Blackhorse Hill, the hill where the baggage wagons were to be left, the supplies minded and the wounded brought. There would be many wounded, most of them beyond helping.

The men, eager and apprehensive all together, ran their thumbs lightly across axe and sword edge, tested bow strings, set arrows loose in the quivers at their hips. Hoisted spears, tapped shields for soundness. Hauberks, for those fortunates who had chain-mail, were pulled on, fitting like a tunic that reached to knee or calf, split from hem to crotch rear and front, the loose skirting laced, for those cavalrymen who preferred it, to form crude breeches. By ill chance, William's hauberk twisted to the left as he brought the mail coat down over his head, ending backwards about his body, the sword slit to his right side, the coif to his front. Men saw and the whisper sped quickly from mouth to mouth. Bad luck? An omen!

William laughed, his head tossed back, a great guffaw of amusement, although inside he was quaking—God's love, but he must turn this thing quickly, in face and word, else he could lose them! He swivelled the mail to its right side, shouting, "see how I turn it from the wrong to the right with such ease? Thus shall I, this day, right Harold's wrongs and turn my duchy into a kingdom!"

They heard and the anxious sweep of superstition fled with a yodelling cheer. The Leopards of Normandy, carried by Turstin, were set in the curve of the hill. Duke William, after signing himself with the cross, sent his men down the slope and into position in the valley beneath the high rising ground, where, upon the ridge, the English stood. Waiting.

21

Sendlach Hill

The English were ranged along the high ridge of Sendlach Hill, a seven-hundred-yard line of men, seven or eight deep. The front rank of more than one thousand men stood in close order, their shields before them, overlapping in place, forming a wall almost as solid as anything that could have been built. In the centre, the area more vulnerable to cavalry attack, were the housecarls—the experienced, elite warriors. On the flanks were the fyrd, protected by the sharp drop of land, forest and marsh to east and west of the ridge. The ridge itself dropped down ahead a full hundred feet in every four hundred yards, before rolling on across a shallow valley towards Telham Hill, more than a mile away. Sendlach was a high, dry watershed for the Brede river and the Asten brook—the sand-bottomed water channel that normally meandered sluggishly across the low-lying ground between the rise of low hills. Only the Asten brook had been dammed with logs, soil, brushwood—the carcass of a dead sheep—anything the English could quickly lay hands on. With its outlet blocked, the water had nowhere to flow across the narrow, flat level, could only seep into the lower ground. For most of the summer—and the summer before that—this ground had been waterlogged, a quagmire of boggy marsh. The surface had only dried out these last few wind-blown and sun-drenched weeks; the grass looked safe, green and lush...until the first of William's men, the Bretons, set foot on it.

It took less than an hour for Duke William to see his men deployed into line. The Bretons were to his left flank, facing what had become bogged, heavy clay ground but a shallower incline; the Franco-Flemish to his right, with firm, dry but perilously steeper ground. In the centre, under William's two half-brothers, the archers with bows and slings waited. Behind, the ranks of infantry and behind them the cavalry. Morale was high and the weather was holding good; rain would have made the ascent of that fearsome slope impossible. Rain, which had fallen so incessantly this year, would have been a Godsend for Harold on this one day.

William sat on his fidgeting horse, gazing out over the mass of men, the sun glinting on armour and weapons, on banners and pennants of blue, green, gold, red. From the position of the sun it was near nine *ante meridiem*; Mass would be beginning in monastery and church, as God's judgement must begin here, William fingered the relic pouch that hung around his neck, then looked to his trumpeters who stood, eyes fixed on their lord duke.

He raised his arm. Let it fall.

"*Ut! Ut! Ut!*" Sword or spear beating upon shields, feet stamping, the noise slammed down from the ridge as the Norman army started to advance. The cries of Harold's own battle call of "*Oli Crosse*" mingling with "*Godemite!*" reverberating between that continued, fearsome "Out! Out! Out!"

The Normans began to fan out sideways and forwards as they marched, the line stretching longer and thinner, filled with foreboding at the views. One hundred and fifty yards ahead, fifty foot higher, rank upon rank of bellowing, spear-edged, axe-sharpened death bringers.

Between the two lines lay green, untrodden grass, dotted with the occasional golden-flowered gorse bush, and pock-marked by the last fading blooms of field speedwell and red campion. To the left, a copse turning autumn russet, the trunks twined about by briars, bearing the last few blackberries. The hedges, all gay with bright berries. A rotting alder tree, tumbled by some past storm, lay aslant halfway up the hill; on one of its skyward-pointing dead branches, oblivious to men and weapons, perched a robin, incongruously piping his territorial song.

Duke William smiled, complacent, as the first wave of arrows arched into the blue sky like a black, hissing storm cloud. And another, and another. And another. One thousand and more archers, each with a full sheaf of four and twenty arrows. The first phase of his planned attack to wrest the crown of England from Harold Godwinesson: archers, to cause maximum casualties, to maim, to kill. Shooting arrow after arrow until their quivers were emptied—and then, as they marched forward, they would gather the spent arrows sent downwards by the English that had missed their targets, and return them in further waves of destruction…only William's plan went awry from the start, for there was no return of arrows. The English were not using their archers. Whether Harold had thought the southern wind too strong for effective shooting, or his archers had been depleted by the fighting in the North—or whether the Englishman had deliberately planned to reduce the quantity of Norman ammunition, William had no way of knowing. The laconic smile hardened as he watched his archers withdrawing from the field, with nothing more to shoot. So, Harold was using his brain, was to make a proper fight of this. That was agreeable to William.

They were nearing now, the infantry, having crossed over the quagmire of the brook and scrabbled up the hill. Using high-held shields, they deflected the missiles raining down from above: stones, rocks, sticks, billets, broken axe heads, clods of earth—then spears and javelins. It was to be expected. The defensive line would remove as many opponents as possible before the Norman infantry came close enough for hand-to-hand fighting; the attackers would then attempt to create breaches for the cavalry to exploit, to crash through the barrier of standing men, inflict their lethal destruction and then pursue those who dropped their weapons and ran…most battles went that way, the fighting usually all over within the hour.

The Bretons had found the crossing of the brook hard work; the sodden ground soon became ankle deep in clay. Caked by mud, the men struggled on; once across, they found the hillside a shallow climb and, unlike in the centre, the debris hurtling down on them was not so substantial. Intent on their own path, the Bretons reached the top and came face to face with the shield wall, intact, for the arrow flights had mostly passed harmlessly overhead. And they were alone, had outpaced the line of men to their right.

Unsupported, uncoordinated, they met with spears and javelins at close range, the men coming behind pushing those in front on to the waiting blades of the English, the dead and dying heaping, one atop the other, before that wall. They tried, they jostled and pushed, swung axes, cursed and spat, but could inflict no damage upon the English. Instead, they were being destroyed with the ease of a man's palm swatting at flies…The centre reached the top of the ridge, found, as had the left wing, an undamaged wall of shields and men with death-tipped blades. The thing was hopeless! The Bretons broke, turned and fled back down the hill.

Confusion and panic spread as fire fanned by a wind. Their flank undefended and exposed, the Norman centre milled in disorder, wavering. The cavalry, coming behind, saw that the Bretons were fleeing and that their own infantry were beginning to turn also, starting to dodge through the excited, almost uncontrollable horses, running back down the hill in fear and terror of those English, standing, the line barely depleted, up on the hill.

Harold's orders had been to stand firm. At all cost. Stand. He had ridden along the length of the ridge, talking to the men, reassuring, jesting, praising, swelling the high morale of battle lust. Repeating, again and again, his order. "Stand firm. If we stand William cannot break through. Unless he can break our line, he can do no great damage to us. Until I give command, stand firm, my brothers, stand firm!" Harold knew the Duke's practised tactics, knew also his own vulnerability of cavalry against infantry. He and the men were tired; they had marched, fought and marched again. Add to that, not all the fyrd were yet here. He had to contain William, hold him back in this peninsula, and to do that, had to let William do all the work. Let him charge up and down to the ridge, let him weary himself on the slope and in the mud at the bottom. The English were going nowhere, were to stand. Firm-footed.

Harold's right wing of fyrd men saw the Bretons running, the Norman centre confused, bleating and threshing like sheep frightened by the stench of a wolf. They heard a roar of victory go up from their own centre, saw the attacking Norman line give ground and begin to retreat.

It was all over! They had won! The Normans were running, were beaten... and the fyrd, experienced militiamen but without the hard-ranked discipline of the housecarls, dropped their shields and erupted from the ridge, down the hill, in pursuit of a broken enemy, jeering and shouting.

Both commanders watched in growing, sickened horror. Two men in their prime, capable and gifted warlords. Two men who claimed the same crown, the same kingdom. Harold, four and forty years of age, six years his opponent's senior, stood surrounded by his personal guard beneath his two standards, set into the high ground to the left of his centre. William, astride his impressive black stallion, observing from the lower slope of Telham Hill.

The rules of engagement were changing as the fight unfolded, here on this battlefield, on this day, the fourteenth of October in the year of Our Lord 1066. Rare it was for battle to last more than an hour or two. Never had mobile cavalry gone against a line of static, immovable infantry. Never had William been beaten.

Without consideration, he clamped his jaw, sat deep into the saddle and spurred his horse from a stand into a gallop. The impatient beast responded with the swiftness and stamina of his breed. He half leapt, half stumbled through the churned quagmire, heading for the turmoil of the Norman cavalry to the left of the centre division. Bellowing and shouting, the Duke turned those riders at the rear, who milled, uncertain.

"Turn back, turn back! Fight, you bastard scum—turn back and fight! Look— they've run out, they're unprotected—ride them down, you whore-poxed fools! Ride them down!"

As Harold well knew, no man on foot, vulnerable and unprotected, could withstand the flying hooves of a galloping horse and its rider with hefted spear. Too late, those Saxon fyrdmen realised why their king had told them to stand, that they had thought wrong, that it was not all over. The Normans were not broken. By leaving the shield wall, the Saxons had isolated themselves. They tried, desperately, to assemble into a wedged formation in the shelter of the trees on that copsed hillock near the Asten brook. Stood with spears, axe and short-sword pointing outwards, with brave hearts and stout courage, tried to defend themselves against the swamping flood tide of battle-crazed, iron-shod horses.

There was nothing the men of the English fyrd could do, nothing, except die.

22

Sendlach Ridge

Defeat had nearly overrun William's army, but by some fortune—by God's grace or his own swift action—the rout had been avoided. The Breton infantry had fled in disarray, the morale of his centre and right flanks was ebbing as fast as a tide could abandon the island monastery of Mont Saint Michel. Leaving the slaughter of the English right-wing fyrdmen to the Breton cavalry, William recalled his army, a tactical withdrawal to gain a respite, gather the wounded and re-form. He was not beaten; it was not ended. Although he was shaken, he could hardly believe that he had come so close to defeat—so uncomfortably close.

The brow of the ridge was clearing of Normans, leaving the litter of battle in the place of troops: broken weapons, lost helmets; the dead, horse and man. As they walked or limped back down the hill, the men collected what they could from the dead. Shields that were less damaged than their own, a tighter-fitting helmet, better-quality boots. Hauberks—a prize indeed! Used their daggers to put a swift end to maimed, dying animals and the occasional comrade; carried with them their wounded.

The commanders were vociferously rallying them, Bishop Odo, Eustace de Boulogne, Robert de Mortain and fitz Osbern, working hard to restore heart and vigour, issuing supplies of arrows, new weapons where needed; sending those with wounds to be patched up by the priests; replacing horses. All the while, William sat on his own horse on the Norman side of the Asten brook, assessing that first attack. What had gone wrong? Why he had failed? More important, how best to send in his men a second time? He could not afford another near disaster. *Merde*, he would never hold these men through a second debacle like this first had been! He began to reorganise his army into three divisions: infantry, cavalry and re-equipped archers. He marshalled them with encouragement, threats and bribes. Told them they were heroes or whoresons. Proffered rewards of land and gold, or retribution that he himself would see to if they again failed him.

For Harold, too, the pause, which lasted half of the hour, came as a thankful respite. The fighting had lasted over an hour; there was no need yet for food, but the passing of the water skins along the lines came welcome to dry-throated, breathless men. With the wounded and the dead lifted shoulder over shoulder to the rear, the line closed ranks. Because of the depleted right wing, the shield line was shortened, but the carcasses of dead horses were hauled closer and topped with dead Normans to create an extra barricade. Those who were not dead, beast and men, were dispatched with a dagger to the throat and added to the gruesome wall.

William made a good general because he used quick, decisive thinking. His first attempt had failed, therefore he must change tactics. This second attack was to be better co-ordinated, the distance between archers and infantry decreased, the cavalry sent in closer. The ranks must arrive together at the ridge of the hill, push forward in a concerted effort, not in a raggle-taggle mess. To do this, and to ensure their courage did not fail, William himself was to lead the advance.

Nearing the eleventh hour of the morning, the Norman trumpets sounded again and the line began to roll slowly forward. Up on the ridge, the Saxon English straightened to attention, tightened their grip on axe, sword and shield. Gyrth and Leofwine, set to right and left of the centre line of housecarls, exchanged a raised hand of salute to each other. Harold himself let out a yell of encouragement that was taken up from man to man, voice to voice: "*Oli Crosse*—Holy Cross! Out! Out! Out!" The rhythm of the war beat thundered on their shields. "*Ut! Ut! Ut!*"

The advance up the hill was slower than before, the quagmire deeper and spreading where the water from the dammed brook was beginning to flood. Gone was the emerald-green grass; the scatter of flowers; the robin. Instead: swathes of blood-puddled mud; the scratched and torn clefts where horses' hooves had gouged as they plunged or fell; the dead, stripped of mail, boots, helmets. Of dignity.

The Saxon line shook, but held. The Norman line pressed and pushed, without wavering, but to the other side of the shield wall. Where one man went down, another leapt in, as savagely determined to hold firm. They tried and tried again to break through that damned impenetrable shield wall. Could not do it.

William drove his black stallion forward with spurs that flecked blood on the animal's lathered flanks. As he rode and fought he bellowed encouragement, goading his men onwards, tongue-lashing the waverers. The stallion was terrified by the noise: the yells, the clash of weapon upon weapon, the cries of the wounded as axe or sword hacked at sinew and gut, the screams of mutilated horses; he was crazed by the anger and the fear, the stench of blood and the raging press of men that battered and jostled his quarters and shoulders. Ears back, eyes rolling white, he trod on the fallen, for those who went down at the front had no chance of getting up. The animal tried to swing round, to escape, but William curbed him, bullying him as hard as he did his men. Fighting his rider, the beautiful animal reared, his hind legs sliding on the slime of gore and gutted entrails. He half toppled, scrabbling with his forelegs to keep his balance, and lurched against the shield wall, his weight, almost half a ton of solid flesh, plunging into the English. But they knew how to deal with any horse or rider who came within range of their long-handled, broad-bladed battleaxes—the terror weapon that could cleave through armour and the man wearing it; could slice off the head of a horse in a single blow.

The black Andalusian was dead in the instant an axe struck downwards behind his ears, severing the skull from the neck. William screamed, kicking his legs free of the stirrups, tried to roll away from the carcass as it fell, was caught, trapped by the lower leg. He lay for a second—seemingly a lifetime—hands cradled over his head, curled into a ball, as the trampling sway of men and horses pummelled at his back and shoulders. Hell was made here, before this shield line at the place of battle! A shout from a yard or two to the left: the shields were giving ground. The Norman line shifted slightly, all effort concentrating on that one small, weak point—and William found himself, for a very brief flurried moment, almost alone down among the dead. He pulled his leg free, though pain shot up from his ankle, crawled and wriggled through the thinned mêlée of men, his hand stamped on by boots, his head reeling from kicks—was surprised to find himself suddenly out in open ground, down behind the Norman line. He loosened the strap of his war helmet and vomited, the inside of his brain whirling with red, muzzy dizziness. Slowly he lurched to his knees, then stood, his body shaking, screeching from the pain of multiple bruises and what felt most assuredly like a broken rib. His ears were ringing, his vision was blurred. Pain thundered down his leg and his arm, where blood also trickled. His face, the front of his chest and his thighs were splattered also, though how much of the blood was his own he would not know until he removed his armour.

Had he moved without realising? Why was he among men again? Why were they passing him? Running—oh, God's curse! That breach could not have been made, they were being repelled, were falling back! He stood, arms lifted, shouting. What could he do, one man standing among so many? Then he heard the cry that was rippling from tongue to tongue:

"*Mort. Le due est mort!*"

"*Où est le duc?*"

Mon Dieu! Non! They were panicking. They thought him dead! William swung his head, ignoring the dizziness that threatened to come upon him again, searched frantically for an unridden horse, saw Eustace de Boulogne astride his grey, beating at the Franco-Flemish right wing, trying to turn them back. The Duke ran to him, at a shuffling, hobbling pace, bellowing for him to dismount.

"*Votre cheval! Vite! Vite!*"

De Boulogne was off, one hand clasping the rein of the maddened beast, the other boosting William into the saddle. The Duke nodded his gratitude and spurred the animal along behind the line. Suddenly he realised the men could not recognise him now that he was not mounted on the black. He yanked at his helmet, exposing his face to full view. Cried out over and over, "*Regardez! C'est moi!* It is I, it is I! *Je vis* I live."

For almost three hours the struggle had continued. The English line swayed and rippled—the occasional breach being sealed instantly—but it held. Only a few from the left wing, again the lesser men of the fyrd, had broken in the same way their comrades had earlier in the day. De Boulogne's men, rallying after they heard Duke William lived, had slaughtered each one of them, but it was not sufficient. Nothing was going to move King Harold's housecarls from the top of that ridge of Sendlach Hill.

William's second assault was crumbling into disarray. He had no choice; his men were exhausted; too many horses were down riderless; swords were broken or blunted, spears all used. If he did not take the decision to withdraw and regroup, then they would surely break and there would be no holding them this time.

Respite was welcomed by everyone except the Duke. It seemed hopeless. A quarter of his men killed, as many horses slain or made useless. How many more men were slipping away unseen? His soldiers sat where they fell on the far side of the morass that had, at first light, been nothing more than a calm brook. Too tired, almost, to drink from wineskins, eat the food that was passed around. Only the commanders were active, for William had called his captains to gather at his standard. One last try at it. Once more only and they had to use it to their best advantage. Looking out over the men, some weeping, others numb to feelings, all of them nursing sword or wound, William de Warenne, who had once asked his duke about England, wondered how they were going to get them up on their feet again. How they were going to make them go back up that foul and stinking slope that led direct to the devil's hell.

23

Sendlach—The Shield Wall

Morale was running high among the English; twice, now, had they beaten off the Norman whoresons; their casualties—even counting those fool men of the fyrd who had not heeded the King's orders—amounting to less than half the Norman dead strewn over the battlefield. Aye, the line had dwindled to only two or three men deep in places, but shortened, gathered in towards the centre, they ought to be able to withstand a third assault.

Food and drink were passed from man to man, those women who had come—wives, mostly, who had no children to care for—issuing flat-baked barley cakes, wheaten bread and recent-picked sweet and juicy apples. It was from the women, too, and the priests, that the wounded sought aid, hobbling, being carried or supported to the safety of the baggage line. Not that there was much that could be done for many of them, beyond the comfort of a clasped hand or a pretty smile and the offering of prayers.

Harold threaded his way to the front of the wall, clasping men by the hand, gripping their shoulders as he passed, praising, encouraging or sympathising with those who sported minor wounds.

Pointing to a bloodied rent in one man's byrnie, he exclaimed, "Godfin! Is that a wound to your side?"

"Nay, my Lord, 'tis nothing serious. An arrow poke to me belly. Could 'ave been worse 'ad it been lower. Might have nipped me in the family tool department, eh!"

Godfin offered a skin of ale to his king, with a laugh and nod of appreciation. Harold accepted, lifted the pig's bladder to his mouth and drank a mouthful. It was strong-brewed ale, stuff for men.

"By the Christ," Harold jested, wiping his lips and handing it on to another man, "we ought give some of this to those bastards down there—it's strong enough to blow their balls off!"

It was easier to laugh and joke, for the terrible carnage at the front of the line would be too sickening if there were not something to balance its horror. The stench was appalling. A horse wandered, broken reins trailing, lamed in the foreleg by an axe stroke that had gouged part of his lower shoulder away; another stood, head lowered, bewildered that he could no longer see, for a sword had slashed across his face; a third struggled to rise, not understanding that he no longer had a hind leg…Not four yards from the shield line, a man lay, moaning, calling piteously for water, his stomach and entrails exposed, black blood oozing. Already the ravens were circling the field. One, more brazen than its companions, landed a few feet from the dying man, hopped closer, its beak preparing to pick at the exposed flesh. They went for the eyes, these nauseating scavengers. The soft flesh of the eyes, not caring whether a man or beast still lived…Thrusting aside two of the men who stood in the front rank, Harold pushed his way through to the open hillside, his dagger in his hand. A ruffle of unease spread through the men as he stepped out of their protected shielding, but he ignored it. He waved his hand menacingly, chasing the obnoxious bird away, bent and touched the man's shoulder. A Norman, a young lad, no older than his second son, Edmund.

"Give me water, my Lord!" he croaked in French, and Harold answered him in his own tongue.

"There'll be water in plenty awaiting you, son." With his dagger, he slashed neat and quick across the boy's throat. Aye, he was a Norman, but no one deserved to die that way. Except perhaps William himself…No—Harold, shouldering his men aside, returned behind the lines, dismissing the thought from his mind—no, not even Duke William, for if he thought that, then he was no better than him. Uncaring, unfeeling. Ordering this day of death, causing this mighty pain and suffering for no reason except his own wanting of something that could not, by any lawful right, be his. No, Harold was not like that.

"See to those beasts," he ordered. "End their torment." He made his way back, all the while exchanging cheerful banter. All the while driving and driving away the thought that hammered and screamed in his mind: *My brothers are dead. Both my beloved brothers, both are dead!* Gyrth, killed by a spear through his throat, Leofwine, a Norman sword slicing through his stomach as he had raised his axe to strike. Both Harold's brothers slain and left among the dead, for during those hours of furious fighting there had been no opportunity to help with the wounded or to remove the corpses. Harold halted as he cleared the straggle of ranked men. Looked over his shoulder, along the lines. Men standing, sitting, lying. Leaning on spears, eating, resting, drinking. Hurting, wounded. Nigh on exhausted. Was it worth it? This death, this carnage?

Ah, no! No crown was worth this dreadful taking of life—but then, no crown ought to be surrendered without it, especially not to a man who could so casually cause it all.

"They will come again," Harold said to those who could hear, knowing his words would be repeated along the line of sprawled men. "A last time, William will try for us again. It will be worse. I can guarantee." He forced an encouraging smile, raised his fist in a gesture of victorious defiance. Shouted, "But then for them, we shall make it worse still!"

They answered him with cheers.

"The day goes well for us, my friends, my heroes!" he called as he walked back down behind the line, heading for the baggage and the wounded. He had to keep up the talk. Show he had energy yet to spend, that he had no doubts. That his confidence and pride were unsullied. How good an actor, then, must a king be!

"I am proud of you! Take your rest while you may, my brothers—though we are not as tired or exhausted as they, the poor fools that they are, tramping up and down that damned hill all day. I almost feel sorry for the bite of the blisters to their heels!" The men laughed, appreciating his humour, as he knew they would. A few clattered their swords on to their shields, others hefting their axes and spears in salute. Not one man in those ranked lines of the shield wall atop that ridge wondered what in the name of hell he was doing there—why he was taking part in such a God-awful, bloody day. There was no need to question, for they knew, each and every one of them, fyrdman or housecarl, nobleman or freeborn farmer.

They were there for their King. For Harold.

Quietly, in an aside to one of his most trusted captains, Harold said, "Fetch me as soon as there is movement from down there. I go to see my mother."

Removing his helmet he glanced again briefly at his loyal, brave army. Aye, they were all tired, but the battle lust was thundering through their veins and they were good for a while yet. By God's mercy and the vows that he had made on that day of his anointing, but he was proud of them!

It was quieter back among the shade of the woodland trees; darker, too, for the sky was clouding over, the warmth of the day fading, the promise of rain in the air. Too late for their benefit, though. It would fall, perhaps, during the night or on the morrow. Had it rained this day...ah, but it was no use thinking of the ifs and buts. It was what it was, would be what it would be. Harold ducked under a low branch, came out into a clearing. At least the rain would wash away the blood. Would set this hill clean again.

A few tents had been pitched, fires lit. Cauldrons of water steamed, dangling suspended from tripods. Within one or two a thin gruel was bubbling. The wounded were laid in rows, some covered by blankets or cloaks, most as they had come from the battlefield, sweat-grimed and bloodied.

Beneath an oak, away to the left, a woman was kneeling beside a white-haired, elderly man. She looked up, saw Harold making his way towards her, attempted a wan smile as she brushed stray hair from her eyes, leaving a smear of blood across her forehead. Her veil was askew, her gown stained and sodden in places near the hem.

He took a while to reach her, for he stopped at nigh on every man, to pass a word of comfort or praise. Beside one or two he squatted down, laid a hand on chest or head or arm. There was nothing he could do to ease the pain, to stop the march of death, but a personal word from the King, their beloved lord, was all they asked. They were content, after Harold had passed by, to go to God.

"Where is my mother?" he asked Edyth as he hunkered down on the other side of the man she was tending. A broken spear shaft poked from his chest, his breath coming in bubbled gasps as the lifeblood and spittle seeped from him. Harold laid his hand on his shoulder. "Go with God, my old friend, you have served both Him and me well this day."

With a cough, the old man attempted a grin. "I have spoken to two of the greatest kings now, my Lord, As a lad Cnut once praised me for my quick-running legs and now you, God go with you, my Lord." He closed his eyes. Died.

Harold sighed, dipped his head as he lifted the unlaced byrnie over the man's wrinkled face. Why had the old fool not stayed at home? At his age he had no need to come. None, save perhaps that of pride, which burnt so fiercely in the hearts of so many of these gloriously brave men.

Edyth choked back tears. She dared not cry, for if she allowed just one to fall, she would not be able to stop. The weeping would come later, when there would be nothing else to do but to remember this day, these men. To remember how young many of them were; their names, their kindred. Their ending.

"Countess Gytha is over yonder," she said, tipping her head towards the makeshift tents, "she watches over your brothers."

Harold massaged his face, his cheeks, chin, nose. Brought his hand up through the sweat streaks of his damp hair. Closed his eyes to squeeze back his own tears. "Three sons has she now lost in as many weeks. Wulfnoth, too, is perhaps dead—I doubt William has allowed him his life after this."

Edyth reached across the body of the old grandfather, touched Harold's hand, her thoughts screaming: *Let it not be four sons! Please, let it not be four!* She said in a voice that belied her terror, "Your nephew, too. Hakon is dead. He was slain in the first hour of fighting—he was so determined to fight in the front line, to avenge those years of missed freedom."

"At least he is free now." Harold's hand tightened around hers, the grip intense, desperate. Not Hakon as well, God no…"Ah, Edyth, Gyrth and Leofwine gone—so many good men gone with them." He lifted his eyes, stared into hers. "Is it justified? All this? All this spilt blood?"

She did not answer him immediately. What could she say? She shrugged her shoulders, tried with, "Would you then rather let William rule England? Give these men, your men, over to the ways of Normandy, without at least a chance to fight for what is our own?"

He let go her hand, pushed himself upright. The joint-ache in his knee was paining him, but then his whole body felt stiff and sore. He would most assuredly sleep for the month around after this day.

"You are right, my Willow-bud, as ever you are. I must go see my mother, and then return to the line." He turned to go, paused, swung back to her. Stepping around the dead, he took her to him in an embrace that was brief but more eloquent than any spoken word. He touched his lips to her forehead, spun round and walked abruptly away.

She saw him again, some few minutes later, making his way back across the clearing, heading through the trees to the ridge. She was kneeling beside a boy who felt no pain from the neck down, his spine being severed. He had told her that he came from Wessex, from Bosham itself, that his father had been Earl Godwine's man, that he was proud that one son should serve the other. That his four brothers were here also, somewhere.

Harold stopped before he left the cover of the woods, glanced back at her. He raised his right hand, palm outward, fingers slightly bent. It was how he always waved farewell to her, whenever he left the manor. He would rein in his horse before the gateway, turn, raise his hand…when Edyth looked down, the boy had died. Perhaps it was as well he had not lingered long; he would not be alone in his journey to the other side, for all of his brothers had gone ahead, were gone before him.

24

Sendlach

Duke William allowed five minutes under the hour to rest, and then the war horns blared for the third time. Again, he had spent the precious respite planning. For this third try, they were deployed under his own command in one single force, not three divisions. He had lost many men, more horses—knights would be fighting on foot, for the remounts were all used. Their position was desperate, the outcome uncertain, but there was no choice but to go for this one last assault. Were they to withdraw, where would they go? The English would hunt them down, finish them like game at bay. Whether they fled or fought, death waited. Better to die fighting than running like a whipped hound, to be hanged or burnt or starved...but then, for William, if captured, death was a certainty. That Harold might allow him and his followers their liberty did not occur to him.

William's survival depended on his men destroying that shield wall. Harold's on holding it firm.

Two things made the Duke the leader that he was: his determination to win and his ability to recognise mistakes and to change tactics. Harold had placed his army in the most appropriate formation, had chosen his ground well and had commanded with skill and precision. That fact William had conceded after his first assault had been so easily deflected. Both men were worthy generals, but only one could win. Skill no longer seemed to come into it. Luck would be playing a lead role in the outcome of this day, but William was not going to risk what was left him on the chance roll of a die. This attack would be different and, if they did not win through, then perhaps they were deserving of death.

Harold watched almost dispassionately as the tidal wave of men rolled forward again. The front line of cavalry and infantry were protected with high-held shields; archers were placed at the rear. Slower on this occasion, not tiring themselves, respecting the disrupted state of the ground, the slope of the hill and their own exhaustion, they trundled nearer. It would take a while for them to reach the top—could something be done to slow them more?

"He is a formidable man." Harold admitted to his personal bodyguard. "And a rare one, for he uses his brain to seek solutions to a problem. Pass word that we will at last require our archers—set them to the front—but they are to be ready to step back as soon as the line is approached. The shield wall must be held!"

The abuse hurled by the English was as searing as any barbed arrow, but words could not maim or injure, unlike the hail of missiles that was propelled downwards. Arrows first, then anything that could be thrown. Clods of turf, severed limbs, dead men's boots. The head of a horse, even apple cores and empty ale skins. Anything, everything to deflect the attention of the Norman ranks. A man would duck his head, raise his shield arm at something that flew through the air from a waiting battle line. It might only be the harmless, shrivelled core of an apple, but then again, it could be a dagger blade...

The Norman advance shook, but only briefly; it came onwards. The English reset their shields, braced their legs and shoulders, and waited.

Needing to distract the attention of the front line, to sow confusion so that the cavalry and infantry could come in close without danger, the Norman archers had come to a standstill—were aiming—let loose their arrows in a high, wide trajectory to fall from above. How many men would be fool enough to look up as that cloud of hissing, whining shafts sped overhead? Enough? Would enough stop an arrow in the vulnerable, unprotected flesh of the face? Enough to do damage to the shield wall? And how many had instinctively ducked, cowering from the death-tipped cloud, had crouched, exposing their shoulders and backs to the same spitting barbs?

Clever! thought Harold, as he watched, listening to the screams of his wounded men. *For all I think of him, I admit Duke William is indeed a capable man.*

They joined, Norman breath heating on English faces. Eye to eye, sword to sword. The front line was weakened—but holding. Hand-to-hand fighting, the weight of the Norman advance crashing against the shield wall, as if some great devil-driven sea storm was mercilessly battering at a shoreline. The defence coming as desperate and brutal.

The Duke appeared to be everywhere at once—to the fore, to the rear. To left, right, to centre. Shouting, urging, cursing. His horse was killed from under him—two now had he lost. He leapt clear as the animal crashed downwards, screamed at the nearest rider to dismount, took the animal for himself. He must be mounted, must be seen! Must drive these cur-sons on!

For one whole hour they fought. So rarely did a battle last this long—nearly the whole of the day had they fought here, up on this ridge seven miles from the coast at Hastings. Harold himself was now fighting, had come nearer the front with the best of his housecarls. The line that had held so long was beginning to break and to crumble; too many were dying; not enough were there to take their places.

And then the breaches came, great gaps of dead men, and the Norman cavalry were through, the advantage, suddenly, exultantly, swinging towards the Normans. William's helmet was dented by an axe blow; Robert fitz Erneis rode for Harold's standard, intent upon seizing it, killed several men with his sword before being cut down by the cold metal of English axes.

The mêlée was man against man, group against group, nothing left of that wall that had stood, unshakeable, since the ninth hour of the morning. Naught Harold could do, save stand and fight. Hope and pray that they could last out until darkness fell. It was not now a matter of winning, but of staying alive. The light was fading, soon the sun would be down. The housecarls fighting for their king at the centre of the ridge were growing smaller in number, gathering closer around the two royal standards. There was no time to think, to analyse, to feel. Only once, briefly, did Harold wonder that perhaps he ought to lay down his great death-edged axe and surrender. But he remembered Dinan. No, this was the better way to die.

Four mounted men were closing in, two of whom had a personal grudge against this Saxon King: Eustace de Boulogne, who had suffered humiliation at the hands of Godwine his father, and Guy de Ponthieu, who had lost the hope of a chest of gold. With them were Hugh de Montfort and Walter Gifford, all from the Franco-Flemish side, now forcing their way inwards from the eastern end of the ridge. They showed no mercy to the dying or the wounded as they hacked their way through towards Harold with a bitter thirst for revenge that had taken hold along with the unstoppable fever of bloodlust? The King's guard tried to protect their lord, but there was nothing, nothing they could do to stop the vicious tide of bloody death. Nothing they could do to save England's last Saxon-born King.

To the western end Duke William had been unhorsed a third time. He remounted more leisurely, for all his army were now upon the ridge and the English were broken, beginning to run. He rode at a walk, issuing commands, encouraging that last, final push. Could not believe his fortune.

The shout went up in French, spread, was repeated, clarioned from mouth to mouth. William spurred his horse to a gallop to where Harold had stood, where the standards of England had, all the day through, fluttered...

"*Le roi anglais est mort! Le roi est fini!* The English King is dead!"

Epilogue

The Battle Place—15 October 1066

More than 600 horses and 4,000 men lay dead along the 600-yard ridge of Sendlach Hill, the place of battle. The place of death. In the drizzle-misted dawn of the fifteenth of October the carnage and destruction were unfathomable. Had it taken so much death to achieve such a little kingdom?

William stood, exhausted and unshaven, near to where Harold's standard had flown proud until the moment that everything had ended for the English. He had not slept during the hours of darkness—had not sought a bed until after the midnight had passed and then his mind had whirled with thoughts that would not, would not, be banished. Thoughts of how close he had come to defeat, of how many had died and in what manner. The unbelievable realisation that he had won. Harold was dead and the crown of England was his for the taking. But the winning was empty, the nightmares had been there instead, hammering with galloping hooves behind his eyes, trampling his brain, howling with the cries of the dead and the dying. Harold was dead, but William now knew the manner of his dying and it would haunt him until the day of his own passing. He knew how Harold had died. How brutally he had died.

Walter Gifford had struck the first blow, slicing his sword through Harold's left thigh, shattering the bone. As the King had staggered, half fallen, de Montfort's lance had pierced his shield, penetrating through to his chest. Harold's axe had remained in his hand; he had attempted to rise, the ground drenching with his blood; he had fought on. Bleeding, dying, he had fought on. Eustace de Boulogne's sword had slashed through his neck, below where his helmet had protected him; he was already dead as the Norman removed his head from his body, and as Guy de Ponthieu, with deliberate savagery, disembowelled and dismembered England's King before also hacking at those English housecarls who had fought to their deaths to protect him.

Few of the Norman army had slept well, because of that dishonourable death. They had curled beneath their cloaks where they had dropped, unable to carry their aching limbs far from the carnage of the battlefield. Too many crowding, weeping spirits walked over-close at heel for easy rest.

By flaring torchlight they had searched through the bodies, heaped several deep, around the standard of Wessex, looking for Harold. Could not find his head, could not identify what remained.

Angry, the Duke had thrust his face closer to de Montfort's, had stabbed his finger into the older man's broad chest. "I suggest, my friend, that you search again, and keep searching, until you find it!" Incompetents and fools! Why was he surrounded by such? He must have Harold's body, to prove he was dead.

Come morning, the anger had increased, fuelled by the lack of sleep and the first insidious stirrings of conscience. He had not undressed to sleep, but had lain, clothed, on his cot. As the sun rose and the day began, he strode from his tent that they had erected to the leeward side of Telham Hill and looked up at where, yesterday, they had fought. He would build an abbey, he thought, up there on the ridge, where the victory had been his. An altar could cover where Harold had fallen. A small voice flickered to the back of his mind. Was thrust immediately aside as he bellowed for his horse to be brought up. The voice of honesty: To honour a victory! Or to honour a king whom you had no right to kill?

Someone touched his arm. He spun round, a gasp half leaving his lips, almost expecting to see Harold's headless corpse standing there. No ghost, only William fitz Osbern, his face haggard with fatigue. "My Lord, there are two women asking to have audience with you."

Irritated, William snapped, "I have no time for the weeping of widows—tell them they may take their husbands' remains and be gone. I have more important things to tend, Will."

"Sir, these are no ordinary women. One is Countess Gytha, Lord Harold's mother, the other is his concubine, Edyth the Fair."

William raised an eyebrow. They have come to bargain with me? What is it they want? My protection? Tell them I intend no harm to women who do not oppose me."

Fitz Osbern said nothing for a moment. The appalling savagery that he had witnessed—participated in—since their ships had beached on the bay at Pevensey sickened even him, a seasoned warrior. He had believed this campaign to be right, that Edward had promised the throne to William, that Harold had thrown a given oath into the wind and deserved punishment. But not like this. Not with the slaughter of the innocent. Of women and infants. Nor with the cowardly mutilation that had happened up on that ridge, "Sir, the Countess asks for naught but her eldest son's body. She has offered its weight in gold, were you to return it to her for Christian burial."

"And where would that be, think you? This Christian burial?" William snorted.

Fitz Osbern shrugged; he did not know, had not asked. "Winchester, I assume, where I believe his father, Godwine of Wessex lies. Or Westminster, within the cathedral that King Edward had built, where he rests."

Duke William ran his gaze over the sprawl of the Norman dead, beginning to be gathered by those who had survived. Looked further, to the crest of the hill, where the Saxon women were still walking, searching for the remains of husbands, fathers or sons. So many dead, and all for the arrogance of one who thought he could take that which was not his—Harold had caused all this, Harold, who had called himself king—and they wanted to bury him beside other, lawful kings? *Non. Jamais.* That he would not permit! But these women could prove useful for his own purpose.

"Tell them I will consider their request, but first they must find what they want. This Edyth, if she is Harold's whore, she will be able to identify him for us."

≈≈

The night had passed with bitter slowness for Edyth. All those men who could walk, limp or hobble had drifted away, silent, into the darkness, making for their own homes, to try to forget what they had witnessed; to rest, to heal. To be ready to fight again, if they were wanted, another day. Those who were left, the wounded who had no strength for walking, lay waiting for death. Most of them had not survived the night of cold rain. The women had made their way among them throughout the night, collecting up those they knew for burial, helping those few who remained alive to the tents in the woods to be comforted and bandaged as best they could.

Strange, but Edyth's tears would not come. They were there, screaming in her throat, in her head, but they would not reach her eyes. And beyond that silent scream there was nothing else. Nothing, only a blankness and that last view of Harold as he had stood beneath the trees, one hand raised in a salute of farewell...

The sounds of that ending had carried through the forest, tossed by the wind moaning through the autumn-coloured leaves of the trees. She had heard that last cry, that desolate howl of defeat, the bewildered silence that had followed.

They had gone up to the ridge, Gytha and she, with the other women, once the dark had settled and the Normans had gone back down to their side of the valley beyond the brook. Had carried a torch, eerie in the blackness, that had flared and hissed as the rain spat into the pitch. The rain…if only the rain had come earlier! They had looked for Harold, but had not found him.

She thought she would not be able to do this thing, to walk up and down the lines of what had once—only yesterday—been men. The Normans had gathered those who had fallen beside the standards together, laid them in a row along the gory ridge. So much blood, the rain had not yet washed it clean. They had all been stripped naked, their hauberks and tunics stolen, everything that belonged to one man of value to another. So many of them were without limbs or heads, their bellies slit open, their innards pulled out…She tried not to look at the details as she walked from one corpse to another. She recognised the faces, distorted in the agony or surprise of death. These were—had been—Harold's housecarls, his loyal men who had given everything to serve him, some of them since he had become Earl of East Anglia, on through his being Earl of Wessex and King. Some had even served Godwine before Harold.

It was no use looking at those who had faces to recognise. She would not find Harold by his familiar face or by the colour of his hair. They had hewed his head from his neck. William, the Duke, had told her so as he had come up on the ridge escorted by that other man, fitz Osbern. How he had looked at her, spoken to her! As if she were something a boot had trodden in. He had stood, legs spread, fists resting on his hips, his head, with the hair shaven in the style of all his kind, tipped backwards, bloated with arrogance.

"So you are his whore," he had said.

Edyth had looked at him, eye to eye, her pride the more dignified, the more honourable. "I would rather be whore to a good man like Harold than duchess to a man who commands murder to satisfy his ambition."

She found Harold towards the end of the row. Recognised him by the faded, distinctive scar that swerved across his shoulder. And by the others on the upper arm, the right thigh, the small V shape on the hip. Scars, honourably won in skirmish and battle, in fight and feud. It was the one on the shoulder, though, that she reached out for. Her trembling fingers stretched forward but did not touch. She remembered her dog, his brother's dagger making this wound. The killing of her dog and the kindling of their love.

"Is this it? Is this him?" The voice, the eager words in French, startled her. William stood behind her, ordering men to take away what remained of the body. His men began carrying it down the slope towards the Norman encampment.

"*Monseigneur!*" she cried, coming to life, running after William who was starting to walk away. She caught hold of his tunic sleeve; he snatched it from her grasp as if stung, a hiss of anger leaving his lips.

"*Monseigneur*, the body is for my Lord's mother! Did you not say she could take it? She is with the English wounded, not down yonder. We would give my Lord proper burial."

William glowered at her, unused to being questioned. "Do you think I shall not ensure it, madame? He shall be buried, but where no one will know or tell of it. By the sea, I think. *Oui*, he can guard the coast he failed to defend. *Allons-y*." He hurried the men forward, flicking his hand impatiently at the woman who stood stunned, disbelieving, as they took what remained of her beloved away.

The woman forgotten, William called to one of his lesser commanders who was making his way obliquely across the sloping, scarred hillside. "Malet! William Malet!"

The man raised his head at the shout, trotted to meet his lord duke, listened gravely to his orders. Already he had been charged with the burial of all these dead—the Norman dead, the English could look to their own. Mass graves, he had decided, would be best, pits dug away to the east where the ground appeared softer. Now he had this other grave to dig. By the shore, the Duke said. That would mean a journey back to the coast—as if he had not enough to do this day! But so be it. The Duke had commanded it.

Edyth sank to her knees. There on the blood-mired trampled grass, she covered her face with her hands. He was gone. Harold, her lord, her lover. Harold, husband, father, earl and king, was gone from her for ever. The tears were coming and now that they fell, it would be so hard to stop them.

Down on the slope, a robin fluttered to the highest branch of a fallen tree. He lifted his head and sang, proclaiming his territory.

A far sweeter song than the bloodied one that had been carolled here but yesterday.

Author's Note

⤎⤏

The year 1066 is probably the most famous date in English history. It marks a decisive battle that dramatically altered English history, literally overnight—but English history did not begin in 1066. The Saxon kings—Harold II among them—were civilised, educated men. English law and chronicles were recorded and written, the administrative work of government highly sophisticated and well organised. William's *Domesday Book*, a list of all the taxable commodities in England, was compiled so quickly and accurately because the information was already there. It only had to be updated.

The majority of what is known about the sequence of events that led to two such remarkable men—Harold and William—facing each other across a battlefield, seven or so miles from Hastings, was recorded after the event by the victors. Propaganda we would call it today—hardly a good starting point for accuracy. There was a keen need to hide or at least bend certain facts: that William had no right whatsoever to the English throne being one of them.

I Am the Chosen King is a novel. I have based it on fact, but cannot claim that the details of the events and circumstances are all historically accurate; it is, after all, only an interpretation. There are too many disagreements, even among the experts, ever to be able to state categorically that anything in history is undisputed fact. Unless we were there to see for ourselves, we will never know, and even then the truth can often be elaborated or exaggerated.

As with many events this far back into the past, we *know* what happened, often *where*, occasionally *when* but rarely the *why* or the *how*. Much of our information about the Norman Conquest comes from the Bayeux Tapestry, an embroidery (not, in fact, a tapestry) which was probably commissioned by Duke William's half-brother, Bishop Odo of Bayeux. Being of Norman origin and showing only "cartoon-like" illustrations, it leaves much open to conjecture. For example, it shows us Harold leaving Bosham by sea and being captured by Guy de Ponthieu, of his being a "guest" of William—but why he went to

Normandy is entirely unknown. It is in the tapestry that Harold rescues two men from drowning; that a woman named as Ælfgyva appears (who she was, we do not know; I have conjectured that she was Agatha, William's daughter); Halley's comet is there; and the consecration of a barely completed Westminster Abbey—we see a man putting the weather vane on the roof. And, of course, William's preparations for invasion, the sea voyage and the battle itself—all strictly from the Norman view.

The main characters of my novel existed; I have merely invented some of the "bit parts" and added colour and animation. One practical problem was with their Saxon names, often similar or the same, or with spelling unfamiliar to a modern reader. I decided to use a variety of spellings to differentiate between characters sharing the same name—for example the three "Edith's": Edith, Harold's sister; Edyth, his concubine; and Alditha his formal wife—as I have also used Edward and Ædward, Godwine and Goddwin. Canute—of turning the tide fame—is the more well-known spelling, but "Cnut" the more correct, and as he is a central character in my novel devoted to Queen Emma, I considered he ought to be so honoured.

We know that Queen Edith, Harold's sister, never had a child and that later writers declared Edward to be intentionally celibate. This seems unlikely as it was the duty of a king to provide heirs who would become "throne-worthy." It was never written that Edith was barren, with the blame put openly on her, therefore it seems more probable that the truth was shielded: that Edward was either impotent or homosexual. I have not used King Edward's later title—the Confessor—as this was not applied until his politically manufactured canonisation in 1161.

Some minor dates I have slightly altered to fit the convenience of narrative. For instance, Tostig was more probably married in 1052. His wife, Judith, I have placed as sister to William's wife. Some authoritative works place her as Mathilda's step-aunt, but as I needed my characters to be similar in age, a sister fitted better.

With a story that covers more than twenty years, it is difficult to know how or where unobtrusively to indicate the passing of years. Within the narrative is clumsy and artificial; as chapter headings, a risk of reading as a chronology. I believe the majority of readers wish to know where and when the action is happening, but without being distracted. I hope the eventual compromise is a suitable solution.

Specific dates mentioned within the narrative are actual known dates as recorded in the *Anglo-Saxon Chronicle* and similar documents.

Most sources imply that Ædward the Exile returned to London by mid–April 1057, but some believe it was later in the year—whatever the date, the event happened: Ædward died within a few days of reaching England before ever seeing Edward. The question remains, however, did he die of natural causes or not…? His son Edgar was hastily declared King after Hastings, but was, as Harold and the Council had feared, too young to be an effective leader against a man like William. He was forced to capitulate to the Duke when London surrendered late in 1066. Edgar returned to Normandy with William in 1067, probably not by choice. He did eventually attempt to raise a rebellion, but it was too late, the Normans were too firmly entrenched. His sister Margaret fled to Scotland, where she married King Malcolm and later became canonised as Saint Margaret. Their daughter married William's son, Henry I of England.

There is no substantial evidence that Harold was descended from Cerdic through Alfred the Great, nor, of course, that he was the mythical King Arthur's son, but I wanted some small and tenuous link with my Arthurian trilogy and this one suited nicely.

For those readers who are interested in the details of what is real and what is imaginary: Swegn did abduct the Abbess from Leominster Abbey and did murder his kinsman; Godwine and his family were exiled but clawed their way back into favour as I have described it; Harold did surprise Gruffydd at Rhuddlan at Christmas. I have invented the location of Harold's manor house, but he definitely founded Waltham Abbey after being taken ill and Edyth, his concubine, was forced to identify his mutilated torso after the great battle. His mother pleaded with William to exchange his remains for their weight in gold. The Duke refused.

As for Harold's resting place, that remains open to conjecture and personal preference. William ordered his remains to be buried by the sea—that is all we know for certain. Waltham Abbey lays stout claim to his body, as does the marked place of the high altar at Battle Abbey. The skeleton of a man's headless torso placed in an unmarked but expensive coffin was discovered beneath the Chancel Arch of Bosham Church in 1954. Some say this was Godwine's body—but he was buried at Winchester with public honours. And even if his body was placed at Bosham, why in an unmarked grave? Earl Godwine died in his bed at Winchester, three days after suffering a mortal seizure having declared his innocence of murder before God. Harold was hacked to pieces on the battlefield. With apologies to my local town of Waltham Abbey, I believe that it *is*, Harold's body that rests at Bosham. His mother, Countess Gytha, remained there a while before she fled abroad—and Bosham is, after all, by the sea...perhaps poor William Malet just did not have the time to go back to Hastings to bury a body; perhaps he took a bribe from a wealthy Countess instead? Who knows?

Harold was the first English King to be crowned in Westminster Abbey, though William, arrogantly declaring Harold's anointing as king void, later claimed that accolade for himself when he was crowned there on Christmas Day 1066.

My interpretation of the battles may be open to debate—but here again I would emphasise that this is a novel, although my ideas are based on the theories of those with a far greater historical knowledge and intellect than I possess. I have merely woven opinion into a story. With regard to sea battles: the Vikings were the most experienced and skilled seamen ever to have sailed the waters of this world. Trade ships and merchantmen were deep-draughted, slow-moving sailing ships—but the sleek, narrow-keeled longship, the true dragon ship, was manoeuvred by skilled oarsmen. William had to wait for the wind because the majority of his ships were merchant craft, relying on sail not oar. There is plentiful evidence that seafarers of this time were perfectly able to fight from shipboard. The English of Harold's time remained closely connected to their Danish sea ancestry, and had a worthy fleet of ships. Harold's own grandfather was renowned as a sea pirate. Remembering that the surviving accounts of William's invasion of England were written by the Normans, we have no information on or details of what went wrong. We can only ask questions and guess at the answers. Did William make sail earlier than was admitted? We know that many of his ships *were* destroyed somewhere between Dives and Saint Valéry, and that he had the bodies of dead sailors buried in secret so as not to spread alarm. Why? We are told that the damage was caused by bad weather—but was it? If storms were the cause, why not just give reassurance that they would wait for a fair wind? The advantage of being a novelist is that the original story can be unravelled and re-spun to a different pattern, using the very same yarn. Eadric the Steersman *did* exist—he was one of the few men immediately banished into exile by William after the conquest.

The use of cavalry at Stamford Bridge was highly probable. Horses must have been ridden on Harold's incredible march north; infantry could not have maintained that pace and fought immediately upon their arrival and the widespread historians' declaration that the Saxons only fought on foot is nonsense. If this was so, why was the explicitly bred *warhorse* so highly valued? There are many instances of such horses being left to beneficiaries in wills. Any old nag could be used as transport. So why did Harold not fight William on horseback at

Hastings? Ann Hyland, in her excellent work *The Medieval Warhorse*, suggests the most likely reason: the forced march north, and back again, took its toll on the horses; many had been killed on the battlefield in Yorkshire and of those remaining, many were probably lame or exhausted.

One other argument for the Saxons being able to fight on horseback is their perfect ability to fight *against* cavalry. The men in Harold's shield wall knew very well how to defend against a cavalry charge. Using an axe to take off a horse's head with one blow is not something that you discover by accident during the heat of battle!

After 1066, most references to King Harold were obliterated or ignored. His title in the *Domesday Book*, for instance, reverts to Earl Harold. Queen Edith surrendered Winchester to William, who subsequently gave her full respect as a king's widow. She died in 1075. Alditha was given no such similar honour. She gave birth to a son, Harold, at Chester some time after Hastings; she may have remained there, or returned to Wales. Neither she nor her son or daughter is mentioned again.

Harold's mother eventually fled to Flanders; his brother Wulfnoth remained in captivity in Normandy for over thirty years—he was never to return to England. Harold's sons by Edyth tried to raise a rebellion, but were repulsed and fled abroad—William was either too feared or had settled himself too tightly to be dislodged. One son, either Edmund or Magnus, was killed during a raid, probably on Bristol. Ulf, the youngest, was imprisoned by William.

Harold's daughter Gunnhild remained at Wilton Nunnery and Gytha (I have called her Algytha to differentiate her from her grandmother) travelled, possibly with her surviving brothers, to Smolensk to marry the Russian prince Vladimir, who in essence became the first Tsar of Russia. Their first-born son was known in the Danish world as Harold. She died on 7 May 1107. Her great-grandson was King Vlademar I of Denmark, from whom the present queens of Denmark and Great Britain are descended. Elizabeth II, therefore, carries the blood of Harold in her veins, as well as Duke William's.

Eustace de Boulogne's grandson made an attempt at invading England, but failed. Eventually Bishop Odo turned against William—as did Robert, the Duke's eldest son. William died alone in 1087 and was buried within his abbey at Caen—his corpulent body bursting open as the attendants attempted to squeeze it into the stone coffin.

As for Edyth Swann hæls, she had apparently remained in possession of much land when the *Domesday Book* was compiled in 1085–6, but where she lived, where she went...we do not know.

One last matter of conjecture: was Harold killed by an arrow in his eye? The evidence for this is based upon a scene in the Bayeux Tapestry: the wording "here Harold is killed" extends above a soldier with an arrow apparently in his eye, and also over a man falling from a sword wound to his leg. Which one is meant to be Harold? I do not support the arrow theory on the grounds that such a terrible wound would more likely kill a man outright, either through shock or by piercing into the brain, and we do know that Harold, although mortally wounded, continued to fight until he was decapitated.

1066 is known as the Norman Conquest, but it is worth remembering that although William had himself crowned king, and while most of the male English aristocracy were replaced by Normans, the ordinary English—the Saxons—*remained* English. England was *ruled* by Normans but never became Norman—if that had happened, we would be speaking French, not English.

Writing is the art of turning imagination into reality—

Harold was our last *English* king.

I have written what I imagine to have been his story.

An Excerpt from

The Forever Queen

I

⚜

Canterbury—April 1002

Emma was uncertain whether it was a growing need to visit the privy or the remaining queasiness of *mal de mer*, seasickness, that was making her feel so utterly dreadful. Or was it the man assessing her with narrowed eyes from where he stood at the top of the steps? A man she had never seen until this moment, who was four and thirty years to her three and ten, spoke a language she barely understood, and who, from the morrow, was to be her wedded husband.

Did he approve of what he saw? Her sun-gold hair, blue eyes, and fair skin? Maybe, but Emma was uncomfortably aware that he was more probably thinking her nose was too large, her chin too pointed, and her bosoms not yet firm and rounded.

Her eldest sister had laughed when Emma confided that this Æthelred of England might be disappointed with his bride. "Pleasure him in bed, *ma chérie*," had been the answer. "In bed, no husband will remain disappointed for long." Here in England, Emma remained unconvinced.

Hiding her discomfort as well as she could, she stared at this King's sun-weathered face. His blond hair, curling to his shoulders, had silver streaks running through it. His moustache trailed down each side of his mouth into a beard flecked with grey hair. He looked so old!

Her long fingers, with their bitten, uneven nails, rested with a slight tremble on her brother's left hand. Unlike her, Richard appeared unperturbed as they ascended the steps leading up to the great open-swung doors of Canterbury Cathedral. But why would he not be at ease? It was not he, after all, who was to wed a stranger and be crowned as England's anointed Queen.

She was aware that Richard of Normandy had agreed to this marriage of alliance for reasons of his own gain. He ruled Normandy and his brood of sisters with an iron will that imaged their father's ruthless determination—their father Emma had adored; her brother, who thought only of his self-advancement and little else, she did not.

The drizzling rain had eased as their Norman entourage had ridden through Canterbury's gates; the mist, hanging like ill-fitted curtaining across the Kent countryside had not deterred the common folk from running out of their hovels to inspect her. England and the English might not hold much liking for the Normans and their sea-roving Viking cousins, but still they had laughed and applauded as she passed by. They wanted peace, an end to the incessant *i-víking* raiding and pirating, to the killing and bloodshed. If a union between England and Normandy was the way to achieve it, then God's good blessings be upon the happy couple. Whether this marriage would be of lasting benefit and achieve that ultimate aim no one yet knew. The Northmen, with their lust for plunder, were not easy to dissuade, and the substantial wealth of England was a potent lure. For a while, though, when Richard, in consequence of this wedding denied winter access to his Norman harbours, the raiders would search elsewhere for their ill-gotten gain or stay at home. Unless, of course, they elected to offer Richard a higher incentive than the one King Æthelred of England had paid.

If Emma minded being so blatantly used for political gain, it was of no consequence to anyone. Except to Emma herself. *What if I am not a pleasing wife? What if he does not like me?* The questions had tumbled round and around in Emma's mind these three months since being told of the arrangement, had haunted her by night and day. She knew she had to be wed; it was a woman's duty to be a wife, to bear sons. Either that or drown in the monotonous daily misery of the nunnery, but there would be no Abbess's veil for her. Her brother needed the alliances his sisters brought, the silver and the land. Normandy was a new young duchy with no family honour or pride to fall back upon, only the hope of a future, which Richard was too impatient to wait for. This, Emma had understood from the day their father died. Richard wanted all he could get, and he wanted it not tomorrow or next year, but now. One by one his sisters had been paired to noble marriages, but they were all so much older than Emma. She had not expected to be bargained away so soon.

About the Author

Paul Reed

Helen Hollick lives in northeast London on the edge of Epping Forest with her husband, adult daughter, and a variety of pets, which include several horses, cats, and a dog. She has two major interests: Roman/Saxon Britain and the Golden Age of Piracy—the early eighteenth century. Her particular pleasure is researching the facts behind the small glimpses of history and bringing the characters behind those facts to full and glorious life. She has an honours diploma in early medieval history and may one day, if ever she finds the time, go on to obtain her full degree.

For up-to-date information, you are invited to visit www.helenhollick.net and www.helenhollick.blogspot.com.